TORRANCE

Scars of Tomorrow
Book I

A NOVEL BY TOM CALEN

*For the Truth Seekers,
the Diggers for Answers,
the Conspiracy Theorists of the World.*

*In all of history, never was a saint more loved,
nor sinner more hated,
than the man from the woods.*

Marcus Seton
Grand Historian

TABLE OF CONTENTS

Note To the Reader	10
Chapter One	14
Chapter Two	19
Chapter Three	27
Chapter Four	36
Chapter Five	43
Chapter Six	51
Chapter Seven	57
Chapter Eight	66
Chapter Nine	71
Chapter Ten	77
Chapter Eleven	87
Chapter Twelve	93
Chapter Thirteen	106
Chapter Fourteen	113
Chapter Fifteen	121
Chapter Sixteen	128
Chapter Seventeen	135
Chapter Eighteen	143
Chapter Nineteen	149
Chapter Twenty	157
Chapter Twenty-One	164
Chapter Twenty-Two	172
Chapter Twenty-Three	181
Chapter Twenty-Four	188
Chapter Twenty-Five	193
Chapter Twenty-Six	203
Chapter Twenty-Seven	211
Chapter Twenty-Eight	215
Chapter Twenty-Nine	220
What Followed After	227

NOTE TO THE READER

ON WRITING OF TORRANCE

I do not write this tale as a recrimination of those that have already been penned. Though, much of the histories of Torrance suffer from a lack of primary knowledge regarding the principle. Rather, I put these words to page in a selfish attempt to remember, or perhaps reclaim, my own past. In the years since the revolution, I have reflected on the events with which my life became so entwined. I have sought out those who survived to aide in filling the gaps in my memory and experience. Certainly, as a boy of only thirteen years, and sheltered as those years were, I had limited cognizance of the world. And far less awareness of how drastically the man from the woods would change all that I knew. All that we all knew.

Nor do I transcribe the happenings of Torrance in an effort to discredit either the infamy or devotion now attached to his name. The history books declare he was born to be a hero and the salvation of mankind. But, like the histories of all great men, the distance of time has muddied the clearer waters of truth. When I first met him, he seemed more likely to steal from the blind than rescue humanity; unless, of course, he could find some personal gain in the endeavor. I smile when I hear the oft repeated tale of Torrance pulling an enemy onto the safety of his escaping aerocycle while bullets rained down upon him. Many cite the incident as an example of Torrance's legendary heroism. They willingly ignore the fact that two kilometers later Torrance unceremoniously kicked the bullet-filled corpse from the bike. He simply no longer had need of a human shield.

Torrance was neither saint nor redeemer sent by the disavowed gods. He was human. Human and, like all of us, marred by that very humanity. To me, that makes his deeds more laudable than if he had been truly a blessed savior. Quick tempered, too fond of drinks and whores, the man from the woods was faulted and flawed in incalculable ways. But those stains on his character were an intrinsic part of him and I would bear the guilt of negligence to tell the story of Torrance and overlook his darkness in order to preserve your sanitized knowledge. No, I will tell it all, and tell it true, for only in that way can I honor the man to whom I owe my life.

If one willingly and impartially examines all the parts of Torrance's tale as, dear reader, I ask you to do, then a truly informed answer may satisfy the question that has plagued me over these many decades. *Did Torrance, the man from the woods, in fact save humanity? Or did he simply deliver us from one Hell to another?*

ON PRE-ALLIANCE EVENTS

One cannot begin to explore the man without first understanding the world in which he lived. While in truth the machinations that led to the creation of the

Global Alliance stretch back millennia to the founding of nations and religions, the most marked movements to one-world-rule occurred in the twenty-first century. The preceding hundred years brought organizations such as the United Nations, World Trade Organization, World Health Organization, the World Bank, and the International Monetary Fund to the forefront of global dealings. All seemingly benign in nature, and vociferously defended as such, the establishment of these institutions was the first overt step in unifying the various nations under one flag. In fact, the term "new world order" began to spice the propaganda speeches of leaders from the former countries of the United States of America and her ally-enemy, Russia. But, as I said, it was during the twenty-first century that the final pieces were carefully placed; and, as always, under the guise of easing the human condition.

The West's aggression in the Middle East continued and expanded until finally the battle lines of the third world war were drawn in the year 2016. The usual allies and foes took stalwart stands against each other for nearly a decade. As troops and missiles fell, the nations of North America and Europe found themselves without the necessary fuel to power their weapons. The flow of oil had been stilled. Stronger alliances, based on full disclosure of energy technologies, were forged. As has often been seen in the history of mankind, necessity preceded innovation. Upon the American discovery of a stable and renewable fuel source, the oil rich sands of the Middle East lost their ransom power. Thus, the West ended hostilities with cataclysmic dominance.

The dust-covered, yellowing diaries of those that witnessed the bombings on television (this was, of course, before global media was completely under state control) paint vivid portraits of the carnage. One witness wrote:

> Our family sat around the television and we watched the broadcast. What we saw. . .it was just horrible, sickening. Clouds of black smoke raced into the sky above domes of fire. The news anchor switched from several different camera views; Egypt, Iran, Pakistan, Libya, Syria, and more. Finally, a map came on the screen; red dots indicated where the bombs had dropped. As I counted the dots, ten, twenty, fifty, I thought to myself, "My God! How many have just died?"

By the end of the bombing, well over one hundred million souls were lost. In the weeks and months that followed, the estimated death toll rose another eighty-five million. In total, more than half the Middle East's population was killed in the final days of World War III. On April 27, 2026, the Western Alliance accepted the unconditional surrender of the desert countries. It was the last major conflict of the twenty-first century.

Years passed and other dangers threatened the global community. Famine. Financial collapse. Disease. Each peril was quickly met with multinational intervention. Each intervention slowly eroded the personal freedoms of the world's citizens. But, who could complain? After all, the governments had its citizens' best interests in mind . . . according to the propaganda.

With that excuse at the forefront, the Global Alliance was formed in the year 2060. Individual nations ceased to exist, borders were blurred, different currencies were abandoned . . . and the new world order was complete. And the dominion of the Five Families began.

On the Sub-dermal Implant Device (SID)

" . . . the sub-dermal implantable device is the ultimate defense against identity theft. Injected into the right palm, the device serves as the bearer's financial center. All commerce can be conducted through the SID thus removing the risk of unauthorized purchasing."

- M. Clemorsant, June 2022

Even amidst the turmoil of the first half of the century, the technological world continued its unbridled sprint forward. The introduction of the personal chip was initially met with wary skepticism. While the corporate elite understood the promised benefit of greater security, middle and lower income families, with few assets to protect, were slower to adopt the claims. Only once the old governments mandated its use, and assumed the cost of implantation, did the SID begin to see widespread use.

Grocery stores, banks, cinemas, and gas stations no longer needed to process credit cards, or even maintain a cash register. With just the swipe of the hand, consumers were able to purchase goods with ease. One never had to worry about forgetting one's wallet; "Don't leave home without it" quickly became "You can't leave home without it."

There were, of course, the outraged voices of civil libertarians who argued the device allowed the government an exorbitant amount of surveillance capabilities. Not only could buying habits be tracked and catalogued, but so too could every person's whereabouts be accessed and pinpointed. The United States of America, the first nation to adopt the SID and the home of its creation, immediately responded to the concerns with a familiar tactic: fear. Endless statistics were released, and awareness campaigns were quickly rolled out, highlighting the government's ability to use the SID to track and apprehend criminals. The faces of children previously abducted and killed were flashed across billboards. Wasn't the sacrifice of some personal freedom worth protecting innocent children? If you were against the SID, you were against safety. In the end, of course, the voices of dissent were shouted down (and in some cases mysteriously silenced) and the adoption of the SID spread across the world.

To be fair in my account, collected evidence did indeed show a significant reduction in global crime rates. In fact, by the year 2075, most territories of the Global Alliance boasted the near elimination of all major crime. Few were foolish enough to engage in illegal activity when apprehension was all but guaranteed. Even more naïve were those that removed the SID in an attempt to blind authorities to their location. "Justice," in those cases, was swift and fatal.

On Personal Involvement

This was the world which gave birth to Torrance. His faults (and they were many), as well as his accolades, are a direct result of the environment and circumstances which forced his creation. And forced it was. The corruption of the Global Alliance, the SID, and the Five Families could only have continued its perpetration for a finite time. If not Torrance, another would have risen to take his place, though albeit for likely different reasons. He was the first, however, for as you will see, dear reader, no other living man at that time was so perfectly suited to the task.

For much of this tale, I was near at hand; while in other places I have been forced to rely on research and rumor. In order to more closely align with the constructs of a documented history, I will refrain from referring to myself directly. Though, I hope you will forgive an old man if at times in my ramblings my voice becomes present. This is, after all, not only the story of Torrance, but also a retelling of my own life.

-M.S.

CHAPTER ONE

Phillip Seton

"Danica Marie Seton, if you're not downstairs in the next five minutes . . .," Beth Seton, mother of the ever-tardy teenager whom she addressed, shouted with stark warning as she busily set out a simple breakfast for her children. After a summer of leisure, this first morning of the school year was proving to be a difficult adjustment for all four members of the Seton clan. Readying herself for a repeated call to her daughter, Beth swallowed the words as she heard the familiar sullen thumping of feet from the floor above.

"Sounds like you woke the beast," Phillip mused humorously as he panned through the morning holo-news. He responded to his wife's withering look with the smile with which she had long since fallen in love.

Topping off his white ceramic mug with the remaining coffee, Mrs. Seton admonished, "Smile all you want, Phil. But, if she misses the bus, you're going to have to drive her. I have to be at Marcus's school for Parents Welcome Day."

Marcus Seton, the youngest of the family, was beginning his final year of primary school. The first-year teenager had woken early that morning; unable to sleep due to the eager nerves which tumbled within his stomach. Favoring his father with sandy brown hair and nose that was just a bit too wide for his narrow face, the youth sat hunched over his bowl of oatmeal at the kitchen's breakfast bar. Though he had spent much of the summer months engaged in activities with his core group of friends, he was keen to reconnect with the larger circle of his school peers.

"Mom, you really don't need to come today," Marcus implored his mother once again. At thirteen, he preferred to think of himself as an adult and was decidedly against having his mother present for the first day of school. "Palin and Drew's parent aren't going."

"Good for them," the family's matriarch replied as she pinned a set of small diamond studs to her ears. "I already took the day off, so you'll have to suffer through my presence for a few hours." Though her husband's work with the government more than provided a sufficient income, Beth Seton had returned to the workforce once Marcus had entered the fourth grade. Her work at a local antiques shop provided a rewarding outlet for her interest in forgotten craftsmanship.

Marcus was forming another futile argument when the entrance of his sister ended the debate. Only a few months past her eighteenth birthday, Danica would today begin her final year of high school. Unlike her brother, she would have willingly postponed the start of the new school year indefinitely. Her auburn hair, still wet from a hasty shower, was gathered in a ponytail which stretched to the middle of her back.

"Aren't you going to dry your hair?" Mrs. Seton asked upon seeing the expanding wet mark on her daughter's shirt.

"It'll dry on the way," Danica replied sullenly as she slumped into a dark wood kitchen chair. Attired in the regulated school uniform, white short-sleeved crew neck shirt and gray pleated skirt, she still managed to accessorize her individuality with twine bracelets of varying colors and clunky black boots which ended midway up her calf.

With a relenting sigh and roll of her eyes, Beth moved on and asked, "Did you load your books?"

Waving her right hand in a reply which carried an unspoken and exasperated "yes," Danica sipped some orange juice before eating a few spoons of oatmeal. Unlike her brother, Danica's looks had certainly been inherited from her mother's genetics. At five-foot-nine, she stood taller than most of her gender. The high school basketball coach had often asked her to try for the team, but she always declined; preferring the independence of track and field. Neither of her parents had been runners, so it was a surprise to them when their daughter announced in her freshman year that she had joined the team. In truth, they had been surprised she had joined anything at all.

Though far from antisocial, Danica Seton had always been somewhat removed from those around her. Her own circle of friends was small; consisting of two other girls, Janey Martin and Valen West, with whom she had formed a bond in middle school. To her parents' knowledge, Danica had not yet expressed interest in any of the boys at her school, though her athletic build and flawless cream coloring certainly placed her near the top of the list of "most attractive" in her school. For Dani, as her friends called her, the boys of her year seemed to compete for the crown of immaturity. If wishes were granted, hers would be to skip over the next year and begin college.

The soft voice of Bera, the home's Integrated Family Management System, announced, *"Bus 23 to Mayfield Academy is approximately three minutes away."*

Once a luxury, IFaMS were now commonplace in most homes. The system, an unseen assistant, served households in a variety of ways. Everything from home security, appointment scheduler, information retrieval, alarm clock, banking and bill payment, and telecommunications were accessed through IFaMS. The Setons, like most families across the world, relied heavily on the system to keep their home and lifestyle functioning properly.

Finishing the last of her juice, Danica heeded the IFaMS pronouncement and rose from the kitchen table before proceeding to the front door. "I put lunch credits on your SID," Mrs. Seton called out to her daughter.

"Thanks," she responded as she closed the door behind her and walked down the length of the winding driveway.

"How much longer until graduation?" Philip Seton asked with a tease as he rinsed the few coffee grinds from the bottom of his mug.

Glancing to Marcus and finding him entirely engrossed in one of his comics,

Mrs. Seton replied, "You can't really blame her. Eighteen, a senior, and taking the bus to school?" In the quiet nights of the summer, as husband and wife talked in the last moments before sleep, they had debated the topic of buying Danica a podcar of her own. The previous agreement had been to purchase the vehicle for Danica on her eighteenth birthday if she achieved straight A's on her end-of-year report. With a B+ in economics, Mr. Seton felt strongly that his daughter had not maintained her side of the bargain.

"What's the point of making a deal if we're going to reward her no matter what?" Philip again espoused his view on the matter. Raised in a family far stricter than that of his wife's childhood home, he steadfastly believed in instilling their children with the concept of hard work and reward.

"I know," Beth countered, "But, at what point do we stop spiting ourselves? We're the ones driving her to practice, meets, her friends'."

In previous discussions, his wife had always argued the point in terms of their daughter. Mr. Seton had not truly thought of the inconvenience his wife incurred by denying Danica her own podcar. Beth had been kind enough to use "we," but Phillip knew it was Beth that bore the burden of chauffeuring the children to their various activities. He smiled inwardly at his wife's clever strategy. Rarely did she abuse the total devotion he felt towards her. If Beth was willing to bring out the big gun, as he saw it, then perhaps he needed to reconsider his unyielding stance.

"When I get home tonight, let's talk about it. Maybe we can make it a Christmas present," he allowed.

"An early Christmas present?" Beth asked with a face of loving pleading.

"You're evil, you know that? Pure evil," he told her before he kissed her gently. As he turned towards the garage door, Beth aimed a playful swat at his rear. With a shake of his head, Philip knew he had lost the months-old debate. "I might be late tonight. We have to finish the presentation for Friday."

"Try not to be too late, though," his wife responded. "I'm making salmon and it won't be as good reheated."

"I'll try."

"Bye, Dad," Marcus called to him from the kitchen bar.

"Be good, Marcus. Don't drive your new teacher crazy on the first day," father cautioned son.

"I won't."

Crossing the concrete floor of the spacious garage, Philip slid into the open hatch door of the two-seater podcar. The recent model had improved amenities from previous versions. Both seats offered a nearly full recline for longer drives, though Mr. Seton relied on the vehicle solely for the short journey to and from work. The feature he used most often, however, was the full screen display on the oblong windshield. The elder Seton found checking his work messages during the drive prepared him for whatever events awaited at the office.

"Directly to the office, sir? Or will there be stops along the way?" Bera's all-too-human voice surrounded him from the pod's many speakers.

"Just the office, Bera," Philip informed the IFaMS.

"Very well." With a soft rush of air, the hatch door rotated downward and Mr. Seton heard the compressed, metallic click of pod and door sealing together. The garage door lifted and the podcar turned on its three wheels, two rear and one front, before making its silent exit into the morning light. Minutes later, the automated vehicle had travelled beyond the residential neighborhood and joined the steady stream of traffic along the motorway.

Scanning the messages displayed before him, Mr. Seton sighed with predictive disappointment at the day ahead, and what was likely to be a challenging week. As managing director of the project, the pending roll-out of the next generation Subdermal Implant Device, or SID as they were commonly known, weighed heavily upon his shoulders. The last product launch of this nature occurred nearly twenty-five years ago and had been marred by a fair number of glitches and hiccups. Recently elevated to his title, Seton was aware of how keenly the eyes of his superiors were watching his control of the project. With a global population nearing twelve billion, any endeavor to upgrade the SIDs was an arduous task at best. From supply, to shipping, to implantation, Seton had been tasked with ensuring a smooth worldwide transition to the upgraded SID. Success all but guaranteed a future of wealth and comfort for him and his family.

Most of the correspondence was from the various team leaders he had selected to oversee product distribution. Shipments had begun three weeks earlier and the digital holograph of Gregor Tarasov, Seton's assistant managing director, informed him that sixty-two percent of the deliveries had reached their respective destinations around the world.

"By week's end, we should see well over eighty percent delivered, with the remaining shipments completed a week after that," Gregor's image explained in his typically stoic Russian-influenced accent. Seton had worked with the man for seven years and never had he known Gregor to break from his leveled tone and serious expression.

The news, however, delighted Seton. Even if Gregor's estimates were off, which he doubted they were, the shipments would be in place well ahead of schedule. "Bera," Seton instructed once his colleague's message finished, "record reply to Tarasov, Gregor."

"Please begin your reply at the tone."

A deep harpsichord note sounded, and Seton focused his eyes at the small camera lens embedded in the pod's instrumentation. "Gregor, thanks for the update. Sometime this morning, send me a breakdown of delivery locations completed, as well as locations still outstanding. Also, get your people to prepare an insert to Friday's presentation reflecting the new numbers. I don't mind going with the sixty-two percent, but it'd be great if we can include results from end-of-day Thursday. Oh, and Gregor . . . remind me to buy you a drink. If everything runs this smoothly, we'll both earn long vacations. End reply."

"Recording completed. Would you like me to replay your message?"

"No, Bera, you can send it."

"Message sent to Tarasov, Gregor at 7:45."

During the remaining portion of the drive to the office, Philip Seton moved through another three messages. The first two pertained to the advertising campaign encouraging the vast citizenry of the Global Alliance to schedule their implant appointments in accordance with their allotted timeframe. The announcement of the SID upgrade had been met with near universal disdain, at least from the portion of the populace that was old enough to recall the previous upgrade debacle. Long lines, a shortage of skilled implant technicians, and mismanaged supply streams had left a memory of understandable dissatisfaction.

For the last two months, an outreach campaign had been in place to alleviate public concern of a repeat performance. Not well-versed in the nuance of advertising, Seton relied heavily on the company he had contracted to develop the campaign. The Pacer Group had come highly recommended; having won awards for the launch of a podcar line (the same make in which Seton himself now rode), as well as several blockbuster films and musical acts. The prevailing wisdom had been to reach the public through entertaining adverts rather than dry service announcements. Polling showed the effort was beginning to change the negative discourse. For the first time since the upgrade was announced, the gap between positive and negative was beginning to close. With one month until the launch, Seton hoped the numbers continued their shift.

The final message Philip watched, with more than a little surprise, was from Dr. Sonje Nysgaard. One of the researchers who had aided in the development of the new SID, he had not spoken with Nysgaard since the chip's final analysis had been completed nearly six months prior. Every bit as Scandinavian in appearance as her name implied, Sonje Nysgaard would have found equal success wearing couture on a Parisian runway as she had with a white coat in a lab. Perhaps fearing her remarkable beauty detracted from her prestige as a scientist, the doctor wore her blonde locks in a tight bun at the back of her head. A hairstyle potentially severe on others, only worked to highlight the crystal blue eyes and defined angles of her face.

"Herr Seton," her image began, "my apologies for intruding on you during what I am sure is a very hectic time. But, I have discovered . . . I have discovered, ah, that my niece will be traveling to the Americas, and I was hoping you could recommend some sights to see. She leaves shortly, ah, so if you could, please contact me immediately."

The message from the young scientist ended and Philip Seton was left with confusion. Though he had worked with Nysgaard, as well as a dozen other researchers during the new SID's development, the two had never before communicated in a social context. Perhaps more disconcerting, however, was the absence of her usually pleasant demeanor and free smile. Shaking his head with a smile of his own, Seton wondered how much of the change in Dr. Nysgaard's temperament resulted from worry over her niece travelling abroad. Even with safety records of the highest rank, some people still fretted over air transportation. With no crashes in nearly a quarter century, Seton found it difficult to understand the apprehension.

"Bera, return the call to Nysgaard, Sonje."

"Sir, we have arrived at the office. Would you still like me to place the call?"

A quick look about showed Philip Seton that not only had he arrived at the office, Bera had already navigated through the parking lot and deposited the podcar in his assigned parking spot. "No, Bera, that's fine. I'll make the call inside."

"Very well, sir. Have a good day."

As the hatch door slid open, Seton could feel the warm air of the late-summer morning against his face. Stepping from the pod, his attention was immediately drawn to the short figure that was briskly approaching from the office building's direction. If his assistant, the dour Maggie Evert, was meeting him in the lot, it only could mean the day was indeed going to be long.

"Good morning, Maggie," he said to her once their paths met.

"Good morning, sir. We just received word that the execs are rescheduling the presentation to Wednesday," the middle-aged woman informed him with a bite at her lip.

"Of course they are," Philip Seton sighed. All thoughts of Dr. Sonje Nysgaard and her niece fell from his mind as he ran through the logistical nightmare of moving the presentation up two days.

CHAPTER TWO

Dr. Sonje Nysgaard

Nothing had changed in the data displayed on the massive panel which served as the focal point of her stare. Yet each time she studied the complex diagrams and formulations, the shock of the discovery boiled anew. The discovery had been pure happenstance; a seemingly cosmic alignment of events and chance which riled her scientific mind. It had begun with a phone call two days earlier.

"What are you doing tonight?" her sister, Gretchen Nysgaard, asked as soon as the holographic digitized. Younger than Sonje, Gretchen was in her late twenties and still clung to her youthful days of late-night parties and poorly selected boyfriends. Sonje could not understand how a bright, successful third-year surgical intern failed to see the error of her freewheeling inclinations.

"I'm not going to a party, I know that much, Gretch," Sonje replied. It was barely past dawn and she doubted her sister had yet been to bed. By no means a bore, Sonje accepted, and in fact enjoyed, her marriage to her work. Whereas her sister longed for weekends to engage in one type of debauchery or another, Sonje used her brief time outside the lab for the completion of routine tasks of laundry, groceries, and perhaps a few pages in the hefty stack of scientific journals that towered precariously in her living room.

"What a surprise!" Gretchen retorted with melodramatic shock. "But, that's not what I meant. I ran into a guy I went to university with. He's an M.E. in Uppsala. Single, tall, and boring – just your type. He's in Stockholm for a conference and I told him you'd meet him for dinner tonight."

In addition to Gretchen's predilections for raucousness, she had adopted a side hobby aimed towards setting Sonje up on a string of doomed blind dates. From the "one-day-I'll-be-a-rockstar" street performer, to the "Edge-abusing junkie/artist" (though Sonje had admitted his canvases were quite remarkable), to most recently the "I-shoplift-for-the-thrill" clothing model, Sonje wished she could forget the dates her sister had orchestrated. Wanting to say no, she knew, however, Gretchen was unlikely to accept a refusal.

"A medical examiner?" she asked. "Is that Gretchen-speak for 'has a fetish for nurses?'"

"No. He spends his days surrounded by dead bodies. Which means he's used to mute stiffs . . . you're a perfect match," Gretchen snarked back with humor.

With a glance around her scantly-furnished bedroom, and a failed attempt to recall when last a man had set foot in the room, Sonje turned back to her sister's image. "What's his name? And when and where am I meeting him?"

A triumphant smile crossed Gretchen's face as she ran through the details. "His name is Alvar. There's a new restaurant in Söldermalm . . ."

After the call with her sister, Sonje made a weak effort to return to sleep. Her mind was such, however, that once active it was a losing trial to quiet the thoughts, tabulations, and figures which occupied her concentration. Surrendering to the start of the day, Sonje padded across the wood floor of the bedroom and enjoyed the penetrating heat of a shower.

The restaurant Gretchen selected had, of course, been easy to find. Profiled in last Sunday's holo-news, Rōd Sammet (Red Velvet) was the "hot spot du jour" for the high ego crowd. Her ability to obtain reservations was a testament to Gretchen's friend-of-a-friend connections to bartenders and maître d's across Stockholm. If perhaps lacking friends in positions of true power, Sonje's sister certainly could boast a network of pop culture powerhouses.

"Then you must know Dr. Jonam Lindfors," Alvar said excitedly upon learning Sonje received her doctorate at Karolinska Institutet.

"Dr. Lindfors! I had him in second year. His work in biorobotics is legendary. Half the reason I went to Karolinska was for the chance to hear him lecture. How do you know him?" Sonje asked. Once again she reminded herself to thank Gretchen for her matchmaking. When Sonje had been escorted to the table and first spied Alvar, her knees weakened at the sight. Broad shouldered and standing at six feet-three inches, Alvar Falen seemed a sculpture carved by one of the masters. Neatly groomed hair, so blond it almost appeared white, framed a masculine face of blue eyes and a gleaming smile. His hand was strong yet gentle when he had risen from his seat to introduce himself. Thirty minutes in and barely finishing their appetizers, the two had talked easily of shared interests.

"He's my father," Sonje's date informed. "My parents split when I was young and my mother changed my name to hers.

"Oh, I'm sorry."

"Don't be. It was a long time ago. It was messy at first, but as I got older they learned how to be in the same room without imagining homicide," Alvar waved off her apology with a laugh. "Now instead of complaining about her, my father complains about my 'slacking,'" he added.

"Slacking?"

"When you're the son of the esteemed Dr. Jonam Lindfors, a simple MD is considered slacking," he explained.

"Oh no," Sonje laughed for not the first time that evening.

Nodding, Alvar continued, "Oh yes! All I hear is 'What can you learn in a morgue? What great discoveries are waiting in a freezer for corpses?' In a way I know he's right. But, there are discoveries. Nothing that will get me on the cover of a journal, but there are still discoveries."

"Discovering cause of death. Which probably means more to the family of the departed than what's on this month's journal covers," Sonje intuited. To many, the conversation would likely have been considered morbid and rather inappropriate for a dinner date. For Sonje, however, the dialogue had her entranced. Outside of the laboratory, it was difficult to find those who shared her love affair with science. Those she did know (and she was aware how superficial her thoughts were) looked much like people who were having a love affair with science.

"Exactly," Alvar smiled in response. "Take this case I have on my table now. White male, thirty-seven years old, non-smoker, non-drinker, works as a foreman, no history of medical problems, full battery of testing six months ago . . . dies three days ago. For the life of me, I can't pinpoint cause of death other than a sudden myocardial infarction."

"Heart attack," Sonje translated.

"Yup, but I've found no signs of previous damage to the heart tissue, no blockages, etc. The guy was simply healthy as a horse one minute, next minute he drops dead."

Feeling the familiar bite of a mystery, Sonje then asked, "Foul play? There are poisons that could . . ."

"Tox-screen came back negative. Twice."

"Environmental factors . . . stress, panic?"

"None to speak of. His wife said they were relaxing at home. There were no issues at his employment."

"Hmm," she mumbled as her thoughts traced other possibilities. For a silent moment the pair sat across from each other, busying themselves with the last remnants of their appetizers. It was the first time since they had shaken hands that conversation seemed stalled.

"So . . . ," Alvar said, drawing out the syllable.

"So . . . ," Sonje repeated.

Hesitating, he asked, "Want to get our dinners to go and go back to my lab?"

"Yes!" Sonje answered too quickly as Alvar signaled for the waiter.

She was not sure about whom the evening revealed more, Gretchen or herself. But, Sonje, hair pulled back as she always wore it for work, latex gloves snugly over her hands, and the body of Alvar's quandary before her, could not deny that this was perhaps the best date which she had been on in quite some time. The previous men with whom her sister had set her up had certainly not engaged Sonje's mind and interest as Alvar now did.

Once their meals were packed and purchased (a request which clearly insulted their waiter), Alvar had gallantly offered his hand to steady her as she slipped in the passenger seat of his podcar. During the hour long drive, the two studied the notes Alvar had called up on the vehicle's glass front. Sonje could imagine her mother's reaction when she learned of her evening. "Last night? Oh, last night I got into a strange man's car to see a corpse." Chiding herself for the humor, she knew her overly-concerned mother would be apoplectic.

"You sure you're okay with this?" Alvar asked her as he slid open the containment unit in the lab.

"I work in biorobotics. I've seen my fair share of mangled limbs and blood. Plus, I trained on cadavers at university," Sonje assured him, though she warmed at his concern.

Without pause, Alvar gently rolled the heavy white covering down the body's torso. His respect for the deceased further increased Sonje's opinion of him. She knew of some fellow colleagues that treated living subjects with less courtesy. Working opposite each other, Alvar guided her through his initial findings, pointing out various aspects of organs that should have offered some clue to the reason for the man's sudden demise. Yet, as Alvar had attested earlier, the biological evidence failed to provide causation.

As the lab held no windows, the dawning sun crept into the sky beyond Sonje's sight. Only when Alvar mentioned the early hour did she realize how long the two had spent studying and reviewing. Triggered by the realization, Sonje caught herself in a rather unattractive yawn, which she quickly tried to conceal behind the back of her hand.

"I'm sorry I've kept you out this late," Alvar offered with apparent sincerity.

Shaking her head, she replied, "Not at all. I've had a great time."

Alvar's unassuming confidence slipped visibly for a fraction of a second. In that time, Sonje believed she saw a fleeting glimpse of the boy he had been. His awkward smile reminded her of the many boys who had vied for her attention in grade school – the sheepish grin twitching with nerves, hands in a constant fidget perfectly matching the feet that slid against one another, and of course the eyes, round as saucers caught in headlights.

"Listen," Alvar began; a slight crack marred his deep baritone. "I live a few blocks over. Would you want to grab coffee . . . or I could make breakfast . . ."

Though a rule of the opposite had been always set in stone, Sonje found herself agreeing to return to a man's home on the first date. Oh, how her mother would have fainted!

If he had been unsure in delivering the invitation, all traces of fumbling vanished once breakfast had finished and Sonje found herself in Alvar's bed. They had gently and deftly explored each other's body, slowly rising to an intense crescendo which left her gasping for breath. Wrapped warmly in his arms, the soft skin of her back pressed against his well-defined chest, Sonje drifted in a sheltered calm she had not experienced in far too long a time. Usually her mind resisted stillness. Her work always filled the empty idle moments of quiet. But, with Alvar, Sonje's thoughts were as clear and serene as the mid-morning sky beyond the bedroom window.

Shortly before noon, Alvar Falen drove her back to her home. They shared a longing kiss and made plans to dine together later in the week before Sonje slipped through the open hatch door on the passenger side. She smiled as he gallantly waited for her to enter the front door before disappearing into the stream of podcars at the end of the block.

Not surprisingly, Laris, her IFaMS unit, informed her that several messages awaited her review. Sonje was sure more than one would be from her sister, eager to receive a recap of the previous night's events. Feeling the need for a shower before facing Gretchen's endlessly interrogating stream of questions, Sonje slipped out of her dress and refreshed herself in an overly long cleanse. Though only managing a few hours of sleep at Alvar's, the shower proved invigorating; as did the dancing thoughts of future times she would spend with the man. Sonje allowed herself a few more moments to enjoy the possibilities of new romance before settling into her home office and letting work return to prominence in her thoughts. She skipped over Gretchen's messages, knowing her sibling's pestering would tarnish the golden memory of last night. Instead, she called up the case file Alvar had sent of the enigmatic man she had studied in the medical examiner's lab. Without the welcome distraction of Alvar's presence, she could let her mind delve deeper into the mystery of the other man's death.

"Laris," she addressed the IFaMS, "when was the patient's last medical exam?"

Searching the file and responding faster than any human could have, the program's voice replied, "*Patient 243-A received a complete medical examination on March 13, 2161.*"

Six months, Sonje quantified in her head. "Results of the exam?"

"*Patient 243-A was declared in higher than average health for similar subjects in his peer group.*"

"Who was the administering physician?" Sonje asked. Even if the patient's doctor had overlooked something in the man's physiology, it would not explain the lack of evidence in the cadaver. But, Sonje Nysgaard was, if nothing else, thorough.

"*The administering physician was Dr. Emil Blomkvin.*"

The name immediately caught Sonje's attention. "Laris, repeat." Again, the IFaMS identified Emil Blomkvin. The theory of the doctor passing over vital information diminished to the point of impossibility. Blomkvin was not only the top physician in Sweden, the man was nearly world renowned in the field of medicine. His considerable expertise, and well-earned fame, had made him a prime choice in the Beta testing of the new SID chip. Several dozen doctors across the globe had been selected (and well rewarded through honoraria) for participation in the program.

Six months, Sonje repeated silently. The timeframe fit.

"Laris, crosscheck Patient 243-A with the list of subjects which received the upgraded SID."

Again with remarkable speed, Laris answered, "*Patient 243-A is listed as a recipient of SID v3.*"

Those who received the new chip had been monitored for three months for any signs of biological rejection of the implant. It was an unlikely possibility, as the revised model had been based on its two predecessors, but the Global Alliance had insisted on the measure. Upon the completion of the monitoring period, the Beta version of the chip had proven successful; no adverse effects from the implantation had been reported. Statistically, Sonje knew it was likely some of the nearly twenty-five hundred subjects in the program could expire from causes outside of implantation. Alvar's patient, however, and his lack of evident causation stirred Sonje's scientifically-trained mind.

"Laris, how many of the subjects from the Beta program have died?"

"*To date, all recipients of the SID v3 Beta are active.*"

"Laris, repeat."

"*To date, all recipients of the SID v3 Beta are active.*"

Even though Alvar's patient had suffered the fatal heart attack only days earlier, the SID system was updated hourly. Any deaths in the population were immediately crossed referenced with both doctor and Peacekeeper (PK) reports. Deaths unaccounted for were investigated straightaway by a local Peacekeeper division. It was one of the many benefits of the SID program. No longer would bodies languish for days, even weeks, without the notification of the proper authorities. For a patient such as 243-A to be listed as alive days after expiring was incredulous.

Sonje instructed the IFaMS to state the time of the most recent SID system update. As intended, the system had been refreshed at the start of the current hour. Assuming a technical glitch in the system, she waited anxiously until the next update and rechecked the status of Patient 243-A. Once again, the SID database listed him as active.

Tempted to contact the local PK station, Sonje hesitated with indecision. Identity theft, a rampant problem in the twenty-first century's technological adolescence, had declined considerably over the last hundred years. True, there were still those who trafficked in the field on the black market, but even those operations were few and far between. The PKs had far more tools at their disposal to investigate such a crime, but Sonje disdained surrendering control of the mystery. The chip involved was one on which she had worked, and she felt a proprietary ownership of the situation.

Applying a scientific approach to the investigation, Sonje selected a random sample of subjects from the SID v3 implantation roster and began to crosscheck the names and respective statuses with death notices in distant locales across the world. If not for the processing power and speed of the IFaMS, the task would have required a number of people and many days to complete. For Sonje, her searching lasted but two hours. She would never understand the minority which protested the technology as an overreach of the government.

While the endeavor went smoothly, the results it produced forced a deep furrow into Sonje's brow and wracked her temple with a dull ache. Of the eighty subjects she had researched, twelve had been eulogized in their hometown holo-news. None of those twelve, however, were listed as deceased in the SID database. Unable to access coroner reports, she was forced to expand her search for any mention of cause of death. Not a common anecdote in an obituary, Sonje did manage to find three which attributed the loved one's sudden passing to a massive myocardial infarction.

"Sixteen percent," Sonje spoke to the empty office. Sixteen percent of her random selection had died, all after the three month monitoring period, and none had a status change in the SID system. A moment of extrapolation and Sonje estimated nearly four hundred subjects may possibly be incorrectly classified. Distasteful as the mathematical error was, Sonje's unease focused on the inordinately elevated mortality rate. Any substance, whether pharmacological or biorobotic, with a sixteen percent mortality rate would never have reached the public. At least not in its current formulation. The SIDs, however, were scheduled for global implantation in mere weeks.

"Laris, call Seton, Philip."

Retrieving the contact information from Sonje's records, the IFaMS unit proceeded to place the call. Unanswered, the image of Mr. Seton appeared requesting the caller to leave a brief message which he would return at his earliest convenience. Cursing the time difference between Sweden and America, Sonje began her message.

"Herr Seton, my apologies for intruding on you during what I am sure is a very hectic time. But, I have discovered . . . ," Sonje paused. Of the irregularity she was certain; however, a flicker of foreboding, the soft prickling of skin for reasons unknown, gripped her. Deciding against detailing her findings in a recording, Sonje quickly shifted to less momentous excuse for contacting the doctor. It was a decision that would save her life.

"I have discovered, ah, that my niece will be travelling to the Americas, and I was hoping you could recommend some sites to see. She leaves shortly, ah, so if you could, please contact me immediately."

Completing the message to Seton, she then instructed Laris to contact Alvar. As with the previous call, Sonje sat anxiously through a series of rings before being greeted with the medical examiner's away message. Ending the call without leaving a message of her own, Sonje quickly gathered the loose pages on which she had scribbled various details from the recent hours of research. The door to her apartment closed behind her and she heard the automatic locks as she hurried down the flight of stairs.

Her podcar waited idly in the building's parking lot. Swiping her right hand over the older vehicle's scanner, Sonje waited the brief second as the system identified its owner. As the hatch door made its vertical lift, the podcar's mechanical voice greeted her.

"Good evening, Dr. Nysgaard." Though certainly able to afford the latest IFaMS system, which integrated home and vehicles, Sonje had yet to find time to order the new unit. Like so much in her personal life, it was a task she had delayed in sacrifice to her research. She provided the address of her destination and was quickly on her way to Uppsala.

As with all podcars, Sonje's vehicle maneuvered itself through traffic with skill and precision. Though licensed to operate the vehicle manually (any driver wishing to obtain a license was required to prove proficiency in both the automatic and self-steering capabilities), it had been many years since she had truly driven a car. Obeying all speed limits, merging and yielding in safety, the pace of the vehicle was far slower than Sonje's racing pulse. Swallowing back the temptation to override the system's navigation software, she forced herself to recline and wait patiently during the hour long journey.

Stopping first at Alvar's residence, Sonje knocked somewhat aggressively at the man's door. She had tried calling him repeatedly during the drive, but still had been unable to reach him. Abandoning the home, she returned to her podcar and traveled the short distance to Alvar's employment. The night before, when she had first walked the foreign hallways of Alvar's office, excited tumbles of nerves and flirtation warmed her stomach. Now, though, the same organ was unsettled with uncertainty and worry.

As it was a Sunday, no receptionist waited at the front desk. In fact, there was no soul to be found as she made her way through the building. It had only been one date, albeit one that stretched for hours, but Sonje knew Alvar would be working tirelessly, despite the weekend. Once down in the level below the offices, she called out to the medical examiner.

Four rooms built for autopsies and freezer storage branched off from the main hall. The cloud of heady romance had blurred her memory, and Sonje could not recall in which of the rooms she and Alvar had worked. Pressing gently on the first set of swinging doors, Sonje slipped her head inside and scanned the empty room, but did not see the man. Moving to the second, and then the third room, she finally found him sitting in a chair at his desk.

"Alvar," she said, voice echoing on the sterile chamber. Slumped with his back to her, Sonje smiled as she walked towards him. *I'd be exhausted, too,* she thought, if not for the worry. Speaking his name again, with a touch greater volume, Sonje experienced a chill not attributable to the facility's low temperature. *The building was unlocked,* her mind finally noticed.

Dread was not an unfamiliar sensation. Four years earlier, when a midnight call broke her sleep, Sonje had stumbled with haste from her bed to the phone station in the kitchen. Before the tear-streaked face of her mother had even appeared, she had a witch's sense of ill tidings. Felled with a stroke, Sonje's father had been rushed to the hospital. She could recall the misery in her soul as the podcar had moved silently through the darkened streets. Not yet an hour had passed after the call had come in when Sonje reached the white building. She had missed his passing by minutes.

Now, as then, the same feelings gripped her. Her shaking hand reached out and slowly came to rest on Alvar's shoulder. Gently angling the swivel chair towards her, the lifeless face of the medical examiner came into focus. A garish red hole at his temple marred the once perfect features. The thin trickle of blood ended slightly below the sightless left eye. Not twenty-four hours had passed since she had proudly proclaimed her iron stomach, yet seeing the blue-tinged coloring of the man's skin turned her stomach.

"Oh my Truth!"

There was no inclination to alert the authorities. Years of scientific exploration demanded she reject coincidence. Stepping back with legs that barely followed her brain's commands, Sonje turned and ran up the stairs and into the fading light of dusk. Slowing to a brisk walk, too many eyes would notice and remember a frantic woman, Sonje crossed the half-block distance to her podcar.

"*Destination?*" the serene voice inquired.

It was difficult to sort the cascading thoughts and impulses of her mind. Only one option returned again and again with a trace of viability. "The airport," she shivered in response. With the podcar gliding steadily along, Sonje made arrangements for the next flight to Washington, DC. She needed to reach Philip Seton. A question nagged, though. Could she trust him?

CHAPTER THREE

Kerwen Garrott

"Thank you, thank you," his commanding voice sounded through the acoustic system. The crowd of dignitaries, their sycophantic followers, and an assemblage of media elites in attendance continued their applause. With proper humility, Kerwen Garrott bowed his head at the adulation. Seated behind him, and far more stoic than the audience, were the other members of the Council of Five. True, they brought their hands together and forced smiles onto stony visages. But, today was his day and he knew the rankled jealousy which hid behind their façades.

Though the London skies were traced with gray and streets splashed with rain, under the glass dome of the stadium the excited expectation warmed him far more than the strength of a tropical sun. And why should it not? Today he would unveil the most significant achievement of his career. The history of humanity would forever be altered, and he would not let the petty jealousies of his brethren detract from *his* moment. He let the applause stretch a moment longer before raising his hands for silence.

"Since the dawn of time, mankind has been forced to shed its own blood in order to protect that which they hold dear. Criminals and doers of evil traded on the fear of injury and death. The days when we must sacrifice life to preserve life have come to an end!" Timed to the last word, massive white sheets were lifted skyward from the venue's flanks by unseen cables revealing the security of his family's position on the Council. Row upon row, four full battalions of Peacekeepers stood motionless as another wave of cheers and applause reverberated.

The bright lights of the stadium danced along the soldiers' polished metallic silver armor. The contrast against the black plating comprising the remainder of the machines' exterior proved a powerful effect. For decades, industries across the spectrum had implemented and grown dependent on the use of robotics. Security and defense, however, had long struggled with developing an efficient bi-pedal humanoid which could function at the same level of living soldiers.

Kerwen's father, who had preceded him on the Council of Five, had begun the research in earnest when Kerwen was a young boy. Simple tasks such as climbing stairs had been the first obstacle, but by the time of the elder Garrott's death, great strides had been made in android stability and functionality. Upon assuming his father's place as head of the Family and member of the Council, Kerwen had tirelessly worked towards completing his predecessor's dream. Now, some thirteen years later, the dream had been realized. Far short of true artificial intelligence, an understandable concern of the Council, the Peacekeeper drones were programmed to identify and manage a wide variety of security concerns.

Again, Kerwen motioned the crowd to silence. "I give you . . . the twenty-second century's solution to crime! Over the coming days and weeks, models just like the ones before you will begin integration with local Peacekeeper stations across the world. In time, as production expands, our sons and daughters, our mothers, fathers, brothers, and sisters will no longer be placed in harm's way in order to keep our streets safe. Two generations of the Garrott family have dedicated endless hours and incalculable funds to actualize what once only existed in my father's imagination. The Garrotts are but servants to the world, and today I am proud to walk with you into our bright future."

The small voice of his conscience moaned at his dramatic hyperbole. One of his aides had drafted the brief comments, but it was Kerwen who added the "servants of the world" bit. Too long had the Garrott name been in the dusty recesses of the people's minds. The last war had ended decades ago, thus diminishing the need, and likewise appreciation, of global defense and security. The other four Families were an integral and daily part of everyday life, but the Garrotts were quietly slipping into antiquated superfluity. His discreetly placed agents constantly relayed the rumors and plottings of the other Families. They were moving to consolidate their power; planning a future without the Garrotts. This morning's event, however, cemented his standing on the Council of Five. It would take bold, overt action to move against him now. And as manipulative and cunning as the Families were, they preferred subtlety; machinations in shadow, rather than light.

The program ended with a simple display of the PK-drones' maneuverability, to which the crowd offered another round of thunderous cheers. Leaving the dais, the heads of the other Families grudgingly congratulated him.

"Quite the morning for you, Kerwen," Abdul-Basir Fawzan offered in a thick-tongued accent as he clasped Kerwen's hand. The Arab's family was the oldest bloodline to sit on the Council. It had been a Fawzan ancestor who had betrayed his land by working with the Americans to develop an alternative to oil fuel. A wise decision. As the shahs and emirs lost their energy influence on the world, the Fawzans grew rich in money and power and survived the Last War. Abdul-Basir's grandfather had been one of the original Five at the founding of the Global Alliance. A Fawzan had held the seat ever since.

"Shukran gazelan, Caput Basir," Kerwen thanked him. Though the blood of his ancestors had betrayed his people, Basir was the only Caput on the Council with whom Kerwen placed a fraction of trust. "It is a great day for the all the Families."

The slightest arch of a brow was the only emotion on the brown skin of the other man's unreadable face. "Yes, today you will have made many allies, which will likely create many foes." The cryptic comment provided no indication to which category Fawzan himself was placed. *A fraction of trust indeed,* Kerwen reminded himself.

Once Fawzan moved away in a rustling flourish of his white robes, Graziano De Luca bustled forward. Kerwen's slight understanding of Italian was enough to know Graziano's name translated to "pleasing" or "agreeable," but the man before him was anything but. Nearing one hundred-sixty kilos, the many-chinned shame of the Council usually only spoke to voice complaint. De Luca had adopted the Middle Eastern garb of loose fitting robes, likely to avoid the appearance of a walrus stuffed into suit. Though where Fawzan's robes were a simple white, the Italian's attire was hemmed and slashed in gold thread work. The De Luca Caput extended a bejeweled hand (Kerwen wondered how many assistants it required to force the rings onto the man's sausage fingers). Even though the plump man's grip was school-girl loose, Kerwen could still feel the slick oil of massive amounts of lotion.

Breathing through his mouth to avoid the nauseating perfumes emanating from the Caput, Kerwen said, "Caput De Luca, it pleases me to see you today. I know what a strain on your health this must have been." *If only,* Kerwen thought. De Luca still ruled his Family with the iron fist of a man half his age.

"I would not miss such a momentous spectacle, Caput Garrott," the glistening behemoth replied in broken English. "Though, truthfully, I found the event somewhat lacking in excitement."

Of course you did, you fat bastard, Kerwen sneered in his mind. De Luca's garish appearance suitably fit his Family's monopoly. House De Luca prided itself on providing the citizens of the Global Alliance with the amenities of civilization. Everything from clothing, cars, music, videogames, and prostitutes, the De Luca Family ensured the public was well occupied. There had been some grumbles on the Council when the man had introduced the narcotic "Edge." The measure had passed the Council with a one vote majority; Kerwen and another Family had thrown their support behind the plan. De Luca benefited from the sales of the illegal drug, and Kerwen benefited from Peacekeeper actions to bust the dealers. It was an uneasy alliance, but a profitable one nonetheless.

"Not everyone can have the flair you possess, Caput De Luca," Kerwen offered. Grunting a wordless reply which jiggled the thick flabs of skin at his neck, De Luca waddled off to the right, accompanied by the flock of attendants who fawned over him. Kerwen could almost see the aura of overwhelming scent slide along with the man. Distasteful as he was, the head of the Garrott Family knew the Italian Caput was harmless; vain and blindingly ornate, but harmless. Quite unlike the next two Caputs to approach Kerwen.

Yin Xian Hu was the notorious schemer on the Council. Thirty-one years old, the man's diminutive form, barely reaching Kerwen's shoulder, belied his deadly nature. Known as "The Viper," a name never said to his face, but one Hu likely coined himself, had risen to power after a string of assassinations. None of which, of course, could be linked to the man or his Family directly. With his control of the world's food supply, the Council turned a blind eye, swallowed their objections, and accepted Hu's ascension to the Five.

Bowing, or more accurately inclining his head a few degrees, Hu raised his stare to meet Kerwen's eyes. "Today is a day of many achievements," the shorter man said.

No word of congratulations, Kerwen noted. *And no indication of his feelings.* Before Kerwen had a chance to respond, the Asian fellow turned on his heel and rejoined his Family. *Seven words,* Caput Garrott muttered without voice. *Seven words and I'll spend as many days trying to root out some meaning in them.*

Last to present himself to Kerwen was the only other native English-speaker on the Council. Alexavier Cambrie was, in most things, the direct opposite of Caput Hu - tall, wide-shouldered, and possessing a booming voice which he employed with frequency. In deception and vengeance, however, Cambrie and Hu had been born of the same womb. It was Cambrie who had cast the deciding vote allowing the sale of Edge. Kerwen had yet to discover what benefit the American, whose

Family had amassed a fortune in the medical field, gained from the distribution of an illegal narcotic.

"Don't listen to De Luca," the brown haired man told him in an accent common to the western coast of his continent. "It was a well-done presentation. And a well-deserved triumph. Your father would be proud."

Smiling almost sincerely, Kerwen thanked Caput Cambrie. "It's been a long road, but worth it in the end. I think."

"Indeed. I'll be in London for a few days before returning home. Perhaps your schedule will allow us to share a meal?"

Controlling his facial muscles to disguise his surprise, Kerwen offered a non-committing reply. "The next few days will be hectic, but I will see if my assistant can find a time."

Clasping hands in parting, the American Caput's voice adopted an uncharacteristic drop in volume, yet the weight of the tone would have been impossible to miss. "Please do, Kerwen." As abruptly as the message had been delivered, Cambrie stepped back to his Family. With the American out of view, Kerwen found the penetrating stare of Caput De Luca whose brows were knitted in intense scrutiny. Close enough to have heard the brief conversation, De Luca had likely caught the unmistakably conspiratorial request for a meeting. As layers of intrigue built steadily in his mind, Kerwen Garrott could feel the self-satisfaction of the morning's success ebbing away.

Only a short break for the afternoon meal provided relief from the monotony of the media interviews. What should have been hours of feeding his ego and boosting the Family name had become a tedious task. He had agreed to a thirty-minute sit-down with each of the continental media groups. By the fourth interview, Kerwen was regretting the decision. The questions were repetitive and the beautiful but dim women that had occupied the opposite chair were incapable of understanding the complexity of the PK-drones. It was a challenge to keep his voice light while he listened to their irksome banality. He made a mental note to speak with the Office of Communications at the Global Alliance. Whoever had hired these simpletons to disseminate information to the masses needed to be reprimanded. In truth, though, Kerwen knew the source of his ire.

Cambrie and his damned request!

Shooting his aide, Alain, a silent command, the younger man swept forward and brought the final interview to a much delayed finish. "Thank you, Pashnea, but I have to steal Caput Garrott away. He is expected on a conference call." Once the reporter and her crew exited the sitting room, Kerwen sighed loudly as he loosened the narrow length of his tie.

"Remind me to never schedule that many interviews in a row again," he said as he accepted the etched glass of whiskey the aide offered.

"Yes, sir."

The warmth of the earthy liquid filled his chest and he could feel a slight relaxation in his stiff back. "I need to speak with Liam."

"At once, sir," the aide responded before leaving the room. As he waited for his chief advisor, Kerwen rose from the chair and made a slow crossing to the far wall. Glass from wall to wall and ceiling to floor, the clear window offered a calming view of the northern gardens of the estate. Dozens of lush willows, downward arching branches of green, stirred in the gentle breeze outside while further in the distance tall oaks rose proudly to the sky. Unlike the other, more manicured gardens, the North Field was largely untamed. His wife could not understand his affection for its wildness, but she allowed him the indulgence as long as the Family's entertaining was hosted in the other gardens.

Having slipped noiselessly into the room, Kerwen flinched when his advisor spoke. "You needed to see me?" rasped the balding man.

Liam Walford had served as chief counsel since Kerwen's late father had assumed the Council seat decades earlier. A second cousin (*Or was it a great-uncle?* he asked himself. Kerwen had little interest in the Family's genealogy.), Liam had a keen mind, able to see hidden snares which would have otherwise ended the Garrott line many times over. Even Kerwen did not know just how many agents, placed within the other Families and the Alliance, whispered secrets to the man. Nor did he care to know. The aging man's sources, and the information they provided, had long since proven invaluable, and that was all that mattered to Kerwen Garrott.

"Cambrie has requested a meeting," the Caput informed him as he turned from the window.

"I know."

Kerwen smiled. His father had always expressed light-hearted frustration with the advisor's seeming omniscience. "What do you make of it?" he asked.

Clearing his throat, Liam began, "It seems Caput Cambrie has twice met with Caputs De Luca and Hu. Separately, of course. All four occasions have occurred since the last convening of the Council of Five."

Kerwen mulled the information. Two meetings apiece in two months' time was not necessarily cause for alarm, but with Cambrie any moves were suspect. "Any details from those meetings?"

"Not as of yet. I am aware that Caput De Luca had eyes and ears trained to your conversation with the American."

"Yes. I caught his stare once Cambrie moved away. Do we know of his reaction?" he questioned his advisor.

"Only that he was unaware the Caput would approach you with the request. He is, of course, quite keen to hear what will be discussed when the meeting occurs. If it occurs."

Unthreatening as he was, De Luca suffered from a near debilitating need to have knowledge of even the smallest of minutiae. A private meeting between two Caputs was sure to have the rotund man's preening nature itching with curiosity.

"You don't think I should meet with him?"

Raising his palms in ambivalence, Liam explained, "Until I receive more information, I cannot say. By denying the request, you risk the offense of a very dangerous Family. In accepting the meeting, with Caput De Luca sure to gossip of its occurrence, the risk lies with raising the suspicion of the other Families."

"Isn't that always the case," Kerwen sighed in half statement, half question.

"True, but with the launch of the PK-drones, the Garrott name is likely to have already raised the hackles of the other Caputs. Today's success all but guarantees the security of the Family and the others know that. The target on your back may well have grown, and there are now more archers drawing a bow."

Laughing mirthlessly, Kerwen acknowledged, "Antiquated and poetic, but likely true in the end, Liam."

Raising the glass to his lips and letting the last of its contents play across his tongue before swallowing, he dismissed the old advisor with two commands. "Learn what you can about the reason for this meeting and Cambrie's recent dealings with Hu and De Luca. I will have to answer his request by tomorrow morning. In the meantime, begin complementing the Family guard with two companies of the drones."

A target he may be. But if Cambrie, or any of the Caputs, planned to make a move against him, they would find him to be a very deadly target.

The moon had risen twice since the unveiling; set twice since Kerwen had received the ambiguous request from Alexavier Cambrie. In that time Liam had been unable to unearth any significant details aside from Graziano De Luca postponing his return to Italy. Ostensibly the Caput wished to explore several new Mayfair restaurants. A reasoning Kerwen could believe if not for the man's knowledge of Cambrie's request. In the end, Caput Garrott and his advisor agreed security was best served by meeting with the American.

Though Cambrie had not mentioned a need for secrecy, Kerwen assumed the verbally delivered invitation served the same purpose. Liam, however, had suggested less subterfuge in the arrangements. "Caput De Luca is already aware of the invitation, and therefore we can assume the other Families have been alerted as well. Attempts to hide the meeting only work to increase suspicion," the advisor had cautioned.

En route to the Buckingham, once the seat of monarchial power in England but now one of the world's most elite hotels, Kerwen sat comfortably in the sleek black podcar. Unlike the standard pods of the working class, this machine stretched closer to the size of the antique limousines of the twenty-first century, and boasted a height which allowed a full-grown man to stand. Soft leather seats circled the perimeter of the interior; a smooth chrome and glass table was bolted to the floor at the vehicle's center. Seated with him were his eldest son and Heir, Tilden, the Family's finance officer, Morgan Sears, and of course, Liam Walford. A pair each of human and mechanical guards filled the remaining spaces. A formal meeting would have required the presence of his wife, Roslyn, but given the lack of official protocol, he had instructed his wife to remain at the estate.

Kerwen studied the fast-passing sights outside the podcar while the other three men discussed the meeting. He had always enjoyed the view of London as dusk settled quietly over the bustling city. Though his vision was somewhat blocked by the motorcade which surrounded the podcar, Kerwen still caught glimpses of the exquisite architecture of the buildings streaking past the window.

"You will remember to hold your tongue, Tilden," Liam admonished sternly. The respect with which the advisor addressed the senior Garrott did not extend to the Heir, despite his twenty-nine years of age.

"I'm fully aware of how to conduct myself," the son responded icily to the Family's chief counsel.

Breaking from his pleasant distraction, Kerwen turned to his eldest child. "Liam is right. You are to sit and observe. Don't doubt that I'll have the guards usher you home should you speak a syllable beyond 'hello,' 'goodbye,' and 'thank you.' Your presence is solely to remind Cambrie that I have five children, and all of an age to succeed me."

"Yes, sir," Tilden bowed his head in respect. He had not intended to speak in so harsh a tone to his son, but Kerwen could not manage to calm his anxiety. He eyed the bottle of whiskey at the podcar's small bar, but discounted it almost immediately. Cambrie may be boisterous, but his volume only masked the subtle venom of his mind. Kerwen needed to have as clear a head as possible this night.

"I have a man in the kitchens, but we must assume Caput Cambrie does as well. Your meals will be presented to me and I will scan them for poisons. Accept nothing that has not passed my scrutiny," Liam instructed them all, though the message was clearly meant as another reminder for Tilden.

Beyond official engagements, tonight would mark Tilden's first involvement in the actual management of the Family. A realization which further soured Kerwen's dark mood. Yes, his son had been involved in the operations of the Garrott's businesses, but there were other, less simple, duties for which a Caput was responsible. Kerwen had hoped to keep his son beyond the tangled realm of intrigue and manipulations for a few years more. But, as Liam had said, the introduction of the PK-drones had catapulted the Family from the brink of dissolution to the glaring lights of center stage. And the heat from those lights could be fatal.

"We're here," one of the guards announced. With practiced skill, attesting to the extensive military training, the guards from Kerwen's podcar as well as those from the rest of the motorcade formed a tight perimeter at the palace entrance. Liveried attendants in the employ of the facility stood at attention just beyond the wall of his armored men. Once the twin doors of the podcar slid apart, Kerwen, followed closely by his son and Liam, stepped down to the paved ground.

"Caput Garrott!" sounded the shrill voice of Reginald Norshire. A thin-framed man (Kerwen had always thought he looked more rodent than human) with sharp-nose and only small tufts of white hair above his ears, Norshire was the epitome of a bootlicker. Constantly under heel when dignitaries were present, words of praise fell from his tongue as frequently as drool from a slobbering pup. Kerwen wondered how many bruises Norshire's workers had earned in the rush to prepare for the meeting of two Caputs.

"Caput Garrott," the man shrieked again, "so good to see you this evening. It has been too long since the Caput has dined beneath this roof." Kerwen returned only the barest of smiles, lest the manager presume too familiar a connection with the Caput. Liam sidestepped quickly and led Norshire by the arm before he could impede the party's progression. Kerwen could hear Liam's hushed voice inquire about the arrangements. The manager may be a slobbering dog of platitudes, but frequent invitations to the city's premiere events ensured he was a loyal dog. He was only one of a few of Liam's sources Kerwen could name.

Attendants led Kerwen and his retinue through the Grand Hall. Guests and visitors spoke in muted voices as they gaped at the impressive procession of a Caput and his guards. Despite the grandeur of architecture, which Kerwen had studied extensively, the crowds were more overawed by his presence. Finally reaching the State Dining Room, Kerwen paused to allow servants to open the ornate double doors and announce his arrival.

"His Excellency, the Honorable Caput Kerwen of House Garrott," a booming voice echoed across the chamber. Cambrie's own entourage had already arrived and respectfully rose at the proclamation. Men in fine cut suits of black, Cambrie's personal guard, lined the left side of the room, providing an impressive contrast against the rich red paint of the walls. As Kerwen crossed the distance to greet his peer, the Garrott family guards assumed their positions on the opposite wall.

Though the monarchy of England had long since been removed, little had changed in the room's décor. A thick carpet, lush with a color matching the painted walls, stretched across the dining hall. The high ceiling was embellished with moldings of soft cream and gold, forming intricate designs which awed the eyes. Two marble hearths filled the room with the warm glow of well-constructed fires, and reflected their dancing light along the high-polished wood table that sat at the room's center. Save for the old murals of past monarchs (now replaced with images of The Five), the State Dining Hall, as did much of the palace, held the echoes of its storied past.

Alexavier Cambrie, standing before the seat at the table's far end, extended his right hand in greeting. "Kerwen, very good to see you again. You remember my cousin, Erroll."

"My pleasure, Alex. Yes, of course. How are you, Erroll?" Kerwen said, shaking each man's hand in turn.

"Very well, Your Grace," the man replied. Erroll Diadem, an imposing figure in his late forties, served the Cambries in a role similar to that of Liam Walford – chief advisor and Family spymaster.

Kerwen was slightly jarred by the absence of additional Cambrie dignitaries. Having brought his son, Liam, and Morgan Sears, he wondered if the act would be seen as a show of strength or cowardice. He would have to closely observe Cambrie's tone and mannerisms and adjust his own to compensate if it was the latter. Placing the caution to the back of his mind, Kerwen reciprocated with his introductions, before taking his seat opposite the American Caput.

In a ballet of silent synchronization, tuxedoed servants quickly filed out from the kitchen and began placing pieces of fine china laden with food before each of the seated men. Kerwen cleared his throat gently as he saw Liam attempt to rise. A subtle shake of the head delivered a wordless instruction to the advisor. Scanning for poisons now, with Cambrie present with but one retainer, would only serve to mark Kerwen as overly paranoid. Liam's scowl at the change of plans expressed his concern.

"I'll seek no insult if you wish to have your man test for poisons, Kerwen," Cambrie projected. "I'm told his devotion to Garrott security is quite thorough."

"Ah, yes," Kerwen laughed. "Liam's nose for foul play is but one of many skills which endears him to the Family." *Read what you will into that, Cambrie,* he added in thought.

"Such a man is to be cherished. I often find myself with too few. If ever you wish to change employment, Mr. Walford, the Cambries would be honored."

"Thank you, Your Grace. But, I have served the Garrotts my entire life and I am too old now to learn a new Family," the spymaster replied coolly.

Lifting a fork to his mouth, the American replied, "Well said, sir."

As the gathering dined on the appetizers, intermittent conversation passed smoothly across the table; with much of the discussion focused on the launch of the PK-drones. Kerwen spoke vaguely of the specifics as he savored the Gleneagles Pate before him. The slightly chilled pate of smoked fish, salmon, trout, and mackerel held soft hints of basil and was accented with crisp cucumber slices. It was his favorite dish at Buckingham and Kerwen smiled thinking, *If I'm to die by poisoned food, this would be the last meal of choice.*

The servants soon returned and removed the empty plates from the table. While they waited for the main course—thick cuts of roasted lamb in dark gravy with servings of root vegetables—Kerwen, Cambrie, and their Family dignitaries sipped wine from crystal goblets. Though the other Caput drank deeply, and grew louder with each refill, Kerwen took only the occasional swallow.

"I hear you have been enjoying the company of that Hollywood starlet, Master Garrott," Cambrie addressed Tilden. "What is her name, Erroll?"

"Isla Carene, sir."

"Yes! Isla Carene. Quite the beauty she is. Though given her profession, I assume conversation is a struggle," Cambrie joked before taking another long draught.

Though he had not heard of his son's dalliance, Kerwen immediately saw the rising tension in the Garrott Heir. Thus far, Tilden had adhered to Liam's prohibition against speaking. "Conversation is an intrigue of older men. Don't you think, Alex? Perhaps before the servants return, you might engage in the conversation you wished to hold this evening?" Kerwen supplied before his son could speak.

Turning his eyes to Kerwen, Cambrie studied the man for a few seconds before answering, "So, the time for business is at hand?"

"Unless this invitation was purely social. Which given your recent visits to Hu and De Luca, one might think you have a new interest in socializing with fellow Caputs," Kerwen said as he studied the other man's reaction.

The thin line of a grin was the only trace of emotion he could read. Gesturing dismissively to Liam, the tall Caput spoke with a hint of amusement. "Your man is truly skilled to learn of such visits. But, you are right. This is not a social call. So, here it is – Hu is moving against De Luca."

Kerwen had to work quickly to mask his shock. He had expected Cambrie to propose a business deal or partnership of some sort, or perhaps Kerwen's support in an upcoming Council vote. Certainly not the announcement of one Caput seeking to oust another. Maneuvering amongst the Families was an open secret, a shadow sport all accepted but none openly acknowledged. To do so technically fell under the auspice of treason. Even Cambrie's foreknowledge of such an event could bring disaster to his own Family.

Stalling for time as his thoughts veered in many directions, Kerwen said, "That's a bold accusation."

Shrugging with an air of negligence, Cambrie simply stated, "But a true one."

"And why are you telling me this?"

"Two reasons. First, your cooperation would ensure success. Second, insurance for me," the dark-haired American told him.

Was that a hint of a smile? Kerwen wondered.

"The Viper, among many things, is determined to consolidate power among The Five. He is not foolish enough to think to rule completely, but he does believe the Council can survive a one member reduction. But, the man is equally fickle. The Garrotts were his first target. Forgive my saying, but until late your family had a rather weak position among The Five. The introduction of the new PKs, however, has shifted Hu's attention to De Luca. The fat Italian is now the weakest of us. His monopoly is vast and rich. Hu approached me, thus my meetings with him, to work with him to remove De Luca. If you also joined our plans, De Luca can be defeated and his monopoly split among us."

Kerwen stole a glance towards Liam, but his advisor kept his head slightly bowed. *Choose your words carefully,* Kerwen warned himself. "And insurance for you?"

"Ah, yes. While the prospect of annexing a share of the Italian's interests is tempting, I do not trust Hu. He is as likely to honor my alliance as he is to send an assassin to slit my throat. A third party, namely the Garrotts, reduces the risk of a Viper double-cross. I'd rather take a third and live, than half and die. Hu wouldn't dare move against three families at once, nor does he have the power to do so."

As the words of treason hung in the air, servants returned to the State Dining Room with the main course. *I either join in treason, or risk becoming Hu's next target,* Kerwen quietly assessed. *The Viper is unlikely to accept my refusal now that I know of his plans.* Looking at the dish of finely spiced lamb, he pondered the animal's final moments.

How blindly it must have followed the butcher to the slaughter!

CHAPTER FOUR

Milo Chance

The presentation, a holographic projection filling the entirety of the small stage, had droned on for the better part of an hour. It had contained little information Corporal Milo Chance had not already studied, and studied again, over the past month. Already disgruntled with his selection for the program, he bristled further due to the time wasted during the presentation.

"The brass sure do like their ceremonies," Harrison Peters muttered at his left. Milo knew little of the man from a station in a neighboring city, save for sharing a similar rank with Milo. And, that Peters evidently mirrored his impatience.

"Any chance they can to get in front of the cameras," CPL Chance said in a voice meant only for Peters.

The pilot program had been announced several months earlier. Initially accepting volunteers, his commanding officer had been forced to select participants once it was clear no one on the force was stepping forward. Milo could still recall the pity in the eyes of his squad when his name had been drawn. True, they had slapped him on the back and joked in good nature, some even going as far as congratulating him, but he knew the thoughts the actions hid. Better him than me.

Since early in his youth, Milo had dreamed of joining the Peacekeepers. While others enrolled as a way to escape broken homes, poverty, or criminal penalties, he had enlisted with a clear sense of duty. His middle-class parents could not understand the decision, but they did not withhold their support. Five years in uniform, Milo had settled into a pleasant routine, formed strong bonds with his brothers and sisters in arms, and not once had he regretted his career choice. Until, of course, the morning his CO had drawn his name.

The latest military advancement from House Garrott, the PK-drones were seen by the public as the next logical measure in twenty-second century law enforcement. For the PKs, the artificial soldiers represented future lay-offs and unemployment once the machines were mainstreamed into the force. Why pay the yearly salary of a human when you could purchase a PK-drone for a one-time fee?

"Finally!" Peters's voice broke through Milo's thoughts. While his mind wandered, the production had concluded. With obligatory acceptance, he rose with the crowd and brought his hands together in half-hearted cheer.

A small reception followed the presentation, though unlike the other PKs, Milo filtered out of the hall and sought the seclusion of the station's squad room. He was expected to present himself for interviews with local press, but he wanted a few minutes alone before forcing a smile on his face and speaking insincere words of his excitement and enthusiasm. On any given day, the squad room would have been bustling with activity. With the so-called festivities one floor below, Milo was able to slip into a seat, close his eyes, and ready himself for the bombardment of media questions.

"Good morning, Corporal Milo Chance."

Startled by the intrusion, Milo raised his head to find the black and silver form of a PK-drone standing at the doorway.

"What do you want?" he asked the machine.

"I have been assigned to serve as your partner in the Peacekeeper Force of Philadelphia," the words emanated from the mouth-less metallic face. "Our presence has been requested in Room 134 for an interview with the Philadelphia Ledger."

As much as he detested this new development in his service, Milo could not deny the impressive sight of the drone. Though the voice held a hint of mechanics, the rest of the machine could easily pass for human. Armored as a cross between ninja and soldier, the PK-drone stood at the height of an average male, with its metal shell cut to mimic the musculature of a well-defined human. While the majority of its exterior was sleekly black, chest, shoulders, shins, and forearms held bright silver overlays which reminded Milo of medieval knights. The head was helmeted; more silver than black, with a five-centimeter wide rectangle of red stretching across the "face" at eye level.

"Yeah, I'm coming," Milo sighed as he lifted himself from the chair. "So much for a quiet moment," he muttered inaudibly.

"My apologies for disturbing you, Corporal Milo Chance."

Damn, Milo blinked. *It could hear that?* "You don't have to use my full name and rank every time you speak to me," he instructed as he approached the drone.

"My apologies. I will update my programming to address you as Milo."

"Only my mother calls me that. Chance is fine. And don't apologize in every sentence."

"Your instructions have been registered, Chance. My programmed name is Godwin," the drone informed him as it extended a hand in greeting.

Milo looked down at the outstretched hand, and reluctantly he met it with his own. An unnerving shiver passed through him as he felt the strength of the machine's grip.

Sleep had been most welcome once Milo returned home after the interviews at the station. Though most of the reporters' inquiries had been directed to the drone, Milo felt he had talked more that afternoon than he had in a month. How did he feel about being chosen for the program? What was he most looking forward to in working with a PK-drone? How did he think it would benefit the city? The questions seemed repetitiously endless; each reporter asking them in different variations. By the end, the rote responses fell from his lips without thought. He wondered if he had sounded as programmed as the drone.

With a reheated plate of take-out leftovers, Milo sprawled himself on the living room couch. The apartment was small, consisting only of three rooms, but he found the space adequate to his needs. He could not rationalize paying higher rent on a larger place when most of his waking hours were spent at work. The one indulgence he did allow himself was the investment in a comfortable bed and the latest in entertainment technology.

"Holoset on," he spoke to the empty room. Obeying the verbal command, the IFaMS unit activated the system. Barely visible projectors attached to the walls sparked to life and digitized the three-dimensional image of the local evening news. Milo moaned when the image dissolved into an interview he had completed a few hours earlier. Directing the IFaMS to one of the sports channels, he began to eat as the Phillies game unfolded before him.

His parents had questioned the extravagance of the holoset, its platform consuming most of the living room's floor space, but Milo enjoyed every inch his credits had purchased. The life-sized figures of the players on the field allowed him to immerse himself in the game.

At the end of the sixth inning, with the Caracas Ganadors up by five, Milo retrieved another beer from the kitchen. A personalized advertisement, touting the new De Luca sedan podcar (and the reasons Milo simply had to buy one), greeted him upon his return to the couch.

"With seating for four, the Cenaro is the perfect automobile as you begin to plan a family, Milo," the saleswoman's enticing voice implored.

"You're a bit behind," he said sullenly. Not long after he had proposed to his girlfriend, the ads had transitioned from appealing to a twenty-five year old bachelor to those supposedly essential to a newly engaged man.

Julia, tears rolling down her cheeks, had returned the ring to him only yesterday over dinner. Clearly, the commercials had not yet synthesized the end of his year-long betrothal.

He had sensed at the onset of the meal that Julia was distressed. When she had begun to discuss the long hours he spent on the job, a continuing thorn in an otherwise smooth relationship, Milo knew the end was at hand. Each time the argument had arisen in the past year, he had made sincere attempts to cut back his hours. But, without fail, after a week or a month, the squad saw more of him than Julia did.

"I love you, Milo," she had told him in the pained voice of the brokenhearted. "You know that. But, I can't plan a future with someone who is never around."

He had only nodded in understanding. In the past, he had assured her of change, but the guilt of disappointing her had grown too heavy. They both knew he assigned greater priority to his work than any other part of his life. And each had finally come to accept it. He had watched with silent inevitability as Julia slipped the diamond from her finger, placed it on the table, and left the apartment. The memory of her departure replayed in his mind as the baseball game resumed.

"And we're back as the Phillies take the field. It's going to be difficult for them to make a comeback . . . ," the announcer postulated.

Milo took a deep drink from the bottle.

"Do you have hobbies, Chance?" the drone asked as Milo steered the patrol pod along the congested morning traffic of downtown Philadelphia.

"Do I ha . . . ? Yea, I have hobbies. Why?" he responded. Two hours into their first shift together, Milo was already mentally updating his resume. Or at least he tried; his heavy head ached with a hangover.

"I am programmed with a wide variety of information beyond law enforcement. Knowledge of your interests will better equip me to engage in conversation."

"I'm not much in the mood for conversation," Milo replied flatly.

Unrelenting, the machine continued, "It is my understanding that Peacekeeper partners routinely engage in conversation to assuage the monotony of patroling."

Turning onto a side street infamous for Edge trafficking, Milo retorted, "Human partners do that. Not drones. And people don't drop words like 'assuage' in normal conversation."

"Your personnel file lists your intelligence quotient as one hundred thirty-three. Such a score places you in the category of gifted. If you would prefer, however, I can downgrade my speech capacity to a lower level."

As it was most mornings, Lugar Street held the usual array of criminal personalities. The patrol pod's sensors scanned the SIDs of the various people milling about and scrolled the list across the lower section of the glass windshield. Milo was quite familiar with most of the names; having repeatedly busted many on different occasions. The drone's words, however, cut into his study.

"You know my IQ?" he asked incredulously.

"Yes. The contents of your personnel file were uploaded to my system once I was assigned as your partner. Do not worry. The file is protected as confidential and I am unable to discuss the information with unauthorized personnel."

They left that part out of the brochure, he groused. Uncomforted by the drone's assurance of confidentiality, Milo wanted to inquire what other personal information his new partner had been programmed with when the name he had been searching for appeared on the display.

"Alright, it's business time. But, we're gonna talk about my file later," Milo informed the drone. Directing the patrol pod towards the left side street curb, he tapped his finger on one of the control panels and the driver side window slid horizontally.

Banhen, the street name for Esteban Siler, stood at the center of a small grouping of teens and young men. Likely, most of those surrounding him should have been in school, but Milo ignored the infraction.

"Looks like you're up to no good, Banhen," Milo called out from the cruiser, causing the street tough to emerge from his followers.

The stretching white skin of the puckered scar that marred the right side of Banhen's face, a result of an abusive father with a fetish for pyromania, had earned him the nickname of the Chinese word for "fire." The damage, however, had not prevented a rising career in the criminal underworld. Shorter than Milo, Banhen's coloring and features were an indicator of the many ethnicities which comprised the man's genes. The young man wore the current gangland fashion of a leather bracer, marked with identifying colors, tightly secured to his right forearm.

"Hey, man, why you always thinking I'm into some shit?" Banhen replied as he walked towards the patrol pod. His accomplices eyed the vehicle warily.

"How many times have I busted you?" the corporal teased dryly.

"This month?"

"Exactly," Milo answered.

Resting his forearms against the window frame, Banhen peered over to the drone. "Shit man, you got yourself a robo-pig." Seemingly within minutes of the announcement of the PK-drone's development, the street had developed the slur.

"Harassment of a Peacekeeper is a violation of Article Four Section D of the Global Alliance Security Charter. Conviction of such a crime is punishable with a minimum three-year sentence," the drone warned from the passenger seat.

"Meet Godwin," Milo laughed. "My new partner is real strict with the protocols, Banhen. You better watch yourself." Lowering his tone, he added, "What'd ya got for me?"

Keeping his one functioning eye on Milo's partner, the drug runner shared his new information. "Word's been Muerte is using an abandoned house on South Main. Least that's what I heard two days ago. He's got his usual troops with him."

Muerte was one of the chief kingpins in the city. Cruel to the point of sadistic, the drug lord's reputation had kept him safe from loose tongues. Milo had seen the man's most recent vengeance when one of his exes had talked to the PKs. Muerte had personally skinned the girl's face from neck to hairline. Even with advanced medical treatment, her face was a ruin. Unable to deal with the disfigurement, she had hung herself in the hospital. Milo knew the danger faced by those who turned on Muerte—which made Banhen an invaluable asset.

"Address?" Milo asked.

"239."

"All right. Keep your nose clean," he told the young thug to end the conversation.

Straightening from his lean, Banhen stretched his arms in a gesture of innocence, saying, "You know me, man. I walk the narrow."

Slowly driving the cruiser down the street, Milo instructed the computer to transfer two hundred dollars to Banhen's SID chip. Upon hearing the direction, Godwin asked, *"Esteban 'Banhen' Siler is an informant?"*

"That he is," Milo answered.

"His file does not reflect such status."

"We're pretty sure some of the big-timers have moles within the PKs," he explained to his partner. "For protection, most of the informants we use aren't listed in the system."

The drone remained silent for the minutes-long drive to South Main Street. Though most leads ended cold, Milo continued to hope a break in the pursuit would eventually materialize. Muerte had eluded the PKs for the better part of three years; leaving a trail of bloodshed throughout Philadelphia. Like most of the underworld chiefs, he had been able to afford the illegal removal of the SID implanted in his hand at birth. The PKs were eager to collar Muerte, not only to reduce the traffic of the instantly addictive drug Edge, but also for the information the sadist could provide. Somewhere in the darkest recesses of the black market, a man specialized in the removal of SIDs and identity replacement. Nameless and faceless, the PKs had unearthed only the faintest whispers of his existence. But, Suspect X, as the department referred to him, sat atop the list of the city's most wanted. Rookies and gnarled veterans alike fantasized of his apprehension.

Turning onto the street of their destination, Godwin broke his mute companionship. *"You intend to investigate the location the informant provided without backup?"* he asked.

While the drone was extremely advanced in many areas, Milo also understood the machine's naiveté in the knowledge and instincts only years of field work could provide. "By the time we hear about one of Muerte's hideouts, the place has been empty for two or three days. We'll search the house, tag and bag some evidence and hope he left something helpful behind. Besides, I've got a super soldier for a partner. How much more backup do I need?"

"Your tone suggests sarcasm," Godwin interpreted.

Ignoring the comment, Milo studied the console. The cruiser's sensors detected no SIDs present in the dilapidated building. *Which means nothing,* he quietly understood. Both driver and passenger door panels rotated open, allowing the pair to step from the patrol pod. Not surprisingly, Milo found the street devoid of human activity. Located in the city's most derelict area, residents had steadily left the neighborhood over the past decade in favor of the newer, more cost-efficient homes and apartments across town. The municipal government had debated plans in recent years aimed towards rebuilding the area, but red tape and self-interests had derailed the project. The result created a hotbed for squatters and the crime they attracted. Instinctively drawing his sidearm from its holster, Milo climbed the concave concrete steps leading up to the three-story home.

Beyond the front door, unsurprisingly unlocked, he found a hodgepodge of trash and debris. Tell-tale signs of graffiti vandals adorned the faded blue walls. Milo recognized several gang symbols amidst the various tags and impromptu artwork. His eyes scanned the markings for the skull logo of Muerte and his crew, but failed to locate the mark. The floor which stretched the length of the railroad-styled dwelling was littered with containers and bags from local fast-food eateries.

Though he did not expect to stumble upon the kingpin himself, Milo kept his service arm ready at his side. He may have snarked about the drone's presence, but the corporal admitted a sense of security with the machine closely following his steps. As many times as he declared he had joined the PKs out of a sense of duty, the adrenaline rush of being in the field, tracking a murderous drug-trafficker, exploring abandoned homes in dangerous neighborhoods, had addicted him the first time he'd donned the uniform.

A short search of the first floor offered no indications Muerte had recently used the home for a temporary base of operations. With two more levels to search, Milo began the climb up the wooden staircase. Several of the horizontal boards were missing, forcing him to stretch himself into a forward lunge to reach the next available step. The second story consisted of a half dozen small rooms; some still containing bedroom furniture and rodent-chewed mattresses. A small bathroom connected two of the rooms, and another was located in the master suite. It was in the latter sleeping quarters Milo noticed discrepancies. While the floor was largely covered in trash, the uncluttered areas of the wood floor held no trace of the dust which had accumulated in the other sections of the house. Squatters did not typically clean a shelter before occupying it; caring more for the roof above their heads than the tidiness of the interior. Stooping, Milo ran a finger across a floorboard, collecting the barest hint of dirt.

"Looks like Banhen was right," he told the drone. "The garbage in the room was cleared out and replaced once Muerte was done here."

"In an attempt to hide his presence," Godwin added.

Impressed with the mechanical PK's deduction, Milo affirmed, "Exactly. But, it's tough to put back years of dust. Do a scan for fingerprints, Godwin."

Milo's partner nodded his metallic head and began to slowly walk the perimeter of the room; passing his "eye" over each wall and piece of furniture. As he waited, the corporal rifled through some of the rubbish on the floor. Burger wrappers, chicken buckets, and beer bottles were in greater numbers than any real clue to Muerte's next location.

"Chance, I have identified fifty-seven distinct prints."

Milo audibly groaned at the number. Transient squatters always made fingerprinting abandoned homes an aggravating process of elimination game.

"Six of the prints belong to individuals registered as the previous residents of the home. Seven are listed in the database as realtors once having contracts to show the property. Nineteen prints belong to individuals with prior records for truancy, vandalism, and/or illegal occupation of an abandoned home. Twelve are

associated with violators currently incarcerated in correctional facilities. Of the remaining thirteen prints, eleven are linked with outstanding warrants for murder, drug trafficking, robbery, and various racketeering charges."

Unable to hide his smile, Milo felt a slight decrease in his negative emotions regarding a drone partner. What Godwin had completed in minutes would likely have taken him a handful of hours. "Those last eleven are our guys," he said to the drone. "Who are the other two?"

"One is a woman with three arrests for prostitution."

"Muerte's got himself a new girl."

"The final print belongs to Benjamin Hopkins, a physician at Philadelphia General Hospital. Dr. Hopkins has no criminal record."

A doctor? Milo thought. "How old is that print?"

"Based on the fingerprint's electrical charge and the oil penetration into the wall's surface, it is likely the print was left within the last two to five days," Godwin delivered.

While not an exact science, the technique of fingerprint dating using an electrostatic charge had advanced tremendously since its initial discovery in the early twenty-first century. Continued development of the technology had stalled once SID chips allowed for a more rapid identification system.

What was a doctor doing here with Muerte and company? he asked silently. The physician could have been a victim of Edge addiction; Milo had seen the drug ravage the highest and lowest members of society. *But Muerte doesn't deal with individual users,* Milo reasoned, *he operates large scale sales.* Hopkins could be in the drug lord's service, though; patching up Muerte's minions when the need arises. Either way, the man was a living link to Muerte and therefore warranted a visit.

"All right, Godwin, I think Dr. Hopkins has some explaining to do," Milo said.

The smell of the sewer was nearly unbearable, despite the thick fabric which covered his nose and mouth. Granted the location was temporary, but the stench only added to his frustration with being forced underground. Red-eyed rats scurried near his feet; most kept a safe distance, but occasionally one ventured too close. The soles of his boots were slick with the blood and gore which had erupted from the rodents when he crushed the life from them. It was a small, but satisfactory, diversion as he waited for his guest to arrive. Based on the whimpering echoing through the tunnel, the wait was nearly over.

Only minutes later, two men dragged the struggling figure into his sight. Even gagged, the scarred young man strained his voice in a muffled pitch of screaming. He could not truly blame him—facing death could be terrifying. But, the struggling fellow his men restrained surely knew death was still many painful hours away.

"Remove the gag," he ordered.

Once the man's mouth was free to form words, humiliating pleas gushed forth. "Muerte, please, man, I didn't say shit! I swear! I would never rat on you, man!" As he begged, a dark wet stain spread across the front of his pants.

"I've heard differently." Motioning to an unseen shadow, Muerte continued, "They say smell is the strongest sense for memory. A familiar scent can bring back memories from years past. Tell me, Banhen, do you remember the scent of your own burning flesh?"

From the darkness, one of his men emerged and handed Muerte a welding torch. As the steel blue dagger of flame cast its eerie light on the kingpin's face, Banhen's eyes grew wild and wide. For long hours, hellish screams rang through the tunnels of the sewer.

CHAPTER FIVE

Philip Seton

    The hollow ache in his stomach reminded him he had worked straight through lunch. Much of Philip's morning had passed in an exhausting blur from the moment his assistant, Maggie, greeted him in the parking lot. Looking at the other faces in the room, it was clear the rest of the team shared his fatigue. Philip had tried to start the morning off with a pep talk, but the words rang false, even to his own ears. Losing two days of preparation for the presentation nearly bordered on catastrophic. Regardless, his team needed a momentary reprieve from the chaos.
    "Okay, folks, let's break for lunch," he addressed the room. "Take an hour, get something to eat, refresh yourselves." From their responses one would have thought he had announced the end of a decades-long war. Tired feet shuffled flagging bodies out the conference room doors. Collapsing into the high-backed, leather executive chair, Philip counted silently. He had not yet reached four, when the ever-attentive Maggie stepped into the room.
    "Maggie, if I survive this month . . . hell, if I survive this week, I'm going to get myself very, very drunk," he sighed while he rubbed weary eyes with the heels of his palms.
    "You keep this pace up and you're not going to make it to the end of the day without a breakdown," she admonished him. Though she was but a few years older than he, Maggie Evert carried herself with the matronly rigidity of a boarding house schoolmarm. Her clothing, tastefully demure and well-tailored, was usually of a dark hue which added to the effect. Prematurely graying, she had rejected the dyes and coloring most other women would have eagerly applied to hide the signs of aging.
    Philip had hired her as his assistant when he began his career at Global Tech, the government division overseeing SIDs. Over the last eleven years, Maggie had done more to keep him employed than any of the people on his team. A sharp mind combined with a seemingly preternatural sense of predicting his needs, often long before he even knew what he needed, had made Maggie much sought after by other executives with the company. As loyal as she was irreplaceable, she had rejected all attempts to poach her from his office.

"I'd welcome the hospital stay," he joked.

"Hospital? The launch is a month away. They'd move a bed into your office and stick an IV in your arm," Maggie returned in kind. Sadly, Philip thought the comment was all too true. "Your wife called to remind you about dinner, but I told her about the change in dates for the presentation so she knows you're likely going to be late. And I have a Dr. Nysgaard waiting for you."

Nysgaard again, Philip thought. All intentions of returning her earlier call had fallen from his mind once the work day crashed over him. He hated putting her off again, but a sightseeing niece of an acquaintance was currently quite low on his priority list.

"Tell her I'll call back later."

Shaking her head, Maggie responded, "Sorry, I mean she's waiting here, in the lounge."

"Dr. Nysgaard is here?" Philip asked with bafflement. He did not recall a mention of being in the states in her message.

Nodding in affirmation, his assistant added, "And looking worse for the wear. She insisted on waiting until you were free. Should I bring her in?"

"Yes, please," he replied.

Maggie ducked out and returned shortly with Dr. Nysgaard. Philip immediately saw his assistant's appraisal of the doctor's appearance had been overly diplomatic. In past dealings with the woman, Philip had known her to be acutely polished and refined. The woman before him now was attired in rumpled clothing; previously fresh creases sagging with extended wear. A failed attempt at styling her hair was noticeable in the loose strands falling sporadically from a ponytail. Most disconcerting, however, were the dark circles of worry and exhaustion beneath her usually sparkling eyes.

"Sonje," Philip addressed her as he rose in greeting. "Good to see you again. Though, this is quite a surprise. I didn't realize you were in the states when you called." When she met his extended hand, he felt a cold tremor in the delicate grip.

"I wasn't," she answered. "I'm very sorry to show up so unexpectedly, but . . . ," she paused as she glanced hesitantly towards Maggie who waited in the doorway, "but there's an urgent matter I need to discuss with you . . . privately."

Philip met his assistant's eyes and tilted his head slightly in dismissal. Once the door closed behind Maggie, he offered the doctor a seat.

"Please, sit. Can I get you any . . ."

Cutting him short, she said, "Perhaps we could go outside to speak."

Her tone indicated the words were more demand than request. *So much for lunch,* he thought dejectedly. Philip led them out of the conference room and through the halls to the elevator. During the six-floor descent and the short walk across the marbled lobby of the building, Dr. Nysgaard remained mute. Though her voice was idle, the woman's eyes furtively scanned each passerby until the pair finally exited into the thick summer air.

"Is everything okay with your niece?" Philip probed.

Confusion crossed her face briefly before she replied, "I don't have a niece, Philip. I couldn't risk explaining in the message. Something's happened . . . I've discovered something."

"And you're sure it's all linked to the SIDs?" he asked her. They had spent the last half-hour on a nearby park bench huddled in quiet conversation. With vigilant eyes, Sonje Nysgaard had detailed the events of her previous two days. The tale was fantastical, and he would have dismissed it easily if any other had shared it. The doctor, however, possessed a brilliant mind and Philip had never known her to be less than scientific in her conclusions.

"It's the only common variable I can find," she told him. He could see she had already traveled the same road of doubt down which he now stumbled. Her body language and tone held a sense of desperation. *Desperate for me to believe her?* he wondered. *Or for me to provide another conclusion?* "I believe the new SIDs have a defect . . . and someone is trying to cover it up."

"*If* there is a defect," he placed intentional stress on the word, "it would be discovered once the chips were implanted. No one could cover up a sixteen percent global death rate."

The slight lifting of Sonje's eyebrows forced him to admit how foolish a declaration he had made. The history books were littered with such incidents. Many terrorist attacks had been orchestrated to serve the needs of the supposedly targeted nations. Several natural disasters, earthquakes and tsunamis mainly, had eventually been attributed to the testing of new weapons of mass destruction. Even some of the viral pandemics, which had taken the lives of millions, had been intentionally developed and spread across the world. Today, people could not help but shudder at any mention of Africa – the Dead Continent.

Philip could feel the shifting click in his mind. "So what are you suggesting we do? If your friend, the medical examiner, was indeed murdered, won't the same happen to us if we talk?"

"Probably," she calmly replied. *Too calm,* Philip realized. "Any search of my IFaMS will show them what I know."

She's already accepted herself as a target, he understood. *My Truth, she believes they will come after her!* "But, who are *they*?" he asked.

"I don't know. Whoever's behind the cover-up had to program the system to ignore the deaths of the test subjects."

The heavy burden of comprehension suddenly crashed to his shoulders. "And I have the clearance to see who accessed the system. That's why you came to me."

Sonje offered him an apologetic lowering of her head. "I'm sorry. I just didn't know whom I could trust."

"How do you know I'm not part of it?"

"I don't," she said honestly. "It was a risk, a calculated one, but still a risk. But if I'm right, over a billion people will die. I had to trust someone."

Lifting himself from the bench, Philip helped Dr. Nysgaard to her feet. "All right. I need to get back. We're preparing for a Wednesday presentation to the Council. I might be able to dig around tonight without drawing too much attention. We've been in and out of the system all day as it is."

Relieved, Sonje replied, "Thank you."

"Don't thank me yet, Sonje," he cautioned. "If this is truly happening, I'm sure those behind it have covered their tracks well. It's unlikely I'll find anything. Do you have a place to stay?"

"Not yet. I came to you directly from the airport. I usually stay at the Churchill, so try me there. Otherwise, I'll call you to let you know which hotel." Philip could not help but notice the minute easing of tension in the doctor's face. *She traveled halfway around the world with this secret,* he thought, *and now that she has shared it, her burden is lifted. And placed on me.*

Maggie thoughtfully had a lunch ordered and waiting by the time Philip returned to the office. He picked distractedly at the salad, mixed greens with tender slices of grilled chicken, but his appetite lacked. The members of his team had crowded back into the conference room and were continuing their work on the presentation. Philip, interjecting only when necessary, did not doubt they sensed his drastic change in temperament. Try as he might, his mind wandered from the looming deadline and tunneled its focus on Dr. Nysgaard's revelatory visitation.

"Philip?"

Startled by the sounding of his name, the fork slipped from his hand and loudly clattered on the table. "Yeah," he replied as he tried to divert attention from his unease.

"The forecasts. Do you want to include them? We won't have more accurate numbers until after the presentation," Gregor Tarasov repeated his question. The project's assistant managing director looked to Philip with visible concern.

"The forecasts . . . yes," Philip forced his thoughts back to the present. "Leave a placeholder for revised numbers. First thing Wednesday we can drop in whatever delivery estimates come in from the shippers." Though Gregor accepted the instruction, his faced indicated Philip had not sufficiently answered the question.

The remaining hours of the workday crept along in similar fashion. Philip fighting vainly to keep his attention on the project, answering questions he had not heard, and hoping his team could compensate for his distraction. When the clock ticked to seven, he finally surrendered and ordered a halt to the day's work; surprising the team which had expected to toil well into the early morning hours. The decision marked the first time he had allowed a slackening in the rigor since he assumed control of the SID project. Moving quickly, lest their boss reconsider the pronouncement, the team hurriedly gathered papers and belongings before exiting. Gregor, however, remained.

"What's wrong?" he asked.

Imitating levity, Philip attempted to disguise his anxiety. "Nothing. I promised Beth I'd make it home for dinner at a reasonable hour. Plus, it was the kids first day back to school."

Unconvinced, the tall Russian replied, "Last month you worked through your son's birthday. Now, two days before the biggest presentation of your career you're rushing home for dinner?"

Not trusting eyes and face to hold his secret, Philip turned away from the other man and made an overlong effort collecting the browning remnants of his lunch. "The team is burned out tonight. We can pick up again tomorrow with fresh minds."

"Philip, what's wrong?" Gregor asked again with greater intensity. "Since Dr. Nysgaard showed up you've been distracted. You told Leo to delay the data from the Australian implementation."

Philip silently cursed himself for stumbling at the mention of Sonje's name. "Leo? He's not even running the Australian rollout."

"Exactly," Gregor returned, believing his point proven. "I corrected it, but you've never misspoken before. You know every name and every detail backwards. So, what's the matter?"

He understood the relief Sonje had felt once she had shared her knowledge. Philip could feel the twisting of his nerves and he had only been aware of the situation for a few hours. *And there wasn't a dead body for me to discover,* he added. Weighing the moment, knowing Gregor would not easily be put off, yet hesitant to draw the man into potentially unfounded paranoia, Philip struggled for a plausible, but vague, explanation.

"Dr. Nysgaard had some concerns with the implantation process," he explained. "I'm just running through the plans to make sure we covered all contingencies."

"What concerns? We've planned this launch for months, considered every scenario. If you want, I can run another check to . . ."

"No," Philip replied with haste. "There's no need. Listen, go home, get some sleep," he added as he moved through the doorway.

"Philip . . ."

Meeting the other man's eyes, he said, "Gregor, trust me. It's nothing."

The drive home permitted the private reflection he could not reach in the office. The distance in time, it had been hours since he had met with Dr. Nysgaard, returned the initial doubt he had experienced upon first hearing the woman's wild claims. *Perhaps this is a simple computer error,* he silently rationalized. Sonje was likely in the early stages of grief. Her friend had been murdered, after all. Maybe this was only her attempt to make peace with loss; apply reason to tragedy. Even as the thoughts shuffled in his mind, Philip could feel their hollow foundations. He would have given anything to not believe the doctor was right.

As he had on the last school day before summer vacation, his son Marcus rushed to meet Philip at the front door. A jumble of information, details about his new teacher, new classroom, new classmates, flew in a dizzying bombardment from the boy. Marcus moved from topic to topic without regard for segue or transition. Somber as he was, Philip could not help to smile at his son's enthusiasm.

". . . and Mrs. Havert said we get to pick our own topic for the science fair. I think I want to do mine on podcars, or maybe PK vehicles. Mom says that is too general, though. What do you think? We have to have our topics in by the end of next week if we want to participate in the fair. Jace already picked his – the moon mining base. But, that's only because his father is a transporter and will give him all the information. They have a whole collection of rock fragments his dad collected."

"Marcus, let your father get in the door before you attack him with your day," Philip's wife admonished from the kitchen. The youth acquiesced with a roll of his eyes.

Stepping into the kitchen, where the family's activity began and ended each day, he inhaled the pleasant aromas of a cooking meal. Pink portions of salmon sizzled in light traces of oil in a sauté pan while Mrs. Seton diced tomatoes for the salad. "Good timing," she said after welcoming her husband home with a kiss. "We're just about to sit down. I didn't expect you until later. Maggie told me about the presentation."

Removing a pitcher of filtered water from the refrigerator, Philip filled the tall glass set by his usual seat at the kitchen table. "We needed a break," he explained with half-truth.

"Bera, tell Danica we're ready to eat," Beth instructed the IFaMS as she combined tomatoes and crisp leaves of baby spinach. "Did they say why they moved up the date?"

"I've learned not to ask," Philip laughed. In his years at the company, he had grown accustomed to the unexpected whims of his superiors. Once, an entire conference had to be rescheduled at the last minute to accommodate the president of marketing's decision to extend his yachting trip. Now, Philip preferred not to seek reasons since more often than not the reasons only led to greater frustration.

With her usual aura of perceived annoyance at an interruption of her solitude, Danica marched into the room and took her seat. Philip was helping his wife set the meal to table when their elder child groaned, "Ugh, are we having fish?"

"Unless cows have grown gills," Beth replied. "And before you start complaining about dinner, you could say hello to your father."

"Hello, father," Danica said with the dry sarcasm of a teenager. Philip wondered if he had been as a great a challenge to his own parents at that age.

"Hello, daughter," he returned, trying to match her tone. "How was the first day?"

"Fine," the girl answered as she poked at the salmon with disgust.

"What about your classes?" he tried once more to draw her into a conversation.

"What about them?"

No, Philip thought, *I was never this difficult.* "What do you think of them?"

"They're fine."

Dismayed, he looked to his wife who shrugged with understanding empathy. Without prompting, Marcus jumped in to fill the gap of speech. And managed to talk for the rest of the meal.

~

Late in the night, both children asleep and his wife dozing peacefully next to him, Philip stepped softly out of the bedroom and into his study. He had decided against checking Sonje's beliefs at the office; there were always a few company owls working with the moon.

Hearing his request, Bera connected him to the office system. He accessed the command protocols for the SID verification program and found the expected long list of names. With a system as advanced as the SID, it necessitated maintenance by dozens of authorized personnel. *Finding one specific entry among thousands in the last three to six months would be nearly impossible,* Philip reconciled pessimistically.

"Bera, call the Churchill Hotel," he commanded.

Seconds later, a woman, brighter eyed than the late hour should have allowed, greeted him, "Churchill Hotel. Good evening, Mr. Seton. How may I be of service?"

I forgot to block my ID, he winced. "Ah, yes, can you connect me with Sonje Nysgaard's room, please?"

"One moment," the woman at the front desk replied before the image dissolved into the hotel's logo. Tapping his foot with impatience and worry, Philip exhaled deeply once Sonje's face appeared.

"I was getting worried," the doctor said. Since he had seen her last, Sonje had once again resumed her usually impeccable appearance.

"I didn't want to risk someone walking in at the office," Philip explained. "I'm in the system now, and there are several thousand entries. If someone is trying to hide the deaths, they'd have had to go in each time a test subject died. Give me some of the dates and I can crosscheck that with the entry log."

"I'll do you one better," Sonje told him. Within a heartbeat, the woman's files appeared on holo-platform atop his desk.

"One second." Issuing a series of verbal commands, Philip instructed the system to isolate the entry log to dates corresponding with the deaths of the patients. Even narrowed to the twelve dates, close to three hundred entries were still cataloged.

Assessing the next step for a moment, he then said, "Remove entries for scheduled maintenance." The list shrunk slightly, but what remained offered no answers.

"Anything?" Sonje asked.

"Nothing obvious."

"Try isolating entries specific to the names of the subjects," she suggested.

Relaying her recommendation to the system, Philip watched as the columns of listed entries slowly faded until only twelve posts remained. All from the same account. The hairs of his arms rose as a chill puckered his skin. He tried to swallow, as if the act would change the revelation, but a desert of disbelief dried his saliva.

"Philip . . . what is it? What did you find?" Dr. Nysgaard beseeched with worry.

It was an effort to connect mind and tongue, to speak aloud the name repeated before his eyes. "Beckett. Joseph Beckett."

Six levels above Philip, Joseph Beckett was the head of Global Tech and a cousin through marriage to the Garrott family.

"Are you sure? Can you see if he changed the statuses?" Sonje asked, trying to break through Philip's shock.

"No," he muttered. "I don't have clearance to access his entries. Sonje . . . what do we do? This is too big for us. I mean, this is a member of one of the Five Families. These are powerful people."

"Those are just rumors," she replied, but he could see the memory of her dead friend in her eyes. "Listen. Make a copy of what you found. Meet me tomorrow morning at the fountain in Dupont Circle. We can figure out what to do then."

Nodding his understanding, he said, "Okay. I'll be there at eight." Ending the call with the doctor, Philip then transferred his research onto a thin, blank holocard drive. He could have added the information to his SID chip, but his stomach clenched with the thought of having that kind of data so closely linked to him. When the brief period of uploading the files to the holocard was complete, Philip removed the device, similar in size to the now outdated credit cards of the previous century, and moved into the living room.

A small wet bar was built into a series of bookcases which lined the west wall. Hoping to ease the shaking nerves, he poured himself a generous glass of scotch. Finishing the spirit with one large swallow, he was quickly reminded why he disliked the beverage as a stinging burn expanded in his chest. He battled the temptation for another drink, knowing the second would be easier than the first, but a glance at the digital clock dissuaded him.

Entering the kitchen to place the empty glass in the sink, a confusing shift in the midnight silence caught his ear. The unseen, and typically unnoticed, hum of appliances and electricity disappeared, leaving only the true emptiness of the dark. *Power's out*, his mind realized.

His reaction was involuntary and instantaneous, a primal instinct buried in the oldest strands of genetic coding. The cool metal handle of the chef's knife, pulled from the wooden block atop the counter, was in the tight grip of his fist before the next breath. Sliding quietly across the floor of the kitchen, and then the hall, Philip knew he had little time before they came for him. *Unless they're inside already?* his mind flashed in panic. Reaching the second floor, he rushed to his sleeping wife, covering her mouth as he whispered urgently.

"Beth! Beth!" he said, shaking her awake. Roused from slumber, she blinked her eyes open and panicked when her skin sensed the hand blocking her lips.

"Shh, don't talk. There's someone in the house. Get Dani!"

The same urgency driving him was mirrored in his wife as she tossed the coverlet aside and ran to their daughter's bedroom. Philip followed behind her and slipped into Marcus's room where he lifted the boy from the mattress, careful to keep the blade from his skin. Returning to the master suite, Beth was dragging a groggy Danica by the hand.

Philip fought back the self-loathing which bubbled beneath the panic over bringing this mortal calamity to his family.

"Dad, what's going on?" both children, awake and confused, asked him. Philip weighed surrendering himself, perhaps sparing his wife and children, but opting against risking their safety on the mercy of the intruders. *They'll take us all,* his thoughts screamed.

"Philip, call the PKs," Beth suggested. How could he explain it was likely corrupt PKs invading their home? A soft creak of wood, a foot placed on an unfamiliar step, spurred him into decisive action.

He pulled his wife's right hand to his chest, he warned in a hush, "We have to take out the SIDs." Philip felt her pull back her arm in shocked revulsion, but his hold was too tight for her to break free. "I'm so sorry," he told her in broken anguish as the tip of the knife pierced her palm. Pain and astonishment prevented Beth from sounding more than a whimper. Working by the dim light from the moon and street outside the window, Philip felt more than saw the exposed chip and pulled the blood-slick device from her body.

The detection of a SID being deactivated brought a thundering of boots up the stairs. Knowing he was out of time, Philip placed the handle of the knife in his daughter's shaking hand. "Cut out your SIDs and run," he told the girl. Memory flashed the image of the holocard he had placed in the pocket of his sweatpants. He fished the slim drive out and gave it to Danica. "Find Sonje Nysgaard. Give this to her, and no one else!" He wanted to say more, to tell his wife and children how much he loved them, how sorry he was for the decisions he had made which had led to this moment, but further chance to speak was cut off abruptly as the bedroom door was violently kicked in.

Philip Seton could not see the shapes in the darkness which threatened his family. Instead, he threw himself blindly at the shattered remnants of the door, only finding the trespassers once his body crashed into them. Tumbling to the floor, he heard his wife scream out and saw three amber flashes as silent gunshots tore through the air. He had never been the strongest physically, yet his muscles flexed with predatory strength. Wrestling with the shadow below him, Philip's hands closed like a vice around the figure's throat. The other man threw wild punches to Philip's side in defense. Hands pulled at his arms, trying to lift him away from the attack. He resisted their efforts and continued the assault until the back of his head exploded in a swirl of white pain. Sense and awareness thinned into wisps of smoke to which he vainly tried to hold. White turned to empty black, and consciousness faded to darkness.

CHAPTER SIX

Danica Seton

The dream was nonsensical, at one point there were flying bears, and its confusion had still shrouded her mind when her mother's panicked voice brought about its unfinished end. The next moment was a hazy blur, being pulled from her bed, cautioned against making any sound. It was not until her father sliced into her mother's hand that her thoughts fully reached wakeful clarity. And then a new, more dire, confusion settled upon her.

Staring with terror at the knife her father had just handed her, and the holocard he had placed in her other hand, Danica battled through the questions racing in her mind. He had given her instructions, to hide, to run, to find a woman whose name was unfamiliar to her. A second away from demanding some answers, the door to her parents' bedroom split from the jamb; several splinters of wood ricocheting into her tangled hair. Her mother screamed, pushing Danica and her brother towards the walk-in closet of the master suite. The press of Beth Seton's hands, cold and shaking yet strong, spurred Danica forward into the dark confines of the smaller room. Short bursts of orange-red light briefly lit the air behind her before those hands disappeared from her shoulders.

She wanted to turn back, to reclaim the reassuring presence of her mother, but the loud rush of men storming into the bedroom sapped her courage. Danica reached out for her brother and pulled him to the far wall of the closet. Pushing aside hanger-hung dresses and overcoats, her hand found the latch to the small door leading to the crawl space above the garage. After ushering her brother through, his body rigid with fear, Danica pressed in behind him and closed the mini-door. *Hide,* her father had told her. *And run.*

"Marcus, give me your right hand," she murmured into the black. Having seen the act performed on their mother, the boy pulled away in apprehension. Danica wrapped her arms around him, confining his back to her chest. "Don't scream," she breathed the words against his ear. With no light to guide her, Danica ran her thumb across his palm until she found the barely raised skin which covered the rice-sized SID chip. The size of the knife and Marcus's struggling made the incision sloppy, yet to his credit her brother bit back the cry of pain she caused him.

Danica tried to ignore the warm wetness of his blood on her fingers as they dug into his flesh to extract the chip. The procedure completed, she turned the knife on herself and bit the fabric of her tee shirt while removing her own SID. The pain was brief, and surprisingly minimal, anesthetized by adrenaline.

Discarding the chip, Danica moved forward across the thin plywood floor in search of the drop-down stairs leading to the garage. Bare toes stubbed against the folded steps. Bending low, she spread out unseen hands and located the metal lock holding the contraption in place. A barely audible compression of air from the hydraulic pistons was the only indication the staircase had lowered. The windowless garage offered no additional light. As a child, she and her friends had often climbed and descended the steps in playful games of hide-and-seek. Now though, in a thick fog of darkness and danger, Danica's legs shook as each foot sought the next step down. The cold concrete of the garage floor meeting her soles was a welcome relief. Wordlessly, Marcus scrambled down the planks and drew close to Danica.

"When we go out the door, run as fast as you can for the trees," she told him.

"Okay," Marcus acknowledged through a tearful muffle.

Hand on her mother's podcar, Danica navigated them to the side door of the garage. Above her, she could hear the heavy feet of the men in her parents' bedroom. She knew it would not take the invaders long to find the small entrance to the crawl space. Danica held her breath as she turned the dead bolt. She could not recall seeing any signs of power in the brief moments since her sleep had been interrupted. If the power was indeed on, Bera, the family's IFaMS unit, would alert the intruders to the door opening. When the soft metallic click of the lock disengaging was met with silence, Danica said a silent word of thanks. Easing the door inward, opening the slightest crack to the world outside, she scanned her eyes for any signs of movement. Seeing none, Danica reminded her brother to remain silent and make for the trees lining the edge of their property.

"They're in the garage!" a voice bellowed from the opening in the ceiling.

"Go!" she commanded as she pulled the door fully open.

The paved driveway was hard and cold, and the slapping of bare feet running echoed against the house. Men's voices, equally hard and cold, shouted behind them. The glow of interspersed street lamps illuminated their path as they dashed for the trees. Danica heard her brother breathing in nervous desperation beside her. Stride for stride, they matched each other until pinching needles and branches lashed at their faces.

Her parents had always drilled into her mind the correct course of action in an emergency. Run to a neighbor. Run into a store. Run to someone. Her father's parting words, however, had demanded the opposite. No one else. Whatever was happening, whatever reason her family was being hunted, Philip Seton had believed only Sonje Nys-something could be trusted. Though it went against the teachings of her youth, Danica ignored the other homes in the tony neighborhood on the outskirts of DC.

Turning down random streets, cutting across various well-tended landscaped yards, Danica kept only one direction permanent – away. Several times, she could hear the treetops rustling from the strong winds of PK hoverpods searching from above. When the near-silent crafts approached, she would pull Marcus to a halt and hide behind a wide oak trunk, a metal work shed, anything near enough to keep them from view. Once, she caught a fleeting glimpse of the black metal vehicle, the stubbed wings which branched from the bulky bus-like hull pivoted and angled keeping the craft aloft with powerful streams of air. Armored troops poised for immediate action lined the open interior.

"It's a HALO," Marcus whispered beside her.

"Shh," she hissed at him. Like many boys his age, Marcus held an inquisitive fascination with the advanced technology of the Peacekeeper forces. The shelves of his bedroom displayed numerous models of military vehicles, including a replica HALO-pod, or Hovering Air and Land Operations pod. In that moment, Danica did not care about the correct name for the craft. To her its presence only signified danger.

Nearly forgotten, her hand tightened around the handle of the large knife her father had given her. If not as frightened as she was, Danica might have laughed. A kitchen knife against a squad of PKs, her thoughts calculated the dismal odds. Still, though, as the HALO continued its lingering, the presence of the blade offered some strength. Eventually, the craft moved along, and Danica and Marcus resumed their wandering flight.

Though the destination had been chosen without intent, the siblings soon found themselves entering the western woods of Rock Creek Park. Covering just over seven square kilometers, the area was a living oasis of flora and fauna abutted by urbania on all sides. Frequently used in her track team's practices, Danica was familiar with the various trails and fields within the park. Trusting to instinct, she led her brother forward, hoping the park was large enough to hide them until she could figure out their next actions.

Fearful of further HALO searches, Danica brought them to Boulder Bridge, a short expanse over a shallow stream. There was a time, decades earlier, when many such structures were a highlight of the park. Boulder Bridge, however, was now the only span that had survived both flooding and modernity.

Huddled beneath the low stone arch, the two found a small section of dry ground which spared them the dampness of the stream. The break in their running allowed Danica to feel the chill of the night air. Clad only in a thin tee shirt and loose pajama pants, she shivered from cold, fear, and confusion.

"Let me see your hand," she said to Marcus. Her own ached dully, but the bleeding had thankfully decreased to a trickle. The wound in her brother's hand proved to be less butchered than she had originally believed. After instructing him to wash the cut in the water, Danica used the knife to shear two strips of fabric from the bottom of her drawstring pants. Once his incision was cleaned and dried, she tied the makeshift bandage across his palm causing him to flinch slightly. The cold water of the stream made her wince as she saw to treating her own self-inflicted gash.

"Dani," her brother asked, speaking for the first time since fleeing the garage.

"Keep your voice down," she cautioned him gently.

Dropping his volume, Marcus continued, "What happened to Mom and Dad?"

It was one of the same questions which had raced through her mind during the brief escape into the night. The answer to which only added to her fear. Even before the appearance of the HALO, Danica had concluded the men in her home to be no ordinary intruders. The amber bolts which had sliced through the air could have only come from a particle gun – the standard issue weapon of a PK soldier. More damaging than a metal bullet, the shot, essentially a charged matter particle, would not only pierce most substances, but would also leave a devastating burn in its wake. Such weapons were forbidden to the general public.

"I don't know," she answered honestly. "I think they were taken . . . arrested." But for what?

"They shot Mom," Marcus said flatly, shock continuing to prevent emotion.

"I know."

The younger Seton sat quietly for a moment. "She's dead, isn't she?"

The charges had flown so close to Danica, the scent of the burning air still clung to her nose. Their mother's hands had simply disappeared from her back even as the glow faded back into darkness. Unwilling to confirm Marcus's suspicions, whether out of mercy for his emotions or hers Danica did not know, she simply replied, "No." Sitting together, Marcus clinging tightly, she wished her tone had held more certainty.

They spoke no more. In time, Danica heard her brother's breath steady and shallow as he drifted to sleep. The warmth his body offered kept her shivering at bay while she sat vigil in the moonlight. Her father had told her a name, and given her a holocard to deliver. Whatever danger surrounded them, Danica knew the drive held the answers. Those answers, the reason she had woken to a nightmare, would have to wait, though. While the bridge provided shelter that night, once the sun rose she and her brother had to move on, find clothing and food. But, without their SIDs, the pair was penniless.

Her school lay less than a kilometer to the southwest. With only one day into the school year, however, her locker had yet to accumulate the random articles of clothing which would have been present in a few weeks' time. She could try to find her girlfriends as they entered in the morning, but Danica wondered if they would be willing to assist a fugitive. *That's what I am now,* she realized. Even if some mistake had been made, if her father had been confused for someone else, removing the SIDS marked them as criminals. *Besides,* Danica thought, *regardless if Janey and Valen helped us, they'd never be able to keep it a secret.* She loved her friends, but she knew their propensity for gossip. And the PKs were likely to be watching the school anyway.

With that avenue of aid discarded, Danica silently pursued potential alternatives. Theft was an option she quickly discarded. Years ago, on a dare, she had tried to shoplift a bag of chocolate candies. The caper had ended with tearful apologies to her parents and the store owner who had caught her within seconds of pocketing the goods. Another dead end.

The city proper held numerous locations for clothing donations - large metal deposit boxes - to help the less fortunate. A pajama-wearing, barefoot teen and her similarly dressed younger brother, both sporting fabric bandages on their hands, were sure to stand out in the throng of morning commuters. Even if they could reach a shelter, the missing SIDs would raise eyebrows and set tongues wagging. *No,* Danica decided, *the city was out.*

Much as the park itself seemingly appeared in answer, so now did a possible means of escape materialize in her thoughts. Not a kilometer north of their location ran the Beltway, the interstate highway surrounding the DC area. The loop connected with the famed Interstate 95, the long span which reached to the northern and southern extremes of the country. A major shipping and trucking route, Danica thought sneaking aboard one of the large freight-pods might be the only safe way to escape the city. Her maternal grandparents, lifelong residents of New York City, would not turn away their frightened, and possibly orphaned, grandchildren.

She had seen movies in which stowaways managed to gain access to the typically unmanned freighters. While she doubted the actual act was as easy as the films depicted, she and her brother might be able to gain access to one while it paused at the fuel recharging station. It was a bold plan, she knew, but the possibility of getting out of DC was too tempting to resist. Unwilling to waste the protection of the night's black sky, Danica nudged Marcus awake. Mumbling incoherently at first, she felt the boy tense with fear once the memory of their shared plight broke over him.

"What . . . Dani, what's wrong?" he asked trembling.

"Shh, nothing. We're going to move," she told him. With her athletic conditioning and familiarity with the park, she knew she could cross the distance with relative speed; despite her lack of footwear. Marcus, however, while in good shape, would require a slower pace. Even so, Danica believed they might reach the interstate in less than an hour – still allowing time to gain entry to a freighter long before dawn. She explained the plan quickly; hoping the promise of safety energized him as it did her.

Checking the pocket of her pajama pants and finding the holocard still tucked inside, Danica retrieved the knife from the ground, gripping the handle in her left hand, point towards the earth. With the other, she grasped her brother's smaller hand. The contact pulsed with warmth and emotional strength. Joined together, the night seemed less oppressive, the fear less consuming, their fates less lonely.

They maintained a steady pace, halting briefly at the first sight of airborne search lights. *They're beginning to search the park,* she silently accepted as more HALO-pod mounted beams filled the sky. *Get out of the city, get out of the city,* the mantra repeated in her mind, spurring her with purpose. Another thought, however, was growing with panic inside her. *How far will they hunt us?*

Before the wondering grew incapacitating, the trees before them thinned and she saw the bright lights of the Beltway. Hulking freights and smaller personal pods zoomed along, carrying cargo and passengers to destinations unknown. Except for the searching HALOs, the vehicles traveling in the night were the first signs of normality Danica had seen since fleeing the house. A confusing moment of realization shocked her. The world had not ended when men had stormed the Seton home. This night was unchanged for everyone else. Only she and her brother had been torn from peaceful naiveté and thrust into a new reality.

For long minutes, the pair followed the interstate west, careful to keep a safe distance from unwanted eyes. Danica began to dismay when no signs of the charging station emerged along their path. Memory refused to reveal how many kilometers still separated them from their goal. *It can't be much further,* she hoped with waning self-encouragement. Marcus remained silent, his hand still entwined with hers as they jogged along. Offering a gentle squeeze of his palm, Danica wondered if his lack of speech stemmed from doubt or trust.

She estimated they had paralleled the interstate for a few kilometers before her bare feet forced a halt. In the moonlight, she saw rocks and twigs had torn the skin of her soles, opening shallow wounds now packed with dirt and blood. Without a proper bandage, there was little to be done to ease the stinging and prevent further cuts.

"How are you doing?" she asked Marcus who leaned against a tree beside her.

"My feet hurt, and I'm thirsty," he said with more fact than complaint. "How much further to the station?"

"Not much further," came her hopeful lie. *It can't be,* Danica calculated, though having already misjudged the distance, she began to distrust her own plan. "Come on. If we stop for too long, we'll just get more tired."

They toiled over another three-and-a-half arduous kilometers before finally reaching the fuel recharging station. Some two dozen freighters, varying in colors and brand logos, sat idle in the large lot, while a line of others waited for service. Men in brown uniforms handled thick cables, attaching them to the freighters' tanks for the recharging. Danica's chemistry teacher had taught them generalities regarding the power source which fueled the world's industries. Though she had passed the lesson's exam, Danica could only recall the process was similar to the PKs' particle weaponry.

Inching forward, yet still hugging tightly to shadows, her eyes searched the station for opportunity. Unseen initially, Danica's gaze fell on a stationary HALO-pod at the far right of the lot. A squad of soldiers milled about the vehicle while one of them, Danica assumed it to be the group's commanding officer, spoke with one of the station workers. Skin tingling with fear, she jerked her head back out of the soldiers' line of sight. Her breath came in heavier gasps than when she had been running through the park. *We're never going to escape,* panic screamed in her brain.

Her thoughts frantic, believing their only means to safety was now blocked, Danica found one freighter a few yards away which they might be able to reach without the PKs spotting them. Motioning to Marcus, she wordlessly relayed the objective. It was an effort to force her body to break through the icy terror. Legs and arms resisted her control, paralyzed in self-preservation. Only Marcus's soft whisper of her name allowed her mind to reclaim dominance. Trapping the air in her lungs with a clenched jaw, Danica pulled them forward and sprinted for the freighter; expecting to hear the shout of alarm with each stride.

Safely behind the vehicle, and with no alarm sounded, she immediately slid her hands along the metal surface in search of an unlocked hatch. Bay after bay, only secured doors met her probing. In her desperation, Danica failed to hear the footstep behind her until a strong hand on her shoulder spun her around.

"Hey, what are you doing?" a gruff voice demanded.

Instinctively, she shoved Marcus behind her with her right arm, while her left stretched out towards the man, threatening him with the quivering knife. She wondered how she and her brother appeared to the station worker. Even with the blade, Danica doubted they managed any believable vision of intimidation, disheveled and bloodied as they were.

Stealing a glance to her side, Danica anticipated the PKs to descend upon them at any moment. "Please," she gasped, her voice fraught in supplication.

The figure in brown studied them for a long moment, judgment weighing in his eyes. Finally he broke his stare and stepped towards the freighter. Passing his right hand over a scanner mounted on the vehicle, he motioned them towards the now-open compartment. Danica hesitated, unsure if she read his intentions with accuracy.

"It's a tight fit," he whispered, again gesturing for them to enter the opening. "She's bound for Philly. Won't stop again until then."

With the knife still directed at the man, Danica silently urged Marcus sideways. He lifted himself into the open hatch and tugged Danica to follow him. Backing her way in, clumsily positioning herself among the various emergency repair instruments and tools, she shuddered as the man stepped forward. If it was a trap, she knew she had voluntarily entered it. He made no lunge for them, nor did he call out to the nearby soldiers. Instead, the uniformed man simply passed his SID across the scanner's sensors. Danica said a silent "thank you" as the steel hatch slid closed.

CHAPTER SEVEN

Kerwen Garrott

"So you agreed?" his wife asked from the couch. Kerwen, standing at the study's window wall with a glass tumbler in hand, had just finished detailing the unsettling meeting with Caput Cambrie.

"Could I have refused?" he questioned in return as he stared into the fields. "Either decision would have created an enemy. Aligning with De Luca wouldn't stop Hu from moving against him. It would only place the Family in Hu's sights. By agreeing, we at least allied ourselves with the victor."

"Mmm," Roslyn Garrott contemplated. Unlike the other Caput`es, the honorific stylization for the wives of the five heads of the Families who were more enamored with the wealth and privilege the station brought, Roslyn was considered a near equal with her husband. As cunning as she was beautiful, Kerwen valued her opinions with greater weight than any of his other advisors, Liam Walford included. Thirty-four years ago, when Kerwen bent one knee in proposal, Roslyn had accepted with one condition. "I'll not be meek," she had warned him then. In all their years together, she had never failed to keep that promise.

Turning to his Caput`e, Kerwen pressed, "You don't agree?"

"Cambrie and Hu are dangerous enemies. But, they might prove more treacherous allies. Simply by informing you of their plans, Cambrie tangled us in a web, and he knew it. As for the Viper . . . he has earned the name well. The man has plots within plots within plots."

"We are not as weak as we were a year ago," he reminded her.

"Nor did we have as much to lose," Roslyn countered. "It's been what, fifteen years since the last war of the Families? Even Hu's recent ascension was relatively peaceful. Removing an entire Family from the Council will be bloody . . . and costly. What of Fawzan? Where does he factor in all this?"

Basir Fawzan had been one cause of Kerwen's reluctance to join in the treason. The Arab Caput was typically removed from the inter-Family squabbling. His past votes in the Council had greatly benefitted the Garrotts. Maneuvering behind Fawzan's back, especially in something of this magnitude, made Kerwen uneasy, even dishonorable.

"He won't know of it until the work is done."

Roslyn, keenly attuned to Kerwen's varying emotions, likely sensed her husband's inquietude. "And after? How damaged will that relationship be? As I said, this war will have costs – many of them unknown."

"And many benefits. I've already agreed to it, Roslyn," he said in resignation.

Her eyes considered him for a moment, then the gaze shifted to unspoken acceptance. "How will it be done?"

What other misgivings she may have had would be left unsaid. His wife was practical. The decision, for ill or gain, had been forced upon the Family and the Caput'e would not waste further discussion airing concerns with which she knew her husband also wrestled. *Asking for her hand was the best decision I've ever made,* Kerwen acknowledged.

"A company of PK-drones will be gifted to each Family," he began.

"An expensive gift," Roslyn interjected. While not a serious hazard to the Family's wealth, the "donation" of four hundred drones would cost billions.

"Yes," Kerwen agreed before continuing. "One of the drones will be outfitted with a compressed nuclear device. De Luca will likely have the drones scanned for such a thing, so the bomb will be placed in one given to Hu. A meeting will be called between De Luca and Hu, at which time that drone will be swapped into De Luca's company."

Roslyn tilted her head in a fashion which warned of argument. "So, the Family's greatest achievement will become a weapon turned against another Family. You're supplying the drones, Hu is planting the bomb, and Cambrie? Are his hands to remain unsoiled?"

"Alexavier has used his connections in the Dead Continent to smuggle in several warlords," he explained. "They've been charged with harassing De Luca, seizing shipments, assassinating lower members of his Family, and such. When the bomb is detonated, the obvious conclusion will be that the warlords are responsible."

"A people that can barely feed themselves will possess such a weapon?" the Caput'e asked with doubt.

"They're savages, Roslyn. Their very existence is reliant on the black market. It's not entirely beyond possible." Kerwen recalled his last tour of the continent, on the fiftieth anniversary of the militarized quarantine. Scattered tribes, ruled by warlords who reigned and died in rapid succession, dotted the vast stretches of desert and jungle. Flying above, safely ensconced in a private jet, he had seen the straw and mud huts the people of the Dead Continent called homes. He often wondered if simply exterminating the civilization, if that term even applied, would have been more merciful than the quarantine which allowed them to slowly depopulate over time.

Knowing Roslyn's strong opinions on the topic, Kerwen quickly pivoted the subject. "How long has Tilden been seeing an actress?"

Smiling knowingly, but allowing the segue, she replied, "They've made a few appearances together in the last month or so."

Frowning, Kerwen admonished, "And you didn't think to tell me?"

Rising from the couch, the soft satin of her long cobalt dress flowed alluringly with each step she took toward him; the cut of the fabric highlighting the womanly curves of her slender frame. "What would you have said? That an actress is not suitable for a Caput's Heir? They're treated as royalty among the people, you know."

"Which says a great deal about the people," he grumbled, but the press of her warmth against him softened his argument. "She is well-liked then?"

"The next big thing. This century's Marilyn, if one believes the critics. She's been staying in London while filming her next movie."

The comparison did little to boost his opinion of the girl. Still, Kerwen considered her potential value. "Have Tilden bring her to the gala tomorrow."

Roslyn pulled back from her husband's embrace, mocking shock written on her face. "What's this? Kerwen Garrott encouraging his son's interest in, what do you say, oh, yes . . . a fool of Hollywood?"

"Certainly not!" he replied with feigned insult. "But until this business with the Council is over, I see no harm in keeping our name linked to some cinema darling. The more the people love us, the tougher it will be for Cambrie or Hu to attempt a double cross."

"Tilden will not like you using his private affairs in such a way," the Caput'e cautioned.

"The sacrifice for being the Heir," Kerwen stated.

As a matter of course, Caput Garrott held little favor for the extravagant fetes which consumed the social calendars of the Alliance's ruling elite. He found the posturing and preening of his supposed peers unbelievably tiresome. Brightly garbed men and women, eager to show off their taste and influence, did as much dancing with their words as they did with their feet. The scenes always reminded him of oversexed peacocks strutting their feathered arses for political mating. His secretary had strict instructions to limit the events he attended to the barest minimum. Tonight, however, was different. For this fete was in celebration of the Family's launch of the PK-drones. Tonight, the Garrotts were the object of everyone's desire.

The endless stream of luxury pods had begun arriving and depositing the invited guests at the manor an hour earlier. From the window of his dressing room, Kerwen watched the process as attendants finished dressing him. Though these events were usually a dizzying display of bright colors, he had opted for a simple black military-cut tuxedo. The points of the closed-ring collar ended just above the black panel which stretched from each shoulder and down to his waist, forming a sort of fabric breastplate. Knee-high leather boots, adding the only hint of shine to the ensemble, tightly hugged his well-formed claves. Hair, as black as the clothing, was slicked back to emphasize the intricately drawn lines of black which decorated his eyes. The only ornamentation had been placed on his left index finger; the heavy sliver ring of a House Caput. Stark and imposing, the look had been deliberate. *Let them act the fools,* Kerwen mused, *as they parade around in their foppish dressings.*

The second reason for the somber choice in clothing entered the dressing chamber and stole the breath from his chest. On a simple day, Roslyn Garrott was a woman whose beauty could make jealous even the most dispassionate hearts. Outfitted as she was now, the aura of elegance and power was nearly blinding. A deep red skirt swept to the floor, curving upwards at the hem, and was adorned with a complex weaving of silver at the waist. Long strands of diamond and rubies traced up the center of her navel to reach the crimson metal covering her ample breasts. A collar of Ancient Egyptian design circled neck, nape and shoulders; dazzling with white and red gems. Her blond tresses had been woven into a delicate, yet powerfully striking, Medusa-crown headdress made of the same colored metal. False gloves sewn with a fortune of more diamonds and rubies stretched to her elbows. *Queen and goddess,* Kerwen reflected.

"The heavens are envious," he said when the ability to speak returned.

Soft chimes of laughter preceded her reply. "They wouldn't be if they knew how long it took to put on." A wicked humor flashed in her eyes; their blueness was surrounded by scroll work matching his own.

"Worth every minute . . . and clearly every penny," Kerwen assured when he kissed his wife's cheek. "How much did . . ."

"Trust me, darling, you don't want to know. Tilden and Isla are at the receiving line. Shall we greet our guests?" Kerwen offered the Caput`e his arm and the pair strolled out of the chamber, a bevy of formally dressed attendants and House guards flocked forward with them.

Though several hundred more continued to arrive, the guests already present were being entertained in the main hall of the manor. Servants moved about the privileged mass, offering drinks and hors d'oeuvres, while a small orchestra played soft tunes. Kerwen nodded to the two men standing ready to open the doors to the grand ballroom. The towering gilt ingresses were pulled simultaneously inward. Tilden and his Hollywood date took their places at the doorway, and Kerwen and his wife stood further into the room.

The Caput Heir wore an identical attire to mirror his father. Though by no means unfit, Kerwen was forced to admit his son's youth complemented the severe look well. *Let them see his strength,* he thought. *I am not the only Garrott they need to fear.* Standing close to the younger Garrott's side, Isla Carene smiled and greeted each guest in turn. Kerwen hid his smirk as he watched the fawning and stammering which gripped both men and women when they met the actress. Where Roslyn's beauty was enhanced by the stately grace with which she held herself, Isla's attraction owed greater credit to exotic alluring, an innate quality blended of sex and mystery.

Tall, her low heels bringing her to a height equal with Tilden, Kerwen believed the young woman's ancestry contained hints of Asian, Mediterranean, and perhaps Northern European. Each feature of her face showing a distinct heritage, yet they combined in perfection. Her dark hair highlighted the slightly slanted emerald green eyes set in the naturally bronzed skin. The full lips and bosom, with slender waist and delicate hands, were assuredly a sculptor's ideal vision. *Yes,* Kerwen considered, *I can see why he is taken with her. Her career, though, makes the match impossible. A shame, really.*

Once the dignitaries of note, including ambassadors from the other four Families, had processed through the line, Liam signaled discreetly, indicating the end of the receiving line. Kerwen was relieved. After nearly an hour of handshaking and smiling, he was eager to rest hand and lips. Walking to their raised table, the Caput moved beside his son and date. "I realize we have yet to be formally introduced. I am Kerwen Garrott," he offered the beauty.

Isla Carene accepted Kerwen's offered hand, saying, "Isla Carene, Your Grace. It is an honor to meet you. Thank you for inviting me to your home."

"The honor is mine," he added genteelly as he waved an attendant away and slid a chair back for the actress." *My wife has said many wonderful things about you. I do hope you enjoy yourself tonight, which might be a challenge. I'm afraid these events tend towards the more boring side."*

Accepting the seat, Isla smiled in gratitude at the chivalry. "I'm sure I will enjoy the night. Truthfully, I've always had an interest in politics."

Of course you have, Kerwen muttered to himself. Reclining into his chair at the center of the table, with his wife at his left, he hoped his son had not attached himself to one of the Hollywood crowd who decried the government's reach whenever she needed a headline to boost a career. "Really?" he asked flippantly.

"Yes," the woman with the mesmerizing eyes answered. "It seems to share many commonalities with my profession."

Intrigued by the comment, Kerwen prodded, "How so?" Roslyn placed a soft touch to his hand, a clear reminder to be easy with the girl.

"Well, tonight for instance," Isla began the comparison. "Most of your guests presumably hope to gain from your success. They will say what they think you want to hear to entice your favor. They have probably repeated their words over and over, making sure tone and meaning are perfected. And you'll be forced to mask contempt or pleasure, respond with half-truths, vague promises, and the like. The stakes are certainly higher, but I find politics to be another arena for acting. False faces and words, all working from their own scripts."

When she concluded her oration, Kerwen stared in flat surprise. Shifting his gaze to Tilden, he saw apoplexy in the boy's wide eyes. For a long moment, no sound or movement disturbed the uncomfortable silence. Whether feigned or genuine, Isla began to stumble an apology when the realization of her words hit her.

"Your Grace, forgive me," she stammered. "I didn't mean to . . . "

Kerwen sliced through the woman's words with a barking laugh. "I couldn't have described it better myself! Tilden, I toast you for bringing such a refreshing voice to our table."

Raising his glass, Kerwen sipped the chilled wine in amusement. *A bold one*, he assessed Isla as the fragrant taste danced on his tongue. *And insightful! The boy may have found his Roslyn,* Kerwen added silently. "You must save me a dance, Isla."

"Yes, Your Grace," she promised, though the hint of worry still shook her voice. Tilden, however, was smiling proudly, knowing his paramour had made a worthy impression. *Oh, he's taken with this one,* the father understood. His reluctance to the match was slightly mollified.

The meal passed with conversations of far less importance. Roslyn made lighthearted inquiries into the film Isla was currently filming. A period piece, she had explained, set in eighteenth century England. The lady of the house managed a remarkable commentary on the various other actors in the project. Usually disinterested in the goings-on of popular culture icons, Kerwen was certain his wife had educated herself on the topic specifically for this evening.

Eventually, Liam approached the table to usher Kerwen into a small antechamber off the ballroom. Business, even in the midst of the night's merriment, needed attention. Brief meetings with myriad elites filled the following two hours. Governors and businessmen from diverse regions had made the journey to England for reasons more pressing than dining and dancing. Though the initial PK-drones had been donated to the pilot program, eager adopters sought an audience with Kerwen to outline large scale purchases of the machines. For private and public use, the security the drones offered proved too enticing to resist. Vague deals were agreed to, the specifics to be outlined more formally at a future date, and most of the petitioners left pleased.

"Any others?" Kerwen asked after a Chinese executive departed the room. The diminutive man had amassed a sizeable fortune through electronics and had wished to buy twenty units from the Garrotts. Liam had convinced him to invest in a full platoon of fifty.

"Only small purchasers, sir, wanting to buy one or two for personal guards," the advisor informed. "They can be put off without insult."

"Very well," the Caput said, rising from the chair. "See that they meet with either Morgan or yourself before they leave."

"Ah," Liam intoned, "Your son has asked if he might be able to conduct some of the lesser meetings."

Sighing, Kerwen wondered if he should have brought Tilden with him to the antechamber. He did not begrudge the boy his interest in the Family business. In fact, Kerwen was pleased to hear his son wished to participate. He wished, however, Tilden had come to him directly to make the request. "That's fine. But, I want you there as well. Make sure he understands he is not to bind us to any contracts."

"As you wish," Liam nodded. Though the Family's old advisor often set a lashing tongue to Tilden, Kerwen knew the man did so only to train and prepare the Heir for ascension. Kerwen recalled all too well the lectures and reprimands the same source had delivered in his own youth. Having lost his family years earlier, Liam had treated Kerwen, and then Tilden, as the children he had never had. Making a note to discuss Tilden's further integration into the business with Liam, Caput Garrott walked out the door held open by one of the House guards.

One of the modern waltzes, which had fast become a favorite among the upper classes, resonated along the high ceiling of the ballroom. Partners spun and slid across the marble floor, deftly shifting limbs to the music's time. Kerwen spotted Tilden and Isla among the gliding sea, moving in harmony at the hall's far corner. He wondered how many men were stealing glances at the holo-screen beauty.

For his part, the scene was a tranquil relief from the guarded parsing of words and gestures of business. Splashes of color, reds and blues, yellows and greens, shades found in nature, others the creation of expertly mixed dyes, seemed to float in unison - a rainbow of cascading and twirling movement. Women smiled in sincere delight as their men lifted them into the air, the trains of a hundred gowns fanning out behind them. Still several hours from completion, Kerwen knew the evening was a resounding success, likely to be the topic of high society for some time. *Well, at least until another fancy stole into their minds,* Kerwen smiled in thought.

Roslyn intercepted him before he could escape to the Family table. Taking his hand, she pulled him into the whirling dance. His skill was not lacking, but he had never found comfort twirling about in the complicated footwork. Her smile, however, was a welcome balm.

"Done for the night?" she asked as the dance brought them together.

"Liam and Morgan can handle the rest."

One dance became two, and then three, and Kerwen found himself in step with Isla, while wife and son shared a dance nearby. He could sense the young woman was still worried over her earlier commentary. "Are you enjoying yourself tonight?" he asked her.

"Very much, sir. And you?"

"Too much acting for me," he joked and saw a slight easing of tension in her eyes as she laughed with him. In a rousing crescendo of brass and strings, the song came to a close. Breathless, Kerwen brought the woman's hand to his lips in the old fashion. Isla gracefully dipped in return, thanking him for the dance. His place was quickly filled by Tilden once Kerwen escorted his wife back to the table.

"You approve of her," Roslyn stated as the orchestra stirred into another piece.

"More so than yesterday," he admitted. A stutter in the music caught his ear while he waited for the Caput`e's reply.

"Kerwen . . ." The edge in her voice raised his hackles and he followed the direction of her worried stare.

From each entrance of the vast room, House guards - drone and human alike - streamed into the ballroom. The music continued to break; the orchestra's members distracted from their instruments as they watched the hurried movement of the guards.

"Kerwen Garrott!" shouted a voice from the crowd. The Caput sought the caller which was easily done as men and women backed away, opening a wide circle around the figure. Kerwen did not recognize the man. Dressed formally in Eastern garb, the man stared coldly.

The House guards rushed forward, weapons drawn. The unfamiliar man's voice boomed again as he raised his right hand, which tightly grasped a small metallic cylinder, to shoulder level

"Sic semper tyrannis!"

Caput Garrott felt his men pull him to the floor as the ballroom erupted with a fiery flash and concussive roar. A wave of heat blasted his skin. Confused and disoriented, Kerwen's body seemed to float across the room. Only once the ballroom dissolved into an adjoining hall did he comprehend security was carrying him to safety.

The men around him were shouting commands and Kerwen struggled to free himself from their support. "I can walk! I can walk dammit!" Slowing only enough to allow his feet to touch the ground, the tight mass of guards continued their dash.

"Sir, we're bringing you to the bunker," a guard told him. The words were familiar, but in the tangle of his mind, they held no meaning. He watched, and ran, with detached awareness. A guard flashed a palm across a hidden scanner and a large section of wall slid aside. The assemblage wasted no time as they pushed him forward into the steel compartment. The panel closed and he felt the downward speed of the elevator as it descended.

"Sir, are you hurt?" another guard asked, one of many crowded into the conveyance.

"No . . .," Kerwen managed. He felt no pain - he had no feeling at all. Dropping his chin, the Caput was surprised to find he stood unassisted. He wondered briefly how legs he could not feel managed to support him. Seconds later, the descent ended and the panel slid open once again to reveal a large underground facility. *The bunker,* he remembered.

"Get him into the med-scan," someone ordered.

As they steered him, shock waned and comprehension exploded. "My wife. Where is Roslyn? Tilden, my children?"

The nearest guard touched the mobile comm device in his ear, mumbled, and replied, "We have them. They're bringing them down now, sir."

Kerwen was led to a small room; white and empty save for a waist-high platform resembling a halved-egg. He found no will to struggle as the men lifted him onto the bed.

"Where is he? Where's the Caput?" Roslyn's voice was panicked and commanding.

"We need to scan him, Caput`e," another voice implored. Ignoring the comment, Roslyn Garrott pushed a passage through the men. The headdress which earlier crowned her beauty now hung awkwardly from the side of her head. Several small scrapes and cuts leaked thin trickles of blood down the creamy skin of her arms.

"Kerwen!" she exclaimed, rushing forward and embracing him tightly.

"I'm fine," he soothed.

"Sir," the white-jacketed physician bravely interjected. "We need to run the scan."

Kerwen untangled himself from his wife. "The doctor needs to work," he told her then directed an order to the waiting guards. "See to the Caput`e's injuries!"

Once the room was finally cleared, he reclined on the hard surface of the platform. The room darkened, and then the surface of the medical bed poured a vibrant blue glow onto the sleek walls of white. In the quiet minutes of the scan, Kerwen organized his thoughts. And stoked his vengeance.

"He is likely to lose the eye," Liam intoned regretfully. The Family's chief advisor had continuously updated Kerwen during the two hours since Tilden's body had been rushed into the underground security shelter. Roslyn had cried a gasp of anguish upon seeing the bloodied face of their eldest child. Shrapnel from the blast had scored through Tilden's right eye.

"The optic nerve is intact," Liam continued. "They will implant a bio-prosthetic. He should regain full vision after the procedure."

The only serious injury his Family had sustained, Kerwen knew Tilden's condition could have been much worse. Early reports from above already counted twenty-three fatalities. Nodding, Kerwen addressed one of the guards, "Inform the Caput`e." Voicing obedience, the man hurried from the command room.

Liam assumed his seat at the table, surrounded now by the members of the House council. Assistants swept in and out relaying the latest details from the carnage while wall mounted screens displayed the surveillance video and still images of the ballroom before and after the attack. Seated at the table's head, Kerwen turned to his security chief, Winslow Fabirichi.

"Do we have an identity for the bomber?" he asked the same question again.

Frowning with disappointment, Fabirichi shook his head. "His SID hasn't been found yet, sir. Even then, it's probable the chip will be a false identity. We are still running the facial recognition program, but no matches yet either, Caput."

"I want a name, Winslow!" Kerwen shouted as he slammed his fist against the table.

"Yes, Caput," the security chief replied before rising from the chair and leaving the command room. *Truth help whoever was about to feel that man's wrath*, Kerwen thought.

An assistant stepped into the room and handed Liam a slip of paper. Scanning its contents, the advisor informed Kerwen, "The other four Caputs have called with inquiries, sir."

"The bastards can wait and shite themselves with worry," he growled. The other Families would be wringing their hands, fearing the Garrotts' reaction to the assassination attempt. *How disappointed they must have been when the media announced I still live!* "One of them is behind this."

"Not necessarily, sir," Miah Porter, Kerwen's head of intelligence broke in. "The bomber's words, 'sic semper tyrannis,' 'thus always to tyrants,' is well known as the motto of the Ignota. And they have employed suicide attacks in the past."

Erich DeSoren, Fabirichi's second, countered, "The agitators can barely manage to strategize a mugging. What happened here tonight was too sophisticated for them. False SID, infiltrating a Family's compound, masking explosives from our detection . . ."

"What of the bomb itself?" Kerwen asked.

DeSoren swiped through the panel screen embedded into the table in front of him. Selecting his notes, the security second-in-command called up a hologram from the platform at the table's center. "The device itself was a simple design. Wireless trigger, which he held, detonated the explosives hidden on his body."

Believing his assertion proven, Porter surmised, "A simple device. Not beyond the ability of the terrorists."

Kerwen was certain DeSoren was setting Porter up to look the fool. *Even now*, he thought, *they bicker to impress me*.

"I said the device was simple," DeSoren sprung his wit-trap. "The explosives themselves were highly advanced. Military-grade plasma charges."

"Which brings us back to the other Families," the Caput sighed. Frustrated, he knew the speculation would continue cyclically until the bomber's identity was ascertained. "Liam, work with Erich and Miah to craft responses to the Caputs. I want an update in thirty minutes—with a name. Until then, I'll be with my Family."

CHAPTER EIGHT

Milo Chance

No sooner had he, and his robotic partner, returned to the station house after speaking with Dr. Hopkins that Milo found himself summoned to his CO's office.

"Close the door and sit," Sergeant Anestes barked. The gruff twenty-plus year veteran of the force was sorely lacking in skills of interpersonal communication. And he was well aware of that fact. "Why the hell am I getting a call from the Alliance about you harassing a Dr. Hopkins?"

"The Alliance?" Milo questioned. "Sir, we didn't harass the guy."

"We? There's no 'we' in this, Chance. Your partner's a damn machine. You're the only one making decisions. What the hell were you doing there?" Anestes demanded as he loomed over Milo's seat.

Though the interview was contentious, and he believed himself free of any harassment accusations, the corporeal still selected his words with care. "I was following a lead, sir. An informant provided the location of a Muerte safe-house. We . . . I discovered a fresh print belonging to the doctor so we, I mean I, went to speak with him. There was no harassment. I asked him a few questions, that's all."

"How can I help you, Corporeal Chance?" Dr. Hopkins, who surrounded himself with an aura of self-importance, asked from behind his desk as he offered Milo a seat.

"Thank you," Milo said as he lowered himself to the chair. "We're investigating an open case and your name came to our attention."

The doctor returned a quizzical look. During the drive to the hospital, Milo reviewed Hopkins's file in the patrol pod. Fifty-eight years old, the gray-haired physician specialized in surgical pharmaceuticals; his degree obtained at a premier university on the West Coast. Currently on his third wife, Hopkins had several offspring and was expecting his ninth grandchild within the month. As Godwin stated, Dr. Hopkins had no record of criminal charges. Even claims of malpractice were absent from his history.

"Are you familiar with a home on South Main Street? Specifically number 239?" Milo continued.

Seeming insulted, Hopkins responded, "That'd be in the Ruins, yes?"

Milo nodded affirmation at the man's use of the slang name for the area in which Muerte's recent base was located.

"I live in Chestnut Hill, sir," Hopkins hinted with pride over the typically upper class section of Northern Philadelphia. "I tend to avoid *that* section of the city."

Milo bit back his contempt of the man's snobbery. "Is it possible you were visiting a patient in the area, sir?"

A sniff of indignation puffed through the doctor's nose. "I don't have patients, Corporeal . . . Chance, is it? I head the hospital's research in surgical pharmaceuticals."

"Yes, I read that in your file. Graduate of University of Washington Medical School." Mentioning his perusal of the man's file had the desired effect. Dr. Hopkins's face flashed with anger at the intrusion into his records. Milo hoped the slip in composure might elicit greater truth. *Even if it doesn't,* Milo mused, *at least I got under this pompous prick's skin.*

"Does your research ever cause you to go to *that* part of town?" Milo pressed.

"Like me, the people with whom I associate don't spend time dallying in the Ruins," Hopkins sneered in response.

Unfazed by the man's rising anger, Milo pressed forward. "I ask because during our investigation, your fingerprints were discovered at the scene. Would you happen to know how they got there?"

Dr. Hopkins glared for a fractional second before answering with thinly disguised defensiveness, "No, I would not. Though, I do recall reading several articles about a SID forger running wild in the city. If I'm not mistaken, your people have been unable to apprehend him for quite some time now."

Taking the barb in stride, Milo retorted, "Well, forged SIDs are quite different from fingerprints, Doctor."

Rising from his chair behind the steel desk, Dr. Hopkins crossed the office saying, "I'm afraid I don't know what to tell you, Corporeal. Now, I am late for a meeting. So, if you'll excuse me."

Milo stood and was followed out the office door by Godwin who had remained silently standing during the exchange. "Thank you for your time, Dr. Hopkins. Oh, and don't worry too much about the forger. Sooner or later, all criminals get caught in a mistake."

He could feel the doctor's stare burning into his back as Milo exited the room.

"I asked him a few questions, that's all."

Sergeant Anestes stepped away from his intimidating hunch above Milo. "Well, the doctor didn't see it the same way. Now, I'm getting calls from the Alliance ripping me a new one because of your Truth-damned 'few questions'!"

Feeling a slip of bravery, Milo said, "All due respect, sir, but I was following a plausible lead. The guy's prints were found in the same room as those belonging to Muerte and his men. The drone's scan indicates it was likely the doctor was there at the same time."

Milo could see his CO consider the words. "So, what did you get out of him?"

"Nothing."

"Chance!" Anestes returned to his earlier barking.

"But it was a very emphatic nothing, sir," Milo jumped in before the sergeant could launch a new tirade. "He got agitated when I pressed him, *gently* pressed him," he stressed the correction. "I told him there was an investigation, and a crime scene, and the guy never asked either. You and I both know that's the first thing an innocent suspect asks. He was there with Muerte, sir. You gotta trust me on this one."

Milo watched as Anestes weighed the options. "Officially, you're to drop any further investigation where the doctor is concerned."

"And unofficially?"

"Unofficially, you run the show. I can't authorize any surveillance, taps, tech, etc. It's you and the Truth-forsaken drone. No records, either. And keep your distance from Hopkins. He makes another complaint and it'll be my ass, and you better believe I'll take you down with me!"

"Yes, sir."

"Good. Now get the hell out of my office. And at least try to look reprimanded."

Milo forced the smile from his face and stepped to the door, but turned for another question. "Who called, sir? From the Alliance, I mean."

Already focused on the other business cluttering his desk, Anestes looked up. "House Cambrie. Seems your doctor friend is a big shot with Cambrie Laboratories. A well-funded big shot. You're not dealing with some street toughs, Chance. Or even Muerte. These are powerful people with powerful secrets. Watch your ass out there."

"Yes, sir," Milo repeated and exited the CO's office.

With his shift nearly complete, Milo entered the day's activities into the station log. Normally he would have spent a few extra hours at work, the habit which had ended his engagement, but the corporeal instead sought the solitude of his apartment once the clocked ticked the last minute of his shift. Instructing Godwin to review the Muerte case files during the overnight, Milo bade the drone good evening and headed home, stopping briefly to purchase a medium pizza from the neighborhood shop.

As she had each day since learning of the broken engagement, Milo's mother had called to check on him. Milo listened to the message as he stood in his kitchen, quickly devouring the first slice of the pie. Again, the message ended with an invitation to visit his parents over the weekend.

"Honey, why don't you come up this weekend? Get out of the city, clear your head. You don't need to be alone during a time like this," she said. With each message, the request carried a sharper edge of worry.

Milo smiled ruefully at her words. He had not told his parents about the many months he and Julia had contended with his long, and often voluntary, hours on the job. Thus, the revelation of the split had taken them quite by surprise. And they had taken it quite hard, at that. His mother had sobbed incoherently, while his father had grown silent shaking his head miserably. In fact, Milo was the only one who had failed to react with any degree of upset. He had wondered, briefly, what the lack of emotion indicated, but, as with all things, Milo turned his thoughts to work.

Sergeant Anestes had understandably refused formal assistance in the case; leaving Milo to carry out the investigation independently. Though the commanding officer mentioned the use of the drone, Milo knew he had to limit Godwin's awareness of his actions. The drone, after all, was directly linked to the Alliance, feeding unseen computers and watchers the details of the pair's actions. If he hoped to find the link between the doctor and Muerte, Milo would have to rely on his own skill and wit. A realization which held a distinct allure. He had watched the films of past centuries, when detectives worked cases through interviews, evidence trails, and, often, sheer instinct. There was a classical feel to the procedure, an almost romantic renaissance of mankind's self-reliance.

The pizza slice calmed the hunger in his stomach enough that Milo decided to change out of the PK uniform. Walking down the hall to the closed door of his bedroom, his nose caught an unusual odor. Each step forward intensified the scent, moving from a barely noticeable hint to a powerfully nauseating stench. The depths of his training subconsciously moved his hand to the holster at his right hip. Withdrawing the particle handgun, a PK's most common weapon, Milo shifted into a defensive stance as he gripped the door's handle. The smell moved from nose to tongue and eyes, increasing the sickening clench of his stomach.

Gently pressing the door open, Corporeal Chance slowly passed into the darkened room. Reflex memory brought his fingers to the control panel beside the interior doorframe. Lighting the room, Milo's eyes were immediately pulled to the bed. The shape was unmistakably human, but the similarities ended there. A crackled black hide had replaced the skin which had been burned off the victim. Feeling the bile rise in his throat, Milo forced his eyes away, searching the rest of the room. Gun arm preceded his advance as he checked both closet and bathroom, finding both areas undisturbed. Disassociating himself from the carnage, trying to forget the crime scene was in his home, Milo moved towards the bed, knelt, and scanned its underside. Convinced whoever deposited the corpse was gone and no longer a threat, Milo summoned the IFaMS unit and called in the discovery.

"Based on the charring," the medical examiner explained, "I'd say the vic was alive through most of it."

Milo leaned against the counter in the kitchen as he listened. The past hour had been a swirl of activity as men and women he had worked beside moved through the apartment. Sergeant Anestes had also responded to the call, and stood in the now crowded kitchen with Milo and the medical examiner.

"How do you know?" the sergeant asked.

"The hypocermis is mostly intact. Whoever did it made sure to restrict the burns to the top two layers of skin. They were very careful, very precise. They wanted the victim to feel every minute of it. Whoever your perp is, I'd say he enjoys his work a bit too much. I'll know more when I can open him up on the slab, but my guess is he died from hypovolemic shock. The extent of the injuries brought about a fatal decrease in blood volume."

"Do you have an ID?" Milo forced the question through his clouded thoughts.

The ME shook her head. "SID chip was removed through an incision in the right hand; likely after death. Based on the size . . . adult male, maybe late teens. And no stranger to fire. Beneath the char, I found an old scar, deep, covering the victim's right profile."

"Banhen," Milo muttered. The informant would have certainly met a violent end at some point in the future, but Milo knew working with the PKs had hastened the young man's fate. Another death to lay at Muerte's feet.

Anestes thanked the examiner, who assured the autopsy would top her list of priorities as she took her leave. The sergeant then turned to Milo. "You're thinking this is Muerte's work?"

Milo nodded slowly as he stared at the floor.

"Then I'm assigning you protection."

"Sarge," Milo began in protest.

The commanding officer sternly dismissed the attempt. "Muerte's always been a nasty son of a bitch, Chance. It's a death sentence for anyone who turns on him. But, he's never directly targeted a PK. This was as much a warning for you as it was for the street. You got his attention, and the next time it's gonna be you in that bed. You'll take the Truth-damned protection!"

"How can I investigate Dr. . . .," Milo exclaimed before lowering his voice beyond the reach of unintended ears, "how can I investigate Dr. Hopkins if I've got PKs watching my every move? Muerte's getting personal? Fine. But why? Whatever it is I've stumbled upon, it's clearly hitting too close to home for him. We have to keep the pressure on him, force him into a mistake."

The kingpin had ruled in the shadows too long and Milo knew the sergeant understood the necessity of the risks. Anestes offered a compromise. "You'll move into a safehouse for now. A safe environment we can control and will still allow you to move forward on the case. You set foot aside, and the drone is right behind you. I don't care if you're walking down the block for a cup of coffee! That drone is with you whenever you leave the safehouse."

Milo found no disagreement in the offer. Even once the body was removed from the bedroom, he doubted he would be able to sleep in the room without vomiting from the lingering stench and memory.

"I'll list you in the system as on paid vacation. After tonight, no one will question you taking some time off," Anestes added. "You have one week. After that, I'm shutting you down."

CHAPTER NINE

Sonje Nysgaard

The late night call from Phillip Seton brought a jumble of emotions to her already overworked mind. More than all else, however, Sonje warmed with a sense of relief. Her secret, and the worries and fears with which it mated, was now a shared burden. Whatever course of action was to follow, the decisions would have shared contributions and consequences. Instinct had driven her to contact Seton. And after speaking with him, Sonje believed she had chosen wisely.

Her body, however, still sought clarity as the time difference and the countless hours of activity made mud of her normal routine. Checking the clock, an hour to midnight, Sonje shuffled over to the tea set in the small sitting area of the hotel room. Still warm, she filled a delicate porcelain teacup with the brewed liquid. With luck, the infusion of chamomile would soothe enough to allow a few hours' sleep before the scheduled meeting with Phillip.

Though she held to no naïve conception that any resolution would be simple—leveling a charge of corruption against a man as powerful as Joseph Beckett required irrefutable proof—Sonje did, however, hope her predicament was working towards its end. Phillip could use his position and access to retrieve evidence of Beckett's guilt, and both Seton and she had sufficient government connections to expose the flaw in the chips. Complicated and dangerous, yes, but at least a path forward existed.

Cup in hand, she stepped onto the balcony off the sitting room. Used to a far colder clime, Sonje enjoyed the relative heat of the late summer night. Eight stories up, the dazzling lights of an active city sprawled out below in a woven tapestry of many-colored stars. Even though the Global Alliance had united the disparate nations of the world under one flag, the unity had not diminished the cultural idiosyncrasies enmeshed in the people. America still moved at a breakneck pace; her people maximizing the finite hours in a day. While she enjoyed the comparative idleness of her home, visits to the old empire always proved fascinating.

Drifting her gaze to the street, Sonje caught sight of an unusually high level of activity. Even for an American night. A stream of figures, greater distinction made impossible by the distance, rushed out of several large podcars towards the entrance of the Churchill Hotel. Leaning over the railing, Sonje heard fragments of startlement from the growing crowd of onlookers. The soft breeze on the balcony stirred until she was forced to hold closed the lush hotel robe covering her body. Seeking the source of the sudden gale, Sonje's vision was blinded by a harsh light parallel to the balcony.

"Remain where you are!" a voice commanded with a window-rattling boom. Confusion had her scanning the other balconies for the object of the command when Sonje realized the glaring white light was trained on her, and only her. Clutching the robe's lapels, she backed from the ledge towards the interior of the hotel room.

"Remain where you are!" the voice demanded again. Wind continued to increase as the airborne vehicle moved forward. Panicked, Sonje spun about, legs tangling and bringing her crashing to the carpeted floor. Explosions of amber heat struck the glass doors, the shattered pieces raining on her in sharp pricks. Dragging herself further into the room, Sonje screamed as additional blasts scorched the floor around her prostrate body. She pulled her knees up and launched herself into a run. Abandoning her few personal contents in the hotel room, Sonje scrambled out the door into the hall.

"Freeze!"

Shouting shock, Sonje turned to find several black-uniformed soldiers pouring into the hall at her right. Without pause, she sprinted to the left as the men again called for her surrender. Refusing to turn back, knowing the sight of the soldiers would freeze her with fear, Sonje continued running past the shining metal doors of the elevators. Amber bolts robbed the hallway of its warm yellow glow as the walls erupted in clouds of scorched wood and drywall. Reaching the heavy metal door labeled "stairs," Sonje slammed the exit open. A sharp pain like a burning knife ripped through her left shoulder and the acrid smell of singed flesh sickened her.

Stumbling down the steps, Sonje heard the men shouting from the hall.

"She's in the service stairs!"

"All units to the rear service stairs!"

"Seal the building!"

"I'm tracking her. She's moving down."

The SID! Sonje realized no matter how fast she ran her pursuers could trace her movements as long as the chip remained in her hand. Fearing the stairwell would soon be overrun, she found herself entering the fifth floor of the hotel. Behind her, the heavy trod of soldiers echoed down the stairs.

A surprised man, clad in the old fashioned uniform of a hotel attendant, stood with his mouth agape as he stared at Sonje in her frenzy. Before he could react, she rushed towards him and the room service cart he had been pushing.

"Ma'am, are . . . are you okay?" he asked with concern, unaware of the security forces filling the building. Ignoring the question, Sonje lunged at the silver table knife on the cart. Before she could retrieve the weapon, the attendant gripped her wrist with a powerful hold. With his free hand, the man pulled a small silver gun from his pocket. As he pressed the gun to her open palm, Sonje corrected her understanding. The attendant held no gun, but rather a pressure syringe.

"Seventh door on the right," he said as a he pulled the device's trigger and a small needle pierced her skin. Mystified, Sonje stared blankly at the attendant. Sensing her confusion, the man shoved her violently down the hall. The brief delay allowed the soldiers time to deplete any lead she had in escape.

"She has a gun!" the attendant shouted to the soldiers rushing into the hall.

Baffled by the false claim, Sonje pushed herself from the floor. Though she knew the men were too close for her to possibly avoid capture, fear impelled her to run. As a door opened on her right, Sonje's mind recalled the man's words. *He pushed me into a trap,* her mind screamed in betrayal. Before she could prepare herself to fight off whoever waited behind the door, a shout distinct from those of the soldiers rose above the din. *Latin?* she questioned. The explosion which followed lifted her feet from the floor.

As her eyes blinked against the waking light, Sonje recalled the sensation of flight which had preceded her loss of consciousness. Memory flowed back in a torrent and she lurched from the cot beneath her. The sudden movement brought a stinging pain to her shoulder.

"Easy now. You are safe, Dr. Nysgaard," a voice intoned from the shadows.

Frightened by the close proximity of the unseen speaker, Sonje mustered sufficient strength to question, "Who are you? Where am I?"

"I'm afraid names and locations must remain hidden for the time being," the voice offered apologetically. As her eyes adjusted, she was surprised to find herself alone in a small stone-walled room, a dark metal door the only break in the stone. An inset of mirrored glass confirmed her fearful suspicions. She was in a cell.

"Why am I here?" she asked, though she doubted denials of guilty would diminish the present danger.

"You were brought here for your protection."

"Protection?" Sonje derided. "You tried to kill me!"

A silent moment passed before the disembodied voice returned. "We are not associated with the men who attacked you. I am sorry for the mystery, but we had to move quickly to extract you from the hotel. More information will be provided to you shortly. In the meantime, I must ask you to be patient. Food is being brought to you now."

Cued by the unseen man, a thin rectangular opening slid open at the center of the door. A tray of food was pushed forward, waiting for her to accept it. Distrust lost out to hunger and Sonje stepped from the cot and took the tray in her hands. Whoever held her prisoner had no need to poison the simple fare. Her death would have already been delivered if her captors wished it.

Though the meal was plain, sliced turkey, lettuce, and tomato sandwiched in nearly stale bread, it was adequate to settle the pangs of emptiness in her stomach. Hunger satiated, and head somewhat clearer, Sonje eased the short sleeve of the shirt, presumably provided by her jailers along with loose fitting jeans, to examine the remembered wound. The graze was not deep and had been treated with an accelerant; already the injury puckered into a flat, purple-hued scar. Checking her hand, Sonje found no evidence of the injection the hotel attendant had forced upon her.

Satisfied with the condition of her wound, and wondering what the treatment revealed of her imprisoner's intention, she then set her investigative mind to the cell. The slot through which her meal had been delivered had closed immediately after she accepted it. Upon closer inspection of the walls, Sonje found the material was cinderblock rather than the stone she had initially believed. The cement securing the blocks in place was smooth to her hand, evenly placed and signifying a measure of skill to the masonry. *Cool to the touch,* Dr. Nysgaard assumed she was being held underground.

The ceiling matched the dull gray of the walls and held a square metal grating, approximately two feet to a side. Sonje slid the cot over to the air vent, allowing her to test the grate's strength. A minute of pushing and pulling provided futile; the grate was beyond her ability to pry free.

The exploration of the room revealed a previously unnoticed feature. A steel toilet, lidless but operable, hugged the wall opposite the door. The discovery prompted an urge in her bladder, but Sonje swore off use of the receptacle. Even in the dim light of the cell, she had no intention of exposing herself before unseen eyes.

With no means of obvious escape, and lacking any means of distraction, she returned to the cot. The last two days (*or was it now three?* she wondered) had swept her up in a dizzying tide of events. Tracing through the cause and effect of her predicament, the sound of her own laugh surprised her when it broke the pounding silence of the cell. Gretchen's matchmaking had been the catalyst of the spiraling chaos in which Sonje was trapped. She promised to give her sister a great deal of grief when next she saw her. The next thought brought a chilling fear. *If I see her again.*

A short while later, without windows or clocks Sonje could only estimate an hour's passage, she heard movement beyond the door. Metal slid against metal as a lock-bar was moved aside and the door opened.

The man who entered was dressed in a soldier's fashion, though it was clear the various articles of clothing had been collected from multiple sources. Sonje gauged him to be mid-thirties, perhaps slightly older based on the lines at the corners of his blue eyes and the specks of gray in his short blond beard. Taller than she, the man's body spoke of significant physical strength.

Extending a hand, he said in a voice which identified him as the earlier speaker, "Dr. Nysgaard, I promised you some answers. I am Gavin McAvoy. And I am a member of the Cohors Ignota."

Sonje's eyes widened at the name and pulled her hand free of the man's clasp.

"Judging by the reaction, I trust you're familiar with us," McAvoy offered somewhat sheepishly.

"You're terrorists," Sonje replied. The Cohors Ignota, Latin for Band of the Unknown, had claimed responsibility for a spate of worldwide terror attacks spanning the last two decades. Countless innocents had met brutal ends as a result of the Ignota's suicide bombers and guerilla tactics.

"So the government keeps saying," the man flatly returned, though a glint of humor reflected in his eyes. "Come," he motioned her to follow as he moved toward the door. Fearing to learn what would happen if she refused, Sonje stepped cautiously into the hall. Narrating as they walked, McAvoy provided a brief history.

"A church once sat atop us, back when such things were needed. After the Alliance took control, and Truth replaced faith, the building was torn down, though the lower levels escaped destruction. Through a series of sales, the land deed eventually came into our hands. We fortified what remained underground and established a small base."

"Are we still in DC?" Sonje asked.

"Virginia, actually," McAvoy corrected before stopping at another nondescript door which he then proceeded to open. "It's not much, but it does offer a bit more comfort than where you woke."

The room was constructed much like the cell, yet was nearly double in size and far more furnished. A small wooden table, clearly serving as a desk, four slim folding chairs, a dusty embroidered rug, wall sconces holding thick cylindrical candles, and the several maps on the walls, did little, however, to mask the militaristic utility of the room. Sonje accepted the chair her captor pulled forward.

"Why am I here?" she asked once McAvoy seated himself.

"Because you'd be dead otherwise. It was pure luck that we received information of the attack on your hotel in time to extract you."

"Who were they?"

McAvoy studied her before asking, "Do you need to ask?"

She realized she did not. "Peacekeepers."

He nodded.

"Because of the SIDs. Philip Seton—he and I were working together . . ."

"Unfortunately, Mr. Seton was taken before we could act," McAvoy said. Sonje believed she heard sincere regret in the man's voice. "They stormed his home late last night. His wife, Elizabeth Seton, was killed in the attack. From what we've been able to intercept, his two children seem to have escaped."

"Oh, Truth," Sonje gasped. "Why?"

Gavin McAvoy leaned forward, gently placing his hand on her shoulder in an act of consolation. "We're hoping you can tell us, Dr. Nysgaard."

And so she did. For nearly an hour, Sonje put words to the nightmare which had begun a few short days earlier. McAvoy only listened, nodding occasionally, as she spoke of her date with Alvar Falen, the mystery of his patient, Sonje's discovery of Alvar's murder, her conversations with Philip, and finally the link of the defective SID cover-up to Joseph Beckett, head of Global Tech. When she finished, Sonje wiped the tears which had escaped her eyes.

"I'm sorry for what you've been through, Doctor," McAvoy said. "And this will sound insensitive, but did you make any hardcopies of your findings? A holocard, print-outs?"

Shaking her head, "I had some notes, but they were in my hotel room. My Truth! Two people are dead, and I have no proof of anything!"

A flash of disappointment, quickly masked, covered the man's face. "But you're alive, Doctor. And given the circumstances, that is no small achievement."

She looked at McAvoy. "And what happens to me now? Yes, I'm alive, but for what?"

"If you choose to return, they will eventually find you," he told her. "But, we can offer you protection for as long as you want it. The injection you received in the hotel destroyed the SID. They can't track you anymore. However, if you choose, we can implant you with a new identity and you can try to resume a normal life."

"The man in the hotel . . . the explosion . . . he . . .?" Knowing she was responsible for yet another death was almost unbearable.

"His sacrifice was his decision, Doctor."

"What was his name?" Her guilt demanded she mourn him as more than a stranger. More than a nameless man who had only shared seconds of her history.

"Jamie," the hard-faced militant told her, his voice coldly pained. "Jamie McAvoy. He was my brother."

In years to come, Sonje Nysgaard would point to a handful of decisions which had transformed her life, altered the path of her presumed future, shaping events unimaginable to the fearful woman who had sat in an underground bunker in Virginia.

She told me once, as we huddled together awaiting death in a darkened building, bombs falling around us, that she had never regretted those decisions. She was a mother then and believed if she had chosen differently, walked another path of fate, then the child might never have been. "No," she had said with a mother's accepting love, "I can never regret those decisions."

And so it was that Sonje Nysgaard accepted the offer, and joined the Cohors Ignota.

I cannot help but wonder if she had refused, and instead returned to the world, how many lives might have been spared? But, blind to the future, we make our choices.

-M.S.

CHAPTER TEN

Danica Seton

"Put him in room two," the watch commander ordered, small bits of bagel spraying from his mouth. It had been over four hours since the calamitous raid which had ended with one dead, one in custody, and two on the run. His superiors had harangued him repeatedly for the failure. That the two escapees were children only added to the embarrassment. If he had any hopes of keeping his rank, or even his job, the Seton children had to be found. And quickly.

On his orders, teams of Peacekeepers had scoured the family's neighborhood; the search expanding as more time passed without locating the targets. Thirty minutes ago, the watch commander had ordered a tight net be dropped across the entire city. Billboards flashed digitals of the missing girl and her brother, local PK stations had joined the search, and metro transportation, including the airports, was placed on high alert. The official story, as far as the press and public were concerned, was the girl had abducted her brother after murdering the pair's parents. People were more apt to report sightings of violent offenders than they were simple adolescent runaways.

Wiping his mouth on his sleeve after washing down the bagel with coffee, the watch commander strode across the squad room. The first break in the case awaited questioning in the interrogation room. The man, a recharging station attendant, had initially denied crossing paths with the suspect siblings, but his story had changed after some physical encouragement.

"What's his name?" the watch commander asked the officer guarding the door.

"Brahm, sir. Nathan Brahm," the officer replied formally before opening the door to the room.

Truth! the watch commander cursed silently upon seeing the witness. He had told his men to rough up the attendant, make him more malleable for interrogation. With the blood and bruises covering Brahm's face, it was a wonder the man was still conscious.

"Nathan," the watch commander said, changing his planned approach. "We have a serious problem and we need your help. Those two children are in a lot of trouble. They killed their parents. Now, I know you thought you were helping them, but they tricked you into becoming an accomplice."

The attendant's eyes strained to maintain focus.

"Do you have a wife, Nathan?"

An affirmative grunt was all the man could manage through his shattered jaw and split lips.

"What's her name, Nathan?"

"Brishny."

Translating the mumble, the watch commander continued. "Brittney? I'm sure Brittney is very worried about you. Help us out, and we'll get you fixed up and back home to your wife. Where are the children, Nathan?"

The watch commander could see the other man's struggle for coherence. Finally, after a short moment of deliberation, the fuel worker spoke.

"Fray-er"

"You put them on a freighter?"

Another grunted yes.

"Where was the freighter headed?"

"Phwley."

"You put them on a freighter to Philadelphia?"

The watch commander barely waited long enough for Brahm's confirmation before turning and exiting the room. "Identify any freighters bound for Philadelphia which refueled at that station. Alert the Pennsylvania PK that our suspects have entered their jurisdiction. And get me a transport to Philly," he barked the series of commands to the officers gathered in the squad room.

"Sir, what about Brahm?" one of the soldiers asked.

Jordan Parker, the District's watch commander, wasted no time deciding the fate of the attendant.

"He aided terrorists. Under Alliance Charter Section 41-B he is now considered an enemy combatant and is hereby sentenced to death."

Only once the freight-pod lurched forward did Danica find she could breathe without a fearful shiver shaking her body. The soft hum of the vehicle as its tires spun across the smooth road served as a soothing reminder she and her brother were getting further and further from danger with each passing minute. As long as the freighter was moving, Danica believed they were safe. To avoid thoughts of what challenges lay ahead once they reached their destination, she busied herself by exploring the cargo with which she and Marcus shared the small confines of the compartment. A dim red light provided enough illumination to guide her hands and eyes.

The first container, a metal tool box, offered little benefit apart from a retractable box cutter which she gave to Marcus. Not as substantial a weapon as the kitchen knife she carried, the razor could at least score flesh deep enough for her brother to minimally defend himself. Another box, marked with the recognizable symbol of a red cross, held bandages in varying sizes, a full bottle of peroxide, as well as a small tube of healing accelerant.

Danica helped her brother remove the strip of fabric covering his hand, the coagulated blood pulling away with the cloth and bringing fresh dots of red to the skin. She dabbed a cotton ball soaked in the peroxide on the wound; Marcus flinching as she worked. Finally, she spread a thin line of the accelerant along the incision. If he was careful, the cut would be but a memory in two days' time.

Marcus applied his own bandage while Danica focused on her own hand.

"Dani," Marcus said as he explored the remaining supplies. "I found water! And some food bars!" A day earlier, the excitement in his voice would have been reserved for reaching a new high score in one of his games. Marcus twisted the water bottle cap and upended the container until, four loud gulps later, the plastic was empty.

"Don't drink too much," she warned, though the desert of her mouth pushed her hands to work faster. "We don't know how long we need to make it last."

"Ugh," Marcus replied over the crinkle of foil. "These bars are nasty."

Amused with the boy's reaction, she reminded, "They're meant to keep you alive. They don't have to taste good. Hand me a water."

Ignoring her previous admonition, Danica repeated her brother's gluttony and finished the drink in the span of a breath. The refreshment was fleeting and she had to fight the urge to request one of the remaining four bottles. After confirming Marcus's culinary critique, Danica wished she had saved a bit of the water to wash the taste of the emergency food bar from her mouth. Despite the dry, mealy aftertaste, her stomach felt fuller, and the headache pinching the sides of her temple abated slightly.

"What if Grandma and Grandpa don't help us?" Marcus asked.

"Why wouldn't they help us?" she quickly questioned in response.

Marcus shrugged, but Danica could tell the question had been on his mind for quite some time. "I don't know. If Mom and Dad did something really bad . . . maybe they wouldn't want to help us. Maybe they'd turn us in."

The idea seemed blasphemous, yet it did lead her to another thought. Seeking refuge with their grandparents might be dangerous. Not, of course, for her brother's reasoning, but rather it would put their grandparents at risk, too. It had not been a simple arrest which drove her from her home. Soldiers had cut the power, stormed in with guns drawn, and kicked down doors to reach her parents. Danica was beginning to believe whatever danger hunted them would not be confined to their hometown. PKs might very well be waiting for them in New York, and at the home of all their relatives.

"They wouldn't turn us in," Danica finally addressed her brother's hypothetical. "And Mom and Dad didn't do anything bad." It all had to be some mistake.

"But then why were they— " Marcus began to ask.

"They didn't!" she snapped at him. Immediately regretting the tone, Danica tried to mitigate the moment. "Just get some rest, Marcus. It's less than an hour to Philadelphia."

Her brother, smarting from the rebuke, said nothing else. Searching her mind for words of consolation, Danica disregarded phrase after clichéd phrase; nothing she could conjure even remotely encompassed her emotions. Perhaps no words existed to describe the mixture of fear, anxiety, sorrow, anger, and confusion. *No, that's not true,* she thought. Mom would know exactly what to say. A motto by which to live, some axiom or proverb remembered from youth but perfectly fitting, and of course, doused with enough sap to make Danica's eyes roll. But it would always be right. Thoughts of her mother eventually traced forward, ending with the brilliant flashes of golden red gunfire. If Marcus asked again, she would continue to deny it. A preternatural sense, however, some inexplicable knowledge passed along familial bonds, told Danica her mother was dead. No matter what events were to come, regardless of her efforts to right yesterday's wrongs, her mother was gone.

Though the light in the compartment was dim, any tears she needed to shed would have been seen by Marcus, despite his sullen cold shoulder. Leaving him to his sulk, Danica turned her attention to Philadelphia. Apart from a family tour of the monuments when she was in middle school, Danica had little familiarity with the city. Thus, one direction was as acceptable, and as potentially dangerous, as another, so it mattered little where she and her brother headed once the freighter stopped. And with food and water needs currently met, the next goal on her list was clothing.

Imagining various scenarios through which she and Marcus could obtain more appropriate attire consumed the remaining portion of the journey. Sooner than she would have wished, the freighter-pod came to a halt. Unable to see beyond the compartment, Danica pressed her ear to the hatch door. No voices, or sounds of movement, permeated the thin metal. Tucking the first aid kit under her arm, Marcus had claimed responsibility for the water and food bars, Danica pulled the emergency handle and she pushed the hatch open; the early dawn's light flooding into the compartment.

The change in brightness blinded, but as her eyes adjusted she observed the lot in which the freighter had come to rest. Several other large pods, as well as massive steel containers, filled the otherwise empty area. From the smell tickling her nose, Danica knew a waterway was nearby.

"Come on," she directed to Marcus as she stepped out. Stretching free, her legs sighed with pained pleasure. Part of her wanted to immediately return to the sanctuary of the freighter, but Danica clung to a small spark of courage.

"It smells like dead fish," Marcus complained next to her, nose crinkled from the malodorous assault.

Ignoring the complaint, Danica moved slowly along the freighter's side. In the distance, the sound of machines groaned and jerked. At the front end of the freighter, her field of vision expanded and she could see cargo loaders moving about the other pods, lifting and transporting heavy palettes with their robotic arms. Men in protective helmets sat nestled within each loader, directing their respective machinery's movements. Careful to avoid the operators' notice, she pulled Marcus close as the two cut across the lot.

A few minutes of skulking brought them to a building with cavernous hangars stuffed with more cargo containers. Beyond the structure, Danica saw the river - the Delaware, if her memory of geography class was accurate - and the source of the offending smell. Entering the first hangar, brother and sister quickly ducked behind a tall stack of containers. Wordlessly, Marcus directed her attention to a series of lockers lining the far wall. Motioning him to remain still, Danica crept towards the lockers.

Unlike the assigned lockers at school which were only accessible with a SID, these metal cubbies were nearly ancient; secured by combination locks built into the doors. The first three she tried were sealed, but the fourth yielded to her hands. Explicit images of buxom women in outrageous positions, one had her legs fully spread atop the hood of a sports-pod, lined the locker's interior. The images freed Danica from guilt over looting the owner's belongings. Pulling crumbled articles of clothing into her arms without prejudice, she moved along the wall of lockers; emptying two others before returning to her brother. From the concealment of the containers, the siblings sorted through the stolen collection.

Tall for his age, Marcus had not yet reached his full growth and the jeans and work pants Danica requisitioned proved too large for his frame. Selecting two with the narrowest waists, she instructed him to change. Modesty turned their backs in an attempt for relative privacy. The cuff of the navy pants she pulled to her waist hung several inches past her feet. A few wide rolls shortened the hem to a less cumbersome length. Danica pulled the drawstring cord from her now discarded pajamas and wove it through the pants' belt loops, cinching tightly several inches of extra waistband. Trading the torn and bloody tee for a long-sleeved shirt, Danica was thankful for the absence of a mirror.

"You done?" she whispered to Marcus over her shoulder.

"Yeah," he replied.

It was difficult to stifle laughter as the two turned to see each other's new attire. Even with the smaller sizes, Marcus looked like he had raided their father's closet. That is if their father had owned a tee shirt emblazoned with the logo of a vulgar band more famous for off-stage drunken antics than any musical ability. Danica helped Marcus shorten the jeans, opting to cut off the superfluous material rather than rolling it as she had. A nearby spool of twine provided the boy with a makeshift belt.

As ill-fitting as they were, the clothing was at least alterable. The small selection of footwear, however, proved the greater challenge. For his part, Marcus slipped easily into a heavily scuffed pair of tennis shoes. His large feet, foretelling of future height, had sprouted early and waited for the rest of his body to catch up. Danica was forced to lace on sneakers much too long, even with pieces of balled fabric stuffed into the toes. The result caused her to step awkwardly, though her worn soles appreciated the cushion.

"Now what?" Marcus asked.

Clothing secured, even such as it was, reduced the need to enter the heart of the city. Just as well, Danica thought. She had been justifiably leery of navigating the crowded streets of an unfamiliar metropolis. To her mind, she and Marcus had two options – find a place to hide, or keep moving. "How do you feel?" she asked her brother.

"Tired, but okay." The understatement was glaring. Danica wished she was "tired." It would have been a vast improvement to the consuming exhaustion which had replaced her limbs with leaden weights. Even her skin felt heavy.

"Then we keep going," she decided. *But where?* her mind begged.

The siblings retraced the path which had led them into the hangar. Their movements, though sluggish, were more confident now that they were dressed more suitably. If caught in a passing glance, their appearance should provoke little interest. They were simply two youths in hand-me-down clothes. If anything, pity, not suspicion, would be the sentiment flowing towards them. At least, Danica hoped so.

It took several minutes to reach the perimeter of the facility. The journey allowed her to adapt her gait in compensation of the oversized shoes. Even with the improvement, Danica believed she surely looked like a newly-birthed foal stumbling about. Turning left on the first street beyond the cargo depot, she kept their pace to a measured stroll, fighting the nervous anxiety of being out in the open. Though the knife was bundled in the sweatshirt tucked under her arm, Danica missed the security of its handle in her palm.

Set back from the street were several nondescript industrial buildings; the plain façades masking the activity of the factory workers within. Parking areas of idle podcars surrounded each structure. Occasionally, she saw figures bustling through the lots. Some were walking towards the buildings to begin their shift. Others, which Danica studied with great interest, were ambling from the factories with the weary tread of overnight employees. Most were men, inhaling deeply from cigarettes as they parted from colleagues with calls of "see you later" and "have a good one."

Danica had hitched rides before, a fact which would have sent her parents into a fury had they known. They had always warned of abductors and rapists eager to snare misguided young girls who placed too much trust in the kindness of strangers. She had partially heeded their cautions, only accepting offers from women. Though Marcus had never been with her in the past, Danica hoped a willing motorist would help the pair now.

The first woman they approached had snappishly denied their request before shutting herself securely within her pod. The lady's narrowed eyes of suspicion had Danica wishing she wore her school uniform. People's instincts were often swayed by the studious skirt and shirt. At the next lot, Danica saw an older woman, the short gray hair reminiscent of her grandmother's coif, walking towards a pod.

"Excuse me, ma'am," she called to the woman, adding a saccharine innocence to her tone.

The senior citizen slowed her walk upon hearing Danica.

"Yes?" the woman asked.

Truth, let this work! Danica prayed. "Are you heading over the bridge?" Looming not a half-kilo away, a steel lacework stretched across the Delaware River connecting to New Jersey.

"I am," the old woman responded.

"Could you possibly give me and my brother a ride across?"

The woman looked to the bridge then back to the disheveled pair, studying them. "Where are your parents?" she asked.

With the story hastily prepared, Danica answered. "Our mom's on a business trip. My brother decided to sneak out with some friends and I spent the whole night looking for him. If I call the Peacekeepers or take a bus or cab, she'll find out. And hit him." The last part she added on the fly hoping to appeal to the woman's maternal senses. A claim of abuse might also help to explain the scratches both children bore.

"Uhm . . .," the woman deliberated aloud.

"I understand if not, ma'am. It's just I don't want to be late for school. I have a chemistry test today and I need to get a good grade or my mom will flip out." Danica hoped the woman would not question a test scheduled for the second day of school. *One of the many holes in the story,* Danica mused.

"Where do you live?"

The game was lost. Danica's mind blanked, unable to even recall the state's capital.

"Tabernacle," Marcus interjected.

The woman's face immediately softened at the city's name. "Well, that's where I'm headed. I guess I can drive you."

"Thank you!" Marcus and Danica exclaimed in unison before walking to the passenger door. As they crossed the rear of the blue car, Marcus tugged her sleeve, directing her eyes to the pod's bumper. A digital display on the fender proclaimed, "Tomis Reginon for Tabernacle City Council." Danica mouthed "nice" in appreciation for her brother's quick thinking and the woman's personalization of the podcar.

Marcus took a seat in back as Danica placed herself in the front passenger seat. The podcar was sterilely clean, neither a scrap of paper nor speck of dirt marred the interior. A light vanilla scent permeated the air which was a welcome relief from the lingering smell of the nearby river. Her parents rarely made use of the built-in air fresheners of the family's automobiles; both continually forgetting to refill the receptacle with scented liquids.

"This is really very nice of you, ma'am," Danica said as the pod pulled out of the parking space.

"Oh, I had a sister who liked getting into trouble when we were young," the woman chuckled. "And, please, call me Carla."

"I'm Beth," Danica lied, adopting her mother's name. "And this is my brother, Philip."

Carla turned to "Philip." "It's very dangerous sneaking out at night, Philip. Your sister must have been worried sick. There are a lot of people who wouldn't think twice about harming you."

"Yes, ma'am," Marcus replied with more penitence than Danica thought he could muster.

Believing the youth duly admonished, Carla shifted in her seat and engaged Danica in pleasant conversation. Her questions were mostly concerned with school (Danica was careful to avoid mention of a specific school name), what she planned for post-graduation, a possible major in college, and similar topics. Danica answered amicably, though it was a trial to think of events so commonplace when her world had upended only hours earlier. Not twenty minutes since leaving the factory parking lot, a digital sign welcomed visitors to Tabernacle, New Jersey.

"Where should I drop you?" Carla asked.

"By City Hall is fine," Danica replied. Without knowing the area, a government building was the only generic location available to her.

The pod slowed to city-limit speed and eventually came to a stop alongside a neatly landscaped garden; the brick seat of the city's governing body stood stately down a ruler straight paved walkway.

"Well, here you go," she said after instructing the pod to open the passenger side doors.

"Thank you again, Carla," Danica replied.

"It was nothing. Good luck on your test. And no more sneaking out, young man!" the old woman called to them across the now empty passenger seat.

Danica waved acknowledgement and purposefully strode down the sidewalk to reinforce her belonging in the neighborhood. She only managed a few steps before realizing Marcus was not with her. Turning back she found her brother staring dumbstruck at the city building.

A tree-high holoset platform usually used to inform the community of upcoming activities instead displayed three-dimensional images of Danica and Marcus. A chyron scrolled across the bottom of the spectacle declaring the Seton siblings as fugitives wanted for the murder of their parents.

Even at that early hour, a handful of pedestrians ambled along the city's main thoroughfare. Danica realized, however, all surrounding movement had ceased. Everyone's attention was drawn to the breaking alert. Including Carla.

The kind woman who had transported them across the river turned her head slowly from the holoset to Danica. Their gaze locked, panic mirrored in both sets of eyes. Danica ran forward, pulling Marcus from his stupor and fled with him down the nearest connecting avenue. Carla's voice instructing the podcar's system to contact the local PKs echoed in Danica's ears.

She wanted to feel anger towards the newly-acquainted woman's betrayal; some indolent rage that anyone could believe the lie of the holoset. The only sentiment her mind summoned, however, was defeated acceptance. Their unrelenting pursuers had reached out once again, tracking them across the distance from home to a small New Jersey town. *No matter how fast we run,* she thought, *they're going to find us.*

Some three blocks from the city hall building, Danica unfurled the sweatshirt and rejoined hand and blade. Marcus added his bundle to the sweatshirt and medical kit his sister discarded and withdrew the small razor from his pocket. In the distance, the wailing banshees of Peacekeeper patrol pods tore through the brightening sky.

Danica searched the street, hoping to find an alcove or alley in which they could hide from the searchers. The few businesses on the block had not yet opened, and the residential buildings were sure to be secured. A green sign with white lettering hung from a street pole and its words caught Danica's attention – "Wharton State Park, 1.1 km." They had managed to evade the PKs in the small park back in Washington. Danica wondered if such luck could be repeated.

"I need you to run as fast as you can," she said as she gripped Marcus's shoulders. "Don't stop. Don't look back. Just stay with me. Okay?" Marcus nodded, eyes wide with fear. Danica had meant to encourage, but her brother had easily heard the distress in her voice. The sirens drew closer, perhaps only a block away now. Squeezing his shoulders, she turned them both towards the unseen park.

Before her reality had turned to nightmare, such a short distance would have served as a warm-up in Danica's usual practice routine. Whereas some teammates excelled in the sprints which brought crowds roaring to their feet, she had trained, and succeeded, in events of longer distances. She found the combination of the physical discipline and mental strategy those races required far more stimulating than short-lived explosions of energy. Finding the runner pack which matched her pace, monopolizing the efforts of those ahead as she drafted closely behind them, swinging wide on the straightaways and tucking close to the oval on the curves appealed to her competitive nature. With several laps to plan and maneuver, Danica would set her sights on specific runners; overtaking them with brief surges before opening her stride when the bell of the final lap rang out. Atop her bedroom bureau sat numerous bronze and silver medals, and more than one of gold.

The exhaustion and the clumsy shoes she wore, however, combined to make the current dash a Herculean task. Though his frame was more suited to the tight strength of little league baseball, Marcus did well to keep up with his sister. Their reserves of endurance were bolstered by the ever-nearing sirens. Danica could almost hear her coach's recriminations as she stole a backward glance over her shoulder. Four patrol pods, easily recognized by the intimidating designs of black and red, chased after them unhindered in the empty street. If they did not reach the dirt ground of the park soon, the PKs would be upon them.

With little ceremony, the smooth pavement was replaced with the impact-forgiving sponge of green grass. Picnic tables and an elaborate collection of see-saws, monkey bars, and swings dotted the flat stretch of land. The patrol pods bounced loudly from the street, over the cement curb, and tore deep lines along the lawn. Amber flashes whipped through the air, striking the earth with dirt-churning explosions. A nearby table ripped apart as a bolt struck the wood. The sudden attack proved there would be no attempt at arrest. Thus, Danica knew there could be no surrender.

Breaking from a straightward run, Danica pulled Marcus into a weaving sprint as more shots ate the ground meters from their feet. The earth dipped slightly into a small gully of shallow water moving steadily along the rock bed. Their frantic steps sent up wet splashes, though Danica could feel most of the water seeping into the sneakers' stuffed toes. The added weight dragged her into a stumble; Marcus's reflexive grab the only prevention from a complete fall.

Though the sirens grew distant, Danica heard the communicative shouts as the PKs followed on foot. The onslaught of shots continued as the soldiers sporadically paused to aim and fire their charged rifles at the fleeing quarry. Overhead, limbs of the thickening tree coverage bent and swayed. *HALOs,* Danica registered as she and Marcus scrambled along the ravine. The bordering walls of dirt rapidly steepened and prevented the siblings from leaving the stream. A flat footbridge spanned the divide ahead. Danica, energy lagging despite the urgency, spied an arched opening underneath the bridge. Praying the tunnel was not a dead end, she shouted for her brother to follow inside to avoid the blasts from the pursuing HALOs.

Shielded from the morning sun, the shaft plunged into complete darkness only meters from the entrance. Essentially blind, the two were forced to slow their pace for fear of running into an invisible obstacle.

"Marcus?" Danica called into the darkness. Her heavy breathing and the pounding blood in her ears blocked out the sounds of her brother.

"I'm here," he answered from a shadow closer than Danica expected. "There's a light to the left," the boy added. Initially missed in her frantic sprint, Danica turned to find another long tunnel branching off from the main route; small illuminations evenly distributed along its curved ceiling. To their rear, the natural light at the entrance broke as soldiers breached the tunnel.

"Go," Danica whispered. Seconds later, she saw his silhouette as he reached the first overhead light.

"Come on!" he rasped to her upon realizing his sister had not followed him. The PKs, thin white beams of light shining from their weapons, moved further into the tunnel. Danica pressed herself into a small recess in the wall. Her hand tightly gripped the knife's handle. She had no delusions a teenage girl with a knife could overwhelm a squad of Peacekeepers, but, quite unknowingly, she had made the decision to distract the soldiers in order to allow Marcus time to escape. Maybe even killing one or two in the process. In the haze of fear and adrenaline, the concept of taking a life failed to surprise her when the thought settled into her mind.

The soldiers were only a pace away, and Danica felt her awareness detach from her body. The wall against her back seemed to disappear and a damp chill crept along her spine. A flicker of thought and she wondered if she now felt what others reported after near-death experiences - the surreal out-of-body sensation when events slowed beyond normal human perception. If one was present, would she see the individual beat of a fly's wings? Feel the imperceptible glide of the Earth round its axis?

The first PK stood a breath away. Danica readied the knife, readied herself. The hand of Death clutched at her back and she pushed herself forward. Her vision tilted as her body was pulled in the opposite direction until she collided with the ground. Heat and flesh pressed past her and the soldiers in the tunnel shouted startled cries of alarm. In the dizzying dance of white lights and amber gunfire, Danica watched in confusion as a blurred figure moved within the pack of Peacekeepers. Grunts of pains escaped through strangling voices and Danica heard the sickening snapping of bones. In year-long seconds, the assault moved before her eyes until the charged shots faded and only the disarray of small flashlights, resting unmoved on the ground, lit the tunnel. Three of the idle beams pointed upwards, crisscrossing in dramatic effect to reveal a lone figure standing among the fallen warriors. From his tattered clothing, Danica could see the man was not one of the Peacekeepers.

Questions spiraled in her mind as she tried to separate reality and confusion. Still splayed upon the tunnel floor, Danica worked her mouth around three weak words.

"Who are you?"

The man turned and lowered his gaze. The light irradiated the wildness in his eyes. With a voice graveled from disuse, he answered.

"Torrance."

CHAPTER ELEVEN

Kerwen Garrott

"Thank the Truth you and your Family survived," Abdul-Basir Fawzan condoled. Studying the man's holographic image, Kerwen believed his fellow Caput spoke with sincerity. If not sincerity, the Arab certainly had accuracy. In the final reckoning, the suicide attack had claimed thirty-seven lives, with ten times that number wounded. *The Garrott Family had been very lucky indeed,* Kerwen had thought many times over the last few hours.

"I'm sure that fact will bring much disappointment to the orchestrator," Caput Garrott nearly growled from the desk in his study. *Was that a twitch in Fawzan's eyes?* Kerwen wondered. He had already returned the calls from Caputs De Luca and Hu. The former had seemed more appalled with the ruination of a perfectly fine celebration than the loss of life. Hu, however, had cut his words with surgical precision. Even so, Kerwen could tell the Viper was quite concerned about blind reprisal. "I will break the neck of the snake who dared attack my Family," Garrott had told him; the allusion impossible to miss.

"I hear it was the Ignota," Fawzan said and brought Kerwen's mind back to the present.

"Or made to look like it was," he corrected. "They've never been this bold."

A troubled shadow passed over the man's dark-skinned face. "Our estimations of the Ignota's capabilities may need reassessment, Kerwen. I am loathed to add to your troubles this evening, but there is a situation in Washington, DC. A breach has occurred within Global Tech. The man heading up the SID upgrade, Philip Seton . . . you'll recall him from the presentation a month past . . . he went searching where he should not."

Kerwen did recall the man, although vaguely. Seton had been quite nervous during his first presentation to the Council of Five - an understandable reaction given the long remembered incompetence of the last man to oversee a global SID upgrade. "How bad?" Kerwen asked.

"He and one of the research scientists stumbled upon the discrepancies in the testing results. Echelon moved quickly to contain the situation. Seton is in custody."

"And the scientist?"

"Echelon tracked her to a hotel in Washington but was ambushed before they could apprehend her. It appears the Ignota has no dearth of individuals willing to blow themselves up for their cause. At present, she and her rescuers have vanished," Fawzan explained.

The Caput's voice held a worried edge and Kerwen suspected the entirety of the man's concern had not yet been revealed. "And?" he prompted Fawzan.

"It appears Seton made a copy of their findings. A search of the man's home failed to locate the holocard," Fawzan continued. "His two children have thus escaped our efforts of apprehension and Echelon believes the drive is in their possession."

Kerwen leaned back in his chair, mulling the shock of consecutive failures by Echelon. The elite Peacekeepers carried an aura of near infallibility throughout their decades-long history. "Basir, if that drive reaches the public—"

"An outcome to be avoided at all costs, I agree," the older Caput interjected. "But, combined with the attack on your Family, I believe we must re-evaluate our approach in dealing with the insurgents. To that end, I have called for an emergency gathering of the Five."

"Such an act might be viewed as fear on our part," Kerwen calculated. "It would only give more weight to the threat of the Ignota. The Council cannot be seen to jump at shadows."

"I will defer to your counsel," Fawzan nodded. "Via holophone, then. I will make the arrangements."

"Very well."

Before ending the call, the Arab Caput added, "I am truly grateful you survived this night, Kerwen. I fear this stirring of events as a bird who takes to wing when the storm clouds gather. We must keep our allies close."

In parting, Kerwen offered his thanks for the other man's words, but found himself unsettled by the warning. *Does he know I have aligned with Cambrie and Hu?* he wondered.

Wearied, he rose from the desk, deciding to forego the etiquette of making the final call. Even with the knowledge of the new developments Fawzan had imparted, he still wondered over Cambrie's involvement in the attack. There was some satisfaction in imagining Cambrie's worry when he learned Kerwen had spoken with the other Caputs.

Without intention, Kerwen's path from the study had led him to the grand ballroom. The House guard still picked through the debris, collecting evidence among the crumbled remnants of his triumph. The bodies, and the parts of bodies, had been removed, though the dark smears of blood decorating floor and walls remained. Upon noticing his entrance, the guards straightened to attention, but Kerwen dismissed their strict adherence to protocol with the wave of his hands. *Find me an enemy,* he silently implored.

His feet carried him to the elevator and then to the underground bunker. The manor had been secured, yet the subterranean conference room still buzzed with activity. His various lieutenants had opted to continue their investigation where it had begun. Though his frustration and anger desired it, Kerwen bypassed the room. He had delivered his commands earlier and he knew his presence would only be a distraction. *They'll come to you when they learn something,* he tried to comfort his mood.

Entering a room further down the hall, he found his wife seated beside the bed holding their son. Having shed the elaborate gown, Roslyn was dressed comfortably in clothes a servant had fetched from their chambers. Her hair was pulled back in a long braid and all traces of makeup had been removed. Even now, the blind could see the elegant authority of a Caput`e. Tilden, awake after the surgery, sat propped in the bed, a white bandage looping around his head and covering the wounded eye.

"How do you feel?" Kerwen asked his son while taking a seat across from Roslyn.

"Tired mostly," Tilden answered. "And my head hurts, but the doctors said it's from hitting the floor, not the surgery."

"The surgery was successful," Roslyn added, reiterating Liam's earlier pronouncement. "Do we know who did this?"

"Thus far it looks like the Cohors Ignota," Kerwen said.

"But you think otherwise." his perceptive wife replied.

Raising his hands in an admission of unsubstantiated suspicion, he said, "It could have been another Family, but there is no evidence to support that. Yet. Tomorrow, the Five will discuss a course of action to address the rebels."

The corners of the Caput`e's lips turned up in derision. "And they'll move to blame the attack on the Ignota, and in doing so direct attention away from themselves."

"Perhaps," Kerwen offered. "There was a similar bombing in America tonight, as well. Fawzan seems genuinely worried. He believes the cancer of insurgency is more malignant than we suspect."

"The Council has allowed them to exist for too long," Tilden broke in. Kerwen's brow lifted with surprise at his son's criticism. He had never known Tilden to speak with such vehemence against the Council. "Even if they are not responsible for tonight, the Ignota are terrorists, flouting the law and harassing Alliance operations. Yet, the Five sit idle."

In many ways, the Caput Heir spoke true. The Council had long been aware of the Ignota, the group having formed not long after the world's nations signed the Global Alliance Charter. Since then, Ignota agents had actively worked against the government. Yet, until recently, their efforts had been inconsequential; a nuisance yes, but relatively without much import. With every building they attacked, each bomb they detonated, the citizenry looked to the Alliance for security and direction. Media reported with government bias, depicting the subversive members as coldhearted killers with no claims to human decency. Fear of terrorism created blind devotion to the protector. The Cohors Ignota had done more to bolster Alliance dominance than to undermine it. Thus, the Five saw little need to strike down the rebels. Why waste such an effective tool?

"As I said," Kerwen repeated, "the Five will discuss the situation on the morrow. Now, where is that lovely young woman with whom you're so taken?"

"I don't think he is the only one so taken with her," Roslyn added to assist her husband's change of topic. In all their years together, Kerwen had not even considered being unfaithful to his wife. If he had, both he and the hypothetical mistress would likely have met with an assassin's skill.

Laughing, Kerwen responded, "One lioness in my pride is quite enough."

"I should hope so," the Caput`e said with a warning tone, though her eyes danced with humor. *Oh, those beautiful eyes!* Kerwen thought.

"The guards would not let her down," Tilden explained his date's absence. "Once the guests were cleared, a pod took her back to her hotel. After tonight, I don't think involvement with a Caput Heir is all that appealing to her."

"You'd be surprised," Roslyn said. "Some women are made of tougher stuff than men dare to believe."

"Only foolish men would make such a miscalculation," Kerwen mused and gave his wife a warm smile.

Any meeting of the Council of Five was an event marked by pomp and grandeur. Even now, with each member safely in their respective homes scattered across the globe, the moment sagged with a gravity of purpose. Typically, the Palace de'Caput, once a lavish hotel of twenty-first century design, held the formal, quarterly meetings of the Alliance's governing body. Large enough to house the Families (and keep the more bellicose members well separated), their retainers, media, and countless dignitaries, the Persian Gulf bastion was the most recognizable structure in the world – a symbol of the Council's power.

Other symbols, more subtle than the Palace, were at work this evening. In the pentagonal room of his manor (created for just such a purpose), Kerwen watched with a slight grin as his colleagues joined the conference; their images projected on large holoset platforms. Caput De Luca, in all his rotundity, had selected a room with mirrored walls, gilded ceilings, lacquered furnishings, and bejeweled accoutrements. The opulence of the setting, combined with De Luca's equally garish robes, brought physical pain to Kerwen's eyes. *The man probably shites ostentation,* he rued.

Left of the fat Italian, a more stark contrast could not have existed. Yin Xian Hu sat in a room near as black as his passionless eyes. Tall pillar candles bookended the Caput's image. Their faint light flickered and wavered, adding to the ominous sight. Peering deeply, Kerwen could make out no other detail of the Viper's setting, save for the sigil of House Hu behind him – a five-pointed crimson star, its lines formed by assassin's daggers, on a field of black. *No embarrassment over his Family's infamy,* Kerwen acknowledged.

Cambrie and Fawzan, respectively, appeared in rooms with less deliberate, and thus less overt, displays of power. The former reposed in a chamber of sharp, steel lines and edges. The modern design reflected the Westerner's self-belief in his Family's intrinsic importance to the future of Council and Alliance. Alternatively, Fawzan was surrounded by well-ordered riches, both large and small, from times long past. Centuries old canvases of the masters' greatest works adorned the walls, trinkets and small statues, some dating back millennia, rested on neat shelves and pedestals. The antiquities served to remind that Fawzan's House was the oldest and longest ruling of the Five Families.

Caput Garrott could not deride his contemporaries' representative selections. To the left and right of his chair stood four PK-drones, dramatically lit from above in museum-style. Kerwen hoped their silent presence spoke loudly of his recent gain in status.

"In service to Truth, with remembrance of our duty to the Global Alliance, I convene this gathering of the Council of Five," Fawzan, as the eldest of the Caputs, intoned with all due reverence.

"May our deeds honor Truth," the other Caputs responded in formulaic unison.

"In light of recent events," Fawzan continued, "I move we forego discussion of business not pertaining to the matter at hand."

"Seconded," De Luca said.

With the motion approved, the Arabian Caput pressed forward. "As you all are aware, Caput Garrott was the target of an inexcusable attack yesterday evening."

"And we are relieved the Caput survived such outrage," Cambrie interjected.

Twice that day, he had sought words with Kerwen; both occasions politely rebuffed. *His bowels must be water by now,* Kerwen thought.

"Yes," Fawzan added. "Thank Truth the attempt failed. Yet, even in failure, the Council must worry how such a plot even occurred. Unless new information has come to light, the blame points to the Cohors Ignota." Fawzan looked to Kerwen for agreement.

Clearing his throat, he answered, "No SID has yet been found to identify the bomber, or aid in tracing his history. Facial recognition has likewise proven unsuccessful." Kerwen casually passed his eyes over each Caput, searching for flashes of guilty relief.

"Are we sure Garrott was the target?" De Luca asked through a goblet of wine, a trickle of deep red running down his jowls.

Stunned by the question, Kerwen replied, "They infiltrated my home, killed nearly forty of my guests, and took my son's eye! Is there any doubt to the target?"

In a tone of condescension, De Luca said, "Yet, the detonation occurred some distance from your person. Would not the alleged terrorist wait for a more opportune moment to ensure his mission's success? Beyond a three-word utterance, there is nothing to link the attack to the Ignota. And they have yet to claim responsibility. Rather unlike them, no?"

"Meaning what?" Kerwen spat, anger rising.

"Meaning the Council should avoid myopathy," the Italian cooed with eely guile. "Several of the deceased had, shall we say, questionable allegiance to House Garrott. It would be a clever ruse to blame their removal on the Ignota. Or the other Families."

Cambrie, disgust clear in his voice, accused, "Have you become an Ignota sympathizer, Graziano?"

De Luca fixed the man with a cold stare. "You forget, Brother Cambrie, my House has oft been a target of the terrorists. Though, lately, I find myself besieged with violence from ebony-skinned warlords."

It was a task for Kerwen to force his face to passivity. *He knows Cambrie hired the warriors from the Dead Continent! The fat bastard is not as oblivious as he seems,* Kerwen noted with concern. He wondered if the Italian was also privy to Kerwen's involvement.

"Gentlemen," Fawzan addressed them as he sought to bring order. "We veer from the topic. With only speculation towards other possibilities, the only fact we have is the bomber declared himself an Ignotum before death. Perhaps the rebels have outlived their utility. Their next attack may indeed kill one of us."

Cambrie voiced his agreement. "We have informants embedded in their midst. We know many of their strongholds. I propose we move in force against them. Hu, you have been silent thus far. What say you on the matter?"

All attention seamlessly shifted to the darkened image of the assassin Caput. The man's eyes slid across each Family head in turn before he spoke. His soft tone, little more than a whisper, stirred images of a forked-tongue. "The Cohors Ignota operate in a complex arrangement of cells, mostly independent and unaware of one another. Only one member of each cell possesses the means to contact another cell. Complex, and yet simple. And very effective in protecting their identities. It is unlikely any strike, however large in scale, would completely remove the threat."

Guffawing, Cambrie slammed his hand down on his metal desk. "Two Caputs who lack the will to face a band of insurgent filth!"

"I did not say I opposed an offensive measure, Cambrie," Hu hissed. "I am simply elucidating the likely outcome. We need but look to our recent ancestors to find examples of wars on terror which proved public failures due to unrealistic expectations. True, those actions were strategically necessary to bring about the Alliance, but our forefathers were inept in handling the global perception. A costly mistake, as we well know. Striking the Ignota now, while not eliminating them, will certainly cripple them for a time; perhaps a decade or two. If we operate under that auspice, then I consent."

Fawzan let the Viper's words hang then settle for a moment. "Are we all in agreement, then? We will direct the Peacekeepers to strike against all known Ignota bases and members?"

Vocalizations of assent circled the pentagon.

"Very well. In the name of Truth, it is so ordered," the Council elder affirmed. "There is another matter—"

"Yes," Hu interjected, "the Seton girl and her brother. Pardon any offense, Caput Garrott, but I find this matter far more distressing."

In truth, Kerwen agreed with the Viper – much as it pained him to admit. The Ignota's actions might threaten an individual Family, but the secrets the Seton children possessed were beyond dangerous. If the "defect" in the SID upgrade was exposed, the resulting uprising could cataclysmically destroy the Alliance. The fall of Rome, the empire which had come to the precipice of achieving the goals of the Alliance, would seem but a skirmish in comparison. It had taken two thousand years to redirect the course of that failed history.

"I fear the situation has grown worse," Cambrie said. "Half a dozen PKs attempting to secure the children were slaughtered in a park tunnel. Clearly, two teenagers would not be capable of such a thing, which means they have found assistance."

"The Ignota," Kerwen mulled aloud.

"Most likely," Cambrie nodded.

De Luca, who had uncharacteristically been mute for more than a minute, stated, "Then, the urgency to hit the Ignota is increased. With luck, the siblings will be discovered in our raids."

The remaining minutes of the meeting were filled with continued repetition of the need to retrieve the damning holocard. Before Fawzan concluded the gathering with official words of adjournment, Caput Cambrie shared a pre-planned request. The other three Caputs agreed with vigor, and it was thus decided Kerwen would supply each Family with a company of PK-drones. Kerwen marveled over Cambrie's ability to plot treason in the midst of other such weighty matters. *Not just him*, Kerwen acknowledged as the holosets winked to black. *This treason is now mine as well.*

CHAPTER TWELVE

Danica Seton

Along twists and turns, traversing a path her eyes could barely discern, Danica and Marcus, nearly conjoined, followed the stranger through the underground tunnels. After supplying his name, the stranger had ducked back into the hidden door through which he had miraculously appeared. Though he had yet to speak again, Danica hoped there had been an implicit invitation to follow.

"What if he's some kind of killer? Or rapist?" Marcus whispered. The acoustics of the passage amplified the slightest sound, and while he was many feet ahead of them, Danica knew from the man's exaggerated sniff he could hear the commentary.

"Shh," Danica cautioned her brother. "If he wanted to kill us, he would have done it back there." She prayed such logic was sound.

"Maybe he is a cannibal and is luring us to where he can cook us," the boy continued to voice the wild turnings of his imagination.

As crazed as the suggestions were, Danica could feel the tendrils of fear multiplying each time Marcus shared another scenario. "Then, I hope he starts with you so you'll shut up!

Sometime later, Danica's exhaustion and the tunnel's darkness prevented an accurate measure, the stranger opened a large vault door. What lay beyond the meters-thick steel stole her breath. Blazing sconce-hung torches lit a chamber so cavernous its far walls hid in distant shadows. Mismatched furniture, beds and dressers, desks and chairs, were arranged as if in separate rooms, though no walls divided one from another. Faded rugs and carpet remnants formed a flowing patchwork across the stretching floor.

The most striking detail, however, was the number of books (*Actual books!* Danica thought in amazement) filling every available space. Thousands, perhaps tens of thousands, of bound volumes of all sizes caught the eye at every turn. Save for digitals of old buildings, libraries she remembered the name, Danica had never seen such a vast collection. Most families of even moderate wealth owned one or two books, selected for sentimental or monetary value. Her parents proudly displayed a first edition of a novel titled *Eye of the World*, a classic favorite of her father's from the late twentieth century. For her part, Danica could not see the excitement in its ownership; her SID provided digital access to the same work.

"You live here?" she asked.

"Yes," the man replied. "Close the door."

The siblings complied, exerting the last reserves of their strength to pivot the heavy door into its frame. Unsure of their place, the two stood watching the stranger as he moved about the nearest "room," a kitchen if one was generous in definition. As he went about his task, Danica studied him. In the warm glow of the cave, she saw he did not appear as wild as her first impression. Nearing two meters in height, his towering build was lean yet well-muscled, chest and arms stretching the fabric of a black cotton shirt. His blond hair, thick and reaching to his chin, hung loose and clean except for the few splatters of blood from the earlier battle. The skin of his clean-shaven face, dotted in crimson as well, was unnaturally pale, which Danica attributed to sunless, underground living. Though he seemingly ignored their presence, she did catch a few glimpses of deep-set ice blue eyes. His movements were deliberate, each flex and contraction of muscles a practical and efficient use of energy. *No*, Danica thought, *not a wild man, but extraordinarily intense.*

His gruff voice startled her from her observations. "Eat if you're hungry. I'll be back. Don't wander." *Doesn't waste words either,* she added in silence. Without ceremony, the stranger disappeared through an opening in the cave wall Danica had initially overlooked.

For all his fearful warnings, Marcus was the first to break from their statue-stillness. He wandered towards the small wooden table the stranger had set with chipped plates and metal cups. Tin cans of vegetables and cubed beef, jagged-edged lids lifted upright, and a plastic jug of water had been placed at the table's center. Small beads of condensation were beginning to form around the jug. The long-ignored pangs of hunger roared back with demand, and Danica joined her brother. With the dry food bar their only meal in a day's time, the stranger's offerings seemed a feast to her eyes. Ravenously, and without care for tidiness, they emptied the cans, the food resting but seconds on the plates before reaching their empty stomachs. A loud belch from Marcus caught them both in surprise and the echoing sound sent them into a fit of laughter.

Stopping short of licking the cans' last traces of food, Danica thrice filled and emptied her metal mug; the refreshing water cold despite the apparent lack of a refrigerator. Pushing back from the table, she could feel drowsiness spreading through her. Curiosity, however, kept the sensation at bay, and she began to explore the lit areas of the cavern. Moving through hip-high towers of books, careful to avoid upending the stacks, Danica stood before a wide double-door bureau. Pulling gently on the brass ring on the right door, she gasped at the overwhelming assortment of weapons inside. Knives, crossbows, and bullet guns neatly covered the smooth wood interior. Lower drawers contained endless boxes of ammunition marked with diverse caliber numbers. A smaller compartment held a plain leather cuff with a simple silver finger-ring attached to one end. Danica lifted the ring and discovered it was tethered to the cuff by a clear, retractable length of cord similar to fishing line.

"Don't touch that."

Danica nearly yelped when the stranger's coarse words broke through the shadows. Clumsily, she dropped the cuff back into the compartment. The man emerged from the darkness at her right and closed the drawers and doors of the bureau.

"I'm sorry," she squeaked as she backed away from him. "Where did you go?" she asked.

"Checked the other entrance."

"Did they follow us?"

"No."

He moved past her towards the "kitchen," and hand-over-hand pulled a rope which disappeared into an opening in the floor. Seconds later, a sloshing metal bucket of water rose from the well. Unclasping the container from a hook, he then walked to a table and poured some of the liquid into a bowl. The stranger shrugged out of his shirt, revealing a sculpted back crisscrossed with a lattice of scars; some faint and short, others raised and longer than a hand. As he washed the now-dried blood from his face, Danica saw the strength of his musculature underneath the taut skin. Marcus, eyes wide from the sight of the scarring, stared warily from the table of empty cans. When the man finished cleansing, he turned and slipped into a fresh shirt. Before the clothing fell into place, Danica spied purple blotches of bruises.

"You're hurt," she said.

"I'm fine."

Danica doubted she would have been able to move if her body possessed half as many injuries. "Thank you for rescuing us. And for the food," she added.

"Mhmm," he grunted.

Determined to draw him from his reticence, Danica asked, "How long have you lived here?"

"Always."

"With anyone else?" she prodded.

A flash of emotion, the first she had witnessed from him, flickered briefly across his face. "Not anymore. There are beds. Get some rest." In a dimmer recess of the cavern, the stranger faded from view; only the familiar sound of a body sliding into sheets indicating he had put himself to bed.

Looking to Marcus, who twirled his finger at the side of his head, Danica smiled encouragingly and waved him to follow as she selected a place to sleep.

Her dreams had been troubled, in most she ran from unseen terrors, and in others the images of her parents' dying flashed mercilessly. By the thrashing at her side, Marcus seemed to share her fitful slumber. She had given no argument when he had asked to share her bed. Though well past the years of fearing bogeymen lurking in closets, Danica welcomed the security of his closeness. When sleep faded and her body returned to wakefulness, she laid staring at the unseen cave ceiling; mind burning with worry. Eventually, soft shuffling reached her ears and she slipped free of her still-sleeping brother.

The stranger, Torrance she remembered, dressed as she had last seen him, reclined upon one of the many couches in the cavern. In his lap he held an open book – the leather cover too faded for her to read the title.

"How long was I asleep?" she asked. Though she had not made a sound in her approach, Torrance did not flinch at her appearance.

"Half a day," he replied without lifting his gaze from the pages. With the dull ache of her muscles, Danica would have guessed at a shorter span of time. Doubting an invitation was forthcoming, she sat down in an adjacent cushioned chair.

"My name is—," she began.

"Danica Seton," he finished the sentence.

Taken aback by his foreknowledge, and alarmed at its meaning, she asked,

"How do you know that?"

"Your face is everywhere. You and your brother, Marcus. Wanted for murdering your parents," he answered casually as he turned a page in the dusty tome.

"We didn't kill . . .," Danica nearly shouted. "What do you mean our faces are everywhere? Where did you go?"

Closing the book with agitated resignation, Torrance finally turned his eyes to her. "I went Outside," he explained. Danica heard the pronounced inflection, as if the world beyond the cave was a distinct place like New York or China. "They've offered a reward for your capture."

Given the poverty surrounding her, Danica immediately feared the sway a reward might have on the man. "Will you turn us in?" she asked with trepidation, though she doubted he would admit it if that was his intention.

A few beats of silence passed, his eyes boring deeply into her, before he answered. "No. There'll be no reward. Only a fool makes a deal with the Alliance and expects it to honor the terms. And, I'd have to explain six dead Peacekeepers."

Though the charges against her were fabricated, the man who had rescued her and her brother had indeed committed a grave crime in the eyes of the law. Their mutual criminality, actual or perceived, offered Danica some assurance Torrance spoke truthfully.

"Those soldiers . . . how did you, I mean, where did you learn to fight like that?" she inquired.

Danica was sure the shadow of pain and sorrow which she had witnessed the night before, once again darkened the man's features. "I was taught by the man who raised me," he said in explanation.

"Your father?"

"No," he replied, the tone of his voice cold and dispassionate. "I . . . I never knew my father. Or my mother," Torrance added; the first time he had answered her questions with surplus detail. Danica could see he was as surprised as she by his unguarded confession. In that moment, she felt a thread-thin rapport, a wavering kinship, with the man. Only newly orphaned herself, the easing of such pain was unfathomable. How had Torrance borne that sorrow his entire life?

"I'm sorry" she intoned with weighty understanding. The blond figure rose from the couch, tossing the book down upon the now-empty cushions, and walked into the shadows.

"If you're hungry, there's some food in the cabinets. I've made arrangements for someone to take you in. We leave in two days," his disembodied voice reverberated along the high ceilings. And as quickly as it had been felt, the bond Danica thought had formed shattered; its fragile shards added to the piles of grief and disappointment in her mind.

Torrance's presence in the cavern over the next two days was as limited as his conversation. He came and went at varying intervals, staying only long enough to sleep a few short hours before disappearing once again. When Danica pressed him for an explanation, he replied he was "seeing to things." Though she knew little of the man, and less of his typical routine, she was certain he was avoiding the siblings.

Left to their intrigues, Danica and Marcus passed the intervening hours with exploration. The cavern was even more immense than either had imagined. Removing a torch from the wall, the two walked beyond the visible area and into the shadowy recesses of the lair. The odd arrangements of furniture ended at the lit perimeter, yet it took them another six minutes to reach the furthest end of the chamber. A series of arched openings, three in number, branched from the main part of the man-made cave towards destinations unknown. Danica, while braver than she had been upon first arriving in Torrance's underground home, recalled the man's caution against wandering, and turned back to more familiar territory.

They explored the other "rooms," made a game of hunting for the softest couch and largest bed. Marcus suggested counting the books, but brother and sister grew bored after reaching five thousand, and realizing it was only a fraction of the collection. They ate the food their host had left for them, brought up buckets of water from the well to drink and wash with, and made passing attempts reading selections from the horde of books. Not much for the latter, Danica flipped through old texts, pausing to study digitals, yet finding no real interest in the subjects. Marcus, however, was far more voracious in his perusal of the literary collection. Upon finding an entire section of historical non-fiction (it was Marcus who had discovered the many books were divided into specific groupings), the boy folded his legs on the floor and buried himself in the pages. Occasionally, he would call out a fact he believed Danica simply had to know. She would murmur an appropriate reply, which only encouraged Marcus to share another tidbit from his readings.

By the end of their second day below ground, Danica was twitching with boredom. Engaged as he was in his books, Marcus seemed to disassociate from the conditions of their lives. Danica did not know if his was a healthy response to the death of their parents and their fugitive status, but she found herself envying him regardless. She found no distraction powerful enough to silence the nagging worries whispering in the corners of her mind. Torrance had yet to expand on the identity or location to which he was going to deliver them. His absence, and stone-walled silence in the fleeting moments of his presence, left Danica answerless and frustrated. And forced to remain in hiding prevented her from easing either sentiment. The result was a cyclical pattern of worry to frustration to anger and a return to worry once again to begin the revolution of emotions anew.

On the morning (or at least Torrance told them it was a morning) of their scheduled departure, he presented each of the Setons with a bag of clothing. Since their rescue, both had worn shirts and jeans from Torrance's wardrobe. Given his towering build, the items were of course outsized for Marcus and Danica, but were clean and fresh and an improvement from the pilfered outfits in which they had arrived.

"We need to change your hair," he informed Danica as she examined the apparel in the bag. The long locks of auburn had frequently earned compliments from the girls at school and she was reluctant to part with them. She had never been one to agonize over her appearance, though despite her lack of effort Danica had often been declared a natural beauty. Just like her mother. As Torrance worked the silver shears through her hair, Danica fought back a tear watching the clumps pile around the chair. It was not vanity which pained her, but rather a renewed sense of loss. Each cut further removed the resemblance she had shared with her mother. With the work done, Torrance handed her a bottle of brown dye which she applied with regret over a large tub.

Rinsed and dried, Danica moved behind a tri-fold screen and donned the outfit Torrance had provided. The backless, forest green dress was short, ending at mid-thigh, and was cut deep down her chest. The fashion was modern, reminding her of the celebrity digitals in entertainment digi-zines. Knee-high, black leather boots, with precariously angled heels, finished the look. Observing herself in a full-length mirror, Danica's cheeks warmed scarlet as she saw the immodesty of her attire. Beth Seton would surely have fainted if her daughter had ever dared leave the house in such a manner. The short pixie hair and the revealing dress, however, made it difficult for even Danica to recognize the reflection.

"I don't know if I can wear this," she said after rejoining the two males. Marcus, his own hair trimmed and styled in severe points, wore the clothing of a young pop-star. Lines of thin black scrolled outward from his left eye mimicking an ivy-vine pattern. Foregoing the black on black of his usual attire, Torrance was clad in a pair of fitted crimson pants with a white cavalry shirt. A long black trench, the expense of the leather evident in its soft sheen, hung from his broad shoulders to just above the ankles of his boots.

"It will keep eyes off your face," assured Torrance with an uncharacteristic hint of humor. *And on everything else I'm showing,* Danica protested.

Make-overs complete, Torrance led the small party through a series of dark tunnels. They made so many turns, Danica doubted she would have been able to trace their route even with a map. Her feet had begun to ache, the spiked heels a marked difference from her usual choice of flat boots or running sneakers, when the stone shaft dead-ended. With complaint ready on her tongue, Danica watched Torrance as he worked a network of levers. An unseen seam expanded as the false-wall silently swung inward. Danica shielded her eyes as the long absent light of day flooded into the tunnel.

Torrance urged them forward through the opening. Once her pupils contracted and her vision returned, Danica saw a thick forest of trees and a carpet of autumn leaves on the ground. Turning about, she watched the door close behind them, its edges blending into a rock wall and perfectly camouflaged from detection. A short path led them to a black podcar waiting idle behind a large tree.

"You have a pod?" Danica asked in amazement.

"I do today," their guide answered, lowering himself into the vehicle. She offered a silent apology to the hapless person who would discover his costly pod stolen. Overriding the system's automated navigation, Torrance steered them down a winding dirt road, eventually connecting to a pavement of flowing traffic. The first recognizable feature appeared minutes later as the pod crossed a long bridge over the Delaware River, the tall buildings of Philadelphia rising in the distance.

Danica did not need the pod's clock to confirm they travelled during the morning rush-hour commute. Their pod sped along at an even pace in the middle of the five lane expanse. To the left and right, men and women busied themselves with chat, work, make-up application and a variety of other tasks as pods carried them to their destinations. Surrounded once again by strangers, Danica's stomach fluttered. She had not realized how calming the security of their short days underground had truly been.

Torrance did not speak during the journey. His first words coming a short time after crossing the bridge. "We're here," he said as he turned the pod onto a broad avenue in the heart of Philadelphia, and slipped into an available parking space.

Stepping from the pod, Danica struggled with dress, fighting its efforts to reveal her most delicate of areas. The crowded sidewalks teemed with pedestrians; some in the fine cut suits and dresses of executives, others dressed more similarly to Danica and her two companions. Following Torrance through the throng, she grew increasingly self-conscious as men, and more than a few women, roamed their eyes down her body.

"Stop fidgeting," Torrance corrected her under his breath.

"Easy for you to say," she growled back. *You're not walking around half naked,* she added in her thoughts. Untwining her twisting fingers, Danica dropped her hands to her sides and willed herself to wavering confidence.

Torrance led them to a pair of ornate silver and gold doors guarded by two men whose size made even Torrance seem dwarven. A sign above the entrance named the place as "Angel's Touch." The men offered Torrance a nod of familiarity, and pulled the heavy bar handles of the doors.

Lit dimly with electric candles, the interior was equal parts heaven and hell. The red-tinted floor, made of a mirror-like material, undulated in soft ripples at the contact of their steps. The effect was dizzying as Danica's ripples melded with her brother's before coalescing with Torrance's footfalls. Shiny, unadorned, black-lacquered walls stretched high to a curved ceiling depicting a sky scene; though the blues of nature had been traded for shades of red. It took a second glance to see the clouds moved and expanded across the surface. Twin flights of stairs curved up the sides of the hall to a railed balcony; their silver steps the only break in the red and black motif. Several couches and divans, in dark leather, were scattered across the main level.

If the stares on the sidewalk had been discomforting, the groping leers from the room's occupants had Danica nearly apoplectic. Men and women, clad in the faintest traces of clothing (and some bare of any covering at all), lounged on the furniture. Their bodies were well chiseled, curves and angles in sinful perfection. Those not escorting patrons up the stairs cast seductive looks toward the newly arrived trio. Several touched themselves scandalously in perverse attempts at enticement.

"You brought us to a brothel?!" Danica accused.

"Shut up and keep walking," Torrance commanded.

In contrast to Danica's abhorrence, her brother stared with impropriety at the eroticism which filled the hall. "Marcus!" she snapped his name, repeating it when he failed to acknowledge her.

"What?" he asked. Even with the reprimand, his eyes still grinned with delight.

"Torrance, mmm . . . " cooed the buxom woman behind the long counter at the back of the hall. "Back so soon? If Alanna is losing her touch I'm sure I can find you a girl with more skill. I just hired a pretty little Asian thing, oh yes, and she can do things men only dream . . . "

"I'll stick with the usual, Seraphim," Torrance cut into the woman's sales pitch.

"As you wish. Mmm, and for them? Do they want guys, girls? Maybe both?" she continued as she stared at the siblings with a hungry smile. Danica's jaw dropped at the outlandish suggestion she or her brother would ever engage a hired lover. Her indignation, though, was undercut by Marcus's ogling.

"No," Torrance answered. "They'll stay with me."

Seraphim, whose name Danica took as evidence of the woman's ownership of the establishment, raised a penciled eyebrow. "Mmm, that's a different request for you. Let me see," the woman scanned a screen while running her tongue across cherry lips. "Ah, yes. Alanna's available. Go ahead on up, you know the way. And remember, I have plenty of others if you . . . mmm . . . want to expand your horizons. Ming-sa has been getting rave reviews. Mmm, oh yes. The men love how she can put her legs . . . " The flesh-peddler continued the lurid descriptions of her new employee's abilities despite Torrance leading Danica and Marcus up the left-side staircase.

The uppermost step opened onto a wide corridor, decorated much as the main hall had been. Every few paces, opposing numbered doors (even on the right, odd on the left) broke the continuity of the black walls. From the emanating sounds,

Danica could only guess what activities were shielded from view. Moans and grunts she had expected, but by several doors she heard whip-snapped air followed by cries of pain. Another room shook with the voices of more men and women than she could easily count.

Despite the ordered ban on speaking, Danica brought herself to an abrupt halt, refusing to continue. She had intended to deliver an orderly argument against what she believed Torrance had planned, yet the outcome was closer to a rambling shriek. "That's it! We're leaving. I'm not letting you turn us into . . . into the kind of people who work here. Marcus is only thirteen, for Truth's sake! And I've never . . . . We're not selling ourselves. If the people here want to do that, that's their choice. But . . . but . . . thank you for your help, but we'll make it on our own. If you want we can . . "

Pain.

Caught up in her ill-devised speech, Danica had not seen Torrance's hand until it had already reddened the side of her face. Disbelief and shock gagged her, and she stared speechlessly at the man.

"I told you to shut up, girl," Torrance growled. "Even in a place like this there are cameras; watching and listening." Cold blue eyes burned, and then softened some seconds later. "No one expects you to whore yourself. Alanna has offered to shelter the both of you until things die down. That's all."

Danica stared up at him as she rubbed her assaulted cheek. She tried to match the force of his eyes, a penetrating intensity which quickly withered her resolve. She doubted two suns could hold as much power. "Why can't we stay with you?" she asked.

Torrance looked almost wounded upon hearing the question. His mouth opened, lips curving around words which would go unsaid. As the stoicism returned to his visage, Torrance tightened his jaw, speaking through clenched teeth, "Cause you can't."

Momentarily frozen, she watched him turn and continue down the corridor. It was foolish, she knew, to feel a sting of abandonment from a man who was still little more than a stranger. But, she had read into the wide spaces between his slowly-delivered words. *We can't stay with him,* Danica thought, *because he doesn't want us around.* Marcus entwined his hand with hers, squeezed gently just as she had once done to comfort him, and he pulled her forward.

Eventually coming to the desired door, Torrance knocked twice before turning the brass knob and pushing the door open. Unlike the rest of Angel's Touch, or at least the more public areas she had seen, Danica was surprised to find the room a welcome departure from the overly-sensual red and black colorings.

Soft tones of blue, from nearly white to a calming azure, covered every meter of the room. A canopied bed, dressed in silks and satins, snugged invitingly against the far wall. Nearer to the door, a delicate vanity, its curved Victorian legs thinning downward to small pegged feet, displayed a collection of glass perfume bottles and a silver-plated brush with matching hand mirror. The one-person bench was tufted with a thick cushion. Breathing deep, Danica thought the room even smelled blue; a tension-relieving combination of powder and rain, ocean and hydrangea, and, if possible, the scent of clouds. An unseen breeze gently rustled the sheer curtains hanging before the false-windows. In any place, the chamber would have been beautiful. Located as it was within the sexualized, dungeon-esque Angel's Touch, the bedroom was a majestic paradise.

A section of the mural on the right wall fell back and the mistress of the room entered through the concealed doorway. Instantly, Danica felt foolish for thinking the chamber exquisite; it was lifeless and dull compared to the woman who glided forward. Thick waves of sun-gold hair fell perfectly past her shoulders. The soft features of her face were warm and tender, and impossibly angelic. Her emerald eyes were highlighted by the blonde lashes and unblemished cream skin. Lips of rose-blush formed a perfect kiss even as they parted in a caressing smile. Wearing only a translucent skirt of flowing blue, Alanna's pink-tipped breasts, full and lush, swelled from her chest in flawless formation. Danica had never imagined nature could create such magnificence, nor contain it within one form.[1]

"I've missed you," the goddess said with a voice of pure serenity. She pressed herself to Torrance, tilting her head to reach his lips. Danica would have rolled her eyes had she witnessed her parents engage in a kiss as passionate, but Alanna's perfection had her mesmerized.

Reluctantly breaking from the affection, Torrance said, "Just business today." *He's blushing!* Danica realized. She could see a thawing in his harsh eyes of ice.

The woman traced a finger down his hard jawline and under his chin. "This *is* my business."

"Next time," Torrance told her. Danica wondered how he could manage the will to resist the woman's seductions. "Can you still look after them?"

Stealing a glance at the door, she turned her attention to the siblings, studying brother and sister with her gem eyes. "You made a frightful mess of her hair, Tor. Don't worry, child, we can fix it. The digitals don't do your beauty justice."

Danica's knees almost buckled at the compliment. How could one so perfect find any beauty in her?

"I think you'll become quite the strapping man," Alanna addressed Marcus.

"For now, it will be dangerous for them to be seen," Torrance said. "For you and them."

Alanna nodded. "They can stay in my apartment upstairs. When Seraphim asks, I will tell her they are your children and you asked me to care for them until you can find a proper home. If she questions further, I'll say Danica is thinking about training here. Sera won't ruin an opportunity to add such a face to her roster."

A weak voice in her mind suggested Danica reiterate her earlier protestations. Yet, in the dazzling hypnosis of Alanna's presence, she found herself considering the offer. Torrance, stronger willed and perhaps more accustomed to the woman's power, said what Danica could not. "They are not here to work, Alanna."

"Relax, love. It's only what Sera will be told," she soothed. Then, directing her words to Danica, "Unless of course, you change your mind, child. I would see to your training."

"Alanna—" Torrance warned.

"Oh, very well," the woman gave over. Danica doubted Alanna was often denied a request. "You really are too serious, love."

In a tone of parting, Torrance said, "I'll be back next week with credits to pay for their keep." Before turning to the door, he warned the youths, "Don't go outside. Don't even leave Alanna's apartment."

The woman's voice broke from tranquility, edged with a hint of desperation. "You're leaving so soon, love? Stay. Let me show the children upstairs and then I can entertain you. On the house."

Torrance's stride stopped short. He turned slowly around; eyes narrowed and

---

[1] We would later learn that nature had little to do with her beauty. The men and women who sold their bodies and desires had spent many credits to attain the levels of perfection through an alarmingly high number of surgical procedures. –M.S.

once again chilled. "On the house? You never work for free."

Gliding to him, the curve of her hips visible through the thin fabric of the swaying skirt, Alanna pressed herself to his chest. "'Never' is a word for fools, love," she purred. "Stay with me awhile. Let me thank you for protecting these children." The tones of seduction returning from their momentary lapse as she lifted his hand, pressing it to cup her exposed breast.

Resolute, Torrance asked, "Why?"

Feigning insult, Alanna rose on her toes to whisper breathily into his ear. "Why? Have I ever needed a reason to want you inside me?"

"You've needed credits," he dryly reminded her. The suspicion on Torrance's face flashed to comprehension. "What have you done, Alanna?"

"All I've done is give you my heart, love."

Gripping her wrists in one large hand, Torrance pulled her roughly to him. "What have you done?" he accused again.

Alanna gasped at the sudden display of violence. Danica observed in silent confusion, unsure what scene was playing out before her. She pulled Marcus to her side, fearing the wildness she once suspected within Torrance was soon to emerge.

All trace of alluring calm fled from the woman's voice. "Two million credits. They're going to pay me two million credits," Alanna blurted in a sob.

Betrayal and anger flashed menacingly in his eyes. His words, filled with demonic malevolence, seemed blasphemous in the blue sanctuary.

"Spend it in Hell," he growled. With one fluid motion, Torrance pushed the woman away while his left hand bent beneath the back of his trench, pulling an altered firearm into view. Before Danica could scream, a single bullet sliced the air, passing entirely through Alanna's temple in an explosion of blood. For a frozen moment, the woman's body stood in disbelieving death. Danica's mind reeled as the harmony of the chamber ripped from existence.

"Get down!" Torrance commanded through the fog of her shock. She pulled her brother to the floor as Torrance retrieved a second gun hidden in the folds of the coat. Twin streams of bullets expanded into the room, following the slow circle of Torrance's rotation. Danica heard the shouts of alarm and injury erupting throughout the building; her own screams drowned in the chaotic din. Debris from the room, wood and plaster mixed with torn fabric and pillow feathers, floated in the air, momentarily suspended before falling to the carpet. The enveloping shades of blue quickly paled beneath the dust, leaving visible only the red splashes of Alanna's death.

The air began to sizzle as charged bolts returned through the openings Torrance's onslaught had created in the room's structure. Upon seeing the comet-tailed amber rounds sear walls and floor, Danica slowly understood the lurching shift the world had taken only a moment before. *Alanna sold us out!* her mind shouted. *She had betrayed Torrance for two million credits. And now the Peacekeepers have us cornered!* Refusing to accept capture as inevitable, Danica dragged her brother forward; knees and elbows scraping along the now hazardous flooring. Freeing her feet from the awkward high heels, she sent a silent wish for a pair of jeans and her old, familiar boots.

Reaching the mural-wall, Danica pressed her hand along its base until the disguised door surrendered to her search. A tight-spiraled, metal staircase wound its way up to Alanna's personal apartment. Standing again, Danica looked quickly back to Torrance. The man crouched low behind the thick wood of the bed's headboard, which splintered and smoked from the endless charged blasts from the PKs in the hall. Her eyes locked with his; Danica's stare conveying fear and gratitude. Torrance angled his right hand and sent one of his guns across the room in a low toss. Landing at her feet, Danica bent quickly and gathered the weapon from the floor. Any attempt to thank him was made impossible as the man had already returned his focus to the approaching PKs.

Marcus, halfway up the staircase, called down to his sister. Danica's long, toned legs swallowed three steps a stride as she twisted around the rising spiral. Entering the mistress' apartment seconds behind her brother, her racing heart contracted in a skipped beat. A PK squad, particle rifles aimed forward, filled the small foyer. A man at the group's center, silver eagles pinned to his black Peacekeeper uniform, had his arm wrapped tightly around Marcus's neck, a gun pressed to one side of the boy's head. Remembering the weapon in her own hand, Danica swung the gun up from her side.

"Drop it!" the man restraining Marcus ordered. Indecision turned her stomach in agony. "Don't be a fool, Ms. Seton," he added at her hesitation. Seeing the tears escaping her brother's eyes, Danica's remaining wisp of courage evaporated. Opening her hand, the gun slipped from her grasp. Before it hit the floor, the soldiers surged at her, roughly spinning her around and pulling her arms behind her back. Cold metal encircled her wrists, binding them together.

"She's secure, Colonel," one of the soldiers announced.

"Get them loaded," instructed the man who had held Marcus. "Once the transport's away, converge on their accomplice."

Two men pushed the siblings across the foyer into the larger sitting room. The French doors of one of the room's tall windows opened wide revealing a hovering HALO vessel; a metal plank connecting the vehicle to the apartment. Staring down at the street below, Danica wondered if the three-story fall would be enough to kill her. The option was immediately removed as their escorts shoved her onto the HALO. Forced into fold-out seats, she watched as the colonel, grim face triumphant, stepped across the platform. One of the soldiers called the order to depart, the command relaying to the pilot through the built-in microphone of the PK's helmet. The air swept through the open sides of the HALO as it zoomed forward, and away from Angel's Touch and Torrance.

"Please, let us go," Danica pleaded to the colonel, knowing how foolish the request sounded. "We haven't done anything."

The imposing man stared down at her with a mocking smile. "Let you go? You're the daughter of a traitor, Ms. Seton. Your father betrayed the Alliance. You've stolen State secrets, resisted arrest, allied with a terrorist, and killed a half-dozen Peacekeepers. Those were my men you and your friend slaughtered. You will answer for your crimes."

"My father isn't a traitor!" she spat. "We haven't stolen anything!"

The colonel nodded to one of the soldiers. The PK pulled Danica up from the seat and forcefully ran his hands over her body. One hand slid under the short hem of her dress, groping and searching in equal measure. A tear welled in her eye as the violation continued. "What do we have here?" the soldier hotly breathed against her cheek. The man's hand gripped the hidden holocard, tearing the fabric of her underwear as he pulled it away.

"Haven't stolen anything?" the colonel accused as he held up the drive the PK had handed him.

"I don't know what's on it," Danica said truthfully as the guard pushed her back down into the seat.

"That's not for me to decide," the leader told her. "You're to be delivered to the Council for interrogation. They can be very persuasive, Ms. Seton. I doubt you'll resist as much as you're father."

Danica's eyes widened.

"He's alive?" Marcus asked in adolescent desperation.

The colonel paused before answering; regret for the informative slip darkening his already stern features. "For the time being," he begrudgingly confirmed, and then turned away, ending the interview.

Dad's alive! Danica's mind shouted; the knowledge spreading warm hope from her chest to goose-fleshed skin. There had been little time to grieve for her parents since the nightmare had begun. She had pushed the painful thoughts to the corner of her mind. Always present, always looming, but continually suppressed through denial and distraction. Yet, now knowing Philip Seton still lived allowed the hope that the fate of her and her brother was not definite. *Dad can help us, save us. He can fix this!* Even at eighteen years of age, Danica had found herself childishly believing in the omnipotence of a parent.

"Colonel, we're ten minutes from the base," the second soldier announced.

"Good. What's the status from the whorehouse?"

The soldier repeated the question, and fell silent as he listened to the reply over the communicator. Shaking his head, the man replied, "Mostly chaos. Two explosions from the pro's apartment. Casualties unknown. The reserve team has entered the building, but communications are limited, sir."

The colonel displayed no reaction to the news of casualties, instead inquiring, "And the target?"

"Unclear, sir. Specialist Raines is closing behind us on an aerocycle. He'll have better intel."

Danica felt her stomach knot in grief. Outwardly indifferent, Torrance had risked much in rescuing them in the tunnel, providing refuge, and finally sacrificing himself so that she and Marcus could escape. She knew little of the man, yet the inevitability of his death struck her with surprising profundity. Seated opposite her, Marcus clearly suffered the same sense of loss. His face was a torture of sorrow and fear.

Silent minutes passed. The strong winds created by their airborne speed buffeted Danica with their chill; the thin dress providing little shield from the battering. As the HALO carried them towards fates unknown, Danica clung to the hope of her father's protection. A bodiless voice, sinister and cynical, taunted in her mind – *your father's a prisoner, and soon you will be, as well.*

Attention diverted, she heard one of the soldiers update their commanding officer. "Six minutes out, Colonel. Raines is coming up along our portside now."

The HALO's trajectory shifted slightly as the aerocycle rose into view off the vessel's left bay. Danica fearfully wondered if the arriving PK carried news of Torrance's death. She cast her eyes to the sleek steel craft. Far smaller than the troop-carrying bulk of the HALO, the aerocycle more closely resembled its land-dwelling, two-wheeled motor bike cousin. In place of tires, however, the aerocycle possessed the same hover-technology which propelled the HALO.

Danica blinked as she registered the two bodies straddling the vehicle. At the rear, a uniformed PK slumped limp and unconscious against the driver. The driver with crimson pants. Before Danica's mind processed the unexpected shock, Torrance aimed a particle rifle with his right hand.

The amber bolt slammed into one of the PKs, driving the soldier back and out of the other side of the HALO. The second PK flinched from the searing bullet which had taken his comrade. Recovering quickly, the Peacekeeper hefted his own rifle but his aim went wild as Torrance slammed the aerocycle into the HALO. The jolt knocked Danica from the seat and with her hands bound behind she could not prevent her jaw from colliding painfully with the metal deck. The impact brought small white starbursts to her vision. Blinking through the specks, she glimpsed legs and feet shuffling and entwining.

"Bring 'er down!" the voice of the remaining PK solider shouted; the last word ending in a strangle as Torrance spun the man's neck. Unable to right herself, Danica screamed as the soldier's body dropped; his dead eyes, only centimeters away, stared at her from the floor of the HALO. The sharp angle of his head and the protrusion of bone from his neck brought Danica close to retching. Disorientation returned as the HALO slammed to the street below; forcing her body into a hard bounce against the machine's deck and pushing the air from her lungs.

The chaos, which had been contained within the HALO's bay, poured into the street surrounding the downed craft. Automated pods swerved, tires squealing and smoking, to avoid colliding with the HALO. Pedestrians pointed and gawked, unsure what to make of the emergency landing in the midst of mid-morning traffic. Only a brave few stepped forward from the safety of the sidewalks to check on the HALO's occupants.

Danica struggled to her feet. Her eyes frantically sought her brother. Relief swelled when she saw him rummaging through the dead PK's belongings, clearly searching for the release to their handcuffs. Turning left, she found the colonel's body lying motionless some meters away; his torso on the black pavement, while his legs still perched on the HALO bay's deck. She could not tell if the man was dead or simply unconscious, but Danica stumbled to him regardless. Awkwardly contorting her waist so her still-bound hands could search him, she dug her fingers into the colonel's pants pocket; snatching back the holocard.

Equally successful in his own search, Marcus slid a silver device, no larger than his thumb, into Danica's restraints. "Are you okay?" she hugged him once her bonds fell away.

"Yeah," he answered, "What about you?"

She nodded in reply and wondered when the timbre of Marcus's voice had shifted from adolescence to adulthood. When had he begun to sound like their father? "Where's—"

Danica's question was simultaneously interrupted and answered as one of the HALO pilots burst through the cabin door. The hilt-deep knife in his chest made it quite clear Torrance had taken the battle into the cockpit as soon as the HALO had landed. In further confirmation, he ducked his head beneath the cockpit door and stepped into the bay.

"Injured?" he asked.

"No," Danica replied for both siblings.

"They're closing in. We need to move," Torrance said as he turned back into the cockpit. The Setons moved quickly to join him. With only two seats, and Torrance already occupying the one of the left, Danica lowered herself into the available one on his right. Marcus squeezed into a small open space behind her.

Danica was surprised to find the HALO's controls lacked the technology of even the least expensive podcars. Gears and switches filled the flat metal panel between the two seats, while a confusing series of gauges and dials covered the front dashboard. Excepting the hovercraft advancements, and some alterations to the hull design, she realized the HALO was little different than the old military helicopters displayed in museums.

"You can fly this?" she asked Torrance as he engaged the craft's hovers.

"We'll see," he replied. Danica's knuckles whitened as she gripped the cushion of the seat.

CHAPTER THIRTEEN

Sonje Nysgaard

Three days of travel, never stopping for more than a few hours at safehouses along the way, had her exhausted and disoriented. Gavin had expressed hope their current location, a decommissioned prison in Alabama, would provide an extended respite from their endless running. Weary, Sonje prayed he was correct.

Each stop on the journey south had brought more disheartening news of Peacekeeper raids. Several times, the Ignota cell Gavin headed had been forced to alter the route upon discovering PKs had already struck the next planned stop. On two occasions, the cell learned their last hideout had been attacked hours after their hurried departure. Sonje could see the grim tightness in Gavin's eyes increasing as the list of dead and captured Ignota grew. At last count, eight cells in Virginia and North Carolina had fallen under the Peacekeepers' sudden blitz. Twice that number was rumored to have been invaded in neighboring states. With the exact total of cells across the globe unknown, Sonje wondered how the confirmed loss of eighty members would affect the subversive operation. She also wondered how long Gavin McAvoy would be able to honor his promise of protection.

Upon arriving at the abandoned prison (abandoned except for the two other cells which had already sought its refuge), Sonje was escorted to one of the many available prisoner cells. While the thin mattress on the metal slab bed offered little comfort, Sonje's exhaustion prevailed and she managed a few hours of much needed sleep. Awake now, she wandered through the oppressive halls of the jail, moving quietly to not disturb the other Ignota resting in nearby cells of their own.

The gun Gavin had supplied her, and had warned to keep with her at all times, nuzzled uncomfortably in the rear waistband of her jeans. During a brief pause on the trek, he had shown her how to unload and reload the weapon, a nearly archaic semi-automatic pistol. She had yet to fire the gun, and secretly hoped she need never experience the sensation. The fact she carried it was but one more reminder of how drastically her life had changed.

The aimless stroll brought a familiar voice to her ears. In a small office on the second level, its former use forgotten over the decades, Gavin sat alone, staring blankly at the faded paint of the opposing wall. Sonje knocked gently on the empty door frame.

"Hey," he greeted her. "Come in."

"I don't want to interrupt," Sonje apologized.

"You're not. I was just thinking out loud."

Accepting the offered chair, Sonje bent to sit, but quickly rose again to remove the gun at her back. Smiling with slight embarrassment, she said, "Not used to having this yet."

McAvoy replied, "You will be. Unfortunately."

"Any new updates?" she asked him.

Gavin shook his head in response. "Not since last night. Intel has thinned, which probably means the PKs have raided more cells. I don't know how long this location will remain a secret. I sent Ament and Corey out on reconnaissance."

Though the pair were the two youngest of the cell, both only recently out of their teens, Sonje knew Gavin relied heavily on their superior ability to scout and observe. In fact, it had been Ament and Corey who had brought word of PK movements ahead of the cell's path south.

"Still no word on the Seton kids," Gavin continued, knowing Sonje's interest in her former colleague's children. "And no one has claimed the attack on House Garrott. If it was an Ignota op, they're keeping quiet. There's too much we don't know."

The lack of information proved frustrating for Sonje, and she could only guess how it affected Gavin, the man charged with safely leading the cell. She did, however, find some satisfaction in the absence of news about the children. If the Alliance had captured them, the government would have boasted of it loudly. The hunt for Philip Seton's two children had been widely broadcast; the reward currently at two million credits for information leading to an arrest. The longer Danica and Marcus Seton remained loose, the weaker the PKs and, by proxy, the Alliance, appeared to the world audience. The massive mobilization against the Cohors Ignota had likely been authorized to counter that perception.

"What do the other cells say?" Sonje asked. Though she had gone directly to rest, she knew Gavin had met with the leaders of the two cells already in residence at the prison.

Gavin inhaled a deep sigh. "Marshall suggests we attack an Alliance position, while Camorata thinks we should lay low until the dust settles, then reestablish communications with other cells. They want me to be the tie-breaker."

Sonje did not envy his position. "Which way are you leaning?" she asked, understanding her fate rested with his decision.

A shallow shrug of shoulders expressed Gavin's ambiguity. "Camorata has a point. We don't know how many cells have fallen or how many others will be exposed as a result. Until we can reconnect with the network, we're pretty much running blind in the dark."

"But?" Sonje prodded. Long trained in scientific objectivity and debate, she sensed the man had attached equal deliberation to the other cell leader's proposal.

Smiling thinly at her correct evaluation, Gavin continued, "But, we don't know how long the PKs will continue the assault. They have never before moved against the insurgency with this kind of force. It might last a week, a month, or longer. None of our sources within the Alliance seem to know. The longer we wait to act, the weaker we'll be. A strike against the Alliance might make them pull back. Or, it may just strengthen their resolve."

"And the Ignota would be over," Sonje added when he finished.

"Exactly," Gavin said before asking, "What do *you* think we should do?"

Startled by the question, she stumbled, "Gavin, I'm a doctor, a scientist. I work in a lab. I'm no tactician."

"None of us were tacticians before joining the Ignota, Sonje," he reminded her. "As a doctor, how would you treat someone if a virus was attacking their body?"

"That's not the same thing," Sonje countered.

Gavin's eyebrow rose as he asked, "Isn't it?"

Forced to consider the comparison, she acknowledged the inherent similarities. "If a patient had a virus, I'd recommend a course of anti-virals," she explained, hoping the generality of the answer would suffice.

"So, you'd attack it? Not wait for it to spread? Even if the treatment carried its own risks?"

"Yes, I'd attack it," Sonje replied, realizing the weight of the answer, and the action she was now advising. "If we strike at the Alliance, it might kill us. But, it also could rally the remaining cells, and divert attention away from the PKs hunting for them, and away from the Setons."

Gavin smiled. "Keep it up and you can have my job," he joked. "I'm ready for early retirement!"

"How long have you been with the Ignota?"

"Fourteen years, five months and twelve days," he answered without hesitation.

Knowing a story must lay behind such exact memory, Sonje asked, "What made you join?"

A bitter laugh escaped his mouth. "For that, we're going to need a drink," Gavin chuckled, though there was no mirth in the sound. He reached into the gear bag at his feet and withdrew a metal flask. With practiced dexterity, he slapped the heel of his hand against the container's cap, sending it into an opening spin. After taking a swig of its contents, he handed the flask to Sonje.

"A few weeks after I turned nineteen . . ."

Sonje had been transfixed during Gavin McAvoy's retelling of the compounding events which had led to his enlistment with the Cohors Ignota. Unlike her own evolution, which had begun with the simple agreement to a blind date and then spiraled beyond her control, Gavin and his brother, Jamie, seemed to have been fated from birth to join the underground resistance.

Their father had been a Fifth, an Ignota agent not linked to a cell, but instead serving the movement as an observer and informant. Hiding in plain sight, operating within the very system the Ignota aimed to overthrow, Fifths risked much in their service. To the boys, however, Owen McAvoy was simply their father; a man who trudged each morning to his management job at the local news station and returned each evening to his wife and sons. Gavin freely admitted there was nothing exceptionally remarkable about the man – average build, plain looks, even temper. In fact, if while growing up someone had told him his father was a clandestine operative for an insurgent militia, Gavin would have convulsed with laughter. It was, of course, Owen McAvoy's outward mediocrity which had made him a perfect Fifth.

His position at the station allowed Owen access to internal reports within the Alliance. Though information was well scrubbed and polished before being handed down to the media for dissemination, Owen often obtained raw intel, free from the redaction of the Alliance spin-doctors. Owen would then supply the data to his contact with the local Ignota cell. Only his wife was aware of Owen's life of dead-drops, secret protocols, and midnight liaisons. By the time Gavin learned of his father's espionage, it was too late to ever speak with him about it.

It was during his second year at college, just after his nineteenth birthday, that Gavin had been startled out of sleep by two men loudly knocking on his dorm room's door. Rubbing the dreams from his eyes, Gavin had shuffled to the door with harsh words ready for whichever of his drunken friends had woken him at so late an hour. A pair of unfamiliar faces had stood in the hall, and quickly pushed past Gavin once he had opened the door. They had spoken in hasty whispers, explaining the intrusion in nonsensical terms. His father had been compromised. Peacekeeper agents had discovered his covert operations. They were there to take Gavin underground. Another team was moving his brother to safety. The men told him all of this with a level of severity that Gavin forced a half-hearted laugh at the obvious joke. It was surely some bizarre initiation prank, he remembered thinking. Only when the men, Ignota agents he would later learn, had stuffed some of his belongs into a duffle, and had forcibly ushered him out the residence hall and into their pod, did frightening reality press on him.

A full month later, the brothers had reunited in a small encampment high in the Adirondack Mountains. They had embraced with relief, shed mourning tears for their lost parents, and shared fears of what their futures held.

"I don't think either of us slept without nightmares for the first year," Gavin reflected. His soft voice hinted at the renewed pain of reliving the past. "Sometimes it feels like it all happened to someone else, like a friend's story you've heard so many times you feel part of it, yet at the same time detached."

Sonje took another sip from the flask, adding to the warm lightheadedness in which the strong drink had already enveloped her. More accustomed to wine, the potency of the almond-flavored libation had her bordering on intoxication by the time Gavin had finished the tale.

"I'm so sorry," Sonje, tongue loosened with alcohol, said with a slight slur. "For your father and mother, for Jamie. If I hadn't come here, he wouldn't have died, and—m"

Gavin broke into the apology. "I accepted long ago that Jamie would not live to turn gray. He and I saw the Ignota differently."

The statement seemed to carry much meaning, but before Sonje could inquire further, their conversation was interrupted.

"The boys are back," Adirene Jorner, the only other female member of Gavin's cell, announced from the doorway. In her time with the group, Sonje was already quite sure Adirene took issue with Sonje's enlistment. Most, men especially, would have missed the undertones to the woman's words and body language. Sonje, however, had become very familiar with that type of rejection from her gender. Her sister once said Sonje's looks brought immediate distrust from other women; despite her never having been involved with an unavailable man. Whatever the cause for Adirene's misjudgment, Sonje regretted the impossibility of a friendship between the pair.

Short seconds later, the two scouts filed into the now-cramped office. With only a handful of years as Ignota between them, Ament and Corey had none of the war-weariness possessed by Gavin, Adirene, and the other cell members. They reminded Sonje of the university students who would spend a term interning in her lab; not government-declared terrorist operatives. Though unrelated, they shared a striking likeness of features, which was amplified by the matching buzz cuts and tanned skin. Unlike Adirene, the boys (Sonje could not help but think of them as such) nearly tripped over themselves in welcoming her to the cell. Gavin had jokingly threatened to hose the pair down if they did not keep their hormones in check.

"What'd'ya got, guys?" Gavin asked.

Ament hopped atop the old particle-board desk, wiped the faint sheen of sweat from his brow, and began his debrief. "Not much, to be honest. We couldn't find any Fifths. They may all be compromised, or they're too scared to display the signals. Given what we already knew, I'm thinking they're scared. The only way the Alliance could have moved so quickly is if they had moles within the Ignota."

"And if someone spilled secrets, the Alliance probably knows the Fifth's signals," Gavin conjectured. "I don't blame them for being afraid of exposure."

Still learning how the Cohors Ignota operated, her previous knowledge of the group having been tainted by the government's media, Sonje knew only a few details of Fifths. A series of coded symbols, adopted from the runic tradition of ancient Germanic tribes, were used to alert cells and relay messages. Everything from offers of protection, resupply, and transportation, to warnings of danger and operations, were conveyed through the simple arrangement of lines. Fifths might wear a trinket with a given symbol, or even embed a rune within a company logo or window decoration. There were additional protocols to ensure anonymity, but Sonje struggled to remember them through the haze of Gavin's liquor.

"Exactly," Ament agreed. "The news seems to be downplaying the PK crackdown. The Alliance won't want people thinking the Ignota is widespread. Even so, there are reports of incursions from each of the continental territories. It's not confirmed yet, but there are rumors that the barricade around the Dead Continent has been increased."

"Are there even cells in the D.C.?" Adirene directed the question to Gavin.

"None that I know of are based there," he answered. "Only recruiters."

Continuing his report, Ament said, "The Alliance spokespeople have said the mobilization is a result of the attempt on Caput Garrott. They're sure the attack was an Ignota op; though, they haven't released any evidence supporting the claim. Not that they need to, either. The feeling on the streets is mostly anger towards the Ignota. People may not entirely like the Alliance, but they are blaming us for the PKs sweeping through cities and towns."

"Eroding any support the Ignota might have established among the citizenship," Gavin added. "What did you dig up?" he then asked Corey, the younger of the scouts, who leaned against the door frame.

"A lot of the same. No Fifths and lots of people pissed off. Something's going down in Philly," Corey said.

Ears perking at the mention of the last known location of Philip's children, Sonje asked, "Philadelphia? The Setons?"

Corey shrugged. "Not sure. The news was streaming live coverage of PKs storming a brothel when the whole building blew to bits. After that, the networks quickly switched back to their regular schedules; no explanation."

Apart from the family digitals decorating Philip Seton's desk, Sonje had never met his offspring. Yet, she felt a sense of responsibility towards them; a kinship for two others whose lives were uprooted because of a blind date.

"I did talk with a PK," Corey shared, holding a hand up to stem Gavin's reprimand. "Relax, Gav. I was careful. He told me the brass was getting orders to be on high alert. The bombings at Garrott's and the Washington hotel has the Alliance pretty jumpy. Whatever is going down in Philly will only add to their anxiety."

"At least Jamie died for something," Adirene mumbled just loud enough for the icy words to be heard.

"Adi," Gavin said, his tone was gentle yet filled with warning. The woman clenched her jaw and said no more, but Sonje was beginning to understand the resentment. "All right," Gavin shifted and rose from his chair, "I'll go update the cell leaders. You two go get some rest, you've earned it. Adi, we'll speak when I get back."

Adirene burned a hot glare at Gavin, then nodded her head in bitter assent as she strode defiantly from the room.

"Come with me," the leader said to Sonje. Her head spun as she stood for the first time since she had shared the flask with Gavin. Extending his hand, he helped her steady her feet as they walked through the prison complex.

"Don't let her get to you," Gavin said.

Sonje, attention mostly focused on placing one foot after the other, asked, "They were together? Adirene and your brother?"

"For the last two years," he confirmed. "Part love, and part fervor."

Even in her clouded state, though the walk was working well to lift the fog, Sonje thought the choice of words to describe the relationship was peculiar. Unlike the past women in her life, who believed Sonje would snatch their mates at the first opportunity, she realized Adirene could truly accuse her of that crime. By sacrificing himself to save her, she had irrevocably stolen Jamie from the woman. Sonje doubted she could ever possibly rectify the evident loathing Adirene felt for her.

"She's right to blame me," she confessed.

Gavin stopped and turned to face her. "No, Sonje. She isn't." His stare was warm and intent, and she could see the burgeoning passion behind his eyes. Another drink and she might have surrendered to him. He was attractive, she admitted; a finger width taller than she, with eyes bluer than any she had ever seen, short blond hair, and an impressive build. While his features were stern, she could see the distant memory of laughter in the small lines around eyes and mouth. *Yes*, she thought, *he was someone she would have smiled at across a crowded bar*. But, with all that had changed in the past few days, Sonje could not bring herself to return the emotion in his gaze.

"Gavin, I—," she began, and faltered.

Predicting the words she had not spoken, he smiled with understanding. "Come on. I need to break a tie."

"And you're certain the Alliance is behind the cover-up?" Camorata asked. Initially wondering why Gavin had brought her to a meeting of the three cell leaders, Sonje now understood the purpose. After brief introductions, Gavin had asked her to share her knowledge of the SID defect with the other two men.

"The only two other people I worked with on this are dead," Sonje tried to mask her indignation. "And I would be, too, if Gavin hadn't gotten me out of the hotel."

Even still, the cell leader squinted with skepticism. "Let's say you're correct, and there is a cover-up—"

"There is," she interjected.

Camorata continued unfazed, "*If* there is a cover-up, without proof, there's nothing we can do about it."

"So we get proof!" Marshall, the more militant of the two leaders, exclaimed as he slammed his fist on the table. "Truth-almighty Camorata! We can't just bury our damned heads in the sand. This is the best intel we've had in years. Exposing a scandal like this would rock the Alliance!"

In the hour she had been in the man's presence, Sonje had quickly learned Marshall spoke even the simplest phrases with bombastic inflection. Even his "hello" had boomed like an alarm of attack. Sonje understood Gavin's difficulty in choosing with which man to agree; one would readily burn the house to steal the milk, while the other seemed to only think in terms of truce and appeasement.

"We can't be sure there *is* a scandal to expose," Camorata shot back with no lesser a degree of vehemence in his muted tones.

Breaking his silence since the meeting had begun, Gavin cleared his throat before defending Sonje's information. "Dr. Nysgaard risked her life to uncover the truth. That the Alliance and the PKs were so quick to silence her and her friends only adds credence to the intel. I think we have to work under the assumption that there is in fact a defect in the new SIDs and the government is aware of it."

Marshall harrumphed in vindication.

"But," Gavin mediated, "Camorata is right – without proof it's meaningless."

"Then. We. Get. Proof.," Marshall punctuated. "If their system was hacked into once, we can do it again. Then, we show the world the corruption of the Truth-damned Alliance!"

Camorata sniffed, "They know they were hacked."

Sonje noted the lack of "if" in his words and delivery.

"The evidence is probably destroyed, or it will be buried behind a million fail-safes and firewalls. We don't have the resources to bypass that kind of security. Especially not now after the crackdown. What do you suggest, Marshall? We simply walk in to Global Tech headquarters and ask nicely for the data?"

"Yes." Sonje was surprised to hear her own voice answering the cell leader's rhetorical question. The three men in the room looked to her with quizzical stares. "I worked with Philip Seton's team. I know them. I can get the data."

She would have liked to blame intoxication for the outrageous suggestion. The only remnant of the earlier drinking, however, was a minor ache at the center of her forehead. The ensuing debate, and its eventual conclusion, exponentially expanded the headache's strength. It was no hangover, though, which pounded her skull. But rather the free-swinging cudgels of fear and anxiety.

CHAPTER FOURTEEN

Milo Chance

"So, you don't, you know, sleep or anything?"

"My systems do not require such an activity. I function on a self-recharging power cell."

"Lucky me," Milo mumbled under his breath. Two days in the safehouse, a small one-story home in the Philadelphia outskirts, had done little to lighten his mood. Forty-eight hours into his one week deadline, and Milo had yet to discover even a whisper linking Dr. Hopkins to Muerte, or Edge distribution. A night-time stakeout of the man's home had proven fruitless. As had circumspect conversations with some of the doctor's associates. In order to not arouse suspicion, Milo had been forced to limit the investigation to people with only the loosest, most peripheral connections to his subject of interest. Even those interviews ended when, inevitably, he was asked, "Why are you interested in Dr. Hopkins?"

Two days. And no leads.

With the exception of the rotating shifts of fellow PKs guarding the safehouse, and Godwin's constant presence, Milo had had no interaction with his squad, or even Sgt. Arestes. The guards had initially been friendly, spending a few minutes chatting with him during each hourly perimeter check. Once a city-wide manhunt for a pair of fugitive teen murderers began, the guards did little to hide their resentment. *Who could blame them?* Milo thought. *I'd rather be part of the search than stuck babysitting.* As a result, his only outlet for conversation was his lifeless partner. Even that was strained. Given Godwin's direct link to the Alliance, the true direction of the investigation had to be masked. As far as the drone knew, Milo's sole focus was Muerte.

"I know you don't think, I mean not like humans do," Milo said. "So, how do you make decisions? Like in the field, how do you know what to do?"

Standing across from him in the living room (Milo had initially been put-off by the drone's rigidity. He once had instructed his partner to sit, but the stiff visual was even more absurd), Godwin answered, *"I am programmed with thousands of scenarios compiled from actual interactions with the criminal element. The speed of my operating system allows me to scan the downloaded scenarios and select a* suitable course of action at roughly the same speed as human thought. Each new interaction of each unit is incorporated into all our systems."

"But, where we act on impulse, you base your movements on stats and data," Milo added.

"That is only partially correct. What humans consider 'impulse' is actually reaction based on previous experience. When a child learning to walk first stumbles, he will not know how to break his fall, or even that such an act is possible. Upon discovering, either through observation or primary experience, that reaching out for a support can prevent the incident, the child will then repeat the action with each future stumble, to varying degrees of success."

Milo recalled a similar explanation from his college classes. "A learned behavior," he offered. "Like the guy with the dogs."

"You are referring to Dr. Ivan Pavlov, the physiologist. Such a comparison is not incorrect."

"But, even with prior knowledge, humans still make mistakes."

"Not all situations are the same. Thus applying an experience-based reaction will have dissimilar outcomes. Theoretically, even Peacekeeper-drones have the ability to act incorrectly, despite our vastly greater range of incorporated experiences to guide our decisions. Though, the statistical likelihood of error is less than one half of one percent."

Amazed by his engagement in the conversation, Milo asked, "Then, after enough time and interactions with humans, couldn't you eventually become perfect?"

Godwin shook his head; the humanity of the gesture was more than slightly unnerving. "Only if the population of the world did not alter. Each human birth introduces a new psyche, thus creating original actions and reactions for Peacekeeper-drones to learn."

Milo found the drones' inability for perfection and correlating possibility of error, however minute the chance, oddly comforting. The concept of an infallible being, even one man-made, was more than unsettling.

The soft tone of an incoming call prevented further discussion. At first, Milo was confused by the sound. The phone had not rung once during his occupancy, nor did he expect it to. Even his parents were ignorant of his location; though he did call them before he had relocated. He had hoped to prevent the predictable hysterics once his mother learned of the incident at his apartment. The effort had failed miserably.

Unlike his home, the safehouse was equipped with Omni technology which allowed him to answer the call without being confined to a call station. Upon his command, the IFaMS unit projected the holograph onto the oval coffee table. Milo assumed the system was malfunctioning when the displayed image formed a featureless black cube.

"Do not attempt to trace the call, Corporeal Chance," a computer-altered voice said from the darkness.

Immediately on edge, Milo demanded, "Who is this?" *Only Anestes and the guards know I'm here,* his mind panicked.

"An ally. You may call me the Soothsayer," the voice replied. "You have been asking dangerous questions, Corporeal Chance. Do you have the courage to find the answers?"

"If you're an ally, why hide yourself?" Milo asked. He had some training in dealing with anonymous informants, and knew the longer he kept the caller on the line, the more information he might be able to gather.

The voice did not reply. During the pause, Milo focused his hearing on the background noise. A passing airplane, street traffic, even a muffled conversation might help him identify the caller.

"Ask again and our business is done," the haunting voice finally answered. "What are you willing to risk to find the answers?"

Unwilling to force the stranger's disappearance, Milo replied, "Whatever it takes."

"Even those closest to you?"

Angered by the insinuation, he accused, "Are you threatening my family?"

"You have already put them at risk, Corporeal. If you cease your investigation now, they are likely to remain unharmed. Choose to continue, and their fate will be tied with your own."

Milo hesitated. Sgt. Anestes had warned of the stakes, though Milo never imagined his parents would be drawn into the deadly game. Trusting his CO to provide security for his family, he answered, "I'll continue."

"Talk to Naesha O'Geron of the *Ledger*. Tell anyone about this call and I will know. And your parents' blood will be on your hands."

As abruptly as it had appeared, the projection vanished.

He was tempted to request the drone replay the message, but after seven repetitions Milo had the interaction cemented in memory. And he doubted a replay would result in anything but further frustration. Godwin was unable to match the caller with any known voice print in the PK system (due to the digital alteration), nor was Milo's partner able to detect background noise. *The guy covered his tracks pretty well - if it even is a guy,* his mind added silently. Skipping another listening, Milo directed the IFaMS to display the file on Naesha O'Geron.

A young beat reporter for the digi-news' justice desk, the woman had amassed a sizeable collection of by-lines over her three years with the *Philadelphia Ledger*. Though none of her stories had advanced beyond the eighth page, Milo found her writing skills strong in the few pieces he scanned. O'Geron had not simply rephrased the court reporters' notes, as commonly done by her peers and predecessors. Instead, she drew her readers into the larger cases, made them feel as if they had watched the court proceedings firsthand – an impressive feat given the limited column centimeters she was given.

Milo conducted a few searches; cross-checking Muerte and Dr. Hopkins with the reporter's stories. Except for brief mentions of low-level enforcers from Muerte's crew, mostly petty theft and possession convictions, there was nothing in the articles indicating O'Geron had any familiarity with the subjects of his investigation. Milo deliberated if the caller was indeed an ally, or simply sending Milo on a goose chase to divert his attention. His instincts, however, believed the strange voice was credible. After the philosophy discussion with Godwin, Milo worried if his "instincts" could be trusted. Checking his watch, the day not yet half over, Milo decided to pay a visit to O'Geron. Quickly calling Sgt. Anestes, who ranted about a slight to his jurisdiction over the manhunt for the teen murderers, Milo convinced his CO to place his parents under protective watch. Milo had not mentioned the caller, and hoped the request was not breaking the rules.

Leaving the safehouse, and receiving sneers from the PK guards, Milo and Godwin settled into the former's pod and headed to the Ledger's offices. The city's center was a chaotic jumble of closed streets and diverted routes. A few blocks from his destination, Milo saw black smoke billowing from the downtown area; a section infamous for its high-end brothels. Patrol pods and HALOs raced past him in an earsplitting cacophony of sirens. Only through a battle of will did Milo ignore the urge to follow his brethren towards the commotion. *Stay focused on Muerte,* he reminded himself.

"I need to speak with Naesha O'Geron," Milo informed the receptionist in the lobby of the Ledger building. Large screens on the side walls showed choppy footage of the nearby explosion.

"Do you have an appointment?" the woman asked dismissively without turning away from the live feed.

"No, but my partner does," Milo responded.

The receptionist's eyes grew wide when she finally broke from her stare and saw the PK-drone at his side. "Uhm, flourth foor . . . I mean fourth floor," she gulped. Milo offered her a toothy grin; he truly enjoyed the reactions Godwin's presence elicited.

The elevator's short ascent delivered the partners to a maze of cubicles and confusion. Pages and interns were running in all directions, answering the barked orders of frenzied reporters. The events downtown had the media in an understandable lather. Three explosions in a week's time was a raw meat gift to the fourth estate. The past days had seen wall-to-wall coverage of the attacks in DC and England. Even the entertainment and style reporters managed to fill columns and airwaves noting which designer labels had been worn by the dead at the House Garrott gala. Distasteful, yet readers and viewers gorged themselves on every last detail.

Milo grabbed a shell-shocked intern who pointed him towards O'Geron's desk. Dodging his way through the mayhem, he eventually reached her cubicle. Seeing her in person, Milo assumed the digital in the coffee-skinned reporter's file had been taken on a better day. Her dark hair was pulled back in a messy ponytail, exposing the small swells of exhaustion beneath her eyes. Clad in a mismatch of crumbled jeans and silk blouse, Naesha O'Geron had the look of someone running solely on caffeine and sugar.

"Naesha O'Geron," Milo said.

Looking up from her computer, she studied the two figures standing just outside her cube. Either too tired or simply unimpressed, Naesha seemed unfazed by the sight of Godwin. "What do you need, Officers?" she asked impatiently before taking a drink from an over-sized mug.

"I need to ask you a few questions."

"Do it quick. As soon as they make an arrest, I need to get down to the PK station," Naesha responded and tilted her head towards the small holoset platform adjacent to her desk. No longer a live broadcast, the set showed a team of PKs storming into the smoking building. Milo guessed the footage was coming directly from a camera crew at the scene.

"I thought you covered court cases," he said.

"I do. But, a story like this can put me on a real beat," she replied with a slightly jaded sense of aspiration.

"Not a fan of the justice system?" Milo lightly joked.

Expressing her impatience with an incline of her head, the reporter retorted, "You here to ask about my career goals, Officer?"

Though a few years her senior, Milo found himself floundering under the woman's blunt, and mildly abrasive, style. The media and law enforcement historically had a tenuous relationship. With only a few words exchanged between them, Milo understood why. "Ah, no. Your name was suggested during an investigation I'm working. I found some articles of yours covering a few of Muerte's henchmen. You ever report on him directly?"

Naesha replied, "I only report on people you guys arrest and charge."

Sensitive to the jibe, as were most of the city's PKs, Milo was ready to bid farewell to the caustic reporter. But, as she was the first new lead (*Only lead!* he reminded himself) in his pursuit of Muerte, Milo brushed the insult aside. Abandoning the circumlocutory approach, he adopted a different tact – one more direct.

"Here's the deal, Ms. O'Geron. I'm working off the books for the next few days; focusing solely on Muerte. An informant, a *confidential* informant, seems to think you have information which could lead me to an arrest," Milo surrendered as much of the truth as he thought safe. And added, "A story like that could get you off page eight."

Milo prided himself in his ability to read people. Yet as the woman stared at him, with no change in eyes, mouth, anything at all, he could not tell if the face displayed curiosity or dismissal. With such stoicism, he wondered if she had even heard him.

"I want exclusivity," she finally said.

Got her! his mind nearly cartwheeled. "Done."

"And access. Whatever you know, I'll know. I'm not going to bust my ass and have you keep me in the dark at every turn," she added.

"You got it," he agreed.

"Married? Live alone?" she asked.

Staggered by the unrelated questions, Milo answered, "Uhm, yes. I mean, no, I'm not married, and yes, I live alone. But, why do you—"

"Good. Write down your address and I'll bring my stuff over tonight," she said, handing him a pad and pen.

"Your stuff? What do you—"

"While we work the case, I'll be staying with you."

Hours later, having returned with Godwin to the safehouse, Milo sat on the couch; his brow furrowed in bafflement. "I don't . . . I don't understand. I went there, she was rude, really rude, and now she's moving in? Who does that? How did I agree to that?"

"Perhaps Ms. O'Geron intends to mate with you," Godwin offered with clinical sobriety.

"I . . .," Milo looked at the drone with shock, "I'm not going to *mate* with her, Godwin."

"My analysis of her physical dimensions and facial symmetry indicates she is of considerable attractiveness. Do not humans select mates based on these calculations? Do you not find Ms. O'Geron attractive?"

"Yes, of course she is attractive, but . . .," Milo began. "No, stop, I am not having this conversation! A week ago I was home watching a game. Now, I'm living with a drone and some woman I don't know. There's no way I'm talking to you about mating!"

As if summoned by the conversation, the guards (whom Milo had informed of the new house guest) escorted Naesha O'Geron through the front door. Carrying several bags of varying sizes, the reporter brusquely thanked the guards and dropped her luggage to the floor. "Nice place," she assessed. "What're you guys up to?"

"Corporeal Chance and I were discussing the mat—"

"Godwin!" Milo snapped. "Nothing. Just sitting here and *not* talking. Listen, I don't know how . . . all this," he pointed to her bags, "came about. But, you living here might not be the best idea."

From her expression, Milo might have easily suggested aliens were living in the couch. "Of course it is," she explained. "You said you only have five days until your boss pulls the plug. We're going to be working around the clock and can't afford to waste time commuting back and forth."

Makes sense, Milo begrudgingly admitted. "What about your work?"

"Taken care of," Naesha replied. "I told my editor I got a tip I need to follow. Everyone is so wrapped up in what happened today, he gave me the days off. He probably didn't even know what he was agreeing to."

"I know how he feels," Milo muttered as he scratched his head.

An empty pizza box and a few drained beer bottles sat discarded on the floor beside the coffee table. Milo had removed the bland paintings from the large west wall of the living room, and the IFaMS filled the space with projections of PK case files and Naesha's shorthand notes. They had studied each page, each word, for hours, and had found nothing of interest. As they had waited for the pizza delivery, Milo had shared the backstory with the reporter (omitting mentions of Dr. Hopkins since Godwin was present), rehashing the search of Muerte's abandoned hideout, the grisly discovery of Banhen's body, and the mysterious call leading him to seek her out. He assumed since the Soothsayer had named Naesha directly, the disclosure was permitted. "Sounds like you really stepped in it," she had replied after the retelling.

"Another beer?" Naesha asked as she uncurled herself from the floor.

"Yeah," he answered. Milo rotated his head and rolled his shoulders. The soft popping of joints attested to his exhaustion. The last time he looked at his watch, the display read 1:27 A.M.. He dared not look at it again, knowing his heavy eyes would demand rest. He envied his artificial partner's freedom from sleep requirements.

"Maybe we're looking at this the wrong way," Naesha called from the kitchen. Milo could hear the soft clink as she popped open the bottles' caps.

"How so?"

Returning with the cold beverages, and handing one to Milo, she hypothesized, "Well, we've been pouring over the statements and testimonies of Muerte's street thugs, searching for something they said to lead us to their boss. But, they knew he'd kill them if they sold him out. Each one refused to admit any association with Muerte. Serving a year or two beats a slit throat."

"Okay?" Milo tried to temper the frustration in his voice, but hours of dead-ends had taken their toll.

Tipping the bottle to her lips, Naesha took a long swallow. "What if what we're looking for isn't in what they said?"

"So, you want to investigate what they didn't say?"

Mostly ignoring the sarcasm, she answered, "No, jackass. I mean maybe we need to look at the cases themselves, the big picture."

Forcing himself to renewed vitality, Milo called out a series of commands to the IFaMS. Projected documents shifted, and re-shifted, with each directive. Over the last two years, nearly four dozen suspected Muerte associates had been convicted of crimes ranging from illegal weapons possession, larceny, and drug trafficking, to rape and murder. The locations of the arrests were spread throughout the city in no discernible pattern. The offenders, expectedly sharing similar backgrounds of poverty and minimal education, had long histories of prior incarcerations. If the answer hid among the cases, the canvas was too vast for Milo to identify it.

"They're all nobodies, small-timers," Milo declared. "Locking them up didn't even put a dent in Muerte's operation. They're so low on the totem most of them probably never met him."

"What about the bigger fish?" Naesha asked.

"Too well protected. His inner circle is as much of a ghost as he is. The few we've managed to collar hire Javen Redwine, a sleaze attorney bankrolled by Muerte, and they walk. A few years ago, we jammed up Chinga, believed to be Muerte's right hand man, on two counts of murders. Case got dismissed on a technicality."

The reporter chewed the corner of her lip as she pondered. "Can't link Redwine to the syndicate?"

Milo laughed as he placed the empty bottle with its fellows. "He hides behind the wall of attorney-client privilege. All right, I'm beat. You want the couch or the bed?"

Eyes glued to the array of documents on the wall, Naesha absently answered, "Take the bed. I'm going to stay up a bit longer."

Needing no further encouragement, Milo dragged his feet towards the bedroom. *She's worse than me,* he thought as he glanced back to the reporter engrossed in her study.

After what seemed only a few minutes sleep, he felt a small hand shaking his bare shoulder. "Milo . . . wake up," a voice whispered.

Groaning an incoherent reply, Milo buried his head underneath the pillow.

"Milo," the woman's voice. *Naesha's,* he realized in his half-dream, called to him again with more insistence. "Wake up!"

"You realize I carry a gun, right?" he voiced the empty threat through the feather-filled cushion. He immediately regretted acknowledging his awareness of her interruption.

"Yea, I'm terrified. Now, get up. I think I found something. And put some clothes on," she added as she left the room.

Growling his vexation, Milo slid from the bed and pulled on a pair of shorts and a white tee shirt. He reminded himself he need not be embarrassed by the woman finding him as she did. *It's my room, in my house,* he silently argued. *I'll sleep however I want.* Still, though, his cheeks flushed despite his effort.

"Good morning, *Chance,*" Godwin greeted as Milo stumbled across the house into the living room. Milo grunted a wordless reply.

"Here," Naesha handed him a hot mug of coffee. Feeling spiteful from the intrusive wake-up call, Milo offered her no thanks for the much needed drink. She failed to acknowledge his purposeful ill manners before launching excitedly into her discovery. "When you mentioned Chinga, it got me thinking. We've only been going over the convictions."

Deeply inhaling the aromatic vapors rising from the mug, Milo could feel the last traces of sleep recede from the stimulant. Each morning he relished the first sip; the welcome expansion of the liquid warmth flowing from tongue to throat to chest. It could be the hottest morning of the Philadelphia summer, but that sip's sensation was a momentary glimpse of Heaven. *Hi, I'm Milo, and I'm a coffee-aholic,* he amused himself. Swallowing, savoring, and inevitably returning to the more mundane, he said, "We haven't looked at the ones that got away."

"And those cases, my friend, are much more interesting," Naesha teased. Using a remote she conducted a symphony of cases on the living room wall. "I started with Chinga. Represented by Redwine, prosecuted by Assistant District Attorney Willem Roberts, with Judge Sampkin presiding. Two other cases, both involving higher level Muerte enforcers, and both dismissed before going to trial, have the same trio: Redwine, Roberts, Sampkin."

Intrigued, but aware the pattern was merely circumstantial, he responded, "A corrupt judge and a dirty ADA. Disgusting, unethical, but not surprising. And not proven simply because they were all attached to the same case."

"Agreed," Naesha continued. Milo realized she was leading him through the logic and reasoning, rather than just revealing her conclusions. "But, if we assume the pattern is correct . . ."

"Then we can look at cases, otherwise not associated with Muerte, but where the same characters come into play," Milo, having inched closer to the couch's edge, finished her thought.

Naesha grinned in genuine approval. "Of which there are none."

Confused, and his own proud smile sliding off, Milo said, "Well, that was anticlimactic."

"That's what I thought, too. Until I remembered the defendants would be people we haven't yet linked to Muerte," Naesha replied, clearly waiting for him to make the next leap. Milo could only offer an expression of bewilderment. "Thus, they wouldn't have an attorney who everyone knows *is* linked to a drug kingpin."

"But, that doesn't fit the pattern you just created."

"Screw the pattern! We're not looking to bust a judge and an ADA. The first pattern leads us to a larger one."

Utterly lost in the woman's process, Milo waved his hands for her to continue.

"There were too many cases with both Roberts and Sampkin. So, I excluded prosecutorial wins." The IFaMS projection shuffled the display, leaving several dozen cases from the original hundreds. "Narrowing the field to cases with mistrials, or pre-trial dismissals, and . . ." The projection sorted again. " . . . we're left with these seven cases."

Studying the display, Milo was impressed. "All with the same defense attorney – Joliet Killiandare."

Naesha nodded. "And it gets better. It seems Ms. Killiandare is a member of The Stratum Group. As are Roberts, Sampkin, and Redwine."

A high society think-tank, The Stratum Group was a global organization which boasted an exclusive member list comprised of politicians, bankers, military leaders, and corporate behemoths. During the sixty years since its founding, the group's closed door meetings provided a great deal of fodder for conspiracy theorists who believed malignant forces operated in the shadows. Milo did not put much stock in the claims of subterfuge and manipulation. In his experience, the elite class seemed to thrive on the validation offered through membership to closed circles of wealth.

"Do you have access to the group's roster?" he asked.

"It's the only really public thing they put out," Naesha replied. "Everyone wants to brag about being a member."

At her direction, a long list of alphabetized names covered the wall. Milo scanned the projection; quickly finding the one he had hoped would appear. Dr. Hopkins. Though by no means definitive proof of the doctor's guilt, Milo sensed a shift in the investigation. And for the first time, the shift was in his favor.

CHAPTER FIFTEEN

Danica Seton

Torrance gripped a lever at his left and Danica heard the HALO's large rotors stir to life. The machine rose and lurched, briefly colliding with the brick building to their right before bouncing back into the wide street. Wincing at the crunch of metal and stone, she looked to Torrance, but the man's attention was drilled to the controls. With his right hand, he angled another lever, which reminded Danica of a joystick, and the HALO propelled down the avenue. Standers-by pointed and ducked as the hulking mass passed only meters above their heads.

In the distance ahead, her eyes registered several fast-approaching specks above the traffic. Within seconds, the objects drew close enough for her to recognize three HALOs and nearly a dozen aerocycles. Her warning to Torrance caught in her throat as he steered the craft onto a connecting side street. Danica could feel her internal organs slamming together with sickening pressure from the sharp angle of the turn. Torrance pulled the joystick and the wing rotors pivoted, driving the HALO higher into the air. Another adjustment to the throttle, and the ship's speed increased, blurring the buildings on the other side. Amber bolts streaked past, indiscriminately exploding pods and façades.

"They're shooting at us!" Danica screeched.

"I noticed," Torrance replied with a calm voice.

"Then do something!" she demanded.

Torrance kept the HALO in a pendulum, swinging left and right to avoid a direct hit. "You're in the gunner's seat," he informed her.

Danica stared at the panel of controls. Numbered switches and lights stared back in a confusing array. Twin screens displayed the rear and front views, the former filled with pursuing PKs, but she had no idea how to engage the HALO's weapons systems. Selecting random controls, Danica jumped as a pair of flashes flew from the front of the ship, igniting unintended targets in mushrooming clouds of fire and smoke.

"They'd be behind us," Torrance said as he struggled to dodge the debris Danica's shots created. Before she could snap a reply, Marcus called out behind her seatback.

"It's just like Street Assault!"

Danica's only knowledge of the mentioned game came from the incessant discussions in which the boys of her year engaged. High scores, hidden levels, and weapon collections enthralled them far more than any other topic.

"Move over," Marcus instructed, though not waiting for her to comply. Lean as she was, the HALO seat had not been constructed to accommodate two. Danica pressed herself against the side as her brother climbed into the remaining space. She watched as his hands glided over the control panel with a composer's grace. In the left screen, rust-colored blasts sped backwards. Three shots connected with PK aerocycles; the riders taken by the unexpected return fire. Danica shook her head in surprise. Her brother's hours of game-play, often in defiance of their parents, had proven unimaginably useful.

"Good job, kid," Torrance offered in an uncharacteristic declaration of praise. Marcus did not respond, instead continuing his focus on their defense. Speeding above countless streets, Torrance's control of the HALO much improved, the trio left a wake of carnage in their path. Yet, the PKs still pursued; their numbers increasing despite Marcus's rookie accuracy. Even with their small victories, Danica feared a total escape was impossible.

Torrance's face, however, showed none of Danica's concern. "When I tell you, kid, I want you to blast straight down," he told Marcus, who acknowledged the command.

"Get ready . . . now!" The rear view screen burned blindingly and quickly blackened as the camera's lens was engulfed in thick black smoke. The image cleared once Torrance turned the HALO down the next side-street. Trusting there was a purpose behind the action, Danica remained silent. Torrance maneuvered another last-second turn and the HALO was retracing a previous path through the city. Never a fan of amusement park rides, Danica knew adrenaline was all that kept her stomach from emptying.

Undaunted, a veritable fleet of aerial PK units dogged close behind. A deafening explosion roared through the HALO as one of the pursuers managed a hit. The craft dipped dangerously to the right, wing tip sparking as it scored along the buildings. Torrance cursed while he fought to regain control; both hands tightly gripping controls, beads of sweat running down his face. Through the thick glass of the cockpit, Danica could see flames billowing from the damaged rotor wing.

"Come on, you bitch," Torrance pleaded. "Just a bit longer."

With one rotor destroyed, the HALO made a wide arc through the next turn; the still-functioning wing glancing buildings before Torrance corrected the trajectory. "Aim for street level. Take out every pod you can."

Marcus made immediate adjustments to the weapon controls, and the street behind them flared with concussive booms. Danica watched the screen, stunned as pod after pod burst into flames. The destruction was unthinkable, beyond even the most violent movies she had seen. She tried convincing herself the vehicles were empty, abandoned by their drivers after the first passing of the HALO. She knew, however, the mayhem on the screen had claimed countless casualties. The realization was far more sickening than the jostling and careening of the HALO.

"Get ready to move," Torrance's voice cut through the horror. He angled the controls down, and the craft dipped toward the street; the black pavement rushing forward. The HALO's underside caught a podcar roof, sending the machine into a wild tailspin. Danica screamed as images of street and buildings flashed along the cockpit window in tornadic speed. She could hear Torrance shouting commands, but the grinding collision of metals drowned out his words. Sparks showered in all directions once the HALO slammed into the road. The friction fractionally slowed their spin, as did the pods through which the HALO barreled.

Confusing vertigo lingered even after the ship skidded to a halt. The cockpit still spun in her vision, only slowing when Torrance's face entered her sight. A profusion of blood flowed from his temple, the redness made brighter by the pallor of his skin. She could feel his hands pulling her up from the gunnery seat; her legs unsteady as she was forced to stand. Through a will not her own, she followed him out of the cockpit into the bay. Marcus, already exited from the cockpit, was pulling a particle rifle from a rack on the bay's wall.

"No," Torrance reprimanded. "Their guns have tracers." She watched, trying to regain sense of reality, as her brother dropped the weapon in sudden revulsion.

Torrance helped the siblings down from the sharply-angled wreckage, directing them towards the craterous hole in the street's center. Smoke and steam still wafted from the opening Marcus had created during the first pass down the road. Peering into the underground, Danica saw the twisted remnants of pipes and thick, corded cabling. Enough awareness had returned to her, and she heeded Torrance's caution of finding sure footing as she lowered herself into the pit – no easy task given the sunken piles of macadam slabs.

She had been prepared for the overwhelming stench of sewage, but Danica was surprised to find the damp air held only a slight sour hint. With a splash, she jumped the last meter into the ankle-deep water flowing along the center of the drain tunnel. Torrance and her brother joined her seconds later.

"We need to move fast," he instructed the siblings, then broke into a loping jog. Barefoot, Danica tried to ignore the numerous jabs her soles encountered as she followed behind him. The jabs were less disconcerting than the squishing bursts too frequently exploding under her step. She was sure the last one had been covered in fur.

Torrance paused only once, briefly studying a fork in of the canal passage before selecting the left tunnel, but Danica noticed his pace was erratic, and twice her eyes caught him stumbling. "We need to slow down," she suggested at his side.

"Can't," he replied through a labored breath. "They'll be . . . all over . . . the tunnels soon." He had navigated them along a handful of turns, and Danica could not determine the distance of their pursuers; though they were undoubtedly following.

As the trio raced along, Danica used the intermittent emergency lights along the tunnel wall to sneak half-second glances at their rescuer. The right side of his face was masked in a steady flow of blood from the deep gash in his scalp. Though he continually wiped the fluid from his squinting eye, it took only seconds until he was blinded again. She knew he was right, they could not stop running, but she doubted he could maintain the strenuous push much longer. Her fears were confirmed when Torrance stumbled again. Danica grabbed his arm but was unable to prevent the fall and his body splashed hard into the water.

Brother and sister struggled to lift his weight, slinging his arms across their shoulders. The filthy stream temporarily cleared the blood from his face, and Danica cringed at the sight of the exposed bone-white skull in his wound. With their support, Torrance managed a few more steps before his legs completely buckled. They pulled him to the curved wall, gently propping his back against it.

"Torrance." Danica pleaded, fearing the man was dead. His eyes rolled up, only white visible in the open lids. She called his name again, relieved when irises, glazed and unfocused, returned. "Torrance, we need to get you help! Tell us where to go."

"Alanna," he weakly mumbled as he stared at her. "I had to . . . forgive me . . . loved you."

"I'm not . . ." Danica began but the words trailed off as Marcus grabbed her wrist.

"Don't confuse him," her brother warned.

Swallowing the guilt of manipulation, she said, "Torrance, it's Alanna. You need to help me get to safety."

He considered her, and Danica prepared to repeat the request, when he said, "Abandoned junction . . . follow . . . green marks." His head dipped into unconsciousness with the last word. Danica prayed his directions were not delivered in delirium.

"We have to carry him," she told Marcus. Torrance's stature made the process difficult and the Setons staggered, dragging him between them. They passed three tunnel connections, yet found no green marks to guide them. Hopelessness pulled heavily on Danica's mind; without direction, they were wandering aimlessly beneath the city – every lost minute bringing them closer to capture.

At the fourth connection, a broad stroke of faded green paint slashed across the entrance's stone arch. The discovery sparked a resurgence of untapped strength, and the pair's pace quickened despite the burden of Torrance's limp body. Long minutes ticked, and another green mark post appeared, followed by another, then three more until the path ended at a steep flight of stone steps behind an iron gate. Shifting the man's weight, Danica reached a free hand to the rusted handle, and pushed the barrier open; a dull squeal of disused hinges echoed along the tunnel. Aligning themselves diagonally along the stairs, Danica and Marcus descended carefully; each step precarious as they struggled to carry Torrance. The stairwell turned on itself three times before they reached the lowest level.

The square chamber was only a few strides wide, and its thin, dank air never quite filled the lungs of the panting siblings. On each of the four walls, small tunnels, narrow and only tall enough for an average man's height, moved off into darkness. Seeing little in way of protection, and no additional green indicators, Danica worried they had followed the markings incorrectly.

Equally dismayed, Marcus asked, "Now what?"

Craning her neck to the perimeters, Danica searched for any way to determine which tunnel led to safety. Passing her gaze from right to left, she flashed a double-take at a rectangular shadow on the far wall. Her eyes narrowed until she was sure the darkness was indeed a door. "This way," she announced.

Unadorned and easily overlooked to all but the most desperate of searchers, the door opened into an adjacent room, far smaller than the junction chamber. "Look for a light," she told Marcus after the pair lowered Torrance to the floor. Hands fumbled in near total darkness until her fingers found a cool cylinder on the edge of a barely visible shelf. Powering on the flashlight, the white beam illuminated the cramped space, revealing it to be more closet than room.

A small military cot of thin, olive green canvas unfolded against one of the longer walls, while the other supported a wire shelving unit filled with nondescript boxes and containers. Off a hook attached to the third shelf, a medium-sized electric lantern offered more substantial lighting. After trading flashlight for lantern, Danica closed the metal door; pulling a heavy handle to slide the bar-locks into place.

"Help me get him on the cot," she told her brother. Still unconscious, Torrance's limpness made flipping him atop the cot easier, even if the process was rather indelicately completed. Recalling the distant memory of her high school health class, she pressed fingers to his neck searching for a pulse – adjusting their placement until finally feeling a weak thrump.

"Is he . . .?" Marcus asked.

"He's alive," Danica said. *Barely,* she added. If they did not stop the bleeding, she doubted he would stay so much longer. "Check the boxes for a medical kit, or something we can use to close the cut on his head." If this was truly the refuge he had directed them to find, Torrance had likely stocked the shelter with emergency supplies.

"Anything?" she impatiently asked as her brother searched the shelves.

"Food . . . water . . . bullets . . . here! I got it!"

With minimal space, Marcus placed the kit on Torrance's chest, quickly opening the plastic lid and rummaging through its contents. Pulling a fresh tube of accelerant from the box, he handed it to Danica.

"We need to clean it first before sealing it," she told him. The brackish water Torrance had fallen in had certainly deposited untold amounts of bacteria into the wound. Taking the bottle of isopropyl alcohol from Marcus, Danica instructed him to gather the flashlight and direct its beam at the gash. Removing the cap, she tipped the bottle close to the cut, desperately trying to ignore the visible bone. Only a brief stream poured before Torrance jerked violently awake, his right hand tightly wrapped around Marcus's throat. The boy released a strangled gasp as he ineffectively tried to remove the man's far-stronger grip.

Danica shouted, jumping quickly to her feet, adding her limited strength to the struggle. As her brother fought for air, his facing darkening to crimson, she screamed, "Torrance! Stop!"

His beast-wild eyes flashed with menace, the hard muscle of his outstretched forearm flexing to crush his victim's neck and windpipe. Danica furiously beat at his face, fearing the bone-snapping sound which would signal her brother's death. As brutally fast as the assault had come, recognition flooded Torrance's eyes and he released Marcus, who collapsed to the floor. Danica dropped to her knees, enfolding her brother in her arms as he painfully wheezed life back into his lungs. Even in the dim light of the lantern, Danica could see the bruised impression Torrance's hand had left on the boy's throat.

"You're okay," she told him in a sob. "You're okay."

"I'm sorry," Torrance murmured from the cot.

Spinning feverishly, Danica resumed her earlier barrage, striking him with fists and slaps; heedless of the man's feeble state. Weakened as he was, Torrance still blocked most of the blows, defending himself without harming her. The bottled fury amassed since men had stormed into her home exploded out of her in an unrelenting storm.

"You could've killed him!" she cried.

Having pulled himself from the floor, Marcus wrapped strong arms around her in restraint. "Dani, I'm all right," he repeated over and again until his words broke through her uncontrolled rage. "I'm all right," he said again softly when her body slumped weakly in his grasp.

Through her tears, she saw the stricken look on Torrance's face; fresh blood seeping from his head. "I'm sorry," he offered again. Never before had Danica heard him speak with the volume of pain now filling his voice. Calmed in exhaustion, she drew a shuddering breath as Marcus freed her.

Embarrassed by her outburst, and understanding the reason behind Torrance's own, she bent to collect the scattered medical supplies in an attempt to mask her guilt and shame. Reading the obvious motive of her actions, Torrance touched her arm gently.

"Hey," he said. "Your brother was in danger. You did good. But, we're gonna have to work on your boxing skills," he added with a faint smile.

Emotions jumbled, Danica replied with an expected nervous laugh. Acceptance and empathy passed between them in a brief meeting of eyes. "You're head—" she began.

"Hurts," Torrance finished for her.

Assessing the damage of the struggle, she said, "There's only a little alcohol left. Most of it spilled out."

"It's enough," he told her as he lowered his back onto the cot. Danica poured the remaining solution on the wound. Gritting tightly, Torrance asked, "Which shelter are we in?"

"The one you told us to go to," Marcus answered, absently massaging his injured throat.

"What color?"

While dabbing the area with a sterile pad, Danica supplied, "Green markers." Uncapping the tube of accelerant, she pinched the separated skin together, the cut deeper than it was long, and applied a thin line of the compound. She held her fingers still as the bonding agent connected to the skin tissue. The wound warranted more comprehensive care, but the accelerant would at least stem the loss of blood. Even if they were not trapped underground, three un-chipped people could not walk into a hospital without raising immediate suspicions.

"Green," Torrance repeated. "We're about a half-mile from the river drainage, then."

Testing the application, and finding it sufficiently stiff to her touch, Danica placed a fresh gauze pad over the wound. A few strips of white medical tape secured the bandage in place. As she returned the supplies to the kit, Torrance attempted to stand, only to sway at the first step. For a man of action, Danica knew he was frustrated with his incapacitation. Marcus retrieved the water bottle Torrance had been trying to reach.

"Are we safe here?" Danica asked after the man drained the bottle in one quenching gulp.

"Should be," he replied in a stretching yawn. "For a little while, at least."

There was more she wanted to ask, more she needed to tell him, but the exertion from his brief spate of consciousness was evident in his eyes. Torrance drifted into dreams, with Marcus soon following, and Danica eventually found sleep as well, with worry chewing at her mind as she sat on the cool, hard stone floor.

"You should be lying down," she said. Her neck ached from the awkward sleeping position, and her left arm pricked and tingled with fading numbness. Torrance was working quietly in the corner, draping a sheet down from the side of the shelves.

Stepping down from a small box, he turned into the dim light. His coloring had improved, at least by his pale standards, and he moved with the tight intensity of his former self. "There's a toilet there," he said, indicating the corner behind the newly-hung sheet.

Cued by the mention, Danica realized she needed to relieve herself. Rising from the floor, she slid past Torrance in the cramped closet and dropped the curtain behind her. A small portable toilet, much like the one her father and brother used on their camping trips, sat low to the ground. Though grateful for the thin barrier of privacy Torrance had erected for her, it still took a moment for her nervous discomfort to subside. When her water finished, Danica pulled the plain undergarment back up under her dress. She returned to find Torrance sitting on the cot; Marcus sleeping in a ball beside it.

Lowering herself to the empty spot beside him, Danica whispered, "I'm sorry we got you into this. If we hadn't, Alanna would still be alive and . . ."

Staring down at his hands, Torrance said, "I shouldn't have trusted her."

"You loved her," Danica replied, speaking before thought. Torrance turned his head sharply as if accused. "You mumbled it, in the tunnels."

His eyes moved into the distance. "I did," he answered with revelatory wonderment. Danica doubted he had ever confessed those feelings to the Angel's Touch mistress. "But, that doesn't matter now," he added coldly, conclusively.

"Because she betrayed you?"

"Yes. She made a choice. And one of us would have died because of it. I don't regret that it was her and not me."

There was no anger in his voice, just detached reason. Danica's heart filled with pity for the man. She now understood the wildness within him. Raised in isolation, apart from society, Torrance was the lone wolf, hardened and untamed; actions guided by self-preserving necessity, not intrinsic violence. Perhaps pity was misplaced, she pondered. Perhaps she should envy him.

"I don't know if I could live like that," she said aloud.

"You may have to one day," he told her; the regret in his voice unmistakable.

Daring to hope, Danica said, "They have my father. He's alive."

Torrance sat silent as the words, and the unspoken request, thickened the heavy gloom of the small underground shelter. She had forced him to surrender the security of his life, the isolation he had protected and prized. The woman he loved had fallen to his own bullet because two teenagers stumbled into his world. Could she truly expect him to risk more when walking away would be far easier?

He shifted on the cot, lifting his eyes to hers once again. As his mouth moved to speak, Danica steeled herself for rejection.

"Then, we get him out," he promised.

CHAPTER SIXTEEN

Kerwen Garrott

It was prideful, he knew. But, even for Kerwen Garrott, the sight of four full companies of Peacekeeper-drones, standing in statuesque formation, was overawing. Two generations of faith and funding had eventually born perfected fruit. A lesser man might have dismayed, abandoned the project when the first prototype failed, or perhaps the fifth, most certainly by the fifteenth. Kerwen Garrott, however, had refused defeat. He had watched his Family's wealth, and subsequently its status among the Five, diminish. He had suffered the snickering; the pitying looks from Caputs and Caput'es both. "His obsession will be his undoing," they had whispered. And salivated. Looking out from the factory balcony, his vengeance arrayed in sharply aligned rows and columns of black and red steel, Kerwen welcomed his moment of pride.

"Impressive, are they not, sir?" intoned Dr. Rupert Thompson, chief engineer of Garrott Industries. A relic from the late Keanan Garrott's reign, older than even Liam Walford, Thompson had resolutely held the unwavering belief that the Family's dream would one day be realized.

"That they are, Rupert," Kerwen replied to the withered man at his side. "Ready for shipment?"

Nodding through the hacking cough, Thompson wiped a trail of spittle from his lips with a pocket cloth. "Awaiting your order, sir."

Kerwen frowned at the engineer's frail health. "You have worked yourself too hard, Rupert."

Waving away the concern with an old man's nonchalance, the man said, "Bah, at my age taking a piss is hard work. I'll have all eternity to rest."

The Caput laughed at the man's frank admission. Like Liam, Rupert Thompson had known Kerwen since he was an underfoot scamp, running through the factory in wide-eyed wonder - and finding himself in more than a little mischief. The man had seemed old even then, though he had been spry enough to catch the young Garrott by the shirt collar to settle him down. "Truth willing, that rest is far off," Kerwen returned.

"Eh, it comes when it comes. 'Til then I'll keep a pretty young thing on my lap and a stout in my hand," the engineer replied, laughing through another spasm. Out living four wives, each younger than the last, and currently on his fifth, Thompson made no excuse for his vices. Kerwen had long since lost count how many children the man had sired; he wondered if the old coot even remembered them all.

"And the special request?" Kerwen asked.

"Nasty bit of work, that one. But, we managed – had to remove some of the more advanced operating systems to fit the explosive. Undetectable though; unless someone disassembles the unit."

Thompson had asked no questions upon receiving the order to outfit a drone with a high-grade bomb. He had only nodded, and assured Kerwen he would personally make the alterations.

"Very well," Kerwen said. "You have the order to begin shipment. How are the advancements coming along?"

"Eh, not as fast as I'd like. I brought in a few new engineers to work on the project, though," Thompson replied, shuffling along the catwalk. Kerwen followed, offering his arm to aid the engineer's unsteady gait across the metal pathway. Stubborn as he may be, Thompson accepted the assistance without complaint.

"We're still struggling with the weight," he explained as they walked to another section of the immense factory. "The thrust required to lift nearly four hundred kilos is the trouble. The first design was too bulky, making the unit unbalanced. The smaller version allowed more maneuverability, but only provided a few meters of lift."

Before the first operable PK-drones came off the line, Garrott Industries had already begun to design the second class of the machines. While the current model was greatly superior to its human equivalent, Kerwen wanted to develop an aerial line of drones. The project, however, was proving nearly as difficult as the decades-long development of the initial drone.

Stepping into the testing facility, a high-roofed hangar filled with various diagnostic machines, Kerwen saw several teams gauging and evaluating their respective drones. The nearest grouping surrounded a PK-drone harnessed with a large winged pack. Kerwen's eyes widened at the wingspan.

"Bulky would be an understatement," he said to the engineer.

"Six meters across to fit the hovers. They get it off the ground, but they're clumsy. A fraction of a degree puts the whole damn thing into a spin. Which makes maneuvering close to impossible."

Looking up, Kerwen added, "That would explain the hole in the roof?" A large patch of metal had been affixed to the arched covering.

"Aye. One of the operators was a bit over zealous," the engineer replied. "There were a fair amount of mishaps in your father's day, too."

Regretting his unintended recrimination, Kerwen smiled, "Oh, I remember." As a child, he had often heard his father grumbling and cussing after returning from a visit to the factory campus. A building on the eastern perimeter had been entirely rebuilt after an overlooked miscalculation burned the original to ashes. While grateful none of the staff had been harmed, Keanan Garrott had ranted over the incident well into the evening.

"Though the looks on the boys' faces when that drone crashed right through the ceiling—I damn near choked on the laughter," Thompson shared with humor. "Scrambling outside to see where the bloody thing landed!"

Kerwen could not help but chuckle; imagining a team of reserved scientists and engineers dashing about after a runaway drone. He spoke with Rupert Thompson for several more minutes, asking to be notified when the shipments had been delivered, and then Kerwen bid the engineer farewell. A complement of house guards, drones and humans, fell in behind him as he exited the building. Outside, HALOs idled on the landing pad, waiting to bear the Caput home.

Absently returning the gesture of the saluting guards, Kerwen climbed aboard the craft. While the tour of the factory had been successful, the puzzle of the aerial drones still teased his thoughts. His wife would have scolded him, reminding him to appreciate the success of his life's work, rather than quickly jumping to unravel the next "impossible." *And she'd be right,* Caput Garrott mused. *My legacy will be the creation of the drones. Let Tilden's legacy be to make them fly.*

"Directly home, Your Grace ?" asked one of his captains.

A cloudless sky and bright sun beckoned; a rare treat in the usual gray dampness of the country. "Home, yes," Kerwen ordered. "But, let's take the long way."

"Yes, Your Grace ," the captain responded and moved into the cockpit to relay the command.

Looking out the window[2], Kerwen watched as the hover-blades in the right wing slowly began to turn. The rotation sped to a blur; dirt and dust collecting in a cloud beneath the wings, and then the craft smoothly left the hard ground surface. A pair of HALOs on either side of the Caput's ship rose to secure positions on the flanks. Once sufficient altitude had been reached, the wings pivoted several degrees propelling the HALO forward.

The small town of Sheerness, a port city opening to the North Sea, had once been as famed for its seaside resorts as for its industrial complexes. It had been Kerwen's grandfather who acquired control of the town, and reshaped it into the unofficial seat of House Garrott's power. Though the Family had factories across the globe, all greatness began at Sheerness. Every prototype, both those leading to private failure and as well as public success, had been conceived in the factory town. Some thirty-thousand citizens called Sheerness home, and all were contracted with Garrott Industries. It was the diamond in the House's crown.

Sheerness receded into the distance as the convoy travelled towards London above the River Thames. Minutes rounded and the familiar landmarks of the great city sprawled out below. Acquainted with Kerwen's architectural appetite, the pilot brought them past the Parliament and its fabled clock tower, then the twin gothic risings of Westminster Abbey – the final home to some of history's greatest minds, poets and leaders alike. His own father was interred in the abbey, and Kerwen would one day join him there. He was humbled to think his legacy was equaled to Darwin, Kipling, and Newton.

Eventually the eagle's height tour drew to a close, and the HALOs continued northwest to the Family's residence. The physical House Garrott, once named Windsor Castle, was a medieval masterpiece painted on over a dozen acres. From the time he could walk, Kerwen had explored with wild excitement the towers and wards, and the countless chambers and levels of his home. An only child, he had often played with the children and grandchildren of the higher servants. His closest friends, Alember Winshire, grandson of the Housekeeper, and Logan, the youngest child of the House Constable had joined him in the imaginative games of youth. They had also shared his many scoldings when boredom encouraged them to taunt the stiff-faced House guards. *Simpler times then,* Kerwen thought nostalgically as the HALOs descended to the lawn off the North Terrace.

Guards moved with hurried steps towards the settled crafts, forming a protective

---

2 For security purposes, HALOs used to transport dignitaries had covered sides rather than the open bays of the standard model. –M.S.

pair of lines alongside the Caput's ship. Liam waited patiently in the midst for his master to emerge. Stepping from the HALO, Kerwen enjoyed the unseasonable warmth of the midday sun on his face.

"I trust your tour of the factory went well, Your Grace?" his chief advisor asked as he fell into step beside him. Instinctively, Kerwen moderated his pace to accommodate the older man's slower walk. With Rupert's frailty fresh in his memory, Kerwen briefly mourned his son's eventual future without the two long serving members of the House. *Tilden will have to find his own Liam and Rupert,* he thought. *If such men still exist,* a quiet voice mocked.

"It did," Kerwen replied. "As you surely already know." During the hour flight back, Liam had likely learned the details of each conversation the Caput had had while away from the manor. "What news?" he asked.

"The raids continue," Liam said. "The latest count lists one hundred twelve Ignota cells which have been either destroyed or taken into custody. Three were discovered in London, and the surviving members are being questioned regarding any involvement in the attempt on your life."

"Are they talking?"

"Not yet, sir. But, they will," Liam assured as they entered the manor. Kerwen regretted the use of torture, yet the drastic measure often yielded valuable intelligence. "Philadelphia," the advisor continued, "is still in disarray. Damage estimates have already climbed into the hundreds of billions."

Prior to leaving for the factory, Kerwen had seen footage of the disastrous chase through the streets of the historic American city. *Half the world saw the damn feed,* he sneered. Even with their control of the media, the Alliance had few options in directing the story. Naturally, the destruction had been attributed to the Cohors Ignota. Mention of the Seton children was purposefully removed – it was tremendously embarrassing to admit terrorists had run wild, much less announce mere children had caused the carnage. And continued to elude Peacekeepers.

"When might Cambrie take control of the situation? It is his territory after all," Kerwen inquired.

"There has been no indication he will directly involve himself," Liam supplied. "And I would caution against such action, sir. A Caput embroiled in the conflict would only imply the situation is out of control."

Kerwen stopped mid-stride. "The situation is out of control!" he shouted. "Those two children have been on the run for days, killing PKs, and now burning half a city! Where do you see Alliance control in that?"

The old advisor to House Garrott held his tongue, knowing silence was best until his Caput's angry tirade subsided. Kerwen glared, realized the man's ruse, and resumed the walk forward.

Liam continued the update. "A name has emerged. The Setons are believed to be in the company of a man called Torrance."

Forcing his focus onto the only seemingly positive outcome of the botched raid, he asked, "What do we know about him?"

Liam paused and cleared his voice before responding. "Nothing, sir."

Kerwen could feel his blood boil anew as his chief counsel activated a hand-held holo-tablet. A six inch projection, slowly rotating, displayed the image of a blurred figure riding a Peacekeeper aerocycle.

"Beyond a preference for a certain whore, whom he killed, the man has not existed until yesterday. No cameras were able to lock on him, thus thwarting facial recognition. He likely has a device which blocks the signal."

Studying the image as he walked, Kerwen said, "An Ignota, then?"

"Possibly. Though, the insurgents in custody claim no knowledge of him, but, as we are discovering, their global network is vast. The name Torrance, however, may well be false. If he is not already an Ignotum, they will certainly seek to add him to their ranks."

Disgusted, Kerwen added, "They're probably in their hovels praising his name."

They had reached his formal office, known as the Crimson Drawing Room in the time when monarchs still existed, and a liveried servant stood beside a small table topped with the silver tray holding his midday meal.

"You've read my mind, Alain," Kerwen said as the enticing aromas excited his stomach.

"Your Grace might wish to lunch with the Caput`e and the Heir," Liam suggested, slipping easily into the formal address he used when others were present. "Isla Carene arrived a short time ago, and is being hosted in the Caput`e's study."

Surprised to hear the actress had so quickly overcome the fright of the gala, Kerwen answered, "Truly? Yes, I'll join them. Roslyn must be eager to gloat over being right—again."

Liam nodded dismissal to the attendant, who proceeded to collect the tray and exit out a small door at the rear of the office.

"Care to join us, Liam?" Kerwen asked.

The advisor demurred as the Caput had expected. "Thank you, but no, sir. I would not want to intrude on the Family's personal engagements. And, there are things I must see to." The man took his leave with a slight, respectful bow. Kerwen smiled as he made his own exit into the hall. Present or not, the old spymaster would know the exact weight of every forkful lifted during the small luncheon gathering.

The sound of renovation echoed along the high ceilings and marble floors as Kerwen walked across the long stretch of the manor. Once his security personnel had cleared the ballroom, crews had immediately begun repairing the substantial damage. The Superintendent of the House, an ornery old fellow for whom Kerwen held little fondness (and would have dismissed years ago if not for the man's flawless management of the House's functions), had instructed the crews to work round the clock until the project was complete. Kerwen saw no reason for the haste – it would be quite some time before another ball could be successfully hosted at House Garrott. Though their attentions flitted in all directions, the collective memories of the society class were less ephemeral. Perhaps there was *some* luck to be found in the assassination attempt. He would not have to entertain the boors and fools for some time!

Wind chimes of feminine laughter brought his mind back to the present. Off the Family's dining room, the doors to Roslyn's study sat open; protected, of course, by a half-dozen of the House Guard. The men saluted rigidly upon seeing the Caput's approach. He nodded in acknowledgement as he passed.

"Kerwen! I'd hoped you would return in time," Roslyn smiled as she rose to greet him. Tilden and the actress stood as well despite the informal setting.

His son's injuries were mending well. The physicians had removed the bandages from the prosthetic eye, and, excepting of a few healing scars, Tilden's face showed little of the damage it had incurred.

"I would have come sooner had I known," Kerwen replied, extending his hand to Isla Carene.

The young woman wore a simple knee-length dress of green slashed with white; the dominant color adding to the pronounced sparkle of her eyes. Though less ornate than when Kerwen had last seen her at the ball, Ms. Carene was still a remarkable beauty. Dipping into a practiced curtsy, she said, "Your Grace."

"Ms. Carene, when a friend of my son is nearly killed in my home, she has earned the right to call me by name," Kerwen corrected, beckoning everyone to sit.

"Thank you, sir," the actress replied.

"Have you eaten?" his wife asked once the party had resettled. Kerwen shook his head, prompting Roslyn to make a small motion to an attendant. "All well in Sheerness?"

"Rupert is as tenacious as ever," Kerwen laughed. "The man is truly a force of nature."

"Father's chief engineer," Tilden explained for Isla. "He has designed everything from particle guns to HALOs, and now the drones. He's older than dirt."

"And just as coarse," Roslyn tasked playfully.

Isla laughed at the discourse. "Sounds like my grandfather. Tilden has told me some of the Family's history with Sheerness. Amazing that such a small town has grown into the world's center of military technology. It was your grandfather who began its modern development?"

Sipping from a wine glass, Kerwen nodded. "Yes. The Family was not yet on the Council when he invested in Sheerness; House Swayton held the seat then. But, my grandfather gambled everything to build an industrial empire in the hope it would force the Council to elevate the Garrotts. He had already gained much fame when House Swayton was charged with treason and subsequently divested, losing the seat. Shortly thereafter, the Family was elevated, and my grandfather became our first Caput."

"A proud history," Roslyn complimented.

"Quite so," he replied, raising his glass in toast. "I feared we had scared you off, Isla, after the tragedy. A savage bombing does not make the best of first impressions. My wife thinks your spine might be as steely as her own."

Blushing at the comment, she said, "Well, I thank the Caput'e for the comparison. But, in truth I was quite rattled. Filming even the most convincing action scenes was no preparation for the real thing. I am so sorry for the losses your Family suffered."

"Some of Father's closest advisors fell to that butcher's bomb," Tilden intoned with bite. Kerwen hoped his son had enough sense not to spew an angry rant over the Cohors Ignota while the young woman was present. "The PKs should string up every last one of those terrorists," his Heir continued.

So much for sense, Kerwen thought.

"A rather unsettling topic over lunch, dear" Roslyn said. Though her tone was soft, the command it contained was razor-edged. Kerwen was quite glad he was not the intended recipient. Tilden seemed ready to argue, but once Isla laced her fingers with his, the rising tension in the room dissipated.

Recalling Roslyn's many tricks to curb his own rages, Kerwen smiled inwardly at his son's predicament. *How willingly we fall into the loving webs of these magnificent creatures!* he mused.

"How is your filming going?" he asked.

"Production was suspended after the incident," Isla informed him. "But, we begin again tomorrow. There's perhaps another month of shooting before it wraps. I look forward to the days when I don't have to be laced into a corset for eighteen hours straight."

Roslyn, who usually required more time to warm to strangers, laughed. "Dreadful things! Years ago, I made the mistake of selecting one for a masquerade. I could barely breathe, much less dance."

"Do you have more projects on the horizon?" Kerwen queried.

"Mmhmm," Isla replied as she took a drink from her glass. "Excuse me. Yes, I'm signed on for two, but thankfully the first doesn't begin until after the holidays. It will be the longest stretch I've had between films in the last four years."

"Perhaps you would consider spending some of that time at the House," the Caput offered. He knew Roslyn was wondering if the suggestion came from the favor the starlet's presence would bring the Family, or from genuine congeniality. Silently, he admitted to a bit of both.

"That's very generous of you, sir," Isla responded. "I'd be honored."

"Actually, Father," Tilden interjected, "Isla has some time next week, and I was hoping to give her a tour of Sheerness."

Kerwen considered the suggestion, and found no problem with the proposal. Tilden had been a rare sight at the factory campus and it would do well for the employees to see the House Heir. *And perhaps the future Caput`e?* his mind questioned. Though, he had not yet embraced the match entirely, Kerwen's initial objections had diminished. *I must hear Roslyn's thoughts on the matter.*

"I don't see a problem with that, but clear it with Liam first," Kerwen said. The old spy had likely conducted a thorough search of the girl's history, and would have already informed him of any concerns, but the Caput relied heavily on the man's instincts.

From the doorway, Roslyn's head butler cleared his throat and announced, "Your Grace, Caput`e, lunch awaits you in the dining room."

CHAPTER SEVENTEEN

Sonje Nysgaard

"Well, you're . . . getting better," Gavin McAvoy encouraged. For the last three hours, he had overseen Sonje's target practice. Beyond weary arms, she had little to show for his troubles.

Casting him a withering look, she replied, "For a clandestine agent, you're a terrible liar." She had mastered the mechanics of loading the firearm, even exhibited impressive skill in assembling the gun from its parts, but actually hitting the target (a boxer's heavy bag) a dozen meters away had proven frustratingly problematic. Only three shots of the several dozen rounds had grazed the edges of the dangling target.

"You'll get it sooner or later," he offered.

Laughing, she said, "Until then, I better hope my attacker is standing right in front of me. Besides, I won't be armed inside Global Tech."

Mention of the mission brought serious concern to Gavin's face. "I still don't like the idea of you going in. You don't have enough training to face PKs."

The cell leader had first voiced his opposition to the plan during the meeting with Camorata and Marshall. Since then, he had made repeated attempts of dissuasion. There was logic and reason in every one, but Sonje had inherited the Nysgaard genes of intractability.

Appreciative of his concern, she gently reiterated her argument. "The public doesn't know I'm wanted. If your gadget can get me past security, I'll be able to reach one of Philip's colleagues."

"Assuming they agree to help you."

Of the people working in Seton's department, Sonje was most familiar with Gregor Tarasov, an assistant managing director. Philip had often mentioned his belief in the Russian man's indispensable involvement in the project. She hoped it meant Tarasov also held his supervisor's trust. "He will," she said.

"And if a PK recognizes you first?" Gavin challenged.

Sonje knew that was the biggest risk. Even with the cuff Gavin had shown her, embedded with a false SID identity and frequency block for the cameras scanning every face, there was a high probability the Peacekeepers assigned to the complex had been given her likeness. "Then, as my father used to say, we're 'ha samlag med.'"

Laughing, Gavin replied, "I don't know Swedish, but I think I get that one. All right, if I can't change your mind, then let's forget the gun practice and work on some hand-to-hand combat instead."

Though preferring to work on resting her sore arms, Sonje accepted his offer. The brave front was little more than skin deep, and she wanted as much preparation for the mission as possible. She stowed the handgun on the nearby bench before joining Gavin on the thin mat covering a section of the hard stone floor.

"You're taller than most women, and you have long arms which will give you a good reach, but the PKs will outweigh you. And you better believe the ones guarding a government building, especially that government building, will be very well trained. But, I can show you a few things, how to use their size against them, momentum leverages, etc. I assume you know the fastest way to bring a guy down?"

"Knee to the groin?" Sonje suggested.

Gavin contorted his face into an expression of exaggerated relief. "Good, then we don't have to practice that one," he said as he mimed wiping sweat from his temple. "We'll skip throat attacks, too, since PK armor protects the area. Let's start with a frontal attack."

While exponentially more tiring than target practice, Sonje thrilled with renewed energy each time Gavin introduced another maneuver. He showed her basic skills to break free from wrist grabs, bear hugs, and choke holds; demonstrated the proper stance to keep her base level and balanced; and detailed the weak points of Peacekeeper armor. Unlike the humiliating debacle with the handgun, Sonje discovered she possessed a significant aptitude for physical battle.

They sparred for hours. Teacher and student were oblivious to the passage of time as they grappled back and forth across the blue mat; Gavin driven by his desire to ensure her safety, Sonje by the exhilaration of the lessons. Though he was obviously holding back, she knew there were several times he had been taken off guard by an unexpected blow or well-timed feint. Both would certainly bear many bruises tomorrow, but Sonje had earned her mementos early in the session. She measured her progress by the continually decreasing frequency with which Gavin slipped past her guard. The small successes provided a sorely needed boost to her confidence. *If only I had a month to train, rather than a week,* she silently lamented at the end of the session.

Gavin remained panting on the floor after Sonje swept his legs in their last encounter. A "V" of perspiration darkened the chest of his blue shirt. "I think you broke me," he groaned.

Sitting on a bench, blonde ponytail hanging over her shoulder in a damp clump, she laughed through deep breaths. "You? I'll be lucky if I can walk tomorrow."

"Does that mean you don't want to train tomorrow?" he asked as he pulled himself from the ground.

Sonje tossed him a bottle of water. "You're not getting off that easy," she teased.

"I was afraid you'd say that," Gavin replied.

Stopping first at her cell to collect a change of clothes, Sonje followed Gavin's directions to the facility's showers in the Block C. Much as she expected, the room was dimly lit with floor and walls covered in alternating tan and brown chipped tiles. A dozen spouts were evenly spaced along the three walls. Stripping of the sweat-drenched clothes, Sonje selected the third showerhead and turned the knobs. Water hit her skin with painful force, liquid daggers trying to pierce her flesh, forcing her to hop backwards with a startled yelp. Longing for the massage of her home's shower, Sonje eased herself into the torrent. Though the sensation of pounding nails continued, the pleasure from the stream of heat outweighed any discomfort.

Letting the warmth penetrate, muscles sighing with relief, Sonje lathered her body with a new bar of white soap. While lacking the floral fragrance to which she was accustomed, the cleanser did leave a scent of fresh clean on her skin. Once the last traces of white suds were rinsed away, she bent to retrieve the razor and shaving cream Gavin had provided. Without a perch to steady her, Sonje assumed an awkward position and proceeded to remove the light stubble from her legs. It had seemed an odd concern, but the result imparted a feeling of normalcy. Finally, she worked a generous dollop of shampoo through her long tresses.

Sonje spun the knobs off and padded across the slick tiles to the neat pile of her towel and dry clothes. The cloth was thin, saturated before she even tried to dry her hair. She gathered the locks, twisting them into a self-securing bun on the back of her head.

"Whatever you're planning won't work," a woman's voice sounded from her left. Sonje jumped at the sound, snatching the wet towel to cover her nakedness as she turned to find the speaker.

"Adirene," she said, relaxing, and then tensing again. "Oh Truth, you startled me. Did . . . did you need something?"

Leaning against a round column, the other woman sneered. "You think because *he* is tripping over his tongue for you that the rest of us don't see what you're doing?"

Sonje tried to hide a shiver, telling herself it was damp skin and wet hair, and not Adirene's aggressive tone and posture, tingling up her spine. "I . . . I don't know what you mean? I'm not doing anything."

Moving forward with deliberate steps, the veteran Ignotum spat in return, "No? Since you've been here how many cells have been destroyed? How many have died? You worked for the Alliance! And I know you still do! I heard how it was your idea to go back to DC. How many PKs will be waiting for us? What will they give you once you lead us into their trap?"

"I'm not working for the Alliance, Adirene," Sonje promised, cursing the fear in her voice. "They tried to kill me! Believe me, I want to get back at them as much as you do. I'm so sorry about Jamie. I know you lov—"

The hours of training with Gavin fled with the same speed as Adirene's lashing hand. The woman gripped Sonje's neck and slammed her back against the tile wall; exploding a flash of white pain in her head. Dropping the towel, Sonje fumbled fruitlessly to remove the hand choking off her lungs.

"Don't say his name!" Adirene hissed, breath hot against Sonje's face. "Don't you ever say his name, bitch!" With a final squeeze, the Ignotum released her grasp and receded from Sonje's flecked vision.

Shaking, she slid down the wall and wrapped her arms around her drawn-up legs. Sonje fought back the tears, allowing only a few to escape, as the concept of safety shattered in her mind.

It had been several long minutes after Adirene departed before Sonje's legs could support a quiverless stand. With the immediate danger removed from her presence, the fear which had clamped to her heart eventually gave way to outrage – with herself. She had spoken with such assured bravado when convincing the cell leaders she was mission-ready; so much so, Sonje had begun to actually believe herself prepared. Yet at the first occasion of violence, she had crumbled in cowardice.

Even now, dressed and in the relative security of her appointed cell, the memory of those moments brought heat to her veins. Her hair was absorbing the larger share of her mood as she forcefully pulled a brush down the length of her mane. Replaying the shower scene, the clarity of hindsight pointed to the many reactions she could have returned. Swing an arm this way to break the hold, propel forward from the wall, kick out a knee—anything would have been better than wide-eyed cowering.

There was no doubt that had she fought back, Adirene, with years of training, would have pummeled her. Possibly even killed her. But, Sonje knew passivity and fear carried a high cost, as well. Despite the year, the fields of science and engineering were still heavily male dominated. First at university, then later in the early stages of her career, the men around her had assumed feminine weakness. They expected her to fail, and, when she did, embarrass them with an emotional breakdown. She had rewarded them . . . once.

After a particularly harsh reprimand from her doctorate advisor had cracked her strength, Sonje had been unable to stave off her tears. From then on, whenever he offered a critique of her work, he would preface with, "I don't want to upset you . . ." That one momentary display of frailty had defined her in his eyes. Never mind that he had been screaming at her until his face was cherry red and both his beard and desk were speckled with spittle. Sonje, because of her gender, was thereafter the "emotional one." A costly lesson.[3]

Adirene had gotten the better of her, exposing both fear and weakness. The woman may well be unhinged, but Sonje could not deny the frustration of playing into her hands. Though the altercation had stunned Sonje with its unforeseen fury, she was not concerned by the grieving woman's accusations. Jaime's death was still too recent for Adirene to feel much beyond anger. And blame. In the days following her father's passing, Sonje had been cross with both friends and family; lashing out had been easier than accepting his death. *Time*, Sonje recalled, *Adirene needs time.* While the two would likely never gossip together over a late-night bottle of wine, Sonje hoped time might at least ease open hostilities. *Until then,* she thought, *Gavin'll have to train the hell out of me.*

"Knock, knock," Corey called to her from the cell's entrance. "You missed dinner, so I figured I'd deliver." The young scout had a cafeteria tray resting on his right palm, and waited for Sonje to invite him forward.

"Is it really that late?" she asked. Confined to the subterranean levels of the prison complex, time seemed to stall and speed at its own preference. "Come in. Thank you, Corey."

Placing the tray on the small end table, he laughed, "Ament did tonight's cooking, so don't thank me yet."

While the offering smelled enticing, its appearance offended a different sense. Divided into the three sections, Sonje could not distinguish a distinct ingredient in the trio of gelatinous blobs; one green, one yellow, and the largest dressed in

---

[3] Sonje admitted to smug self-satisfaction when, years later, both she and her former professor were the final two candidates for a substantial research grant. Sonje won the grant. –M.S.

brown. The Ignota scout easily read her expression.

"He's big on blending," he said in explanation. "It definitely tastes better than it looks. So, don't look at it."

Laughing at his encouraging warning, she asked him to sit and keep her company while she ate. As promised, the mysterious spoonfuls tasted far better than her eyes had imagined. "Mind if I ask how someone your age ends up with the Ignota?" she asked.

"It's pretty simple, really. If I wasn't here, I'd be locked up." Corey replied, and then elaborated on his background. "I grew up pretty rough. Dad walked out when I was little, Mom could barely take care of herself, never mind a kid. I started hanging with the wrong crowd. Pickpocketing led to stealing cars, and eventually I was fifteen years old and running SID credit scams. Got pinched when I was seventeen, sentenced to thirty years. That's when Gavin found me."

Sonje would never have guessed the boy had such a history. "Gavin got you out of prison?" she inquired.

"Yeah. I was being transported to prison when he ambushed the patrol pod, busted me out. A week later he transferred my info onto the SID of some kid who had OD'ed in a drug house. 'Corey Branson' was declared dead, and I've been with the Ignota ever since."

Realizing the food had slid off the spoon held midway to her mouth, Sonje gathered another serving. Sheltered in adolescence, and truthfully in adulthood as well until recent events, she had been mesmerized by the boy's tale. Swallowing the green substance, a pleasing combination of spinach and spice, she pointed to the chain around Corey's neck. "The medallion. It's a rune symbol?"

Corey lifted the small metal circle from his chest and fingered the engraved upward arrow on its surface. "The Tiwaz," he identified the name for her. "Ignota scouts wear it. Means bravery, I think. A Fifth won't share intelligence unless they see one of the symbols."

Intrigued by the system of codes, Sonje asked, "How many are there?"

Slipping a paper pad and pen from his pocket, the scout began drawing the ancient symbols. "There are twenty-four basic symbols. But, there are a lot of variations depending on the message. Like this one," he indicated one which looked to Sonje like an hourglass on its side. "It means there is a new mission. Put a dot inside the first triangle, and the message changes, saying help is needed for the mission. One in the right triangle means the mission is already underway. One in each says the mission is occurring in multiple places."

The meal forgotten, Sonje surrendered to fascination as Corey led her through the various runes and their meanings. The education was dizzying. There was an entire language which she had never known. She wondered how many times she had passed a store, spoken with a stranger, perhaps even a friend, and had not noticed the markings of the underground resistance. Her sister Gretchen, who spent most of her nights cavorting with society's fringe element, would have delighted in the lesson. Recognizing one of the symbols, an oddly angled S shape, from a tattoo on Adirene's wrist, Sonje asked, "What about this one?"

Corey frowned, seeming reluctant to expound. "That one's for the crazies."

"The crazies?"

Her young teacher nodded. "Least that's what most call 'em. They prefer Sowilo, though."

"Why do you call them cra—"

"Corey," Gavin's voice sounded. "I asked you to bring Dr. Nysgaard her dinner, not keep her from getting rest."

Sonje sensed the cell leader's displeasure had little to do with any deprivation of sleep. *What doesn't he want me to know?* she wondered. "Corey was teaching me some of the Ignota codes. The system is fascinating."

Gavin returned an empty smile. "It's late. And you have a lot of training tomorrow."

Heeding the unsaid order, Corey rose from his seat, apologized for keeping her awake, and exited the cell. As he brushed past Gavin, the cell leader fixed the scout with a clear look of admonishment.

"Gavin," Sonje started to say, but let the attempt die on her tongue as the man turned and walked away.

The next morning, declared such by the few clocks in the sunless prison, Sonje walked with a stiff limp to the mess for breakfast. In her old life, she had been an intermittent attendee of the local gym. Genetics kept her naturally lean, a gift from her father's side, and the occasional kilometer or two on the treadmill in her home had been more than adequate for her cardiovascular needs. If asked, she would have considered herself in a condition of fitness. The current cramps and aches in her muscles proved that to be a laughable delusion. From toes to ears, every part of her was tender to the touch. Moving with the snail pace of one twice her age, she was relieved when, tray in hand, she lowered herself to a seat at the table.

The apparent rifts and tensions among the members of the cell were thicker than the watery mixture of oatmeal. Adirene glowered, slamming a tin cup to the table, when Sonje joined the group. In contrast, Gavin kept his gaze in every direction but hers, while Corey hung his head low like a scolded pup. The others sipped from their bowls in silence, none daring to step onto the minefield of hot tempers. For her part, Sonje was a jumble of discordant emotions: confusion and disappointment with Gavin's icy demeanor; frustration and residual anger towards Adirene; and Corey, poor Corey earned her pity.

Sonje saw wisdom in following the majority's example of silence. She decided the dynamics of the cell, the interplays of its various personalities, were best observed before blindly diving into its murky waters. With a scientific eye, she studied the group as she would any project in her laboratory. Biorobotics required diligent attention to nerve endings, artificial receptors and transmitters, and microscopic nuances which could shift the balance between success and failure. Between absentminded swallows of oatmeal, Sonje discretely applied her years of training to the assembly.

All ten members of the cell (Sonje was slowly beginning to count herself as one) sat along the long table. Yet, only Adirene, with her short brown hair and dagger stare, had an empty seat to either side. Even the simplest organism instinctively isolates a malignant entity. If the tattoo indeed marked Adirene as one of these "Sowilo," perhaps the others shared Corey's negative assessment of the individuals. Though she did not wish to get the scout in further trouble, Sonje was determined to ask him more about the rune symbol's meaning.

Corey's own behavior was far easier to read. The youngest of the cell, he clearly felt shame over whatever offense Gavin had accused him. Given his youth, and understandable sense of arrearage to the leader for sparing him an eternity in prison, Corey presumably viewed Gavin as the patriarch long-absent from his life. Sonje wondered if such dedication would prohibit Corey from willingly providing the information she sought.

At his side sat his fellow scout, Ament. A few years older than Corey, Ament seemed to cast looks of irritation toward the cell leader. Sonje had rarely seen the pair separated in her time with the Ignota. Intuition whispered, and she presumed Ament's mood a reaction to Gavin reprimanding his friend. If Corey was not forthcoming, perhaps the older scout would be less reticent?

The remaining members of the cell appeared ready to run should the fragile silence erupt into conflict. Ol' Ben, whose perpetual cynicism, not his age, had earned him the nickname, occupied the seat at Gavin's right. Close-cropped chestnut hair framed a once-handsome face now marred by a thick scar running from his left ear to the corner of his thin lips. Sonje had previously noticed his habit of tracing the old wound with his knuckles; an act in which he was currently engaged. Though she had yet to determine Ol' Ben's function in the cell, she rather enjoyed the few conversations she had had with the rough-tongued man. Sour he may be, but Sonje was sure he was a first-in/last-out soldier.

On her left and right, sat Adetokunbo Fofana and Match Quentin. The former was assuredly the darkest individual Sonje had ever met. His ebony skin, with its natural sheen, suggested that, unlike most of the world, there had been no race-blending in his ancestry. Along with the coloring, Kunbo had a distinctive accent which marked him as a refugee from the Dead Continent. Sonje had only seen digitals of the poor wretches slowly fading into extinction on the D.C.. Dressed in a civilized manner, Kunbo did not look as barbaric as the grass-skirted, war-painted "Deaders" depicted in the digi-mags.

Tall, quiet, and reserved, the man had offered little conversation during Sonje's time with the Ignota. As the cell's weapons master, Kunbo passed most of his days repairing, maintaining, and customizing the group's arsenal. Sonje wondered if her unease had been noticed, thus keeping him distant. Years of rationalized bias were harder to shed than she suspected. *Surely, all those stories aren't true,* her mind considered. *Not even Deaders would eat their . . .* the sickening thought forced her to focus observations on Match.

Garrulous, salacious, and incredibly boastful. It had been Sonje's initial impression of the former Peacekeeper, and there had been little to warrant a revision. A year or two her junior, Match's rakish charm and boyish good looks helped soften any offense his uninhibited personality might convey. In truth, Sonje found the cell's operations technician amusing, and rather harmless. She did, however, decline his offer of "companionship any night you need it"; apparently it was an invitation he extended to every member of the cell. Sonje assumed she would be working closely with Match in the coming days, as he outfitted her with the various gadgets and devices required to infiltrate Global Tech.

Sonje turned her inspection to the last two members of the cell, Patton Rivera and Lance Holton. Where Match was wiry and impish, the men seated across from her were pillars of brawn. There was no confusion as to their roles in the cell. From the hard muscular coils of chests and arms, to the intense, ever-aware gazes, Patton and Lance were clearly warriors. A finger's width shorter than she, Patton had thick, nearly black hair cut just above his chin, and unblemished honey chestnut skin; both attesting to a strong Latino heritage. Lance Holton, however, hair and eyes of brown and a slightly tanned complexion, lacked a visible ethnic history; a common occurrence in the blended genes of North America. She had spoken with both men intermittently over the past days; finding each pleasantly amicable, and incontrovertibly loyal to the cell leader.

Eight individuals, nine if she included herself, from varying backgrounds, offering diverse skills, and most certainly possessing several dissimilar dispositions, yet bound together with Gavin McAvoy as their leader. If the Ignota cell was to be viewed as an organism, he was its nucleus. *What kind of man was needed to maintain control over such an assemblage?* she wondered. Sonje had led research teams with some level of success, but she had never asked them to follow her in a coup d'état.

An Ignotum for nearly fifteen years, Gavin was still younger than some in his command. Yet, Sonje had seen those same men follow his directives with the reverence due a starred general. She wondered if, like Corey and herself, Gavin had rescued the other members of the cell from equally dire fates. Had their allegiance begun as honorable obligation?

With each inspection, Sonje found more questions than answers. The process, however, was one with which she was intimately familiar. The moment she had first peered into a microscope in a high school lab, the scientific exploration, the journey of discovery, which was both reward and punishment, had proven intoxicating. Studying the members, despite the illogic of her situation, her mind thrilled at the challenge of understanding this complex organism, this cell of the Cohors Ignota.

CHAPTER EIGHTEEN

Milo Chance

The first time had been accidental. And, really, the cramped kitchen was to blame. It was not as if he had purposely inhaled as she had slipped past him to reach the refrigerator. He certainly had not tried to breathe in the soft hints of lavender and vanilla which had reminded him of a summer meadow. *No. Purely accidental. And meaningless. Very, very meaningless,* his mind repeated as Naesha worked the intricate knotting of his bow tie. *Then why are you holding your breath?* a silent voice asked.

For two days they had secluded themselves within the safehouse. Combining resources, Milo and the reporter had scrutinized endless pages and files, anything with even the smallest connection to their investigation. Their initial presumption regarding the judge, assistant district attorney, and defense lawyer was essentially proven. Shortly before the criminal cases in question, each had received large amounts of credits. The payments had been moved through a series of corporations, some with no known listing of employees or even a physical address, before eventually landing in the respective accounts of the dirty trio. Milo and Naesha had yet to determine from where the credits had originated. He doubted a local kingpin like Muerte had the means to establish such an intricate network. Naesha was convinced they were on the scent of a much larger quarry; perhaps a regional, or even national Edge trafficker. It was at her insistence they had crafted this evening's plans.

"There," she said as she finished retying his neck piece. "Don't mess it up this time."

Milo gently pulled at the shirt collar with his finger. He would have been far more comfortable in his PK uniform and armor than the old-fashioned tuxedo. Naesha, however, insisted the attire was appropriate; the Stratum Group apparently had a fondness for outdated fashion.

"I still don't see what you think we'll discover tonight," he said, breathing freely once the reporter stepped away. After selecting one of the many society events of the week (Milo wondered when these people had time to work), Naesha had contacted a hacker friend who added the pair to the guest list.

"Won't know until we're there," she replied, waiting for him at the front door. The woman's red dress dulled his hearing so he was only vaguely aware she had responded. Catching himself staring, Milo coughed and turned away. *Was she smirking?* "Everyone we're looking into will be in the same place. Think of it as observing wildlife in its natural habitat."

Doubting he would enjoy the safari, Milo followed her out of the safehouse. Godwin stood silently by the podcar, waiting for the two humans to enter before maneuvering himself inside the vehicle. The drone would not be attending the event, his presence far too conspicuous, but he had agreed to remain in the pod while they investigated. Though a technological impossibility, Godwin had seemed almost disappointed to learn he would not be able to protect his partner.

The event, a charity fundraiser for some supposed concern of the wealthy, was being hosted by Judge Sampkin at his family's estate in the Gladwyne community north of Philadelphia. Only twenty kilometers away, the journey should have been relatively short. Security across the city, however, had tightened noticeably since the terrorist attacks two days earlier. *Whoever this Torrance person was, the man had bombed his way to the top of the Alliance's most wanted list. Just my luck,* Milo thought, *I'll catch Muerte and no one will care as long as this new maniac is on the loose.*

An hour later, and a dozen checkpoints cleared, their podcar slowly rolled up to the massive gates at the entrance to the judge's home. A steady line of pods, all models from elite lines Milo knew he could never afford, paused beneath a decorative arch. After the arch scanned each pod, and confirmed the occupants' SIDs, guards waved the arrivals through.

Next in the queue, Milo said, "I hope your guy didn't screw this up."

In mock annoyance, the reporter replied, "He's good."

"How good?" he asked, unable to ignore his PK instincts.

Naesha rolled her eyes. "He lives in his parents' basement. He's not stealing government secrets, so you don't have to bust him."

"Welcome Corporeal Milo Chance and Naesha O'Geron. With your permission, I will assume control on your automobile's navigation and direct it to the receiving line."

"Uhm," Milo muttered, unwilling to surrender control of the pod to the interrupting voice.

"Yes, thank you," Naesha answered for him.

Turning to her, he asked, "So, if we need a quick getaway?"

"Most estates have it now. No one gets in or out without the security system's approval. A few days ago, I would have said it was just more of their typical paranoia, but with the recent attacks, who can blame them?"

"And only someone with bad intentions would complain," Milo added with understanding. As he had learned in his PK service, security often required the sacrifice of personal freedom. Tonight, he found himself on the wrong side of that doctrine.

Down a winding, tree-shrouded driveway, the Sampkin home rose into view. Nearly twice as large as his apartment's entire building, the manse shocked him with its vast size and sprawling beauty. With a range confined to inner city investigations, Milo never had occasion to breach the physical boundaries of the wealthy. In his childhood, the Chance family had driven through elite neighborhoods, sightseeing the homes of unlikely futures. Set far back from the road, behind evergreens and stone walls, the manors and estates had been as far beyond his vision as they were from his possibilities.

"When we're inside, it'd help if you looked like you belong," Naesha scolded.

Embarrassed to be caught gawking, Milo immediately settled his face into stoic professionalism. Lacking both uniform and weapon, it was a challenge to assume the PK demeanor he had developed over years of service. Naesha, apparently the more skilled actor, stepped from the idling pod with poise and nonchalance. She nodded with thinly disguised superiority at the white-gloved attendant who helped her to her feet. Milo saw no trace of the mismatched, tired-eyed journalist he had met in the Ledger's office. The woman on his arm, strolling with him down the plush red runner, was every bit a lady of society.

A twenty minute pattern of a few steps then wait, few steps then wait, eventually brought the couple to the front of the receiving line. A shiny-skinned man leaned toward the host and hostess, whispering the identities of the next set of guests. Judge Sampkin looked to his aide with confusion. Milo caught a hasty "how did they get on the list," but the magistrate recovered quickly to greet the PK and journalist.

"Corporeal Chance," he offered his hand, "Thank you for coming tonight. And Ms. O'Geron, so wonderful to see you outside of the courtroom. Please, enjoy yourselves." Sampkin's wife, who made no attempt to feign recognition, smiled, complimented Naesha's dress, and turned to the next set of arrivals.

"See, I told you the dress was worth it," Naesha teased as she tugged him forward. Costing him nearly a month's pay, his hand had actually quivered over the SID scanner when he had finalized the purchase. The gown, along with the far cheaper tuxedo, had arrived at the safehouse a few hours later via a delivery pod. Even as stunning as Naesha looked in the crimson dress, he found it difficult to excuse such needless extravagance. Any guilt he had over splurging on his home holo-system (which cost barely a tenth of the gown) was quickly assuaged.

"These people spent more on dresses, jewels, food, servants, and musicians than this charity will even raise," Milo replied. "They'd save a lot of time if they just donated that money."

Naesha chuckled, "But, then the world wouldn't see them looking beautiful as they donated a handful of credits. For most of them being rich isn't as satisfying as being *known* as rich. They need to feel adored. And they believe we *need* to adore them."

"And do you? Adore them?" he asked.

"My mother was a servant for forty years before she died," Naesha told him with a hint of anger in her voice. "I've seen what these people are really like. Adoration is the last sentiment I feel for them."

He had only known her two days, yet in that brief time Naesha had never spoken with such open hostility. Her words dangerously mirrored the grievances expressed by the Cohors Ignota. His companion's intense devotion to their investigation began to take new meaning – bitter resentment was driving Naesha as much as a chance of career advancement. Milo knew the hazards of such motivation. As a Peacekeeper, each investigation, every criminal who had escaped justice, threatened to become a personal affront. Only vigilant detachment kept that sentiment from consuming him. His broken engagement was consequential evidence of a lapse in vigilance.

"Over to the right, past the orchestra, Willem Roberts," Naesha softly interrupted his thoughts. Slowly shifting his gaze, Milo ran his eyes over the seated musicians of the small chamber orchestra, and found the assistant district attorney engaged in serious conversation at the far end of the large hall. A fluctuation in the thick crowd revealed the prosecutor's dialogue partner, Dr. Hopkins.

"Looks like Roberts and your doctor are not getting along," Naesha added.

Milo nodded, then stunned as her words set in. "My doc—? How'd you know?" he asked, forgoing the pretense of denial.

Winking, she said, "I'm a reporter, I notice things. And you didn't hide your interest very well. Shall we move a bit closer?"

Milo watched her glide through the revelers, never pausing to see if he followed. Flummoxed by the casual way she had exposed his secret, he ground his teeth and quick stepped after her. The soft strings and flute of the music did little to mitigate his frustration. From the moment he had met her, Naesha O'Geron had managed to keep his head in a constant spin.

Still several meters from Roberts and Hopkins, she stopped and rummaged through the small purse in her hand. Reaching her as she began to freshen her lipstick, Milo said, "We're still too far to hear anything."

Ignoring his comment, Naesha replied mid-application, "You know, you did agree to tell me everything. That was the deal you made. How do I know if you're keeping back anything else?"

Sighing, he explained, "The Alliance contacted my CO and ordered me to back off Hopkins. I didn't tell you because Godwin would have heard and transmitted what we're doing."

"Don't you think he transmitted the rest of the investigation?" she asked, switching from lipstick to a silver compact. "Don't you think the Alliance already knows what we're doing?"

The questions tightened his chest. He had been so focused on avoiding displays of overt interest in the doctor while the drone was present (which had clearly not been enough to fool Naesha), he had not thought how investigating Sampkin and the others was as equally revealing. If the Alliance was protecting Hopkins, surely the same protection extended to his conspirators. Chilled by the revelation, Milo expected swarms of security to race towards them.

Sensing his sudden alarm, Naesha said, "I doubt they'd let us get this far only to cause a scene in the middle of the party."

Sorely removed from the familiarity of his world experience, and now seeing threat in every face despite Naesha's apparent calm, Milo wished for the comforting grip of his sidearm.

Closing the compact, the reporter warned, "Don't say anything stupid."

"Wha—"

"Corporeal Chance," a familiar voice called. While lost in his worried thoughts, Milo had not seen the end of the conversation between Roberts and Hopkins. Nor had he noticed the doctor's approach.

"Dr. Hopkins," Milo stammered and accepted the man's offered hand. The formal attire of the soiree only added to the gray-haired physician's air of superiority.

"I don't recall seeing you at one of these events before," Hopkins stated with tender suspicion. Milo easily heard the hidden accusation. Before he could reply though, Naesha pulled the focus of both men.

"Milo gets so intimidated by these gatherings. If he had his way, I'd spend every evening on a couch with a beer," she said. "Naesha O'Geron," she added in introduction. Milo registered the doctor's slight jitter upon hearing the name.

"Ah, forgive me, Ms. O'Geron," the doctor apologized. "It's been so long I hardly recognized you How is your mother?"

Smoothly, and with none of the former ire when last she last spoke of the woman, Naesha replied, "She passed a year ago; killed during a home invasion."

Dr. Hopkins frowned in false sympathy. "How tragic! I hope the perpetrator was brought to justice."

Dagger-sharp danger flashed in her eyes when she answered, "Sadly, only the man who fired the gun was arrested and convicted."

Gypsy seers and fortune readers snared innocents with their claimed gifts of supernatural perception. Milo, however, needed no extra sense to detect the powerful undercurrents surging between doctor and journalist. Though Naesha's face held a smooth smile, her body pulsed with tense aggression. Some of the doctor's arrogance had dimmed during the exchange; replaced by self-surprising wariness. Whatever history the two shared, Milo feared the slightest ill-placed word would unleash their barely contained loathing.

Hopkins allowed his locked stare to linger a few seconds longer before redirecting his words to the Peacekeeper. "Are you still investigating my stolen identity?"

Responding truthfully, Milo said, "No. In fact, I've been on vacation the past few days, clearing my head and getting perspective. I apologize for the confusion in your office. My exhaustion was getting the better of me."

"Ah, yes," Hopkins replied. "Sometimes we are all guilty of jumping at ghosts, Corporeal. If you'll excuse me, I see some colleagues arriving." Not waiting for a return of farewell, the doctor brushed past Milo, and drifted towards the reception line.

"Care to tell me what that was about?" Milo asked Naesha.

"No," she replied, eyes still aflame.

Having recently been accused of withholding information, Milo refused to accept the answer. "Bullshit! That's not good enough," he told her. "You have a history with our suspects and it's clearly tainting your objectivity. Why were you so eager to take on this case?"

Naesha's tongue slipped over her bottom lip, white teeth nervously biting the red fullness. He could see the debate in her mind as she considered how much of her past she was willing to reveal. Her mouth opened to speak, but the intended words changed in the second before she voiced them. "I need to splash some water on my face," she said as she stepped away into the crowd. Milo watched her cross the room, stopping briefly to ask a servant for the nearest restroom, and then disappearing down a connecting hall.

He had not wanted to add to her upset, but he could not allow personal conflict to jeopardize the investigation. Left with his frustration, Milo lifted a glass of champagne from the silver tray of a passing waiter. Decorum prevented him from upending the crystal flute in one swallow, though his sour mood craved an intoxicant. Sipping instead, the soft effervescence tickled his nose as he waited for Naesha's return.

Long minutes passed while he observed the finely dressed men and women of the room. Most faces were unfamiliar, though he did recognize a few from the covers of dig-zines. A business executive chatted nearby, regaling the small crowd around him with tales of his company's latest product. The listeners oohed and aahed at the appropriate times, swelling the man's evident ego, and encouraging further boasts. At his side, a young model stared blankly, all her effort directed to maintaining the pouted lips of her surgically-enhanced smile. Milo could spot the dazed expression of an Edge user a kilometer away.

At the entrance, a regional magistrate and his husband were being greeted by the Sampkinses. From the judge's fawning, it was clear the guest held power over Sampkin's future rise in the court systems. Along the far wall, a Hollywood couple expressed embarrassment over requests for posed digitals, yet managed to smile through their feigned humility. Closer to Milo, a trio discussed the success of recent investments and acquisitions. Power plays and manipulations mixed with innuendos and overtures to create a heavy fog which tasted bitter to Milo's simplistic preferences. The mass of wealth and status set his skin crawling far worse than any criminal he had incarcerated.

Midway through a second glass of champagne, and Naesha still not returned from the facilities, Milo decided to seek her out. While not the most eloquent apologizer, he had learned during his doomed engagement to initiate reconciliation to soothe whatever offense his words had offered. Following her path, Milo turned into the hall off the ball room. Two women were exiting what he assumed was a powder room.

"Excuse me," he interjected into the duo's near-drunken giggles. "Could one of you check on my date? She's been in there a while, and I just want to make sure she's okay."

The women stumbled to a stop, laughing and holding to each other to steady their steps. The shorter of the two, clad in a daringly sheer black dress, replied through a slur, "There's nu..noblody . . . nobody in there." The comment apparently was humorous enough to send both into another fit of laughter.

Checking his irritation, he said, "Are you sure? She's brown-skinned, wearing a red gown."

Black Dress lurched forward, avoiding a fall only by Milo's quick reflexes. She pressed herself against him, dropping her voice to a husky tone, "If gour yirl's gone, maybe I can take her prace." The woman emphasized her word-stumbling offer with a groping fondle of his crotch.

Milo gripped her wrist and stepped back. "Not tonight," he replied in a dismissive growl. The woman's lip curled with insult and pulled free of his grasp. With several muttered vulgarities, the pair staggered back into the main room.

Doubting his witnesses, he knocked on the door of the powder room. "Naesha?" he called through the polished wood. Turning the knob, Milo opened the door enough to slide his head in. "Hello? Anyone in here? Naesha?"

No response.

Risking further exploration, Milo fully entered the rose-colored washroom. A set of arched divans were centered on the carpeted floor and four pedestal sinks sat in front of a massive mirrored wall. Two delicate doors opened into softly lit toilet rooms – and both were empty.

He had kept a steady watch during Naesha's absence, and he believed it unlikely she had slipped back into the ball room unnoticed. *If she's snooping around and didn't tell me . . . ,* the thought stoking his already significant anger. Pulling the mobile comm from inside his jacket, Milo said, "Godwin, locate Naesha's SID."

Almost immediately the drone's voice replied, *"I am unable to detect Ms. O'Geron's SID."*

The wealthy may invest heavily in advanced security features, but blocking PK scanner's was highly illegal. "Godwin, are you picking up my location?"

"Affirmative, Chance. Would you like me to provide your exact coordinates?"

"No, try finding Naesha again."

"Ms. O'Geron's SID went offline at 20:38 local time," his partner replied.

Checking the time, Milo swallowed hard. *Almost ten minutes,* he calculated. Even if she had decided to investigate the mansion on her own, Naesha would not have been able to cloak her signal. Unless her hacker friend was more advanced than she had acknowledged. For all his professed adherence to compartmentalizing emotion, operating with objectivity, Milo now struggled to think clearly. Fearing his instincts had been compromised, but unable to shut out the image of the charred remains of his last informant, Milo willed himself to act.

"Godwin, issue a ten-thirty-five at the Sampkin estate. All available units are to respond and seal all exits. And get yourself in here, partner."

CHAPTER NINETEEN

Danica Seton

While it was a relief to be in something more substantial than the too-short dress, Danica longed for a return to times when clothes actually fit. The emergency shelter beneath the city was stocked with an ample supply of food, water, medical supplies, and assorted weaponry. It did, however, lack diversity in clothing selection. Several sets of Torrance's typical black on black shirt and pants meant Danica once again was forced to roll the cuffs and cinch the waist of borrowed, oversized items.

Sitting cross-legged on the thin military cot, she picked at a loose thread along the vertical seam of the pants. The centimeters long strand had been the focus of her attention for more minutes than she cared to count. Thumb and forefinger twisted it clockwise until the thread tightened into a ball, then counter clockwise to unravel, then back again. She debated pulling it free; but then what would pass the time? Danica was rapidly understanding what caused people to snap into insanity. Three people crowded into a glorified closet for two days seemed a believable stimulus for a breakdown.

The first hours in isolation had passed with relative peace. Torrance had eventually gotten to his feet without assistance. She had helped him redress the head wound; a purplish scar had already begun to form where the accelerant had knitted the torn flesh. Several times, Danica had caught him in a wince when he had absentmindedly brushed a hand across the tender spot. Given the mosaic of scars she had seen on his back, she knew the man had overcome more significant injuries.

There had been little conversation among the three; Marcus favoring his sore voice box, and Torrance continuing his habit of silent reflection. The long stretches of soundless idling permitted unwanted worry to occupy her mind. The relief over knowing her father was alive faded with each passing minute. Did his heart still beat? Would the PKs punish him for the destruction his children had created? Or would they kill him as carelessly as they had her mother?

Danica tried to force the thoughts from her mind, but their dark seeds had already been planted. Once, while Marcus was asleep, she had shared her questions with Torrance. He believed as long as the siblings remained beyond their reach, the PKs were likely to keep her father alive. "Leverage," he had told her. It was painful to think of her father in such terms.

By the second day, the walls of the too small shelter seemed every bit as wicked as the men hunting her. The flat stone surfaces, cool and damp to the touch, kept her from reaching her father. Their sterile lifelessness mocked her, constantly reminding her that while she sheltered within them, her father remained a prisoner. Correspondingly, as the proprietor of the underground hideout, Torrance began to represent the same obstacles. Whenever she had questioned the length of their stay, the man had only reiterated the need to wait. His outward calm, the long hours he spent merely sitting and staring at the walls, caused her further frustration. The kinship she had started to feel, the empathic link to another who had been denied a father, turned to resentment. *He never had a father,* her mind accused. *He doesn't know how this feels!*

Thus, as the time slugged along with glacial drifting, anxiety inclined towards simmering, seething pique. Of an age to understand the provenience of her mood, and the inanity of those self-same reasons, Danica's misplaced ire bred further frustration. And an encore of anger began a new cycle.

"Dani, did you see how fast I did it this time?" Marcus asked. Since waking, Torrance had been teaching her brother how to disassemble and rebuild a nine millimeter handgun and a large black rifle. From the speed of the metallic clicks, and Marcus's frequent exclamations, Danica assumed the youth had improved.

"How much longer are we going to sit down here?" she asked petulantly through her sulk.

"Until it is safe," Torrance replied. His tone had grown increasingly aggravated each time he answered the question.

Plucking the thread, Danica said, "When will that be? How will we even know if we're hiding in a sewer? You said you'd help us rescue our father!"

Torrance slammed the magazine into the butt of the gun. "And I will. But, I'm not going to rush in and get us killed simply because you're bored. For now their search will have been confined to the city. Another day and it will be assumed we've moved outside Philly."

"Then what?"

"Then, I contact a resource."

"Great, another one of your resources we can *trust*, right?" In her agitation, Danica did not care how deeply the words stung; nor did she care if they sounded as peevish as she believed they must. Her parents had often accused her of passive aggression, but with no room in which to retreat, and no door to slam, the present company could not be spared her venom.

Impervious to the obvious baiting, Torrance replied, "No, this one's different. I know not to trust him."

"Want me to show you how to put the gun together?" Marcus offered in an attempt to cool the heated tension of the shelter. Even with the bruises on his throat still visible, the boy had developed an idolization of their protector. For him, Torrance was a holo-game hero made flesh; a true to life guardian who could do no wrong. Twice already he had voiced his support of Torrance against Danica's repeated urgings for action.

She spat, "No. I don't feel like playing, Marcus." With melodramatic flair, Danica turned her back to the pair and found another dangling thread to pick. Seemingly unfazed by her outburst, Torrance and her brother turned attention back to the weapons. Their easy dismissal fueled her pout through the remainder of the day, through both the lunch and evening meals, until emotions finally tired and her eyes grew heavy.

"Keep your mouth shut when we're in there," Torrance threatened. Danica rubbed the side of her face with the memory of the last time she failed to heed that particular reprimand. "He's dangerous, violent, and, well, not entirely sane," he reminded the Seton siblings.

During the early dusk hours of the third day underground, Torrance had announced, without warning, it was time to leave and seek his contact Outside. The moment for which she had argued had finally arrived. Having been so focused on convincing Torrance to begin the mission to rescue her father, she had confined to the corners of her thoughts the reality and dangers lurking beyond the shelter door. Both had come rushing back once Torrance had unsealed the exit.

Adding to her new set of worries, their reclusive guide had detailed for Danica and Marcus the character of the man they sought. Perhaps the dark tunnels of the sewer system amplified the horror, but she almost turned back several times during Torrance's description.

Genkei Yakuza was the owner of several exclusive nightclubs in the city's entertainment district. Over twenty years, he had amassed a sizable fortune catering to the vanity of the wealthy elite. On any given night, his establishments hosted celebrities and dignitaries by the scores; offering the glamour of status and discretion to those who could afford entrance. It was, however, Yakuza's involvement in weapons trafficking which generated billions of credits; all secured in well hidden accounts across the world. To protect his illegal empire, the man had casually ordered the deaths of any who threatened his interests. According to Torrance, Genkei Yakuza cast a long shadow in the criminal underworld.

Surfacing through a manhole, Torrance led the siblings down a narrow back alley. Forced to walk single-file, they slipped past a series of trash bins which echoed with the scurrying of scavenging rats. Despite the dangers she had already overcome, the close proximity of the rodents chilled her skin, and she pressed close to Torrance's back. The pounding of amplified bass grew stronger the further they moved along the dimly-lit passage until Torrance stopped and banged his fist against a metal door. She heard the scrap of several locks and bolts before the door swung open. Three men, matching Torrance's all black attire, stood just inside; their faces as grim and deadly as the automatic rifles in their hands.

"*Watashi ha Genkei wo sanshou suru hitsuyou gaaru,*" Torrance said in a commanding rasp.

The middle guard returned a dismissive laugh.

"*Genkei ha houmonsha wo ukeire teimasen.*"

His message delivered, the guard pulled the door's handle to shut out the visitors. Torrance caught the door with his hand, locking his elbow to keep the gap open.

"*Watashi wa genkan no doa o kayotte kuru baai wa, 10-bu de heiwa iji butai o motte irudeshou. Karera wa watashi o sagashite hanarete kono basho o hikisakuceshou. Dono yó ni shite Genkei ga sonoyóni naru to omoimasu ka?*" Torrance growled.

Whatever scenario he had threatened, the guards considered his words briefly before allowing the door to swing out again. Inside, the men pushed the trio into a line; the muzzles of their guns never lowering from chest aim.

"Let them frisk you," Torrance told the Setons as he lifted his arms up. Danica flinched as their rough hands ran across her limbs and chest, but none repeated the molesting of the PK on the HALO. Satisfied the three were unarmed (though she had seen Torrance stash several knives before they left the shelter), the guards motioned them forward. One spat fast words into a mobile comm, likely alerting Yakuza to their arrival.

As they walked through a busy kitchen, Danica asked, "You speak Chinese?"

"Yes," Torrance replied. "But, that was Japanese. And why are you talking?"

Clamping her mouth shut, and ignoring Marcus's smirk, Danica followed. The kitchen workers kept their eyes averted; either intent on their tasks, or unwilling to witness what they should not. Through a pair of swinging doors at the far end of kitchen, the group passed into the club itself.

Plush couches and small cocktail tables were tucked into dark recesses, forming a perimeter around the expansive room. On the dance floor, countless bodies throbbed and swayed to the hypnotic rhythms of bass and treble. A dizzying array of laser and holo-beam lights swept through the smoky air, reminding Danica of an imagined journey through the far reaches of space, nebulas and comets cascading, enveloping the celebrants. She wondered how the effects were interpreted by the intoxicated minds of the hundreds filling the room. Looking up, she saw several levels of railed balconies stretching towards a mirrored ceiling only glimpsed in brief flashes of light.

On the uppermost level, the guards handed off their burden to a dozen of their brothers-in-arms. Once again, Danica and her companions submitted to the indignity of a physical search; ensuring no weapon had come into their possession during the short journey from the rear door. And once again, the weapons she was certain Torrance had placed on his body remained undetected. Finally, a massive guard, so tall even Torrance was forced to tilt his neck, led the three up a short spiral staircase pressed against the corner of the balcony.

The brightly lit lounge at the top of the steps covered the entire width and length of the dance floor five stories below, which was visible through the translucent tiles lining the lounge's own floor. Danica startled when the pneumatic door slid shut behind her, entirely muting the cacophonous sounds of the thriving nightclub.

"Torrance," a thin voice greeted, "I thought by now you'd be shackled in a PK prison." From the description provided her, Danica recognized the speaker with the faint Eastern accent as the infamous weapons dealer.

"You're not that lucky, Genkei," the man at her side replied with half-mirth.

"Indeed. Please, come in, make yourselves comfortable."

Danica and Marcus followed behind Torrance, though she could not match his confident stride. She fully expected the glass floor to crack and shatter like an early winter lake. Their host read her foolish hesitation, and assured, "It's quite strong, child. Not even a particle gun could mar its surface."

Lowering himself onto the curved couch, Torrance remarked, "Few more guards than usual, Genkei." Only then did Danica notice the armed men standing statue-still along each wall of the room.

Frowning, Yakuza replied, "A necessary precaution given the upheaval you unleashed. The Alliance has moved in force against the Ignota, and PKs have nearly declared martial law in the city."

"Surely no one would accuse you of sympathizing with insurgents," Torrance said, waving off a servant offering refreshments.

"Certainly not. The status quo is far more profitable. Though, if these terrorists continue, there may be some gain in doing business with them. They'll be crushed, of course, but perhaps a few credits might be earned before the inevitable."

Danica could see calculations spinning inside the man's shrewd mind.

"And you? Have you joined their ranks?" Yakuza asked as he peered over the pyramid of his hands.

"You know me better than that."

Yakuza hummed. "Yet, the lone moth has emerged from his cocoon. And protects the prize both sides seek." There was little doubt who he viewed as the prize. Danica feared Torrance had erred in confining them within Yakuza's reach – a man whose motivations were based solely on reward and return. She doubted even Torrance could overcome the many guards at Yakuza's disposal.

"I need your help, Genkei," Torrance said, ignoring the other man's musings.

"Clearly."

"Their father is being held in a PK facility. I need to know where."

The small man raised his brows in humor. "And you intend to set him free? As skilled as you are, Torrance, you'll find that task impossible."

"So you know the location?"

"Of course," Yakuza replied. "We can only benefit from the events we know."

Torrance leveled his stare. "How much?"

"Perhaps more than you can afford. Even then it might not be enough to make it worth my while. I would be owed many favors were I to turn the three of you over to the Alliance. Dead or alive."

Danica cringed at the casual manner in which the man considered their fate. She quickly moved her hand to Marcus's arm; his shivers voicing his fear. Torrance, however, remained still, unmoved by Yakuza's threat.

"True, but how long will it take you to replace you're most important client?"

Yakuza's derisive laughter echoed menacingly through the office lounge. "A long-standing client, yes. But, my friend, you are far from my most important."

A small, twitch of a smile turned the corners of Torrance's mouth. "Oh, I know. That honor falls to Aemon Rothschild. Followed by Patrick Helmsmen of The Syndicate, followed by the Tigre Bandidos cartel. Though, if you charged your normal rates, several of the warlords on the D. C. would surpass them all. I was really impressed when I reviewed your client list. A list, complete with shipment dates and locations, which will automatically be distributed to PK stations throughout the Alliance if I don't walk out of here in the next thirty minutes completely satisfied."

His tone never threatened, nor did his volume rise above civil conversation, as Torrance explained the situation to their host. Yakuza, however, was visibly shaken; the smug grin slipped further from his face with each word.

"So you've come to blackmail me into assisting you?" Yakuza said. Danica sensed the man was unused to negotiating at a disadvantage.

Torrance continued to clarify the bargain. "Not at all. We've done business together too long for me to disrespect you. The list is simply encouragement for you to agree to the transaction. I intend to pay you. Half a billion credits seems more than fair, no?"

Danica drew a sharp breath upon hearing the sum. How could a man separated from society, living in subterranean caverns, possibly possess that amount of credits?

"Half a billion. For a location?" the arms dealer inquired.

"No," Torrance replied. "I also want an untraceable podcar. And weapons."

Yakuza narrowed his eyes and met Torrance's open stare. The index finger of his left hand drummed on the arm of the wing-back chair as he considered the arrangement as one might roll a sip of wine across the tongue. Finding the vintage to his liking, he shifted his gaze to one of the guards, and nodded.

The bodyguard moved to a wall-mounted SID scanner. With a pass of his palm, the scanner registered his identity. Danica heard the heavy shifting of mechanized movement which culminated in a section of the wall recessing several inches before sliding from view. Lights cascaded to life in backward procession to illuminate a sizeable hidden room of glaring white walls, ceiling, and floor. At her distance, Danica could just make out the thin outlines of cabinets and drawers along the walls' surface.

"Shouzo-san will assist your weapons selection," Yakuza announced. While in no way gregarious prior to the negotiations, Yakuza's current deportment was entirely grim contempt. Danica prayed he held his rage until Torrance had them safely away.

"Then Shouzo-san needs to open a different vault," Torrance said. "I'll be leaving with four particle handguns, and one particle rifle."

He's going to get us killed, Danica's fear screamed in her mind. *It'd be safer to poke a rabid lion—even a pride of rabid lions!*

Yakuza shook his head. "Two handguns, one rifle. And even that is a gift."

"I can't infiltrate an Alliance facility with that. Four and one, the podcar and location, and I'll add another quarter billion," Torrance countered.

"If I sold you a HALO, you still could not free the Seton fellow," the trafficker said. "But, I will agree to the terms. It will be worth it to see your arrogance finally defeated."

Within minutes, guards placed three cases on the steel table; the smaller cases each containing a pair of handguns, while the larger held the rifle. Torrance briefly examined the weapons before offering his approval. Yakuza then revealed the location – a Peacekeeper base in Washington, DC – where her father was being held.

"The podcar will be waiting for you behind the building," one of the guards said, handing Torrance a small remote to access the vehicle.

"And now the payment," Yakuza prompted.

Torrance unclasped the leather cuff on his wrist, tossing it to a guard. The man moved the cuff across a handheld scanner to confirm the embedded SID held the agreed upon payment of credits. Once the transfer was complete, the guard moved to return the wristlet.

"Keep it," Torrance said. "That identity is officially broke now." Danica wondered how many counterfeit SIDs he possessed, and how much wealth Torrance had stockpiled on them.

"I believe our business is concluded," Yakuza said as he rose from the chair. "My men will escort you out."

Torrance motioned the siblings to collect the two smaller cases; Danica was surprised to find hers unexpectedly light. Lifting the rifle case from the table, he said, "Until next time, Genkei."

Dismissing his unwanted guests, Yakuza replied, "I doubt there will be a next time."

Shrugging his shoulders, Torrance said, "You might be right."

Guards led them from the lounge back into the pounding atmosphere of the club. Consumed by drink and dance, the patrons paid no notice to the trio's laden exit. Once again in the rear alley, relief flooded through Danica. She had half-expected Yakuza to reconsider the agreement, and decide killing them was more rewarding.

As promised, a podcar blocked the west end of the alley. Torrance, however, ignored the glossy black vehicle. Looking back, Danica asked, "Isn't that the pod?"

"Yep," he replied as he led them further away from it.

"But we're not taking it?"

"Nope."

Confused, she continued to question, "Because . . .?"

Not slowing the brisk pace, Torrance explained, "Yakuza had no intention of letting us live. The pod'll be wired. We might have gotten a block, maybe two, before it blew. If I didn't ask for the pod, he'd have had us shot as soon as the credits were transferred. This way he'd still be able to kill us, and not have to clean up after."

"How did you know?" Marcus asked.

"Because I know Yakuza."

Nervously glancing back over her shoulder at the pod now a half-street away, Danica wish their hurried walk was a sprint. At their current distance, it was unlikely an explosion still threatened their safety; but she did not want to test that theory.

With complete trust in their protector, Marcus said, "But if the pod doesn't explode, won't he come after us?"

For several strides, Torrance did not respond. When they reached the streets' intersection, he dropped to one knee, and removed a thumb-size device from his boot heel. After returning to a stand, he pressed a finger to the device. A soft click and the sky behind them immediately erupted into carnage. Danica felt the flames' heat burn through the air as glass shards shattered to the pavement. Fire and smoke poured from the nightclub's uppermost level – the level of Genkei Yakuza's personal lounge. Tossing the remote detonator into the street, Torrance directed them to resume walking.

"The people . . . the people in the club," Danica stammered through horrific shock.

"The floor," Torrance said.

Yakuza's words emerged from her memory. "Not even a particle gun could mar its surface," he had boasted. She realized Torrance had orchestrated every aspect of the meeting with the arms trader; the client list, the podcar . . . and the cuff. He had planned to offer the quarter billion credit increase all along! It provided the perfect excuse to discard the cuff; leaving behind the bomb. Danica could almost feel pity for Yakuza. His fate had been ordained the moment the guards let Torrance in the building.

Several blocks from the club, yet still close enough to hear the wailing sirens responding to the explosion, Torrance ushered them into a multi-story parking garage. Danica and Marcus followed silently behind him. She assumed he was selecting a pod to steal, but his gaze and pace were too intent to allow him much time to search. Three flights up, they came to a silver pod sedan; its sleek, aerodynamic body, seamlessly covering even the wheels, impressed an image of a launched missile. While unfamiliar with most makes and models, Danica recognized the pouncing jungle cat emblem, and knew the price tag of the vehicle was staggering. She was about to question the logic in pirating such an expensive pod (*If I owned it, I would not sleep 'til it was found,* Danica thought), when Torrance boosted Marcus toward a small crevice where support column met ceiling.

"Got it," Marcus declared.

Torrance eased the boy back to the cement, taking a remote from his hand. The pod hummed as the large doors on either side pulled back a few centimeters, and then pivoted upwards. The spacious interior, offering twin rows of inward facing seats, was encircled with a light bar glowing in warm, blue shades. Danica was reminded of the trendy European lounges featured in the celebrity holo-zines in which her mother had secretly indulged.

Stowing the weapons cases in a rear compartment, the trio eased into the seats. Torrance engaged the pod's operating system, lowered the doors, and set the navigation to DC. As the pod moved into the streets, Danica finally surrendered to one of the many questions burning her mind. "How do you have all this?" she asked. The inquiry was perhaps impolite, but she doubted etiquette rules still applied to her circumstances.

Expecting the usual half-answer, which in the past had only added to the man's mystery, Danica was astonished when Torrance answered in length. "Some of it I've acquired over the years, but most belonged to the man who raised me. He never told me how he came into it, and I eventually stopped asking. He'd just say it was necessary in order to 'place ourselves beyond the possibility of defeat.' It was the philosophy of Sun Tzu, an ancient general. Most of my questions were answered with quotes from the general. Some I understood immediately, others I had to work out, and there are still others I have not yet deciphered."

"I know what that's like," she muttered. Hoping to capitalize on his forthcoming mood, she questioned further. "He trained you to fight, taught you languages, kept you hidden from the Alliance, why?"

His expression showed the question was one of the undeciphered riddles. "'In peace prepare for war, in war prepare for peace' – another saying. I don't know which he believed we're in, war or peace. Maybe it doesn't matter. War is linked to both."

Danica felt uncomfortable with the cyclical logic. It disturbed her to believe war always loomed on the horizon. Yet, had her life not proved its validity? Could she truly describe her situation as anything but war? After the attack on her home, the murder of her mother, and the arrest of her father, she had secretly believed events might be corrected. The right words could be said, the truthful evidence revealed, and the knot of terror would be unraveled. Her heart ached as the realization of her naiveté set in. Even if they managed to free her father, what then? They'd be fugitives, constantly running, hiding, waiting for the next stranger to betray them to the PKs. She *was* in a war – one not of her choosing, and beyond her understanding, but the end of innocence required neither.

"And we can't win," she despaired aloud.

Almost tenderly, he replied, "That depends on how you define victory."

"Going back to the way things were?" Danica proposed.

Torrance shook his head. "Impossible. Even during times of peace, events move forward, not back. Our lives, the world, it's all in constant flux. You'll never find victory fighting against that truth."

Challenging him to bolster their hope, Marcus asked, "So, what is our victory?"

"You tell me."

"Rescuing Dad," he stated with certainty.

Torrance looked from the boy to his sister; waiting for her to complete the puzzle of reasoning he had laid out.

"But," she said, slowly comprehending what he needed her to see, "it won't end there. I mean, that's not the victory, is it? They'll keep coming after us. It'll just be one battle, one battle in a war."

The man nodded. "And who knows what comes after."

CHAPTER TWENTY

Kerwen Garrott

Kerwen sat behind the desk, rehearsing the conversation as he waited for Liam to arrive. He had anticipated the request. Even prepared himself to deny it. Yet, with the moment at hand, the Caput of House Garrott could feel his resolve weakening. Too many events were afoot, too many unknowns lurking in the shadows. This was not the time to be without his chief council, but hadn't Liam earned this indulgence? The spymaster had sacrificed decades in service to the Family. Could he really deny the old man's request? However foolhardy it may be. When Liam finally entered the office, Kerwen was as certain of his decision as he was the flip of a coin.

"You have news?" Kerwen asked.

Liam Walford inclined his head and waited for his master to invite him to sit. "Yes, sir. Yesterday, Tilden approached me about scheduling a tour of the Sheerness facilities for him and Ms. Carene. I conducted a second search of the lady's background, and finding nothing amiss, I scheduled the tour."

The man must be slipping! Certainly there were other, less flimsy, pretenses to request this meeting. Unable to hide his smile, Kerwen said, "Very well. Though, I don't think you needed to schedule an appointment to tell me that."

Admitting defeat, Liam replied, "True, sir. There is another matter I wish to discuss."

"A trip to America."

"Yes."

Inhaling deeply for effect, Kerwen asked, "Do you really think it necessary? Isn't it more likely to be a coincidence?"

"Perhaps. But, given the treachery of which we already know, is it not possible she is capable of this, too?"

Old grievances boiled over. "I am no longer you're student, Liam! Do not play Socrates with me, answering in questions, leading me by the nose to a conclusion of your choosing! Do you have any evidence to support your suspicions?"

Stung by the rebuke, Liam bowed his head. "Only circumstantial, Your Grace."

"If even that!" Kerwen snapped. "I've seen the same reports, Liam. Even with all your whisperers and shadows, there is next to nothing to encourage this thinking. Tell me, if I faced the same choice, how would you advise me?"

Kerwen wondered, and worried, if his advisor could see his way to objectivity. He was being overly harsh, he knew, but who else could make the man see reason? Liam's station in the Family was of a height that even Tilden, the Caput Heir, would not dare speak with such invective.

The spymaster answered, "I would advise against it, sir. I would point it out as folly."

"Then why can't—"

"Yet, I would understand the desire all the same," Liam cut into the Caput's words.

Desire. Emotion. The lives of men, and too often their deaths, hinged on how they dealt with emotion. Cut it off completely, and one was blind. Surrender to it, let emotion overtake reason, and disaster fell. Liam had ingrained that lesson; taught him to master mind and heart to the proper balance. How often had a young Kerwen listened to those lectures? He found no joy in the reversing roles of teacher and pupil.

"The enmity you harbor for the Ignota is understandable, old friend," the Caput tempered his tone. "But, I fear this path only leads to pain. If your theory is wrong, old wounds reopen. And if you're correct, if she . . . what then?"

"I do not know, Your Grace."

The Caput studied him intently. Under his tutelage, Kerwen had lived and died by the praise or recrimination Liam had delivered. His strives towards success had been as much about pleasing the House advisor as pleasing his own father. As an adult, Kerwen had often thought the man would have made a better Caput than he could ever hope to become. Such a man, such an indomitable force, was Liam Walford.

"Two days. No longer," Kerwen commanded.

Rising from the seat, Liam offered his relieved gratitude. "Thank you, Your Grace. Thank you, Kerwen."

Watching his councilor walk slowly from the office, the Caput could see every day, every minute, of the man's seventy-three years[4] pressing down on once-strong shoulders. Time had been the only foe capable of matching Liam's grit. For the first time, Kerwen saw the battle had shifted against the Chief Advisor of House Garrott.

Rotating his chair to face the window wall behind him, Kerwen's thoughts made the natural progression to his own mortality. Unlike many, he did not fear death. He had been raised to never fear the inevitable, but rather, prepare for it. What did gnaw at his peace of mind, however, was death's too early arrival. His father had died well before his time; leaving a young son, green with inexperience, to inherit the Family. Upon Kerwen's last birthday, he had seen two years more life than his father. *There's still so much more to be done,* he mused. *Another two decades, and maybe then I'll be satisfied. Maybe.*

He had no desire to cling to power. In fact, he intended to willingly step down, help his son transition to Caputhood. But, only once the Family's position was secure. Too well did he recall his own succession; days of chaos, months of missteps, and years of working to confound expectations. Keanan Garrott had suffered a devastating, fatal, and wholly unexpected, heart attack. The vultures

---

4   Discrepancies still exist regarding Liam Walford's year of birth. The most prolific accounts date his birth to the year 2093, while a small minority place it two years earlier. For the purpose of this history, I selected the more common year of 2093. –M.S.

had quickly swarmed, both in and outside the Family, seeking to monopolize on Kerwen's youth and presumed inability. They were not too far wrong in their assessment of him either. Only through Liam's guidance, and Roslyn's support, had he managed to stabilize House Garrott. Even then, it was some time before the other Caputs regarded him as an equal. Those memories drove him to ensure his son faced an easier elevation.

Kerwen had no doubts of Tilden's ability. The Heir was smart and enigmatic, though at times a tad impetuous. But, the latter would fade with age and maturity. Though he would not have Liam at his side, Tilden would have his brothers and sisters for guidance and counsel. *The Family will be in capable hands.*

"Alain," he called to the attendant waiting outside the office.

The servant dutifully entered upon the Caput's call. "Your Grace?"

"Is Tilden about?"

"The Heir went riding a short while ago, Your Grace," Alain informed. "Shall I send word for him to return?"

Thoughts of successions, past and future, had triggered a melancholy mood, and Kerwen decided an hour or two on horseback might be an ideal remedy. "No, I think I'll join him," he told the attendant.

"Very well, Your Grace. I will inform the stables."

By the time he had reached his chambers, a riding outfit had already been laid out on his bed. The snug breeches served to remind him how long it had been since last he had taken out the white gelding. Nevertheless, the muscular beast nickered affectionately, angling its ears forward and whisking its tail upon Kerwen's arrival in the stable.

Gently stroking the horse's nose, he said, "I've missed you, too, Gaspar."

"He's been missing you, he has, Your Grace," the stable master intoned.

"And I him," the Caput told him. "He's been well, Cordy?"

Adjusting the billet strap, the stable master replied, "Aye, Your Grace. Still the strongest of the lot, he is."

Ignoring the mounting stool on the ground, Kerwen hoisted himself onto the saddle, muscles contracting and flexing from memory. A groom passed over the reins, and Kerwen clucked twice to urge the mount forward into the damp autumn air.

Low clouds hid all trace of sun, darkening the sky to appear much later than the true hour. Though the leather kept the chill from his body, Kerwen's cheeks steadily tinged pink as he rode across the northern fields. He preferred this weather (a lucky thing for a Londoner) – an overcast sky, a thin, sound muffling fog, and just enough cold to speed the blood. Kerwen let out the reins, and the intuitive horse moved from trot to canter.

Far too long, the Caput thought. For months the launch of the PK-drones had consumed every spare minute, each free thought, so that he had forgotten the pleasure of riding. Coursing across land to the steady hooves-on-earth rhythm, Kerwen could almost fool himself to freedom. Ignore the echoing gaits of the mounted House Guard following behind him. Avert the eyes from the movements ahead where other guards scouted in the woods. Yes, the illusion was almost believable.

Quite sure which trail his son had taken, Kerwen slowed and led the party along its twisting path until Tilden and his own retinue came into view.

"When they said my father was riding to us, I was sure it was a jest," Tilden greeted from the saddle. The Heir's mount, a red roan mare, snorted testily as it sidestepped to allow the arrivals into the grove.

"I think Cordy was just as surprised," Kerwen replied with a laugh. "The stable hands even put out a stool."

"Which I'm sure your pride refused," his son mocked.

"Of course."

Travelling slowly along the trail, the guards keeping a respectful distance, Kerwen asked, "How's the eye?"

"The soreness has faded, thank Truth," his son answered. "The skin is still a bit tender to the touch, but even that is lessened each day. It's somewhat strange to know there's a machine in my socket. Though, I guess I'll never need glasses; at least not for that eye."

Kerwen knew it was not uncommon for recipients of artificial limbs to require a great deal of time to emotionally adjust to a prosthetic. Often, their minds struggled more than their bodies to acclimate to the physical alteration. Tilden was fortunate his prosthetic was essentially removed from sight.

"So, what brings you out today, Father?" Tilden asked.

"A sour mood," he answered.

"Lucky me," Tilden joked.

Cresting a small rise, the Garrotts entered a thick cluster of sky-reaching pines. The ground already held the first layer of browning needles shed from the tall, slender trees. By month's end, the trail would have a soft carpet of them, centimeters deep and cushioning even the heaviest step.

"I've spent all these years working to secure the Family's future, Tilden," the Caput explained. "But, today I began to wonder *who* is the Family's future."

"Father . . ."

Understanding how his words might be misinterpreted, Kerwen quickly clarified, "I don't mean you. You'll make a fine Caput, son. But, for you to achieve greatness, you need to surround yourself with greatness. I was fortunate to have Liam at my side; Rupert at Sheerness; even old Cordy to manage the stables. But, I inherited them from your grandfather. When you become Caput, who will you have? Who will be the ones to keep you from error as they did with me?"

Kerwen felt a twinge of guilt; low spirits had settled in his thoughts, and now he had imposed the gloom on his son. The current and future heads of House Garrott let the horses carry them through the next minutes in silence. At their right, a startled flock of collared doves burst through the underbrush, wings flapping in frantic beats to carry them aloft. Too distant to be the cause, the Caput wondered what lurking predator had forced the birds to abandon their foraging. He watched the frightened creatures circle to high perches; white feathers contrasting with the greens and wood brown. One dove, too focused on escape to see the dangers of safety, settled on a branch already occupied. With slow-moving majesty, the golden eagle unfolded its wide wings, thrusting itself at the intruder. The dove realized its mistake and attempted to dive away, but the power and speed of the eagle was too great, its talons too sharp, too merciless. The small corpse hit the ground with a muted thud. Making no effort to claim its prize, the bird of prey resettled itself into a camouflage of motionless vigilance.

"A fitting analogy," he said to Tilden.

The Heir nodded. "When the time comes, I had thought to install Aubrey in Liam's place."

As cunning as the woman who bore her, Kerwen's second child possessed a keen, disciplined mind. Just two years younger than the Heir, Aubrey Garrott was an interesting selection to inherit the spymaster's mantle.

While Kerwen secretly approved, he wished to hear his son's reasoning. "What led you to that decision?"

Tilden laughed. "Don't pretend to disagree, Father. She's as calculating as they come, a match even for Liam. Aubrey would never consent to a marriage of political benefit, and woe to the man she does wed. Her gender will cause our enemies to underestimate her, which she'll only see as an amusing challenge."

"Agreed," Kerwen replied, adding, "From the time she learned to speak, Aubrey's had me wrapped around her finger!"

"And Liam. And Mother, as well."

At the mention of Roslyn, the Caput asked, "What of Ms. Carene? Do you foresee her in the Family's future?"

Visibly turning rigid, Tilden answered, "I know you don't approve of her. Or at least you did not at first. But, you don't know her like I do, Father. Yes, she works in an industry of vapid minds and social self-importance, but she's more than that. She is kind, loving, and more intelligent than any of the women who have tried to gain my affection. I intend to propose with the new year."

Kerwen rode, considering Tilden's words. "And if I tried to dissuade you?"

In a voice more determined than he had heard before, the Caput's Heir said, "I'd listen. But, it'd not change my mind, Father."

Smiling, he returned, "Well, it seems my powers of persuasion are falling short today."

Tilden cast him a questioning look.

"Liam has gone to America on a fool's errand."

"Because of the Ignota's actions?" Tilden asked.

Kerwen debated how much of Liam's motivations to reveal to his son. "Yes," he replied, though his tone suggested no further questions on the topic would be answered.

Father and son continued the ride in relative silence, speaking only of trivial matters. The afternoon sun was just beginning its westward descent when they returned to the stables.

"I heard you joined Tilden on his ride today," Roslyn said from across the dining table.

Seconds earlier, servants had finished serving the gathered Family an appetizer of steamed mussels coated with a light garlic sauce. Caput and Caput'e sat in the customary places at either end of the table, with the children (minus Tilden who claimed an engagement in the city) filling the sides. The nineteen year-old twins, Kendal and Kinsey, youngest of the Garrott clan, eyed the small plates of fish morsels with disgust; neither shared their parents' fondness for shellfish. To Kerwen's immediate right was Aubrey, looking every bit the memory of her mother in youth. Next to his daughter, sat Saunders, the middle child at twenty-two. The proclaimed rogue of the Family, Saunders kept his black hair long, several thick strands hanging forward blocking the perpetual sulk on his face.

"Yes," Kerwen answered his wife as he selected the short-tined salad fork. "I felt the need for some fresh air."

"Enjoyable?" she asked.

Savoring the first taste of the mussels, Kerwen nodded. "Very much so. I didn't realize how long it had been. Though, my legs are beginning to remind me."

"I tried to go out last week but froze after only a few minutes," Aubrey shared. "The forecasters are calling for an early winter."

Saunders snorted, "They call for that every year. And every year the people rush out to purchase what they don't need."

"Not everything is a conspiracy, Saun," Aubrey replied with a roll of her eyes.

"That's the worst conspiracy of them all; to make you doubt there are any conspiracies!" Saunders countered.

While in many ways his son was correct, Kerwen spent too many hours hatching and unraveling them to spend dinner discussing secrets and rumors. "Enough, you two," he warned the pair away from the topic.

Saunders suspicion might have made him an apt prospect for Liam's post, but the constancy of his distrust would have him fettering out mysteries where none existed. *No,* the Caput thought, *Aubrey's evenness would serve the Family better.* In any event, Saunders interests directed him towards the arts, with which he apparently had some skill. Kerwen, however, had never understood the convoluted canvases his son created.

"Early winter or no," Roslyn said with a weighty stare, "it is good for you to get out of the office. Those pressures can take their toll."

He knew his wife too well to miss her meaning. The plot against De Luca had left her unsettled. *And understandably so,* a voice in his mind added, *the dark waters we sail are treacherous.* In two days' time, the act would be carried out and the matter will be behind him, though he wished the event had already past.

"Some can't be avoided," he reminded the Capute. Turning to the twins, Kerwen asked, "And, how did you pass the day?"

Throughout their youth, Kerwen had made every effort to regard his youngest children as individuals, not simply "twins." Yet, as they grew, and their personalities formed, it became clear the pair shared a connection beyond brother and sister. Beyond the completing of each other's thoughts, as was often described of twins, Kendal and Kinsey seemed one soul dwelling within two bodies.

"Class in the morning," Kendal offered.

" . . . then free the rest of the day since Liam is away," her brother finished.

Despite the privilege of the Family's wealth and status, Kerwen had insisted his children obtain degrees. Only one would become Caput, and he wanted the others in careers, not merely living spoiled off the Family's riches. Each child had progressed through the holographic classes of one of Oxford's programs. The twins were but a year away from completing their respective degrees.

In the opposite corner, a service door opened, and Kerwen saw the grim visage of his security chief, Winslow Fabirichi, and another fellow whom he did not recognize. Both men, however, panted lightly with flush faces. Excusing himself in a mumble, Kerwen walked to them, readying himself for whatever new worry they carried.

"What's wrong?" he hushed.

Fabirichi spoke first. "Your Grace, this is Lieutenant Trover from the security detail at Sheerness."

The young man flinched back from Kerwen's demanding stare. Swallowing anxiety, Trover, stuttered, "Your Grace, Dr. Thompson is missing."

"What do you mean he's missing?"

"He was not present at the factory today, Your Grace. In the past, on occasion, he has worked from home. An hour ago, his security team was due to change shifts. When they arrived, they discovered the bodies of the day team and Dr.

Thompson missing. They also found this stabbed to the door."

Kerwen took the paper from the guard. "WS JC 1.2.19," he read it aloud. "What is it? A code? A date?"

Fabirichi said, "In a manner of speaking, sir. It's from a favorite text of the Ignota. I believe it is a reference to Shakespeare's Julius Caesar, specifically, Act One, Scene Two, Line Nineteen."

"Which says?" the Caput asked.

"'A soothsayer bids you beware the Ides of March.'"

CHAPTER TWENTY-ONE

Sonje Nysgaard

She had only just begun to familiarize herself with the prison camp when the time to move came once again. *That's the toughest part,* Sonje thought as she stepped out of the older model podcar. Since leaving Sweden, she had sheltered in more places than she wished to remember; some for a few hours, others, like the prison, for a few days. But, departure always loomed. Living nomadically for a little over a week, Sonje could already feel the effects of the transience on her mind and body.

Limbs and joints ached from the constant change in sleep surfaces – perhaps a bed here, then the pod at the next stop, or maybe the cold dirt of the ground. The position which worked for one rarely worked for another. She assumed the ever present aches would eventually subside. *That, or it'll just become normal,* she mused. The pacing of their travel also worked against comfort. Gavin rarely allowed more than a few hours respite in a given location before ordering the company onward. The cell leader would have preferred a non-stop return to DC, but the stops, of course, were necessary to obtain information and supplies.

To reach the prison in Alabama, the group had hugged the eastern seaboard until turning west in South Carolina. Their current route, however, moved them north through Tennessee and Kentucky, then further to Indiana. It was a long, indirect course, but Gavin hoped to make contact with other cells along the way. For every cell they discovered, they had learned of two more destroyed by the Peacekeepers. Sonje had quickly come to recognize the slanted runic "H" warning of danger. The mark had been spray-painted on town welcome signs, sides of buildings, and highway overpasses. Once, they even found it carved into the door of home in a quiet residential neighborhood. Such overt placement indicated extreme desperation. The mood of her companions grew bleaker with each discovery.

The gypsy travel also assaulted her mind; instilling a buzzing anxiety which prevented any rejuvenation during the brief rests. Sonje found herself increasingly sharp-tongued during the rare occasions of conversation. Gavin continued his distant attitude, even assigning Kunbo to oversee her combat training. The scouts still sulked, though Corey offered sporadic smiles and quips. And Adirene, well,

Adirene maintained her obvious hate, sneering and glaring so often Sonje wondered if the woman's expression was permanently fixed in contempt. Sonje was thankful the woman had chosen to travel with Ol'Ben, Patton, Lance, and Match in the other pod.

With the other two cells, under Camorata and Marshall, traveling different routes, and planning to reform the triad in Washington, Sonje was forced to subsist solely on interactions with the members of her cell. Surprisingly, her sessions with the quiet Deader proved the most enjoyable. As an instructor, Kunbo was strict, but never harsh. He unapologetically pushed her hard, and, unlike Gavin, was unrestrained in his teaching.

"In my country," he had told her, "we must fight for food, water. Even children must learn to kill in order to survive." That he saw Sonje as a child was clear, but the perception was not meant as insult.

Though sparing in his speech, Kunbo did share some of his history with her. His brother, a powerful warlord in Uganda, had grown feverishly suspicious members of his family plotted to unseat him. An order of execution was issued, and most of Kunbo's relatives were slaughtered. Elders and newborns, women and men, were indiscriminately murdered by the warlord's death squads; the lucky few were shot, while the greater number was butchered in the streets. Kunbo and two cousins managed to flee, but his brother, incensed by their escape, pursued them relentlessly. Bounties of weapons and food were offered to any who returned the heads of the refugees. Word spread, and the Dead Continent no longer held a cave or forest beyond the warlord's reach. Only through an accidental meeting with an Ignotum was Kunbo successfully smuggled off the D.C.. By that time, though, his two cousins had fallen to the familicide.

"And what of your brother?" she had asked upon conclusion of the horrific tale.

"Over the last three years, he has expanded his territory," Kunbo had said. "I pray one day he will face justice."

"Have you ever thought of going back to . . . to kill him?"

Kunbo had shaken his head with resolve. "No. I owe my life to the Ignota. The success of their mission will do more for my people than satisfying my vengeance. If he is to ever pay for his crimes, it must come at the hand of another."

Sonje still marveled at the man's peace. She had known people to express calm in chaos though turmoil raged beneath the surface of the façade. Kunbo, however, had internalized that serenity, reaching an enlightenment few could imagine. The abominations of his past were immutable and thus to be accepted. In their sessions, as he was teaching her to kill, the harmony of his mind penetrated the tangle of her emotions, momentarily soothing her anxiety.

Free from the confines of the podcar, Sonje followed the rest of the cell across an uneven stretch of earth. Shouldering the pack containing her sleeping bag and few personal items, she sighed when they reached the small campsite Gavin had rented for the evening. *Another night on the ground,* her mind mumbled over the inevitable discomfort. With so many cells exposed, finding an accommodating safehouse had proven impossible.

The owner of the campground had haggled over the price more out of habit than any true attempt to increase profit. This late in the season, a party of ten seeking a stay was an unexpected boon. The squat little man narrowed his eyes upon seeing Kunbo; the African's pitch dark skin was an anomaly outside the genetically pure Dead Continent. The prospect of income overcame his distrust, and the owner handed Gavin a map marked with the location of the large camp site.

With her camping expertise only beginning days earlier, Sonje struggled to assemble the single-person tent. As he had twice before, Corey aided her after erecting the tent he shared with his fellow scout. Normally, she would have faced the challenge until she prevailed, refusing assistance in order to master the task. Her mental fatigue was such, however, that she readily surrendered the chore to more capable hands.

"Thank you," she said when the work was finished. Corey only smiled and nodded, apparently concerned Gavin might think he said what he should not. Biting back a scream of frustration as the scout walked away, Sonje tossed her gear into the tent. She was tempted to seal herself inside, block out the agitators with the thin canvas, but the small quarters would surely amplify her feeling of isolation. Instead, she turned and headed toward one of the trails branching off the site.

Wandering through the trees, careful not to venture too far from the security of the cell, Sonje took several long breaths of the unpolluted freshness. Her sister had often extolled the healing powers of nature, recommending Sonje spend less time secluded in her lab. *Oh, Gretch, I wish you were here now!* If there was a Nysgaard daughter better suited to the complexities of Sonje's new reality, her sister was the obvious choice. Sonje always viewed her sibling's care free outlook as too undisciplined, a lingering element of adolescence Gretchen should have abandoned long ago. She understood now, though, it was not a sign of immaturity, but rather adaptability.

Thoughts of her sister reminded Sonje of the chaos she had left behind. She had never gone this long without speaking to either Gretchen or their mother. Sonje knew the risks in attempting to contact them. The PKs would certainly be monitoring her family's actions and communications in the hopes Sonje would reach out to them. For now, it was best if Sonje was simply missing. There was another, far darker, thought which she forced away from her mind. When the Alliance moved against Philip Seton, they had not only taken him. The PKs had gone after his family as well. *If Gretchen and Mom—no.* She could not allow the idea to take root.

Kicking a small rock, Sonje muttered, "Calming effects of nature my ass!"

"Nature is always calm, Dr. Sonje," a baritone voice spoke behind her, "even during storms. We can only share in its peace if we are opened to receive it."

The intrusion had taken her by surprise, yet Sonje was pleased to discover her body had instinctively assumed a defensive posture in turning to the speaker. *Less than a week, and I'm already acting like a soldier,* she gloated.

Kunbo, the only cell member to address her as Dr. Sonje, eyed her stance – the shoulder's width spacing of her slightly bent legs, the turned-away angle of her chest, the hands raised to protect neck and face. His assessment complete, her instructor said, "Are you being attacked by a squirrel?"

Deflated, Sonje maintained her position as Kunbo explained her errors.

"Elbows must be tucked in. What good to protect your head when the enemy has a clear shot at your heart? Plant the rear foot perpendicular. Good. Lower your head slightly. Use your chin to guard your throat. Good."

Adjusting to each critique, she asked, "Did I do anything right?"

"You turned around," he replied with a wide smile, the white teeth gleaming against the black skin. Lowering a small bundle to the ground, Kunbo said, "I thought we might try something new tonight."

The man unfolded the bundle's leather wrapping to reveal four pairs of knives in varying sizes; the longest set measuring a meter of blade and handle, the shortest barely the span of her hand.

"You will not be able to carry a firearm into Global Tech, but these will pass undetected," he explained.

Sonje crouched to examine the weapons. Black blades and black handles were seamlessly joined, molded together in one solid piece. Lifting one, she marveled over its lightness. She gently ran a finger along the blade, the deceptively sharp edge drawing a thin line of blood.

"They're not metal," she said.

"No. Fiberglass and plastic," Kunbo explained. "They will not rust or crack, and they hold their edge well. Shall we?"

Nodding, Sonje stood with the knife. The African patiently led her through the basic positions and thrusts of knife fighting. "When you move to stab, do not hesitate. Follow through with your weight and use the moment to inflict as much damage as you can. Move quickly and combine attacks. Strike the abdomen, then move to the neck. Strike the neck and move to the thigh. Once you're inside their guard strike fast and repeatedly before they can recover."

Sonje listened and practiced, listened and practiced, until her worries faded from her mind and all that remained was Kunbo's voice.

"Control their attacks. Your opponents will be stronger and bigger," he repeated Gavin's earlier advice. "But, strong and big must still breathe, still pump blood. If you interfere with either one, your opponents will fall."

Beads of sweat ran down her back despite the cooling of dusk. Kunbo produced a pair of practice knives, edges dull and safe for sparring. He challenged her to strike him. Her first attempts were clumsy, and he easily disarmed her each time.

"You're hesitating," he told her as she stooped to retrieve the knife he had sent flying from her hand. Though she knew the blade was harmless, she was still drawing back when she came near to his flesh. "You will not injury me. Imagine I am one you hate."

Easy enough, she thought. Her list of enemies had grown long in the past week. First, she pictured the nameless PKs who had stormed the Churchill to kill her. She circled Kunbo in the clearing, feet moving through the patches of dried leaves, the practice knife tight in her right hand. Feinting left, then lunging forward, Sonje thrust the knife under his guard. Kunbo swung his free hand up to close on her wrist. Spinning, he hoisted Sonje from her feet along his back and sent her crashing to the ground; knife tip pressing on her throat.

"You're dead," he said. "Again."

Rising, Sonje assumed the defensive position. The pair circled and she fixed the image of Adirene in her mind; recalling the anger she felt after the attack in the showers. Kunbo lashed out, striking a punch to side. Before his knife mimicked a killing stroke, Sonje drove her elbow upwards to his throat. Though he blocked the full weight of the blow, the strike allowed her to pivot away from his knife.

"Good," he said.

Falling back to a safe distance, Sonje studied her instructor as he had taught her. "Every enemy has a weakness. Every guard has an opening," he had said during their first training session. She felt foolish trying to spy a flaw in his defense; the man was a skilled warrior from top to toe. Chest protected. Blade drawn in. Knees balanced. There was nothing she could find to—his foot! Just as she had at the start, Kunbo's rear foot was improperly planted. Moving quickly before he could correct it, Sonje pushed forward and spun low. Extending one leg in the spin, Sonje felt her shin collide with his leg. Unbalanced, Kunbo lurched unsteadily as she slashed her knife across his stomach. A true blade would have spilled his guts to the dirt floor.

"Very good," Kunbo complimented.

Knowing the accomplishment was not fully earned, Sonje replied, "You purposely placed your foot wrong."

Nodding, he said, "Yes, I did. But, the lesson was for you to notice, which you did. Openings will not always be so obvious, but your mind is training. In time, it will detect the contraction of a muscle, the shifting of eyes, so you can predict your opponent's move."

Recalling a lesson from her father, Sonje offered, "Like in chess. You have to know more than a player's next move. You have to know what they will do in three or four more moves."

"It is no accident many great leaders were skilled at the game," Kunbo agreed. "Do you play?"

"As a child. But not in many years," he replied. Sonje detected a rare expression of sentimentality. Unwilling to force him to somber memories, she shifted the conversation.

"Thank you, Kunbo," she said. "For teaching me. Without these lessons, I think I'd go crazy."

After returning the practice knives to a pouch on his belt, Kunbo carefully placed the black knives into the leather sleeve. "When I came to the Ignota, I had already lived a life of war. All that changed for me was the name of my enemy. Yours is a more difficult transition."

"Especially with the others avoiding me like the plague," she answered, then added, "Gavin seems to have ordered me into isolation."

Sitting atop a large stone, Kunbo said, "That was not the order I received."

Not intending to include him among those she perceived as wronging her, Sonje quickly apologized. "I'm sorry. I didn't mean you, Kunbo. Some of the others are— wait. 'That was not the order you received.' What order did you receive?"

"I am to protect you," he responded.

"Protect me? Like a bodyguard? Why just me? If the PKs find us, we're all going to need protection."

Kunbo paused briefly before replying. "It is not just the soldiers of the Alliance who threaten. Your guard must always be ready, Dr. Sonje. When you eat, when you sleep, when you *shower*."

Noting the emphasis, she asked, "You know about that? About Adirene?"

Kunbo nodded.

Preferring not to know how he was aware of the incident, naked as she had been during it, Sonje instead inquired, "What are the Sowilo?"

"That tale is long," he said as he gestured for Sonje to sit beside him. When she settled onto the stone, Kunbo continued.

"For thousands of years, humankind looked to the sky to find meaning. They needed a purpose, an explanation of the unknown, a reason for suffering. From that need religion was born. Civilizations throughout history, despite differences in time and place, believed a transcendent power existed beyond their perception. Ra, Odin, Zeus, Brahman, El, Yahweh, the Light, God, Wakan Tanka, Allah. The names changed through the millennia, but the foundation remained. There *was* meaning. There *was* purpose."

"And then came the Great Revelation[5]," Sonje, the scientist, added.

Kunbo seemed amused. "An ironic name. Science disproving thousands of years of religious doctrine was nearly cataclysmic. Alliance schools do not teach

---

5 The Great Revelation occurred on July 17, 2048.

the crisis of faith which swept across the world. It is amazing what can be forgotten in a hundred years' time if a government wishes it so. My people, however, who once again rely on oral histories, remember the unrest, the darkness. Many in my culture believe that unrest helped allow the Alliance to form."

The suggestion that the greatest achievements of her professional predecessors in anyway aided the Alliance offended her. Perhaps more sharply than she intended, Sonje asked, "How?"

"The Alliance filled the void faith left behind. Advances in medicine, technology, entertainment all combined to distract the people from their grief, alleviate their suffering. It is a debate for another time, Dr. Sonje. You asked about the Sowilo, and the Great Revelation is part of the origin."

Reminding herself Kunbo was providing more information than any in the cell had been willing to share, Sonje swallowed the argument. "You're right. I did. Please, continue."

"The Ignota was formed in opposition to the Alliance. The founders penetrated the veil; saw the Alliance's true nature. Because of that, the allure of the government's offerings did not satisfy the emptiness. Most, like myself, like Gavin McAvoy, found fulfillment in the quest for justice. Others, though, sought comfort in belief."

"The Sowilo," Sonje said. "It's a religious group?"

Kunbo lifted his hands in ambivalence. "In a manner of speaking, yes. They believe a savior will come and lead them to victory over the Alliance. No, they don't believe this savior is a god," he added before Sonje could ask. "Their fervor, however, is no less potent. Nor less dangerous. They will sacrifice everything, their own lives, if it furthered the cause. For them, there is honor in the act."

"Like Jamie did when you rescued me," she added. "If the Sowilo view suicide as honor wouldn't Adirene, I don't know, not hate me as much as she does?"

"Ah, and now we come to vipers' nest," the African intoned. "Borrowing from past myth and belief, the Sowilo hold that their savior will descend from the founders. Adirene believed Jamie was that descendant."

Shocked to be hearing tales of myth and legend in the modern world, Sonje said, "The McAvoys were founders."

"Jamie and Gavin's great-grandfather Seamus helped form the resistance," Kunbo continued with an affirming nod. "The Ignota were a small band at the onset, counting no more than thirty members. They knew remaining one unit risked complete annihilation if they were discovered. Thus, the founders dispersed in pairs, establishing operations across the world, and increasing their number."

"Adirene hates me not just because she loved Jamie," Sonje realized with dread, only half-hearing Kunbo's last words. "By dying to save me, he proved her belief wrong. To her, I'm the reason her savior died."

"She was dangerous before," the man said. "Gavin would have sent her away long ago if not for his brother. And now he won't because of the child she carries."

Sonje's stomach twisted. "She's pregnant."

Kunbo placed his strong hand on hers in consolation. "That is why you must be careful, Dr. Sonje. Adirene believes you brought the death of one savior. She will be as fierce as a lioness to protect her unborn child. A child with the blood of a founder."

Incredulous, Sonje shook her head. "How can anyone return to these primitive beliefs? With all we now know? How many died in the name of religion before the Great Revelation?"

"And how many were saved in its name?"

Sonje raised her eyes to his. "You're a believer?" she asked without accusation.

He replied, "Not in the way of the Sowilo. But, my home largely escaped the pain created by the fall from faith. Many of the old customs are still practiced among my people. Another reason the Alliance cordons off the continent, allowing it to slowly die from disease and bloodshed."

"This just all seems so—I don't know," she struggled to define her emotions. "It's as if I've stepped into some fairytale. Saviors and Sowilo, rune symbols and prophecies."

"The past is never truly gone. The old finds ways to become new," Kunbo offered with reverent sagacity. The pair was close in age, yet Sonje felt naïve compared to his tones of wisdom and foresight.

"Will you be reprimanded for telling me this?" she asked. "Gavin clearly tried to keep this from me."

"He charged me with protecting you," Kunbo replied. "I believe knowing who our enemies are, and what motivates them, is protection."

Rising from the stone, Sonje laid an affectionate hand on his shoulder. "Thank you, Kunbo. It is good to know who our friends are, as well."

Smiling, he handed her the leather-wrapped set of knives. "These are yours, Dr. Sonje. When you are finished speaking with him, come to me and I will show you how to hide the blades on your body."

Nodding at his insight, Sonje thanked him once again and walked back to the camp site. The sun had set in the hours she had trained and listened, and a small fire burned in the pit at the center of the tents. Ol'Ben hunched over a steaming pot, arguing with Patton as the two prepared the evening meal.

"Anymore salt and the whole damned thing will dry up," the old man grouched.

"Better than the flavorless crap you cook," Patton retorted.

Ol'Ben spat on the ground. "Boy, I've been cooking on a fire since before you left your momma's tit."

The two bantered in play, urged on by the scouts who sat on the log bench. Lance and Match Quentin leaned against another felled trunk, passing a bottle between them and laughing at the interaction. As usual, Adirene sat apart from the group, wrapped in a dark blanket and staring at the fire – the dancing flames reflected in her pale eyes. Even idle, the woman appeared menacing. *She will be as fierce as a lioness to protect her unborn child.* While grateful for Kunbo's honesty, the knowledge caused Sonje to fear the woman all the more.

Several paces away, sitting crossed legged by his tent, Gavin ran a lightly oiled cloth along the components of his disassembled firearm. Ignoring the guarded stares as the others watched her, Sonje walked over to the cell leader. She was not yet certain of her words; apologize for doubting him, castigate him for keeping so much secret, or simply thank him for his attempts to protect her.

The fire behind cast her shadow across Gavin's work area, yet he did not move his eyes from the task.

"We need to talk," she said.

Slowly placing the cloth aside, he replied, "I know."

"You were already dealing with enough," he said before she asked. "I didn't want to add to it. The government is trying to kill you; oh, and by the way, my dead brother's woman, widow I guess, thinks she's pregnant with some holy child and that you'll try to kill it."

They had moved beyond the hearing of the camp, into a cluster of trees still thick with leaves to block out the night sky. Sonje had stepped close behind the cell leader as her eyes were not accustomed to the darkness. More surefooted, Gavin had led them to the grove without the aid of light.

An unexpected laugh escaped her lips. "Wouldn't have been the best of introductions," she admitted.

"That's how I saw it," he said. His faint smile was just visible in the consuming night. "I made a judgment call, and maybe it was the wrong one. If it was, I'm sorry."

Letting the last traces of anger ebb, she said, "I understand—now. And, I guess I should apologize, too. You saved my life. You're hiding me from the Alliance. Instead of being grateful, I was selfish. I have no right to expect more of you, of any of you. All of this," Sonje swept her arms wide, "it's so new. So confusing."

"I understand how hard it is," he offered in empathy. "To wake up one morning and find the world turned on its end. I still get angry sometimes – wish I could go back to . . . to being happily oblivious. But, it gets easier, Sonje."

Hearing the first hopeful words in some time, she sighed, "Does it?"

"No, not really," Gavin replied with deadpan gravity.

Sonje's hand flew up to cover the embarrassing snort of laughter which was the trademark of the Nysgaard women. Initially remaining a gentleman, Gavin held back his own mirth until her second snort sounded into the night. Though he had just dashed that briefest glimmer of hope, she felt more at ease as they shared the humor. Wiping newly sprung tears from the corners of her eyes, she said, "Oh, Truth, I don't think I've laughed this hard in a long time."

Catching his breath, the cell leader agreed, "Me either. So, you and me, we're okay?"

"Yeah. We're good," she smiled with the words.

"Good," Gavin said as he stepped toward her, fingering back a stray lock of hair from the side of her face. His eyes searched hers for rejection, but this time she offered none. Sonje titled her head back as he leaned in and pressed his mouth to her parted lips. The chill of the night forgotten, Sonje allowed herself to be sheltered in his arms, warmed by his embrace, carried away with his passion. There were no thoughts of Ignota or Alliance, Adirene or the Sowilo. In those few, too short moments, Sonje allowed herself to forget what waited ahead on the morning after next.

CHAPTER TWENTY-TWO

Milo Chance

In the short walk back to the ballroom, Milo could already hear the shocked gasps and murmurs of confused excitement from the gala's guests. *Godwin must have run here,* he thought. Shuffling his badge from the inside breast pocket of the tuxedo jacket, and wondering how much longer the badge would be his, Milo entered the arching room. As suspected, the PK-drone stood imposingly at the entranceway. Milo flinched upon seeing his partner leveling a particle gun at the startled crowd.

Holding his identification aloft, Milo boomed his voice over the din. "Excuse me, ladies and gentlemen!" In slow-motion unison, every head turned toward him as the orchestra's music faded mid-note. Trying to work some moisture back into his suddenly arid mouth, Milo continued, "Ah . . . There's no need to be alarmed. Everyone please remain where you are. This is a Peacekeeper matter." The blank faces of the elite made him wonder if he had spoken at all.

Judge Sampkin barreled through the throng with a look of utter contempt. "Just what do you think you're doing?" the man growled when he reached Milo's side.

Refusing to wither under the man's impossible stare, the Peacekeeper replied, "I'm Corporeal Chance, sir. A situation has occurred and I need you and your guests to remain in the ballroom."

Dissatisfied with the vague explanation, Sampkin demanded, "What situation?"

"I believe there has been an abduction, Your Honor."

"An abduct—this is ridiculous! You bring that *thing* into my home," the enraged justice pointed to Godwin, "and threaten my guests! Leave now or I'll have you courtmartialed!"

"With all due respect, sir, you don't have that authority," Milo replied and hoped he was correct. "Now, if you'll stand aside and—"

Sampkin nearly foamed, "I'll do no such thing! Who is your superior? With one call, I will make you wish they never accepted your enlistment! What is his name?"

Seeing the increasing number of blue lights through the ornate windows (even trained in rapid deployment, the response was inordinately fast), Milo's courage heightened. "Sergeant Ken Anestes. And you can save the call; he'll be here in a minute. Until then, why don't you step back or I'll have that *thing* restrain you."

Unaccustomed to being disregarded by those he considered inferior, Judge Sampkin's jaw lowered in shock. "You wouldn't dare!"

A week prior, the corrupt official would have been correct. Milo, however, had just anteed his entire career, and had no intention of folding his cards until Naesha was found. Marshaling his limited authority, Milo flatly retorted, "Try me."

Before the judge could respond, Milo brushed past him and headed to his partner. Either genuinely intimidated, or simply curious to witness professional suicide firsthand, the eyes of the rich and powerful silently followed his movements.

"*Corporeal Chance, I have secured the entrance,*" Godwin announced as Milo drew close.

"Lower your gun," he whispered through a clenched jaw. The drone complied without comment. Instructing his partner to remain stationed at the entrance, Milo stepped out to the open air of the manicured lawns. When he had issued the ten-thirty-five, the PK coding for a major crime alert, Milo had not expected the response he saw before him.

Two dozen patrol pods, twice as many aerocycles, and no less than four HALOs had converged on the Sampkin estate. The last hovered low to disperse the many PK squads piled into the crafts' open bays, and then lifted skyward to flood the area with light.

"You the one who called it in?" a gruff voice shouted. Turning to the speaker, Milo raised his hand to shield his eyes from the passing brightness of a HALO lingering just long enough to reflect off the insignia on the speaker's uniform.

Silver leaves, Milo's mind groaned.

"Yes, Lieutenant Colonel," he replied in formal salute. "Corporeal Chance reporting, sir."

"What's the situation, son?" the seasoned officer asked.

"An abduction, sir. A SID went offline approximately fifteen minutes ago."

The officer's gray brows knit together in consternation. "You called in a ten-thirty-five for an abduction?"

"Uhm, yes sir."

Offering Milo an excuse for declaring such a high level alarm, the Lieutenant Colonel asked, "Terrorist involvement?"

"I don't believe so, sir," Milo answered.

Before the superior officer could reply, Sgt. Anestes's voice entered the rapidly devolving conversation. "Corporeal Chance is a bit overzealous, Colonel."

"He one of yours, Anestes?"

"Yes, sir," Milo's CO acknowledged. Stepping into view, the man fixed Milo a reproving glare. "He's been investigating a high-value target – the drug lord Muerte."

Musing aloud, the colonel said, "Muerte, eh? There'd certainly be a medal for his capture. But, that still doesn't warrant pulling in these resources, Sergeant. We've got a terrorist out there responsible for blowing up half the city. I can't have my men running around looking for a drug pusher!"

"I understand, sir," Anestes replied with slight apology. "It is possible, however, Muerte has information regarding the whereabouts of the terrorist Torrance. The city's not big enough for those two not to cross paths in the underworld."

Milo watched as the man calculated the potential link. "Very well," the colonel announced. "Tell us what you know," he said to Milo. After receiving Naesha's description and last known location, the senior officer instructed his men to initiate the search.

Pulling the Peacekeeper aside out of earshot, Anestes barked, "This is keeping a low profile? You've got a full Truth-damned battalion searching a district judge's estate!"

"I'm sorry, sir," Milo answered. "But, I know this—"

Anestes waved off the apology. "Sorry or not, Chance, I can't protect you. I warned you to be circumspect and instead you did this! When this blows up, and trust me it will, you'll be lucky if you only receive a dishonorable discharge."

"Sir, I—"

"No! Enough, you've said enough, Chance," Anestes said, then turned to address another Peacekeeper. "Private, escort Corporeal Chance back to the station and put him in holding until I return."

Numb and dazed, Milo was escorted into a patrol pod. Clearly uneasy arresting a fellow PK, and one of higher rank, the private struggled to avoid eye contact with the unlikely prisoner. Through the window of the departing pod, Milo stared at the military activity buzzing across the vast grounds of the Sampkin estate. He wondered how many laughs the judge and his associates would share over the demise of Corporeal Milo Chance.

Halfway back to the station, and his inevitable detention, Milo replayed the past week's events in his mind. When had the investigation gotten away from him? Which moment, which choice, had sent him down the path to self-implosion? Thoughts turned to Julia and the tears his blindness had brought to her face. He had never imagined giving everything to his work would leave him with nothing in the end. *Just as the Soothsayer warned.*

Shifting in the rear seat, an object pressed into Milo's side through the material of his tuxedo jacket. Reaching into the left hip pocket, his hand closed around a slim disc. Exposed to the dim lights inside the pod, the object was revealed as Naesha's compact. *When did she give me this?* he wondered. His eyes widened at the next thought.

Retrieving his mobile comm, Milo hushed into the device, "Godwin, get back to the station as fast as you can."

"Excuse me, sir?" the private asked from the front of the patrol pod.

"Uh..nothing. Just talking to myself."

Pacing the chipped tiles of the holding cell, Milo waited impatiently for the drone to arrive. The private had courteously left him with his belongs, an act sure to get the young Peacekeeper a stern reprimand in the future, and Milo studied the compact as he walked. Eyes and hands found nothing beyond ordinary, but he was certain the item had significance. Naesha had used it during the doctor's conversation with Roberts. *Could it be a recorder?* It was a great effort to keep from disassembling the compact. Milo, however, knew the task should fall to Godwin's far more exacting hands.

"And where the hell is he?" he said out loud.

"Have you been arrested, Chance?" the drone's false voice asked from the hall.

Finally! "Not totally," Milo replied, not wanting to force his partner into an ethical dilemma. *Especially one his programming won't let me win,* he added to himself. "It's more for my protection." *Yeah, protecting me from making another* stupid decision!

"Any update on Naesha?" he asked to move the drone along.

"Negative. Her SID has remained offline."

Truth, let her be alive! "Godwin, listen," he said as he slid the compact through the bars. "Naesha passed this to me before she disappeared. There has to be something on it, maybe a recording, or a message, something to help us find her!"

Godwin turned the circular make-up holder in his inhuman hands. "Perhaps she thought you needed to freshen up."

"What—seriously? Jokes, now?" he replied once the words took meaning.

"My system shows humans often use humor to lighten tense or difficult moments," Godwin responded.

"Scan my expression. What's your system telling you now?" he growled back.

The cycloptic red sensor of the artificial PK's helmet flashed. "It would seem humor would, perhaps, be not well received. My apologies. You are, however, correct, Chance. There appears to be a camera and recording mechanism contained within Ms. O'Geron's personal affect."

"Can you access it?" Milo asked.

"Certainly." Godwin replied before turning about and exiting the station's holding area. Gone long enough for Milo to doubt his return, the drone eventually reentered the cells with a portable computer cart. Milo watched as Godwin separated the halves of the compact, connecting the mirrored section to an open port on the mobile tech center. Entering a series of commands on the holograph keyboard, he accessed the recording. A small projection of Dr. Hopkins and Roberts formed on the platform.

"There's no sound," Milo complained.

"Patience, Chance," the drone advised as he continued to watch the video to its conclusion. "I have analyzed the conversation and applied an automated lip reading program. Seventy-eight point four nine percent of the conversation has been decoded."

Impressed, Milo said, "You can lip—never mind. What are they saying?"

In response, Godwin replayed the video, though now captions appeared at the bottom of the display.

" . . . prints was a foolish mistake, Benji."

"It's handled. The PK's investigation has been hamstringed. He is on a short leash – UNREADABLE - to end his questioning in a matter of days."

"Then why is he here with a reporter?"

"She's hardly an investigative journalist, Willem."

"She needs to be removed."

"That will only raise more questions. – UNREADABLE – and he'll keep digging."

"It should never have gotten this far! As soon as you knew there was a risk, it should have been eliminated. O'Geron has a score to settle."

"You worry too – UNREADABLE. But, if it will put your mind at – UNREADABLE – take care of her. Tonight."

"No theatrics?"

"There's a reputation to uphold. Muerte is known to be ruthless, a fact which keeps the operation secure."

"You enjoy your work too much."

The projection blinked out. A memory itched in Milo's mind. "Godwin, replay the last few seconds."

"You enjoy your work too much."

"Again."

"You enjoy your work too much."

A dam of comprehension burst with sickening clarity. In Milo's apartment, the medical examiner had said nearly the same phrase in describing the informant Banhen's death. He had had it right from the beginning. Finding the doctor's fingerprints at the safehouse would lead to Muerte. The error he had made, however, was assuming Hopkins worked for the drug lord.

"Godwin," Milo said, dread for Naesha's fate exploding. "Dr. Hopkins *is* Muerte."

"I would agree with your hypothesis, Chance."

"Where is he now?"

The drone paused, then replied, *"Dr. Hopkins's SID is currently at 2121 State Street."*

"The Ruins. Son of a bitch! He's got Naesha. Godwin, can you get me out of here?"

"As you are not 'totally' under arrest," Godwin answered as he flashed his palm across the cell's lock scanner.

Once the bars slid open, Milo rushed forward, instructing his partner to follow to the elevator. Pressing the button with repeated anxiety, they waited for the conveyance to descend to the sublevels.

"Chance, it would be prudent for you to request I transport you to Dr. Hopkins's location."

Confused, Milo inquired, "Why?"

Without explaining, the drone asked, *"Do you wish me to transport you?"*

Before he could reply, the elevator toned a soft bing as the doors swept aside. The private who had escorted Milo from the Sampkin estate stood agape, an unopened bottle of water in his hand.

Milo whispered an answer to his partner's question. "Yes."

"Wha . . . what are you doing?" the private, rightfully alarmed, turned the question to the waiting pair.

"I have received instructions to transport Corporeal Chance to another location," Godwin supplied. Milo cast his eyes down in an appropriate display of contrition, though mostly he hoped to cover his smirk. The private, unsettled by Godwin, openly struggled to decide the correct protocol.

"Is Sergeant Anestes aware of the transfer?" he stammered.

Godwin tilted his head in all-too-human disregard. *"Who do you think issued the order, Private?"*

"Right. Okay," the junior officer replied warily as he stepped back to allow Milo and Godwin onto the elevator.

The ascent from the lower level was wordless. Milo kept his eyes lowered, but still caught the nervous glances of the private. Silently urging the elevator speed, he hoped the younger man would not realize Godwin's manipulation. The Peacekeeper bit back a sigh when the doors finally parted on the main floor. Only once they exited the building, the private staring at their departure, did Milo risk speech.

"That was damn near close to lying," he said.

Continuing a steady pace to a patrol pod, Godwin replied, *"It seemed necessary. Private Laertes would not have allowed you to leave otherwise."*

Milo smiled and shook his head. *Truth, I'm corrupting him,* his thoughts teased.

The patrol pod's vertical doors lowered, and Milo directed the navigation system to the address Godwin identified. Removing a spare particle rifle from the auto's arsenal locker, he checked the weapon's readiness.

"Any other SIDs at the location?" he asked Godwin.

"*Negative.*"

"Hopkins's . . . Muerte's men probably aren't chipped," Milo said, reminded of the target's true identity. He wished he could scan the house with infrared, but the technology had been sacrificed decades earlier due to its disruption with SID transmission. *We're going in blind,* he thought with unease.

The patrol pod was waved through the city's various checkpoints without question. Milo said a silent offering of gratitude; he doubted Godwin's explanations would have survived deeper scrutiny. He briefly contemplated alerting Anestes, summoning back-up, but worried a large and loud assault would allow Muerte the needed seconds to escape. And kill Naesha, if she was not already dead. *I have to believe she's alive. He likes to torture, he won't kill her outright.* There was little consolation in the thought.

Arriving at the intersection of State and 4th, Milo directed the pod to halt. "We walk from here," he told Godwin. "Surprise is the only thing on our side. He won't hesitate to kill Naesha if he has the chance." *Please let her be alive!* "We take out his men as quietly as we can."

"*Understood.*"

The street was nearly empty, save for three teens loitering outside the corner house. The sight of the patrol pod, and the two PKs emerging from it, sent them indoors in a rush, though they tried to intimate nonchalance. *You're getting a pass tonight, kids. You can Edge yourselves all you want.*

"The house is ten meters ahead," Godwin informed with minimal volume. "it appears to be unguarded. Though my audio scans detect human presence approximately two meters behind the door."

Recalling his scant perusal of the Peacekeeper-drone logistics packet, Milo knew, at this distance, his companion could perceive elevated breathing at least as far as the front rooms of the abandoned home. "His SID still here?"

Godwin nodded.

Wiping the sheen of sweat from his hand, Milo adjusted his grip on the rifle. Motioning Godwin forward, Milo felt none of the romanticized glory he had imagined in finally apprehending Muerte. The tactical plan they had quickly hashed together during the drive seemed suddenly flawed and ill-prepared as Milo slowly rounded the side of the concrete stoop. The rules of his training, secure the perimeter, seal possible exits, screamed for obeisance in his mind. Urgency and inadequate resources forced them aside. Milo motioned Godwin to proceed.

Gripping the brick and mortar façade, the drone expertly hoisted himself alongside the door; artificial strength and dexterity the only justifications for the feat. With his partner in place, Milo angled the rifle up to scratch softly at the base of the wood door. Waiting, but hearing no movement, he repeated the action. On the third attempt, the noise was noticed and heavy footfalls moved inside. Milo swallowed hard, tucking into the shadow of the stoop, as the door opened.

First a basic semi-automatic gun, then an arm, emerged from the dark interior. Breathless, Milo waited for Godwin to act. Sweeping his hand from the bricks with impossible speed, the drone closed his fingers around the guard's neck; cutting off the man's ability to alert others. Seizing on his shock, Milo pulled himself up on the railing to disarm him.

"He can either choke you out, or snap your neck," Milo whispered into the guard's ear "The choice is entirely yours. Do you understand?"

Nearly lifted off his feet by Godwin's strength, the man managed a slight nod through the strangle hold.

"Is she alive?"

Another nod.

"Up or down?"

Muerte's security man dramatically lowered his eyes to the steps.

"How many men? Blink the number."

One, two, three . . . seven, Milo counted. There was a chance the number was purposely altered lower, but the expanding puddle beneath the guard's shoes indicated he was too frightened to deceive.

"Sweet dreams. See you when you wake up," the PK patted the captive's cheek. Godwin shifted his grip slightly and within seconds the guard's head lolled unconsciously to the right. Once on the ground, Milo secured hands and feet with the durable plasticuffs he had carried from the patrol pod.

Falling in behind Godwin, the drone's night vision one of their few advantages, Milo moved blindly through the indiscernible rooms. Twice, his foot collided with some unseen obstruction on the floor; thankfully the resulting noises were muffled and faint. Eyes finally adjusted to the darkness by the time they reached the kitchen in the back of the railroad-style home. Tapping Godwin's shoulder, momentarily forgetting his partner's composition and finding surprise in the unyielding exterior shell, Milo pointed towards a door at the rear of the kitchen table.

Approaching the door, Milo extended a hand to the old-fashioned knob; the rifle butt couched in the crook of his bent elbow. He mouthed a silent curse when the door pushed open with more force than he intended. *Barely touched the damn—* he thought before realizing the door had been not pushed but *pulled*. Instinct brought his fist to where the second guard's face should have been. The shadow, however, was ready and Milo only managed to clip his knuckles across the right ear. Unbalanced from the misaim, he could do nothing to avoid the down-swinging blow of the guard's fist. The strike caught him along the jaw, and Milo's head ricocheted off the sideway.

"PKs!" the guard shouted a fractured second before the close quarters flared in amber. A sickening crack and pop preceded a splash of warm liquid on Milo's face. In the afterglow of Godwin's shot, he saw the guard, head only beginning at the bridge of his nose, crumple backwards down the staircase. Loud voices below proved the guard's warning had been heard.

Naesha! Milo charged after the still tumbling body; legs tangling with the limbs of the pinwheeling corpse. A return volley of particle bullets flashed wildly. Dodging as he ran-fell down the steps, Milo's footing was eventually defeated, and he slid down the remaining stairs head first. His shoulder flared painfully as it struck the concrete landing. Instinctively angling the rifle, he fired three rounds into the basement as Godwin leapt over him.

The only light came from a small room to the left. From his upended vantage, Milo saw Naesha inside grappling with Hopkins-Muerte as the latter dragged the reporter backwards, pressing a gun to her head.

Godwin engaged with four unseen guards; golden brown streaks crisscrossing with a sizzle through the dank air. The drone's position behind a round support pole left him partially exposed. While the machine's armor could withstand standard bullets, particle shots would cut through it just as easily as flesh. Already, one of Godwin's legs bore a deep, sparking gash where a well-aimed shot had found its mark.

"Get cover!" Milo shouted to his partner as he hauled himself free of the dead guard pinning his legs. Crouching low, using the body as a shield, he aimed the rifle and joined the gun battle. In his periphery, Milo could see Naesha succumbing to the strength of the three men holding her. She loosed a shattering scream as they pulled her through an exterior door.

"Go, Chance," Godwin commanded. Loyalties warred within him. Even though made of metal and circuits, Milo agonized leaving his partner while under heavy fire. The drone, however, forced the decision. Godwin stepped from behind the pole, twin particle guns orchestrating a brief spate of safety. *A human life,* Milo reminded himself. *The human life has to come first.* Pushing himself away, he ran low, diving and tumbling into the side room. Milo looked back just as a series of bullets staggered his partner.

A primal scream erupted from Milo, and he sprinted after Naesha and her captors. Scanning left and right across the rows of backyards, he saw night-lit movements three yards over. Hurdling the squat fence dividers, most grown thick with thorny unkempt brush, Milo hoped to gain sufficient ground before his quarry realized they were being pursued. Distance closing, he saw no signs of life from the limp figure the men carried.

Finally within range of his accuracy, he dropped to a knee, steadied the rifle, and squeezed the trigger. The night brightened and dulled, but Milo's marksmanship cut true; felling one of the guards with a searing bolt through the chest. The suddenness of Naesha's full weight burdening the other man caused him to stumble. Milo could not risk another shot. Lurching forward, he instead fired above the huddle, preventing further escape as he moved in.

"Freeze!" Milo shouted across the few meters of separation.

Hopkins-Muerte spun and leveled his weapon at Milo. The guard rose slowly from the ground. His thick arm tightly wrapped around his hostage's neck – and his particle gun digging into her temple. Using her body to shield himself, only a few centimeters of the man's head were visible.

"Drop your weapons!"

Moonlight glinted off the drug lord's toothy sneer. "I don't think so, Corporeal Chance," he said with eerie calm. "The odds are in *my* favor. You pull that trigger, she's dead. And chances are, I'll get a shot off as well. Then, we all die."

Milo could find no error in the man's assessment of the stand-off. *Stall,* the mind directed. *For what?* he asked back. "There's no way out, Hopkins. Even if you kill me, the same video which led me to you will lead others. Muerte's exposed. You can't run from that."

Mention of the video brought flickering consternation to the doctor's face. His words, however, still held triumphant tones. "What you fail to understand, Peacekeeper, is the level of protection I have. The forces you serve, shelter me."

"I serve the Alliance," Milo returned, still searching for a slim opening to turn the tides.

Hopkins-Muerte smiled. "Exactly."

A buzz of heat burned past his ear into the fractionally exposed section of the guard's head. Reacting quickly, Milo dove to his left just as the doctor fired. Reflexes spared his heart from the fatal shot, but the bullet still ripped through the side of his unarmored chest. Before his body hit the earth, he unleashed two rounds of his own.

The world pitched and spun in reverse as Milo fought to fill his air with lungs. His right side seethed and shrieked in pain with each inhalation. Training turned him to check the target was neutralized, though he knew there was little he could do if it was not. The doctor's body lay motionless on the ground; the smoking wounds in his chest declaring him dead. Another form dragged along the ground towards Milo.

"Naesha," he said.

The reporter's face came into his vision. One of her eyes was swollen shut, and there was a mild burn where the particle bullet grazed her forehead. "Oh my Truth, you're shot!" she exclaimed through tears as she inspected his injuries.

"Collapsed . . . lung," he bit out in pain.

"Godwin!" she shouted.

A shuffling crunch of leaves and grass signaled the drone's approach. Milo shifted as best he could until his eyes focused to the towering figure of his partner. So riddled with rents and tears and the dangling remnants of sheared wiring, Milo was amazed Godwin still functioned.

"Nice shot," Milo gasped.

The vertical bar of his red eye flashed. *"In the future, you need to move faster."*

Coughing a laugh through a grin, Milo replied, "And we need . . . to work on your . . . jokes."

As an approaching chorus of sirens filled the night like wild banshees, Milo let his head slip back to the ground. There would be questions in need of answering, decisions requiring explanations, and quite probably, more than a few lecturing reprimands. He had served long enough to predict the coming bureaucracy. For now, though, he allowed only one thought in his mind. *We got him. We got Muerte.*

CHAPTER TWENTY-THREE

Danica Seton

"How many more times are we going to do this?" she asked, careful to keep even the hint of a whine from her voice. The drive south had not been overly long, but Torrance insisted on scouting the Peacekeeper base. Now on their third lazy circuit around the perimeter of the facility, Danica was eager to stretch her legs. The luxury model podcar, with its full reclining seats, had been spaciously accommodating at the start of the trek, but the space dwindled with each passing minute. The study of the military installation was running nearly as long as the drive to DC. The base itself only added to the discomfort.

Stretching across nearly thirty acres, Fort Rotterdam's[6] fortifications seemed to mock the trio's intentions. The main gate was secured by two squads of soldiers, each with access to a HALO a few meters behind the gate, and a pair of green-brown camouflaged tanks. Even idle, the particle cannon turrets atop each steel behemoth threatened immediate destruction. During their first pass of the entrance, Torrance had commented the heightened security was an advantage. Danica did not see how that was possible, and she did not ask.

Other access points along the outer lines of Rotterdam were no less imposing. The sections between the entrances and exits appeared to offer an easier means of breaching the base. When she had voiced that opinion, Torrance pointed out the innumerable cameras and motion activated weapons systems mounted on trees and poles. Deeper into the facility, dozens of buildings, some narrow and tall, others low flat structures larger than several football fields, served to backdrop the endless activity on the ground. Full companies of Peacekeepers marched in formation as the troops engaged in various drills. The precision of their steps, the laser focus of their movements, reminded her of Torrance. Hundreds of Torrances.

"There," Torrance finally said. "Same thing each time."

Beyond watching yet another pod pass through the security installation at the

---

[6] Prior to the founding of the Global Alliance, Rotterdam was called Fort Lesley J. McNair. The post was rededicated in 2061 to honor Manuel Rotterdam, the first general installed under the new regime.

smaller west gate, Danica witnessed nothing outwardly remarkable. "What's the same thing each time?" she asked.

"See those camera guns running down the street," he explained. "When a pod pulls to the gate, they automatically shift to cover the entrance. Once the pod is waved through, the cameras restart their individual cycles. It takes fifty-three seconds before the cameras return to their original positions to view the entire area. That's fifty-three seconds of blind spots. And that's how we get in."

"We're going to break into a Peacekeeper base in a minute?" she asked. Danica would have laughed if anyone else had made the suggestion, but she doubted Torrance had ever told a joke in his life.

"No. In fifty-three seconds."

She turned to her brother, expecting him to share her bewilderment. Blinded in his hero-worship, the young teen simply nodded confidently to imply the time frame was perfectly reasonable. Danica rolled her eyes in frustration.

The surveillance apparently completed, Torrance manually steered the pod away from the military compound. As the day drew late, the traffic in and out of the city increased as business men and women began their commutes home. Longing tugged at Danica's heart as they passed the highway exit which led to her own home. She wondered how it looked now, a week since . . . since her mother had been killed. The PKs had probably turned the house on its end in their search for the holocard. She imagined it would look like the digitals she had seen after storms and tornadoes moved through quiet neighborhoods. Memories and debris mixed together, indistinguishable.

Had the neighbors watched? Had they shaken their heads while muttering the obligatory platitudes one often heard from those acquainted with both suspect and victim. Danica had not seen the portrayals of her family in the media, though she was sure the depictions were unflattering. After all, she was "responsible" for a double homicide. There were likely more than a few quotes highlighting her loner tendency, which would, of course, be used as motive for her supposed crimes.

She knew it should not bother her, what people she probably would never see again said. But, it did. From a young age, Danica's parents had nurtured and encouraged their daughter's independence so that in maturity she was unconcerned with what people thought of her. The potential accusations of poor parenting, some error Philip and Beth Seton had made to raise a murderer, did knot her stomach. Their mother had died protecting her children, but who would ever know that truth now?

"Where are we going?" Marcus asked.

Returning to the present, Danica looked out the window to find the iconic landscape of central DC expanding across the windshield dome. Though much of the old grandeur of the former American empire's capital had faded since the founding of the Global Alliance, many still flocked to the city to admire its Neoclassical architecture. The white structures, with their great domes and towering columns, shone brightly in the twilight sky. Atop each, the flag of the Global Alliance, a deep blue star and five red circles on a striped field of gray and white, stirred softly in the gentle fall breeze.

"We need to find a place for you to stay tonight," Torrance replied.

"Us?" Danica asked him with a slight edge of worry. "What about you?"

Maintaining his focus on the flow of traffic, he said, "I'm going back to study the base."

"Why can't we go with you?" Marcus asked for them both.

"Because I need to concentrate."

Danica slammed her foot down again. Again shuddering in disgust at the crunching sound beneath her boot sole. If the manager of the motel charged the roaches for occupancy, he would have been a very wealthy man. *Maybe then he could afford teeth,* she thought grimly as she wiped her shoe across the stained carpet.

The lodgings Torrance had rented for the evening perfectly mirrored the decay of the surrounding neighborhood. Homeless bundles of rank clothes and weary skin littered the sidewalk outside the Rose Motel. The only upright pedestrians openly hawked a variety of illegal narcotics and sexual pleasures. If the smell of the street burned her nose, the motel's "lobby" was enough to make her retch.

Behind the desk in the small lobby, lit by inconstant, flickering lights, a living corpse had greeted the trio with a disturbed, rot-toothed smile. A series of pussing sores decorated the manager's mouth so that his lips seemed twice as large as they were. The redness of the cracked skin at the base of his nostrils matched the color of his bloodshot eyes. Upon seeing Torrance and the children enter, the man had pushed away from a kneeling woman, and tucked his sex back into filthy pants.

"How long you want?" he had asked Torrance.

"The whole night," their guardian had responded.

Clearly accustomed to hourly rentals, the manager calculated quickly before requesting two hundred credits. Torrance had placed his hand on the scanner; the cuff stored in the podcar providing a new identity and source of funds.

"Room fifteen. Up two flights, second on the left." As they had walked away, Danica heard the manager instruct the woman to resume her efforts.

Once they were settled in the room, Torrance left to continue his surveillance of the base where Philip Seton was being held.

"This place is disgusting," she exclaimed after finishing the previously purchased fast food burger and fries, and flushing the wrappers down the grime-caked toilet to keep the roaches at bay.

"It's only for a night," Marcus reminded through a mouthful of his meal.

"Yeah, a sleepless night," she countered, eying the unmade bed of tangled sheets still splotched with dampness from the previous occupants. The siblings were forced to find some form of comfort in the pair of wooden chairs which completed the room's sparse furnishings. With uneven legs, the seat tipped and rocked with the slightest of movements. Not that Danica would have been able to sleep if the chair was steady. Her skin crawled with imagined insects. Given the multitude scrambling along the floor, she hoped the ones "on" her skin remained imaginary.

"Tomorrow night we'll be with Dad, and Torrance will find us a better place to stay," he said.

Danica wished she shared a fraction of her brother's optimism. *Did he see the same base I did?* Guards and tanks, cameras and weapons, at every turn. She was beginning to think Yakuza was right. *Even if we had a HALO, there's no way we're getting in.* But Marcus believed in Torrance and his plan of fifty-three seconds, and Danica did not share her doubts with him.

It was a strange thing – expecting to die. She thought the feeling should have been more unsettling, more troubling. Yet, Danica found she was oddly calm. She was not eager for her end, but rather she had come to accept it. Their father was imprisoned, being tortured, and they had to rescue him. Or, at least try. It was simply that . . . well, simple. Love and morality required the attempt, and Torrance's leadership provided their best chances. Failure, she believed, was inevitable. Perhaps they had somehow cheated fate when Danica and Marcus escaped from their home, and tomorrow night that cosmic imbalance would be rectified.

"I don't think you should come with us," she said.

"Where?"

"To the base. Tomorrow night."

Misreading her concern, Marcus snapped, "I'm not a baby, Dani! You saw how I helped on the HALO. I can help Dad just as much as you can!"

Cutting into his defense, she said, "I don't think you're a baby. But, rescuing Dad'll be dangerous. And if something goes wrong—I mean maybe Torrance can give you a fake SID and you can hide somewhere, or . . ."

"I know it's dangerous. And I know you don't think Torrance can do it, but I do! We met him for a reason, Dani. Can't you see that? What were the chances we'd run into some super-soldier who lives in a cave? One in a million? A billion? There's gotta be a reason for it."

Danica let her brother have the final word of the debate. How strange it was for two people to feel the hand of Fate guiding their actions, yet envision such divergent outcomes. Pointing the remote at the room's small holoset (Danica had not seen one of the technological relics since she had padded around in diapers), she absentmindedly scanned through the many channels – not caring what was on, but seeking a distraction from her thoughts. Finally settling on a raunchy sitcom, one her parents had barred their children from watching in the past, she let the characters' bizarre antics fill the slow minutes until Torrance returned.

In the hall, and through the apparently wafer-thin walls, Danica heard guests arrive and depart with the steady hum of bees, briefly stopping to conduct their business before flitting off to other interests. In days past, Danica would have blushed to hear the not-too-private moans and groans of the motel's lodgers. Though brother and sister had an undeclared vow of mutual silence, neither could hide their laughter when a guest in an adjacent room unleashed a hilarious string of gasping expletives.

The holoset program ended, and a brief set of commercials, tailored to Torrance's current identity of "Edmund Killian," preceded the next show. Danica lost track of time until the familiar face of the late night news anchor appeared.

"Good evening. I'm Clarice Pentari and you're watching Global News at 11. Our top story tonight continues to be the government's worldwide terrorist crackdown. Cities across the globe are seeing increased Peacekeeper activity as the Global Alliance strikes the very heart of the group known as the Cohors Ignota. Joining me in studio is retired-General Logan McAllister, and via satellite Badri Kadam, Information Secretary for the Alliance. Thank you for being here, gentlemen. General McAllister, let me start with you. Many have said this is an unprecedented military action; with some even calling it a 'new war on terror.' What are your views?"

"Thank you for having me, Clarice. Unfortunately, there is nothing 'new' about terrorism. It has been the cancer of every civilization in history. We've had a long stretch of peace and security, but we need only look at the early twenty-first century to see how devastating terrorist motivations can be. I applaud the Alliance for finally mobilizing. In fact, I think it is long overdue. I do, however, wish the Council would be more aggressive in this war."

"Mr. Secretary, let me bring you into the conversation."

"Thanks, Clarice. Let me start by saying the Global Alliance appreciates Gen. McAllister's insights and honored service. I would disagree, though, with the

characterization of 'long overdue.' Protecting its citizens has always been the Alliance's top priority. What we're seeing now is the result of decades of intelligence gathering, surveillance, and infiltration into these terrorist cells. While the recent attacks in Washington and Philadelphia were tragic, they were soft targets; which shows the desperation of the Ignota. The Peacekeepers, brave men and women serving our great Alliance, have been crippling the terrorist network over a long period of time. I think it is fair to say the Ignota is in its final throes."

"With all due respect, Mr. Secretary, I don't think we can classify Caput Garrott as a soft target."

"Certainly not, Clarice. But, the incident in London has not yet been claimed by the Ignota. Nor is there any indication Caput Garrott was the target. The investigation is ongoing, and until such time when we have clear evidence of an orchestrated plot, empty speculation has no value."

"How does the Alliance respond to the idea of this being a 'new war on terror?'"

"Using terms like 'cancer' and 'war' gives these terrorists more strength than they deserve. We're talking about a relatively small group who see the freedoms guaranteed by the Global Alliance Charter as a threat. The general is right when he says every civilization has faced a similar group of dissidents. But, history also shows these radicals never prevail."

"So, this is not a war?"

"No. The Alliance views this as a military action. One of many conducted over the years to ensure the safety of our way of life."

"General, is this a war?"

"Well, Clarice, I don't get the same briefings I used to, so I can't really speak to the totality of actions the Peacekeepers are taking. What is clear, though, and I agree with the Secretary on this, the Alliance has the Ignota on the run. Now, that may cause an escalation in the violence as the terrorists lash out before their final defeat. Such a spike is to be expected, but it will also be brief."

"And, that will have to be the last word for now. Gentlemen, thank you both for your time. We turn now to Dr. Mi Sun Rang, clinical psychologist, to help us understand how subversive groups, like the Cohors Ignota, attract followers. Doctor, over the past week we have seen two high profile cases of terrorist recruiting. Let's start with the first, Danica Seton, daughter of Global Tech project manager Philip Seton."

Danica's jaw dropped as her senior yearbook digital appeared in the right-hand corner of the holograph image.

Breaking their pact of silence, Marcus exclaimed, "Dani, that's you!"

"Shh," she replied as the psychologist began to speak.

"This is a sad situation, but not uncommon. We have an impressionable teen, an outsider by most accounts, who has clearly fallen prey to Ignota propaganda. We see this in inner-city gangs – a weak-minded loner susceptible to the perceived acceptance and kinship offered by fringe groups. The Ignota likely targeted her for recruitment given her father's employment with the Alliance."

"It sounds like you're talking about brainwashing. Is Ms. Seton, then, not responsible for murdering her family?"

"Don't get me wrong. She may have been a victim at first, but her actions are her own. She chose to join a terrorist group. And she chose to murder."

It was a challenge not to shout at the holoset. Very little of the past week had been any of Danica's choosing.

"What of the Swedish woman? Clearly she can't be considered a loner or outsider. Dr. Sonje Nysgaard was a well-respected biroboticist, and had actually *worked with Philip Seton on the new SID upgrade."*

"That's her!" Danica did shout when her own digital was replaced with that of a beautiful woman with tightly drawn blonde hair. "That's the name Dad said when he gave me the holocard!"

"She's a terrorist?" Marcus asked.

"According to them, so am I," she replied sarcastically as she turned her ears back to the three dimensional news.

". . . dissatisfied with her employment. The second possibility is Dr. Nysgaard was involved with the Ignota all along, using her access and research to assist the group's activities. I lean towards the latter. It is beyond coincidence she was in Washington on the same night a man she had worked with was murdered. When all the facts emerge, Clarice, I think we will find Dr. Nysgaard is directly linked to the Seton homicides."

The news anchor and her guest conversed a few minutes longer, but Danica heard little after the mention of Washington. The tumult of the past week had forced her father's hastily spoken instructions to slip from the fore of her memory. Confronted with them now, and knowing Sonje Nysgaard was in Washington, or had been a week ago, Danica wondered how their current course of action might be impacted. Should they wait? Should they seek out the woman before attempting the rescue? A dozen other questions dervish-danced in her already overworked mind; joining with the insectile infestation to remove all possibility of sleep.

Another two long hours passed before Torrance returned to the motel room. Marcus dozed in his chair, slouching low with his legs stretched before him, while Danica stared dully at the holoset. Her eyes itched with exhaustion. She had forgotten what exactly she watched until each commercial break ended and she was reminded once more. Never before had she sat through such a night-spanning stretch of holoset consumption.

"You should be sleeping," Torrance told her.

Finally registering his presence, Danica turned from the holoset, and drily replied, "Bed was already occupied."

Torrance looked confused, but shrugged as he tossed her a bag. "Clothes for tomorrow night," he informed her.

Danica opened the parcel enough to see a shirt and pants in Torrance's preferred color. *Be happy it's not another dress*, her inner voice said. Placing the bag of clothes to the side, she sat up in her chair and told Torrance about what she discovered from the news broadcast.

"So," she asked, "what do you think?"

Torrance, who had patiently listened at the foot of the defiled bed, replied, "I think we move ahead as planned."

Expecting some greater response, Danica said, "But, maybe we should find her. My father told me to . . ."

"And he may have told them. That broadcast may have been staged so you'll surface and seek her out."

"He'd never tell them anything!" Danica argued back, her volume rousing Marcus from sleep.

Torrance's expression softened slightly. "Under torture, he might. If he didn't, this Nysgaard woman has had a week to run. She could be anywhere by now."

Falling silent, Danica knew he was right. If the Alliance did not have her father in custody, she would have stayed as far from the city as possible. What kind of fool would return to the center of the hunt?

"Did you figure out how to get in?" Marcus asked.

Taking a tattered scrap of paper from a pocket, Torrance handed the boy what appeared to be a hand-drawn map of Fort Rotterdam's west gate. "It'll be tight, but if we follow that route, we should be able to get past the cameras before they cycle back to their sweeps. If Yakuza's intel is accurate, your father is being held here," Torrance pointed to a black X on the map. "The base is on high alert because a VIP from one of the Families arrived this afternoon. So, we need to get in and out as quickly as possible."

"How do we know where in the building?" Danica inquired.

"The most I was able to pick up is that there is a sublevel for high-priority prisoners, but we won't know exactly where your father is until we're inside," he told the siblings. "The buildings will have sensors to detect any weapon discharge, so a gun fight is the last resort. If they go into a lockdown, it'll be nearly impossible for us to get back out."

"Won't there be cameras inside, too?" the younger Seton asked.

Nodding in appreciation of the boy's acumen, Torrance exposed his right wrist and said, "Yes. But, the cuff will block the signal when we're within range."

"Why don't we just use the cuff to block the cameras outside?" she followed with hopeful logic.

"Different systems. Disrupt one of the camera-guns outside, and the others will immediately lock to that location. It'd be the same as knocking on the front door."

Returning to an earlier statement, Danica asked, "Is the VIP here for our father?"

"Couldn't tell from the chatter," Torrance supplied. She wondered how he had learned what he had. "The arrival was unexpected, though. That much was clear. If it is linked to your father, I don't know."

Rising from the edge of the bed, Torrance walked to the bathroom. "Study the map. You need to memorize the path. And then, get some sleep. You'll need it for tonight."

Their guardian closed the bathroom door behind him, and Danica heard the turn of rusty shower knobs. Looking at the clock on the wall, she saw the time was a few minutes past midnight. A new day had already begun. Before it ended, she would likely be dead.

CHAPTER TWENTY-FOUR

Kerwen Garrott

Much of the day had been spent receiving unrewarding updates in the search for Rupert Thompson. There had been no messages from the Ignota, save for the Shakespearean quote discovered at the scene of the abduction. Kerwen did not expect a ransom request; the terrorists' modus operandi was murder and assignation, not kidnapping. He had ordered the investigation be conducted with complete stealth. The other Families did not need to learn of yet another successful attack against the Garrotts. He had been blessedly free of incoming communication from the Caputs. *That will change tomorrow,* he reminded himself. De Luca's death would send the Council into brief, but certain pandemonium. *Which is why I need no other distractions!*

"Your Grace?" Liam's assistant repeated. Fenton was a capable man, but Kerwen wished his chief counsel was not foolishly chasing shadows across the ocean. He had spoken with Liam twice since the old spymaster had left. Both times, the advice had been to move cautiously. *Like I didn't bloody well know that already.*

"The Heir's tour of Sheerness. Do you wish me to cancel it, Your Grace?" Fenton prompted.

"No," Kerwen replied with a heavy touch of impatience. "Cancelling will raise too many questions. As far as anyone knows, Rupert left for a family emergency. Let the tour move as planned. But, I want my son's security doubled. Use the bombing as an excuse for the additional guards."

"As you wish, Your Grace," Fenton dipped his head.

"Anything else?" Kerwen asked. The agitation crawling beneath his skin was rising to a slow boil.

"Only that the news segment with Secretary Kadam ended a short while ago. Both the Secretary and General McAllister did as instructed."

The interview had been Fawzan's brainchild. There were signs of disquiet among the citizenry regarding the Peacekeeper mobilization. Kadam had been directed to tamp down the perceived Ignota threat, while the General would encourage a greater response. If the confrontation with the terrorists was protracted, it would be easier for the Alliance if the people rallied in support.

"Good," the Caput said. "And what of this 'Ides of March' business?" Only mildly cryptic, Kerwen viewed the message as a warning of impending Ignota attacks.

"Unfortunately, the movements against the Ignota have severely damaged their communication network, thus hampering our own intelligence gathering," Fenton informed. "It is possible they intended another attack against the Family. Yet, their operations may be so degraded that such an attack could not be carried out."

"Do you suggest we operate under that theory?" Kerwen asked. In the span of days, the Ignota had infiltrated his home and taken his chief engineer. He would not risk the Family on speculative presumptions.

Fearfully, Fenton responded, "No, Your Grace. I was simply—"

Kerwen released the rein on his temper. "I am the Caput of House Garrott!" he shouted as he rose from the chair of his desk. "How is it that with all my resources I still have no answers for, not one, but two attacks against this Family? What in the name of Truth are you people doing? Get me answers, Fenton, or so help me I'll have you fed to the dogs! Get out!"

Quivering, the junior advisor gathered his belongings and nearly ran out the office door. Through rage-filled vision, Kerwen watched his wife glide forward into the room.

"You realize we don't have dogs?" she said evenly as she walked to a table and poured a glass of scotch from the crystal decanter.

"I'm not in the mood, Roslyn," he growled.

Placing the drink on the desk, the Caput`e replied, "No, you'd rather scream and rant at the people who work for you."

"They're hardly working."

"Perhaps your head is so far up your ass you can't see how hard they are working," Roslyn suggested. Kerwen was always amazed how the woman could sound so alluring even while deriding him. "You're not the only member of this House to be worried, Kerwen. These attacks were against them, too. And they are doing their best."

Staring into her eyes, Kerwen felt himself losing the battle to remain angered. "It was supposed to be easier," he said after a long sigh. "We should still be enjoying the success of the drone launch, not recovering from two terrorist attacks and plotting treason."

Roslyn offered her husband a sympathetic smile. "It will get better. For now, though, I asked the kitchen to serve dinner in my sitting room. The children have other arrangements, so you and I can be alone for the evening."

The seductive purr in her voice worked to sedate the frustrations aching in his mind. Kerwen let her guide him by the hand from the office. "Isn't it a bit early for dinner?" he asked.

"I thought we'd start with dessert."

The soft rap on the door was duplicated in his dream – which was strange, since he had dreamed himself atop a craggy mountain, looking down over the lower hills and flat stretches of fields and farms. When the knock sounded again, the vista dissolved to beige linen, the cold thin breeze on his cheek became a pillow, and the mountaineer, unrestrained by gravity and altitude, shifted back to Kerwen Garrott.

"Come," he called out while shifting to rest his back against the tufted headboard. Enough sunlight broke through the heavy drapery to show Roslyn had already risen. The double doors leading from the sitting room to the Caput`e bedchamber opened, and two figures stood in the rectangle of light.

"I apologize for disturbing you, Your Grace," Fenton said. From the man's sheepish tone, Liam's assistant was clearly still cautious of another outburst from the Caput.

"What time is it?" Kerwen asked.

"Almost nine, Your Grace," came the second voice. Alain, his personal valet, was less fearful of his master's mercurial moods. *He's used to them,* Kerwen mused. "The Caput`e instructed the staff not to disturb your rest."

Frowning, Kerwen replied, "Did she now?" *That woman . . . I'll deal with her later,* he thought with affectionate frustration. "And yet, here you both are breaking her orders. What's happened?"

"An emergency session of the Council has been called, Your Grace," Fenton replied. "It will convene in one hour's time. I have taken the liberty of preparing the Council Room."

An emergency session. Kerwen knew the reason for the meeting, though the plan had been for the assassination to occur that evening. Perhaps the timing had to be altered. *More like Cambrie wanting to control events. And why an hour's wait?* "Anything on the news? Any intelligence for why the Five will meet?" he asked.

"No, Your Grace," Fenton responded. Kerwen was sure he heard the man's voice crack. He made a note to speak with Liam; the spymaster needed to stiffen the spine of his assistants.

The Caput had not anticipated information to be leaking just yet. An "unexpected" event of this magnitude, the death of an entire Family, would be tightly held by the Council until it agreed on a plan of action. Word of an explosion would spread quickly though, rumors at first, then wild suppositions.

"Very well," Kerwen said as he cast aside the bed sheets. "Alain, find me something appropriate for a Council meeting." Opening the mural door to the passage connecting his chambers with those of his wife, the Caput cringed as the cold stone chilled his bare feet.

Bathing quickly, Kerwen removed the short stubble from his face. Staring into the gilded mirror of the marble bathroom, he practiced an expression of shock. His demeanor must be balanced on a razor's edge; sufficient grief for the death of a Caput, yet nothing overly dramatic. After all, De Luca was never a friend. Outrage, however, would be allowable – such an attack against the Alliance deserved no less. Satisfied he could feign the needed emotions, Kerwen moved into the dressing room were Alain waited.

The valet had selected a white paneled dress shirt with buttons of polished silver, and simple black pants. Once Alain finished the tedious task of securing the numerous fastenings of the shirt, he asked the Caput if he wished for a jacket.

"No," he answered, "this is fine." While he knew the importance of the meeting, his dress should reflect no such knowledge. "Where is my wife?"

"The Caput`e is in her study, Your Grace. Shall I send someone for her?" Alain asked.

Shaking his head, Kerwen replied, "Inform her of the meeting." *She'll know what is coming,* he added. "And Tilden?"

"He and Ms. Carene left for Sheerness early this morning."

Kerwen would have preferred his son be closer at hand, especially with Liam several thousand kilometers away. Had he known the assassination had been moved up, Kerwen would have requested the Heir remain within the manor. *If wishes were horses,* he recited the old adage. The Council would likely meet for some time in any event, and Tilden would return by then. Slipping on the freshly shined black leather shoes, the Caput thanked Alain for his service, and left his chambers.

A pair of guards, both drones, flanked him as he moved through the manor. Kerwen briefly wondered why his normal security was absent, but then recalled his order to increase Tilden's protection for the trip to the engineering town. The errant thoughts running through his mind stilled abruptly when he reached the door to the Council Room.

Beyond simply determining the Council's official response to the assassination, another more private and far greater deliberation was soon to occur. The other Caputs were sure to press for their own interests as De Luca's holdings were divided. He would have to be forceful if he was to carve out a substantial reward for House Garrott. The Family's fortune was about to increase exponentially, and Kerwen prepared himself for the moment.

Checking his watch, he stepped into the five-sided room; empty except for his desk and chair, and the four holoset platforms at the base of each wall. Kerwen took his seat and waited for the final two minutes to pass. He had instructed the guards to remain outside. There was no need to remind the other Caputs of his newly achieved status when the spoils were allocated.

Cambrie was the first to appear, followed immediately by Hu. Neither of his co-conspirators spoke, though the American did dip his head in informal greeting. The third platform lit to form the bloated, and very much alive, face of Graziano De Luca. Kerwen felt the corners of his eyes twitch as he fought to keep the shock from his expression.

So it hasn't happened yet, he spoke. *At least Liam and Tilden will be here when it does.* While there was some relief in that realization, Kerwen wondered what had transpired overnight to necessitate the emergency meeting.

The thought concluded just as the final holoset projected Bashir Fawzan. New, tight grim lines of stress aged the Arab's already weathered features. The Council elder spoke the opening rites. "In service to Truth, with remembrance of our duty to the Global Alliance, I convene this gathering of the Council."

"May our deeds honor Truth." As Kerwen joined the others in reciting the response, he thought he detected an alteration in Fawzan's delivery. The ritual had become so perfunctory he had not fully paid attention, and thus was unable to pinpoint the variation.

"I regret the precipitous fashion in which this meeting was called," Fawzan began. "But, the situation necessitated immediate action. Kerwen, I have already consulted with Caput Cambrie, Caput Hu, and Caput De Luca on the matter."

Kerwen nodded, surprised by Fawzan's blending of formal and informal address.

"Upon receiving the company of PK-drones you sent to each Caput, a disturbing anomaly was detected," the man continued. "One of the units delivered to me contained an explosive device of such magnitude the detonation would have be devastating. Are you aware of this device, Kerwen?"

"Certainly not!" Kerwen replied faster than he would have preferred. Cambrie had double-crossed him! The American's face was placid, but Kerwen could see smug satisfaction in his eyes. Thoughts of revenge flooded his mind. *Not now,* he warned himself. *The bastard doesn't have me cornered just yet.* "I will conduct a thorough investigation, Fawzan. If there is an Ignota in Sheerness, he will be brought to swift justice. I shall oversee the investigation personally to ensure—"

Fawzan raised a tired hand. "I have already looked into the matter. Two days ago, I ordered the arrest of your chief engineer, Rupert Thompson."

A sudden chill gripped Kerwen's bones.

"He has been questioned – thoroughly. In his interrogation, your chief engineer declared the orders for implanting the bomb came directly from you."

Feeling the flood waters rising, Kerwen replied with as much composure as he could gather, "Then Thompson is Ignota, seeking to divide the Houses, pit them against each other."

"His statements have been verified through a battery of scientific measures, Kerwen," Fawzan replied. "Do you still claim innocence in this plot?"

"Of course I do!"

"Very well. The Council has voted, and orders of arrest have been issued for you and your Family, at which time all will be placed in seclusion and interrogated—to the fullest extent possible."

Caput Hu spoke then, "A confession would spare your relations from that . . . discomfort."

All efforts of moderation were cast aside. "You will not lay a finger on my Family! This is their doing," Kerwen pointed to Cambrie and Hu. "They have conspired against me! Against you!"

Fawzan's expression shifted. "Are you implicating another Caput in this crime?"

"I . . . they . . . ," Kerwen stammered with rage. Any attempt to reveal Cambrie and Hu's collusion forced him to admit his own guilt. Even then, Roslyn and the children would still be tortured in the name of justice. The waters had reached his head and the few pockets of air were quickly disappearing. He could only see one course to ensure the survival of the House.

"I gave the order," Kerwen Garrott announced in cold acceptance. *Let them execute me. Tilden will take my Seat and the Family will continue.*

Sorrow and regret stole into Fawzan's eyes. "Before the Council, in the name of Truth, do you, Kerwen Garrott, admit to treason?"

Rising from his seat, Kerwen replied, "I do."

"Then before the Council, you are condemned," the man intoned. "It has been decided the Alliance's defense industry is too great for one House to control. You are hereby stripped of all titles and all claims to a Council Seat. Garrott Industries will be divided among the Council of Four."

Disbelief turned his tongue to stone. *That was the change*, his mind teased. *Fawzan had not said the "Council of Five" when he convened the meeting. The sentence had already been decided!*

"House Garrott is hereby disbanded. Lest a generation of vengeance be born to threaten the Alliance, all members of your family are thus sentenced to immediate execution."

No! I confessed! I confessed to spare them!

"Spare my Family or you will have war! My drones will tear your Houses down!" he shouted at the four projected faces in the room.

"Prior to his death, Dr. Thompson provided the Council with control of the drones. The facility at Sheerness has been secured," Fawzan said.

Sheerness. Tilden!

The contrast of the holosets blurred as light behind Kerwen flooded into the room. Turning, he saw the silhouettes of the twin guards standing in the frame of the double doors.

A flash of amber.

Kerwen gasped as the particle bolt burned through his chest, searing nerves and arteries. Suddenly he was kneeling, though he could not recall the fall.

The fall.

The Fall.

How far this Fall.

The faces of the Council of Four blinked to darkness as the last Caput of House Garrott took his dying breath.

CHAPTER TWENTY-FIVE

Tilden Garrott

"I promise you it's safe," he tried to assure her. Isla had known they would be travelling by HALO to Sheerness, but Tilden had felt her tense immediately upon seeing the idling aircraft. While he attempted to dispel her misgivings, he hid a quiet smile. In their time together, he had never seen her so overtly anxious – including during the aftermath of the ill-fated gala. To him, her current fear of HALO flight was endearing; though he would never make such an admission. *Never point out a woman's insecurities,* Tilden recalled the advice of his father from years earlier. *But, always be willing to tell her yours* had been the second part of the lesson. Father and son had never talked more about personal relationships than was necessary but Tilden viewed his parents' marriage as a fine example.

"I know it is safe," Isla replied. "It just looks . . . clumsy."

Tilden had grown up around the machines, as well as the other creations of Garrott Industries. Like his father, the Heir's eyes saw the complex construction of hover blades, wings, and cockpit as a marvel of technology. The lines of aerodynamics were as finely sculpted as any of the Great Masters' works of art. Botticelli's angels never had wings so beautiful.

He tried to see the HALO through Isla's fresh eyes, but still could not bring himself to define the craft as clumsy. It was one of the things he cherished about her, though; the newness she brought to everything he perceived as commonplace. He had dated women from his world, society debutantes who could fill an entire day with gossip and fashion. Those relationships had stagnated quickly. In some cases, not quick enough. Isla challenged him to understand the views he held, the opinions his status expected him to hold. She made the others seem silly girls who only saw the title, Heir of House Garrott. Isla, however, saw Tilden the man. For that alone, she had already won his heart.

"Are you sure we can't simply drive to Sheerness?" she asked.

"We could," he replied, "but it would take three times as long." Perhaps more given the additional security the Caput had assigned to his detail. Tilden believed the supplemental guards unnecessary, yet understood his father's reasons and did not balk at the order. In truth, he was just grateful the Caput had approved the trip. Isla was not the woman his parents had envisioned for him. The tour was a good sign of their acceptance, and Tilden valued that highly.

"Come on. Once we're up, you'll wish you always travelled by HALO," he encouraged as he led her to the ramp.

"I really don't see that happening," she replied.

The pilot greeted them and helped the Heir's paramour secure the seat's safety harness across chest and waist. With passengers fastened, the pilot, Captain Philinor returned to the cockpit and engaged the HALO's thrust controls. Isla gripped her armrests with white knuckled fingers as the craft lifted from the paved landing pad. Two other HALOs, troops filling the open bays, joined the launch.

"This might not be the best time to tell you this," Isla said, "but I have a slight fear of flying."

"You don't say?" Tilden teased. "You fly to film locations all over the world. How can you still be afraid of flying?"

She replied, "I'm usually heavily medicated for those trips."

The laugh which escaped from his lips earned a withering look from Isla.

"We'll be there before you know it," Tilden promised. "Look out the window. You can see all of London beneath us."

Shaking her head, Isla declined through gritting teeth. "I'm fine, thanks. I prefer to look up at buildings, not down."

Tilden smiled and placed an affectionate hand on her arm. He attempted to distract Isla from her anxiety; sharing stories from his own experiences flying. Though it seemed she appreciated the effort, Isla responded with short monosyllabic answers. Only when the HALO began its descent a short while later did her downward stare lift to the window. The slight bounce of landing gear meeting pavement drained the last remaining traces of color from her face.

"See? Here before you knew it," Tilden said while unbuckling his harness.

"Mmm, and I only feel ten years older," Isla replied with the first smile of the morning.

As expected, a team of researchers and engineers had gathered to welcome the Heir to the facility. From the unusual tidiness of their hair and clothing, Tilden knew the visit had been declared an official occasion of state. *Liam's work, no doubt,* the Heir assumed. He had hoped the tour would include less pomp to keep Isla more at ease. She was still new to the formalities and protocol forced upon his station. Settling into the uncomfortable mantle of Heir of House Garrott, Tilden stood to help Isla from her seat. A touch unsteady on her feet, Tilden felt her lean her insubstantial weight on his offered arm.

"This will be a bit stuffier than I planned," he warned apologetically as the ramp lowered.

She replied, "I would have worn something different if I knew I had to curtsy."

Arching an eyebrow, Tilden made a pronounced examination of the tight black leather pants and fitted red sweater perfectly accentuating her figure. With a suggestive smile, he corrected her assessment of clothing choice. "At Garrott Industries, we appreciate flawless lines and curves. But, I'd be more than happy to help you change into something else later."

Further banter was preempted once the House guard formed rigid lines on either side of the HALO ramp. A tall fellow with muted auburn hair stepped from the waiting party of Sheerness employees. Stopping at the end of the incline, the white-coated man bowed his head.

"Your Lordship," he greeted Tilden with the official style. "Welcome to Sheerness. I am Dr. Sunjay Banerjee, First Assistant to Dr. Thompson. If it pleases His

Lordship, I will be guiding your tour this morning."

Escorting Isla down the ramp, her legs seeming to regain some balance, Tilden extended his free right hand. "Pleasure to see you again, Dr. Banerjee," he said. He had met Thompson's second a few times, but the doctor's manners required him to reintroduce himself in the event Tilden did not recall the man. Apparently, Heirs to the Great Houses were not expected to remember those in service to them. Even a man as renowned as Banerjee.

"I appreciate you taking the time," Tilden continued, untwining his arm from Isla's. "Doctor, this is Isla Carene."

Banerjee bowed again, although slightly shallower, and said, "It is an honor to meet you, Ms. Carene."

Shaking the man's hand, Isla replied, "And you as well, Doctor. Tilden has told me about some of the amazing work you do here. The Garrotts regard you and Dr. Thompson quite highly."

Tilden turned a smile inward hearing her well-worded response. He imagined the grace and poise she would exhibit as the House Caput`e.

"You are too kind, Ms. Carene," Banerjee demurred. "I am fortunate to serve House Garrott. Dr. Thompson would surely wish to be here, but as Your Lordship is aware, he was called away on family business."

If only that were true, Tilden replied. The abduction of the Family's chief engineer had only added to his father's already high level of stress. When last he had spoken with the Caput, during the unexpected accompaniment on horseback, Tilden could see the strain recent events had taken on the man. Kerwen Garrott had shielded his son from much of the Family's operations, and previously Tilden had welcomed that distance. Only lately had he pushed for greater involvement. With so much unsettled, he wondered if the time had come for him to immerse himself fully into the Family's management.

"While Rupert is surely missed, I am certain you will prove equally capable in keeping me from blowing up the facility," Tilden joked. "Shall we begin?"

"As you wish, Your Lordship," Banerjee said, turning to escort the pair into the main building.

Craning her neck to reach Tilden's ear, Isla whispered, "As you wish, Your Lordship."

"Shush," he growled, giving her backside a discrete swat.

Tilden had not been to the engineering town since the successful testing of the final PK-drone prototype. Even then, the visit had been brief and mostly confined to a field designed for such events on the western perimeter of the sprawling complex. He could not recall when last he had made a deliberate accounting of the facility and the many projects currently in development by Garrott Industries. In many ways, some of the technologies within the walls of Sheerness would be as new to his eyes as they were to Isla's.

The doctor first led the group to a semicircular room with a forested scene projected across the curved wall. Little in Sheerness was small, and the chamber easily accommodated the Heir's retinue of guards, researchers, and engineers. A four-member team stood ready to begin the first exhibit.

"This is our longest running project," Banerjee orated while the team assumed their positions. "And Dr. Thompson's personal albatross; though he has other more *descriptive* words for it."

Quite familiar with the salt which seasoned the chief engineer's language, Tilden laughed and replied, "I'm sure he does. So, what is Rupert's torment?"

"Adaptive Optical Camouflage Armor. A-OCA," Banerjee replied in the respectful tone reserved to describe a cunning opponent. "As you know, the technology has long been incorporated into nearly all higher-end military models – X-T.E.M. fighter jets, HALOs, Jag tanks. The outer shells are composed of panels which project the surrounding terrain, essentially rendering the crafts invisible. Our goal is to transfer that ability to individual armor. The process, however, has proved unsuccessful."

Banerjee nodded to commence the demonstration. The four researchers, each dressed in the uniform of elite PKs, activated the control panel on the forearm of their armor. In turn, the members of the quartet seemingly blinked out of existence. Though he stared directly at their last visible location ten meters away, Tilden strained, and failed, to pinpoint the human forms.

Sharing his astonishment, Isla commented, "Amazing! But, why did you say it was unsuccessful? Even knowing where they're standing, I can't see them."

"It is only because they are standing, or rather, standing still I should say, that we can't see them," the First Assistant replied. "Once they move . . ."

With Banerjee's directive, the four invisible figures began walking in opposite directions. While never fully returning to sight, Tilden could see a disruption in the optical camouflage – slight, intermittent flickers breaking the stillness of the landscape. The effect, similar to the shimmering waves of heat rising from a road, induced a queasy sensation as he stared.

"What you're seeing is the areas of the armor segmented to allow movement: knees, elbows, etc. Because of the necessary flexibility of the segments, the projected image appears 'folded'. Only the solid pieces of the armor properly reflect the terrain."

Grateful for the deactivation of the nauseating flicker, Tilden theorized, "And a fully solid suit would make them little more than statues."

"Just so," Banerjee affirmed. "We've had greater success implementing A-OCA into the next line of drones. The "folding" is less noticeable with the more seamless composition of their exterior.

"Wouldn't the drones negate the need for advancing troop armor?" Isla questioned. "I mean, isn't the eventual goal to convert the Peacekeepers to an entirely drone force?"

Tilden had worried Isla would have little interest in the tour, but was pleased to find her genuinely inquisitive. "Father believes there will always be a need for human PKs; though on a much smaller scale than present," he explained. "As advanced as the drones are, he sees the human thought process as essential to the protection of the Alliance."

Isla smiled and joked, "Good to know we're not completely obsolete."

"What do you have for us next, Dr. Banerjee?" the Heir asked.

"If Your Lordship approves, we will move on."

Over the next two hours, the doctor led the party to various departments in the complex. A presentation of next generation HALOs, equipped with upgraded weapons systems was conducted in a vast hangar at the facility's northernmost wing. From there, the Heir and his consort were brought to the armory laboratories where several researchers detailed the advancements in small arms manufacturing. Tilden and Isla engaged in a brief target competition, and he was forced to admit Isla had the better aim. A discovery he knew she would ruthlessly tease him over later.

They wandered through displays of behemoth tanks, and their smaller cousins, and aerial combat vehicles, before venturing out to the dockyard to observe the construction of a sleek warship. Though they walked several kilometers along the way, Isla voiced no complaint, nor expressed any hint of fatigue. She talked comfortably with Banerjee, asking questions which would have made even the Caput smile. The doctor answered, clearly taken with the actress. Tilden smiled to himself as he was quite familiar with her captivating charm. Returning indoors for the conclusion of the tour, the party entered the patched-ceiling bay of the drone labs. There was much more to see in Sheerness, but such areas were restricted to all but the highest personnel.

At Banerjee's command, the drones repeated the exercises first seen at the unveiling event a week earlier. The machines ran and jumped, climbed and crawled, seeming every bit as alive as their human creators. Comparisons ended there, though when the drones displayed their superior strength. Podcars and metal slabs, weighing several tons each, were lifted and moved with incredible ease. Feats requiring ten men, twenty, were accomplished by one tireless drone.

"Simply incredible," Isla whispered softly at his side. Tilden could not help but share her awe, even having already seen the drones' capabilities.

"Now, a demonstration of weapon accuracy," Banerjee directed one of the technicians.

The bespectacled woman, a rarity in gender at the facility, entered a series of codes into the holograph console displayed at her cluttered work station. Tilden turned his gaze back to the pair of drones below. Stationary targets stood several dozen meters from the drones; a distance no human could fire a particle handgun across with any type of accuracy. Idle seconds passed as the party waited for the drones to begin the exposition.

When half a minute ticked off, and the drones still were motionless, Banerjee cleared his throat at the technician. Taking the cue, the woman reentered the coded sequence. The metal statues did not respond.

Though mediated by the Heir's presence, the doctor's voice grew stern. "Is there a problem, Agnes?"

Flustered, the woman adjusted her glasses to avoid meeting Banerjee's stare. "No, sir. The codes don't seem to be working."

"Then perhaps you are entering the wrong codes."

Isla shifted uncomfortably at the rising tension between the pair. Winking as he placed his hand on the small of her back, Tilden hoped the scene would quickly resolve. Unfortunately, he had grown accustomed to the agitation expressed by members of the House when errors occurred in the Family's presence. No one wished such embarrassment, and often subordinates bore the brunt of the blame – deservedly or not. Though never in the presence of the Family, it was well known Liam Walford had, more than once, physically "confronted" a failing member of his staff. Tilden did not think Dr. Banerjee as cruel a supervisor, but Agnes the technician would likely receive harsh words after the Heir departed.

Attempting to absolve the woman, Tilden lightheartedly offered, "Technology always has its quirks." He immediately regretted the comment when the doctor launched into an exhaustive apology. In speaking at all, Tilden had made Banerjee aware that *he* was aware of the problem. *Sorry, Agnes,* the Heir said.

". . . for the delay, Your Lordship," the doctor continued. "Here, Warner Ramsden will be able to rectify the situation."

One of the retinue's members, a balding man in a short white lab coat, stepped forward. Agnes meekly surrendered her seat, probably expecting she would soon have to surrender her credentials, and allowed Ramsden access to the console. Furry fingers swept across the projected controls. As one, the party turned back to the drones. Nothing.

"Dr. Ramsden," Banerjee began; frustration barely concealed.

"Sir . . . I'm . . . I'm locked out."

The First Assistant's placid voice rose, "What do you mean you're locked out? Are you entering—"

"I mean I'm locked out! The drones aren't responding to our—"

"Look, they're moving now," Isla directed the attention to the bay's ground floor.

Relieved with the resolution, Tilden watched as the drones turned from facing the targets and raised their red-bar sights to the observation level. The Heir's eyes widened as the drones aimed the particle guns at the group.

"Get down!" shouted a nearby voice. Tilden felt innumerable hands grip and pull him to the floor. The static swoosh of particle bolts flew past his ear as he fell to the metal grating. The shots tore through two guards directly behind where he had been standing. An amber wave of charged bullets swept over the railings. Between the bodies and limbs shielding him from the onslaught, Tilden saw every drone in the bay spring into offensive maneuvers. Under the unrelenting gunfire, the observation deck groaned and listed as the bullets degraded its stability.

Tilden screamed out for Isla, but the explosions and panicked human cries drowned his voice beyond even his own hearing. Seconds after the attack began, the surviving guards pulled him across the deck towards the exit. Fighting their efforts, Tilden frantically searched for Isla in the retreating chaos.

"Isla!" he called again in throat-straining volume.

"I'm here! I'm here," her voice reached him. Looking forward, he saw her entangled with the guards hustling him into the connecting hallway. Finding his footing as the huddle ran, Tilden pulled himself to Isla and wrapped his arms around her thin frame.

"Are you okay?" he asked.

"Yes."

The path behind them erupted in a screech of twisting metal as the observation deck finally broke from its supports. "Sir, we have to get you to the HALOs," one of the guards commanded over the din.

"Negative," another corrected while holding a finger to his earpiece. "The HALOs are down!"

Time refused to be quantified. Tilden could not tell if a minute or an hour had passed since the start of the drone malfunction. The clouded blooms of dust sent up from the collapse of the observation deck filled Tilden's hearing with thick silence. The screaming of victims and the gunfire of their attackers failed to pass through the settling debris. *No. That's not right,* an inner voice warned. There were no screams, no gunfire, to be heard.

"Is it over?" he scattered the question to those nearest him. "The malfunction . . . did they stop it?"

Blank faces and furrowed brows puzzled at him, tilting their chins as if his words had been spoken in a foreign tongue. Addressing the most senior officer, Tilden asked again, "Is the malfunction over?"

"Sir," the sergeant began, "this is an attack. Not a malfunction."

Punctuating the enlisted man's pronouncement, a flight of particle bolts shattered the brief lull. Splatters of blood flecked skin and walls as three guards immediately fell. At the end of the hall, drones charged forward. The remaining guards reformed the circle of protection around Isla and the Heir; returning fire as they back-stepped. Outnumbered and outmatched, retreat was the only option.

The group, now only numbering six, turned down the first available corridor to break the drones' line of sight. While the machines could only reach running speeds comparable to humans, they would not tire, and thus had a distinct advantage.

"Up!" the sergeant directed as he pulled open the door to a stairwell. Taking steps in pairs, Tilden held Isla's hand tight. Twice now her life had been in danger simply by being in his presence. *She'd be crazy to stay with you after this,* his thoughts mocked. *If there is an after,* he replied.

"Sarge! Come on!" a guard Tilden could not name shouted down to the squad's leader. Defiantly, the sergeant remained firm in his position at the door two flights below. His particle rifle seemed to glow as he fired blast after blast at the pursuing drones in the hall.

"Get the Heir out!" the squad leader yelled back. Before Tilden comprehended the man's intent of self-sacrifice, a drone appeared behind him and delivered a spine-shattering blow to the sergeant's unprotected back. The drone's fist had actually penetrated flesh, and the senior officer twitched in death, suspended upright on the machine's limb. The guards pushed Tilden forward, and unleashed their rifles until the drone was smoking and sparking.

No longer held at bay, the full force of drones quickly capitalized on the opening in their targets' defense. One of the three surviving guards called out a litany of epithets while surrendering to the hot-blooded battle craze. His two fellow soldiers struggled to pull him back from the railing, but his adrenaline proved stronger. He did not flinch or break from returning fire when first one, then two, then a half-dozen bullets burned into his body. Tilden, Isla, and their two guards had run well down the hallway before the soldier's rage was finally silenced.

Pausing briefly to identify their location, Tilden found his emotions had tangled and collided so that all that remained was illimitable numbness. As a member of a Family, he had known the men and women charged with protecting him were expected to offer their lives to spare his. Until the past week he had never witnessed a guard's final moment of devotion to service. Now that he had, the full weight of his station felt oppressive.

"Truth, mate! What're we gonna do?" blurted the young guard at Tilden's left; eyes as wide as the harvest moon. He had seen the look before; on the few occasions the Heir had been forced to join his father on a hunting excursion. When a prey had been cornered, whether deer or duck, their eyes had held the same sharp terror – a fear of death and the awareness of its inevitability. "What're we gonna do?"

"Sarge said we go for the roof," the other guard replied. "They've got to be sending air support, right?"

"The roof? We'll never make it that far! Oh, fuck me, I hear them!"

Though he could not blame the guards, Tilden realized the final two members of his protection detail were quickly unraveling. Little in his past had prepared Tilden for this moment. Matters of state, the finely tuned craft of negotiation, and methods of skilled corporate subterfuge had been the focus of his education. While a Caput headed his Family, there was no expectation of leading men into actual battle.

"Do you love me?" Isla asked.

Bewildered by the odd timing of the question, and the strange look on her face, Tilden covered her hands with his. "With all my heart," he told her. *She's so calm, even now,* the Heir mourned.

"Do you trust me?" she asked next.

The sound of drones searching the third story echoed along the walls. Staring up at him, Isla's expression seemed somewhat disjointed from the emotions he assumed she would feel as their mechanical death drew nearer. Nodding with an undefined comprehension that he was agreeing to more than her simple question, Tilden said, "Yes."

The sibilant ending barely left his lips when he felt a sharp pain in the palm of his right hand. Blood-tipped knife in hand, Isla turned to the guards. "The armory labs are one level down. We need to go there and get as many weapons as we can carry," she said with natural command.

"Go down?" the younger guard laughed in panic. "You want us to go back? We'll die for sure! If we get to the roof—"

"We'll die waiting there," she countered. "Listen to me, there's no help coming. We're on our own. And unless you want to feel your spine crushed in a drone's hand, you'll do what I tell you."

The force of her delivery, the crisp cut to each word, reminded Tilden of his father; orders were issued with the expectation of submission. The arguing guard stepped threateningly towards Isla, who responded with fluid motion as she hooked his arm with a painful twist while driving her foot into the back of his knee. Slipping the handgun from the man's grip, she swung the weapon's butt into the guards head, rendering him unconscious.

"Down!" she shouted, barely pausing for Tilden and the second guard to comply before rapidly firing into the group of drones now turning into the hallway. The foremost drone exploded in a shower of sparks, knocking back those to the rear in a domino effect. Isla grabbed the collar of Tilden's shirt, pulling him with her as she ran.

"Who the hell are you?" was the only question his confusion allowed.

The woman did not answer him. Instead, she directed the guard stumbling along behind to remove his SID. Trained to follow orders from his superiors, and Isla's words and actions had clearly placed her in that category, the guard pulled a small knife from his belt, scoring his palm to expose the device. Tilden looked to his own hand and found a thin trail of blood where Isla had seconds before performed the same operation on him.

In the temporary disruption of the drones' pursuit, Isla led them through the twisting corridors of the Sheerness complex until finally reaching another stairwell. The guard looked up in brief deliberation before following the pair down the narrow steps. The second level was filled with confused researchers abandoned by the facility's security who had rushed to respond to the crisis in the drone hangar.

"Open the lab," she ordered a frightened man in a white lab coat. The Garrott Industries employee immediately complied, never questioning why a Hollywood starlet was issuing commands. "Get your people inside," she told him. The specialist nodded and began ushering the others in behind Tilden, Isla, and their remaining guard.

Addressing the guard, she said, "Keep them calm. Don't resist the drones. They're not after you."

Understanding her intention to leave him behind, the guard protested, "I'm sworn to protect the Heir."

"I can get him out. These people need you more than he does."

Sensing the guard faltering from his previous blind acceptance of Isla's authority, Tilden found himself assuring the man he approved her decision. "You've served well. When this is over, my father will award you for your dedication. House Garrott owes you a great debt."

Torn between duty and obeying the Heir's command, the guard reluctantly settled on the latter, and assumed a rigid posture as he saluted Tilden.

"Let's go," Isla interjected, passing him one of the weapons she had collected from a nearby stand. Tilden accepted the double-triggered particle rifle awkwardly, unfamiliar with its weight and operation. Reading his befuddlement, she explained, "Top trigger for small rounds, second one for explosive bursts. Those take longer to charge, so use them sparingly."

"They're coming!" the guard yelled to them from the door. Missing his SID, the guard stepped back to allow the specialist access to activate the door's control panel. A centimeters-thick steel panel slid into place, sealing the laboratory.

Without delay, Isla guided Tilden deeper into the lab, past countless work stations where new technology and advancements had only moments earlier occupied the researchers' attention. It would take the drones little time to override the controls, or simply force their way forward, but the delay allowed the pair to reach another exit at the far end of the cavernous room. Amazed by Isla's ready knowledge of the facility's layout, Tilden focused on maintaining the brisk pace of her sprint.

"We're eight minutes from the dockyard. I need that extraction ready," Isla angrily announced. "For two. Just do it!"

Realizing she was communicating through a mobile comm, Tilden felt a flash of anger. He had believed Isla previously unattached to the Family, yet clearly she served as an agent assigned to his security detail. He felt foolish to wonder over matters of the heart while trying to escape with his life, but one thought continued to cross his mind as he ran. *Does she love me, or was she just following orders?*

Rounding a corner, Isla skidded to a halt as a trio of drones, only meters away, lifted their weapons. Before they could release any shots, she fired a devastating wave of charged bolts from her rifle. Tilden was slower to react; adding to Isla's rounds several seconds after she had pulled the trigger. The drones were injured, mostly by Isla's superior aim, but still threatened. Sliding his finger to the lower trigger, Tilden squeezed and a massive flash of amber pulsed from the weapon. The center drone exploded entirely, while the one on its left fell to the floor with a sheared arm. The concussive blast staggered the third, forcing it into the wall.

Isla turned her weapon to the nearest door, tearing it from the hinges with an explosive round of her own, leaving only a jagged, smoldering frame. She pulled Tilden into the room; a small researcher's office occupied by a man and woman cringing behind the desk. Ignoring the pair, Isla tugged the strap of her rifle so the gun was at her back, leaving her arms unobstructed. Removing a smaller firearm from her waist belt, she aimed at the floor; a razor-sharp, multi-pronged hook tore deep into the tiles. Testing the strength of the thick corded metal tether linking hook to gun, Isla pulled him into an embrace.

"Don't let go," she cautioned before she fired her weapon at the window. Fearing the coming plunge, Tilden held her tightly as they leapt into the open air. The descent was brief; first a dropping rush, then a controlled lowering as the grappling gun slowed their fall.

Feet again on solid ground, Tilden eased his crushing hold on Isla. The dockyard was a short distance away, and the pair wasted little time crossing to it. At the far end of one pier, he saw a small boat waiting. The men on the craft were the only signs of life in the hastily deserted dockyard.

With safety only meters away, and no drones in pursuit, Tilden's tongue loosened. "Why? Why didn't you tell me you work for my father?" he asked as their feet pounded along the wooden planks.

"Tilden," she replied.

Before she could respond completely, the Heir jumped wildly onto the boat's deck. The men reached out their arms to steady him; their vice grips holding him even after his balance was restored.

"I'm fine," he told them, attempting to remove himself from their hands. Staring at their grim-set faces, Tilden took sight of their clothing – distressed and mismatched, with no emblem of rank or House.

Following him onto the boat, Isla offered him a look of pained apology. "Tilden . . . I don't work for your father."

"You don't work for—" he began, finally understanding why the group of ragtag men still clutched him. One word hissed from his lips. "Ignota."

The craft's engines roared loudly, churning the dark murky water as the docks slipped further into the distance. Tilden was roughly brought to his knees, arms pulled behind him as one of the men secured his wrists. Seawater splashed and misted over the sides of the boat to quickly drench him. Tilden shivered from fear as much as cold.

"Commander," another man moved to speak with Isla. "Are you sure bringing him is wise?"

Steady wind toyed with the long locks of Isla's hair. Though her appearance had not changed, Tilden found he no longer recognized the woman. The authority in her voice as she responded marked her as the leader of the group. "If the Alliance wants him dead, we need to know why. He's an asset—now."

Tilden wondered what he had been considered before that morning.

"It's a big risk," the man replied. Studying him, Tilden found the man's gray hair and weathered face, the veteran lines surrounding his eyes, reminded him of Liam. "The Council won't stop looking for him. He's a Caput now."

Flinching from the words, Tilden shouted over wind and engine. "What's happened to my father?"

The grizzled man looked down at Tilden with a mix of contempt and pity. "He's dead, son. You're the last of your Family."

He could summon neither tears nor words. He did not resist when another man, another of the Ignota terrorists holding him prisoner, stepped forward to inject him with a powerful sedative. The drugged coursed quickly through his veins, relaxing his body and blurring mind and sight. The ice in his blood conquered the warmth of all emotions, save one. Vengeance. *I'll kill them. The Ignota, the Council—all of them! I'll kill . . .*

Slipping into unconsciousness, Tilden Garrott did manage one final word.

"Isla."

CHAPTER TWENTY-SIX

Sonje Nysgaard

"We're in position."

Sonje had been standing at the far end of the courtyard outside the Global Tech building for twenty minutes waiting for the signal. Gavin's voice finally coming over the mobile comm earpiece, however, still managed to startle her. Except for a handful of uniformed custodial workers stealing final drags of their cigarettes before heading into work, the concrete pavilion of decorative trees and flower beds was mostly empty. Sonje acknowledged the message in a whisper and began walking towards the building's glass entrance. Avoiding the soft lights interspersed along the courtyard's perimeter, she kept her head slightly lowered as she approached.

The plan originally had called for her to seek Gregor Tarasov shortly after the morning rush. Once her face had been splashed across the previous night's newscast, the mission had been delayed until this evening. Gavin had wanted to cancel it entirely, citing the increased risk of her being recognized, but Sonje had insisted on moving forward. She wore her hair down, blonde waves hiding the edges of her face, hoping the change was sufficiently dissimilar to the digital used on the broadcast.

Motion sensors triggered the glass doors to slide open, and Sonje's heart raced as she stepped in the lobby. Without hesitation, she went directly to the visitor desk; fighting rising fear as her eyes counted the Peacekeepers standing at attention around the spacious entrance. Gavin's repeated reminders to avoid overlong stares drummed in her mind. Forcing a smile to her mouth, Sonje greeted the receptionist.

"Good evening," she said in a practiced mimic of an American accent. "Can you tell me what floor Gregor Tarasov is on?"

The man at the desk turned away from the small holoset projection he had been watching. "Do you have an appointment?" he asked while entering Tarasov's name into his computer.

"I don't," she replied. No one among the three Ignota cells could access Global Tech's system to schedule Sonje a meeting with Gregor. If there was any hope of getting past this first obstacle, it would fall to her creativity. "I didn't expect to be in the city overnight, but my flight was cancelled. Greg's an old college friend, and I was hoping he'd be free for a drink."

"I can't let you in without an appointment, Miss . . . ?" the attendant replied.

"Pierce. Marlee Pierce," she supplied the identity the Ignota had uploaded onto her SID. "Is there any way you could call up to him? If it's not too much trouble, of course."

She flashed her best coy smile; at least she hoped it was coy. Flirting had never been her forte. Unlike her gregarious, and shameless, sister, Sonje was more accustomed to the confines of a sterile lab. For all she knew, the look she was giving could be closer to derangement than desire. Either way, it seemed to be working.

The attendant lowered his eyes back to the console, lingering noticeably at Sonje's breasts as he did, and entered Tarasov's number into the comm. "Mr. Tarasov, Bryon at the desk. Sorry to disturb you, sir, but there is a woman here to see you. She doesn't have an appointment. A Miss . . ."

"Marlee Pierce," Sonje reminded, "from Pomoshch' University."

"Marlee Pierce," Bryon the attendant repeated.

"From Pomoshch' University," she added. She hoped her pronunciation of the Russian word was accurate – and that Gregor would understand its significance. Bryon added the detail to his conversation. Sonje held her breath as she waited for the attendant to relay Gregor's response.

"Very well, sir," the man said into the headset's mouthpiece. "Mr. Tarasov's office is on the fifth floor. Please step to the scanner." His task complete, the attendant returned his focus to the holoset.

Thank Truth! Sonje thought with relief. Moving to her left, she placed her hand on the glass surface to log her entry, and then one of the guards waved her towards the body scan. Trusting Kunbo was correct and the knives concealed on her body would not trigger the metal detectors, Sonje walked through the adjacent oval. The guard studied the output on his console, found nothing amiss, and pointed her towards the bank of elevators at the far end of the lobby.

"I'm in," she whispered as she waited.

"Nice job," Gavin's voice replied. "We're beginning the strike now. Get to the others as soon as you've got what we need."

"Be careful," Sonje cautioned. Since their carnal surrendering in the woods, she could not keep Gavin from her thoughts. Her skin tingled as her mind recalled the warmth of his body pressed against hers, his caressing hands running through her hair. They had briefly slipped the bonds of time and reality during those moments of boundless passion. Eager and hungry, gentle and unguarded, she had given herself to him, and he to her. Returning to the camp, Sonje had blushed under the teasingly knowing looks of the other cell members. Adirene's burning animus had been the only tarnish of that night.

The mellow tone of the arriving elevator car stirred her from reflection. Stepping inside, Sonje pressed the silver "5" button. Just as the doors slid closed, a woman with short brown hair and a dangerous glower walked into the lobby. The glimpse was brief, but Sonje could recognize the stalking aura of Adirene.

What is she doing in here? The Sowilo woman was supposed to remain with the others - Kunbo, Ol'Ben, and the scouts – in the event the plan failed and Sonje needed extraction. Gavin had reluctantly assigned her to Sonje's protection; unwilling to endanger his late-brother's unborn child in the second, and sufficiently more hazardous, measure of the night's strategy.

"Kunbo," Sonje hailed the weapons master over the mobile comm.

Silence.

"Kunbo, come in."

The elevator rose past the first and second floors, yet there was still no reply. *Maybe the elevator is blocking the signal*, she wished.

"Gavin, are you still—" she tried to mask her panic.

"I'm here," he cut in, the background sounds of gunfire almost overpowering his voice. "I'm not getting a response from them either. Where are you?"

"In the elevator. Almost at the fifth floor," she replied. "Gavin, I saw Adirene . . . in the lobby."

There was a slight pause before Gavin's voice returned to the mobile comm. "Sonje, get out," he told her. "Abort the mission!"

"Why? What's happening?"

"I can't reach Kunbo or the boys," he said, but Sonje heard the reticence in his tone.

The elevator slowed as it reached its destination. "What about Ol'Ben?" she asked.

"His SID just went offline."

Sonje had worked too long in SID research to miss the implication. The old Ignota had either removed the implant, or . . . he was dead. The unexpected appearance of Adirene in the Global Tech building immediately formed meaning.

"You need to get out," Gavin ordered again.

Deciding quickly, she answered, "No. We're too close. I won't turn back now."

"Sonje! Then, I'm coming to you."

"You're too far away," she reminded him. "By the time you get here whatever's going to happen will have happened. We have to do this, Gavin. You know we do. I'll meet you at the rendezvous." Without her backup, though, she wondered how she would fulfill that promise. Gavin's continued protestations faded from her cognizance as the elevator's door swept open to reveal Philip Seton's assistant manager waiting with folded arms. The man's usual sour expression turned to shock as he recognized "Marlee Pierce."

"Dr. Nysgaard?" he nearly gasped.

Using his wide frame to block her from the view of his colleagues, any of which would recognize her as quickly as he had, she said, "I don't have a lot of time, Gregor. And I can't be seen."

Dazed, but thankfully comprehending her plea, the man guided her to the nearest unoccupied office. Sonje was surprised how few employees were still working, especially with the approaching launch of the upgraded SID. Closing the door behind them, he turned to ask, "What are you doing here? You're—the PKs are looking for you!"

"I know," she replied. In a rush, Sonje unfolded the events of the past week; Gregor's eyes widening with each detail. The discovery of the SID malfunction. The murder of the medical examiner, Alvar Falen. The raid of the Seton's home. The attack on her hotel. And, lastly, her rescue by the Ignota. Through the telling, Sonje kept watch of the elevator visible through the blinds in the office's interior windows. *No sign of Adirene.* But Sonje was not foolish enough to believe the woman had failed to get past the security desk.

"If we can access the system," she concluded, "I can get the evidence again."

"Philip's alive?" Gregor said through his evident incredulity. "Dr. Nysgaard, I can't—"

Pleading, she said, "I know this sounds crazy. And you don't have to believe me now, but if you help me, I can show you what Philip and I found. Please, Gregor,

I . . ."

"Yes, it all sounds impossible. But, the day you showed up here, after you talked to Philip, he was upset, worried. He said it was nothing, but I could tell. And when we found out he—I just couldn't believe his daughter would do that. Tonight, when security said 'Pomoshch',' I thought maybe it was Danica Seton who was asking for 'help'. Is she with you? Is Philip?"

Sonje shook her head. "No. We believe he is still being held by the Alliance. I know only what the news says about Danica, that she's in Philadelphia, but even that may be a lie. Will you help me, Gregor?"

"I can't," he said again.

"If you believe—"

"I do believe you. What I'm saying is, I *can't* help," he stressed the word. "They told us the team would be at risk if we still had access to the project – that we'd be the Ignota's next target. The day after Philip died they cancelled our security clearance."

Sonje felt the tenuous strands of hope, which had sustained her over the past week, snap and shatter; the shards slicing through her mind. The idea to risk the exposure of three Ignota cells had been her own, and now all its purpose had been ripped away. The loss gripped her heart, matching the crushing force of the moment she had been told of her father's death. She had been too late then. Too late to say goodbye. Too late to save Alvar. Too late again.

"I'm sorry, Dr. Nysgaard," Gregor apologized.

Thinking swiftly of the now futile efforts in which Gavin and the other Ignota currently engaged, she called out to the cell leader. "Gavin, do you read me?"

" . . . read you," he replied; the words broken by battle. "Are . . . all right?"

"Gavin, we can't get into the system," she fought to keep from shouting. "Fall back from the attack! We can't get into the system! Fall back!"

"Can't . . . back. There's others . . . aking in. I think . . . ica Set . . ."

The transmission over the mobile comm ended with an ear-ringing pop.

"Gavin!" she did shout then. Reaching to Gregor in frantic desperation, she asked, "Do you have a podcar? I need to get to—"

"Are you proud of this?"

Sonje spun at the sound of Adirene's voice, realizing as she did the woman was speaking through the mobile comm.

"I told them you could not be trusted. I told them you would betray us. You killed Jamie. And now you've sent his brother to die in your trap. But, you will not murder my son, Betrayer. He will lead us to victory over you and your Alliance."

Sonje realized in fear that whatever struggling grasp the Sowilo had on sanity had finally loosened. Recalling Kunbo's analogy of the lioness, it was clear the woman had no intention of letting Sonje escape this night alive.

Barely afloat in the punishing tides of his confusion, Gregor asked, "Dr. Nysgaard, what's wrong?"

Pulling the mobile comm from her ear to deny Adirene any further advantage, Sonje replied, "We need to get out of here. There's someone coming."

"The PKs?"

"No," she said. "Worse. Much worse."

With no regard for the risk to her pseudonymity, Sonje pulled open the office door and charged towards the elevators. Gregor's much heavier footfalls easily matched her long strides. The floor was even emptier than when she had arrived, and those few remaining paid no attention to the odd scene. Tapping repeatedly on the elevator's call button, Sonje cursed the system's protocol which returned empty cars to the lobby until needed. As she scanned the corridor and offices behind them, wondering if Adirene had already reached the fifth floor, Sonje slipped two knives from her calf-hugging, high-heel boots.

"Oh, Truth!" Gregor exclaimed upon seeing the blades; the danger sliding deeper into his reality. Sonje handed him one of the knives, which he accepted with a worrying shake of his head. Four other knives were tucked away, two on her back and two sheathed on her forearms. Her lessons with Kunbo had only just begun, and Sonje had no experience fighting with two blades. *Truth, I barely have experience fighting with one!* Her skills would be sorely, and most probably fatally, outmatched if forced to engage the Sowilo directly. To live, she must escape Global Tech before Adirene could close in.

Once again, the elevator's arrival was announced by a soft tone; the sound no less stirring than a battlefield bugle. Sonje poised herself ready in case Adirene stood on the other side of the opening doors. Finding the car empty, the pair boarded just as a scream was thrown up behind them. Spinning, she saw Adirene racing towards them; a particle gun leveled before her. Sonje pressed the button for the lobby willing the doors to close. The dozen meters separating hunter and hunted decreased faster than the slow-ticking seconds. The doors finally responded, narrowing Adirene's target. The searing flash of amber reflected in blinding brightness inside the burnished metal interior of the elevator. Doors sealed, the lift began its descent to the lobby.

Relieved, Sonje turned to her companion. Her eyes traced the smear of blood down the back wall until falling on Gregor. Slumped on the floor, the man held his side as a ring of crimson slowly expanded across his white shirt.

"Gregor!" she screamed, dropping to kneel at his side.

Face already paling, he weakly raised his head. "She shot me," he said with disbelief.

Sonje placed her hand over his, applying more pressure to the wound. "You're going to be all right," she tried to comfort. "Hospital, I'll get you to a hospital and . . . and . . . you'll be okay."

"You can't. Too dangerous . . . for you," he replied fighting pain and unconsciousness.

Though she knew he was correct, she could find no other option. She had placed his life in jeopardy the moment she had stepped on to the elevator. Too many had already died because of her; she would not add Gregor to the list.

"I don't care about that. I'm not going to leave you behind."

"No!" he said with more force than she had thought remained in him. "You have to help Philip; Danica. I'll stay—help from inside."

If you live, Sonje added silently and saw the same thought reflected in his eyes.

The debate was decided once the elevator reached the lobby and opened its door. All the PKs which had earlier been positioned around the lobby were now crowded in front of the elevator; guns at the ready.

"Don't move!" one shouted as two others stepped into the small car.

Thoughts spinning, Sonje pleaded, "Please, help him! There's a woman upstairs with a gun! She shot him!"

The soldiers studied the pair warily before deciding a wounded man and a frightened woman posed no immediate threat. The PK who had barked first lifted a handheld comm from his belt.

"Shots fired at Global Tech. At least one wounded. Need immediate medical assist."

A PK lowered his weapon and pushed past Sonje to reach Gregor. The guard pulled several emergency field instruments from a pouch at his hip and started tending to the wound. Gregor squeezed her hand and mouthed the word "go." Unsure when her tears had begun, Sonje nodded through watered vision and released the man's hand.

The squad leader was delivering commands to his team; directing them to seal the building and kill the power to the elevators. With their attention focused on the threat several floors above, Sonje slipped out of the elevator and quietly crossed the marble floor to the exit. Her legs twitched with the desire to run, but she fought the urge. The Peacekeepers' attention might too quickly return if she appeared to be attempting an escape. Reaching the glass doors, she was forced to stop. Sonje looked up to the lifeless motion sensor; realizing in alarm the PKs had already initiated the lockdown procedures.

"Hey!" a PK called out.

About-facing, she watched helplessly as the guard hurried to apprehend her. As she lifted her hands in a sign of surrender, movement to her right caught her eye. Stepping out from the door leading to the emergency stairwell, Adirene stalked forward with a rage-filled stare.

Knowing the Sowilo would not hesitate to shoot, Sonje lunged left. The glass doors shattered under the consecutive rounds Adirene sent after her. The PK dropped behind the security desk as the new threat was unveiled. Sonje placed herself behind one of the lobby's columns as she searched for a more protected place to hide. Gunfire erupted as the remaining guards in the lobby opened fire at Adirene. The lobby was bathed in an amber glow until a PK called for a cease fire. Blocked from view, Sonje could not see if the Sowilo had been brought down.

Having hidden her knife beneath Gregor when the elevator had opened, Sonje freed a new blade from the sheath under her sleeve. The now-glassless doors no longer barred her exit, though she would have to risk exposure if she was to reach them. Slipping the impracticable boots from her feet, Sonje marshaled courage with a deep inhalation. Pushing off from the column, she raced to the doors.

Adrenaline dulled the pain of the glass shards tearing through the thin fabric covering her feet. The flight of particle bolts once again burned through the air. She wondered if she would feel their pain burn through her, or would death be instant. With distant awareness, Sonje found herself offering a prayer to the deities of Kunbo's people. She did not know their names, if many were worshipped or just one, but she still begged for their protection.

Diving across the threshold of the entrance, Sonje curled herself into a roll as Gavin, and then Kunbo, had taught her. The concrete was hard, and she could feel its fine grip tear through the skin of her shoulder. No pain, just pressure. Momentum carried her a few meters beyond the building until friction overpowered and she skidded to a halt. A voice inside her head ordered her to keep moving despite the desire to rest. *Stillness means death*, the voice said, and she was surprised to find her subconscious speaking with Kunbo's voice. The remembered tale of his flight from the D.C. strengthened her failing legs. Sonje rose from the ground. *Run,* the Kunbo-voice commanded.

She took one faltering step, then another, and soon she *was* running. Hope was beginning to rebirth inside her when her ears caught a faint sound from behind. Pivoting as she had in the woods of the campground, Sonje planted her feet as she had been trained. She held the black-bladed knife in her right hand and met Adirene's stare.

Her first realization was the Sowilo was unarmed, but she knew the absence of a weapon did not make the woman any less deadly. They circled and stalked, studying each other, searching for weakness. Adirene was the first to attack, lashing out with a furious blur of fists, one of which knocked the knife from Sonje's hands. Sparing a second to mourn the loss of the blade, she blocked the blows with greater success than either woman expected. The Sowilo broke from the attack and drew back. She could see in Adirene's eyes the woman was reassessing Sonje's abilities. While Adirene might believe her opponent more trained than initially assumed, Sonje doubted she could continue to resist the Sowilo's more extensive training.

Feinting left, then spinning opposite, Adirene directed a high roundhouse kick to Sonje's head. Only managing to counter and deflect a fractional second before contact, Sonje faltered from the explosion of pain in her skull. Blinking through the throbbing cloud in her mind, she ducked and rolled before Adirene moved in for a second strike. The Sowilo punched at empty air as Sonje uncurled and resumed a defensive posture a meter away.

Adirene snarled her contempt over the evasion and drove forward for a third attack. Struggling to keep pace with the woman's fast-flying kicks and punches, Sonje diverted the force of the blows to her shins and forearms. Panting, her body was swiftly growing weary under the avalanche. Adirene seemed tireless as she continued to break through Sonje's guard. Knowing the fight would not be won if she remained on the defense, Sonje dropped her right hand to deliver a strike to the Sowilo's side, leaving her guard half-open. Adirene ignored the momentary opening and tucked to protect her side while lowering her elbow. White pain flared as her fist met unyielding arm bone and not the soft flesh of the woman's abdomen. Adirene cried out with matching distress.

Mirroring Sonje's earlier withdrawal, the brown-haired woman spun away holding her side. Recalling Kunbo's instruction to capitalize on an injured enemy's retreat, Sonje advanced hoping to maintain her newly won advantage. Dropping for a leg sweep, she threw her arm to the ground to support her body. Adirene foresaw the maneuver and did not ignore the opening in Sonje's guard a second time.

Propelling herself to a jump, the Sowilo avoided the attack, letting Sonje's legs pass harmlessly beneath her. Sonje tried to move from the woman's reach and reclaim her guard, but Adirene's instincts were better honed. With feet barely returned to the ground, the woman kicked hard at Sonje's side. Though surviving childhood without serious injury, Sonje knew the popping tear inside her chest was the pain of fracturing ribs.

Sonje rolled along the concrete as she gasped for air with lungs which refused to fill. In seconds, Adirene dropped down upon her and wrapped her hands around Sonje's neck, further restricting the battle for oxygen. Clawing and punching the face of her attacker, the edges of her vision were slowly blurring. Adirene kept her strong, unbreakable grip despite Sonje's wild bucking; smiling as she watched Sonje vainly struggle for life.

Abandoning the fruitless attempt to dislodge herself, Sonje cast her arms to the ground; sweeping her hands across the concrete in search of a weapon. Memory flared with promise and Sonje reached beneath her body to wrap her fingers around the handle of the knife strapped to her back. Knowing it would be her last chance at escape, and that failure's price was death, she slipped the blade free of its sheath. With all the strength still in her possession, Sonje slammed the knife hilt-deep into the Sowilo's side. Enveloped by her frenzy, Adirene's attack continued with no sign of weakening.

Strike fast and repeatedly, the Kunbo-voice returned in her thoughts. Sonje pulled the blade free with a twist and plunged it into flesh again, and again. Eyes widening in shock and disbelief, Adirene's hold finally slackened. With a grunt,

Sonje pushed the woman off and rolled away. Though her broken ribs screamed in agony with every breath, air had never tasted as sweet.

Sonje dragged herself further away from Adirene, even though the other woman no longer moved. Disoriented, she raised her head; relieved to find the Global Tech building far in the distance, and no sign of PKs in pursuit. Using a nearby tree, Sonje fought the pain in her chest as she pulled herself to stand. The street she had reached before Adirene's attack was deserted, save for the line of empty podcars parked along the sidewalk's curbs. She stared hatefully at the vehicles, which all seemed to tease her, knowing she could not access any of them to reach the rendezvous.

As she worked up the strength to find a more suitable place to rest, and decide what to do next, a pair of headlights turned wildly onto the street. *Peacekeepers*, her mind wearily acknowledged; the inner voice once again her own. With nowhere to run, Sonje tightened her grip on the knife. If it would not have hurt, she would have laughed at the idea of fending off a squad of trained soldiers. *I'll fall with the first step!*

The vehicle screeched to a dead stop as she raised her arm to block the glare from the lights. Doors angled open and she could see dark figures quickly move onto the street.

"Dr. Sonje!" Kunbo cried out as he ran forward.

Whether imagined or real, Sonje did not resist when the man lifted her into his strong arms and carried her back to the pod. The doors had barely closed behind them before Corey propelled the vehicle into motion.

"I thought you were dead," she said.

"She gassed us," Kunbo replied. "Ol'Ben tried to stop her, but—"

"You're bleeding," Ament cut in as he tried to locate the wound responsible for the wet, red stains on her clothing.

"It's not my blood. Least not most of it," Sonje said under their heavy stares before adding, "She's dead."

Kunbo lowered his eyes and began to chant low murmured words in a foreign tongue; the mournful cadence marked it an elegy for Adirene and her unborn child. Unable to find the same respectful sorrow within herself, Sonje asked after Gavin and the other cells.

"We're going to the rendezvous point now," Ament replied. Sonje noted with dread the scout had not answered her question.

CHAPTER TWENTY-SEVEN

Danica Seton

Danica struggled with the unfamiliar encumbrance of carrying a particle gun while sprinting in the dark. After waiting nearly thirty minutes crouched behind a dumpster across from the PK base, a podcar had finally approached the west gate entrance. Torrance had held them back until the gun-cameras swept to cover the arrival before leading them forward. Counting the seconds as they made their bizarre run, cutting back, veering right, dashing forward, they had almost reached beyond the security system when a series of explosions flared in every direction. Cursing, Torrance abandoned the planned route and led them directly for the nearest building.

"What was that?" she asked as the trio leaned against the tall exterior wall. Alarms sounded across the base, and blinding floodlights lit the night to false midday brightness.

"Bad luck," Torrance replied.

"Was it us?" her brother asked.

Shaking his head, the solitary warrior answered, "No. Someone else is attacking the base. Getting to your father just got a lot tougher."

A pair of HALOs cut through the air overhead to emphasize the understatement. Wherever she looked, the amber flashing of particle guns burned and faded, burned and faded. Indistinct shouts and commands filled the brief moments of silence between each round of fire. Faster than she would have believed, the night boomed with the sights and sounds of pitched battle.

"Now what?" she asked; hating herself for the half-hope Torrance would decide retreat was best. For the first time, their guardian looked openly worried and uncertain. The assured manner in which Torrance had always moved was missing, and its absence made her even more frightened.

"Guerilla tactics," he said, squinting as he studied the area; talking to himself more than the Seton siblings. "They'll attack and fallback, then attack another point. Can't know where they'll move next."

A thundering blast rocked the air; erupting a distant mushroom of black smoke and fire over the horizon of the buildings to their left. The jolt seemed to force Torrance into action, and he ordered brother and sister to follow him in the direction of the supposed prison holding their father.

The scream of a massive craft, easily thrice as large as a HALO, echoed painfully in her ears as it rocketed toward the site of the large explosion. Dozens of charged particles flew from each of the down-tipped wings on either side of the jet as it neared its target. Danica could not name it, though Marcus undoubtedly recognized the aerial fighter from his many hours of gameplay.

"Stay close," Torrance cautioned. All pretense of stealth was forfeited as they crossed the brightly lit grounds of the PK military outpost. Soldiers poured out of the barrack buildings; intent on reaching the front lines of the sudden attack, and largely ignoring the three infiltrators already within the base. With so many only partially dressed in uniform, Danica assumed she and her two companions were being mistaken for fellow Peacekeepers. If any took a closer inspection, she was sure Marcus's obvious youth would betray the unintended, yet fortuitous, ruse.

Their half-jog brought them to a squat, one-story building unadorned except for the Global Alliance flag rising from a pole on the roof. A squad of PKs kept a wary watch in front of the sealed doors. Torrance slowed to a walk as he approached the soldiers; casually slinging the rifle to his back.

"Look scared, and don't saying anything," he instructed under his breath. Danica was sure the first part of the request was already accomplished.

"I've been ordered to escort these two to a safe location," he announced to the squad as he tipped his head to indicate the children at his side. A Peacekeeper with a series of silver bars decorating each shoulder stepped forward and studied the Setons.

"Who are they?" he asked.

Shrugging, Torrance replied, "Relatives of one of the brass, I think. Don't know and don't care. Soon as they're off my hands, I'm going back to the fight."

"This building is sealed – no one in or out," the PK said, still eyeing brother and sister.

Grumbling with annoyance, Torrance pressed the request. "What am I supposed to do? Take a VIP's family into a gun fight?"

Finally breaking his stare, the PK turned to Torrance. "VIP? Thought you didn't know who they were?"

"Who else would they be?" Torrance turned the question aside. "Only someone from the Families would have PKs babysitting when all hell's breaking loose."

Another explosion, equally as large as its predecessor and much closer, shook the ground. The immediacy of the threat seemed to lessen the soldier's reluctance, and he ordered his men to let Torrance and the children pass. Danica heard the man speak into his mobile comm as they moved toward the door.

"I got three coming in to you," he said. "The two kids are . . ." The rest of his command was overpowered by the flight of two large jets racing to the second explosion.

There was a brief wait before the door, or rather the steel blast door covering the actual entrance, slowly rose into an above recess. Danica realized they would never have been able to breach the secured building if not for Torrance's quickly-formed lie. The lock-down returned after they passed through the entrance, and all sounds of the battle raging outside cut off as the blast door once again sealed shut.

The first room within the building was a five-meter cube; walls, floor, and ceiling all glaringly white. Devoid of any furnishings, the pencil-thin seam of a doorframe on the opposite wall was the only break in the monotonous chamber. Though brightly lit, Danica was unable to find a source for the light; the illumination seeming to simply emanate from the flat surfaces. White flashed to blue in the short span of an eye blink, and then returned to its original color.

"Even with a HALO," Torrance growled, repeating the words of the Philadelphia arms dealer, Yakuza.

"Wha—" Danica asked as a voice filled the cubic chamber.

"Your weapons have been disabled. Place them on the ground and slide them forward."

Shaking, she looked at the man who had sheltered them from so many dangers. "Torrance, what's happening?" she asked even as knowing tears filled her eyes.

"Do what they say," he replied without looking at her. Unslinging the rifle at his back, Torrance tossed the weapon away; repeating the action with the twin handguns holstered on his hips. "Do it!" he shouted abruptly at the motionless siblings.

Startled by the vehemence in his voice, first Marcus, then Danica slid their weapons across the floor.

"Do not move," the voice instructed.

The wide door on the far wall slid away, and Danica's tears fell as she saw the countless Peacekeepers waiting on the other side. Like a wave breaking on the shore, the soldiers rushed forward to surround them; roughly placing restraints around their wrists. Danica sobbed as the shock of reality burned in her thoughts. *We got so far!* her mind cried.

Once the prisoners were secured, a thin, pinched-face PK approached Danica. Cold, bony fingers grabbed her chin, turning her face side to side as he examined her. He moved next to Marcus. Through her tears, she watched as her young brother met the PK with a defiant stare.

"It's them," the man announced with a barely hidden edge of victory. Turning to Torrance, the PK said, "I didn't think you could be trusted."

"I told you I'd deliver them," he calmly replied; tone muted but threatening. "The deal was I'd get immunity. What's with the cuffs?"

Now, the PK made no attempt to mask his smirking gloat. "Ah, yes. While I appreciated your offer to win me the honor of capturing these two, you see there's been a bit of renegotiation since your visit last night. As it happens, there's someone who has come a long way to meet you. And the honor gained from arranging that far outweighed our original bargain."

Through the jumble of her freewheeling thoughts, Danica struggled to understand the two men's exchange. *Bargain? Immunity?* A shiver of comprehension prickled her skin. *He . . . he . . .*

"You lied!" she screamed. "You lied to save yourself!" Danica threw herself at Torrance, but managed just one step before the PKs around her pulled her back. Blinded with rage and betrayal, she kicked and screamed, biting at the hands and arms trying to subdue her outburst.

"Get them downstairs!" the skeletal PK ordered.

"We trusted you!" she cried over and over as the men dragged her away. Danica was only barely aware of Marcus's escort pushing him forward; the boy's face still and emotionless. Despairing, she begged her emotions for serenity, a temporary calm to allow her the strength to comfort him. They had placed their lives in the hands of Torrance, Marcus lifting him above the worth of other men, and now the stranger's true nature was unveiled. She found some small measure of satisfaction in knowing Torrance had been betrayed in turn, and he would likely share their fate.

While travelling to the lower levels, and the siblings' eventual cell, Danica had managed to end the screaming accusations; more from a painful scratch in her throat than any real control over emotions. The dam holding back her tears had only just begun to rebuild when the PKs shoved the pair into a cell and her eyes fell on the man inside.

Thinner than she remembered, far too thin for only a week's time, Philip Seton sat in the corner with his arms wrapped around the knees drawn up to his chest. The fingers of his left hand were swollen purple, and bent with the odd angles of severely broken bones. His face was a swirl of color and pain - yellow where older bruises healed under the blue and violet of fresh injuries. At the corners of his mouth, streams of blood had dried and were beginning to flake. Even with all the visible damage to his body, it was her father's eyes which truly clawed her heart.

Staring at his children without recognition, Philip's eyes had the vacancy of death in their shallow depths. At work, Danica's father had a reputation of strict professionalism, but she had grown up knowing a different man - a man who spent a great many hours at the office, but returned home each evening with an easy smile and a ready joke. True, she had lately found his silly antics irksome, though at eighteen that was a requirement. She would have given anything to catch a glimmer of his former sparkle now. Instead, his eyes held . . . nothing.

"Daddy?" she whispered the name she had not used in several years. "It's me, Dani, and Marcus."

The children took a step closer, but their father only flinched and scrambled into a corner; shrinking even tighter into himself. *Truth, what have they done to him?* she cried. She wanted to run to him, feel the protection of his arms around her. The protection only a father's strength could offer. His fearful trembling, however, forced her to keep the distance.

"It'll be okay," Marcus said as he twined his hand in hers. "He'll rescue us."

She first thought he meant their father, then quickly realized Marcus spoke of Torrance. "He sold us to them, Marcus," Danica replied with venom; shocked the boy could still believe in the man who had readily delivered them to the PKs. "He lied to us to save himself!"

"Don't you remember what he said?" Marcus asked. "'Only a fool makes a deal with the Alliance and expects it to honor the terms.' He knew they wouldn't let him go. He knew. And he'll rescue us."

She recognized his trust in the man was unwavering even now. Danica wondered if the pity she felt for her brother was misplaced. *Perhaps it was better to die still holding to hope? Even if that hope was impossible?*

CHAPTER TWENTY-EIGHT

Liam Walford

He had gained mastery of his emotions decades ago. One could not serve a House as he had, now under his third Caput, without extreme discipline. The decisions he had been forced to make had required total objectivity – the needs of the Family always placed before his own. Many called him ruthless, deadly, yet none would dare believe him unwise. Some compared him to Caput Hu, the Viper of the Council, who had murdered and manipulated his way to a Seat. Yet, the Asian was rash; acting in anger as often as strategy. Liam had seen those same impulses topple great men from even greater heights. *No,* he mused, *one must be calculating. Free from the bonds of whim and passion.* Only once had Liam Walford allowed his heart to lead his mind. Only once, and it had cost him dearly. Staring through the one-way glass, he practiced the Eastern meditations to still the building storm of his thoughts.

"I will speak with him alone," he announced to the attending guard.

"Sir," the guard replied. Liam doubted the man had ever been in the presence of an official as highly ranked as the Chief Advisor to House Garrott. He would use that inexperience to his advantage. *Always find the advantage,* he smiled. Withdrawing the pen from his pants pocket, Liam placed the instrument on the table, and turned to the guard.

"I will speak to him alone, Peacekeeper," Liam repeated, "or you'll spend the remaining days of your service in the desolation of the Dead Continent."

Swallowing, the PK acquiesced. "Yes, sir," he said and ordered the squadron out of the cell.

Liam waited a short moment before turning from the glass and entering the room.

"Bring me a seat," he said over his shoulder. A PK rushed in to place a metal folding chair directly in front of the prisoner. Looking at the glass, a mirror on this side, and the men he knew stood behind it, Liam ordered, "Turn off the audio. No one in this facility has the security clearance to hear these words."

Partly true, he admitted. Not even the general of the base neared Liam's rank. Matters of state, however, were not on his agenda this night. Well-trained ears caught the nearly imperceptible extinguishing of the recorder's electronic hum. Satisfied with the new level of privacy, Liam lowered himself into the chair.

The prisoner, clad in the deepest of blacks, sat opposite him; wrists and ankles secured under thick metal straps. Blond hair hung carelessly down to a rigid, stone-cut jawline; defiance etched into the sharp angles. His cold blue eyes stared at Liam with a penetrating calm; stirring old memories. The eyes erased any doubt he may have had.

"You are the one who calls himself Torrance. I am Liam Walford," the advisor said. Not expecting a response, and receiving none, he continued. "It is said that until only a few days ago, you never existed. No chip in your palm, no image captured on camera. An amazing feat for a man of your age. How old are you? I'd guess . . . thirty-four, thirty-five. Do you even know?"

The prisoner did not move, did not blink.

"I see you have no fear, and that is admirable. But, I assure you I have ways of making you talk. There are drugs which will loosen your tongue. Though, I prefer other methods. I prefer letting a man choose to speak, to let him make the conscious decision to end his pain and speak."

"I don't intend to be here long enough for a conversation," the other man said flatly; not boasting, just stating fact as one might state a preference for one particular color over another.

Nodding, Liam replied, "That was your intention all along, wasn't it? Surrendering yourself so you could rescue the Seton fellow. What is it about that family? Why emerge from anonymity now to save one man?"

Again, the cold stare.

"They say you're one of the Ignota, in league with Mr. Seton. But, I think I know better."

"Do you?" the prisoner said; a smirk twitching at the edges of his mouth.

"Yes," Liam replied. "I think it is not the man for whom you care. Rather, it is his children. Perhaps you hope to spare them from the orphaned life you have known."

The advisor caught a slight narrowing of the prisoner's eyes; the briefest flash of anger before returning to placidity. *Impressive control*, Liam acknowledged. *They taught him well. I must tread carefully or his mind will shut like a steel trap. Let him believe he is manipulating me.*

"You see, Ignotum," the word burned his tongue, "I know more about you than you might think."

"I thought you didn't believe I was an Ignotum?" the man returned.

An untrained interrogator might have missed the millimeter shifting of the man's right foot; the quickened breathing, still calm but fractionally faster; or the tension in his hands as he fought the desire to clench them. But, Liam Walford was far from untrained.

"There are those who choose the Ignota," Liam explained, selecting his words carefully to slip beneath the prisoner's confidence. "And others are born to it."

He let the tease hang in silence. Counting the passing seconds, Liam watched as the prisoner waged an internal battle. *He wants to know more, but won't compromise his position. Desire wars against his training. The training will win out, though. They will have made sure of that. A little longer. Patience. Let the struggle swell. Now.*

"He never told you his name, did he? The man who raised you?" Liam dangled another temptation. "That would have defeated the purpose. They needed a weapon; a sword forged of vengeance, hardened steel ready for them to wield. But, then he died. And you were left alone. Hidden so well that no one sought you out – for only he knew of your existence. He must have taken such pains to hide you away as he trained you, forged you, to be his revenge. Those selfsame measures, however, betrayed his plans when he died. His plans to use you."

Liam knew the man across from him would have been raised completely loyal to his guardian. Only by undermining that bond, could he undo so many years of brainwashing.

"Who?" the prisoner rasped, and Liam knew he had claimed the first victory.

"His name was Nolan McAvoy, and he was the son of an Ignota founder," Liam shared. "A cold man, as I'm sure you know, his dedication to the cause was so blinding he would have paid any price if it gained even the smallest advantage. Even risking the lives of his children. Or, in your case, his grandchildren."

Not allowing a moment for the prisoner to recover from the revelation, Liam pressed on.

"He raised both his children to serve the Ignota. First his son, Owen, then his daughter Regan—your mother. The latter he sent to infiltrate one of the Five Families; House Garrott to be exact. Her task was to insinuate herself into the upper echelons of the Family – even marry if she must. Which she did," Liam paused. He had not expected the memory to sting so sharply.

"For the first two years, she served her father well. Relaying information, providing the Ignota with as many secrets as she could unearth. When she found herself pregnant, though, it seems she began to question the path of her life. With the birth drawing close, she came to her husband . . . she came to me, and revealed herself." Liam silently cursed the crack in his voice.

Blocking away the ancient grief again, he continued. "She hoped the child might bring unity. The blood of House Garrott and the blood of a Founder. Betrayed, I could not see through my anger. And so, I cast her out. By the morning my temper had cooled and I went to find her, exchange our forgiveness, and bring her home. But, I was too late. 'Complications from an early birth,' the doctors said. They showed me two bodies; hers and yours. Until two days ago, I had no reason to suspect the evidence was a well-supported fabrication."

Liam fell silent to gauge the man's reaction.

"Why now?" the prisoner, his son, asked.

"I first met Regan, though she called herself Riall then, while on business in California," Liam replied as the memory of their introduction played in his mind. "She wanted to name you after the city of our meeting. Torrance."

Searching the man's eyes, it was clear he did not doubt Liam's testimony; there was no skepticism in those twin pools of deep sapphire. *His mother's eyes – though hers had never held such ice.*

"Do you expect me to feel some allegiance to you now?" the son asked his father with the first hint of emotion in his voice. "Because I don't. Whatever blood we share, you're not my father. I have no father."

"You have no father because the McAvoys denied you one. He denied you a life of wealth and leisure, of unimaginable opportunity, in order to keep you locked away so he could train you, guide you to patricide and nurse his wounded vanity. When you leave here, you must decide with whom the greater blame lies – the father who cast you out, or the grandfather who hid you from the world."

"When I leave?"

Now there's suspicion, Liam thought. *How much distrust must course in his veins, in his genes?*

"Yes," he replied. "I have already arranged for your escape. Before entering, I left a device with a timed-release neurotoxin. Small dispersal, but quite potent. The

PKs on the other side of this wall have been dead for several minutes now. Most of the others have already been sent to defend the base. So, you are free to go."

"With the Setons," the prisoner returned. It was not a question.

Liam tested him, "I'm offering you a chance to live, Torrance."

"*I* won't abandon *them*," he replied. Liam did not miss the intended accusation shallowly buried within the man's words.

"Very well. I can tell you where they are, but that is all." He had anticipated the demand, knowing the decades of McAvoy training would allow Torrance little choice. The release of the Setons would be unfortunate, but not crippling. Liam did not fear the secrets Philip Seton had learned. Not as the Council did, at least. If the knowledge was made public, there would be advantages from the resulting scandal. Advantages he could leverage for his Caput and House.

Confident the prisoner would not harm him, Liam bent to free the man from the restraints. Torrance rose, making no effort to rub the bright marks of red on his wrists. Liam opened the door with a swipe of his hand across the scanner. Warily eyeing the exit, the unshackled prisoner held back.

Understanding the hesitation, Liam said, "The ventilation system has removed any lingering traces of the toxin from the air." He took a long, deep inhalation to bolster the assertion. An empty gesture in many ways since he had long ago built his immunity to the agent. "The Setons are two levels up – the family together in one cell." *An arrangement of my devising,* he added.

Torrance stepped into the room of dead Peacekeepers; quickly swapping his clothes with a guard of matching size. A moment of paternal pride warmed Liam as he watched the man, now smartly dressed in a PK uniform, move among the bodies to retrieve whatever weapons and accoutrements Torrance expected to need.

Before the man departed, Liam offered one last message.

"I did not expect you to feel allegiance to me, son; for I feel none towards you. I'm releasing you because I believe every man deserves a chance to decide when he knows all the truth. Should you choose to know me, I am easily found. If, however, you decide the Ignota blood in your veins sounds the stronger call, I shall count you as an enemy. And I will kill you as I killed your grandfather."

"All the truth?" Torrance repeated.

Smiling, the Chief Advisor of House Garrott conceded, "As much as I can tell you now. There is always more truth to be learned."

Turning without comment, Torrance exited the room through another door and took the first steps along the journey Liam had crafted. Rare was the occasion when he could not foresee the unfolding of events which he had set in motion. Normally, Liam would have despised such a situation, avoided it entirely if possible, but he found this one particularly intriguing. Whether or not his prodigal son would return to him, he did not know. He would, however, enjoy watching the game play out.

"Why are you lurking in the shadows, Mitchall?" Liam asked his aide, one of the many spies in his employ.

Stepping into visibility, the man said, "I thought it better if—"

"If you hid from him?" Liam neared a laugh. "He detected you even before I did."

The uncharacteristic worry on the younger man's wan face immediately erased his smile. "What is it?" Liam asked.

Faltering, Mitchall replied, "Our sources say the Council, sir, the Garrotts—the Garrotts have been executed."

Even Liam's well-honed stoicism could not withstand the destructive force of such a pronouncement.

"Executed?" his tongue struggled to form the word. "All of them?"

"I don't know, sir. It occurred only moments ago. The Council has taken control of Sheerness, and the droids. We're still—" The man cut his words abruptly, tilting his head as he listened to the mobile comm earpiece. "The Caput and Caput'e and the three youngest children have been confirmed dead, sir. No word on the Heir or Aubrey Garrott."

Tilden was going to Sheerness today, Liam recalled in dread.

"Sir, we must get you to safety," Mitchall intoned.

Mouth twisting with irony, he replied, "Safety just walked out the door, Mitchall."

"Yes, sir. But if the Garrotts are dead, sir, in the line of succession, you are—"

"I am Chief Advisor," Liam answered. *Truth, let one still live! I've no wish to be Caput!* "But, you're correct. We must leave here."

Liam let the younger man guide him through the facility, and beyond the small war burning around the military base, as he turned scenarios in his head.

If all the Garrotts are dead—an impossible thought—but if they are? Then, Liam remembered Riall's dream. *An intriguing game indeed.*

CHAPTER TWENTY-NINE

Danica Seton

Though he still cringed and shied away from her touch, Danica's father had relaxed enough to let his children occupy the floor on either side of his shielded, and broken, body. His eyes had yet to display recognition despite her repeated attempts to jog his memory. A week spent trying to reach her father, and now that she had, he seemingly remained a world away.

" . . . and Marcus got sick from eating too much cotton candy, and Mom had to buy him new clothes after we got off the roller coaster," she continued the reminiscence of their family vacation of two summers ago. Danica hoped the memory, more pleasant than the current reality, would trigger the return of his mind. "She was so mad, she almost made us leave and go back to the hotel. But, then Marcus started crying—"

"No, I didn't," her brother indignantly denied the accusation.

" . . . and you convinced her to let us stay."

If their father understood, or even heard, he gave no sign. Marcus, who clearly had been listening, continued his unwavering stare through the thick glass divider barring their exit. At first she thought he was unwilling to look at their injured father. When his eyes followed the guards' every movement, however, she knew the reason for his intense watch. He was waiting for Torrance.

Anger bubbled beneath her skin. They were with their father; their horribly damaged father who had been tortured to protect them, and Marcus focused his attention waiting for the man who had betrayed them. Danica felt her brother's slight as the second betrayal of the day.

"You're not even trying to help him," she hissed, her voice unintentionally lowered to a conspiring whisper. Close as they were, Philip Seton could have heard them breathe, if he heard at all.

"It's not working anyway," Marcus replied. "Maybe you shouldn't be talking to him about Mom. Remembering what happened to her might make him worse."

Danica silently admitted the integrity of his suggestion. If pain had forced their father's mind into retreat, reminders of his deceased wife could further force him away. Searching her memories for events which did not include Beth Seton, Danica found her hands empty. She did not have the camping trips, the hours of hologame play, the shared interest in horror movies which father and son had experienced in happier times. Danica had never fit the role of "daddy's little girl." Nor had she been the "dress-up princess" for which her mother had so earnestly hoped. For the first five years of her life, Danica had been an only child. Her parents doting had not required her to assume a particular role. They had simply thrilled over her every action. Attention had been split when Marcus arrived, shifted disproportionately at first as he was a newborn. She held no resentment, felt no slight, over her parents' divided focus. In many ways, it had been a gift. Danica had been allowed to find her own way and develop her own interests with independence. It had been different for Marcus. Truly seeing him now, she realized *he* was different.

Their difference in age had precluded the possibility of common interests. She had been entering high school while he had still been playing with toys. Their parents always claimed maturity would bridge that gap, but for now the five-year gulf seemed impossibly vast. What interactions they had had in the past were usually marred by the mutual antagonism of "big sister" and "baby brother." Over the last week, Danica had seen the story of their relationship rewritten.

Lately, talking to him made her feel as if she was the younger sibling. She had cried, lashed out, panicked, and openly feared, and through it all Marcus had remained composed. When she had faltered, he had been confident. The little boy who had teased and tormented was gone. If not for the staggering changes in their father, she would have doubted Marcus's own metamorphosis could have occurred in a week's time.

"So, what do we do then?" she asked with barely measured sarcasm.

"We wait."

Frustrated, she shot back, "For what? Them to kill us?"

A broad smile broke across his face as he nodded towards the glass.

"No," he said. "For him."

Turning her head to the point of his amusement, Danica saw the same four guards who had earlier positioned themselves just outside the cell. A fifth PK was walking down the short hall to join his brethren.

"Get ready," Marcus advised.

"Get ready?" she absently repeated. Studying the scene again, searching for whatever hope had inspired her brother, her eyes focused on the approaching guard. Chin-long blond hair snuck out beneath the Peacekeeper beret the man had angled on his lowered head. It was his taut and deliberate walk, however, which confirmed his identity.

Before she could voice her excitement, Torrance threw his arms out with a flash of razor-sharp metal. The blades sunk deep into the throats of the two guards leaning against the glass partition; the knife tips clinking on the surface from the back of the men's necks. Torrance engaged the remaining PKs directly. Both foolishly tried to draw their firearms which allowed Torrance the seconds needed to advance and snap the first man's neck. Torrance kicked high, letting the dead man drop, and knocked the particle gun from the hand of the only living guard. Disarmed, the PK attempted to strike with his fist, but Torrance caught the wrist in one hand while driving the other down to the man's elbow. Danica flinched at the crunch of bone as the PK's arm bent in an unnatural angle. The guard's cry of pain doubled when Torrance kicked again, low to shatter a knee. His torment mercifully ceased as their rescuer twisted the PK's head with vicious force.

Unfazed by his own acts of violence, Torrance stepped to one of the bleeding guards slumped against the glass. Red spittle bubbled from the PK's lips as

Torrance dragged him to the scanner. The glass immediately parted at the swipe of the man's weak hand; he was cast away once his use had expired.

"Can he walk?" Torrance asked as he stepped into the cell.

"We can carry him," Marcus answered for them both.

Torrance hesitated, calculated, then nodded his consent.

Confused, but understanding, Danica helped her brother lift their father from the floor. He fought their touch at first, but his depleted strength was easily overpowered. Slinging an arm across each of their shoulders, the siblings dragged him forward after Torrance.

"Do you have the drive?" he asked.

"The . . . yes! They never searched us," she exclaimed as she remembered the forgotten holocard drive still tucked safely in the sole of her left boot.

"Guess not everybody's in on that secret," Torrance said. Danica noticed his tone suggested another meaning. The undertone nearly prompted her to ask how he had managed to win himself free, but she swallowed the question in light of their circumstance.

Instead, she asked, "How are we going to get out?"

"There's a way. Two levels down. Can you two make it with him?" he asked with an incline to her father.

"Do we have a choice?" she returned.

With a wry grin, Torrance replied, "Not really. Come on. I don't know how much time he bought us."

Wondering who Torrance meant, Danica tucked the question away for later inquiry, and helped her brother maneuver their shared burden down the hall after Torrance. Stumbling down the first flight of stairs, she was already feeling the strain of carrying their father. Whether unconscious or unaware, the man was incapable of assisting in his own escape. Battling her will, Danica narrowed her focus to each individual step. Thoughts of how many more were to come would have forced her to her knees.

Torrance guided them down to a lower level, then down one more, until they were finally running along a different set of halls and corridors. *If this counts as a run,* her thoughts corrected. The moment nearly mirrored the event days before when brother and sister carried an unconscious Torrance to safety.

Through their entire flight, Danica had not spied a single soul beyond their haggard quartet. No Peacekeepers standing guard, no sentries roaming about. *This is the worst secured prison in the world,* she assessed. Even if the attack still raged on outside, she thought prisoners of their seeming importance would have been better watched. Again, she wondered who the "he" was who had bought them time to escape.

"Through here," Torrance directed. Pushing open the already-ajar door, he revealed a long, narrow, dimly-lit tunnel. "It will connect with another building, closer to the perimeter of the base."

Danica and Marcus adjusted their stance to fit into the smaller space. The catalog of unanswered mysteries increased as she wondered how Torrance had bypassed the lock's scanner. *Brothels and tunnels, brothels and tunnels. He always has us in brothels and tunnels!*

The endless length of the passage was impossible for her exhaustion to ignore. She desperately wanted to plead for a rest, but she knew their guardian well enough not to voice the request. From the rhythm of his breath, Marcus was also struggling with the effort.

Perhaps sensing the siblings' distress, Torrance encouraged, "Almost there."

Philip Seton began mumbling incoherently as his children carried him along. It was the first sounds their father had made since they had found him, and the only indication he was awake.

"It'll be okay, Dad," she offered. "We're going to get you out of here."

Nearing the limit of her endurance, Danica felt an incremental resurgence when Torrance announced they had reached the exit. Another door sat open along the right wall, and the group eagerly passed through it.

Unlike the prison facility from which they had escaped, this room held several Peacekeeper soldiers. Posing no threat, the uniformed guards lay scattered across the floor. She would have believed them sleeping if not for the absence of the rise and fall of breathing chests. Following Torrance's warning, Danica held her breath until they were well clear of the room; fearing whatever poison had killed the PKs.

They passed through other rooms and halls, similarly occupied by dead PKs, before finally exiting the building. Sounds of battle rang in the night, though the intensity was markedly less than before. As promised, the border of the military base lay a short distance ahead. Far from total safety, seeing the proximity of the base's end did restore some of Danica's flagging hope.

Small pockets of gunfight still lingered in the darkness. Torrance selected a relatively calm point some meters away as their exit destination. Moving across the uneven terrain in the dark posed a significantly greater challenge than the smooth floors of the facilities. Twice, Danica had to fight for balance when her steps encountered unseen obstacles in the soft grass. If camera-guns tracking their movements were hidden in the nearby trees, they were mercifully idle.

"Get down!" Torrance shouted, pushing Marcus to the ground. Entangled as they were, Danica and her father easily succumbed to Marcus's fall, and joined him in a heap on the forgiving earth.

Torrance cut left, drawing fire away from the Setons, while returning amber bullets to the PKs racing forward. The night hid their number, but she guessed they were many based on the endless cascade of the charged bolts flying through the air. *Too many!* her mind shouted. Worse yet, the residual ambient glow of the exchange reflected off the armor of several soldiers. There had been enough news coverage in the past weeks for Danica to recognize the distinct features of PK-drones. Weaponless, she knew the only defense was Torrance and his efforts to keep the soldiers focus on him.

"We have to keep moving," she whispered to Marcus. "Can you crawl and drag Dad with me?"

"I think so," his strained voice replied.

Unsure how long Torrance could keep the PKs distracted, Danica dared herself to rise up on knees and hands. It seemed a slow lifetime just to cross a meter along the grass and dirt. Even with Marcus's help, pulling their father while staying as low as possible was incredibly difficult. Realizing they would never reach safety in time, Danica knew they would have to risk a run.

Eyeing a clustered knot of trees ahead, she said, "We have to run."

Marcus made no reply, but Danica felt him readjusting his hold on their father in preparation. She slid her father's limp arm over her shoulder, hoping the position would support his weight when they broke for the trees.

"Ready?" she asked.

"Yeah."

"1 . . . 2 . . . 3!"

Danica extended her legs, pulling her father up with her, and pushed off with her right foot. The movement was as near to a sprinter's start as she could mimic. She tried to ignore the deadly difference in the guns triggering this race. Legs pumped and turned, eating the ground with each awkward stride. Marcus, stronger yet not as fast as she, grunted under their shared strain.

They reached the stand of trees, but not before their movements were noticed. Bark splintered and exploded as PKs fired their powerful weapons into the small grove. Danica felt jagged pieces of timber tear into her face. Her hand involuntarily released its grip on her father's wrist to shield her eyes; the unexpected shift in weight nearly bringing her down. Fighting the imbalance, she quickly tried to recover.

"Dani!" Marcus cried out in warning.

In her brief second of distraction, she collided with low branches which had seemingly burst from the trunk of the nearest tree. The impact stole the breath from her lungs in a white flash of pain and pressure. Knees buckling, Danica threw her hand out to help break the fall. A fall which did not come. The branches multiplied, pulling and grabbing until she was further into the grove. A warm, wet hand closed over her mouth. She tried kicking herself free, understanding it was arms, not branches, which held her tight.

"Shh," a man's voice whispered. "Don't move."

Whether caught by friend or foe, Danica did not know, but fear froze her nonetheless. The hand across her face relaxed once her body ceased its struggle. Beyond the pounding of her heart, she heard cautious footsteps entering the copse. Danica squinted into the darkness searching for brother and father; finding only shadows upon shadows. The footsteps were nearer now. *The other side of the tree,* her mind judged. The shadows of the grove moved as one, drawing in on whoever approached. Muffled sounds of skirmish were born and died in a heartbeat.

"All clear," another voice hushed. Three men stepped into the dim light. One had her father draped lifelessly over his shoulder like a rolled carpet. Between the two others stood Marcus; face expressionless save for the eerie serenity he had acquired over the past days.

The man behind her gently shifted Danica to the side. "You're Danica Seton, aren't you?" he asked.

Unsure of the man's allegiance, she held back the confirming answer.

"It's okay. We can get you to safety," he promised. "Match, how's the father?"

The man supporting her father replied, "Alive, but pretty beat up. Dr. Nysgaard can probably do more than I can do here."

The name broke the dam of Danica's mistrust. Her father had directed her to seek out the woman. He had said to trust only her. "Dr. Nysgaard? Sonje Nysgaard is here?"

"Not here, but she's close," the man corrected. A marked tone of worry filled his words. "Let's move out," he said to the waiting men. Danica assumed he was their leader.

"Wait," Marcus's voice interjected. "We have to get Torrance."

"No, you don't."

Danica jumped at the nearness of the man's voice. Standing directly behind her, particle gun drawn to a hair's width from the leader's head, Torrance stared at the other men. Their reaction was rapid; leveling their own weapons to protect their commander.

"You move quietly, friend," the leader said calmly despite the sudden standoff.

"You left your back unprotected, *friend*," Torrance replied in a snarl. "Now, tell your men to lower their weapons."

"Even if I gave that order, they wouldn't follow it as long as there's a gun pointed at my head."

Danica could see the calculation in Torrance's eyes. Recalling how effortlessly he had killed the four PKs in the prison, she tried to talk him down from an encore. "Torrance, they know Sonje Nysgaard. She can help my father. He told us we could trust her."

His blue eyes shifted to her.

"It's them I don't trust." There was a heat in his voice she had never heard from him before. Even in the faint light, she saw his finger flex on the gun's trigger.

"Please, Torrance," Danica said. "Please."

The tension stretched and she held her breath against the expectation of gunfire. Finally, Torrance bent his arm; pulling the weapon back toward the side of his face. The other men watched warily, ready to react to any treachery. With a nod, the leader directed his men to lower their guns.

"We have a pod a half kilometer away," he said, dismissing the taut anxiety of just seconds before.

The party encountered no resistance as it escaped the final spans of the military base. She wondered how much of it was luck, and how much was owed to whoever had assisted Torrance in the facility. Free from the charge of carrying her father, Danica was able to keep the brisk pace the group's leader set. Still, she was relieved when they did eventually reach the podcar. Just large enough to hold the four men, the doubling of bodies made comfort impossible. Danica took one of the rear seats; Marcus settling onto her lap. Mind and body were so numb, the crush of his weight went unfelt.

Her father's persistent mumbling was the only break in silence as the leader drove the pod further from the base. The man called Match continued to assess Philip Seton's condition. Though, crammed as they were in the vehicle, his ministrations were forcibly limited. Torrance and the other two men kept a vigilant watch out the windows for any signs of pursuit.

Danica's thoughts were erratic. Hope had come and gone, and returned again so frequently over the last hours she could not identify her present emotion. Only exhaustion was easily understood. Resting her head against her brother's back, the respite allowed the adrenaline to recede from her body; its absence amplifying the weariness.

"We're going to be okay," Marcus whispered to her over his shoulder.

"We're going to be okay," she repeated in reply. For the first time in too long, the words sounded true.

She had not realized she had dozed, or for what length of time, when the podcar came to a gentle stop. Waking with a jolt, Danica tensed in anticipation of some new danger. Through the window, she saw they had entered a garage – abandoned, if the dust and cobwebs was any indication. Another pod, one of the larger models designed for families, was parked alongside their own.

The leader did not wait for the podcar's doors to fully open before he jumped out; running towards a woman lying on the ground surrounded by three men. Once Marcus lifted himself off, Danica followed him out of the vehicle.

"—ken ribs. I'm fine," she caught the prone woman say as the leader gently pulled her into his arms. The men around her stepped back to allow privacy. "Gavin, I'm sorry. I killed her . . . I had to . . . the baby . . ."

The leader, identified for Danica as Gavin, hushed the woman's pain. "I know," he said. "It's all right. It's all right."

Danica moved closer until she had a clearer view of the woman's face. Though bruised and marked with dirt and blood, she was just able to recognize the woman from the digital on the news. Bending to tug off her boot, Danica pulled the holocard drive from beneath the inner sole. As much as she feared intruding into the obvious moment of emotion, the need to be free of her burden overcame all else.

"Dr. Nysgaard," she said as she lowered herself to kneel next to the woman. "My father's hurt, but he wanted me to give this to you."

"Who—" the doctor began, turning the drive over in her hand, then cut off as her eyes grew wide. "Danica?"

"Yes."

Dr. Nysgaard grunted in pain as she wrapped trembling arms around Danica. Breaking the embrace, the woman turned to Gavin, "Help me to him."

As the men brought the doctor to unsteady feet, Danica stepped aside and stood next to Marcus and Torrance. The siblings watched in silence while Dr. Nysgaard tended to their father. Her brother took her hand; saying a thousand words with a gentle squeeze. She could only reply with a tear running down the side of her cheek.

"We can't stay here long," the leader said as he approached the trio. He was nearly as tall as Torrance, and evenly matched across the shoulders. Both men had the same gem-blue eyes, though the former's held none of the ice present in Torrance's stare. "We'll need to reconnect with the other two cells from tonight's attack."

"Ignota cells," Torrance said.

"Yeah," the man replied. "Torrance, we lost a man tonight. And, I've seen what you did in Philly. You must know there's a war coming. I could use someone like you."

"I'm not one of the Ignota, *friend*."

"But you could be. Think about it before you say no," the leader said in return. Smiling, he offered his hand in introduction. "And my name's Gavin. Gavin McAvoy."

Danica watched as Torrance accepted the other man's outstretched hand. While his body maintained the near constant preternatural calm, she caught the flash in his eyes. Danica shuddered involuntarily with memory. She had seen the same look before – in the second between Torrance realizing Alanna's betrayal and firing a bullet into her skull.

WHAT FOLLOWED AFTER

"And then there were four," Yin Xian Hu said, his projected image smiling. Even such a small grin seemed unnatural on the man. Too much had gone wrong for Caput Cambrie to share the Viper's victorious mood.

"How long will that last with Tilden Garrott still alive?" Cambrie replied. The intervention of the Ignota had been unexpected, and greatly marred the well-planned plot against House Garrott. It would have been a minor misfortune if one of the younger children had survived. But, the Heir himself escaping might prove disastrous.

Hu raised a placating hand. "He is in the hands of the Ignota. Their enmity is even greater than ours. Tilden Garrott will likely wish he had died at Sheerness rather than falling into the hands of his enemy."

"Should he decide to join them," Cambrie suggested, "if they manage to turn him to their cause, the Council's secrets will also be in the hands of the Ignota."

The Viper replied, "The terrorists are crippled, Cambrie. How many cells has the Alliance already rooted out? Two hundred? Three? The Garrott Heir can tell them everything, and it will not matter. Their numbers are scattered, dwindling each day. The Ignota will soon become an irrelevant footnote."

Cambrie withheld his strong disagreement. While it was true the Alliance had many successes in the past week against the Ignota, he found no evidence the subversive group was nearing extinction. If anything, the previous night's attack on the Peacekeeper base in Washington, DC, was evidence to the contrary. Either Hu was blind, or the man hid his true intentions behind the boast of inevitable Alliance triumph. Cambrie suspected the latter.

"You still intend to marry the girl?" he asked.

"As soon as she arrives."

Foolish, Cambrie thought. *Better to kill the entire line and remove all threat of reprisal.*

Whether vanity or vengeance, the matter had been an intractable part of the bargain securing Hu's participation in the Garrott plot. The Viper, however, had named his price, and Cambrie had agreed. He did not believe Hu's claims of some archaic right of conquest. Nor, did he see what value existed in marrying the only surviving daughter of an outlawed House. Hu was impulsive, but there was always motive behind his actions. Wedding Aubrey Garrott must have some gain Cambrie had not yet discovered. And that lack of revelation troubled him.

"Fawzan intends to focus our resources toward the Seton affair," Cambrie segued into another matter of concern. He knew the other Caputs placed the debacle's blame at his feet. *Not wholly without reason,* he admitted. The events had occurred within his territory, and he could not well use the distraction of plotting treason as an excuse.

"Our esteemed elder worries more than he should," Hu countered. "If this supposed "defect" is made public, it will be considered just that – a defect. The Alliance can claim to *fix* the malfunction. Doing so will only delay our plans for a few months at most. Any widespread concern after such time will be muted once we start limiting the efficacy of the current SID. People will be forced to the upgrade if they wish to continue buying food, driving, working, etc."

Cambrie nodded. "A few months delay."

"At most," Hu replied. "A short span of time when compared with the millennia which has finally led us here. Where others have failed, we will succeed. The Culling will happen, Cambrie. And we will be its engineers."

"How long has she been awake?" the doctor asked the nurse at his side as they walked down the hospital hall. She was one of the few who shared his secret.

"Only a few minutes, Doctor," she replied. "I came to find you as soon as she was conscious."

The surgery had been successful despite the severity of the woman's injuries. It had been a far more difficult task keeping her beyond his colleagues' attention. Hospital protocol required any evidence of SID removal to be reported to the PKs immediately. Only through a stroke of luck had the woman's wrist tattoo been recognized by an intern in the emergency room.

"Has she said anything? Her name?" he asked.

"No, sir."

The private room was located at the far end of the fifth floor. Soft lights helped dim the harsh sterility of its white walls. A lone figure lay tucked in bed; thin, life-supporting tubes running into her arms. Still weak from the operation and sedation, the woman tried to push herself away once the doctor and nurse reached the bed.

"You're among friends, Sowilo," he told her as he lifted the sleeve of his white laboratory coat. The watch on his wrist was unremarkable except for the rune drawn into its face. Sight of the mark visibly reduced the woman's fear.

"Can you tell me your name?" he asked.

Through dry, cracked lips, the woman rasped, "Adirene."

"Adirene, you're very lucky to be alive. If a passer-by had not found you when he did, your wounds would have been fatal. I've repaired most of the damage, but you'll need a few days before you'll be back on your feet."

"The baby . . .," she whispered, drawing her hand to her abdomen.

Frowning, the doctor replied, "I'm sorry. I did all I could, but I couldn't save him."

Both doctor and nurse cringed back as the woman loosed an endless shriek of horrific grief.

Grunting, Milo padded across the cold kitchen floor. Only two days out of the hospital, and the calls had not relented. Most were from his PK brothers and sisters offering congratulatory wishes, hopes for a speedy recovery, and more than a few quips to brighten his spirits. Of course, his parents had called, almost hourly the first day, to check on his health and healing.

Thankfully, his mother had stopped crying each time she saw his image. Milo did not think he looked all that bad considering, but her tears fell regardless. She had finally managed to maintain composure today when she had called. Every time she had called. *She must be dehydrated by now,* he joked. While she had been an over-soaked sponge of emotion, Milo's father had beamed with pride; somehow managing to link every word he spoke back to the arrests. If Milo mentioned an aching head, his father would say, "I bet Muerte and his goons have a real bad headache right now." *Goons,* Milo smiled, *who says that anymore?* He hoped they would be able to behave during tomorrow's promotion ceremony.

Dropping to the couch, Milo answered the call.

"Hello?" he asked the blank projection.

"Good evening, Corporeal Chance," replied an altered voice. "Though I guess after tomorrow it will be Sergeant Chance."

Sighing with the lost hope he was free of the Soothsayer, Milo said, "I was sleeping."

"My apologies," the Soothsayer's digital voice offered. "I wanted to congratulate you on your success. A drug lord, a judge, an assistant district attorney – a success indeed. Philadelphia's great hero."

"Yeah, well thanks, but I'm going back to—"

"A hero, though, never rests on his laurels. Surely, you must have questions. Benjamin Hopkins was but a pawn. Our work has just begun. I have another task for you, Sergeant Chance," the Soothsayer cut in. "There is another who has caught my interest. I assume you have heard of—"

"Look, I don't know who you are or why you—"

". . . Torrance?"

During the brief recuperation period in the hospital, Milo had updated himself on the world events he had missed while focused on the Muerte case. Cohors Ignota attacks, one of the Five Families executed for treason, a restructuring of the Council—and Torrance. The terrorist had left a burning scar across the city. Milo's city.

"Yes, I have," Milo admitted, knowing the Soothsayer had played on his intrigue.

"I want you to find him. And when you do, I want you to bring him to me."

"To you?" he asked. Milo knew his voice displayed his interest. *Capturing Torrance* and *finding out who the Soothsayer is,* he mused.

"Yes," the blank screen replied. "I will see that you are outfitted with another PK-drone for this investi—"

"I want Godwin," Milo interrupted.

"Your previous drone was severely damaged. A new drone will be just as competent, I assure you."

Feeling foolish for his attachment to what was essentially a computer with legs, Milo still refused. "No. Either fix him, or . . . I don't know, put his *mind* into another drone. But, I want Godwin. It's Godwin, or no deal."

The screen remained silent for several seconds.

"Very well," the Soothsayer finally replied before the empty projection disappeared.

"Why do I feel like I'm going to be visiting you in a hospital again?" Naesha said from across the room. With a smile, his eyes travelled the length of her body.

Dressed only in one of his shirts, the sight stoked his desires. She had not yet shared with him the stories of her past, and he had not asked. *When she's ready*, he said in his mind.

"Come on," he teased as he crossed to her. "You know I look good in a hospital gown."

End of the First Book of Scars of Tomorrow

THE EPIC CONTINUES IN:
THE IGNOTA

THE IGNOTA

Scars of Tomorrow
Book II

A NOVEL BY TOM CALEN

For the authors who inspire me every day.

From the prophecy of the Sowilo:

*"From the darkness,
hidden from the world,
the Founder's Blood will come.
Trumpets of Fire announce
the arrival of the Dagaz."*

TABLE OF CONTENTS

Note to the Reader	236
Chapter One	238
Chapter Two	247
Chapter Three	254
Chapter Four	260
Chapter Five	265
Chapter Six	272
Chapter Seven	281
Chapter Eight	290
Chapter Nine	296
Chapter Ten	302
Chapter Eleven	306
Chapter Twelve	314
Chapter Thirteen	320
Chapter Fourteen	333
Chapter Fifteen	341
Chapter Sixteen	352
Chapter Seventeen	359
Chapter Eighteen	374
Chapter Nineteen	381
Chapter Twenty	387
Chapter Twenty-One	395
Chapter Twenty-Two	403
Chapter Twenty-Three	409
Chapter Twenty-Four	413
Chapter Twenty-Five	420
Chapter Twenty-Six	441
Chapter Twenty-Seven	450
Chapter Twenty-Eight	461
What Followed After	468

NOTE TO THE READER

Constructing a Genesis

Tracing the factual origins of any subversive group is a challenge for even the ablest of historians. Unlike countries and corporations, insurgencies rarely have official dates of formation. Some of my contemporaries in the field assign the point of genesis to the counter group's first formal act or declaration. As you might have guessed, I do not agree.

History provides many examples of an insurgent movement conceived well before its first shot was fired. The American Revolution, La Cosa Nostra, the Irish Republican Army, the Palestinian Liberation Organization, and Al Qaeda all began as small sparks before their bonfires of maturity became known to the world. And so it was with the Cohors Ignota.

Adding to the difficulty of mapping the Ignota's conception is the disinformation supplied by the group itself. In order to protect its fragile infancy, the Ignota not only hid the identity of its members, but also intentionally leaked false names and bases of operation. A sagacious strategy to be sure, but one that creates a formidable obstacle for sociological investigation.

I have been fortunate enough to enjoy a long life of good health; thus allowing me decades to peel away the many layers of shadow and secrecy surrounding the Ignota. Combining my own experiences, conversations with the principle players, and a thorough post-war study of diaries, records, and official archives, I have compiled the most complete, but in no way definitive, exploration of the Cohors Ignota's founding and subsequent rise to global prominence.

Criticisms on Objectivity

Quite expectedly, I received a great deal of . . . I'll call it *feedback* . . . regarding the first volume of this historical narrative. Readers and critics of *Torrance* fell into two categories.

One group, comprised of those who spit and curse at the very mention of the man from the woods, hurled at me accusations of being a "sympathizer." They claim my view of Torrance, and his actions, paint too rosy a picture. I might concede their point if not for the second, and equally large, camp of detractors.

Those who revere Torrance near to deification have been no less critical of my initial volume. To them, I have created a depiction of their hero inconsistent with the mythology and, for some, their own memories of the man.

In my opinion, such strong reaction from both sides is proof of my objectivity. Having known the man—as much as one could, and perhaps better than any others—I am confident in the impartial accuracy of my narrative.

Personal Changes

In writing this second volume, *The Ignota,* I found myself relying on third party accounts—which should, but likely won't, please my critics. After the events retold in *Torrance,* I had become more aware of the inexplicable . . . changes . . . occurring with me. Only thirteen at the time, I had no immediate reference to help guide me through the metamorphosis. However, even though it was some seventy years ago, I do not recall fearing those *changes*. Perhaps if I had known what it meant, what bearing it would have on who and what I was to become, I would have been frightened. But, that tale is still to be told.

I mention it now only to better explain my increased reliance on secondary, and in some cases tertiary, sources to write this work. As I was struggling to understand my internal transformation, I had withdrawn from those around me; spending most of my time in quiet reflection. As a result, I was not present for many of the conversations and deliberations contained in this text.

My research, however, has helped me reconstruct those events from which I was absent.

-Marcus Seton
Grand Historian

CHAPTER ONE

Danica Seton

Rubbing the sleep from her eyes, Danica squinted as her vision adjusted to the muted glow of the oil lamp sitting atop the desk in the corner of the small room. Faint sounds echoed in the hall marking the morning stirrings of the many others living in the underground safehouse. Danica arched her back to relieve the familiar stiffness earned from yet another night spent sleeping in the stiff, unyielding chair. Out of habit, and perhaps some residual hope, she turned her eyes to the bed.

No change.

For nearly seven weeks, she had repeated the morning ritual. And for nearly seven weeks, her mornings had begun with disappointment. Though the wounds had long since healed with barely a visible scar (much was owed to Dr. Nysgaard and her medical skill), her father, Philip Seton, had yet to rouse from his overlong slumber. His color had returned once nutrients and medication had flowed into his stomach and veins. The swelling in his shattered hand had subsided; though Dr. Nysgaard doubted the extremity would ever function properly again.

"He'll need a biorobotic prosthetic," the blonde doctor had said, promising to perform the surgery once the Ignota obtained such a device. Living as they were, underground and on the run, Danica knew such a find was unlikely.

Checking the IV running into his arm, Danica whispered, "Good morning, Dad." If he heard the words, he gave no sign. "It's Friday." At least she thought it was. Keeping track of the days had become a painful reminder of just how long the coma continued to last.

"I'm going to shower and grab breakfast," she told him as she rose from the chair, "but I'll be back soon. I'll bring Marcus with me, too."

As of late, her younger brother had been an infrequent visitor to their father's bedside. While she could understand the boy's reluctance, Danica could not help resenting the absence. She had assumed the role of nurse and guardian in the weeks since rescuing their father, and Danica wished she could share the burden.

Marcus instead chose to spend his time with Torrance, their dark and brooding champion from the Pennsylvania woods. Grateful for the benevolence the man had shown them, Danica still struggled to understand her brother's fascination. Torrance was far from a conversationalist, yet Marcus managed to pass hours in silent reflection with him.

At first, Danica believed the boy's devotion was inspired by juvenile hero-worship. Lately, however, she had begun to sense a different motivation. It seemed as though Marcus was engaged in a deep study of the man from the woods – something more akin to an astronomer observing a new phenomenon in the far reaches of space. A philosopher, perhaps, in search of hidden truth. Whichever, it was a bizarre condition for a thirteen year old boy. But then, Marcus himself had grown . . . different.

First realized when they shared a cell in an Alliance military complex, Danica had watched as Marcus slipped further from the brother she once had known. He had adopted Torrance's near-constant silence, speaking only when necessary, and even then in clipped cryptic phrases. It was not the sparse, enigmatic speaking that bothered her. Marcus had become detached. Detached from her. Detached from their father. Detached from everything and everyone. *Everyone except Torrance, of course,* she concluded the thought as she walked into the hall.

Danica kept her head lowered as she navigated the interweaving passages of the underground safehouse. Located in the northern Ohio town of Oberlin, the Ignota camp was a large complex of tunnels and rooms dug beneath the town over the last several decades. Oberlin itself was quite familiar with masking fugitives from sight, having once served as part of the Underground Railroad[1] in the early years of the old American Empire. Eleven Ignota cells were in residence; twice as many as the facility could support. With the expanding intensity of the Alliance crackdown, the overcrowding was unfortunate and unavoidable.

With a preference for anonymity, Danica often took her meals back to her father's room. Due to his condition, Philip Seton was afforded one of the few solitary sleeping quarters. Danica had expected complaints once the population grew and space became a premium. She learned, however, that her name had a near celebrity status among the Ignota. The events from two months' past, when Torrance had led the siblings through an explosive escape from Philadelphia and a subsequent assault on an Alliance base, had become a rallying event for the besieged rebellion.

Her presumed familiarity with Torrance had also elevated her in the eyes of the Ignota. As each new cell had arrived in Oberlin, its members had sought her out and peppered her with questions about the man. When her answers fell short of their expectations, they assumed she was protecting Torrance – thus adding to the mystery. And while Danica did indeed believe her knowledge of him to be private, the truth was that her knowledge was very limited. Even if she had wished to, Danica would not have been able to answer the majority of the questions with

---

1 The Underground Railroad was the name given to the series of safehouses used by escaping black slaves. Estimates claim over 100,000 slaves used the system to reach freedom. – M.S.

any accuracy. Recently, and much to her relief, the interrogations had ebbed to a manageable degree.

One question in particular, however, had yet to wane in its abundance. Each morning without fail, and without a change in her reply, they would ask, "How is your father?"

Their concern was genuine. She could see the emotion in their eyes; hear it in the hushed tones. She appreciated the sentiment, but the question stung each time it was asked. Her father's condition had not changed in seven weeks, and Danica hated the repeated reminder. Sometimes she wanted to scream out, "He's the same! If he was awake, would I be walking with my head down fighting back tears?"

More frustrating was that Marcus should be the one asking, and he was the only one who never did. Last week, after a night of too little sleep, Danica had erupted in anger with her brother. She had hurled harsh accusations at the boy; questioned his familial love.

Calm faced and even toned, Marcus had replied, "He's not ready to wake up, Dani. Everything's changing, and we need to be prepared for it. That's what Dad would want; not for us to sit and watch him sleep."

That was the last time she had spoken to Marcus beyond the pleasantries of "hello" and "goodbye." Not that she saw much of him anyway, devoted as he was to all things Torrance. In fact, the sole person Danica spoke with at any great length was Dr. Nysgaard. The tall Nordic woman seemed to understand Danica's feelings of loss and despondence. Thus, it was no surprise Danica found this morning's thought-filled wanderings had led her to the woman's quarters.

"Morning," Danica said as she hovered just outside the door.

Lost inside her own musings, the doctor took a moment before registering Danica's presence. "Good morning, Danica," Dr. Nysgaard replied, gesturing for the girl to enter.

Like Danica, Dr. Nysgaard had been ordained with an unspoken degree of preeminence among the forces gathered at Oberlin. The news had splashed her digital across the networks, labelling her a prime target of the Global Alliance. Moreover, Danica suspected the doctor's relationship with the cell leader, Gavin McAvoy, added to her importance.

"Did you sleep well?" the woman asked once Danica took a seat on the worn two-seater couch. Dr. Nysgaard's room was larger than most, and allowed for a small sitting area just before the arched divider leading to a "bedroom." Stacks of paper, mostly maps and blueprints, cluttered the small table and dominated much of the floor.

"Yes," Danica lied.

Smiling her awareness of the untruth, Dr. Nysgaard cautioned, "You need to take care of yourself, Danica. Down here, it's pretty much every man for himself. I can't have you collapsing on me. Are you eating?"

"I was on my way to get breakfast," she said. "And Corey brought me dinner last night."

"Oh really?" Dr. Nysgaard teased. "I'm jealous. He used to bring me my meals, you know. I guess he's got his eye on you now."

Normally Danica would have blushed if an adult had made such a hint, but she felt at ease with the doctor. Despite the difference in age, Dr. Nysgaard treated her as an equal.

"I doubt it," Danica replied with a roll of her eyes. She could understand why Corey, or any man for that matter, would desire the doctor. Now that the bruises had faded, Dr. Nysgaard once again resembled the digital Danica had seen on the news. Tall and lithe, with long waves of blonde tresses and skin as smooth as white marble, the doctor was the fantasy of most men. Danica judged her own appearance to be inferior.

In his efforts to disguise her, Torrance had hacked off great lengths of Danica's once auburn hair. The dye he had used had faded over the weeks, leaving her with centimeters of reddish roots ending in an equal measure of black strands. Though the pixie cut was growing out, it would take a year or more before her hair reached its former length.

Fingering the short strands, Danica thought, *At least now I have clothes that fit.*

"I think you looked beautiful with your hair short," Dr. Nysgaard announced as if reading Danica's mind. "I wish I had the guts to cut mine off," she added. "Long hair isn't really manageable when you're a wanted terrorist. Not a lot of salons in the underground, you know?"

Danica enjoyed a genuine laugh. This was why she appreciated the doctor's friendship. For a brief time, she could escape the sullen thoughts that plagued her mind. Dr. Nysgaard never asked about the girl's father. The omission was in no way malicious; she had spent meticulous hours attending to Philip Seton's recovery. The woman knew more about the condition of Danica's father than anyone else, and therefore did not need to burden Danica with well-intentioned inquiries regarding his status.

"Don't complain," Danica said with mock frustration. "Your hair is one color. I'm walking around with a two-toned mess!"

With almost child-like energy, Dr. Nysgaard jumped from her chair and exclaimed, "I say we fix it!"

"What? You mean, right now?"

Crossing to a small desk, the doctor shuffled papers aside and produced a silver-sleek pair of shears. "Yes, right now," she answered. "I have some time before the morning briefing. My sister and I used to do each other's hair. We can at least trim off the black and shape the rest."

Seconds after agreeing, Danica traded the couch for a chair and watched as short wisps of black floated down to decorate both the floor and her lap.

They talked of silly things as the scissors clicked and snipped in steady cadence: mutual enjoyment of popular holovision shows, movies each had seen before the chaos had entered their lives. And, of course, boys. No matter how well Danica steered the conversation in a different direction, Dr. Nysgaard worked Corey Branson back into the amiable chatter.

"You have to admit he's attractive, in a charming boyish way," the woman cajoled. "He's not much older than you."

Seeing no way to further avoid the admission, Danica relented. She did indeed find the Ignota scout good-looking; an opinion formed the first time she had seen him. Well, perhaps not the first time, given the bedlam of the situation. But, once events had settled (strange how fugitives in a safehouse now felt "settled" to her), Danica recognized Corey's appeal.

"It doesn't matter anyway," she said as the doctor made some final adjustments. "With my dad still . . . asleep, and Marcus doing whatever Marcus is doing, and the whole world falling apart, what should I do? Start dating?"

Dr. Nysgaard crouched low in front of her and enveloped Danica's hands in her own. "Danica, I lost my father a few years ago and it nearly killed me. So, I can't say I'd be doing anything different if I were in your place. But, your father is alive. And not just medically. From every test I was able to run, there's no reason to believe he won't wake up. I've seen similar cases when a person has suffered extreme trauma. Sometimes the brain just needs time to recover."

"He's not ready to wake up," Danica repeated her brother's words while fighting the heavy wetness in her eyes. "Marcus said that to me last week."

"I think your brother is right. When I said 'it's every man for himself' before, it means finding your own ways to be happy, too. I know your dad, and he would not want you running yourself down waiting for something you can't speed up. You're right. The world is falling apart. But, if you can find something, someone who makes it a little less scary then you should allow yourself that."

Now, the tears did run.

"Like you have with Gavin?" Danica asked.

Dr. Nysgaard's milk perfect skin reddened at the cheeks as she smiled. "Yes, like I have with Gavin."

"Have what with Gavin?" As if the mentioned name was a summons, the man himself passed through the open door. His brows lifted in confusion once his eyes surveyed the unusual scene. "You running a spa on the side?"

"Just a little girl time," Dr. Nysgaard replied. Danica noticed the glow of the woman's features when she addressed the cell leader. To Danica she said, "Oh, you have a bit of hair here," and wiped away the remaining tears from the girl's face.

"Meeting's about to start," Gavin said, gallantly ignoring the emotions of the room.

Lifting herself up, Dr. Nysgaard asked, "Danica, when was the last time you went outside?"

It took a moment to recall, and with surprise she replied, "Not since we got here."

"Gavin, would it be safe if Corey took Danica up to get some fresh air and sunlight?" the doctor asked as she gave Danica a mischievous wink.

After a hasty shower, rushed more due to the lukewarm water than any real time constraint, Danica took a moment to examine her newly shorn hair. While short, the look was a vast improvement over the inexperienced styling skills of Torrance. She made a mental note to thank Dr. Nysgaard when next the two were together. Selecting a laundered pair of dark denim and a lightweight gray knit sweater, Danica dressed and set out to meet Corey Branson at the main entrance to the underground complex.

The Ignota scout smiled as she approached. Having none of the muscular bulk of Torrance or the cell leader Gavin McAvoy, Corey possessed a build somewhere between lanky and athletic. Some centimeters taller than she, Danica imagined the young man's appearance would have been quite common on a college campus. *College,* Danica laughed to herself, *I guess that's off the list now, too.*

"All set?" he asked in greeting. *Was there a slight catch of nerves in his voice?*

"I think so," she replied. "Do I need a . . . I don't know, a gun or something? Whenever people go up, I see them take guns. So, I wasn't sure if I should have one. I've only held a gun a few times. And I've never fired one, so even if I took one with me, I don't know that it'd be much good."

Oh my Truth! Stop rambling and shut up!

Corey smiled and shook his head. "No. Oberlin is still pretty safe. For now, at least. There was an Alliance patrol two towns over a few weeks back, but nothing within fifty kilometers."

"Oh, good then," Danica returned, still berating herself for her nervous chatter.

"Follow me."

A short metal staircase, wide enough for three people across, sat at the far end of the tunnel. Ducking low once they neared the top, Corey rapped a sequence of knocks on the heavy wood slab covering the passage. Hazy lines of dust fell from the seams as unseen hands lifted the panel from above. Familiar faces welcomed them "topside," as if the pair was emerging from a ship.

"How's it looking today?" Corey asked one of the men.

"Skies'a'cleah," the Ignota guard replied. His heavy Texan accent delivered the answer in one word.

Nodding, Corey informed, "We'll be about an hour," and then led Danica forward.

Still dazed when she had first arrived at the town and its hidden shelter, she had not realized how well disguised the entrance had been. The room itself, situated in the basement of a small home, was furnished much like any common family room. A small holovision platform in one corner, comfortable –looking couches and chairs along the perimeter, and shelves decorated with family digitals of the house's occupants. By the time Danica reached the stairwell rising to the first floor, the men had replaced the shelter's hatch door, unfurled an ornate rug, and placed a low coffee table at its center. No sign of a terrorist shelter remained, even to her aware eyes.

Passing through the upstairs kitchen and out the home's rear door, Danica frowned at the dark clouds and the steady rain they poured down.

"I thought he said the skies were clear?" she asked.

Corey lifted an umbrella above their heads, and replied, "Clear of patrols."

Though his tone held no condescension, Danica felt foolish. *Genius, why would a guard be giving weather reports?*

"If you don't want to be out in the rain, we can go back," he offered with noticeable disappointment.

Even if such a thought had crossed her mind, the first breath of fresh air was too intoxicating to resist. Once a distance runner for her high school's track and field team, Danica was used to training in less than agreeable weather. In fact, she rather enjoyed it. On a kilometers-long run, rain was a welcome coolant to the heat of exertion. And, again, there was the air.

Seven weeks below ground had tricked her senses into believing the staleness of the shelter was the norm. Breathing the fresh crisp scent of late fall, with its sweet musk of falling leaves and slight chill, was a baptism of nature. Swooning, Danica said, "No, this is perfect."

The fear of discovery faded as the two walked along the paved sidewalks of the small town. Her past forays into populated areas had not ended well. Perhaps sensing her initial unease, Corey detailed some of Oberlin's long history with the Ignota.

"Gavin's great-grandfather, Seamus, was a Founder of the Ignota. He established his first cell in Oberlin. Now, most of the families living here are descendants of that cell."

"An Ignota city," Danica added. It was challenging to maintain her focus on Corey's words. Huddled close under the umbrella, the aura of his youthful strength was as heady as the air.

"Pretty much. And even though not everyone's an active member, they're proud of their history and keep the secret. Hey, you hungry?"

Realizing the morning's unexpected events had preempted her breakfast, Danica confessed to being rather starved. Declaring the café four blocks over had the best blueberry waffles she would ever taste, Corey switched his grasp of the umbrella and took her hand. An electric spark of excitement coursed through her at the small gesture.

Unbeknownst to her parents, Danica had gone on a handful of dates over the previous year. Though none had been worthy of much celebration, she was not inexperienced in terms of sex. Or, at least, the intimate acts which often led to intercourse. Her two closest girlfriends has boasted of "doing it" with their respective boyfriends. Danica, however, had twice declined the same opportunity. Her restraint owed nothing to old-fashioned views of virginity, but instead a lack of self-esteem.

"I'm telling you, best waffles ever," Corey said as he closed the umbrella and held the café door open for her. Blushing at her distracting thoughts, Danica stepped into the quaint eatery.

Henney's Twenties, as the three-dimensional holograph projected above the rear wall named it, was decorated in the style of forty years past. Tables and chairs, booths and fixtures, all in a milky opal, contrasted with the nostalgic lighted walls. Shades of green, blue, and yellow, and all the hues in between them, were fading and melding in steady progression along the panels; giving *Henney's Twenties* a sort of visual pulse and rhythmic throb.

A more than plump, middle-aged woman, with enough extra weight to jiggle as she walked, left the table of customers nearest the kitchen and made her way over to Corey and Danica.

"Well, took three days, but I guess someone's stomach made him return," the woman said in a voice too soft and childlike to accommodate her years and size.

Raising his hands in a show of playful remorse and self-defense, Danica's escort answered, "Henney, you fed me so much last time I didn't get hungry again until today!"

Filling two glasses with orange juice, the proprietress cocked a brow and made quick study of Corey. "Please, you're still just skin and bones. But, we'll fix that this morning. And who's this lovely . . . oh! Ms. Seton, I almost didn't recognize you without your long hair. You're even prettier in person. That's why I hate digitals. They never do a person justice. And I always end up looking fat!"

Danica stumbled with a reply.

"That was a joke, dear. You can't be famous for your waffles and be skinny at the same time."

Forcing a nervous laugh, Danica said, "I guess that's true. Oh, I don't mean that's why you're fat! I mean not that you're fat! I mean, with the waffles and the syrup, and . . ." *Stop talking! Stop talking right now!* Her brain obeyed and forced her jaw to snap shut.

Laughing, Henney said, "As nervous as a virgin on her honeymoon. Sweet, too. No wonder Corey keeps talking about you."

Having been drinking his juice during Danica's torment, Corey gagged and sputtered at the woman's last words. Danica tried to hide her smile behind her hand as she watched him fumble with a napkin to wipe the beverage from his face.

"Well, that should even it up," the woman said with a grin. "Batter's fresh, so order when you're ready." With that, she waddled her way over to another table of diners, leaving the pair in their mutual embarrassment.

Struggling to recover some dignity, Corey said, "So, now you've met Henney."

Danica, feeling much emboldened by the exchange, said, "You've been talking about me, huh?" Tanned as his skin was, she could still see his cheeks color. *Now it's even,* she thought in amusement.

"Well, I, um," he said before clearing his throat. "I've probably mentioned you before. You know, in passing once or twice."

Believing Corey had suffered enough, Danica looked down at the menu in the glass tabletop. The small town café had limited offerings: burgers and sandwiches for later meals, and the much-acclaimed selection of waffles for breakfast. Tapping the glass to place her order, Danica chose a serving of blueberry waffles with a side of bacon. The digitals of each item set her mouth to watering.

A few brief moments of awkward silence passed before Henney delivered the dishes to their table. From the first bite, Danica discovered Corey's description of the waffles was not misplaced boast. Even if the meals prepared in the Ignota shelter had not been bland, she still would have thought the waffles heavenly.

"Wow," she said through a full mouth.

"I told you," Corey laughed, pleased she was enjoying the breakfast.

Recalling her manners, Danica swallowed and asked, "How long have you been coming to Oberlin?"

"Couple years. When I joined the Ignota, Gavin brought me here to train. Any time we need to lay low for a long stretch, we come to Oberlin."

Danica wondered if her future included similar stays in Oberlin, or perhaps permanent residency. There had been ongoing debate among the cells, and especially between Gavin McAvoy and Torrance, over the resistance's next actions. Some urged action, while others advocated patience. On any given day, McAvoy (and by default Dr. Nysgaard) and Torrance voiced support for both ideas, usually in opposition to the other man. More than once, the tension between the two men had nearly come to physical confrontation. Unsure of her own status, guest of the Ignota or full member, Danica feared she would be forced to one day choose between the two factions. Follow Torrance who had risked his life to protect the Seton siblings, or Dr. Nysgaard who had been treating their father for almost two months? *And then there's him*, she added as she looked at Corey.

Some change in her expression caused the scout to ask, "Something wrong?"

Dispelling the worrisome thoughts, she forced a smile and replied, "No, I just . . . it's nothing." Would she be one of those girls who make decisions based on a few smiles from a boy?

Accepting her ruse, he began to ask, "So what do you—"

"Corey," Henney's girlish voice broke in from the kitchen. Bustling towards the table in what might have been a comical jog if not for her dire expression, the woman said, "My sister in Lorain just called. She said PKs just entered the city."

"How many?" he inquired. The tone of his voice had dropped all of its soft charm, and reminded Danica of the older, more hardened men of the Ignota.

"All she said was 'the milk's gone sour.' It's our code. But, from her voice I could tell she was nervous."

"Lorain's less than twenty kilometers from here," the scout replied, worry now edging into his words. "They've never been that close before. If they sweep south, the PKs can reach Oberlin in less than a half hour. Henney, get word to Gavin and the others. Tell them I'm heading up to scout. Can you make sure Danica gets back to the shelter?"

"I can go with you," Danica announced. *You can what?* the wiser part of her mind shouted.

"No," Corey said. "It's too dangerous."

"You're just going to scout, right? I snuck onto a PK military base with Torrance. And if something happens to you, someone needs to get back here to let the others know what's happening in Lorain."

In his eyes, she could see him struggling with indecision. Whatever swayed him—her words, his feelings, or the ticking clock—Corey nodded his agreement. Not two minutes later, the pair was seated in a podcar and traveling north out of Oberlin.

CHAPTER TWO

Sonje Nysgaard

It had been a simple thing, the brief time spent trimming the girl's hair, but for Sonje the interaction had been a soothing balm to her worried mind. Despite the surroundings, despite the situation, the world had almost felt right once again. Almost.

"How's she doing?" Gavin asked as they walked from her room.

Shrugging, she replied, "Considering everything she's been through, I'd say she's holding up pretty well. Her mother is dead, her father's unresponsive, and she's been in hiding for months. Danica's young, but tougher than she thinks."

Ignota going about their daily tasks filled the halls of the overcrowded safehouse. One need not be empathic to detect the growing restlessness among the men and women living underground. Sonje knew it was not uncommon for soldiers, trained for battle, for action, to suffer when kept idle for too long. The results of the daily cell leader briefings would generate a buzz of excitement until the dismay of further inaction came along.

"And the boy?" Gavin asked while nodding acknowledgement to fellow Ignota.

"He's . . . odd. Very quiet, very withdrawn. I met him twice while working with Philip, so I don't know if it's trauma or just his normal personality. He's been spending most of his time with Torrance."

"Reason enough to be traumatized," the cell leader muttered.

Though Gavin had suggested Torrance join the Ignota, he had come to regret the offer. There had been a noticeable tension between the two men quite early on. They tested and prodded each other, much as two alphas might vie for control of the pack. Sonje, however, did not believe Torrance had any desire to join the Ignota, much less lead one of its cells. The man seemed to distrust the group as a whole, while reserving particular animosity for Gavin. Sonje hoped this morning's briefing would be less contentious.

Gavin resented the other man's presence at the meetings, but could voice no complaint. Sonje was not a cell leader, yet the group had likewise extended an invitation to her.

"You can't let him get to you," she cautioned, knowing it was as useful as teaching a pig to fly. If Gavin intended to reply, the moment was lost once they walked into the briefing.

Seven cell leaders had already taken their seats around the large oval table. The remaining chairs filled as Sonje, Gavin, the final three leaders, and Torrance filed into the room. Sonje, placing herself between Gavin and Torrance, smile at two men across the table. Camorata and Marshall, as opposite in outlook as they were in appearance, had been part of the assault on the PK base. Thus, Sonje felt an easy kinship with the men. *We went to battle together, and survived,* she thought.

"What do we have for updates?" Thompson Fielder asked from one end of the table. A few thin wisps of gray covered the man's nearly bald head, and even those grew only along the sides and back. Nearing sixty years of age, his skin bore the deep creases of worry and stress. Sonje could see the beginnings of a thick scar on his cheek before it disappeared into a full beard. The most senior of the gathered group, Fielder had become its unofficial commander.

Marshall was the first to answer, his voice booming as always. "My scouts returned last night. Three cells in Missouri have been taken. But, they did make contact with two in Indiana. Both have gone underground. The few Fifths my men discovered had little intel on the PKs' movements, save that they're pressing inland from each coast."

It had become difficult to find Fifths, the Ignota operatives living and working in the world while funneling information to cells. Whether already rounded up by Peacekeeper troops, or in fear of exposure, the Fifths, and by proxy the Ignota's communication network, had gone dark.

"Pretty much the same in the South," added cell leader Peter Yan. "More cells destroyed than found. The Fifths are still fairly active down there though. We've got about a dozen names of Alliance agents overseeing the SID implantation."

After failing to retrieve the damning evidence Sonje and Philip Seton had compiled, the Global Alliance had announced a delay in the SID upgrade. The government had cited a minor design flaw as the reason for the schedule readjustment. Two days ago, a press conference announced the chips were ready for implantation. In one month's time, the upgrade process would commence. While the delay had been a minor victory for the Ignota, Sonje doubted any recalibration of the SIDs had occurred in the interim.

"What about you, Sam?" Fielder asked the lone female cell leader. Samitha Borden had sent her trio of scouts west to California weeks ago, and the team was now two days overdue in its return.

"No word, yet," she replied.

"We have to assume they're lost," Marshall added. "Which means our location might be compromised."

Sam Borden said, "My people won't talk! If they saw capture as inevitable, they . . . they would have taken appropriate measures."

Suicide, Sonje understood. Among the Ignota there existed an unspoken creed of "death before capture." The identities and locations of cell members were too valuable to risk divulging under the Alliance's expert torture. *These are hard people,* she thought, wondering if she could take her own life if faced with the decision.

The other leaders shared their respective updates, most detailing similar findings from their scouting patrols. Sonje feared she would grow numb to hearing the same disheartening news each day. Even scientifically trained, it was a challenge to think of lost cells with objective abstraction. *Every day starts with the news of more dead Ignota.*

"The only actionable intel we have then," Gavin said, "is these Alliance agents. Pete, you said we have a dozen names? Then, we should greenlight targeted assassinations. Taking out those agents will delay the SID implantations in those areas."

Several cell leaders voiced agreement until Torrance murmured, "For a day."

Sonje steeled herself for the impending argument.

"Excuse me?" Gavin asked leaning forward to address the man at Sonje's right.

Making no move to meet the other man's hot stare, Torrance instead directed his reply to Fielder. "Taking out twelve people won't stop the Alliance. They'll simply fill the position in an hour's time. If that. You want to know why your spies aren't talking? They see no reason to. It's been two months since you people made any kind of noise. Two months for the Alliance to report on the success of dismantling your operation."

Sonje was very aware of the man's use of "you" and "your." *He doesn't see himself as one of us.*

"What do you suggest?" Fielder asked. His tone suggested a deep respect for the solitary man. *Gavin's right. They see him as a hero. But, he has no real ties to us. If we fail, if we die, he'll just go back to living in his caves.*

"Hit the supplies, not the suppliers," Torrance responded with command.

Gavin delivered a sarcastic guffaw. "Every report we have says those SIDs are more heavily guarded than the Council itself. We don't have the manpower or the weaponry for a direct assault of that scale."

"As long as your cells are scattered, you never will," Torrance snapped back. That assessment of the Ignota's modus operandi sent the room into loud conflict.

Camorata, fearful of any overt action without a guarantee of complete success, shouted, "The Ignota has survived because it is scattered! The Founders knew the risks of massing as a group was too great. Our success is owed to their wisdom!"

"What success?" Sonje heard Torrance mutter beneath the din, too low for the others to hear.

Marshall lent his support to the other cell leader's protest. "Cam's right. If the Ignota cells came together, the Alliance could wipe out the entire resistance with one battle. What you're suggesting is lunacy. It'd be the end of the Ignota!"

Peter Yan and Sam Borden kept their opinions to themselves. Sonje studied the two, wondering if their silence indicated agreement with Torrance, or if they thought the other leaders had sufficiently argued the opposition.

Fielder lifted his voice above the others, managing to overcome even Marshall's overbearing volume. "While there may be some merit to the idea, son, what you're proposing goes against over a hundred years of strategy. Even if the cells wanted to come together, it'd be near to impossible. For every cell we know about, there're likely five more secreted away."

"So you hope," Torrance replied.

Unwilling to consider the possibility of error, Fielder pressed on; his face more tense than before. "There is another issue to address. One I'd prefer to ignore, but that ship has sailed, and sunk. Most of us have members in our cells who believe in certain things."

Sonje's stomach tightened.

"Now, I'm not here to judge the beliefs of others," Fielder spoke as if his tongue danced across a floor of glass shards.

"Sowilo," stated Peter Yan. "You can say the name, Fielder. We are not ashamed of our beliefs."

Sonje had not realized the cell leader was a member of the fanatical sect. During their few interactions, Yan had seemed quite levelheaded, friendly even; nothing at all like Sonje's past experience with Sowilo faithful.

"Very well," Fielder said. "The Sowilo here, and above in Oberlin, have heard pieces of what occurred within your cell, Gavin. There's been talk, obviously, of the two Sowilo who died. For me, cells are like ships. The captain runs his crew, and each ship is sovereign – its internal affairs are its own business. With two months of nothing to do, gossip and rumor have become the favored pastime here. A full account of the events of two months ago might help to quell any growing . . . anxiety."

Sonje wondered what word the man had intended to use at the end. Swallowing and wetting her lips, she was about to respond when Gavin stilled her words by placing his hand atop her own.

"As you said," Gavin began, "a cell's business is its own. The Sowilo have no authority to compel me, or anyone else for that matter," Sonje knew he meant that bit for her, "to discuss past events. If members of my cell have questions, I'd be happy to answer them. Beyond that, there's nothing else to say."

Yan said, "So, we're to get no answers on deaths of the only two Sowilo members of your cell?"

"If the Sowilo are so concerned about death, then maybe they should stop blowing themselves up," Gavin bit back in anger.

Though Sonje flinched at the words, Peter Yan showed no reaction as he replied, "I've heard only one, your brother, made that sacrifice. The rumors suggest Adirene was killed by Dr. Nysgaard."

"Then you should be thanking her," Torrance growled next to Sonje. Startled to hear the man speaking in her defense, she felt a wave of panic when she took in the stare the man leveled at Yan. Lions appeared less predatory, less dangerous. She almost pitied Peter Yan as the cell leader withered under the challenging gaze.

"Your cult member betrayed her cell, killed one member and nearly another, and compromised its mission. I don't know where you're from, man, but I'll be Truth-damned if she didn't get what she deserved. If I were you, I'd be happy no one thinks she represents the intentions of your whole group."

The words, and their implied threat, hung in the air thicker than a heavy morning fog. Yan did his best to meet Torrance's stare, but he conceded the battle and lowered his eyes in defeat. In a near whisper, Fielder signaled the end of the briefing. Even if there had been more business to discuss, the mood of the room had deteriorated beyond repair.

Torrance was the first to rise and exit; his movements measured and precise. Again, the image of a jungle cat stalking through the brush flashed in Sonje's mind. The others made their own departures, with haste. Before Sonje and Gavin reached the door, Fielder placed a hand on her forearm.

""I'm sorry about that, Dr. Nysgaard," the man offered with sincerity. "And you, too, Gavin. I'd hoped the gossip would die down, but—"

"It's okay," Sonje replied. She lowered her voice even though the other cell leaders were well beyond the range of hearing. "I understand. What will Peter and the Sowilo do now?"

"Yan's not as fanatical as some of the others," Fielder explained. "Probably why he was able to form his own cell. No one seems to know what to make of Torrance, but I sure wouldn't want to be the one to cross him. Yan will let it drop; he's smart enough to know we don't need internal divisions. The other Sowilo will follow his lead."

"Let's hope so," Gavin added.

The veteran offered a forlorn smile and took his leave.

"I'm going to check on Philip," Sonje told Gavin. "Meet you for lunch?"

"Sounds good," he replied and give her cheek a soft kiss.

Watching him walk down the hall, she felt a twist of guilt. *It was not a complete lie*, she rationalized. She would stop into Seton's room to review his status, but first she wanted to speak with Torrance. *If Gavin knew her true destination, he would have insisted on accompanying her. And the two of them would have locked horns,* she mused. *This schoolyard feud is getting tiresome!*

Knowing just where to find him, Sonje made her way through the overcrowded complex. Her first explorations below Oberlin had been confusing twists and turns. Now, though, she was able to navigate the halls with little thought. *How quickly we adjust!* She had performed countless surgeries during her residency—attaching biorobotic prosthetic arms and legs—and the speed with which her patients had mastered the new limbs had awed her. *As much as we dislike change, humans can adapt when forced to.*

Correct in her assumption, she found Torrance in the shelter's modest weight room. Crude benches and stacks of black metal free-weights littered the hard concrete floor. Whoever had designed and furnished the facility had had enough foresight to plan for a soldier's needs. At most times, the room was filled with men, and a few women, grunting and sweating through presses, lunges, and curls. Sonje herself had been a frequent visitor due to Kunbo's insistence.

"You have speed, Dr. Sonje," the African weapons master, and her appointed trainer, had said. "But, a child has more strength and endurance."

Recalling her final encounter with Adirene – when the burning exhaustion in her legs, arms, and lungs nearly sealed her doom – Sonje knew the man was right. The first gym sessions had been grueling; Kunbo never seemed to train lightly. But as the weeks wore on, she felt new reserves of strength build within her. The greater surprise, however, was the relief exertion brought. It seemed paradoxical, yet her hours in the gym were more relaxing than the idle time she spent sitting in her quarters.

"When the body is engaged, the mind can be quiet," Kunbo had explained. Once again, the man was right.

Entering the room, placed some distance from where people slept, Sonje found the space deserted save for Torrance. *Not surprising,* she thought. *Everyone's either too scared to be near him, or too respectful to bother him.*

Stripped to the waist, with the barest sheen of sweat beginning to glisten, Torrance had his back to her as he dipped into low squats. The weights he held in each hand looked impossibly heavy. *I'd be lucky if I could lift even one of those dumbbells, using both hands.* And while the weights, and near prefect form, were impressive, it was the man's back that drew Sonje's eyes. Countless scars crisscrossed every inch of skin; shoulder to shoulder, nape to waist. Some were paper thin, but the greater majority was thicker than her finger and twice as long. They were old scars; stretched taut over the years as the body had grown from boyhood and pulled the marks flatter. She had seen the like once before, during a rotation in the emergency room, when a little girl, not yet seven years old, had been rushed in. Now, as then, Sonje wondered, *Who could be so cruel? Who could whip a child so mercilessly?*

"Admiring the view, Doctor?" Torrance's voice cut into her thoughts.

"I . . . how did you know I was here?" she asked, realizing he had not yet turned around.

Returning the dumbbells to their appropriate place, he replied, "If you were trying to sneak up on me, you'll need to walk a lot quieter. And stop using shampoo scented with vanilla."

"I wasn't trying to sneak up on you."

"Clearly," the man returned, turning to face her.

Not for the first time, Sonje thought she caught a fleeting resemblance between Torrance and Gavin. *The same prominent jaw, the same high, defined cheekbones. Even their eyes are the same pale blue color.* But, as much as the eyes matched in hue, the emotions within could not have diverged at a greater angle. The warmth of a clear summer sky filled Gavin's, while the ones studying her from across the room were the child of ice and steel.

"You're staring again, Doctor. Keep it up and people may start to talk," he said.

Sonje had had enough encounters with him, and had heard enough stories related by others, to know this was part of his method—keeping people on edge, unsettled. She was frustrated to admit it was working. A biting reply fought to be unleashed, but Sonje choked it down. *I didn't tell Gavin I was coming here because I didn't want this to be confrontational,* her mind reminded.

"As I learned this morning, there's no shortage of that down here," she said, returning to her original purpose. "I wanted to thank you, for what you said at the briefing. Defending me the way you did, it meant a great deal."

Had she blinked, Sonje would have missed the fractional thawing in the man's eyes. *How sad,* she thought. *He is so damaged, kindness unsettles him.*

"No one else seemed to be defending you," Torrance replied. "They declare themselves at war, but are too afraid to engage the enemy."

Tucking away his first comment for later thought, Sonje countered, "Assassinating Alliance agents *is* engaging the enemy."

A wry sneer broke across Torrance's pale face. "Is that why you were shouting me down with the others?"

"My silence doesn't mean I agreed with you."

"Doesn't it?" he asked. "You're not like them, Doctor. You're not caught up in a hundred years of 'this is how it's always been.' They think existing means success. We both know there's a difference between surviving and succeeding."

As a doctor and a scientist, she understood the point well. Even the most lauded practitioners in her field had experienced informing a patient of a failed procedure. She remembered how hollow the words of encouragement had felt on her tongue; when in truth she was saying, "You'll never walk again, but, hey, at least you're alive." Yes, there was a wide gulf separating survival and success.

"Fielder's right, though. Even if we wanted to, we don't have the resources to attack the SID shipments," Sonje repeated the cell leader's opposing argument.

Torrance nodded, but his eyes never broke away from hers. *Has he even blinked yet?* Everything about him teased cold fingers along her spine. He was not simply standing and speaking with her. He was frozen. There were no hand gestures as he spoke; instead, his arms dangled at his sides. Only the muscles needed to speak, to nod, seemed active. Everything else appeared to be in stasis. Sonje knew it took years, decades, of focus and skill, practice and determination, to master the body in such a manner. Never before had she met a man who could be so disconcerting by standing still.

"One of the first rules of war," Torrance responded, "is to divide the enemy, isolate them. Your lot is saving the Alliance the trouble. There are eleven cells, with eleven leaders who will never agree on one course of action."

"So, the Ignota should all follow one leader? Who then? You?"

Laughing under his breath, Torrance said, "No. Maybe it should be your boy. Everyone's been treating McAvoy like royalty." He spat the surname like a curse.

"Why are you here, Torrance?" Sonje asked with narrowed eyes. "I mean, you don't consider yourself one of us. Danica and Marcus are safe now. Why are you still here?"

The query appeared to catch him off guard, though he recovered enough to change his words. "I haven't chosen who. . . I have my reasons."

"Does it have to do with the man who gave you those scars?" Sonje could not explain why the question fell from her lips, but regret filled her after it did. She was sure the room's temperature had plunged several degrees as an impenetrable barrier of icy distance formed around Torrance. She tried, and failed, to fight a shiver as he stepped close to her, dipping his head so his lips nearly pressed against her ear.

"Careful now, Doctor. Some answers come with a price," he growled. Then added, "Your boy doesn't look too happy."

Shaking, Sonje turned to find Gavin standing just beyond the weight room door. His expression was tight, and very grim. She could only imagine what he made of the scene – Torrance shirtless, pressed close to her, and she caught in a lie. There was no doubt he had heard Gavin's approach, and had used her to antagonize him. *And punish me for prying too deep.* She wanted to scream at her foolishness. *I came to thank him, to be civilized! But he's nothing but a wild dog.*

Gavin kept his voice level as he said, "PKs have been sighted in Lorain. We may need to evacuate. Thought you should know." Message delivered, he turned on his heels and stalked down the hall.

Sonje swallowed hard, refusing to allow Torrance to see the anger in her eyes, and followed after Gavin.

CHAPTER THREE

Tilden Garrott

Removing his fingers from the play-piece, the carved marble bishop produced a soft ting against the chessboard's matching surface; the sound echoing off the stone walls of his prison cell. *Three more moves,* Tilden thought. He had been surprised to find a player among his captors, much less one with better than average skill. Even still, Tilden had to lose the occasional match to keep his opponent interested in future play.

The opponent, an Ignota strongman of French heritage named Etienne, studied the landscape of the chessboard. Tilden hid his smile as he watched the terrorist deliberate. Two options remained; one logical, the other far bolder and the first step in a long play to victory. Lacking even a hint of foresight or guile, Tilden knew which the man would choose. Even before Etienne himself.

Beyond keeping his mind occupied, Tilden used these engagements to collect information on his captors. He was circumspect in his probing. Anything overt and they would have isolated him further. As it was, Tilden had no idea how many days had passed since he had last felt the sun's warmth on his face. His meals arrived at irregular intervals; sometimes lunch and dinner came together, other times it seemed a full day had passed between them. The growth of his patchy beard provided some means of measuring time. Until they began shaving it. Thus, it became impossible to track the passage of time, and he had long since stopped trying.

Even his location was a mystery. The Ignota had moved him five, no, six times now. For each relocation, they had placed a thick hood over his head to block out all light. Tilden suspected more than one of the supposed "relocations" had been staged; driving for hours in a podcar only to return to their point of origin. He would not have believed the denial of time and location could so fray a man's thoughts. The chess matches now also served to keep him sane.

For his part, Etienne was an amiable fellow, if rather coarse. Tilden had attempted to converse in the man's native tongue, but the Ignotum's speech was more of the bastardized Arabic[2] than Tilden's classically trained ear could translate. While the situation (and their respective backgrounds) prevented any true friendship, Tilden found he did enjoy the man's company. *It's a shame he will die,* the last Garrott thought.

Etienne made the predicted move, sacrificing his rook in the hopes to save his queen in a future gambit that would never come. Feigning consternation, Tilden allowed some minutes to pass before positioning his knight. It would be the king's bishop in the end to close the trap of checkmate.

Tilden could relate to the piece; not as powerful as the rook—the strongman, the Etienne, of the board—the bishop was forced to attack from the side. If he were to escape, Tilden would need to do the same. Untrained in combat, he had no delusions of overcoming his guards through raw strength. No, he would come at them from the side. Intellect and patience would be his weapons. Liam Walford, the Family's chief advisor, had spent countless hours instructing the House heir in the art of manipulation and subterfuge. Though there may not be a House to reclaim, Tilden had sworn his oath of vengeance.

The method of his release, however, sickened him. He must become one of them, become an Ignotum. If even in name only, the idea turned his stomach. Liam had also instilled in him a red hatred of the terrorist rebels. But, he would win their trust until all they saw was a dedicated follower. *Correction,* his inner voice reminded, *a dedicated and* indispensable *follower!* He had already begun the con; feeding his captors details, exploitable weaknesses, of the other Families. The remaining members of the Council of Five were as much his enemy as the Ignota. If his information manipulated the two sides into doing each other harm, then all the better.

The sown seeds of his scheme were already beginning to show quick and growth. The various guards who ensured his continued captivity had gone from referring to him as "the prisoner" to calling him "Garrott." Some, like Etienne, even used his given name. Initially silent while on duty, his minders had taken to conversing with each other. They never talked of anything with tactical importance, just idle banter. Lately, they had even included Tilden in the chatter. Also, his meal portions had improved in both quality and quantity. That one was deliberate; conditioning him to enjoy rewards for divulging Council secrets. All small gains, but gains nonetheless.

As for the secrets themselves, he shared nothing that would give the Ignota irrevocable leverage among the world's population. Some of the things he knew were so incredulous, so shocking; their minds could not even conceive the right questions to ask. Thus, he appeared to his Ignota captors as forthcoming, holding nothing back. Once free, however, he would use those well-kept secrets to topple

---

2 After the last surge of Arab immigration into France during the late 21st century, Franco-Arabic (initially considered slang) became an officially recognized language in the year 2104. It was also at this time the crescent moon and star had been added to the French flag. While uncommon in the ruling class, Franco-Arabic is widespread among the lower and middle income citizens of France. – M.S.

the Council. They would see him as the world's savior, and he would bow his head in humble acceptance as they demanded he lead the rudderless Alliance. *That is how I will avenge you, Father. There will be no Council. There will only be the Garrotts!*

Thoughts of his family, and the murderous fate which had befallen them, tightened like a fist around his heart. Turning them aside lest the pain show on his face, Tilden followed Etienne's final move with the long planned placement of his bishop.

"Checkmate," he said to the Ignotum, adding the false shock of success to his voice.

"Ah, you are too good for me, Tilden," the man replied. "You improve while I seem to grow worse by the day."

Tilden made a silent note to lose the next few matches.

"Time for another?" he asked.

"I cannot," Etienne said as he pushed his chair back from the small table that he had brought in for the match. "In fact it will be a few days before we can play again."

"Does it take that long for your wounded pride to heal?" Tilden asked with a laugh. He hoped to draw more out of the man before he left.

"I didn't lose *that* badly," Etienne shared in the humor. "No, in the morning I leave with the next scouting detail."

So, it's evening, Tilden thought. "I trust you will be careful, my friend. I'd miss our games and conversation should you come to harm." He hoped he sounded sincere.

"My involvement is only precautionary. The PKs are still too focused on the cities. It will be some time before they start searching the countryside."

Ah, but what country would that be? Tilden searched for a way to elicit an answer to that question. Miming a shiver, he pressed, "The English countryside this late in the year? Too cold for my liking. Give me a winter in southern Italy instead, please." *Clumsy, but necessary.*

Laughing, the Ignotum rose and declared, "Hah! Even your summers are too cold, Englishman! I'll be relieved once we leave your wind and your cold far behind."

Ah, we are still in England. There was comfort in knowing he remained in the land of his birth. Tilden could have perhaps dug for more information, but he chose to bid adieu to the guard and wish him a safe journey. *Small victories, Til,* he told himself once again. *You must make do with small victories.*

As required, he shuffled to the far corner of the cell to allow Etienne and another guard to remove the small table and two chairs, as well as the lantern that had illuminated the men's chess game. Tilden let a thin smile cross his face, knowing the expanding shadows hid it even if the guards were looking. But they were not looking, and that was why he smiled. Either in trust of their prisoner or confidence in their strength, the guards turned their backs to him.

Not long now, he mused.

The metal door shut with a reverberating clang, and Tilden Garrott was once again alone in the darkness.

Not long now at all.

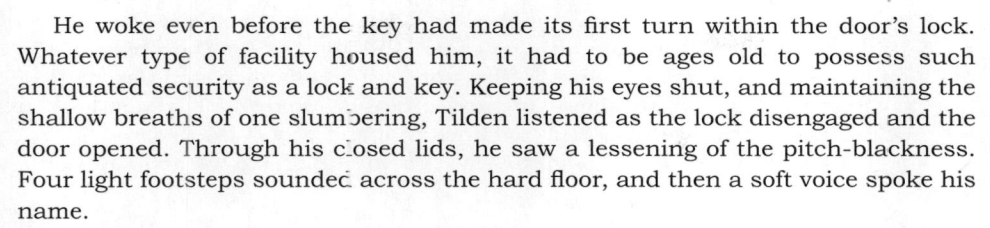

He woke even before the key had made its first turn within the door's lock. Whatever type of facility housed him, it had to be ages old to possess such antiquated security as a lock and key. Keeping his eyes shut, and maintaining the shallow breaths of one slumbering, Tilden listened as the lock disengaged and the door opened. Through his closed lids, he saw a lessening of the pitch-blackness. Four light footsteps sounded across the hard floor, and then a soft voice spoke his name.

"Tilden?"

Exquisite pain burned across his soul at the sound of her voice. He had never known it possible to love a woman so deeply, and yet despise her so entirely. Even with no calendar for accuracy, Tilden knew it had been several days since Isla had last visited him.

"Tilden," her whisper called out to him again. Remaining still, he heard her approach the sturdy cot serving as his bed. He wanted her to touch him, to feel her hand try to rouse him from supposed sleep. He wanted her to remember the many mornings they had shared before she had revealed her true nature.

He would be the first to say his many machinations were elaborate; some even unnecessary. Planning them, however, watching them enacted, reflecting on their efficacy, helped pass the idle hours of dark seclusion. Like chess, these little schemes strengthened his grip on sanity. *I won't let them have my mind, too.*

Letting the mild shaking of his shoulder last for a three count, Tilden opened his eyes. *Truth, but she is beautiful!* he thought upon seeing the actress's face. *Well, former actress,* he assumed. He doubted she had continued leading the double life after his kidnapping.

"Hey," he said, pretending grogginess.

"Hey," she replied in kind; the divide between captor and captive ignored for the moment. "I thought we could talk over breakfast."

"Sounds good to me," Tilden smiled and brought himself upright on the cot. Though loathe to admit it, this role of lovelorn suitor was rather easy to play. Easy and painful. Faced with her exotic beauty—freckled tanned skin, almond-shaped eyes, and glossed raven hair—he wondered if, in time, he might be able to forgive. But the thought faded with a blink. The blink of the eye she had been responsible for him losing. She had delivered the suicide bomber to his home. She had forced his father's attention away from the traps of the Council. She was as responsible as any for the downfall of House Garrott. *And she will pay along with all the others.*

"I've missed you," he said, accepting the square tray holding a plate of scrambled eggs, warm buttered toast, and a glass of chilled orange juice.

Sitting on a chair he had not heard her bring in, Isla Carene cast her eyes down to her lap. "I'd have come sooner, but Cleland thought it best if others took over your questioning."

And why might that be? Tilden asked. *Was he worried your feelings would impair your objectivity? What has changed now to bring you here?*

At first, Tilden had thought Isla the leader of this particular Ignota cell. And while the others jumped to obey, she was only second in command. The actual leader, one Cleland Bain, was a far crueler master. Only recently had the bruises from Bain's ordered beatings begun to fade from Tilden's body. Arrogant and hateful, the man's contempt for Tilden and all things Alliance blinded him. Liam Walford had often spoken of such men during his lectures. "Their power is tied to the fear they instill in others. Remove your fear, and you remove their power," the old Family mentor had said. "They are like storms: fierce, angry, and destructive, but they never last. You must simply endure until their time ends." Tilden wished Bain's time was nearing its end. And he hoped that end was painful.

"I'm glad you stayed away," Tilden told her. "I wouldn't have wanted you to see me that way . . . so broken."

"He shouldn't have done that to you," her voice grew hoarse. "You've been helpful, Tilden. Even Cleland has to admit that."

Laughing, he said, "I don't think that man would admit the sky is blue if he didn't want to. I'm still so new to this world of the Ignota, but I don't understand how such a person managed to rise as a leader. Father always said the best leaders were even-tempered, thinkers with control of their emotions. Probably why he liked you so much."

With a wry grin and crook of a brow, Isla replied, "Your father nearly bit my head off the first time we met."

Recalling the ill-fated gala, Tilden shrugged, "Only because you were an actress." *And what an actress you turned out to be.* "But, he was coming around. He actually approved when I told him I intended to propose. Besides, Mother liked you and he would never have challenged her opinion."

Tilden could barely stomach the blasphemy of speaking of his Family with one responsible for their murders. Even though his ploys were necessary, his soul felt unclean.

"You were going to propose?" she asked in genuine surprise.

Nodding, he said, "Yes. Just after the new year."

"Tilden," she began. Her voice was unsteady, a noticeable crack in her tone. Once the tears welling in her eyes would have mattered to him. Once. "I'm sorry for all of this. For—"

Reaching across the small space between them, Tilden tenderly enclosed her hands in his. "Shh. You never have to say that to me, Isla. You saved my life that day. What little I have left now, I owe to you." *How true!* "I loved you then, and I love you now. Nothing will change that. Not ever." He was impressed with how well he had delivered his lines. *You're not the only actor, darling.*

Isla slipped her right hand from his grasp and cupped the side of his face as tears fell down hers. "You still love me?"

"Yes," he lied. "Always." Then, gambling he was not pressing too far, he added, "And I know you feel the same. I wish we had—"

"What?"

"It's foolish, I know. But, I wish we had run away together before all this. No more Council, no more Ignota. Just you and me."

"If you had asked, I might have said yes, Tilden," Isla admitted through light sobs.

Is it wrong that I'm enjoying this so much?

"No, you wouldn't have. What you're doing here is too important to you, and I love that about you. When they interrogate me, I don't answer because of fear, I answer because I love you. You're all I have left, Isla. If the things I know, some weapons warehouse in the countryside, or a hidden account of credits in a bank, keeps you safe, then I will tell it all."

Too far? he wondered.

Taking back her hand to wipe her eyes, Isla said, "You're amazing, Tilden. I don't deserve you." Shaking the emotions from herself, she continued, "Truth, here I am crying like a fool while your breakfast gets cold. Cleland sent me to ask you questions, not blubber like a schoolgirl."

"Ask away," he smiled while taking a bite of toast.

The first several questions focused on the remaining Families and other various key figures in Council management. Tilden answered each honestly, though he inwardly despaired that his bait had not been successful. Finishing off the last of the meal, he returned the empty plate and glass to the tray.

When he thought the interview nearly concluded, Isla asked, "Is there truly a weapons warehouse in the countryside?"

Every fiber of his self-control fought to keep the smile from his face. *Liam would be proud,* Tilden mused as he spoke of the warehouse at length.

Leaving the chair and tray for the guards to remove, Isla sought her commander, Cleland Bain. Not surprisingly, the man was waiting for her in the room adjacent to Tilden's cell. He had been watching the interactions through the monitor.

"Impressive," he said in his scratched voice. "If that performance had been on the holoscreen, you'd be getting an award. I knew keeping you away from him would help to break him."

"We'll have to verify the existence of the warehouse," she replied.

"Naturally. Kieran and Lars will be out that way to scout. I'll have them check into it," Bain nodded. "But, you've got that man wrapped around your finger. I doubt he could lie to you if he tried. As long as he believes you love him, he'll be more than willing to cooperate. Well done, Isla."

Hearing the dismissal, Isla said, "Thank you, sir," and left the room. The session with Tilden had been relatively brief, but she felt thoroughly exhausted. Lately, exhaustion had become a permanent condition.

It felt like ages ago when Stevan Loranso, the leader of her former cell in Los Angeles, had activated her for the assignment. Four years playing the part of Hollywood starlet, Isla had been more than eager to finally serve a true purpose. The risks had been exhaustively reviewed—discovery meant death—and she had felt herself well prepared for infiltrating one of the Families. It was a slight surprise to learn her target was not a minor House name, but rather the heir to House Garrott himself. The greater surprise, however, was realizing she had developed feelings for the target.

Tilden was caring and kind; so unlike the monster she had assumed all members of a Family must be. Even now, after he had learned of her true allegiance, he looked upon her with love-filled eyes. And she loved him in return.

Perhaps it's not too late for us, she silently hoped. The Alliance had murdered his family, taken his wealth and position. Surely, he must harbor feelings of vengeance for the Council. He certainly had offered detailed intelligence; intelligence which harmed the Council. Perhaps it was not too late. Perhaps she could sway him to join the Ignota. Perhaps . . .

CHAPTER FOUR

Danica Seton

Lorain, Ohio, nuzzled on the southern coast of Lake Erie, was only a short drive north, but Danica found the journey just long enough to begin second-guessing her decision to accompany the Ignota on the scouting mission. She possessed no skills of immediate use, and her face was currently one of the most recognizable throughout the Global Alliance. *Yeah,* she said to herself, *this has bad idea written all over it.*

Crossing into the city itself had the feeling of traveling back in time. Antique homes, none younger than a hundred years old, stood short distances from the tree-lined sidewalks. Small yards, most overgrown and really barely more than patches, decorated the quiet side streets. After passing a half-dozen of them, Danica asked him about the short, wooden posts she spied at the edge of several yards.

"They're mailbox posts. There used to be a box on top and a guy would come around and deliver mail," he said, keeping his eyes alert and forward.

Raised in the affluent modernity of the Washington, DC suburbs, Danica had never seen the remnants of the outdated, and long since abandoned, postal service. It had been a century since one had to wait more than a second for a message to be sent or received.

Turning onto the aptly named street of Broadway, the residential sights quickly gave way to more commercial locales. A florist and a barbershop on the left, a bakery and a diner on the right, caught her eyes first. The names of each business stretched across their respective facades in bright, hand-painted lettering. *No holosigns here,* Danica thought.

Several people moved about, entering and exiting the shops while bundled up against the weather. Like Oberlin, the rain also poured down on its northern neighbor. The difference, Corey explained as the heavy drops drummed on the pod's glass dome, was the strength the Great Lake added to the wind.

Glaring as Lorain's existence in a time long forgotten was, Danica admitted the city had its charm. With no SID chip embedded in her palm, and living the last two months by the light of oil lamps, she felt an internal harmony with the quaint city.

"Truth!" Corey exclaimed.

Redirecting her study of the periphery, Danica gasped as all sense of the idyllic burned away. The wide lanes of Broadway banked left revealing an unbroken view of the city's harbor—now filled with countless Peacekeeper vessels. Great steel ships sat anchored and motionless in the rough chop of the stormy lake. Furthest from the shore were two low-riding aircraft carriers, dozens of HALOs and X.T.E.M fighter jets covering the floating fortresses' decks. Closer, and looking far more deadly, was the endless number of warships formed around each carrier. The sky held threats of its own; hovering HALOs riding the heavy winds like mechanical humming birds.

As the scout guided the podcar to a vacant parking space, he muttered, "Two carrier groups. That's at least fifteen thousand PKs between them. This isn't a patrol."

Nervously, she asked him, "What do we do now?" Her mind screamed, *Please say 'turn back!'*

"We go talk to Henney's sister."

Oh, Truth!

Corey turned down the next side street with all proper adherence to traffic laws. Theirs was the only civilian pod under manual control, and official eyes would spot the slightest variation from the norm. Danica wondered if being pulled over had ever held higher consequences. They traveled a short distance back up Broadway before arriving at the diner Danica had noticed earlier.

"Henney's sister owns a diner, too?" she asked once the pair exited the pod. The wind-driven rain stung her face.

"Yeah, and whatever you do, don't tell Celeste you liked Henney's waffles," he warned with more gravity than Danica thought the comment warranted. Plus, she did not think opinions on cooking would be a pressing concern with an army of PKs stationed down the street.

Grateful for the shelter from the storm, Danica followed the scout inside the diner. More modern in design than *Henney's Twenties,* the establishment was easily twice as large, and held half as many customers. The scout slipped quickly into the first booth past the front door; Danica took the bench on the opposite side of the table.

"Keep your head down," Corey whispered. "Not everyone in Lorain is friendly."

Danica placed her right elbow on the table and hid her face behind her hand. Panicked thoughts raced in her head. *Did anyone look up when we came in? Had someone recognized her? Was someone calling the PKs right now?* She desperately wanted to see if any of the few patrons were looking their way, but she followed Corey's direction. Danica nearly shed her skin when a sudden voice directly at her side greeted them.

"Good morning," the woman said. "This table's menu is acting up a bit. You have to slide your finger just right." The woman leaned forward to assist. "What are you doing here?" she hissed.

"Your sister said your milk's gone bad," Corey murmured his reply, lips hardly twitching.

Perhaps unfairly, Danica had expected at least a passing resemblance between the sisters. There was, however, none. Slender to the point of frailty, Celeste could not have been more than a third of her sister's size. The stark disparity in size made any possible similarities difficult to pinpoint. *And,* Danica added, *this woman's voice has got to be several octaves lower.*

"See, just make sure to swipe the lower corner," Celeste demonstrated in a normal volume, then dropped her tone again, "Exactly. Which is why you shouldn't be here. Especially not with her."

Danica cringed at the words.

"She was with me when we found out. There wasn't any time to get her back to the shelter," Corey lied. From his expression, Danica could see he too was realizing taking her away from Oberlin had been an imprudent and unnecessary risk. "What do you know?"

"Hang on." Celeste said in a huff and hurried off. After placing a brief call on a mobile comm, the woman went about her work paying little heed to the infamous duo in the first booth.

It was not long, though it seemed an eternity to Danica, before the few remaining diners of the breakfast rush finished their meals and departed the café. Ignoring the collection of dirty dishes sitting atop the vacated tables, Celeste instructed the restaurant's Integrated Family Management System to lock the front door. The IFaMS unit complied, and Danica heard the locks engage. *Lorain may be stuck in the past,* Danica mused, *but everyone has an IFaMS.* After hanging a hastily scribbled note declaring the place closed for lunch, Celeste led Danica and Corey past the kitchen into the storeroom.

"You're lucky no one recognized her!" Celeste continued her earlier reprimand; this time adding a slap to the back of Corey's head to emphasize her displeasure. "You hear thousands of PKs are in town and you show up with the Alliance's most wanted? What were you thinking, boy? Does Gavin know about this?"

"I convinced Corey to bring—" Danica tried to defend the scout's action, but Celeste cut her off.

"You shush!" the woman commanded with a sharp, pointed finger that cut through Danica like an arrow. "You don't know any better, so I'm not mad at you . . . yet! And he can make his own excuses!"

Wide-eyed with jaw clamped tightly shut, Danica thought to herself, *Well, there's the resemblance.* She doubted if even Torrance could stand his ground if faced with either of the two sisters.

"We were at Henney's when you called. There wasn't a lot of time. I sent word to Gavin, and then Danica and I drove up," Corey explained. "If I'd known it was more than a PK patrol, I wouldn't have risked the trip."

Visibly dissatisfied with the reasoning, Celeste let the matter drop. "Word spread right as the first ship broke the horizon. When the morning crowd started talking about a whole fleet dropping anchor, I didn't believe it until I checked for myself. As soon as I saw, I called my sister."

"From what I saw it's two carrier strike groups," Corey replied, then clarified for Danica, "Each group has an aircraft carrier, and three each of cruisers, destroyers, and anti-air warships. Plus, other support vessels."

Danica appreciated the additional information, but it did little to further her knowledge. Whatever the difference in the ships' classifications, she still only saw huge ships with huge guns.

"I saw HALOs in the air," the scout continued. "Have any PKs come ashore?"

Celeste raised her hands, palms towards the ceiling. "After the initial sightings, tongues were running wild and there were all sorts of stories. Everything from the Alliance taking the city by force, to them hunting for old Bessie."

"And the truth is probably somewhere in between," added the voice of a man unseen in the shadows at the far end of the dim storeroom. A short figure easily in his late thirties, and dressed in the black and red uniform of a PK, stepped forward. Danica's muscles tensed, ready for another desperate escape, but neither Corey nor Celeste seemed fazed by the arrival of their enemy. In fact, Corey extended a welcoming hand to the soldier.

"Vinsy, how you been?" the scout said with a wide smile.

The PK accepted the handshake, and replied, "Life was a bit easier a few hours ago. You took a big risk coming up here, Corey."

Tsking loudly, Celeste said, "Don't you think he knows that, Alvins? How many years of private school did I pay for, wiping up after other people mind you, for you to come in here and state the obvious? We're all taking risks, doing what we do."

Danica, still shaken by the unexpected and unexplained presence of a PK, noted the marked shift in Celeste's words. Apparently, only she had the right to reprimand Corey and Danica for their decision to investigate Lorain.

"Honey, if you drop your jaw any lower, it'll hit the floor," the café owner commented. "This is my son, Alvins. Alvins, this is..."

"I'm pretty sure I'd recognize her no matter how short her hair is, Mom," the officer replied, light sarcasm lacing the words. "Nice to meet, you, Ms. Seton," he added with an offered handshake of his own.

Wishing she had never left her father's bedside, Danica stammered, "But, you . . . you're a Peacekeeper."

"Oh, Truth, she's as bad as you, Alvins," Celeste snorted through a roll of her eyes. "Yes, honey, he's a Peacekeeper. But, he's one of the good ones. Now, can we get back to what's important? I'm closed for lunch, but I intend to open for dinner!"

It had never occurred to her that there might be Ignota supporters hidden among the PK ranks. *I really don't know anything about the Ignota,* she thought sourly. Relieved to let the others direct the conversation, Danica's mind struggled for clarity amid confusion's whirlwind. She lost that battle once Celeste ushered everyone to the nearby prep station and assigned each a task. Danica, charged with peeling carrots, listened while the scout questioned the Peacekeeper; the pair dicing potatoes and cubing chicken. The scene was too bizarre to even be a dream.

"Our station chief never said anything about it," Alvins, or Vinsy as Corey called him, said. "And from her mood, I don't think she knew they were coming. Their brass showed up at the station house about an hour after the fleet arrived—two rear admirals and a few dozen more junior officers; all staring at us down their superior noses. They met with the chief for ten, maybe fifteen minutes before flying back to the ships."

"Any idea what their intentions are?" Corey asked.

Alvins shook his head. "Nothing concrete. They did tell the chief she would remain in control of the city's PK forces. That's about it, though. But, I don't think we can expect them to leave anytime soon. We haven't seen ships of that size since ... Mom?"

"Oh, probably not since '89 when they expanded the locks and channels," Celeste said, then added, "Your grandfather worked on that project."

"Doesn't sound like they're here for Oberlin," the scout conjectured. "Two battle groups is a bit of overkill when one missile could bury the shelter."

Fingers already stained orange from the carrots, Danica suggested, "Maybe they're looking for that woman, like you said."

"What woman?" her three companions asked in perfect unison.

Faltering under their inquisitive stares, Danica replied, "The woman, Bessie. You said they might be hunting for Bessie."

Stares turned to laughter, and Danica wished the floor would open beneath her.

"Honey," Celeste said, "Bessie is our lake monster. You know, like the one in Scotland."

"Oh." Mortified, Danica forced herself to laugh with the others. *Just keep peeling and shut up,* her mind said behind the false smile.

Corey, who she noticed had not laughed as much as Celeste and her son, said, "Still, though, can it really be just a coincidence that they're here and Oberlin is ten minutes away?"

"Yes and no," the Peacekeeper answered. "I think it's an 'accidentally on purpose' situation. But, there's no way to be sure until it is too late."

Danica listened as the man shared his theory. While she would never claim to be a tactical strategist, she knew what Alvins suggested was a dire gamble. Still, though, they needed to relay the information to the Ignota cells in Oberlin. Unwilling to risk taped or traced calls, Danica and Corey thanked mother and son for their aid and went back into the storm.

The pair traveled in silence; shared concerns of the PK fleet weighing heavily. Danica also worried over another looming conflict. If Celeste's reaction to Danica joining Corey on the scouting mission was stern, she knew a far harsher one awaited her return to the shelter below Oberlin. Gavin McAvoy and Torrance may not agree on much, but Danica was sure the two would find common ground long enough to scold her and Corey both.

This was officially the world's worst first date!

CHAPTER FIVE

Milo Chance

"You know, when you said we were going on a road trip, I wasn't expecting five-star hotels, but I certainly didn't think we'd actually be sleeping on the road itself," Naesha O'Geron complained from the passenger seat. It was not the first time the diginews reporter shared that particular frustration over the past weeks. And Milo was certain it would not be the last.

"I'm so glad you're here," he muttered, not caring if she heard the comment. Five weeks as travel companions, spending every minute together, had soured the new couple's respective moods. Sleeping in a podcar the last eight nights had done little to help the situation. *The podcar you suggested I buy!* He kept that comment to himself.

While the Muerte case had been a certain boon to their careers—Naesha had been nominated for a prestigious journalism award and Milo was promoted to Sergeant—neither had reaped much in the way of financial success. She had turned down several paid interview requests and speaking engagements in order to work with him on the new assignment—a sacrifice of which she reminded him frequently. And Milo had seen only a minor bump in salary with the promotion. Purchasing the new podcar had emptied his modest savings.

Begrudgingly, he admitted (though never in Naesha's hearing) the pod was a necessary investment. Tasked by the faceless Soothsayer to track down the terrorist Torrance, Milo's old one-person podcar would not have been adequate. *Still, I didn't need to buy a DeLuca Corelex RZ!*

The high-end sport utility pod boasted six seats, four of which reclined fully, and a long list of amenities he had yet to master. Engineered for the camping and off-roading driver, the podcar had become a fast favorite among the young and newly rich celebrity crowd, as well as the drug dealers Milo had often busted back in Philadelphia. Owning a Corelex had never been a status symbol Milo had craved. At least not until his recent fame stemming from the Muerte case.

News of the arrests had stayed local; much larger world events had trumped what once would have been a national story. Even still, his name and digital had been in the local press every day for weeks. Despite his best efforts to check his ego, the attention had gotten to him. Thus, the Corelex.

And because I own a Corelex, I can't afford a motel room, Milo concluded. *The ad should say, 'It sleeps four because you'll have no money left to sleep anywhere else.'*

"I'd trade the damn pod for one night alone," Milo complained under his breath.

"What was that?" Naesha challenged.

"Nothing."

"Godwin, what did he just say?" she asked the PK-drone occupying one of the still upright seats.

Before Milo's partner could reply, he warned, "Godwin, if you answer I'll make you sleep outside again!" It was not a punishing penalty as the drone did not sleep, nor would he suffer ill effects from the night's cold weather. He did seem, however, to dislike being excluded from Milo's presence. There were times when Milo wondered if he was dealing with a drone or a child.

"I am sorry, Naesha, but I would prefer to stay in the podcar."

Huffing her displeasure, the reporter snapped, "Typical."

When next he had the chance to speak with his mysterious informant, Milo intended to demand the Soothsayer provide some financial assistance to the investigation. *Well, maybe* request, *not demand*. With each passing day, Milo wondered if he would ever hear the voice again. The last communication he'd had with the Soothsayer had been the call setting the PK and the reporter on the hunt for Torrance. Torrance . . . a man he was beginning to believe was a myth. That was the true source of their frustration.

After accepting the assignment, Milo and Naesha had reviewed the information on the terrorist's rampage through Philadelphia. Or, at least as much as Milo could access with his low-level clearance. Promotion or no, most of the files were restricted several ranks above him. Investigating the attacks in Washington, DC had proven even more difficult. Milo had no connections in the old capital and therefore had no access to PK files there.

Naesha had a bit more luck with the local press. A flash of her newly achieved credentials and reporters became quite eager to share what they knew. Most hoped to share a by-line on her next big story. Unfortunately, little of what they knew had been of use.

Yes, Torrance had been sighted.

Yes, there was an Ignota attack on the PK military base.

No, the Alliance had not released any further details.

He had tried to gain entry onto the base, but was turned away. While all Peacekeepers wear the same uniform, there was a definite separation between those serving locally and those on the global front. With all other avenues closed, Milo and Naesha had spent the last two weeks traveling from one alleged Torrance[3] sighting to another.

The trail, built on rumor and gossip, had taken them through several cities. From Atlanta to Tampa, Jackson to Topeka, Milo, Naesha, and Godwin had chased

---

3 Though sporadic at first, this was the start of the "legend of Torrance." Like the Yeti and chupacabra before him, reported sightings would become a common occurrence in modern folklore. These reports often placed him in two locations concurrently, despite the thousands of kilometers of distance. We do know, however, these initial "sightings" were false as Torrance infrequently left the Oberlin shelter during the weeks following the Washington attacks. And those excursions did not take him any great distance from Oberlin. –M.S.

down every lead until reaching their current location in Lansing, Michigan. A local PK cruiser pod had been bombed, and Torrance had been blamed. Like every other "sighting" they had investigated, the eyewitness accounts had all consisted of "a friend's brother's friend" seeing Torrance at the scene, or a similar third hand account.

One "witness" had even declared, "A few hours before the pod bomb, my girlfriend's holoset was stolen!" Apparently, Torrance and *his* Ignota were responsible for any ill twist of fate someone suffered. Milo had yet to see any evidence linking the man to the terrorist group, much less serving as its leader.

True, the link was likely, but to the average citizen Torrance was Mr. Ignota himself. As for Milo, the more he investigated, the more he grew to doubt the man's existence. Both sides would benefit from his creation. The Ignota would have an indestructible hero the Alliance would never be able to catch or bring to justice. The government would have a boogeyman to justify and, since Torrance could never be caught, prolong their worldwide crackdown. Even Milo, essentially a PK at birth, was surprised with the extent of PK presence.

Each city through which they had traveled had resembled a police state. HALOs darted about, patrolling the air. On most streets, armed Peacekeepers kept a wary vigil; often accompanied by the crushing QuadTrac urban tanks in the busier districts. Whether actual or fictitious, Torrance, and the all-too-real Cohors Ignota, had forced the Alliance to drop a strong, unprecedented net of force across the world.

As soon as the Ignota are stopped, the world will be a safer place, Milo thought.

"Sun's coming up," Milo announced when his eye caught a subtle brightening of the eastern sky. One of the many features of the Corelex was the blackout windshield dome. When engaged, campers could sleep inside uninterrupted by any external light. Eager to begin the day, however, and exit the pod at the earliest opportunity, Milo had left the dome translucent last night.

Instructing the pod's control system to upright her seat, Naesha stretched and arched her back with a weary groan. "How many today?" she asked, their latest tiff forgotten. Or temporarily ignored.

"We have three final witness interviews scheduled today," Godwin informed them. *"The first, with Mrs. Delphine Porter, is scheduled for 9 AM."*

Checking the pod's clock, Milo knew ninety minutes was more than enough to grab a quick breakfast before the first appointment. "Anything major going on?" he asked his partner.

The world had been quiet over the last two months, but Milo did not rely on that peace lasting. In a few days' time, an entire Family had been exposed as Ignota sympathizers, the terrorists had launched a successful attack against a PK military base, and the Alliance had announced the delay in the SID upgrades. Too much had happened in the world for the current quiet to last much longer.

Ever the pessimist, Milo chided himself as he listened to Godwin. There was little to report. The hunt for Torrance and Ignota cells continued with daily successes and few acts of terrorist retaliation. The postponement of the SID implantations was nearing an end; the Alliance planned to begin the process in a month. The Council of Four (Milo was still adjusting to the new number), now sharing control of the deposed House Garrott's former monopoly over the defense industry, had amplified the production of PK-drones. Originally planned to slowly supplement existing forces with the drones, the Ignota conflict pushed the Council to a unanimous decision ordering the immediate manufacturing of an additional ten million units. The process would take close to a year, but when complete it would more than triple the number of PK-drones already in service.

"And the wedding of Caput Yin Xian Hu and Aubrey Garrott occurred a short time ago in Beijing," Godwin said to conclude his update of global affairs. Milo did not understand why a Caput would marry the daughter of a traitor, but then there was little he did understand about *that* world. He assumed Naesha could explain the reasoning. Of course, that would require a discussion of whatever past link she had to the moneyed elite. A discussion Milo dared not start, and one Naesha did not seem inclined to allow.

With instructions to locate the nearest fast food restaurant, the pod's internal navigator directed the vehicle out of the roadside recharge station and into the flow of morning traffic. The two humans tried their best to reach a respectable appearance, with Naesha achieving much better results in Milo's opinion. One of the reporters Naesha had befriended in Lansing had offered them use of the office's showers last night. Though his clothes may be wrinkled, Milo was glad for the cleanse and the chance to shave.

Eating quickly, and pausing to use the restaurant's facilities, PK and reporter were back in the pod and heading towards the home of Mrs. Porter.

Nestled into a quiet suburban neighborhood of leaf-covered lawns and squat bare-limbed trees, they reached the house on Viking Road. A newer construction, as were most of the homes on the block, the oval exterior of the one-story building reminded Milo of an egg which had been halved down its length. Touted as one of the most affordable and energy-efficient of the modern designs, Milo's parents had begun considering purchasing one in preparation for their retirement. Personally, he could not picture his parents living in something so modern however much it saved his credit-pinching father.

Upon stepping from the pod onto the black driveway, a voice crackled with age called out, "Mind the grass!"

Confused, Milo looked down to find a centimeter of his heel had crossed the divide from drive to lawn. He corrected the infraction and flashed Naesha a look of "this is not going to be fun." The smile she returned expressed either her agreement or her pleasure over his scolding. Milo knew on which he would bet.

"We'll be back in a bit, Godwin. Check the chatter for any new sightings," he told the drone. He had discovered early on that Godwin's presence often unsettled the interview subjects, hindering their willingness to talk. Milo regretted the exclusion of his partner from the interviews. The drone's system could detect the slightest increase in the rhythm of human pulse—a walking lie detector.

"*As you wish,*" the drone responded.

Careful to keep to the path of flat paving stones crossing the front lawn, Milo and Naesha approached the front door where their host waited. Sour-faced, the old woman watched their approach with her lips pinched into a tight frown. Age had added a slight forward bend to her posture, furthering shrinking her diminutive frame. Her hands, withered and gnarled like a sundried tree branch, rested atop a silver cane. She had positioned the cane in front of her body, the image resembling a knight and his sword.

"I won't have you tracking mud into my house, so take off your shoes," Mrs. Porter said as she turned away into the foyer. Her tone suggested she was used to being obeyed. As suspected, the cane barely touched the floor as the woman, rather spryly, disappeared into an adjoining room. *It's more of a club than a walking aid.*

Reminding himself to keep an even temper, Milo slipped off his lightweight shoes, supported Naesha as she did the same, and crossed into the living room in search of Mrs. Porter.

The home itself may have been modern in structure, but its furnishings trailed several decades behind. The square cuts and edges of the side chairs, accent tables, and couch clashed with the curved walls and ceiling. Milo's eyes strained to accept the deluge of neon lacquer and fabric covering the furniture.

"You have a lovely home," Naesha offered. *Not quite the word I would have used.*

"Bah, if you like living in a damn bubble," the woman griped. "Why all of a sudden are straight walls a bad thing? That's what I'd like to know! Can you tell me? Of course not. I probably have sheets older than you. No one can leave well enough alone.

"I was perfectly fine in my old house. Grew up there and would've been more than happy to die there. But, no. My great-niece says to me 'Aunt Deli, it's too much house for you.' Never mind that I've outlived everyone who ever slept in that house! Apparently, at my age I no longer know what's good for me." At the end of the prolonged complaint, the old woman added, "Well, you might as well sit yourselves down."

Lowering himself into the nearest cube chair, Milo made his own attempt to cozy up to the woman's good side. "We're very grateful you agreed to meet with us, Mrs. Porter. We've been spending the last few weeks speaking with people who have seen the terrorist called Torrance."

"Oh, I bet you have," she replied. "Your kind's been running around like an under-sexed hound looking for a bitch. Showing up anytime someone as much as breathes that man's name. Yes, I know you're a *Peacekeeper*, Mr. Chance. Even if I didn't see that machine in your pod, I read about you in the digis."

There had been abundant disgust in her tone when she referenced the PKs. Naesha must have detected it as well because she spoke before Milo could respond.

"Would you mind if I record our conversation?" the reporter asked.

With a joyless chuckle, Delphine Porter replied, "I'm surprised you even bothered to ask. By all means, record whatever you want. Farleigh wouldn't want you to, but she didn't even want me to speak with you. 'Aunt Deli' she said, 'it's only going to upset you.' But, she doesn't know why it's so important. Sweet girl, she is, but she doesn't know. So, there'll be no need to go bothering her next."

Milo sat in quiet confusion while Naesha placed the recorder on the center of the coffee table. Smaller than a baseball, the black orb stood on the tripod legs extending from its bottom. The device not only recorded the audio, but it would also capture a three-dimensional rendering they could then replay on any holoset. The playback's precision clarity would allow Godwin to analyze even the slightest shift in the subject's facial expressions.

Due to his lawn-stepping sin and his field of employment, Milo nodded for Naesha to take the lead in the interview. Over the last weeks, the two had developed a shared sense of which of them was best to lead a given session. More accustomed to interrogating suspects, Milo deferred to Naesha's investigative skill when a softer touch was needed. *A feather might not be soft enough with this old bag,* he sneered.

"For the record," she began, "would you please state your name."

"Delphine Angelica Porter."

"Mrs. Porter, are you being paid in any way, receiving any sort of compensation, for the information you are going to share today?"

"No," she replied as if even the suggestion was a stain on her reputation.

"Mrs. Porter, three days ago you told the *Lansing Morning Star* diginews that you had seen, firsthand, the terrorist called Torrance. Correct?"

"No."

Naesha had begun her next question when she caught the negative reply. "I'm sorry. No? You didn't say that or you didn't see him?"

With no trace of malice, the woman said, "I said I saw Torrance. I never said anything about a 'terrorist.'"

Milo could feel a growl trying to escape. *Oh my Truth! I am going to drive donuts in her lawn!*

Naesha smiled insincerely (he had been on the receiving end of the look more than once), and she said, "Thank you for being so precise. Would you please tell us about your Torrance sighting?"

"Which one?" Mrs. Porter asked. Milo swore he saw the corners of the woman's mouth twitch in humor. Frustrated by the idea that an old woman with nothing better to occupy her time was wasting *his* time, he lost his restraint.

"You saw him more than once?" he asked. No one could miss the mocking cut to his words.

Pleased to have riled the PK seated in her living room, Delphine Porter said, "Oh, yes. Dozens of times."

Well, that's a first. None of the other cranks claimed to see him more than once. She's got some stones, this one. Milo placed his hands on the chair arms, ready to lift himself and leave.

"In Lansing?" Naesha asked. She had far deeper reserves of patience than he did.

"No, in Philadelphia," their alleged witness corrected.

The conviction in her voice caught Milo off-guard and the muscles in his arms relaxed to lower him back into the seat. Over the years, through countless investigations, he had heard the same distinctive sound of unwanted certainty. Not from witnesses, though. Or from victims. No, it was the controlled despair reserved for the ones who had ignored the obvious. The mother who had agreed to hide her son, knowing a dark reason must have existed for the request, but had been too protective to refuse. The wife who wondered how her husband could afford the life he had given her, but had been too afraid to ask for fear of what it would mean to the marriage. Their actions, done out of love not gain, haunt them endlessly. For if faced again with the choice, aware of its deficiency and the pain included, they know they would make no changes in their decisions.

"When did you first see him, Mrs. Porter?" he asked. Naesha's face showed her confusion over the sudden shift in his demeanor.

With less defiance, the aged woman replied, "It was June 16, 2134."

"That's almost thirty years ago," Naesha calculated.

"Yes."

Whatever malcontent he had first felt towards the woman, Milo was now intrigued. "When was the last time you saw him?"

"In '48. After my Martin died, I moved back to the family house here in Lansing. By then I was too old for . . . well, too old for my old life I guess you could say." A mist of memories gathered along the lower lid of Delphine Porter's eyes. This was a woman who would not be undone by tears, even her own. Pressing forward, she said, "Now, I see the disappointment in your face. You're saying to yourself, 'We are looking for him now. What good does fourteen year old information do us?' Well, I ask you Sergeant Chance, of the people you interviewed, how many do you think had ever spoken the name Torrance before two months ago? How many claimed to know him when he was just a boy, all smiles and hugs? How many claimed to know him before he was *made* into what he is today?"

That she had orchestrated every second leading to this moment, from the first step out of his podcar, was now clear. He had not realized it then, but now he knew old Delphine Porter had been testing him. He had been fighting a battle for dominance where defeat was the only chance at victory. She had burrowed into his curiosity and started a slow burning flame.

"None," he said in soft surrender.

She gave him the respectful nod of victor to the vanquished, and rose to her feet.

"Well, then, I should probably put on some tea," she announced and, with her cane in hand, walked towards the kitchen.

CHAPTER SIX

Milo Chance

"I'd known I wanted to be a scrub nurse the first time I was placed on a surgery table," Mrs. Porter began after she returned to the living room with a tray of three steaming cups of fresh brewed tea. Milo felt clumsy as he tried to grasp the fragile handle of the porcelain teacup; its daintiness was never meant for his thick fingers. Seated once again, their host continued.

"I was seven years old and was having an emergency appendectomy. Even back then it was a simple procedure; back home the very same day. But, I was scared. That big, sterile room with all the monitors, beeping and flashing. All those shiny tools and instruments. I guess it was pretty clear on my face how frightened I was because before they put me under, one of the nurses took my hand and helped me sit up a bit. He told me what the monitors were for, what instruments the doctor would use—anything and everything I thought to ask, he answered. I forget what exactly he had said, but he said something to make me smile. And from that moment on I was hooked."

For a half-moment, her face slackened with the distant expression of one caught in a long ago memory. And for that half-moment, Milo felt he was reliving the scene right along with Mrs. Porter. The commanding crackle of her aged voice, which earlier had raised his hackles, had now become almost hypnotic. There was secret in her voice.

"For years after, whenever anyone asked what I wanted to be when I grew up, I'd say with all the certainty a child can muster, 'I'm going to be a scrub nurse.' Of course, other fancies stole my heart for a time. But, nursing was the lover I returned to when I entered college and began to build my future. I was overjoyed when Philadelphia General offered me a position. My father wondered why I didn't become a doctor. 'You've got the brains for it, Delphine,' he'd say. And perhaps I would have if it had been the surgeon who had eased the worries of a little girl. But, it had been a nurse, a scrub nurse."

Pausing to sip her tea, Mrs. Porter closed her eyes as the near-black liquid passed her parted lips. She murmured, pleased with the taste, and set the cup back onto the matching saucer.

"Now, all that took place long, long ago; decades before I would meet Torrance. I share it with you because it might make the rest easier to understand. I loved nursing. It was everything to me. When I was in an operating room, I was part of a small group of people responsible for keeping another person alive, supporting the surgeons, anticipating their needs. I was the link between the patient on the table, the life-saving instruments, and the surgeon standing over it all."

Her voice swelled with pride. *And sadness,* Milo thought. *She misses it.*

"I said before nursing was my 'lover.' And it was. My husband and I had a lifetime of wonderful memories, but it was my work that brought me the most pleasure. We never had children because I could not see how to fit them into my life. So, when the time came to retire, I was heartbroken, lost.

"The hospital was kind about it; allowing me to come to the decision on my own. You see, my hands eventually lost their dexterity; my legs couldn't support me through marathon surgeries. I was, and still am, fitter than others my age, but I knew it wasn't enough to continue working. So, at sixty-eight years old, I found myself retired and despairing. Despair turned to depression, and within a few months the fog was so thick it was all I could do to get out of bed each day. Martin was so worried. And I know it hurt him, too; not being able to fill the void, knowing I'd have recovered faster from losing him than losing my career.

"Retired as well, Martin thought we might leave Philadelphia, travel the world, see all the things we had talked about through the years. I couldn't imagine leaving, though. Not so soon after leaving work. I could barely get out of bed, how could I travel the world?"

Milo had a difficult time picturing this woman incapacitated by anything. He was sure the steel-gray of her hair was a perfect match for the metal in her, well, mettle.

"Martin began taking walks. Brief at first, but the longer I closed myself in sorrow, the longer his walks became. He was out on one such walk—it was a beautiful June day—when I heard a knock on our front door. I was in bed as usual, didn't want to see anyone, and assumed whoever it was would eventually go away. After ten minutes of incessant knocking, my anger outweighed my depression, so I drew myself up and prepared a few select words."

I bet you did, Milo thought with an inward smile.

"Whatever I had planned to say died on my tongue as soon as I opened the door," Mrs. Porter said. "My eyes went to the boy first, cradled in the man's arms. The child, no older than six, was pale, too pale, and his face was twisted in pain.

"'He doubled over this morning,' the man said to me. ' His fever keeps rising and he can't keep anything down.' Assuming he was a neighbor I'd never met, or a passer-by, I ran to call an ambulance. 'Put the phone down, Nurse Porter,' the man with the child said. That he knew my name hadn't registered. What did register, though, was the gun he had aimed at me.

"Foolishly, I complied. The shock of that moment mixed with my preexisting struggles, and I couldn't do anything except follow his order. I must have asked him what he wanted, though I doubt my words were that coherent, but he looked at me and said, 'Help the boy.'"

"'I'm not a doctor,' I told him. Beyond that, I was in my home. I certainly did not have the proper equipment to treat anything beyond a stomach bug. Again, he told me to help the child. This time, however, I could hear a small plea in his voice, see it in his eyes. Which was no easy thing, mind you. Despite his age, that man looked every bit like a man who would hold a gun at you in your doorway.

"He kept what little was left of the receding hair cut short; nearly down to the scalp, so you could barely see the grey stubble. His blue eyes were radiant, but their hard coldness robbed them of true beauty. The left side of his face bore a thin scar that began just below the eye and cut through his upper lip so that a thin line of white stood out against the red. He was clearly in excellent shape and his strength had the edge of danger to it. At first guess, I thought him to be in his early fifties. Though, I'd learn later he and I were much closer in age.

"I was about to tell him no again, that the boy needed a doctor, when the child cried out. The sound of a young one crying is bad, but the scream of pain and suffering is unbearable. Heedless of the gun, and the man wielding it, I scooped the boy up from the man's arms and hurried him inside. I examined him as best I could with what I had, and it didn't take long to determine the cause of his pain. It was if the walls closed in and I had been sealed up in a room with Fate."

"Appendicitis," Milo and Naesha breathed together in shared wonder.

"Appendicitis," Mrs. Porter nodded. "In medicine you're trained not to accept coincidence. The body works like a machine, one function linked to another, and to another, so that all are dependent in some form or fashion. Yet, when it comes to the machine of our lives, we don't like to believe all events are dependent on past events, that everything is linked. But then, there he was. A boy no older than I had been when I had required the same surgery, which had then led me on the path where I learned how to perform that surgery.

"The man helped me move the boy to the kitchen table. After forty plus years in the OR, I had seen countless appies performed under all types of conditions and complications. I told the man what I would need and where he could buy the items. He argued at first, saying I should go and he would stay; clearly he thought I'd call the PKs at the first possible chance. Explaining how serious the boy's state was, and how it was worsening with every second of delay, the man finally agreed. Although, he only parted after leveling a series of threats of what would happen should I betray him.

"I sat with the boy, holding his hand tight as he drifted in and out of consciousness. He was never awake for long; the pain would quickly overwhelm him and he'd pass out again. During one spell of awareness, he looked at me with the man's same blue eyes. I knew they must be related; that hue was too distinctive for any other explanation. The boy's eyes, however, were gentle and kind. Yes, they showed his fear, but beneath that, I could see the innocent kindness.

"As I stroked his blond hair, I asked, 'What is your name?'

"'Torrance,' he told me before his eyes rolled back once again.

"The man returned sooner that I had expected, which was good because

Torrance was fading. I called upon every memory of every cut, every maneuver, every twist of finger and hand I'd ever watched, and there on the kitchen table I saved the boy's life. Any surgeon would have been pleased with my work.

"When it was done, I offered, nearly insisted, they stay while the boy recovered. At that point, I had not even thought what Martin might have said had he returned from his walk to find an armed man overseeing a surgery in the kitchen! But, thankfully he didn't come home until much later and by then all evidence that man or boy had ever been there was gone."

"What did he say when he left?" Naesha asked. Milo was amazed she had the wherewithal to even speak, let alone form a query. The story had so engrossed him he had never lifted the teacup from the saucer resting in his palm. The tendrils of steam had long since dissipated. Fearing a perception of impropriety, Milo drank the beverage in one gulp. Bitter, and more than chilled, his tongue cringed at the taste.

"I mean, did he say 'thank you' and just leave? No explanation?" Naesha slipped into investigative mode.

"Oh, he murmured his thanks," the old woman laughed. "Though, I doubt he had ever said the word before. And, in truth, I didn't need to hear it. I had not felt that alive in months. Not since retiring. To have a purpose, to be needed, to feel that rush of surgery . . . I almost thanked him."

"And what of Martin? Did he suspect anything when he came home?"

Shaking her head with a smile, Mrs. Porter replied, "About the surgery, no. But, he was certainly confused. He came home to find a woman he had not seen in months. Poor man must have wondered what had changed; though he was probably worried if he asked it'd be ruined. Besides, it's not as if I could have told him. Even if the man had not threatened me, what could I have said? 'Darling, while you were out a man with a gun stopped by and forced me to remove a little boy's appendix on the kitchen table.' Given the months of my black sulk, he would have thought me crazy and had me committed. No, Martin held his tongue. He walked softly around me for a time, expecting me to relapse. I feared I might as well. But, the return to my former self continued even though I was still retired and without surgeries. I think a part of me knew I'd see the man and Torrance again; that they'd need me and seek me out.

"To that end, I made sure I would be prepared. I purchased medical supplies and stored them in a few boxes tucked away in a corner of the basement. I collected the most recent medical digital texts, studying them with the same fervor as when I trained to be a nurse. I even began volunteering a few days each week at a nearby clinic. I was nearly seventy years old and all but going through medical school.

"Martin may not have gotten the retired life he had hoped for, but he seemed pleased enough to have me back among the living. I'd occasionally join him on his daily walks, explore all the restaurants our friends recommended, and accepted the invitations to dinner parties, and the like. I even agreed to short trips, two to three days at most. I didn't want to be away should the man come knocking again."

"How long before he did?" Naesha asked.

"Almost a year," the woman replied. "It was early spring and the weather had warmed enough for two old folks to walk outside without catching death. Martin and I had just turned back onto our street when I saw the man. He was standing in front of a brownstone a few doors down from ours. I could feel his eyes watching as Martin and I climbed the front steps. Without any real reason to, I had planned for that moment. From the kitchen, I fished out the grocery list I had written months earlier. The ingredients were specific and varied and would take well over an hour to collect. Martin moaned at first, but soon agreed and departed. The man waited a few minutes before knocking. I was worried at first when I opened the door and there was no sign of Torrance.

"'Come with me,' he said.

"Once again my better judgment was muted, and I scribbled some plausible excuse to Martin and followed the man into his podcar."

"You trusted him," Milo said, speaking for the first time since the tale of Mrs. Porter's past had begun.

Wetting her lips as she measured the weight of the word, she then said, "Trust? No, not trust. I think it was more akin to what one who works with wild animals—lions or tigers—must feel. There's a respect for the beasts' power, a respect for the risks, and an understanding that at any moment they could turn on you."

"And still you went?" Milo asked.

The woman fixed him a knowing stare.

"Of course," she said with an arch to the thin line of her penciled brow. The look carried more meaning than the words. *And so would you,* Milo interpreted the expression. He knew she was right.

Continuing, Mrs. Porter said, "He brought me to a house several blocks away, on a street I had walked down with my husband many times. We pulled down into the garage beneath the home and waited for the door to close before leaving the vehicle. I remember wondering if Torrance and the man had been leaving here all the while. Inside, the answer was quite clear. The house was empty—no furniture, no appliances. It was utterly vacant. With one exception. On the third floor of the narrow house was a room to steal your breath. How he managed to do it, I don't know. But, the man had constructed an operating room to rival any hospital. Before I could admire the various machines, which were worth tens of millions of credits, I quickly went to the unconscious boy stretched out on the surgical table.

"The man had already run lines of blood and fluids into the boy's tiny arm, as well as a rather unnecessary amount of morphine. Adjusting the controls to keep the boy from overdosing, I began to examine the obvious injury. Towards the ankle of his left leg, Torrance had sustained a nasty compound fracture; jagged points of both tibia and fibula jutted through the skin.

"'How did this happen?' I asked as sternly as I dared.

"'He fell out of a tree,' the man replied.

"What a boy of seven was doing high enough in a tree to cause this much damage in a fall was beyond me. And I wasn't likely to get much more information from the man. So, I cut off the splint, studied the break and the wound, and mentally ran through the procedure. Unsure how much morphine Torrance had already been given, I decided not to risk anesthesia. If he'd had even thirty minutes of the dosage I had corrected, he'd sleep through the procedure.

"Setting bones is no task for the weak-hearted, I'll tell you," Mrs. Porter said with a shiver and curl of her lip. "After the initial snap of adjusting the bones, there's a grinding sound like no other as you try to position them perfectly. It's not as bad with the little ones whose bones are still ossifying, but it's never a pleasant sound. I gritted my teeth the whole time until I was satisfied with the placement. The next concern was the wound itself. The broken skin held debris, dirt and such, so I feared some of the tissue would need to be cut away. Of course, even if it did, there was a dermal generator on hand. The man had truly thought of everything when outfitting the room. As it turned out, I was able to salvage enough of the boy's own skin to close the wound and seal it with accelerant. Three hours from start to finish.

"While I was cleaning up—I needed to get home before Martin grew worried—I caught the man staring at me. Feeling the high of success, I grew bold and said, 'You could have set a broken leg yourself. Why come to me?'

"He studied me a moment longer before replying, 'It needed to be done right. I could not risk a limp or any imperfection. His future is too important.'"

"'His future is too important?'" Milo interjected. "What did he mean?"

Lifting her shoulders to show her ignorance, Mrs. Porter said, "I thought the same thing. Had I asked, I doubt he would have told me.

"I took it upon myself to check on the boy over the next two days. On the third day, the house was vacant. All that fine equipment had been carried out in the night. But, I knew I'd see the boy again. And I was right. Over the next fourteen years, the man sought my skills more times than I can recall. As Torrance grew, the injuries came more frequently; most during his early teens, then tapering off again as he neared his twenties. By the time he was fifteen, the boy's body had healed more wounds than others would in a lifetime."

"What caused so many wounds?" Naesha asked.

The old woman bit her lower lip for a nervous second. It was the first time Milo had seen any sign of indecision in her. "There were more falls, more broken bones. When he was twelve or thirteen, I removed the first of many bullets. There were cuts and punctures from knives, as well. And . . . and there were other scars. Scars from wounds I was never asked to treat."

"What were they from, Mrs. Porter?" Milo asked her. A perceptible shift in mood had stolen across the room. He recognized this as well from years of investigation. The woman's narration had become a confession.

She responded, "Lashes. From a whip. Someone had been whipping the boy's back."

"Someone?" Milo prodded.

"The man."

"The man," Naesha repeated. "You haven't said his name yet."

"That's because I never knew it. He never offered it. On several occasions, over the years, I'd ask Torrance, but he said he didn't know either."

"And you never wondered why this man and this boy came to you? Why they couldn't go to a hospital? Why a teenager was stabbed, whipped, shot?" Milo asked with accusation.

"Certainly, I did!" Mrs. Porter replied. "I'm not a fool, Sergeant Chance. Whoever the man was, I knew he was hiding from someone, something. Were there times when I thought I should call the authorities? Of course. But, what would that have done? The boy would have been placed into the system and—"

"That's bullshit!" Milo spat.

Shocked by the outburst, Naesha said, "Milo!"

"No, you were being selfish. You didn't tell anyone because then you'd have lost your patient. Your purpose." As much as the woman had drawn him into her tale, Milo could never stomach self-serving rationalizations.

Mrs. Porter's expression flared with indignant anger then subsided. It was she who surrendered now. "Yes, I was being selfish but not only in the way you think. I loved the boy. For years, he'd greet me with a hug and a kiss. 'Nurse Porter!' he'd squeak in a child's angelic voice. Even later, as a young teen, when I only came up to his chin, he'd smile and embrace me. No matter how bad his pain, he'd always brighten when he saw me.

"Towards the end though, he . . . he started to change. Maybe it was gradual. I don't know. When you only see someone every few months, small changes are more noticeable. It was the winter of 2144. Torrance would have been seventeen or so then. The man brought me to an empty house, always a different house each time. Torrance was waiting. I think it was a knife wound that time. His smile was fainter, the embrace more mechanical, more perfunctory.

"I was called upon less at the end. Eight, sometimes nine months would pass before they came to me. Each time, Torrance was more distant, colder. His eyes had begun to match the man's."

The old woman paused before continuing. She stared past Milo and Naesha as she shared the final chapter of her story, reliving it again with each word.

"The last time I saw him was in '48. Torrance came to me then, not the man. We didn't go to a house. Instead, he brought me to Wharton State Park. Or, rather, he brought me underneath it. For the first time since they'd first appeared at my door, I had finally been brought to their home.

"Tunnels and caverns, some man-made others natural, stretched far into the darkness. It seemed impossible that such a place could exist! Torrance led me along until we reached a massive cavern. There were books everywhere; furniture was arranged in open-walled rooms, paintings rested on easels. All of it from different decades, different centuries. It was part museum, part library. In the middle of the visible space lay the man.

"It was a wonder he was still alive. His body was in tatters; particle gun wounds and burns covered him almost entirely. I did what I could, but he was beyond saving. And Torrance knew that when he came for me. In the end, I made the man comfortable so that his last few moments were without pain. I stepped away to allow Torrance to say his goodbyes. He didn't say anything. He just stood by the man until it was over.

"I offered my condolences. As tall and as hard as he was by then, I still remembered the little boy of years ago. I moved closer to comfort him as I had so many times when he was hurt, but he retreated a pace and said, 'There's nothing more for you to do here.'"

Her valiant struggle was lost, and the woman, looking so much older than when Milo had first seen her, let a solitary tear trace down the lines of her face.

"I knew it was over," she said in a tired voice, ignoring the display of sorrow. "And I knew that's why he brought me there. The man was dead. The boy I knew was gone. He could have let me continue waiting. But, instead he gave me closure. I think he let me see his world, his secret home, to thank me. Least that's what I choose to believe."

Emotions warred within. In truth, Milo had not expected anything from the interview, much less the story he had received. There was no doubt in his soul that ever word of it was true. Both he and Naesha sat in the grim paralysis of elegiac silence. This had not been an interview. Rather, a lamentation; a spoken dirge to mourn the man, the boy, and the decades-old sins of Delphine Porter.

"About a month later, I lost Martin to a stroke," the old woman said after a deep, cathartic breath. Her voice carried none of its earlier strength. "The family house had been empty for some time, and with no more ties to Philadelphia, I decided to return to Lansing. I stayed in that house until last year, before it was 'suggested' I downsize."

Finding his voice, Milo asked, "Why did you tell us this? You could have taken your past to the grave."

"Two answers to the same question," she replied. "I broke my silence because whatever happens, if Torrance is caught, people should know the truth about him. The man made him what he is."

"The man," Milo corrected, "and you. Your guilt is just as great, Mrs. Porter."

She nodded, "Yes, it is."

"You're not afraid that I might arrest you? Bring you in for questioning?"

"I'm a couple years shy of one hundred, Sergeant Chance. There's not much I'm afraid of anymore."

"You said there were two answers to the same question," Naesha asked. "What did you mean?"

"You asked *why* I told you this. But, you didn't ask why I told *you* this."

Hearing the changed inflection, Milo said, "Then, why us?"

"When Torrance reemerged in Philadelphia two months ago, I followed the story closely, read all the diginews. Then I saw your story—arresting a judge and an ADA, as well as a doctor from my old hospital—and I was confused. Why, when Peacekeepers from all over the world were searching for Torrance, was a local PK off chasing a drug dealer? At my age there aren't a lot of old friends still around, but there are some. And I called them. I don't claim to know every detail. However, it was clear you were working on your own, with Ms. O'Geron's help of course, but generally free of PK oversight. Even when a member of the Council warned you off the investigation.

"Now, you're traveling the country interviewing anyone who says Torrance's name. Strange how you were not involved when he was blowing up your city, but you are when someone in Miami says he kidnapped their dog."

Milo concentrated on keeping his expression passive. The woman's assumptions, both the ones overt and unspoken, were striking quite close to the mark. *Too close,* he added.

"I don't know that I've ever heard of a city PK defying an order from the Global Alliance and then getting promoted. But then, maybe you're not just a city

Peacekeeper."

More than a little disgruntled, Milo said, "Are you suggesting I am a member of the Cohors Ignota?"

"No, Sergeant Chance. I'm not giving you that much credit."

"Is Torrance? An Ignatum?" he pressed.

"I knew him, and the man, for fourteen years. But, I can honestly say I don't know who they were, what they were. I know the man who raised him believed Torrance had a purpose to fulfill. If his reemergence is part of that purpose, I don't know. Maybe you can discover that, Sergeant Chance."

Delphine Porter slipped a small, folded scrap of paper from the embroidered pocket of her blouse. Leaning forward, Milo extended his arm to accept the offering. There was an intimate second when each held an end of the note. When Milo met the old woman's eyes, her grip loosened. It was so brief Naesha had not caught it. Milo doubted even Godwin's superior functioning would have caught the moment. The power of the instant, however, had not been lost on Milo.

This was her goal all long, he understood without looking at the paper. The balance of power had shifted so fitfully over the past hour, Milo had become lost in the process.

"I only ask one thing," the old woman said. "If ever your paths should cross, if ever his life rests in your hands, I ask that you consider what I've told you today."

Milo could not commit to such a pledge. Not then. *Not ever,* he told himself but feared the hollowness of the thought. Instead, he rose from the chair, nodded to Naesha, who had not realized the interview had concluded, and showed himself out of the old woman's halved-egg home.

When Naesha met him at the pod, she made no effort to hide her bewilderment. "What just happened? Milo, what's on that paper?"

Lowering himself into the podcar, he said, "The location of the entrance to Torrance's home."

They reached Philadelphia the next morning. Finally home after weeks of travel, the pair could not resist the lure of their own bed before resuming the investigation. The reporter was enjoying an extended shower as Milo gave a brief scan of the morning news.

He was not sure why he checked; could not explain the knowing impulse that directed his hand. But, there it was. On the second page of the local Lansing diginews.

The body of Delphine Porter, aged 97, was found last night in her home at 13 Viking Drive. Mrs. Porter, a retired nurse and Lansing native, appears to have died from a self-injected overdose of morphine. At this time, funeral arrangements have . . .

CHAPTER SEVEN

Gavin McAvoy

"This is what you call protecting her?" the man shouted in a cold rage. Gavin understood why the others shied away from confrontation with Torrance. If his silent ominous broods were disquieting, it was nothing compared to the barely contained, raw violence in his raised voice. The cell leader did not share their same fear or awe; Torrance was but one man after all, but Gavin could understand their timidity.

Were the man's skills, his successes against the Alliance, impressive? Certainly. Gavin had recognized that. After all, those very skills had prompted him to invite Torrance to join his Ignota cell. That was before he discovered how detestable the man was.

Beyond his smug arrogance, it had become apparent Torrance's independence was a liability. The man had no sense of cooperation, possessed no concept of how to function as a team. He valued nothing, and therefore stood for nothing. As a fourth generation Ignotum, a descendant of a Founder, Gavin judged that lack with contempt. In war, you needed soldiers you could trust, not ones who served only themselves.

Okay, that's not entirely fair, Gavin added as the other man continued to vent his fury. Torrance may be a lone wolf, but he was also protective of the Seton children. The paradox was confusing. A solitary warrior who seemed solely focused on his own survival, and whatever means ensured said survival, had attached himself to two defenseless kids. And even Gavin was forced to admit there seemed to be no ulterior, selfish motive to Torrance's dedication to Marcus and Danica. The elder sibling was the current cause of the man's wrath.

Not long after word had come of the PKs arrival in Lorain, he had been informed that Corey had gone north to scout with Danica Seton in tow. Before he could voice his own frustration over the knowledge, Torrance had stormed into the emergency gathering of the cell leaders. As much as he detested Torrance, whose life's quest had apparently become disagreeing with Gavin's every word, the cell leader found no argument with Torrance's displeasure. Which made him even more eager to throttle his wayward scout.

"I understand why you're pissed," Gavin said in a tone as level as his mood allowed. "But, Corey's gone out on hundreds of scouts. He's careful. He knows how to handle himself and he won't let anything happen to Danica." *Truth, help us all if he does!*

"He's a damn kid!" Torrance spat back. Then, lowering his volume to a growling seethe, he promised, "If she's hurt in anyway, I swear to you I'll feed him his own guts."

"They'll be fine," Gavin matched him growl for growl. Corey was his solider, and Gavin knew he should be defending the boy with greater vehemence, but his own unspoken anger tempered his words.

"She's an adult, Torrance," Sonje added. "I doubt he dragged her along."

The comment was aimed to deflect some of the blame from Gavin—though as commander, he accepted responsibility for the actions of his Ignota—and he should have appreciated the woman's intention, but Gavin was still sore over whatever it was he had walked in on before.

A life underground had not allowed for relationships. He had *known* women in the past, but those were transactions; services for credits. The only woman he had ever spent any prolonged time with was Adirene. *And she was insane*, he added. *Truth, I hope that's not the norm.* What he felt for Sonje, and had felt since they shared their first words, was a new experience. Seeing her with Torrance, the two of them pressed close together and the latter half-naked, had sparked an unfamiliar emotion within him. Whatever it was, Gavin knew one thing. *It was not jealousy. I am not jealous of Torrance.*

Torrance responded to Sonje's comment with a tight-eyed stare.

"No offense to you and yours, Gavin," Fielder, the senior cell leader, interjected. "But, the situation is bigger than one scout and a civilian. We need to decide what our next move is, people. PKs in Lorain, and potentially more than a patrol, are a clear and present danger to this shelter. Now, it's been over twenty minutes since the call came in which means an attack could be seconds away. What's our plan?"

With a temporary truce accepted by both men, Gavin joined the other cell leaders seated at the table. Torrance moved off into a corner and leaned himself against the wall with arms folded across his now-clothed chest.

"We have a plan in place in the event of an attack," Camorata shared his typical cautious view. "I don't understand why we're wasting time deliberating over something already agreed upon."

"But, it's not an attack," Peter Yan countered. "Or, at least it isn't yet. The plan we created was a response to a *direct* assault on the shelter. We don't yet know what the PKs are doing in Lorain. It may very well be a routine patrol. Acting precipitously may be more of a risk than patience."

"All due respect, Pete," Sam Borden said, "but I think we can say it's more than a patrol. The Fifths in Lorain have been silent since that one call. Whatever is happening there, it is clear our assets fear risking open communication with the shelter."

"I agree," Gavin added. "I've known Henney a lot longer than most of you. There's not a cowardly bone in that woman's body. Same with her sister. If they've gone dark, you can assume there's a reason."

The majority of the leaders nodded and murmured agreement. While not the youngest among them, Gavin knew men like Marshall, Camorata, and Fielder had decades more experience commanding an Ignota cell. Still, those same veterans often voiced harmony with Gavin's pronouncements. *I could probably say the sky is green, and they'd redefine the color just so I'd be right.*

Another might enjoy the value these men placed on his words. Not Gavin. He had never grown accustomed to the inherited prestige that came with descending from a Founder. From the moment a pair of strangers hurried him out of his dormitory in the dark hours of morning, the Ignota had treated him with a respect—a reverence—he never felt he deserved. Even his late brother Jaime, who had adopted the Sowilo's views of the Founders, had never thought himself superior. He had died believing the Ignota's supposed savior would come from another descendant.

There were others around the table who could find in their ancestry a bloodline link to a Founder. Sam Borden, her mother's great aunt's cousin had been a Founder. Peter Yan, Marshall, Fielder, they all had a trace of Founder genes in their DNA. *But that's just it,* Gavin thought. *It's only a trace. Jaime and I were direct descendants—son of a son of a Founder's son.* In a hundred-year-old clandestine operation, marked for death by the government, an unbroken line such as theirs was rare.

"See," Camorata seized on the moment. "Gavin agrees it's an attack. The evacuation order needs to be given! We've lost too much time as it is!"

Marshall, the counterweight to Camorata's faintheartedness, balked. "I didn't hear him say that at all."

"The PKs could be blowing war horns in the next room and you'd choose not to hear it, Marshall!" Camorata mocked.

Stepping in before the two men engaged in one of their infamous exchanges, Fielder steered the discussion towards order. The direction he chose brought the focus back to Gavin.

"What was your suggestion, son?" the eldest leader asked.

Damn you, Gavin's mind cursed. *You know whatever I suggest will be the decided action.* In these meetings, Gavin had always withheld his opinion until the others argued themselves into a consensus. Unless he suggested something reckless—*and perhaps not even then!*—the blood in his veins would bring everyone into agreement. He had accepted his role of cell leader with reluctance; it was no small thing to have the lives of nine others dependent on your decisions. But, with eleven cells gathered, Gavin did not want to be responsible for over a hundred Ignota.

However, Fielder had chosen his words with such care that he had backed Gavin into a corner. The question had been direct. Equivocation now would reflect poorly on him, his leadership, and, more importantly to him, his cell. Founder blood or no, he had to maintain a level of respect with the other leaders.

Hoping to provide them with the grain of salt to devalue his inherited "authority," Gavin said, "I have a man out there now, so my opinion is biased. That said, my vote is to remain here, on full alert, and wait for Corey, and Danica," he added the girl before Torrance could object to the omission, "to return with better intelligence."

When he finished speaking, Gavin was pleased to find the anticipated rush of agreement was more moderate than it had been in the past. Of course, the expected McAvoy "devotees" were quick to agree. The first to voice consent was Samitha. He had worked with her on several missions in the past, and the two shared an easy friendship. Sam was then followed by Peter Yan.

Gavin's heredity outweighed whatever ill will the Sowilo might harbor over the Adirene situation. Before the Alliance crackdown, Gavin knew of two others on the continent possessing a stronger link to the Founders. Unrelated to each other, both were from his father's generation, grandchildren of Founders. Among the Sowilo, such individuals were royalty, or close to it. Gavin wondered if either was still alive. And he wondered what it meant for him if they were not.

Marshall, who would never back down from a fight no matter how slim the chance of victory, had already voiced his support. Not one to miss an opportunity to speak though, he boomed, "Gavin's right! I say we wait for those bastards to come knocking! Then we'll show them what the Ignota can do!"

Not exactly what I meant, Gavin thought behind a small smile. *If they "come knocking" it will be with a bunker buster.*

The other leaders seemed to weigh the situation with a bit more prudence. Gavin was relieved. Seamus McAvoy, his great-grandfather, could have been the only Founder, and it would not mean Gavin's opinions were any more valuable than those of the others at the table. *And it shouldn't.*

"I want to hear what Torrance thinks," Camorata said.

Now that I didn't expect. Camorata, whose position as a cell leader was alone proof against cowardice, was the last Gavin would expect to value Torrance's opinion. Camorata was cautious and adverse to even the smallest risk, whereas the other man was one of action—aggressive, violent action. Just that morning, Camorata had nearly fainted when Torrance proposed attacking the SID shipments.

"So would I," said Ewan Valencia, the youngest of the cell leaders.

"Same here," Marrett "Rett" Sheridan concurred. A few years older than Ewan, Rett was the newest to the position of cell leader. Gavin recalled too well the turbulent anxiety he had felt during his first year of command. He had had Fielder to guide and advise him. Gavin hoped the rookie leader was not looking to Torrance to fill the same role.

The eyes of the gathered cell leaders, and Sonje, turned to the man leaning against the wall. Intentional or not, Torrance's position forced one side of the table to turn in their seats to see him. Given the man's arrogance, Gavin assumed the act was deliberate. *This should be interesting,* Gavin's inner voice said.

Since day one, Torrance had made a sport of challenging and opposing any decision or suggestion Gavin offered. Worse yet, the man managed to find a tactical support for each dissent. Would he continue the trend? Or would Danica's safety trump the man's need for conflict?

In a low hard voice, Torrance spoke first in an Asian tongue, then in translation said, "Thus do many calculations lead to victory, and few calculations to defeat.' You can't calculate without information."

The cell leaders who had withheld their views, and clamored for Torrance to share his, nearly tripped over themselves to be the first to agree.

"He's right," Camorata said. "I agree with Torrance. We should wait for the scout's report."

"I agree," Ewan and Rett said in unison. The three remaining leaders followed them with further votes of support.

This is a dangerous precedent, Gavin considered. Six cell leaders had waited to hear Torrance's opinion, and then rushed to voice their agreement. *He's not one of us. They shouldn't be looking to him for decisions.* He told himself his unease had nothing to do with the others not agreeing when he had suggested the same plan. *Not entirely, anyway. We can't come to rely on an outsider. An outsider who would likely cut and run the moment the winds shifted against them.*

"He's here now, Gavin," Sonje replied when he shared that thought with her. "I don't think anyone can say the winds are in our favor down here."

The meeting of leaders adjourned after they voted to maintain the current course until better intel arrived. Once word spread of the PKs in Lorain, and the order of a condition five alert had been issued, a worried restlessness palpitated through the underground shelter. As overcrowded as it was—one could not move more than a meter without bumping elbows with a comrade—the haven was quiet. *Calm before the storm,* Gavin repeated the old phrase. *Let's hope there is no storm. Corey, where are you?*

Gavin had left word at the shelter's main entrance to be notified upon the scout's arrival. He did not want to imagine the outcome if Torrance got hold of the boy first.

"Yesterday you thought he was an ass, now you're defending him?" the Ignota leader replied.

"I'm not defending him. Truth knows he makes a point of getting under everyone's skin. I'm simply saying it's unfair to suggest he'd 'cut and run' when things got tough. Hell, the man invaded a PK base to rescue Philip Seton."

Torrance's loyalty to the Seton family *was* one of the man's more bizarre character traits. Gavin had not quite puzzled out that anomaly yet.

"Is that what he was doing in the gym? Getting under your skin?" he replied with regret. *Truth, that made me sound jealous.*

Sonje stepped close to him, placing her hands on his chest. The warm vanilla scent of her hair was a soothing salve to his frustration. It seemed so out of place—her scent, her beauty—in the dank confines of the shelter.

"No," she offered. "That was to get under your skin. Which apparently seems to have worked." She said the last part with a teasing grin.

"You said you were going to check on Philip," he responded, though his heart was no longer bruised. *Damn vanilla!*

"I know. I wanted to thank him for defending me at the morning briefing. If I told you where I was going, you would have insisted on coming and I did not want my gratitude ruined by whatever it is you two have against each other. But don't worry. He managed to be an ass without your help."

Why did hearing that bring relief?

"I could have told you that'd happen," Gavin chuckled.

"Still, despite his personality, he is an asset. Even you have to admit he has skills we need. He's like a one man cell."

Gavin had joked with Sonje that one day she would make an excellent cell leader. Over the last two months, that belief had strengthened. She may demur and think herself inadequate for their struggle, but he knew a leader when he met one. Already the others in his cell, and even the other leaders, valued her counsel.

"And an outsider's view might be valuable," she added.

Narrowing his eyes, Gavin asked, "What does that mean?"

"The Ignota has been doing things a certain way for over a hundred years. Sometimes tradition can be good, other times tradition becomes narrow-mindedness," she answered with hesitation slowing her words.

"Really? How so?" he said taking a step back.

"Maybe Torrance is right. Maybe the Ignota cells need to unite."

He did not intend the laugh to be as derisive as it was, but it escaped his throat before he could stop it. "The Ignota operate in cells not because of tradition! This," he cast his arms wide and moved in a circle, "this is why we work as cells. If the Alliance does strike Oberlin, they'll wipe out eleven cells! Even Marshall knows uniting is lunacy! Marshall, the man who, if he had only a slingshot, would be the first to volunteer to assault the Council itself! It's not narrow-mindedness, Sonje. It's a full understanding of what we're facing!"

Gavin would have paid any price for the chance to turn the clock back fifteen seconds. While he believed in the sentiment, he knew the harsh delivery was out of line. Sonje had rolled her lips into her teeth in a physical effort to bite back a sharp-bladed retort.

"Sonje, I—" he began.

"No, you're right," she replied in a tone that implied the opposite. "Well, like I said, I only went to thank him because *he* defended me."

And there's the stab.

He had sensed something had needled her when they had left the morning meeting. More than just Peter Yan's accusations, that is. If anyone under his command had questioned the Adirene event, Gavin would have provided a full-throated defense. But, it had been another cell leader. To dignify the accusations with a response would have given the Sowilo unearned power within the Ignota, it also would have opened the door for leaders to question the internal operation of other cells. *Another dangerous precedent.*

Gavin was about to explain just that when Ament, the second scout in his cell, came through the door.

"Corey just got into town," he informed Gavin.

"And Danica?" Sonje asked.

"She's with him."

"Thank Truth," Gavin said with sincerity. *One crisis averted.*

"Torrance is already waiting at the entrance," Ament added.

Or not.

"Shit," the cell leader spat as he pushed past Ament, and first jogged, then ran to the shelter's main entry.

By the worried pleading of a young female voice ringing along the passage, Gavin knew the altercation he had hoped to bypass had already begun. Sure enough, he turned the hall to find a shocked crowd around Torrance, who was holding the scout against the wall. The boy's toes did not touch the ground, and a thin line of blood was trickling down his chin. A meter to the left, Kunbo, the Dead Continent refugee and Gavin's weapons master, had a semi-automatic handgun leveled at Torrance's head. Danica was crying, and shrieking, as she tried to remove Torrance's hands from Corey's person. Thinking the situation had reached its apex, Ament drew his firearm as soon as he saw his fellow scout's assault.

"I have no wish to harm you, sir," Kunbo said, not a hint of worry to be heard in his African accent. ""I will count to three for you to release my brother. One. Two."

Seeing no indication Torrance was going to comply, and knowing Kunbo never made idle threats, Gavin stepped in to mediate. Keeping his voice calm, but with enough volume to break through the fog of tension these men were in, he said, "Okay, let's not overreact here, guys. Tempers are hot, and I understand that. Kunbo and Ament, you're both going to lower your weapons because, Torrance, I know you're not going to hurt Corey." *Any more than you already have,* he added in thought.

The two men of his cell, while hesitant, began to lower their guns. Even with one of their own threatened, the two would never ignore a direct command from their accepted leader. Torrance, however, had no such compulsion to obey. *And this is why he's a liability, not an asset.*

Playing the lone card Gavin believed left in his deck, he looked to Danica. Upon his arrival with Sonje, the girl's hysterics had made a fractional decrease.

"Danica," he said, "are you all right?"

Simpering, she nodded.

Come on, kid, kind of need you to speak.

"Everyone was very worried about you," Gavin continued. "But, you're okay? Nothing bad happened?"

"I got pod-sick on the way back," the girl said.

So, no, nothing bad happened.

With Danica's well-being established, Gavin addressed Torrance. "Look man, I know you're pissed. So am I. But, they're both back in one piece. Now, I need you to put my man down and step away so *I* can deal with him."

Through it all, Torrance had not taken his eyes from Corey. Gavin wondered if the man had even heard anything. Fearing the inevitability of a violent outcome, Gavin flinched when Torrance broke his pose. Turning his head to Danica, the unpredictable warrior asked, "You're not hurt?"

"I'm not hurt," she assured him.

With obvious reluctance, Torrance released the scout and backed away as

Gavin had asked. For his part, Corey managed to find his footing before sliding to the floor like a ragdoll.

Gavin suppressed a sigh of relief. *No need for everyone to know I thought this would end in a gunfight.*

"Corey, report to the conference room for debrief," he commanded. Torrance may have overstepped, but Gavin still needed to hold the scout accountable for his gross breach in judgment. Corey walked by with his head held low, shrugging away from Danica's attempt at comfort. Gavin could imagine the boy's embarrassment. No amount of formal punishment, or busted lips, could equal a man's shame in being bloodied in front of the girl he's sweet on.

Ament shot a final glare at his friend's attacker before following Corey down the hall. The crowd that had formed had yet to disperse.

"We're still at condition five, people. Get back to your posts," Gavin let his voice boom with emphasis. Murmuring as they went, those gathered obeyed the directive.

Turning to the African, Gavin said, "I'm sure word's already out, but inform the other leaders the meeting is reconvening."

The muscular giant still held himself ready for battle. He stared at Torrance while the man, joined by Sonje, scolded the girl.

"It's done, my friend," Gavin tried to relax the weapons master.

Tilting his head down to meet Gavin's eyes, Kunbo said, "I do not like that man."

With a short laugh, he replied, "That makes two of us."

The pinching vice of a tension headache had now encircled his entire skull. Beyond the understandable anxiety created by the proximity of a large PK force, the conference room choked with lines of animosity. Torrance stared down Corey. Corey returned the same. Sonje had made a point of sitting several seats away from Gavin; and Gavin was quite done with them all. *This is worse than when Adirene was here,* he mulled.

"Vinsy seems to think it's all meant to rattle the Ignota and force us to expose our location," Corey said again. During his entire debrief, the scout had not once looked to Gavin.

"Two carrier groups is a bit of overkill, though, no?" Fielder asked. There was skepticism in his voice, but Gavin knew the man would keep an open mind.

"True," said Peter Yan. "But, then that's the point, isn't it? Put two carrier groups in the Lake, and you'd have cells in a thousand kilometer radius getting antsy. The PKs could just watch for movement and then strike."

Samitha Borden, the lone female leader in the room, was doubtful. "They would have to believe cells have gathered together. Even if one cell did get 'antsy,' who'd notice movement? Ten people could travel in two pods, that's not enough to attract their attention."

"Sam's right," Gavin replied, for once not withholding his opinion until the meeting's end. Part of him hoped speaking early would hasten the meeting's end. This day had seen too many hours crammed into the same room. "If it's a ploy to flush out Ignota, then they must know there's a large grouping of us in the area."

From his seat at the far end of the table—and to the immediate right of Sonje—Torrance guffawed. Gavin had watched with hidden irritation when the man had chosen the seat. Sonje seemed just as annoyed by the arrangement. *Screw it,* Gavin swore. *It's jealousy.*

"I don't know how you people managed to survive for a century," the man said. "We've sat in this room every day for weeks listening to reports of cells that have fallen to the Alliance. And now you think they'd commit two carrier groups to finding a hundred men hiding underground? When all it would take is a handful of PK-drones to bring the roof down? They're not afraid of you; they're winning and they know it. You're the only ones that don't know it yet."

The words filled each corner of the room; suffocating with accusation and truth. It was the argument Torrance had made almost daily. The Ignota were losing. Only now, with an army of PKs *not attacking* did Gavin begin to believe that perhaps the man was right. The force in Lorain had nothing to do with the Ignota hidden just kilometers away.

"The SIDs," Gavin said aloud. *Sonje, Danica, Philip—it's always been about the SIDs.* "It's a defensive force. They're using the carrier groups to deliver the chips to the implantation centers."

"We can't be sure of that," Camorata countered, though his tone suggested agreement.

Nodding, Gavin replied, "There's only one way to find out."

And only one man who can do it, he added in his thoughts as he turned to Torrance.

Meeting the warrior's heavy stare, the cell leader felt uneasy with the amount of trust they would be forced to place in this man . . . this outsider from the woods.

CHAPTER EIGHT

Liam Walford

"If you wish, I can fetch something else, sir," Mitchall Kingston said.

Engrossed in his melancholy thoughts, Liam had nearly forgotten the boy was present. The *boy* was in truth nearing forty years of age, but the aide's ever-youthful face made that fact easy to forget. And, Liam had known him for well over two decades; training him when Mitchall was just a young teen. A skilled pupil, the boy had learned quickly, growing to become one of Liam's most trusted spies. Given all that had occurred, Liam knew he should count himself fortunate to have one such as Mitchall at his side. Yet too much had occurred for him to find any fortune in his world.

Looking down at his dish, Liam understood his aide's comment. He had been pushing the highly salted and overly sauced chicken pieces across the plate with his fork. The Americans had never grasped the subtleties of Asian cuisine. Even if the dinner had been palatable, Liam would have been unable to find his appetite.

"No, it's fine," he told Mitchall, who dipped his chin and let Liam return to his sulk. The aide had grown quite accustomed to his master's dark broods. Though today's was remarkably dim, for the world learned of yet another way he had failed House Garrott.

The Council's swift, and unexpected, attack against the House had crippled Liam's intelligence network far worse than he had thought possible. Still, word of Aubrey Garrott's fate had eventually reached his ears. He had hoped she was alive and in hiding after escaping the raid. Two weeks ago, however, Liam received word the girl was the prisoner of Caput Hu and scheduled to marry him. With little resources, he had tried his best to find some way to remove her from the Viper's grasp.

All in vain, he thought. He had come close to upending the holoset platform when this morning's news reported on the completed nuptials.

Liam Walford, Chief Advisor to House Garrott—*former Chief Advisor,* his mind corrected, *to the former House Garrott*—had spent several decades creating and perfecting a network of spies and informants across the globe. And in the span of a single morning, the Council had all but destroyed his achievement. That pained him as much as his inability to assist Aubrey.

At least, he knew *she* was alive. There had been no word on Tilden, the House's heir, beyond that he had escaped the initial assault. Possibly in the company of an Ignota cell, if that first report had been accurate. *Another failure that,* Liam soured again. If the Alliance-controlled media was to be believed, the actress, Isla Carene, had been an Ignotum. *And you let her get close to the Family!*

It was selfish, and wicked he knew, but in many ways Liam was relieved Kerwen Garrott had not lived to see all of his Chief Advisor's many failures. *Whatever years I may have left to me, I will work to right these many wrongs.*

But how? his mind teased back.

Though it pained him to abandon Aubrey to the Viper's many schemes, Liam knew the priority was locating and rescuing Tilden. Until he had proof otherwise, Tilden was still heir to House Garrott and thus took precedence over the younger sibling. *Forgive me, Aubrey.*

There was some comfort in knowing the girl was likely making Caput Hu regret the forced marriage. Of all the Garrott children, Aubrey had inherited the full measure of her mother's cunning and the father's wisdom. Liam had overseen her instruction and he knew she was quite capable of ensuring her own survival. In fact, he had thought she might one day succeed him as Chief Advisor. *Yes,* he mulled as he forced a bite of the chicken, *she'll be all right for now.*

Tilden, however, was less suited to play the role of hostage. He was softer than his sister. Tilden too had inherited the late Caput's wisdom, but it was tempered by Kerwen's naïve kindness as well. Liam recalled the father's early days after rising to the Council seat; it had become a daily task steering him away from pitfalls and traps. He had grown into the title, though. And in the end, Liam believed Kerwen the greatest Caput in the Family's history.

I must get him away from the Ignota before they ruin him!

Again, the voice of his thoughts mocked, *But how?*

As surely as the Council hunted the heir, they would be searching for Liam as well. His reputation marked him as a loose end too dangerous to leave unsevered. It was a hard won miracle he and Mitchall had eluded the Alliance as long as they have. Most of his aliases and contacts had been compromised, and only a scattering of his most hidden credit accounts remained available to him. The last attempt to obtain intelligence from one of his sources in New York City had ended with a barely achieved escape. Since then, Liam assumed everyone in his network was under surveillance.

At least we managed to obtain the scan-jams. Upon realizing they had been betrayed, Liam had swiped the devices from the contact's hands as Mitchall ran a knife across the man's throat. It was a half-minute before the PKs had swooped in. The PKs would have caught a lesser person, but Liam never entered a situation without ensuring a proper and swift exit existed. The scan-jams disrupted facial recognition software, thus allowing Liam and his aide more freedom in moving about in the open.

Not that one would want to be in the open in New York City. The outer boroughs were still considered livable, but the main island of Manhattan had long since fallen into decay. Beyond the congestion of people and pods that assaulted the senses, the city was a filthy sewer of crime and depravity. The skyscrapers that had once been a beacon of success were now soaring megaplexes offering every type of debauchery and vice a degenerate soul might fancy. Manhattan was a carnival of sin, and thus a major source of Caput De Luca's wealth. The bloated Italian controlled the world's entertainment industry—from the necessity of clothes to the extravagance of the perversions offered in this city. As such, it was the ideal place for two men to hide themselves from notice.

Until we can get ourselves back to England.

Finally quitting the exercise of attempting to eat, easier now that the chicken was cold and the sauce had begun to congeal, Liam rose from the small dining table and tossed the meal into the rubbish bin. The living quarters they had secured were sparsely furnished yet still adequate for their needs. Two small bedrooms, a kitchen, and a large sitting area. The identity Liam had used to rent the space could have afforded far more luxury, but he was hesitant to burn through credits. Only a fool wasted what should be saved. While wise, whoever had coined the old adage had never tasted his meal.

"I don't have much of an appetite," he said to Mitchall. Liam knew the aide would feel responsible if he seemed displeased with the meal. *It's not his fault. I instructed him to avoid anything of higher quality.* The Council would expect him to appease his taste for refinement. *A few more weeks of this and I might.*

"What are the risks of flying?" he asked the younger man and began the ritual once again. It was a process he had adopted as a youth. When faced with a puzzle, Liam preferred to ask questions and evaluate the answers in the hopes of finding a flaw in his own thinking. Mitchall was accustomed to the process and hid whatever frustration he might be feeling with the endless repetition.

Putting his own meal aside, the aide replied, "Normal levels of security are tight. Facial scans, SID scans at multiple checkpoints."

"Which can be bypassed with scan-jams and false identities," Liam said.

"But, the Alliance is currently at a much higher level of security. SID scans will be verifying more than just identities. The identities will need to show an active history: education and employment history, banking records, purchasing history, etc. Anything without an active history will be scrutinized," Mitchall countered.

"Our identities have active histories," the spymaster said. He was amazed when criminals thought a new name, which had never before existed, would be enough to circumvent security systems. True, it was often sufficient for smaller scale crimes—fraud and petty theft—but anything of substance required greater detail. The identities he and Mitchall possessed had complete profiles, down to familial relations and restaurant tabs.

"True. However, we'd still be caught through facial recognition. The scan-jams will block the cameras, but the digitals on our SIDs will also be run through the system. Only two ways around that. One, hack the system itself. Two, alter our facial structure."

Liam was not opposed to the latter option, though he was not keen on relying on a black market surgeon to perform the procedure without complications. *Especially not one in this city.* There was no telling what materials would be used. Plus, even with skin and bone accelerant, the recovery time would be longer than events might allow.

Hacking the system was far simpler. Or, it would have been if the Alliance had not destroyed his network of resources. Three months earlier and Liam could have done it himself from any government-linked terminal. Liam Walford had been Chief Advisor to two Caputs; it had been years since he had been this powerless. And the sensation was grating.

"Sea crossing?" he questioned, dismissing the rising frustration. *What's done is done.*

"Many of the same risks," Mitchall answered. "Passenger ships have the same protocols as airliners. Cargo vessels are a bit less secure, though with the Ignota crackdown PKs are boarding and searching every ship once it reaches port."

"Abandoning the ship before it makes port?"

"We drown," Mitchall said. During their last question-and-answer drill, Liam had argued the possibility of swimming to land after jumping ship. Losing his patience, Mitchall had muttered, albeit under his breath, a rather impolite assessment of his master's advanced age.

Clearing his throat, Liam moved on to the next option: a journey across land. Specifically, crossing the American continent to Alaska, traveling through the tunnel to Russia, then on to mainland Europe, to reach England. While the cost and length of such a trek were not prohibitive, a simple calculation of probability *was* a compelling deterrent.

"Too many checkpoints along the way," Mitchall stated. Pushing his chair back from the table, the aide dropped his empty container into the bin to join Liam's unfinished, and unwanted, meal.

A chill of excited illumination lifted the gray hairs of Liam's forearms.

"Unwanted," he said just above a whisper.

"Sir?"

"We need to be unwanted. We need to be so unwanted that who we are does not matter, but instead *what* we are!" Liam realized his voice had risen to a shout.

"Sir—" Mitchall, always quick to follow Liam's conclusion, began to protest.

"It's the one place in the world the Alliance doesn't keep people from entering." Despite the many risks, there was never a shortage of bleeding heart fools who forsook civilization and booked passage to the Dead Continent. Some went to retrace their ancestors' African roots, but most had some romantic notion of educating the Deaders so that they might rise beyond their suffering. If there were any risk of that occurring, the Alliance would have put an immediate stop to the practice. The majority ended up dead within a few months' time, the rest were lucky to survive a year.

"And it's also the one place in the world the Alliance doesn't let people leave," the aide argued.

"Twaddle! There are smugglers who make their lives' fortune trafficking on the DC. Half the diamonds of House Garrott were 'acquired through discreet channels.'

The ruling class never "bought illegally.'"

Mitchall attempted one final plea for sanity. "Sir, you're suggesting that in order to avoid capture by Peacekeepers, we should travel to a land ruled by tribal warlords who are known to sacrifice and *cannibalize* their young!"

Liam was certain that rumor was untrue. In an effort to gain support for establishing the blockade around the DC, the first Council of Five had begun a propaganda campaign attributing many unsavory stories to the Deaders. Eager to believe the worst, few wondered how anyone still lived on the DC if the inhabitants had been killing their children for the last hundred years. That a man as educated as Mitchall believed such a tale was a testament to the campaign's enduring success. Even still, the Dead Continent was an extremely dangerous place for all but the heartiest warriors.

Which is exactly why the Council would not think to look for us there.

Once decided on a course of action, Liam and his assistant, who had surrendered to the plan with reluctance, spent the following days searching the city's various ports for a ship bound for the DC. Three days, and they were no closer to finding transport. Mitchall hoped the old spymaster would give up the task as captain after captain shook his head and named a different destination. Liam, however, refused to turn aside. *Surely, in this of all cities, there's someone eager to relieve a fool of his credits!* On the fourth day, they met just such a man.

Gervasio Dimas, the captain of the *Espado do Mar,* was a storybook made flesh. Vulgar and surly, Dimas was shouting a string of crude insults as he stood on the dock. The English-Portuguese expletives seemed to be directed to anyone, and everyone, within hearing distance. The brown skin of his exposed chest, arms, and face—tanned even darker by years in the sun—bore intricate patterns tattooed in white ink. It was a centuries-old primitive custom that had seen an inexplicable rebirth several decades past. Now, it was commonplace for Caputs and their wives to paint scrolling designs on their faces for formal events. *Symbols of a warrior's power,* Liam mused on the practice's origin. Unlike a Caput, though, Captain Dimas had likely earned his marks in much the same way as the ancients.

Barrel-chested with short, but muscular, arms and legs, the man reminded Liam of the bulldog breed of his homeland. He wore the thick, curly black hair of his South American ancestry, the kind that shined without moisture, well past his shoulder and secured the locks with a leather cord. If he had an eye patch, Captain Dimas would have fit in the pre-Alliance literature Liam's father had cherished.

"Captain Dimas," Liam said as they drew closer to the man. Looking up from the digital manifest in his hand, Dimas shot an angry look, first to an innocent auburn-haired man a few feet away, then to the two men who were guilty of interrupting his tirade.

"Ex'a risin's 'ready palmed!" he barked, assuming Liam and Mitchall were representatives from the city's port authority come to collect docking fees. Liam was proud at how quickly he was able to translate the sailor's speech; it had been some time since he had done business with the captain's sort. Between the natural evolution of languages combining, and trades developing their own shorthand, two men could both speak English and neither understands the other's words.

"I'm not here to ask you for money, Captain," Liam explained. "Quite the opposite really. My associate and I are seeking—"

"Got no ticks to trash on hawkers. E'en dap'dan ones," the man growled back, spat on the dock, and turned away. Now knowing the men were not government officials, Dimas felt no need for civility.

Raising his voice to reach the departing man, Liam said, "I've no intention of wasting your time, sir. I want to buy passage."

At the mention of credits, the captain slowed his march. He turned back to the two men and re-crossed his steps. "She's full up," he said.

Of course she is. That's why you turned around, you dumb brute. Liam dared not let the smile in his thoughts touch his face. *And now the negotiations.*

"Surely you can find some small corner to place two million credits," Liam replied. The seaman displayed no reaction to the high amount of the opening offer. *So, you're a smuggler, Captain Dimas,* Liam assessed. *Only a smuggler could hear that number and remain stoic. And a smuggler is going to be very cautious.* Negotiating might not be as smooth as he had hoped.

"Can wing to Port fer less," Dimas replied.

"True, but Portugal is not our destination."

"S'mine."

Lifting a brow, Liam pressed, "I've heard you're known to make other stops, Captain. Even ferrying people to the DC for the right price."

The captain's laugh was not much different from his shouting. "You dap'dans'll get dead in'a first tick!"

Mitchall cleared his throat in unsubtle agreement. Dressed and tailored as they were, Liam could understand why the captain doubted the men possessed any skills for survival. *Let him believe we're a pair of wealthy fools.*

"We don't believe the savages are beyond redemption, Captain. With time and patience, and the proper teachers, they can be taught civility. I do, however, appreciate your concern for our safety. Perhaps another million credits would ease whatever guilt you may feel for delivering us to our death."

Dimas studied them. Liam could find nothing in his expression to indicate any temptation by the offer. *Not a man I'd want to play poker with,* the spymaster mused. *It was a rare man indeed who could hide his thoughts from the Chief Advisor of House Garrott. Even Torrance had had his tells,* Liam thought back to the brief encounter with his son. *And he had been well trained.*

Spitting a second splotch of saliva, the captain said, "Dois mill apiece, palmed ahead. N'you share d'cabin."

"Shared cabin, two million credits each—half at departure, half upon arrival—and direct to the DC before Portugal," Liam countered. The price was hundreds of times greater than the journey was worth, and half as much as Liam had been willing to pay to reach home.

Captain Dimas nodded his acceptance of the counter offer and informed them the ship was scheduled to leave in two days, or "risins" as he put it.

Walking back along the dock, Dimas' return to cursing fading in the distance, Mitchall said, "That was rather simple."

"Mmm," Liam replied, his mind already replaying and analyzing the negotiations. "Rather *too* simple. We never gave names, and he never asked. Even the dullest smuggler would want to know who was boarding his ship. And my instincts say Mr. Dimas is far from dull. We'll need to be vigilant throughout the crossing."

"Are you ever not vigilant, sir?" Mitchall asked with a soft laugh.

Liam appreciated the man's loyalty. Even if it was misplaced. *It's my lapse in vigilance which brought us here.*

Neither spymaster nor apprentice, however, noticed the man with red hair following their steps.

CHAPTER NINE

Aubrey Garrott Hu

"Does Your Grace desire anything else?" the old, heart-faced servant asked after placing the ornate silver tray upon the nearby table.

"That will be all," Aubrey replied in a curt chill. The servant may look the part of a sweet, doddering grandmother, but Aubrey knew the woman for what she was: a spy for Caput Hu. *Just like everyone else in this Truth-damned place!*

The servant bowed and withdrew from the room, leaving Aubrey alone with her thoughts once again. The warmly decorated study—the two longer walls held shelves of books from floor to ceiling—offered a breathtaking view of snow-laden trees before ending at the shore of Kunming Lake. Though her mood could not appreciate the vista, she did prefer to pass the time secluded in this study. It was an effort, but there had been times when she lost herself in one of the room's many tomes. The collection was expansive, an equal mix of English and Mandarin texts, and included original copies of works several hundred years old. For a lover of such antiquities, the study was an unexpected paradise. Today, though, as it had been for the last two days, she could not bring herself to enjoy any of its treasures.

Two days, she thought. *Truth, but it feels like a year.*

The wedding ceremony had been a brief, private affair. Hu was wise enough not to risk her denouncing him in public. Not that she would have had the chance arisen. *What purpose would it have served?* The marriage would have been made official regardless. She had resigned herself to that fact as soon as she had been delivered to her future husband. Gnashed teeth and stubborn refusals would not change her predicament. No, the many locks of her prison were too complex. She would need to pick them slowly, and subtly, if she hoped to extricate herself.

And she would have to do it alone.

The Council had spared no one attached to House Garrott. Chefs, guards, and maids had suffered the same fate as the Family. Those images, those horrible memories, brought her screaming from sleep each night. When she had been brought to Beijing, it had been in the company of the enemy—strangers every one. She had learned, however, that the Council's extermination had not been a complete success.

No one had told her directly, but Aubrey had caught enough whispers to learn Tilden still lived. A fact that rankled her new husband; though he as well never spoke of it in her presence. *Whatever Hu's plan, it obviously did not include the heir to House Garrott surviving the strike against the Family.* Which only made her question her value. With Tilden alive, might Hu find her unnecessary? And what of this "Shā Shŏu" she had heard mentioned? Her captors seemed agitated when discussing him. From what she had gathered, "Shā Shŏu" had also avoided the Council's treason. Aubrey had seen the bodies of her parents and three younger brothers, so she knew the name did not reference them. *A cousin, perhaps?* Whoever, she could neither rely on nor expect assistance from either survivor.

Given the levels of security and constant surveillance Hu had placed on her, help from outside sources was doomed to failure. As much as she pretended to be alone in the study, Aubrey was certain hidden cameras were recording every breath and blink. Any excursion beyond the study, whether to return to her chambers or a simple walk down the hall, found her surrounded by no less than twenty guards. That half the force was comprised of drones—her father's grandest achievement—was an insulting test of her composure. But, she persevered.

Her Mother may not have given Aubrey Garrott the gift of exquisite beauty, but she had received Roslyn Garrott's strength and keen intellect. And Liam Walford had tempered and sharpened both traits to a deadly edge. Caput Hu may be known as the Viper, but Aubrey Garrott was . . . was . . . what? *A mongoose?* The comparison brought a long absent laugh to her lips. *Not the most fear-inducing analogy,* she thought. *Nor the most flattering.* Yet, in many ways, it fit.

With eyes just a bit too close together, a proud nose, and thin lips, her looks did not turn heads—either in disgust or in lust. Tall and slender, only an utter craven would find her intimidating. *Well, that's not entirely true,* her mind corrected. She was a member of the Five Families, or had been, and her last name demanded respect and a certain level of fear. Her mother, though, had never needed the name. Roslyn Garrott could have been one of the maids and she would have still set every knee to trembling. Aubrey knew she would never have that ability. *Yes, a mongoose is* quite *fitting.*

With most of her days uninterrupted—she had not seen Hu since the conclusion of the ceremony—Aubrey had a great deal of time to develop a strategy. The interactions with her captors had shifted from glares and harsh words to somewhat indifferent dislike. Another week or two, and she would dampen the hostility to a passable level of civility. Then, wait perhaps a month before initiating a conversation. She *was* a Garrott after all. No one would believe the act if she suddenly befriended her captors. Her "evolution" would have to be slow.

In time, Hu might grant her more freedoms, allow her to move beyond this one floor of the Caput'e's wing of the palace. Within a year, the man could come to trust his ever-less-reluctant wife. It was a difficult thing to ponder the long days between now and then. But, Liam had taught her patience.

True, the opportunity to escape might arrive before then. What would that gain her though? *A life of hiding, that's what.* There was no longer a Family to offer shelter and exact revenge. If Tilden managed to stay alive, he would have no support in reclaiming a Council seat. In some cruel joke, life had placed Aubrey in the perfect position to avenge her Family. However many years it might take.

She would make no efforts to escape, even when Hu arranged such chances. *Which he will, of course. How better to test my loyalty?* Aubrey would also resist the powerful urges to kill the man should such an occasion present itself. Killing him would accomplish nothing. Another member of his Family would succeed him, and then order her execution. House Hu had destroyed her entire Family. Justice required she return the same punishment.

"A wounded enemy is often more dangerous that one unharmed," Liam had once said during a lesson. "For the wounded one might heal and return with double anger. Only an enemy, completely destroyed, poses no threat."

Caput Hu had erred in allowing her to live. When she took her revenge, Aubrey would not make the same mistake.

A servant, dressed in the livery of House Hu, entered through the lacquered doors at the far end of the study. Unannounced, and uninvited, the Asian man did not wait for permission before approaching. She assumed the breach in protocol was a result of her prisoner status. But then, many of the customs she had observed over the last few weeks had differed greatly from her Western experiences. Some had come as quite a shock.

She had nearly screamed when, on her first morning in the palace, two young women had followed her into the shower. It was one thing to have a valet or lady's maid help you dress; quite another to have them offer to bathe you. *It's a shower for Truth's sake! How much help does one need?* Aubrey had learned this land—*my new home*—was a bizarre mixture of the ancient and the modern.

The servant bowed when he reached her. She doubted the gesture was as deep as it should have been for a servant to a Caput`e. Even a captive Caput`e.

"His Grace has ordered you to dine with him tonight," the man said in barely accented English. *No title for me,* she noted. The use of "ordered" told her how truly far she was from even the shadow of power.

Not waiting for a reply, as if she could refuse anyway, the man turned on his heel and left the study. His distaste in having to speak those few words to her was evident in his tone and brusqueness. It mattered little. He was out of her thoughts before he left the room.

Hu had not sought her company but twice since her arrival. Once to "welcome" her and inform her of their pending wedding; then again to speak the words of matrimony at the ceremony. Still unsure what purpose the man had planned for her, Aubrey prepared her wit for the encounter.

Hours later, a trio of maids had whisked her from the study into her chambers. The women spoke in their native tongue as they fussed and primped Aubrey for the dinner. Their words, delivered soft and rapid, had a lyrical quality that worked to soothe her nerves. Or it did until she began to wonder what they were saying about her. At one point, the three broke into a girlish giggle. The sounds seemed a paradox to their ages; the youngest was in her mid-twenties and thus not much younger than Aubrey herself.

The clothes they bustled her into were of modern design, unlike the heavy wrappings of their kimonos. The dress, made of dark gray silk with intricate weaves of crimson threading, had the high collar popular on the world's runways, and plunged to a point midway between her breasts and navel. The fabric of the upper arms clung tightly then flared wide at the elbows into an angel sleeve with cuffs almost touching the floor. The garment's hem did touch the floor, but only just, and had a waist-high slit at the left. As did all the clothes Hu had provided, the dress fit with perfection.

The delicate headpiece held back the raven hair of her father's blood, and draped a small triangular net of diamonds across her forehead. A tear-shaped ruby, the size of her thumb, hung from its lowest point and rested between her brows. Down her chest, one of the maids inked a single line of Asian characters. Their meaning was a mystery to Aubrey, but the artistry of the black marks was exquisite. Her face was painted, with only enough color to sharpen her eyes and highlight the structure of her cheeks.

The maids finished their work by slipping a ruby ring on the third finger of her left hand. A thin string of diamonds reached across the back of her hand and connected the ring to a wide bracelet of larger diamonds. While beautiful, Aubrey thought the piece too reminiscent of a collar and leash.

Giggling once again, the women backed away to allow her to examine their work in the full-length mirror. She was no Roslyn, she knew, but she could not deny the reflection was impressive. A captive she may be, but a Caput`e stared back in the glass.

Sooner than she had strategized, Aubrey offered the three women a small smile as she bowed her head in approval and appreciation.

Beyond the chambers, her usual ring of guards waited to escort her to their master. Venturing further than she had previously been allowed, Aubrey made a quick study of the surroundings as they walked. Again, the mix of old and new caught her eyes as they passed shallow alcoves tucked with heavily lacquered tables and stands. Jade statues, suits of wicker and metal armor, and gleaming swords sat upon the tables. None of the artifacts younger than five centuries. In other places, she saw the technology of the day: holosets and SID scanners. And of course, the PK-drones. If she had thought her Family home held memories of times past, this palace made the Garrott estate young in comparison.

Upon reaching the dining room, two guards slid the paper-paneled door closed behind her, leaving her alone with Hu. She was at first surprised he would meet her unprotected, but then laughed at herself. *What threat do I really pose?* He was the Viper; trained as well as any PK, if not better. *He could subdue me in a blink.*

Rising from the table, Hu slid out a chair for her. Aubrey hesitated as unexpected fear swelled within. *Foolish. If he intended to harm me, he could have had me killed in my sleep dozens of times.* Not the most reassuring thought. Forcing the emotion away, Aubrey walked forward and accepted the offered seat.

Returning to his place, Hu smiled, "You look truly beautiful, Aubrey. As always."

She replied with a thin smile. One that did not reach her eyes. She was still unsure how to play this scene. *Simpering?* If Hu had any knowledge of her, and he certainly must, he knew no one would ever describe her in such a way. *Angry?* Expected, and understandable, but too much hostility would take longer to undo. *Resigned?* Perhaps, but measured. Aubrey had planned to work through his servants first, have his spies report on the changes in her demeanor.

"I trust you have found your quarters acceptable?" he asked as a servant entered with a decanter of wine.

"Yes, Your Grace," she said, careful to keep all emotion from her tone.

Lifting the glass to his nose, Hu inhaled before tasting the small amount the servant had poured. Finding the vintage to his liking, he nodded for the man to fill the glass.

"Aubrey, please call me Xian. We are married now, there's no need to address me so formally." The man's voice smooth, breathy but clear.

"Xian, then," she said as the servant finished pouring her glass. She did not intend to drink the wine. As one servant left, another entered. The new arrival placed a dish of assorted leafy rolls and wraps before each diner. The previous meals served during her captivity had been almost entirely of Eastern cuisine. Aubrey had been surprised how well she had enjoyed the unfamiliar fare.

"I would have done this sooner," he said while sampling the food on his plate. "But, I doubt you're that eager to be near me, much less share a meal."

"I have a strong stomach," Aubrey returned.

Chuckling low, the Caput replied, "Very good, quite clever. You must understand the situation with your father was not personal. In many ways, I liked Kerwen. He was a good man. If perhaps too trusting. I, however, am not as trusting. Control of the drones was far too much power to allow one man, one Family. If I had thought he'd have been willing to share control with the rest of the Council, then such drastic measures could have been avoided."

The candor of his words was unforeseen.

"You make no secret of your treason?" she asked.

"Why should I? You know the truth. What point is there in denying it? Though I do wonder if you consider your late father guilty of treason as well."

Hotly, more hotly than she wished, Aubrey said, "By your own words you admitted to plotting against my father! The accusations of him conspiring with the Ignota to assassinate a Caput are false!"

Furrowing his brow, Hu said, "You don't know, do you?"

Refusing to speak while her temper still flared, Aubrey stared back.

"You are correct that your father did not plot with the *Ignota*. But, he did plot. The bomb discovered in the drone was placed at your father's command. He believed he was working with me and Alexavier Cambrie to remove House De Luca from power. It was a test. Of my design. Had Kerwen refused to participate, your Family would still be alive. By agreeing, he proved himself untrustworthy.

"The only alteration I made was having the drone delivered to Fawzan instead of the Italian. Fawzan and your father were as near to friends as our positions allow. Had the plot been against De Luca, Fawzan might have been more lenient. Learning that his friend, however, had turned against him forced our beloved Council elder to take bolder action."

Hu laid out his treachery with the ease of one chatting up a friend at a pub, even eating and drinking through the confession. Worse, Aubrey found no hint of falsehood in the delivery. *That doesn't matter,* she decided in her mind. Whatever the alleged sins of her Family, she was still a Garrott. And Hu had betrayed her House. The flame of vengeance had not diminished. No, it still burned in her soul.

She searched her mind for a well-chosen reply. Hu, though, had rattled her thoughts. Instinctive memories of Liam Walford's teaching fought through the jumble, and Aubrey worked the meditative technique he had taught her. Within a few heartbeats, the chaos of her mind retreated just enough to let her think.

"And what purpose do I serve? Am I a trophy of your victory?" she asked, her voice once again under her control.

"Partly, yes," Hu answered. "Though a woman has never sat on the Council, you are still the heir to House Garrott."

Keeping her knowledge of Tilden's escape secret, Aubrey asked, "What then? You intend to reinstate my Family? Place me on the Council?"

Hu did not answer. Instead, the man drained the last of the wine from his glass and raised two fingers to signal the servants. Five men entered; two to clear the appetizer plates (of which Aubrey had eaten little), two to serve the main course, and the last to refill the Caput's wine.

"Bring the Capute some water," he instructed the last man. Neither Aubrey nor her new husband spoke while the servants conducted their duties. Instead, the pair sat with their gazes locked in a stare. Hu's was calculating and precise. Aubrey's hard and cold. Both made a penetrating study of the other.

Caput Hu had the coloring of his ancestors; a light butterscotch crème free of blemish or stubble. The angles of his face—the high defined cheekbones and squared jaw—were more Western than most of the Asian men she had known. His narrow nose, tapering to a point at the tip, covered the even distance from the almond-shaped eyes and small naturally pursed lips. Like Aubrey, the man's hair was darker than night, and he wore it well styled with a part on the right. She could read nothing in the gray-hazel eyes. And she hoped he could read nothing in hers.

Once the servants disappeared back into the anteroom, Hu resumed their discussion. "Initially, I *did* hope to see you inherit your father's seat. A challenge to be sure given the more than a century of tradition we'd have to overcome. But, the others insisted Kerwen's removal be explained as an Ignota plot. A suggestion to which I was opposed. I see no purpose in hiding the fact the Houses removed one of our own. Better the people see the act as an internal power struggle rather than a terrorist infiltration. But, alas, I was out-voiced. So, unfortunately, even if the Council managed to break with tradition and seat a woman, they would never agree to seat the daughter of a 'known Ignota traitor'."

"Then, why marry me if I'm of no use?" *Careful, Aubrey,* she cautioned. *No need to prove your futility.*

Shrugging, Hu lifted a glass as if toasting. He smiled and said, "Do you know what Xian means? Roughly translated, it means 'enlightened person.' The future is constantly changing, my lovely bride. Who knows how events might unfold? A day may yet come when a Garrott wife proves valuable. Until then, let us enjoy our meal."

Twice, Aubrey tried reengaging him in conversation, but Hu ate in silence; failing to acknowledge she had spoken, or was even present. Picking at her own dinner, she began to worry if Liam's teachings were enough to contend with the schemes of Yin Xian Hu.

Mongoose? she chided herself. *One newly born at best.* She would have to mature quickly if she wished to live beyond her captivity.

CHAPTER TEN

Danica Seton

Sitting crossed-legged on the cot, Danica was torn between relief and jealously as she watched Dr. Nysgaard prepare for departure. The woman, along with Gavin McAvoy and Torrance, would be leaving on a reconnaissance mission. And regardless how many times Sonje said otherwise, Danica knew success was one degree shy of impossible. But, as much as she worried for her friend's safety, Danica wished she had the opportunity to venture outside the underground shelter.

Her brother had pointed out the irony of the situation. Danica had spent the last months free to explore Oberlin, but had chosen to stay by their father's bedside. Now that she was on "lockdown," she wished for fresh air. *Lockdown,* she thought in frustration. *Who are we kidding? I'm grounded.* She had managed to avoid that particular punishment throughout her adolescence. Yet now, with the world coming apart at the seams, they treated her as if she had broken curfew.

"It's only because we want to keep you safe," Dr. Nysgaard said, reading the girl's expression.

"Oberlin *is* safe," Danica replied. She knew the sulk reinforced the perception of immaturity, but she had not been able to shake the mood over the last two days.

"That's what we thought last time," Sonje replied. "You know, before you decided to investigate an army of PKs in Lorain."

We didn't know it was an army, Danica answered. It was very difficult to be angry when she knew she was in the wrong.

"Once we get a better understanding of the situation, we'll know what's safe and what's not."

Danica nodded and watched the other woman slide a series of black-bladed knives into the various sheaths strapped to her body. Dressed head to toe in the same color, the weapons were indistinguishable from the clothing.

"Can you help me with these?" the doctor asked as she handed Danica a pair of stiff rectangular sheathes. Unfolding her legs, Danica pulled herself to the edge of the cot and buckled a pouch on each of the woman's forearms.

"Little tighter," Sonje corrected, and Danica adjusted the straps. "I don't know why I'm even taking them," the doctor said as she placed three black double-sided spikes into each sheathe. "Kunbo only just started teaching me how to use them."

Danica had observed several of the woman's daily hours-long training sessions. While she was more accurate with the short, flat throwing knives, Sonje still hit the target with the spikes more often than not.

"Are you scared?" Danica asked after the doctor thanked her for the assistance.

Looking into the small mirror on the wall, Sonje finished twisting her long, blonde hair into a wide, flat bun at the back of her head, and then let her arms drop to her sides. From the cot, Danica could see the woman's reflection. Staring at her own image, the beautiful woman looked pensive and forlorn.

"Yes," she replied, seeming to talk to herself more than Danica. "It feels like I've been scared every day for as long as I can remember. I never thought two months could feel this long. It's as if I've always been *this* person, like my old life happened to someone else."

Danica understood the confusion. When memories of school and friends, laughter and happiness, flashed in her mind the images were blurred. The voices and faces of her past were becoming unfamiliar, indistinct. Even her mother's face was now more of a general recollection; like the digitals of celebrities with their features softened, imperfections blended and brushed away. Recognizable, but not a true capturing of reality.

"I'm sorry," Danica apologized to Sonje for asking the question; and to her mother, who was fading from memory.

"It's okay to be scared, Dani," Dr. Nysgaard said, lowering herself onto the cot next to the girl. "Fear doesn't have to be a bad thing. It can drive us, inspire us to do things we never thought possible. We just can't let it cripple us. Everyone down here is scared."

"Not Torrance," Danica said with a wry grin.

Laughing, Sonje put her arm around Danica's shoulders just as her mother once did when she'd had a nightmare. "I wouldn't be so sure of that. When he heard you were in Lorain, I thought he'd single-handedly bring down the entire Alliance. He'd say it was anger, but that kind of anger only comes from worry and fear."

"Lucky me," Danica replied. She said the words, but deep inside she knew she was indeed fortunate. Dangerous and volatile as her world had become, there was comfort in having a guardian with the strength to match it.

With the appointed time at hand, the two women shared a parting hug, Sonje repeating she would be back by morning, and Danica wandered out into the dark halls of the shelter. Though only the doctor, Gavin, and Torrance were the ones intending to board the PK ships, the rest of the cell was traveling north as well in supportive roles. She debated wishing Corey luck, but decided against it.

They had spoken once in the two days since returning from Lorain. She had wanted to apologize for the trouble she had caused the scout by insisting he take her to Lorain. He had not been cold, but there was a definite shift in his personality.

Seeing the swollen lip and purpled bruise around his eye, Danica's guilt boiled over and she told him how sorry she was for Torrance injuring him. That was when Corey mumbled something like, "it's nothing," and made a hasty exit. Whatever feelings he may have had for her were gone.

Can I blame him? she thought in rejection.

With everyone familiar to her leaving, Danica went in search of her brother. She found him sitting with their father. *He doesn't have Torrance to shadow tonight.*

"Hey," she greeted, slumping into the remaining available seat.

"Hi," he replied without taking his eyes from the motionless body of their father. There was a void of emotion in his voice. Studying him, Danica saw how much he had aged over the weeks of their many escapes. The awkward lankiness of a young teen had begun to recede, a result from training with Torrance. *Everyone's training,* she thought.

His light brown hair had grown shaggy and she assumed he was growing it long to match Torrance. Though he had never had a baby face, Marcus did not even have youthful innocence in his expression now. Though, with what they had seen, what they had survived, Danica doubted anyone could have held onto innocence. His eyes made the effect more noticeable.

They were neither haunted nor angry. Either of which would have been understandable. Nor did his eyes hold the icy scowl ever-present in Torrance's stare, despite the endless hours he spent with the man. In her brother's brown irises, Danica saw . . . knowledge. But it was not the knowledge found in the old; the kind earned through experience, and which weighed events with pessimism or optimism because they had seen the like before. His knowledge was more like *awareness*. A detached, observing awareness free of judgment and opinion. *Like the moon watching Earth,* a quiet voice in her mind said. A benign comparison, but it chilled her nonetheless.

"Everyone's going to Lorain," she said to dispel her sudden unease.

"I know," he returned.

Every soul in the shelter knew of the mission, but with Marcus the words sounded more ominous.

Testing a foolish theory that had popped into her thoughts the day before, she asked, "Will they be okay?"

Smiling, he turned his head and looked at her. "I don't know, Dani. I'm not psychic if that's what you're thinking."

She should have been pleased to see the break in his passivity, but his stare was too unnerving. Believing he had provided an opening, she said, "Okay. It's just that . . . you're different lately."

"I know," he said again unblinking. "So are you."

Tough to argue with that, she admitted. "I'm worried about you, Marcus. So is Dr. Nysgaard."

"You shouldn't be."

For the boy who once could rattle on about nothing for hours long past the time she would stop listening, his short responses further highlighted his recent change. There was one other person she knew who spoke with the minimum words required.

"Maybe you shouldn't be spending so much time with Torrance," she suggested. "You could, I don't know, you could . . ."

"Play?" he said.

For the first time, Danica realized how difficult this new life must be on him. At eighteen, it was a struggle to find a place among the men and women living in the shelter—each one a soldier. How would it be for a thirteen year old?

"No, not play, I guess. But, Torrance is, well, kind of dark."

"Torrance is important, Dani," Marcus said. "More important than anyone understands."

It was a discussion they'd had before, while imprisoned with their father in a PK military base. Marcus believed it was not chance which had brought about the intersection of their lives with Torrance's. Then, she had assumed it was the boy's hope for rescue that had inspired his faith.

"What do you mean?" she asked. "How do you know he's so important?"

"I can't explain it," he replied, casting his eyes down as a hint of frustration slipped past his stoicism. It was not directed towards her, but at the doubting questions. Rather, he seemed frustrated with his own inability to give words to his feelings.

"It's just . . . it's just something I know," Marcus added. "Remember when we went to the aquarium and we saw those turtles that *knew* to move to the ocean as soon as they hatched? No one had to show them. They just knew. It's like that."

"Oh," Danica said for the sake of a reply. Nothing her brother had said left her any less concerned for his well-being. *Easier if he was simply psychic.* "Do you . . . are there other things you just know'?"

"Yes."

Steeling herself for further shock and discomfort, she asked, "What else?"

Looking back up, Marcus smiled again, saying, "I know I'm hungry."

Choking and laughing in equal measure, Danica replied, "Very funny, you little brat. Come on. They're probably starting dinner in the mess."

Whatever changes had worked over him, Danica was happy to know a small trace of the boy he had been still remained.

CHAPTER ELEVEN

Sonje Nysgaard

"Remember this is a reconnaissance mission *only*," Gavin stressed for at least the eleventh time. "Kills are to be avoided unless your life is in immediate danger. Leaving behind a string of PK corpses negates any intel gained tonight."

Though he directed the warning to the entire cell, Sonje was sure he meant the words mostly, perhaps solely, for Torrance. Given what they knew of the man, she wondered how effective Gavin's killing ban would be on him.

"It's the ones who can't become corpses I'm more worried about, Gav," admitted Lance Holton, one of the cell's *combies*, or combatants. Tall and wide, Holton and his counterpart Patton Rivera could make even the most fearsome opponent cringe. The pair might not have Kunbo's martial skill, but then the purpose of their brute force was not about finesse. Holton was concerned with facing an enemy that dwarfed even his impressive strength: the drones.

"Ament's scouting this morning confirms no PKs from the fleet, human or machine, have entered the town itself," the cell leader replied. "Unless something has changed, your positions should be secure."

Match Quentin, the rascally op-tech mastermind and former Peacekeeper, caught Gavin's evasion. "All well and good, boss," he said in that charming rasp which always sounded as if he had just left bed. *Which may actually be true in his case,* Sonje added. She had lost count how many Ignota men and women she had seen sneaking from his quarters each morning. "But, I think what Holt's getting at is how are you three going to deal with the drones?"

The three to whom he was referring were Gavin, Torrance, and Sonje herself. The three who'd be boarding one of the PK ships. Torrance had been the first choice for the mission. No one in the shelter came near to rivaling his combination of stealth and combat. And while a single operative was preferable, Gavin's distrust was too great to permit Torrance to act alone. Doubting the two men could function without a referee, Sonje insisted she be included, citing her familiarity with the

SIDs as the reason. *How do I keep volunteering for these things?*

"We're playing that one by ear," Gavin answered. Cutting off further debate, he continued, "Once we get within ten meters of our target ship, we'll go comm silent. I don't want to risk our signals showing up on a scan. Remember, if you don't hear from us ninety minutes after our last transmission you're to get back here and assist in the evacuation. No, and I mean *no* heroic rescue attempts!"

Sonje wished he were not so forceful on that particular point. *Not that it will matter,* she conceded. She and Torrance were still high on the PK's list of priority targets. If they were captured, the Alliance would expend every resource available to prevent an escape. *If they even let us leave longer than a minute.*

"I still don't like it," Holton groused.

"Well, I'm not jumping up and down either, my friend," Gavin replied. "But Torrance says he can get us in and . . . and I believe him."

Though the pause diminished the conviction, Sonje knew how much the words must have stung the cell leader.

"Ten minutes to sunset," Ament advised.

"All right, listen. Before we head out I just want to say I know there's tension, I know we've been stuck down here for too long. Things have been said, things have been done. But tonight's bigger than us, people. If we twist up this mission, it's not just our lives lost. There are ten other cells in this shelter, and a town full of sympathizers above us. Not one of them will live to see dawn if we can't put our personal shit on hold for the next few hours. Am I clear?"

A strong chorus of affirmations filled the room; even Torrance offered a slight nod of agreement. Gavin gave the order to move out, and the cell made its way to the shelter's entrance.

Along the way, the remaining Ignota members lined the hall and voiced somber wishes of success mixed with the occasional boisterous shout. While not involved in the mission, the other cells' next few hours promised to be far from peaceful. Their nerves would be tested as they waited, poised to flee and scatter at a moment's notice.

Sonje appreciated the expressions of solidarity, though she wished the moment felt less like a funeral procession. The mission was fraught with risk and danger, which had prompted Match to compare it to a suicide mission. Gavin had reprimanded him for the offhand comment but the rebuke did not lessen its veracity.

Thompson Fielder, along with the other cell leaders, met the group at the shelter's entrance; their faces carved from dour stone. The senior commander extended his arm to Gavin, and the two men gripped each other's forearms in the ancient way of warriors.

"Order the evac at the first sign of danger," Gavin said.

With greater paternal emotion than Sonje had expected, Fielder replied, "We'll take care of ourselves. You just get your people back safely."

"Yes, sir," Gavin returned.

Men and their emotions, Sonje smiled. Her father had been much the same; masking his feelings behind the fewest possible words, as if brevity was a shield. She had grown to understand that the less he said the more he felt.

As Sonje made her way past Fielder, the man leaned forward and whispered, "Try to keep them from killing each other."

Promising to do her best, she placed a light kiss on the man's cheek. The affection surprised them both, though it was Fielder who blushed scarlet.

"Don't know what I've done to deserve that," he said. "But, I'm glad I did it."

For reminding me of my father, she thought but did not voice, fearing it'd sound too much like goodbye.

They traveled north in two podcars. The three-man recon team and Kunbo, the weapons master, in one; the others in a second pod. Staggering their arrivals by ten minutes, Sonje passed the time studying the massive armada anchored in the lake. Even three kilometers away, the well-lit ships, a floating fortress, loomed in the distance.

Passing the precision binoculars to Gavin, Torrance said, "Same formation. She's still on the portside."

Over the last two days, a rotating team of Ignota scouts had maintained constant surveillance over the two carrier groups. Without deviation, each group's supply ship had remained nestled alongside its respective air carrier, the command ship of a strike group, with all other ships forming a tight defensive perimeter. Everyone had agreed that if SID distribution was indeed the purpose of the fleets' presence, the devices would be located on the supply ship. The well-guarded supply ship.

Gavin handed Sonje the binoculars and then called up the surveillance images on the portable holo platform. As the men manipulated the three dimensional projections, she examined the ship. Though compact and lightweight, the goggle system provided her a clear view. Sonje shuddered to think of the binoculars' cost. *Probably worth more than my podcar.*

The supply ship was nearly as long as the carrier itself, and had a landing pad at the stern where half a dozen HALOs rested. Less sleek than its sister ships, the supplier had several cranes and rigs rising from its deck forming pairs on the port and starboard sides. Adjusting for the shadows created by the artificial lights, the lens zoomed at her touch and she could count the stars of rank on the PKs stationed on the supply ship. To her dismay, most of the figures bore no mark of rank. *Drones,* she thought with a turn of her stomach. Finished with her examination, she offered Kunbo his turn with the device. The weapons master declined so Sonje set the lenses aside and joined the others in their study of the hologram.

"You still haven't said how you're going to sabotage the crane," Gavin said. She detected a hint of temper in his voice. Though when dealing with Torrance, Gavin usually had an edge of irritability. Surprisingly, Torrance answered with a straightforward explanation. *Well, at least by his standards,* she added.

"The cranes' functions are fairly simple," the rogue solider replied. "Up, down. Left, right. It's tougher to override a pod's operating system than those cranes."

Sonje wondered what to make of the marked absence of hostility in the man's current demeanor. Welcome as it may be, she doubted it marked a permanent end to the animosity between the two men. *He's the perfect soldier,* she realized. *However much he might despise Gavin, he is locking those feelings away for the mission.* Even with Gavin's earlier plea for cooperation, the cell leader was struggling to meet his own goal.

She was quite familiar with that flaw in human ability. Though the last few years had found her conducting research in a lab, a bioroboticist spent her developing years honing surgical skills. Avoiding attachment to patients was a constant challenge. "A cold heart and steady hands" was the ideal among her peers, but she had yet to meet one who had managed to reach it.

It was disturbing to think that a brutal killer such as Torrance would have made an amazing surgeon. *He can compartmentalize like a machine.* The image of a PK-drone flashed in her mind.

"Fine," Gavin said. "If . . . when you rig the crane, Sonje and I will meet you here." He indicated a hatch door just beyond the HALO deck.

"Are you sure the port side is the best to climb?" Kunbo asked.

Nodding, Gavin replied. "Yes. I agree with Torrance on that one. It may be closer to the carrier, but that gives us some shadows to move in. Starboard is too exposed and too well lit."

A slow-approaching pair of headlights pulled into the open space behind their pod. There was a brief second of anxiety until Corey came into view exiting the second podcar. Upon seeing the scout, Sonje bit back a nervous chuckle. *That'd be our luck,* she thought. *Being pulled over by a local PK before we even make a move.*

Such a likelihood, however, was minimal. Their contact in Lorain, the PK everyone called Vinsy, had assured them he would keep questioning eyes far from their location. She had never met the man, but she admired his courage. A Fifth working as a Peacekeeper was incredibly dangerous.

"All right," Gavin said. "Let's do this."

Kunbo remained seated as the other three stepped out into the night; Corey taking their place with the weapons master. The cold carried by the strong wind off the lake bit at her face with warning. *"If you think this is cold, wait until you're in the water,"* it seemed to say. Hailing from Sweden as she did, Sonje was not without experience in frigid temperatures. However, she could not understand the rush her friends claimed they gained from ice swimming. *Knullande idiots!* she had called them in her native tongue. *And tonight you're going to be one of them.*

Unwilling to linger long in the streetlight, the trio cut a fast retreat through a thin copse of leafless trees between two ramshackle houses; pulling their hooded masks over their heads as they jogged. Unlike the antiquated night vision technology of generations past, the lenses in the eyeholes of the hood adjusted automatically to the changing subtleties of light and dark. No risk of momentary blindness should a sudden flash of light cut into the night.

Torrance made no sound as he glided along. Instinctively avoiding each twig or loose patch of earth as he slipped from shadow to shadow. Though she knew he was but a few meters away, there were several seconds when the man disappeared from her view.

By comparison, Sonje believed she would make less noise by banging a metal drum with a pipe. *Sorry, Kunbo,* she apologized in her mind. The African had spent tireless hours showing her how to move with stealth. *We'll work on that again tomorrow.* She hoped it was a good sign that she thought there'd be a "tomorrow."

If not quite matching Torrance's silent passage, Gavin was advancing toward the coastline with far less volume than Sonje. Ever the competitor, she forced her eyes to narrow and focus on the path ahead. The disadvantage in that, however, was a decreased vision of her surroundings. Kunbo had said a time would come when her other senses would compensate for the loss of peripheral sight. He had also said, "You're not there yet, Dr. Sonje." Knowing the two men with her had reached that kind of awareness, Sonje trusted them to maintain an alert guard.

The winter had hardened the ground but had spared it from snow. Given their eventual swim, Sonje had traded her familiar heavy boots for a pair of *jika-tabi*. Lighter and more conducive to silent movement, the Asian-styled boots split at the big toe and had a thin, flexible sole of rubber. Though she had worn them while training in the shelter, the feel on open earth was altogether different. Every rock and bump pressed on the bottom of her feet.

They reached the lakeshore without detection. Hugging to the line of massive boulders placed after the destructive storm of 2117, Torrance led them forward. For reasons beyond her novice perception, the man occasionally raised his arm to signal an immediate halt. When each unseen threat passed, he motioned them forward once again.

With effort, and a strict adherence to Kunbo's lessons, Sonje fought the urge to hold her breath; instead concentrating on a steady rhythm of respirations. Minutes wound away and the three interlopers reached the perimeter they dared not pass. Searchlights from the nearest ships swept along the shore.

Shielded from view behind a boulder, Sonje and the men paused to rest before beginning the kilometer long swim to the supply ship. Stealing a quick glance, her worried imagination gave life to the great vessels. It was a fool's thought she knew, but the ships seemed like giant slumbering beasts, hides of metal and particle cannon claws. She half expected one to unfold itself, roar with predatory violence, and charge across the night-darkened water.

"Ready?" Torrance rasped.

Grateful for the mask hiding her apprehension, Sonje, and then Gavin, nodded.

"Stay close and watch the lights. Dive when you can, but surface quietly," he cautioned. "Sound carries on water and will echo off the ships."

Not waiting for replies, Torrance crouched low and moved to the lake's edge. Gavin and Sonje followed on his heels. The cell leader's voice hummed through her mobile comm as he advised the others of the start of comm silence.

"Good luck," Match Quentin replied.

The *jika-tabi*, a thin layer away from bare feet, allowed an easier flight across the sand. Torrance was the first to enter the surf, not slowing as he fought the deepening tides. Adrenaline muted the first spikes of cold as Sonje's feet disappeared in the water. However, by the time the water enveloped her knees, the chill was quite noticeable. A few steps ahead, the black shapes of Gavin and Torrance dove forward and out of sight. The anticipation of full submersion nearly forced her to retreat, but she refused to show weakness.

With the water at her waist, Sonje bent low and pushed off into the water.

The neoprene fabric of her body-hugging wetsuit defended her skin from the icy moisture, and spared her the full effect of the cold. Still, the freezing temperature was all her mind could focus on. *Truth! It'd be like swimming through ice if not for the wetsuit.* And to think some of her friends had been nude for their ice dips!

Fit even before two months of Kunbo's exhausting workouts, Sonje found little struggle slicing her body through the lake's moderate chop. Each time her head crested, Sonje checked her direction through the water-repelling lenses of the mask. She caught sporadic glimpses of her companions; Torrance in the lead, Gavin just behind him. Neither man had greatly outpaced her. *Yet,* her mind teased.

Forced to scan for passing searchlights, Sonje's muscles grew lethargic and disheartened with each viewing. *The ships never look any closer,* an internal voice discouraged. Torrance had warned her against the tricks perception might play. *Just keeping moving,* she argued. *Every second brings you closer.* In time, her silent self-cheers began to ring hollow.

Fatigue is a funny thing. The ships she had dreaded from the shore, the very "beasts" ready to pounce, were now enticing. As her muscles tired and her limbs stiffened, Sonje would have welcomed being swallowed whole by the steel animals. Only once she had passed the outlier warships did she begin to trust the ordeal was nearing its end.

Breathing hard and relying on the added buoyancy provided by the wetsuit, Sonje dove and swam, dove and swam, until reaching the supply ship. The twin masks of Gavin and Torrance bobbed beside her.

"Sixty-seven minutes," Torrance's voice whispered through the mask at her left.

Mostly on schedule, Sonje calculated. They had been prepared for the swim to eat more than twenty minutes from their window of operation. At twenty-three minutes, Sonje was pleased with her first aquatic infiltration. She ignored the itching certainty that the men had slowed their speed to accommodate her. *Torrance probably could have just walked across the water,* she thought with competitive jealousy.

"One minute then latch and climb," he hushed before slipping away beneath the water.

Feeling for the pouch at her belt with fingers numb and stiff, Sonje retrieved the pair of magnetic climbing handles. *Drop these and you're done,* she warned. Even with the handles, she wondered where she would find the strength to pull herself up to the ship's deck. Her arms felt like loosely molded clay, as if the bones had somehow liquefied and seeped through her skin into the lake.

She placed the handles against the ship and activated their magnetic adhesion. Testing the grip, and finding it secure, Sonje looked to Gavin, waiting for his signal to begin their ascent.

"Go," he hissed from the shadows.

Alternating left and right, power on and off, Sonje worked her way up the side of the supply ship. At first, she stretched to cover long lengths, heaving and straining to pull her body along. Soon, it was all she could do to lift her weight a few centimeters at a time. The process was like climbing a ladder, except there were no rungs for her feet. The rubber soles of the *jika-tabi* provided some traction against the hull, but not enough resistance to lessen the effort of her arms.

"Hold!" Gavin's whisper cut through the fog of her fatigue.

With a start, Sonje realized they had climbed to within a meter of the rear deck. If not for the warning, she would have continued upward before Torrance's diversion afforded them some cover. No longer focused on action, she could just feel the start of a quiver in her arms. Her fingers broke through their numbness and now screamed for an easing of their tight grip on the handles. Locking her elbows, Sonje gritted her teeth and swallowed a shout of pain. The quiver of her arms had become a dangerous, vibrating spasm and she knew Torrance's efforts must come soon or she would plunge back down to the icy depths below.

Three sudden, sharp crashes, followed by slashes of air, echoed across the lake. Sonje heard dozens of previously muted voices, subtle at first, then rising to a noticeable panic, shouting and swearing above. Whatever Torrance had done, the crew of the supply ship had stirred to action.

Gavin covered the final span of hull to reach the deck, but Sonje's arms refused to obey. Wide-eyed and fighting her own panic, she gasped with outrage at her deadened limbs. At times, Kunbo had worked her so severely in training it had taken all her will to force her wearied body to comply with her mind. Then, the feeling had been a source of pride, a sign she had worked hard. Now though, unable to deliver herself from danger, Sonje cursed her weakness.

A black-hooded face struck out from the deck, and dropped his arm low. "Take my hand," Gavin said, worry noticeable in his tone.

"Can't," she told him. Can't . . . move."

Straining further, Gavin flattened his body against the deck, pressing himself so his dangling hand brushed against her wrist. Once, twice, his fingers curled around her wrist, but the grip was insufficient. Upon the third attempt, Gavin managed a better grasp. Releasing her hold on the magnetic handles, Sonje entrusted herself to his protection. Grunting, he pulled her up with a shocking surge of strength.

Safely on the deck, he panted and said, "You okay?"

Pins and needles tortured her arms now that muscles and tendons could relax. Intense as it was, the pain was welcome, almost soothing.

"That was not fun," she said.

"Come on," he replied as he rose to his feet, and helped her to her own. Ducking down, they moved to the nearest HALO, hiding beneath its sheltering bulk. Far ahead, well past the midpoint of the port side, dozens of men worked to assess and rectify Torrance's sabotage. On one of the ship's cranes, three large metal pulleys swung freely. Their thick, steel, newly untethered cords still whipping through the air like drunken snakes. Sonje could not help but be impressed by how Torrance had managed to create a diversion which did not indicate an attack.

"Truth, he's good," Gavin murmured to himself. Realizing he had spoken aloud, he tried to recover with a cough. "Let's move," he said.

As planned, the landing deck had cleared as the guards rushed to the damaged crane. These were Peacekeepers, however, and they would restore order once they found no immediate threat. Moving from one HALO to another, Sonje and Gavin stuck close to the few shadows on the well-lit deck. Though the hatch was in sight, her eyes found no sign of Torrance.

Exposed to the light, the final meters to the door offered no means of hiding.

Gambling on the confusion birthed by the damaged crane, Sonje and Gavin walked across the deck. With luck, any curious observers on the neighboring ships would assume the pair to be members of the supply ship's PK force.

"The enemy is less suspicious of what it expects to see," Torrance had said when suggesting the risky maneuver. Sonje hoped he was right.

Walking calmly and confidently, Sonje followed Gavin's lead. Those few steps, unprotected and visible to all, felt as long as the kilometer swim. But no alarm sounded, no voice cried out in warning, and they reached the door unscathed.

"Fifty-nine minutes."

The announcement came from the empty space at her left and startled Sonje into a gasp. Unfolding from a small and nearby shadow, Torrance revealed himself. He had tucked into the darkness so expertly not even her lens-enhanced vision had been able to detect him. Based on Gavin's reflexive posture, she knew he had not seen the man either. *I don't think even Kunbo would have noticed him!*

Pushing past his surprise, frustrated that Torrance had managed to surprise him, Gavin instructed, "Take point. Sonje and I will cover the rear."

Sonje eased a black blade into each hand and slipped behind Torrance as the party stepped through the opening.

CHAPTER TWELVE

Tilden Garrott

"And I didn't get you anything in return," he smiled as Isla secured the heavy metal cuff onto his wrist. The woman tried to hide her grin, but Tilden knew her face too well.

"Comfortable?" she asked.

"Better than a knife at my throat," he replied with a shrug of his shoulders. The cuff, though, was essentially just that. The cell leader, Cleland Bain, insisted on the device and none of his followers had dared argue in opposition. Tilden did not complain.

For the past few days—as best as he could judge the elapsed time—he had been questioned about the weapons cache in the countryside. He endured the interrogations with patience; answering each repetitive question no matter how many times they asked him. When the scouts returned to verify Tilden's initial disclosures, he knew it was only a matter of time. Satisfied the information was credible, Cleland ordered a team to retrieve the weapons. Of course, Tilden had ensured his inclusion in the mission. If the Alliance had not already pillaged the storage facility, Tilden needed to be present for the team to pass the various security measures. Ocular scans, finger and palm printing, and DNA analysis all had to match. Cleland did not like it, but he had little choice if he wanted the weapons. Thus the metal cuff.

Embedded within the device was a lethal dose of a neurotoxin which could be injected by remote trigger should Tilden attempt to escape. He had no such plans. True, he would be arming the enemy, but it was a negligible price if payment gained him the trust of his captors. Only through action, not words, would they come to believe him an ally. And while in the custody of these terrorists, his safety was in their hands. Should the Alliance strike, he preferred his guardians be welled armed.

Seeing Isla frown at the offhand remark, Tilden raised his hand to the side of her face. "I'm joking," he promised. "Cleland doesn't trust me. I understand that, and this," he added and wagged his cuffed wrist. "If I learned anything from my Father, it's that a man in his position must maintain a certain level of paranoia. Unfortunately, my Father was blinded by jumping at every little shadow that he missed the largest threat. It's the curse of men in power."

It pained him to speak disparagingly of Kerwen. Even if there was some truth to the comment. To achieve his goals though, Isla and the others must not only come to trust Tilden, but must also lose confidence in their leader. *So many threads,* he mused on his plan. *Some to be woven, some to be knotted, others to be cut entirely.*

"Cleland's cautious," Isla said in near apology. "But with what you're doing today, the help you're offering, he doesn't forget things like that. He'll come around in time."

Never before in his captivity had the woman expressed words of trust, even ones as veiled as those. Satisfaction bloomed in Tilden's thoughts. *I must still be careful, though,* his mind warned. She is an actress, and Cleland was using her to play on Tilden's emotions. He had yet to decide how much of her tenderness was false, and how much was genuine.

This was the kind of deception Liam Walford had loved. Layers upon layers of manipulation and contrivance. Each side engaged in a battle of the mind, fighting on fronts both overt and unseen. The late Chief Advisor to the Family had lived for it. And died from it. Despite the calamitous end, Tilden knew the man had been a master of the game. *But even a master sometimes falls.*

Tilden had never been the keenest student of conspiracy. His sister, Aubrey, had been far more adept. Even their Father had agreed she would have made a skilled Chief Advisor once Tilden became Caput. They were all gone now: Father, sister, spymaster. All that remained of the Garrott empire was Tilden.

Liam had once said, "Adversity can shape a man, force him to become what he must. But only if he is wise enough to let himself be forged."

"Still with me?" Isla's voice brought him back to the moment.

"Sorry," he said in recovery. "I was thinking about the night we were in Paris. I'd seen the city hundreds of times, but with you there everything felt new, more vibrant." Letting his voice drop to a melancholic mourn, he added, "Things were simpler then, weren't they?"

Cleland Bain's abrupt entry into the cell prevented Isla from replying. "Is the prisoner secured?" he asked.

Putting a respectable distance between them, Isla affirmed the cuff was in place.

"Kieran has the trigger," the terrorist leader said, emphasizing the fact that Isla would not be controlling his fate. While meant as a warning to him, the declaration seemed pointed to the woman as well.

Does Isla not have his complete trust? Tilden wondered. *Or is this more of the charade?*

The larger man stepped close, positioning his face just centimeters from Tilden's. Ignoring the acrid steam of the man's breath, Tilden kept his expression smooth yet with a hint of feigned fear.

"If you so much as blink the wrong way," Cleland growled his expected threat,

"Kieran will drop you. Try to remove the cuff, and the toxin will be injected. If this is a double-cross, or any harm comes to my team, believe me when I say I will find you and I will kill you."

Tilden allowed a beat before replying. "Sir, I owe your team my life. If not for them, the Alliance would have killed me with the rest of my Family. Whatever small assistance I can offer is nothing compared to the debt I owe them."

Narrowing his eyes, Cleland made a point of studying his captive; seeming to believe the stare was more unnerving than it truly was. Tilden let the man have his moment, permitted the sense of superiority this terrorist so needed. Eventually he turned aside, marching out of the cell as he ordered, "I want updates every two hours."

Kieran and Lars, the cell's pair of scouts, stood at the door and motioned Tilden forward. Meekly—he assumed it was the appropriate reaction—he took a few quick steps towards his escort.

They walked a short distance through poorly lit stone halls until arriving in a garage. The space itself was windowless and no trace of daylight seeped through the seams of the large bay door. A white paneled pod, like those used for small deliveries, sat idle with its rear cargo door open.

Etienne stepped into view around the far side of the vehicle. He had not seen his chess partner since the man departed after their last game. It had been Etienne's mention of the countryside that had inspired Tilden's scheme.

Smiling, he said, "So you survived your adventures, Etienne. I'd not realized you'd returned."

"Only just," the Frenchman replied. The blatant cordiality from the prisoner in front of the other terrorists unsettled the man. *They need to see it is not just Isla who is coming to trust me.*

Following the wordless instructions, he climbed into the back of the pod and settled himself on one of the two benches bolted to each side. The others joined him, save Kieran who had already taken the navigation seat at the front of the pod. Double doors slid along their tracks to seal the cargo hold.

Kieran's lyrical voice, emitting through unseen speakers, said, "All right, lads. Hope ya all used the jacks. We got two hours ahead'a'us."

"Just go, Kieran," Isla replied in a manner suggesting she'd often had to redirect the scout's focus.

Tilden felt the pod ease forward, and then turn right. He had hoped to catch some sounds of traffic or itinerant noise to determine their location. However, the heavy drops of rain striking the pod's roof muffled all other exterior sound. If, in fact, any such sounds existed.

For a long while, perhaps an hour or more, no one spoke. *Just as well*, he thought. Cut off from the world as he had been, the drumming rain was a welcome distraction. His grandfather used to joke that rain and English blood were one and the same. One could not be English and not be fond of the rain. Tilden supposed it was true. Closing his eyes, letting the downpour meditate through him, he could almost forget he was the hostage of terrorists and that death was strapped to his wrist.

"How did this farm of your Family escape Alliance notice?" Etienne asked.

Leaving the peace of his moment, Tilden opened his eyes. "It was the home of one of my grandfather's servants," he explained. "When the man's family could no longer afford to keep it, my grandfather purchased it in the servant's name. Over the years, it was shuffled about through various deed swaps and sales. All the Families maintain hidden assets. The Council may be unified in purpose, but there is little trust between the Houses. The assassination of my Family is only the most recent, and more public, maneuvering over the years. Power and wealth do not necessarily guarantee security."

Lars, with whom he'd had little interaction, asked, "Did your Father not suspect something was afoot?"

The question surprised Tilden. They usually interrogated him for answers that might prove useful to the Ignota's aims. This one had a more personal feel.

Nodding, he replied, "He feared the launch of the PK-drones would cause the other Houses to grow jealous. Even though the machines aide the Alliance, the sudden boost to House Garrott's power was sure to worry them. My Family was in definite decline prior to the drones."

Tilden disliked making such an admission to the rebels.

"He knew the Council was likely to move to stem our rise. But, he never expected a coup to be so quickly enacted. Nor one conducted through force. There was no precedent for it. True, there have been 'wars' between the Families, but the weapons then were money and industrial espionage. Very little blood, if any, was spilt during those so-called wars."

"What changed then?" Lars continued. He expected Isla to silence the scout. The conversation was a departure from protocol. However, she made no effort to end the interaction. By failing to do so, she left Tilden the opportunity to further humanize himself in the eyes of his captors.

"Some of it was change," he offered. "But, in many ways, it was an inevitable progression. For over a hundred years, the Families secured their holdings, carved out their empires of business. House Cambrie solidified control of medicine. Houses De Luca and Fawzan respectively monopolized consumerism and energy. Hu governs the world's food supply. And my Family maintains . . . maintained the military might of the Alliance."

As complex as humanity is, Tilden had always marveled how easily its necessities could be divided. There was overlap in some areas, but in the end, a global population needed only five Families to maintain stability. The Council equally oversaw only one area, financial solvency. And that decision was out of distrust more than anything else.

"With everything divvied, and nothing else to conquer, it stands to reason we would turn on each other. Why split by five what can be divided among four? Now that the precedent has been set, I would expect a further dwindling of apportioned control. Perhaps in another century there'll be a Council of Two. Or maybe no Council at all—simply one Family with complete domination."

Tilden was careful to portray disgust over the idea. In truth, he had spent much of his imprisonment fantasizing, and strategizing, how to usher in that exact reality. Reclaiming his Family's seat on the Council, only to return to the status quo, would serve little purpose. The destruction of his House was proof enough against such an effort. No, shared dominion had shown itself to be a failure.

Sensing he still had a captive audience—*or a* captive's *audience,* he punned—Tilden pressed further. "The introduction of the drones provided the perfect excuse for the Families to act. In the past, the Council might have conspired to force my Father to relinquish control of the drones while still keeping his seat. But I'm sure Hu and Cambrie whispered an urgent need for boldness."

"What makes you suspect them more than Fawzan or De Luca?" Isla asked. Etienne and the woman exchanged a brief, but noticeable look. Tilden barely caught it, and it disappeared before he could read it with any certainty.

"Fawzan is wise," he answered, filing the glance away for later thought. "He's the oldest of the Caputs, and is slower to act; preferring to deliberate on outcomes and consequences. As for the Italian, he is too fond of the vices he markets to focus on a plot of high treason. Among the Caputs, he is merely tolerated and mostly disregarded.

"Alexavier Cambrie, however, is another matter. Overly ambitious, and proud of that fault, the man would not shy away from treason if he saw an advantage. And Hu, it is no secret his rise to power came at the tip of an assassin's blade. At birth, he was so far down the line of succession no one bothered to count. Before his eighteenth birthday, rumors already linked him to four deaths. Another ten years and the Viper was third in line, behind his father and older brother. Both of whom, of course, famously succumbed to a mysterious illness. How easy is treason after you've already committed patricide and fratricide?"

Again, Isla and Etienne shared a puzzling look. He let his narrative end, hoping an awkward silence might prompt an explanation. The actress inhaled through her nose while biting her lower lip. Tilden recognized her look of indecision, willing her to speak.

"Tilden, there's—," she began but was cut off by Etienne.

"Cleland gave us orders," the Frenchman reminded her. Whatever the command structure of the cell, Isla was the man's superior.

"I know what he said, Etienne," she replied. "But what difference does it really make? He'll find out sometime."

Tilden hid his pleasure behind a blank face. *So, she's going to defy her leader.* He had not expected cracks in her loyalty to show so soon. *Or is this performance intentionally staged?* another voice countered. Analyzing, and then second-guessing, every word and gesture was becoming a tiring trial. *How* did *Liam manage it for so many years?*

"I take full responsibility for it," Isla said to Etienne. The man nodded in acquiescence.

Turning to face him, she held an expression of guilt and pity. "When the Alliance moved against your Family," she began, "they didn't kill everyone. Aubrey was spared."

Spared. Not escaped, not survived . . . spared. No amount of practiced control could keep the shock from his face. "Aubrey's alive?" Tilden muttered in relieved disbelief. "How? How do you know? Where is she?"

"She was taken into PK custody and she was delivered to Hu."

The spark of joy, which had kindled at knowing his sister still lived, was quickly smothered. Anguish stole over him as he pictured the unending tortures she would endure until the Viper was finished with her.

"Death would have been better," he said, voice cracking in honest pain.

Understanding the meaning of his grief, Isla reached across and pressed a hand to his knee. "It's not what you fear, Til. As far as we can tell, she hasn't been harmed. In fact, just the opposite. They were married a few days ago."

Struck dumb, he managed to repeat, "Married?"

"Yes. In a private ceremony, so we assume it was forced. But, digitals were released and Aubrey seemed uninjured."

"Digitals can be faked. If the Council thinks I'm in hiding, they would try to get me to surface by claiming she's alive," he returned.

"As far as we can tell, it's legitimate," Isla said. "Etienne's mission was to make contact with Ignota operatives."

Tilden looked to the man who gave him a closed-eye nod of confirmation.

"Admittedly, our communications network is in disarray," she continued, drawing back Tilden's attention, "but it's not completely destroyed. Until things settle down, information cannot be definitively verified. However, our sources are confident she's alive and that the marriage was real. Your sister is now the Caput˜e of House Hu."

His thoughts spun, trying to order the overload of information, sorting each detail's importance. Aubrey was alive. And in a position of power, even if in title only. Tilden had wondered how he would rebuild his Family from nothing, but now he might not have to. Working together, he and his sister could seize control of House Hu. Failing that, she would be perfectly placed to kill the Viper as Tilden moved against the other Families. Knowing her as well as he did, Aubrey already had a strategy in the offing.

Does she know I'm alive? Somehow, he must make contact with her before she acted precipitously. Unlike their Father, her temper was cold, but it was just as powerful. *If she thinks I'm dead, her vengeance might ruin the chance for the Garrotts to reclaim power.* Could he convince Isla to send a message through the terrorists' network?

And what of Isla herself? She had defied Cleland's orders. Shown him physical affection in front of her fellows. And even addressed him as "Til." The seeds he had sown had rooted and were growing faster than he had dared to hope. He wished for the isolation of his prison cell, longed to be alone with his tangled thoughts. Kieran's thick brogue, however, cut in to remind him of the immediate task.

"Welcome to Cerne Abbas, lads. Feel free ta'tip yer navigator."

CHAPTER THIRTEEN

Liam Walford

The morning of their departure was warm for the mid-winter date on the calendar. Walking crosstown to the eastside ports in the hours before dawn, Liam was grateful for the unexpected warmth. *It makes the journey slightly bearable,* he complained as he nudged and shoved his way through the crowd.

No matter the weather, time, or day, the streets of the morally decayed city teemed with foot traffic. Some were returning to their rundown apartments after a long, salacious night. Others, however, appeared to have recently risen to begin escapades of their own. Most had the blank stares and shuffling walks of Edge abusers.

Caput De Luca had lobbied the Council to allow the distribution of the highly addictive narcotic. Just one injection of the compound was enough to create dependency, and detoxification was often too intolerable for most to bear. A little over a decade since its introduction, the drug had become a major source of income for the Italian Family. *That will end after The Culling, though.*

At his side, Liam heard the continued mumbling of his protégé. "I still say we could have risked taking a pod to the docks," Mitchall argued.

He had considered the option before discarding the idea. Taxis in the city would have facial scanners. And while their cuffs would disrupt the software's identification, an extended disruption might attract unwanted attention. Liam would rather suffer the indignity of fighting through the throngs on the streets than take such a risk.

"We've only a few more blocks," he reminded his aide. The comment may have silenced Mitchall's complaints, but Liam could still sense the man's agitation.

Crossing a wide avenue, the crowd began to thin, and he caught the first scents of saltwater on the air. It was a welcome relief from the unwashed pungency of the city's inhabitants. White and gray gulls circled above, shouting their screeching calls when they sighted scraps of food, and defecating indiscriminately in their excitement. *Just like the people of this place,* Liam added in his thoughts.

The *Espado do Mar* was docked at the end of a long concrete pier. The ship itself was a long flat freighter with two massive cranes rising up from its decking. Dozens of rectangular metal cargo containers were stacked in neat rows from the bow to the stern's tall bridge. Though Liam had little knowledge of ships, it was clear this vessel had seen more summers than him and Mitchall combined. He hoped its long survival was an indication of its seaworthiness.

Halfway up the portable stairs, Captain Dimas' shouts greeted them from the deck. "Risin's only ticks away! Don't think I's be waitin for ya draggin feet!"

Liam did not need to look at the horizon to know they had arrived well before dawn. Still, he offered the captain an apology for their alleged tardiness and thanked him for his patience.

"Set yer gear n' palm d'fee," Dimas barked, ignoring Liam's reply.

Placing the small satchel with his sparse clothing down on the deck, he placed his hand on the Captain's scanner. Within seconds, he transferred two million credits into the captain's account. If Dimas noticed the cuff at Liam's wrist, he made no indication.

Liam had dealt with his kind before. Dimas likely knew their cover story was a fabrication; just as they knew he was as much a smuggler as the captain of a cargo ship. Theirs would be a delicate dance of mutual distrust. Neither would openly question nor accuse the other of impropriety. Not as long as credits were paid and services rendered.

The transaction was completed without incident; though Dimas did demand proof they had the other half of the negotiated payment available. Which of course they did. In fact, Mitchall's false SID carried an ample amount of credits to pay for their eventual exit from the DC back to England. Satisfied his passengers possessed sufficient funds, the captain directed the pair to a nearby deckhand.

"Points, take'em t'da'cabin," Dimas ordered. "N'get yer laze ass back t'cast off!"

Dismissed, Liam and Mitchall reclaimed their respective packs and headed toward the man called "Points." Lanky and lean, thin ropes of taut muscles stretched the skin of the deckhand's arms. Dressed in a uniform of dark blue coveralls with sleeves cut at the shoulders, the man looked to be in his late twenties. His once white skin had tanned to a golden brown, and in place of hair the man's head bore an elaborate tattoo of an eagle; beak ending at the brow and wings extended down the temples to his cheekbones. Flashing a smile, the meaning of his name became clear.

Each tooth had been filed to a sharp point. The custom had been seen in past centuries, usually among the more primitive people of the Southern hemisphere. Recently, perhaps within the last thirty or forty years, the extreme dental modifications had become common in the regions of Eastern Europe. And only then among the less desirable members of society. Whatever his current occupation, Points most certainly had a gangland past.

"Good morning," Liam offered, careful not to show discomfort with the man's drastic appearance. Mitchall, however, had less tact and tried to muffle a groan.

"Same to you," the sailor replied, offering a cordial hand. "Name's Zlatan, but most everyone calls me Points."

Liam was more than surprised with the man's clear, unaccented speech. Masking his own accent with an unimpeachable Americanized dialect, the spymaster gripped the man's hand. "Jasen Stonewell. This is my assistant, Alec Roames."

"Good to meet you both," Points replied. "Follow me."

As he led them through the unadorned passages below deck, Liam engaged the man in light, probing banter. "How long have you been with Captain Dimas?" he asked.

Chuckling, Points said, "I've survived the Cap longer than the rest of the crew. He caught me sneaking aboard in Poland when I was fifteen. Swearing and shouting the way he was, I was certain he'd hand me over to the PKs. But, instead, he hired me on. I've been part of his crew ever since."

"A merciful act," Liam said.

"Don't let the Cap fool you. He'll stomp and rage, even bloody your face if it's deserved, but he's more bark than bite. He pays fair wages, and rewards your loyalty with his own. I'm lucky I picked the *Espado* to try stowing away."

Intrigued, Liam asked, "You were a stowaway? Not a—"

"Thief?" Points laughed. "No. I was looking for an escape. Well, here we are."

Stopping at the entrance to their cabin, the man waved the passengers forward. "It's not much, but it is private."

Liam nearly commented on the understatement. The cabin was little more than a storage hold, and a small one at that. A flickering exposed light revealed two cots, a hand's span apart, along the walls. And that was all there was to see. The men would have to shuffle single file to enter and exit the tiny quarters.

"We paid for a cabin," Mitchall began to argue.

"It's fine," the spymaster interjected with warning.

Taking no insult at the objection, the sailor said, "You're lucky you booked when you did. The fellow that negotiated yesterday had to accept bunking with Burcu. If he showers more than once a month I'd be amazed."

"Captain Dimas took on another traveler?" Liam asked, keeping suspicion from his tone.

Nodding, Points explained, "Cap can never say no to a large fare. Man's name is Gal, or Gaul, I think. He's got hair like fire, can't miss him. But, I need to get back up before Cap comes looking for me. We should be underway within the hour."

With a dip of his head, the oddly well-spoken, file-toothed Points took his leave.

"Should we leave?" Mitchall asked after placing his pack on a cot.

Liam pressed the tip of his tongue to his upper lip as he considered. "If he's Alliance or an agent of the Council, PKs would have taken us as soon as we reached the docks."

"Surely you don't think it is coincidence?"

Offended by the suggestion, Liam turned a withering look to his assistant. "Certainly not. Whoever this Gal-Gaul person is, his presence is no accident. We've managed to hide longer than I had hoped. But the fact we're still breathing is interesting."

"Your word choice is 'interesting'," Mitchall rejoined.

Ignoring the evident sarcasm, he continued to think aloud. "There are distant cousins in the Family with red hair. He may be a fellow survivor."

"Quite a leap, no? And if he is a Garrott, why not come to us directly?"

"Valid argument," he conceded. "If a spy, then for whom? Which Family? And for what purpose?"

Liam had hoped the trans-Atlantic passage would allow a secure time for him to cultivate future plans; free from the constant distraction of fearing detection. He had been prepared to deal with Dimas, and a surly crew of possible cheats and swindlers. But, a Council spy aboard ship would require greater focus.

"Perhaps," Mitchall suggested, "it would be best to eliminate the threat sooner rather than later."

They had sufficient means with them to conceal a murder.

"A death too close to port might force Dimas to turn back. We'll have to wait three, maybe four days before any radical action. Even then, I'd hate to act precipitously. If this man is a Council operative, he may prove useful to our goals."

The ship's engines groaned and shuddered to life with a thunderous roar. Leaving their packs behind—any snoop would find only a few changes of clothes—the pair headed back to the open air. With luck, their fellow passenger would also take to the deck to view the departure. Liam was eager to unravel this newest development.

Of course, Fortune had decided the men had already received enough of her bounty. The red-haired man was not to be seen on the deck, or in the bridge. Unwilling to display too much interest in locating him, Liam resigned himself to stand with his protégé on the highest level of the bridge and watch the island of Manhattan recede from view. Despite the unease created by the surprise passenger, Liam's tension did feel lessened as the city grew smaller and smaller.

Two months on the run, hiding in hovels and sheltering in slums, had taken its toll on House Garrott's old spymaster. Decades had passed since his duty required any extended fieldwork. He'd had his network of informants funneling information to him for over thirty years. *Truth! Has it been* that *long?* his thoughts asked. The familiar ache in his joints told him it had. He tried to recall his last mission, the last time he had been in the field, but the memory escaped him. There was only a vague recollection of the timeframe. *Not since Regan died.*

Pushing away thoughts of his late wife—her betrayal and the son she had denied him—Liam stepped back from the upper deck's rail. He could not waste his energy on the past. Even Torrance was a distraction with no bearing on the task at hand. He had set the game in motion and now must wait for his son to choose his part in it. Until then, there were more immediate matters to address.

Liam made his way into the bridge where Dimas and a handful of men were overseeing the ship's navigation. For once, the captain appeared subdued, not shouting or barking orders. Arms folded across his barrel chest, the man stared out the glass windows towards the open sea ahead.

"The day seems favorable," Liam commented on the cloudless morning sky.

"Ain't keepin so," Dimas turned to reply. "Der's fierce brewins east."

Mitchall, who had little love for open water, groaned at mention of an impending storm. Both men had been born on the English island, but the younger man found no joy in sailing.

"How far cut?" his assistant asked.

"Dois risins."

"Can't you sail around it?"

Knowing how sensitive captains often were about the management of their ships, Liam apologized for the affront. "Forgive my friend, Captain," he said. "Alec has a strong fear of open water. Even a pitcher of water makes him uneasy."

Captain Dimas and the men on the bridge roared with laughter. A heavyset man seated at the main controls said, "A brown pants!" The comment set off a second round of jeers.

Though his aide looked confused, Liam had heard the old joke of the captain who had requested a red shirt before fighting off a pirate attack. After winning the battle, his men asked about the shirt. If he had been wounded, the captain explained, the shirt would have hidden the blood and his men would not have been discouraged. The next day, when twenty pirate ships appeared for revenge, the captain requested not a red shirt, but brown pants.

Through his laughter, Dimas asked the spymaster, "N'you, fogey? Brown pants, or nappies?"

Smiling, he replied, "I was boarding ships before your father boarded your mother, Captain."

Dimas' eyes widened in shock, and his men stilled their laughs as they waited to see their master's reaction. For a tense second, he thought he might have overstepped with the joke. But then the captain's face broke into a wide grin. "She'd more men on 'er den mos' ships!"

The bridge's crew relaxed and snickered along with their captain. In most company, good manners and meekness worked best. However, Liam knew that rougher men respected better a salty tongue and a bit of cheek. He could already see Dimas holding him in higher esteem. Unfortunately for Mitchall, his measure had fallen beyond repair. *Well, he won't have to worry about remembering his alias. They'll be calling him "Brown Pants" all the way to the DC.*

It had been a risk, jokingly insulting the captain while still strangers, but Liam needed to win over Dimas and his crew. Whatever threat the unknown passenger posed, the spymaster would work to secure the favor of his hosts.

The captain rewarded his audacity by leading them through an extensive tour of the bridge. With a father's pride, he spoke at length about the various controls, systems, and technologies of the *Espado do Mar*. Most of his words came in a flurry, and Liam was unable to translate the sailor shorthand. He nodded along, feigning interest, expressing wonder and awe when Dimas' tone suggested such reactions. Sometimes it was genuine, though not for the right reason. Much of the ship's technology was outdated to the point of archaic. Any wonder lay in the fact the vessel still functioned.

Once he had thoroughly and exhaustively explained the bridge, Dimas guided the pair down to the main deck to lecture them on the twin cranes. A long hour passed before the captain seemed ready to release his audience. Returning to the interior, the three men turned a blind corner and collided with a startled man. A man with a curly mane of shockingly red hair. Years into his craft, Liam caught the flash of recognition when the man's eyes fell on him and his assistant.

"Pardon me, Captain Dimas. I was lost in my own head," the man said with the accent of the American South. Though the diction was precise, Liam knew it to be affectation.

"Steppin' dumb a'ship is a sure fall t'the blue," the captain admonished with a grumble.

"Yes, well, again I apologize. I'll be sure to, ah, step smarter in the future," the ginger replied, offering a weak smile. Shifting his attention, he said, "You must be the other travelers. I'm Gal. Gal Averson."

Accepting the handshake, Liam repeated, "Gaul?"

"Gal. Like doll with a *g*," he corrected.

"Pleasure," the spymaster replied, reciprocating with their own false names.

Fair-skinned, with a constellation of freckles spreading from the bridge of his nose to upper cheeks, Gal was younger than he had expected. Liam would not have been surprised if he was still in his teen years. Surgical skill could reverse the outward signs of aging, but he saw no signs of artifice in the smooth skin. And no amount of credits could buy the naiveté in the man's jade eyes. Naiveté and fear.

The spymaster's befuddlement increased tenfold. *The Council would never send one so clearly inexperienced to assassinate us. Even if the mission was simple reconnaissance, the Caputs would dispatch an Echelon-trained operative. Could Torrance have sent him?* He did not yet know enough about his newly discovered offspring to predict the man's actions. Or who might be in his service. For one who traded in information, Liam detested contending with so many unknowns.

"I hope you'll join us for a drink this evening," he smiled as he invited the young man. "We have a long journey ahead. We should become better acquainted. Don't you agree?"

Hesitating, Gal replied, "Ah, yes. That sounds very good. Well, I'm headed to stretch my legs a bit. I'll see you tonight." Quickly, and nervously, the man slipped through them and walked out onto the main deck.

Captain Dimas took his leave as well and climbed the stairs to the navigation deck. Now able to speak freely, Mitchall asked, "Was that wise?"

"Until we learn his intentions, I'd prefer to keep him close at hand," he answered. "He knows who we are. That much *is* clear. And I think he's more fearful of us than we need to be of him."

"And this drink you offered?" the protégé asked. "Is there a bottle somewhere in your pack?"

Laughing, Liam replied, "We're on a smuggler's ship, Mitchall. There isn't a man aboard that wouldn't part with a bottle or two for the right credits."

The rest of the day drifted lazily along. The squawking birds, which had followed them for most of the morning, had abandoned the ship and returned to the indiscernible shore along the western horizon. Liam and his aide had avoided the cramped space of their quarters in favor of the open deck. With each passing hour, Mitchall's coloring edged closer to a green-tinted pallor. Refusing the midday meal, the man grimaced as he watched Liam eat the bland offering of boiled chicken and broccoli. The spymaster was not looking forward to sharing a cabin with him once the waters turned rough.

Occasionally, they spotted Gal pacing along the ship; his hair a bright beacon impossible to miss. Whenever the man caught sight of them, he would cut a hasty retreat in the opposite direction. Liam made no efforts to follow or engage him. He had the upper hand and would let the boy's anxiety feed upon itself.

As predicted, they secured a bottle of unlabeled whiskey from Points for the sum of five hundred credits. He could have haggled the crewman down, but preferred to let the man come out ahead in the deal.

Mitchall nearly wretched from a whiff of the spirit. Even on the best of days, his stomach reacted poorly to alcohol. For himself, Liam found the tested sip tolerable, though a shade too smoky. As it had come from a sailor's stash, the potency was high. For good measure, Liam doubled the dose of the alcohol-inhibitor he had brought aboard. The two small white pills would prevent any negative effects no matter how much he imbibed.

When he had left England months before, he had not anticipated the need for extensive supplies. A few poisons, a small blade, a garrote, and a compact particle handgun were all he had thought to bring with him. It had taken a few days to acquire a more complete "kit" in New York City's underworld—which was essentially the entire city.

If Gal had any training, and Liam had to operate under that assumption, the man would have his own supply of "intrigues," as they were known in the craft. Among them, the same inhibitors Liam had consumed. *Or we might just get lucky.*

From the bridge, they had watched the sun set in a vibrant kaleidoscope of red and purple, deep orange and bright pink. Or at least Liam had. His assistant sat with his head in hands, staring at the floor. His reaction to the first day of the voyage had done little to change the crew's impression. Once Nature's display ended, the pair followed several members of the crew to the ship's mess.

The cook, a short, gap-toothed fellow from Asia with a name too foreign to pronounce and thus referred to as "Cookie," had prepared a meal of spiced ham and brandied carrots. Dimas' business dealings, both legitimate and not, must have been quite profitable to provide such meals. Liam had traveled on passenger ships with less savory fare. Two months of greasy fast food and overly spiced takeout had also worked to lower his expectations.

The captain took his meals in private, leaving the crew to complain and jest without worry of punishment. Liam and Mitchall took a seat at the long, steel table with Points, Burcu, the fat Trevor who had named Mitchall "Brown Pants," and a pair they had not yet met. Gal, who was already waiting, eyed the spymaster nervously.

With an audience of three passengers, the men of the *Espado do Mar* peppered the dinner talk with an endless string of bawdy jokes. Most were so crude even Mitchall's seasick-coloring managed to blanch.

"Did ya hear the one bout the old sailor 'n the whore?" asked Burcu.

Though he had, Liam shook his head.

"This ol'fucker's missing his days at sea," the man began. "T'rise his spirits he hires himself a whore. He mounts 'er 'n and starts goin at it. A few ticks pass, and the bitch ain't makin no noise. The sailor stops and asks, 'How'em I doin?'

"'Yer doin three knots,' she says t'him.

"'Three knots? Whaddya mean?' he asks.

"'Yer knot hard, yet knot in, 'n yer knot getting yer money back!'"

The joke was old even before Liam was born, but still the men pounded the table with their fists and hooted as though they had heard it for the first time.

"And that's how Burcu met his wife," Points shouted above the din.

Their antics were little better than young schoolboys, and far more crude than his usual company, but Liam found himself enjoying the banter. These men were simple. They led lives free from the webs and snares of power. A clear sky and a full stomach were their strongest desires. He could almost wish he was one of them. Except, he knew how the world worked, how power and influence were the only means to ensure survival. Their profession might spare a few of them from The Culling, but was a simpler life worth the risk?

Liam was pulled from his thoughts when Trevor asked, "So, why the DC? Got a thing for savage meat?"

"Like you never got on a Deader," Cookie accused while leaning against the wall with a dishtowel over his shoulder.

Shrugging and grinning, the other man replied, "I'll never turn down a free ride. But, you gotta be careful and find yourself a clean one. Most got the disease; make your prick fall right off."

Not long into the twenty-first century the epidemic, once known as HIV but now referred to as the "Deader's Plague," had soared well beyond crisis level. One of the first acts of the then-fledgling Global Alliance was establishing the quarantine of the African continent. Medical advances had succeeded in the treatment of cancers, and even achieved some success in an HIV vaccine. However, once a new strain of the virus emerged in Africa, a strain more virulent and deadly than its predecessors, swift action had been required. Some had spoken out against the quarantine, citing moral and humanitarian imperatives. The larger majority, though, accepted the Alliance's propagandized claims of impending death and the threat to civilization. In the end, the measure was enacted, and now, a century later, the quarantine was viewed as sound policy.

Much to the Alliance's chagrin, the population of the DC had not been entirely eradicated. Deprived of outside intervention, large swathes of inhabitants succumbed to infection within decades. Warlords swept in to fill the power vacuum, fighting over land and resources. Their bloody conflicts claimed the lives of millions more. By the turn of the new century, even the most conservative estimates calculated 99.99% of the population had died since the quarantine had been in place. But, on a continent as abundant as the DC, one hundredth of a percent represented nearly twenty million people. Scattered and hidden across the vast land, it was unclear how many more had been breed over the last sixty years.

The Council had debated committing to an offensive, considered directing the

Peacekeeper units maintaining the quarantine to move inland and put a final end to the native survivors. Yet, as with most Council affairs, self-interests had delayed the Caputs decision; the Families opting to focus on their respective industries rather than a minimal threat from savages. So, despite the rich resources of the continent, the consensus had been to wait until after The Culling to reclaim the DC for the Alliance.

"I've lived a rather selfish life," Liam explained to the sailor. "However many years are left to me, I would live them out in service. My friend," he nodded to Mitchall who was gritting his teeth against the tumult of his stomach, "agreed to join me in hopes of some imagined grand adventure. Though, I'm beginning to think he's coming to regret that decision."

His assistant grunted in agreement.

"What about you, Gal?" Liam turned the question to the spy. "One so young must have strong reasons for abandoning the civilized world."

Gal eyed him. "I heard a man could start a new life on the DC. Claim some land, build a home for himself—be answerable to no one."

A murmur of muted chuckles rounded the table. Most of the world believed the DC empty of its former inhabitants. Some made the long journey confident that a world of untapped wealth and opportunity existed beyond the blockade. Only those in power, and smugglers familiar with the region, knew what dangers awaited idealistic wanderers.

"Your family must be very pained by your leaving," Liam pressed in false amicability.

"They understand why I must go," the man replied. There was a distinct noble conviction in his tone, giving Liam the sense that the words, though guarded, were grounded in truth.

Smiling, the spymaster said, "Yes. I'm sure they do. Perhaps they hold out hope you'll survive your actions and return safely to them."

The *Espado* men at the table likely only heard an old man offering elderly advice to one younger and greener. He was certain Gal had heard the warning threat. To his credit, though, the youth masked the fear he had displayed at their first meeting. *He has some training,* Liam acknowledged.

With a word from Cookie, the gathered crew left the table, taking their empty plates and cups to a bin near the kitchen, and returned to their varied posts so the next shift could eat. Gal made no effort to excuse himself, instead remaining with Liam and Mitchall through the second serving. Once again, a chorus of coarse humor filled the mess as the crewmen ate their meal. In time, another round of dishes was deposited in the bin, and the three passengers were left alone at the table while the cook busied himself in the adjacent kitchen.

Placing the bottle of deep brown liquor on the table, he thanked Cookie for the loan of three small glasses and poured the company a shot. The young spy hesitated at first; only drinking once Liam tilted his head back and drank. A pleasant burn seeped through his chest. The minimal warmth of the day had long since dissipated and the whiskey provided a welcome heat.

Mitchall, who had by then surrendered all pretense of seafaring fortitude, forced himself to empty his glass. From his expression, it was clear the medication Liam had provided to treat the seasickness was having little effect. *The alcohol-inhibitor is reducing the efficacy,* the spymaster assumed. He was tempted to suggest the man retire for the evening, but feared Gal would suspect the assistant feigned illness in order to search the spy's quarters. *Sorry, my friend. You'll just have to suffer through this.*

The conversation between the old and young spy was a volley exchange of well-concealed probing. Each asked of the other's family, profession, and the like. Liam searched for hints of the man's true origin; hoping for a slip in accent or idiom. Such clues were sparse, and he could pinpoint only generalities. *Educated in the West,* he decided. *Europe? Or America?*

After the fourth refilling (Mitchall still sipped from his second), Liam forced his tongue to slur, and raised his volume to mimic inebriation. Gal's own words remained steady; his voice even and moderated. Youth may account for the sobriety, but if it continued beyond another few shots, then he would know the spy also had dosed himself with an inhibitor.

Perhaps used to a more disconnected existence, Cookie joined the table after finishing his responsibilities. As one of the few men in the crew who could partake in alcohol without detriment to the ship's safety, the cook assisted in emptying the bottle. Taking over the conversation, the man regaled the passengers with many tales of his time on the sea.

Through it all, Gal maintained a rigid posture. His arms and legs in the position of a wary solider prepared for a hasty defense. From the way his left arm draped on the table, Liam was sure a sizable knife was tucked under the sleeve. He was humble enough to understand that as untrained as the boy appeared, he could still overpower the much older spymaster in a direct confrontation. *I may have half a century more experience, but my martial days ended decades ago.* Which meant he would have to strike first if the need arose.

Hours passed and eventually the bottle ran dry. Cookie was the first to depart, stumbling back from the table, and swaying as he mumbled words of farewell and gratitude. While he was not satisfied with the information elicited, Liam could find no sincere reason to prolong the night. He and Mitchall took to their feet, thanking Gal for an enjoyable time. The red-haired spy replied in kind and turned left out the mess's far door. The pair made the way to their small cabin.

"Perhaps my mind is a bit slow tonight," his protégé said once they were secure behind the steel door of the converted storage space. "But, was anything learned? Beyond the fact that whiskey bought from a smuggler is essentially bleach dressed in brown."

Offering a pitying grin, Liam replied, "Once the inhibitor leaves your system, another dose of meclizine should ease the seasickness. Tell me what you believe was learned tonight."

Lowering himself to a cot, the acolyte slipped off his sturdy boots; curling his toes in happy freedom. "The southern accent is fake," he began as he shrugged out of sweater and shirt. "He may not be England-born, but he spent time there."

"I had assumed Europe. Why specifically England?"

"There were a few times he said 'here' and 'there' without a longer drawl, and with a slight lilt to the *r,*" Mitchall replied. "Each instance was in the middle of a longer reply. People tend to focus on the beginning and end when imitating an accent. They get careless in between."

Impressed, Liam admitted he had not caught the indicative slips. Of the many he had trained through the years, all the various persons in his network, Mitchall was one who had excelled under the spymaster's tutelage. For not the first time, he offered silent thanks the man had been at his side when the Council's might fell upon House Garrott.

"He either has tremendous tolerance or he used an inhibitor," he continued. "Physically, it's apparent he's undergone more than moderate combat instruction. His knuckles bore the signs of one who has worked somewhat extensively with a heavy bag. On his right thumb there was a thin scar which is commonly earned in the lessons of knife throwing." Mitchall held up his own digit as an example of such an injury.

"Certain turns of phrase indicate a higher than average level of education. If his reactions to the crew's jokes were genuine, I'd say he comes from an upper class family. Maybe even one of *the* Families. Though, I doubt there's been any grooming for a position of power. As much as he turned up his nose with the crew, he was too deferential with the captain. And when he looks at you, there's an obvious mixture of awe, fear, and I would say revulsion. He knows your reputation, which lends further support to being from a Family. But, he clearly sees you as superior, thus he is not accustomed to being in the company of someone as high as a Chief Advisor."

Liam allowed himself a small measure of pride over the man's astute observations. Much of it a fatherly pride. A quiet voice within wondered if he had been able to raise Torrance, would it be his true son here with him now, displaying all the skills Liam had taught him? *There is still time for that possibility*, he answered the voice in his head.

"Very well done, Mitchall. Especially given your condition," Liam praised. Still dressed, he sidestepped back to the closed door, and added, "Get some rest."

Confused, the man asked, "Where are you going?"

"When Gal left the mess, which way did he go?" the spymaster responded. "Left or right?"

Searching his memory, Mitchall replied, "Left."

With a grin earned from decades of serving as the master spy for a Family, he said, "And yet a *right* turn would have taken him to the crew's berths. It appears there is still more to learn tonight."

A less experienced man might have followed Gal from the mess after noticing the odd choice of direction. But, Liam knew better. Targets tended towards greater caution during a journey than they did upon reaching the destination. The brief minutes he had spent with his assistant should have been long enough for Gal to believe he had not been followed.

Save for the muted hum of her engines, a slumbering quiet blanketed the ship. The *Espado do Mar's* instrumentation, while not as autonomous as a podcar, required only one crewman to maintain an overnight watch of the navigation. Even still, Liam kept his movements discreet as he slipped through the dim passages. Instinct drew him past the stairs leading to the bridge, and instead directed him out onto the open deck.

Cold slapped his face at the first step into the star-filled night. Unlike the unseasonable warmth of their departure, mid-winter reigned unchallenged on the open seas. With practiced ease, Liam closed his mind to the chill and biting wind. The Eastern trick, once thought to be supernatural, traced its roots back several centuries to warrior monks who had achieved sizable fame through their uncanny ability to withstand pain. Though his own ability paled when compared to the alleged feats of the monks, Liam's skill was enough to mute the icy pain of the frigid temperature.

Slipping a thin blade from the sheath in his boot, he flexed his hand around the hilt until the grip was both familiar and comfortable. The particle gun at his calf offered better protection against a younger and stronger opponent, but he had always been partial to knife-work. In younger days, his ruthless skill had earned him the moniker *Shā Shŏu*. Liam smiled at the thought of the name.

Killer.

Unlike Caput Hu, the infamous Viper who had murdered his way to power, Liam's actions had always been in service to his Family. Even now, when it would have been far easier to slip into obscurity and live out his days in peace, he held to his oath. Perhaps if Tilden and Aubrey had perished with the Family, he might have accepted a forced retirement. But as long as a Garrott still lived, his duty was not ended.

And if they had died, you'd be the heir. With no personal desires for Caputhood, he knew the House would have been finished had such an occasion occurred.

Moving across the deck, slipping between the shadows cast by the cargo containers, he felt the age in his bones. *Seventy-three years old,* he mused. *I should be grooming a successor, preparing the next Chief Advisor. Not skulking about a ship in a winter crossing of the Atlantic!*

As much as he wished to blame the Council and its treachery, he could not absolve himself of guilt. It was his burden to protect the Family, and his blindness to events had instead brought ruin. *Duty and obligation. A heavy weight at any age.*

Nearing mid-deck, a soft whisper on the wind caught his ears. Too far to identify the speaker or discern words, Liam fought to locate its origin. Knowing the deception water had on sound, he tucked into a shadow and stood with eyes closed; stilling one sense to heighten another. Several seconds passed before the whispering again floated to his hearing. *Ahead. Starboard.*

Turning into a narrow corridor between twin stacks of containers, Liam soft-stepped across the width of the ship. Closer now, the voice was male and he thought he heard a brogue sprinkled in the still unintelligible words.

Fool, Liam could not help to scold. *Never drop your cover during an operation.*

Almost at the end of the row, and thus his concealment, he dared another pace forward until he could see around the final container. Gal stood at the railing, his red hair reflecting the light of the half-moon.

"It's not safe, sir. Walford suspects," the man hushed into the darkness.

Definitely Irish. Well done, Mitchall.

Gal fell quiet as whoever spoke to him through the mobile comm in his ear replied.

"I know, but it's two weeks to the DC," the spy countered. "If he decides I'm a threat . . ."

Silence again, then, "Yes, sir. I will try, but . . . yes, sir."

Liam wanted that mobile comm. Three meters separated him from his target. With Gal's back to him, he committed himself to a slow approach. He did not trust his age would allow a rush and tackle. Even if it had, that act was better suited to a killing attack. He preferred to take Gal alive—a dead spy was of little use to him.

Easing one foot forward, he kept the rhythm of his breath steady as he adjusted his weight and balance. Left foot followed the right and he readied the knife.

Gal whirled around. Both men froze in a stutter of shock, but Liam's savvy recovered first and he launched himself across the remaining distance. The battle of strength he had hoped to avoid had forced its way to inevitability.

Remembering the dagger he knew Gal hid on his right arm, Liam focused his force on keeping the spy's left hand immobilized. As they collided, the younger man made no effort to reach his blade. Instead, lifting his free hand to his ear. With a curse, Liam realized his error and watched the mobile comm fly over the rail. Offering no defense to the knife at his throat, Gal submitted in wide-eyed fear as Liam held him against the rail.

"I'm not here to kill you," the youth stammered, the false Southern accent forsaken.

"Then why *are* you here?" the spymaster hissed and pressed the blade's edge just deep enough to draw a thin line of blood.

"I was sent to watch, to follow you."

"Sent by whom?"

"He doesn't have a name. He calls himself the Soothsayer."

He had heard the sobriquet once before. A day ahead of the Council's movement against the Garrotts, Kerwen had contacted his advisor, who was in Washington seeking an impossible truth. The Family's Chief Engineer had been abducted and a cryptic warning was all that had been found in his home. A warning, once delivered to Julius Caesar, to "beware the Ides of March." A warning from a Soothsayer. Neither Emperor nor Caput had heeded the caution. And both had shared the same terrible fate.

Friend or foe, this enigmatic figure had infused himself into cataclysmic events. *But to what end?* Judging by the young spy's actions and words, Liam was inclined to believe he had not been sent as an assassin. Experience, however, told him a new player had entered the game. A clever one who, for the moment, existed beyond Liam's knowledge. That same hard-won experience also warned of the acute danger such a player posed.

CHAPTER FOURTEEN

Milo Chance

"Holy shit."

Grappling with similar shock, Naesha exhaled, "Yeah."

Accompanied by Godwin, the pair had burned through most of the morning in confused wandering. Delphine Porter's written directions had been written many years after her visit to Torrance's lair. Their initial hopes of finding the location without much difficulty had faded as the first hour bled into the second—and then into the third and fourth—and they had still found nothing in the unending darkness.

Twisting and turning through the vast network of underground tunnels, arguments and accusations had nearly forced them to abandon the quest. Even Godwin's systems had failed to be of assistance. The drone had cited a signal disruption in both his navigation and echolocation programs; blaming probable countermeasures installed by Torrance as the cause. Whatever the root, Godwin had been reduced to a more human standard of efficiency.

They had supplied themselves with a stock of iridescent flares before setting out. But, the supply had been exhausted. A dozen times, the party had believed they were making progress only to find themselves back in a tunnel lit with the small, glowing markers. It was through dumb luck, despite Naesha's unwarranted claims to the success, that they had stumbled through the correct series of passages to reach their goal.

What they found stole their breath.

The cavern's size far exceeded even their wildest predictions. *How could a space this massive remain hidden?* Milo thought, squinting into the distance and not seeing an end to the sprawl. More shocking still was the lair's contents. Countless couches, divans, chests, dressers, and cabinets were arranged into false, wall-less rooms. But even the innumerable accents could not match the number of books—

actual bound books!—meeting their eyes at every turn.

Once, as a child, his parents had taken him to the New York Library Museum. A monotone docent had led their tour group through the various sections of the museum. Even for one with as little interest in reading as Milo, the vast, antiquated collection overawed him. Before leaving, the Chance family had stopped into the gift shop and purchased a small, souvenir book chronicling the history of the museum. Now resting on a shelf in his apartment, the tome was the sole printed book in his possession.

"It will take weeks, months to go through all this," Naesha estimated with defeat.

Denied such a luxury of time, he began to despair over finding a clue to Torrance's current location. Milo had never expected to find the man here. But, then he had not expected to discover a stronghold of this magnitude. *Would he really abandon this place? His home?*

They moved towards an area that looked more intimate, more inhabited, than the others. Their steps were cautious; fearing hidden traps and safeguards designed to punish intruders.

Beside an unmade bed, a pile of folded clothes sat on the floor. The original sizes were men's, but someone had cut and rolled the items to fit smaller frames.

"He had the Seton kids down here," he announced.

"There's an empty bottle of hair dye over here," Naesha replied from the kitchen area. "Probably for the girl."

Drifting to another bedroom section, Milo opened the doors of a tall, oak wardrobe. Inside were several long-sleeved shirts, as well as a half dozen pairs of pants. All the same size. And all black. Assuming the space to be Torrance's own sleeping area, he proceeded to examine the contents of the nearby drawers and dressers. Beneath the stacks of well-organized socks—also black—and underwear, he found a thin book. Leather-bound, both cover and spine bore the creases of overuse. Faded silver markings decorated the front. Milo fanned the crisp pages with his thumb; finding Asian lettering on every page.

"There is blood on this shirt," Godwin called out.

Sliding the book into his back pocket, Milo crossed to the drone and took the tattered shirt into his hands. "Can you get a DNA read?" he asked his partner.

"I have already taken a sample," the machine replied. *"But I am unable to access the database. The signal interfering with my navigation systems is also blocking me from all communication. I am . . . disconnected."*

For a machine, there was noticeable discontent, even a hint of worry, in Godwin's "voice." Milo feared anything that could make the resolute drone anxious.

"Run it when we're out," he said. If the bloodstain was indeed from Torrance, a DNA composite would be an incredible asset in their search. From Delphine's tale, it was unlikely the man was sheltering with a relative—if Torrance even knew his relatives. Still, a genetic history could unlock some of the mystery of his origins.

Exploring another "room" of the cavern, Naesha said, "Man certainly likes his guns. And knives . . . and, oh yes, explosives, too. I've got seven cabinets over here with enough weapons for a small army."

While no particle weapons were included in the collection, the arsenal was extensive. Handguns in a wide range of calibers, assault and sniper rifles, several cases of grenades—smoke, flash, and shrapnel—as well as machine guns, and an impressive assortment of shotguns. Milo also found a number of firearms that a gunsmith had modified with the skill of a master.

"He may be a lone wolf, but he's got contacts on the street. Most of these are illegal," he said. "And he isn't lacking for credits." Even with his years in law enforcement, he could not calculate the value of the weapons stash. *Hundreds of millions of credits.*

Milo spent several minutes inspecting the guns, slipping two of the modified sidearms into his belt, while his companions moved off to explore more of the lair. He knew they should be focusing on one area at a time, making a thorough, methodical scrutiny of each space, but their fascination was still too new.

An hour passed before he entered a new area, the seventh in his enthralled wandering. It was another bedroom, but unlike the others before it, a large trunk rested at the foot of the bed. The heavy metal lock sealing the trunk closed drew Milo's eyes. Godwin responded to his summons and tore the lock free with the ease of snapping a stick. Like children with an imagined treasure chest, Peacekeeper and reporter sat cross-legged on the floor.

Naesha lifted a folded bundle of white cloth from the top layer of the open trunk. As she worked to unwrap the fabric, Milo rummaged through the remaining contents.

Disappointment spread as he withdrew various items of dark-colored clothing. Only by accident did he notice the manufacturer's tag inside one of the shirts. With the exception of the clothing they assumed the Setons had discarded, everything else had been of matching size. This shirt, however, was larger. As were the pants. He knew he held the clothes of the man who had brought a young Torrance to Delphine Porter's doorstep.

"Milo," Naesha whispered.

Hearing the pain in her voice, he looked to the unfolded sheet cradled in her lap. Resting atop the white cloth was a curled length of braided leather extending from a thicker handle of the same material.

"It's—"

"Yeah," he said, the word catching in his throat. In disgust, Milo took an edge of the sheet and pulled it over the whip; obscuring it from view. The once giant cavern suddenly felt very small. The borderless rooms no longer enticed him with clues to Torrance in the present. Rather, the space now seemed filled with the past screams of a child being tortured.

Turning to face him, he could see the welled tears in her eyes. "What . . . what is he?" she asked.

Two days ago, he would not have hesitated to say, "Terrorist. Criminal." Now though, he could only shake his head and answer, "I don't know."

Before her guests had left, Delphine had asked him to consider Torrance's past. To understand him and what he had become. Milo had departed her home without making such a promise. As a PK, how could he? The worst death and destruction Philadelphia had seen in decades had been done by Torrance's hand. He had sworn an oath to bring a man like that to justice. *The justice decided by a corrupt judge and district attorney?* his mind asked.

His world of black and white, where those in power were honorable and beyond reproach, had been forced by recent events to accept the gray blurring of distinct lines. Hadn't a ruling House intervened to protect a criminal enterprise? Hadn't the Soothsayer, a faceless man hidden in shadow, offered aid when the Council did not? It went against his very nature, his years of service, to even allow the slim possibility that his judgment of Torrance might be erroneous. *Yet, why didn't I say no to Delphine's request?*

Unwilling to journey down that particular road of thought, Milo replaced the contents of the trunk and helped Naesha to her feet. The trio spent another hour searching the lair. Their previous gusto, however, had waned. He could not shake the feeling they were committing some offense by rifling through the various belongings.

"Godwin, if we leave, can you get us back in without us getting lost again?" he asked upon realizing their collective mood was worsening the longer they spent in the lair.

"Yes, Chance," the drone assured. *"My internal memory is not affected by the countermeasures."*

"All right. Let's pack it in for today. We'll start fresh tomorrow."

Naesha's face offered him a clear expression of relief.

Exiting the underground tunnels was a less arduous task than entering. Godwin took the lead and brought them to the surface. It had been early morning when the party had set out, but now the sun hung low over the trees in the park. *Most of the day was wasted just trying to find the damned place,* he thought.

Parked a short distance away, the podcar hummed to life at his command and lifted its doors for their entry. Hungry from the missed midday meal, he and Naesha discussed a plan for an early dinner.

"I have re-established communication with the mainframe," Godwin cut into the pizza versus burgers debate.

"Okay," Milo replied before defending the pizza option. The drone had a somewhat annoying tendency to inform him of every routine process.

"I have completed the analysis of the blood sample. Do you wish to hear the results?"

After the discovery of the whip, and the gloom that had followed, Milo had forgotten about the sample. Tempted to let the entire matter drop for the evening, he nodded for the drone to proceed.

"I will assume you are not interested in the process—which is quite advanced and certainly impressive—and instead skip directly to the results. Unfortunately, neither maternal nor paternal analysis yielded a precise genetic relationship. In the case of the mother, it is established the woman was a relative, likely a sister, to an Owen McAvoy."

"McAvoy," Milo repeated. The name held a vague echo of familiarity.

"Owen McAvoy was arrested on April 12, 2149, and was executed as an enemy combatant under the Global Alliance's Anti-Terrorism Charter. His sons, Gavin and James, disappeared within hours of their father's arrest. Both men remain at large. It is believed the elder sibling, Gavin, is currently the head of the Cohors Ignota cell responsible for the recent events in Washington, D.C.."

"So Torrance *is* an Ignotum," he said with a small amount of satisfaction. The old woman's tale had almost superseded his well-honed instincts.

"Not necessarily," Naesha retorted. The tone of open challenge in her words surprised him. "His uncle and cousins may be, but there's still no proof he even knew them."

Laughing, he replied, "Come on! The guy was born into a family of Ignota. Truth, Naesha, how much more evidence do you need? Another building blown up? More PKs shot down? I know Delphine's story was powerful. Hell, it got me thinking twice. But, Torrance has terrorism in the blood."

The silent clenching of her jaw as she turned back to Godwin was as loud as the shouting words she left unsaid. "What about the father, Godwin? What are the results?"

"As I mentioned, the analysis did not prove as useful as one may have hoped. Results of the paternal testing came back as classified."

"Classified? What level?" Milo asked.

"The level is classified as well."

Shaken, he said, "The information is classified on a level that's classified?"

"Correct."

Looking to him for an explanation, the reporter asked, "What does that mean?"

Milo paused for a second while the few pieces of the mental puzzle he had thought complete shuffled and scattered. "I've never personally come across it, but I know others who have. We call it 'Five Eyes'."

"Five Eyes?"

"Yeah. When something is beyond top secret—you know, global security type stuff. Only five sets of eyes can see it."

Understanding the reference, she said, "The Council of Five."

He dipped his head with a grimace. "If the father's DNA is classified 'Five Eyes,' then it's almost certain he's a member of a Family. And not a cook or guard or servant, either. Someone with a high rank, a title. Maybe even in the line of succession."

"Okay." Naesha drew the word out as she did whenever she was about to posit a theory. "A girl from the Ignota and a guy from a Family had a kid. Either side would have been eager to hide that fact, which may explain why Torrance was raised in a cave."

"But who raised him? Ignota or Family?"

"Maybe both," the reporter answered. "Maybe his mother *and* his father ran away together. She could have died when Torrance was little. And the man who raised him was actually his father."

Unconvinced he said, "Romeo and Juliet with a kid. Except after Juliet dies, Romeo repeatedly tortures the kid and trains him up as a *super soldier*? I've seen a lot as a PK, but that sounds like a stretch."

Arching a brow she said, "How can you say that? Name one thing that's happened in the last two months that wouldn't have sounded like a stretch a year ago. An entire Family is exposed as Ignota and executed. A guy who has lived underground for over thirty years emerges and successfully attacks a military base. A guy calling himself the Soothsayer pops up and gives you little riddles to solve. And someone from House Cambrie steps in to stop a local PK from busting a drug lord. I don't think we're working in the realm of the logical anymore, Milo."

Confronted with the succinct list of recent events, he was forced to admit the merit of her argument. Little in the past weeks had been grounded in the plausible. Willing to acknowledge Naesha's point, he began, "You're ri—" and then paused. "Wait a minute. House Garrott!"

"House Garrott what?"

"An entire House exposed as Ignota. Torrance's father was a member of a House. What if he's Ignota on *both* sides? Godwin, run a search of diginews articles."

"*Parameters?*" the drone asked.

Energy refreshed from the potential lead, he estimated Torrance's age from Delphine's confession, and replied, "Go back thirty-four to thirty-eight years. Look for any male members of House Garrott who suddenly went missing."

"Or died," Naesha added, following the rapid jumps of his mind.

The drone remained quiet for half a minute before replying, *"No males linked to House Garrott went missing during the specified time frame. However, eight men from the Family did die in those years."*

As his partner reported their names and causes of death, Milo discounted five of the men who had been well into their eighties and nineties at the time of their deaths. Delphine had described Torrance's guardian as appearing in his fifties, but actually closer to seventy. Of the three remaining names, each a distant cousin and far removed from the line of succession, none seemed an answer to the paternity mystery.

Two, both mid-forty, had died together in a boating accident. Though the event had occurred before his birth, Milo's parents still referenced the shocking tragedy that had sparked an outpouring of global grief. While he could not discount the men completely, his gut doubted them as candidates. The last name on the list, a boy of thirteen who had been born with a genetic defect, could not be the man Delphine Porter had met.

Before Milo's frustration could return, the drone said, *"I hope you do not mind, but I took the liberty of expanding the initial parameters of the search. It seemed logical to allow for the possibility that the unidentified mother had married into the Garrott Family."*

Milo jumped in his seat. One of the biggest side stories to the fall of House Garrott had been the involvement of the actress Isla Carene. A Hollywood darling outpacing her peers in the rise to stardom, it had been a great shock to learn she had been an Ignota operative. If the Council had not acted, the woman was rumored to have been close to engagement with the heir, Tilden Garrott. *Of course! If the Garrotts were not Ignota*—it was the first time doubt of the official story had slipped into his mind—*planting a spy among them was certainly a wise tactic.*

"What'd you find?" he asked.

"On November 18, 2128, Riall Walford nee Barnes, wife to Liam Walford, Chief Advisor to House Garrott, died from complications of premature childbirth. The child was declared stillborn."

As Milo ran the dates in his head, Naesha asked, "How far along was she? Could the baby have survived?"

"At the time of her death, Riall Walford was in her eighth month of pregnancy."

"Any connection between Riall and the McAvoys?" he asked in follow-up.

Silent again, the drone performed the search with incredible speed. Milo could not believe there had been at time when he thought having a machine as a partner was anything less than advantageous.

"Much of her history has been classified; a standard practice when an outsider marries into a Family. There are two society articles, published just before the Barnes-Walford wedding, which mention her time with an advertising agency."

Without prompting, Godwin brought one of the articles up on the glass display integrated into the podcar's windshield. In a human touch of the dramatic, the drone selected and enlarged a portion of text. *"You might find the agency's location rather interesting."*

Milo scanned the short paragraph, which highlighted the various regional campaigns the firm had managed for Garrott Industries. Skimming lower, he saw what the drone had teased. The advertising agency was based in Torrance, California.

"Hello, Mom and Dad," he said, half-expecting Naesha to object to his conclusion.

Instead, she revised her earlier theory. "Riall Barnes was in truth a McAvoy, an Ignotum. Working undercover, she was placed in an ad agency that has Garrott Industries as a major client."

"Hang on. I'm not saying I disagree," Milo was careful to open with a caveat of neutrality. "But, you said 'she was placed,' which implies a third-party giving orders. Who?"

Naesha chewed the corner of her lip. "From what we know so far, it's been a family affair, right? Owen McAvoy, Ignota. His sons, Ignota. Riall, which I think we can now assume was Owen's sister, was also Ignota."

"You think Owen McAvoy embedded his sister with the Garrotts," he said.

With a shake of her head, she replied, "It's possible. But he wasn't the one training Torrance. The dates and ages don't match up. Besides, you don't just grow up and one day say, 'Hey sis, I need you to become a spy.' For something like that, it's got to be years of grooming, training. Keeping it in the family, I'd guess Owen and Riall's father raised them as Ignota. And then did the same with his grandson, Torrance."

Though she would likely believe him to be lying, Milo had followed the same reasoning and reached the same presumption. Eager to continue and avoid needless debate, he said, "I think you're right."

"So," she returned to verbal speculation. "Through her job, Riall catches the eye of Liam Walford, the Caput's right-hand man. She marries into the Family; spying and sending intel back to the Ignota. Liam finds out, kills her, but the baby survives . . . and . . . that's where I get a bit murky. Would he really send the baby to Riall's father? If Walford was Ignota, then that makes some sense, but then if he was Ignota, Riall wouldn't have been a spy."

As discomforting as the possibility was, Milo was expanding his doubt of the Alliance's pronouncement linking House Garrott to the Ignota. There was little evidence to support his suspicion, and nearly every aspect of the tale he and Naesha had just concocted was conjecture, but something told him they were right. He'd had a similar feeling, a tickling hunch that had dogged his thoughts, when he had begun the Muerte investigation.

"I don't think Walford was Ignota." *There. Now you've said it out loud.* Naesha seemed too engrossed in her hypothesis to understand the enormity of the admission. *Or maybe it's just not enormous to her. She hasn't spent her adult life as a Peacekeeper, serving Alliance and Council.* Yes, he had heard stories of the Families maneuvering against each other. He had assumed most of the gossip had undergone hefty embellishment by those who enjoyed telling tall tales. But even the worst rumors had never approached as horrific a suggestion as an entire Family slaughtered on false charges. For Milo, accepting such an idea as true was a devastating blow to his very identity. Yet as quickly as the thought had been conceived, that sense of nagging certainty returned. Every instinct within screamed the impossible had become the probable.

"For whatever reason, by whatever method, Torrance was taken in by Riall's father," he added. "He was tortured. And he was trained. Delphine said the man believed Torrance's future was important."

Well versed in human behavior and predictability, Godwin ventured, *"One of the most common motivations behind humans' actions is revenge. Assuming all your previous suppositions are indeed true—and ignoring the fact each is a possibility contingent on another possibility, and another before that—there is a high likelihood Torrance was raised to exact revenge against those his guardian viewed as enemies. In this case the Alliance, and specifically House Garrott."*

"Could he have caused the Council to remove the Garrotts?" Naesha suggested.

They knew too little about him to discount that possibility. However, Torrance had been in Washington, attacking a military base, when House Garrott had fallen an ocean away. An impressive accomplishment if he had been involved in both events.

Milo was torn between cursing Delphine Porter and thanking her. If the woman had not taken her life after their meeting, she'd be well entertained by his frustration. Instead, she had placed herself on the list of those who had known Torrance and were now dead. Delphine. Riall McAvoy. Her father. Liam Walford.

Like a hound, he caught a fresh scent of intrigue. "Godwin," Milo said. "What do we know about Owen McAvoy?"

The drone replied, *"Owen McAvoy was born to single mother Ava in Oberlin, Ohio on May 6, 2109. He attended Cleveland State University, graduating in 2131 with a degree in journalism. A year earlier he married Lillien Pelleiter, and the first of their two children, Gavin McAvoy was born. James McAvoy was born three years later. The McAvoy family remained in Cleveland as the patriarch worked at a local news station. As I previously stated, Owen McAvoy and his wife were arrested and executed in April of 2149."*

"And his sons? Where were they when they disappeared?"

"Gavin McAvoy was a sophomore at Ohio State University in Columbus, Ohio. He was last seen leaving his dormitory in the company of two unidentified men. James McAvoy was sixteen at the time of his parents' arrest and was abducted, also by a pair of unidentified men, from a classmate's home where he was spending the night."

Grinning, Milo turned to Naesha.

With an exhausted sigh, the reporter said, "We're going to Ohio, aren't we?"

CHAPTER FIFTEEN

Gavin McAvoy

For all the confident trust he had projected to the team, or hoped he had projected, he had never convinced himself. *Not even close.* As Torrance led their incursion deeper into the Alliance supply ship, Gavin kept a vigilant watch for signs of betrayal. True, the man had created a diversion allowing the party to board the craft. And thus far, he had helped them avoid detection as they wandered through the ship's belly. But Gavin still could not feel any trust for him. He told himself it was not jealousy tainting his view. *Truth, it's bad enough I'm even admitting to being jealous! Like some damn teenager vying for the prom queen!*

No, it was more than jealousy. He had led men for several years now, celebrated shared victories, and mourned common losses, relied on them and confided in them. Whether an intrinsic gift, or one gained through leadership, his sense of those in his company—their strengths and skills, faults and flaws—had guided him successfully. When others had feared Kunbo Fofana's size and color, he had known the African would be an incomparable ally. Despite their bond of blood, Gavin had seen his brother's unbalanced nature. The suicidal sacrifice had been expected. Even Adirene, whose eventual fanaticism had been much more muted at their first meeting, had raised flags of concern in his mind. When judging character, his internal barometer had proved accurate.

With Torrance, there were flags and sirens and bells and alarms. Danger cried out from every corner of his being whenever the man was present. Or simply mentioned, for that matter. Gavin had never before experienced, not even during Adirene's final days, a more visceral reaction to a man or woman. When he had confessed the sensation to Kunbo, who still held to disproven religion and mysticism, his master-at-arms had named it a "death-warning."

"In my homeland, such strong sensations are considered prophetic," the Dead Continent refugee had explained a few days past. "Our souls feel the souls of others. When in the presence of evil, our souls try to warn our minds. This is what you feel when near Torrance. I know, *ndugu*, because I feel it, too. I have prayed on it, asked God and my ancestors for guidance."

Talk of souls and prayers to dead relatives and nonexistent deities seemed foolish to Gavin, but the strong bond he shared with the African kept him from disrespecting the man's primitive beliefs.

"And what response have you gotten?" he had asked in the privacy of his quarters beneath Oberlin. He placed great value on the weapon master's counsel. If Kunbo wanted to ascribe his insights to a god or two-headed purple zebras with wings of fire, Gavin did not care.

The man had lowered his shaven head and said, "On this, I have been met with silence." The sense of abandonment in his voice pressed into the cell leader's heart.

"I'm sure your god will answer you soon," he had tried to offer with sincerity and cheer. He may not believe as Kunbo did, but he was not immune to the man's distress.

"You misunderstand, *ndugu*," the African had answered; again referring to Gavin with the Swahili word for *brother*. "My worry is not that I have received no answer. But that the silence *is* the answer. That Torrance, and the great evil within him, is necessary to our victory."

Kunbo's dark words hung like storm clouds as Gavin moved close behind Sonje; both following Torrance's silent steps. Twice now, the trio had been forced to alter their course to avoid discovery. Apparently, not all the ship's personnel had responded to the clamor above deck.

Raising a clenched fist to signal a halt, Torrance tapped his hooded ear. The cell leader initially heard nothing to warrant the other man's caution. Then, almost imperceptible sounds—*voices!*—caught his attention. If not for Torrance's signal, he would never have noticed the sound. *How does he do it?* Gavin's thoughts asked once again.

Ducking through an open door, and moving to the shadows, the party found themselves in a sizeable cargo hold. Dozens of containers, perhaps a cubic meter each, were stacked on palettes throughout the hold. At the center of the space, four guards sat around a small holo-platform gaming table. Judging by the "chip pile" projected in the middle, the stakes of the game were rather modest. With a scratch of his bearded chin, the man facing the hidden group studied the palm-sized tablet in his hand.

"Raising it ten," he said. The corresponding amount of holographic chips disappeared from the stack at his side and reappeared in the main pot. The bet was enough to push the next two players out of the hand, while the final guard raised the stakes by another fifty credits. Again, digital chips blinked and reformed in accordance with the play. Smiling at the other man's error, the first player called the bet.

The losing guard cursed when the voice of the gaming table's virtual dealer announced, *"Petty Officer Nadir wins the hand with a king-high straight."*

"Don't you know by now Nadir never bluffs?" teased one of the guards as the next hand was dealt.

With the men engrossed in their game, Torrance motioned for Gavin and Sonje to risk a closer inspection of the containers. Constructed of durable molded plastic and securely sealed, each of the label-less boxes had a small SID-scanner and display screen on the visible side. Stacked atop each other, opening one of the cases would require climbing to the upper most level of the palette.

He watched as Torrance entered a series of coded instructions into the cuff on his wrist. The man had spent long hours teaching Match Quentin how to enhance the devices. Ever the braggart, the cell's tech specialist had surprised everyone by admitting Torrance's skill exceeded his own.

Torrance placed his palm in front of a container's scanner. The guards' banter was loud enough to hide the audible ping of activation. Holding his breath and adjusting his grip on the tranq-gun in his hand, Gavin waited as the cuff worked to bypass the security protocol. If an alarm sounded now, a safe return to shore would be all but impossible. Finally, the container's screen displayed the details of its contents and eventual destination.

Scanning the information, much of it in a technical jargon beyond a layman's understanding, it was clear their theory had been correct. The case, bound for a distribution center in Toronto, Canada, held ten million SID chips. Repeating the hack on the cases within easy reach revealed other destinations: New York, Boston, and Detroit.

Whispering through the black fabric concealing her face, Sonje said, "There must be half a billion SIDs in here."

Nodding, he replied, "Least we know they're not here for an assault on Oberlin." With a check of his own cuff, he added, "Forty-one minutes. If we leave now, I can comm Match from the water and tell them to wait." With luck, they might even reach the shore before the deadline. Pressing tight against the cases so Torrance could pass and lead the retreat, Gavin felt a chill of danger when the other man did not move.

"We need to destroy the chips," Torrance rasped.

With as much command as whispering allowed, he replied, "No. That's not the mission."

Torrance tilted his head. "Then change the mission."

He did not need to see Sonje's face to know her opinion. On several occasions, she had voiced guilt over her involvement with the defective chips. Was he rejecting the idea out of sound reasoning? Or was his dislike of Torrance overwhelming his judgment?

In truth, the suggestion was tempting. The destruction of half a billion SIDs, guarded by two of the Alliance's carrier strike groups, would be one of the greatest operations in the history of the Cohors Ignota.

But, what would be the consequences?

He had never been one to act precipitously, preferring instead to weigh the possible outcomes before committing to action. His task, the one agreed upon by the other cell leaders, was to determine the purpose of the fleets' presence and return to Oberlin.

And what then?

Upon their return, Torrance would likely advocate the destruction of the SIDs. If recent days were any guide, half of the leaders would support the offensive measure. Could a second infiltration be successful? Or was this the extent of their luck?

Offering a different argument, he said, "We're not equipped for it."

Torrance wasted no time in countering the foolish statement. "It's a military ship. Pretty sure it has what we need."

Grateful for the hood covering the worry and indecision he knew was etched in his expression, he again thought of Kunbo's portentous words. *Necessary to our victory.* If only his own long-dead ancestors could advise from their graves. *Don't they?* a small voice asked. Three generations of Ignota had preceded him, each dying in duty to the resistance. His great-grandfather, Seamus McAvoy, a Founder, had been among the first to understand the Alliance had to be stopped no matter the cost. Could he draw counsel from their lives . . . and their deaths?

Yes.

"How do we do it?" he asked Torrance, the question declaring his agreement.

With no trace of smug victory in his voice, the man replied, "These cases are heat resistant. Fire alone won't cut it. We need explosives."

"Won't the guards have grenades?" Sonje asked in a hush.

"Not powerful enough," Gavin explained, then added with an unseen grimace, "We need a warhead."

Unlike the other vessels in a carrier strike group, supply ships had limited armaments, primarily for self-defense rather than offense. However, as a supply ship, it would be *carrying* ammunition for the other craft in the group.

"McAvoy and I will get the bomb," Torrance said to Sonje. "You stay here, stay hidden, and watch the guards. Break comm silence if it's not safe for us to comeback."

The doctor's small shape nodded and whispered "good luck" as the men crept back towards the door. Gavin was reluctant to leave her unprotected, but understood the other man's reasoning.

Moving through the quiet passages of the ship, he said, "Never seen you doubt before."

"If we get caught, she'll need to tell the others about the chips."

The man may claim strategy was behind his motivation, but Gavin was sure he detected sentiment as well. Once again, a wave of adolescent jealousy swept over him. *It's only been a couple of months,* his rational voice tried to break through. *I have no claim over her. Sonje's free to choose whoever she wants.* Chivalrous as the thought might be, one less noble followed it. *As long as she doesn't choose him!*

When Torrance spun on his heel, grabbing Gavin by the shoulders, and slamming him into an alcove, he almost believed the man had heard that last thought. He brought up his arms to break Torrance's hold, then froze midway as the echo of footsteps sung along the metal walls. He relaxed his tension to signal his understanding.

Still pressing his weight against him, Torrance took his hands away, and slipped a curved-blade knife from his waist. The unique inward angle design of the *kukri*, essentially a hand-held guillotine, was itself intimidating. When wielded by Torrance, the weapon seemed even more violent and vicious.

Sliding a finger onto the trigger of his gun, loaded with a dozen rounds of small paralytic darts, Gavin listened as the footsteps drew closer. Close enough to feel the other man's breath through their respective hoods, he heard Torrance say, "Two. Mine."

Before he could object, or confirm the count, Gavin felt the pressure against his chest build and fade in a flash as Torrance pushed off him. In a tight spin, the man overtook the pair of PKs; slashing into the throat of one, while smashing the other's trachea with a hard drive of his elbow. Both guards, stunned and muted, dropped to their knees. With the *kukri's* butt, Torrance delivered a blow to their heads; rendering them unconscious.

Impressed by the accuracy and speed of the assault, Gavin flinched out of his own shock and bent to remove the mobile comms from the guards. He held one of the devices to his ear, tossed the other to Torrance, and listened. The sabotaged crane was still the focus of the crew's chatter, though the initial mayhem he had witnessed on deck had lessened. There was no mention of his team's infiltration of the ship. Careful to keep the blood from the guard's severed vocal chords off the grated floor, they dragged and hid the bodies in a small room of gauges and dials.

Having holstered his weapon while moving the bodies, Gavin rearmed himself with the tactical baton tucked into one of the many pouches at his belt. Though the darts were non-lethal—a signal from a dead guard's SID was an alert they needed to avoid—he did not want to risk a target managing a shout of alarm before the toxin took effect. With a snapping flick of his wrist, the thin metal rod extended to its full length. Torrance tilted his masked head at the movement before nodding in silent approval.

You're not the only with training, Gavin shot back in his mind.

The pair continued on; each turn and hallway almost indistinguishable from the last. He had spent several hours over the previous two days working to memorize the layout. In addition to their collaboration in enhancing the team's op-tech, Match Quentin and Torrance had combined their substantial knowledge and drawn out a thus-far accurate blueprint of the supply ship's interior. Where the latter had gained his information was a mystery, but the former had earned it at great personal risk.

Enlisting with the Peacekeepers the day he turned eighteen, Match had spent a decade rising through the ranks. Operating as a Fifth for much of that time, the Ignota had extracted him after an unfortunate leak destroyed his cover. In his final act before disappearing, Match stole an incredible mass of data and then had uploaded a nasty virus to the Alliance's mainframe network. Four years later, his name was still near the top of the government's list of most wanted. *He must be bumped by now,* Gavin guessed. Torrance, Sonje, and Danica had at least moved him out of the top ten. *If I'm not already, after tonight I'll be up there, too. Assuming we actually pull this off.* He wished he felt more confidence in that belief.

Checking the time—thirty-two minutes remaining—Gavin could feel the cool beads of sweat accumulating under the wetsuit. Nearing the last turn to what should be one of the artillery holds, he pulled up short and hissed to Torrance. When the man turned back, Gavin nodded his head towards the upper corner of the far wall. Through the enhanced lenses of the facemask, he had spotted the mounted camera positioned towards the connecting passage. A few more steps and they would have been within the camera's view. Their cuffs may disrupt facial scans, but the sight of two men clad in black neoprene was certain to raise the alarm of anyone watching the feed. It was more than a little childish he knew, but there was definite satisfaction in detecting something Torrance had missed.

It's not a damn competition, he scolded himself. *At least for tonight you're on the same team.*

Torrance nodded his understanding after turning his eyes towards the warning cue. Speaking through a rapid flash of hand gestures, the man detailed an impromptu plan. Gavin twined his fingers into a platform and boosted Torrance up to the collection of pipes running along the length of the corridor. The meeting of glove and pipe emitted a soft sizzle of steam. Grunting low, he jerked his hand back from the scald. Gavin adjusted to the sudden movement's disruption of his balance, preventing them both from toppling. More cautious in his next selection, Torrance pulled himself free of Gavin's support. Within seconds, the black figure slipped over the side of the piping and made a steady shimmy to the camera.

Waiting and watching their surroundings, the cell leader slipped the PK comm from his pocket. Just a few minutes had passed since his last check, but he needed to be sure Sonje was still safe. The only change in status he heard was a team now worked to repair the damaged crane, and the rest of the crew was returning to their previous tasks. *Getting off the ship just got more difficult.*

Sooner than expected, Torrance was sliding his way back along the pipes. *Could he have really disabled the camera that quickly?* Dropping down, he pressed a finger to his lips and motioned for Gavin to retreat.

"A drone's guarding the hold," he said once they backtracked to the room hiding the unconscious soldiers.

There were other artillery holds in the ship that they could attempt to reach, but Gavin had little doubt they would find a similar obstacle.

"Assuming you don't have some secret way to take down a drone, what's the play?" he asked. He had faced the machine soldiers once before—when his cell, joined by two others, had attacked the PK base in Washington. They had learned standard bullets had no effect on the drones, only bouncing harmlessly off their armor. Particle bolts, however, did inflict damage. Though they both had a particle handgun in their possession, firing one on a ship and destroying a PK-drone was as far opposite stealth as one could get.

Torrance shook his head as he crouched down to examine the uniform of one of the PKs. Looking up, he said, "Drawing it away from the hold would buy us some time. But, it won't take long for the PKs to figure something is up. If this works, we'll have to move fast."

Excluding a direct confrontation, Gavin was certain the plan was their only option. Strangely, aborting the operation did not return in temptation. "And if it doesn't work?"

"Even faster," Torrance said.

His wry tone hinted at the grin hidden behind the mask. Straightening, he pressed the stolen mobile comm to his ear. With a flat voice, forgettable in its blandness, he said, "Conners to the bridge. We've got a couple of crates almost falling over in Hold 12. We need a drone ASAP before these things crash down. Over."

After a few seconds pause, Torrance signaled that the request had been approved. Cargo Hold 12 was a short distance from their present location. If the drone guarding the artillery was the one sent to assist—and there was no guarantee it would be—he and Torrance would have mere minutes to access the hold, remove an explosive device, and return to Sonje. Once the PK-drone reached Hold 12, and found no guards waiting, their ploy would be unraveled. Gavin had no need to calculate their odds of success.

Low. Low. Low.

Heavy dull thuds sounded in measured percussion down the short corridor. Nearer to the door, Gavin stole a careful look from their concealment. A PK-drone marched into an adjoining hall several meters away. Waiting until the metal-on-metal footsteps faded, the men left the confines of the small room and made a quick dash forward. Two turns brought them back beneath the pipes that had attacked Torrance's hand.

Truth, he did kill the camera! Gavin realized as he passed beneath the inactive device.

A massive set of double doors sealed the entrance to the artillery hold. Stretching five meters across, and three in height, these doors were quite different from the standard nautical hatches they had passed. Further proof the schematic Torrance and Match had created was near to perfection.

Wasting no time, Torrance stepped to the SID scanner, holding his palm a few centimeters from the reader. Gavin had used SID-cuffs to bypass security systems before, but had never tested their limits. There were not many systems more sophisticated than one protecting a military ship's artillery hold. He wondered if Torrance was sweating as nervously beneath his wetsuit as he was.

Anxiety itched as the small display panel continued to flash "Authorizing" with the rhythm of a heartbeat. *A heart at rest.* His was contracting as if he was sprinting a kilometer. On the verge of screaming out to relieve his building tension, the display finally changed.

Access granted.

The doors, thicker than the length of his arm, began to slide apart. First Torrance, then Gavin, sidestepped into the hold as soon as the expanding opening yielded sufficient space.

Far larger than the chamber housing the SID chips, the artillery hold was filled with endless crates of ammunition, numerous steel racks holding individual missiles of varying size, as well as several self-contained missile pods which could be attached fully loaded to HALOs and other aircraft. If they needed an explosive more powerful than a handful of grenades to destroy the SIDs, the artillery hold offered myriad options.

"Tell Sonje to run," Torrance ordered.

Turning, he saw the man listening to the mobile comm held to his ear. Fumbling its twin out of his pocket, Gavin's stomach knotted in panic as he heard the chatter over the comm.

" . . . security units to AH-4. Unidentified access. Two men already down."

"Code Bravo. I repeat, we are at Code Bravo. Unknown number of hostiles aboard ship. Proceed with caution. Assailants are to be taken alive."

As he activated his own comm, a deafening siren blared throughout the ship. "Get out!" he shouted to Sonje over the alarm's wailing screech. Her reply was muffled and close to inaudible, but he could just hear her acknowledge the command. With the attention focused on the artillery hold, she had a better chance of escaping the ship.

In response to their far less promising situation, Gavin cut back to the now-fully open doors. Shouts of approaching soldiers reverberated from both directions of the corridor. That he could hear them over the siren proclaimed their proximity. As one hand sought the particle gun holstered at his thigh, the other tapped through a series of instructions on the doors' interior display screen. Slowly—*too slowly,* he cursed—the weighty panels slid closed. Just before sealing, a brief tide of amber bolts flashed and seared into the steel. The bursts of light, muted through the lenses of his suit, failed to inhibit his sight. He returned three rounds, angling the shots into the hall. With a deep boom, the doors met and all sound, save for the alarm, cut off.

Torrance was moving through the room's arsenal, prying open one crate before abandoning it for another.

"That door won't hold 'em for long," Gavin said as he reached him. "I jammed the codes, but they'll be able to override in a minute or two. Maybe less. What are we looking for?"

"Don't know. I'll tell you when I find it," Torrance replied. Pointing a finger up, he added, "And it's that door I'm worried about."

Lifting his eyes, he remembered the PKs would not have to override anything. *It's a damn cargo hold. Loads from the top.* Punctuating the thought, the ceiling moaned as gears engaged and a seam of artificial light, as long as the room itself, began to spread wider.

A few meters away, Torrance called out, "Got it. Follow me." Carrying what seemed to be an over-stuffed black backpack, and not waiting for a reply, the man ducked into a space between two tall stacks of crates. As Gavin ran to follow, several human shapes dropped down into the hold. The light reflecting off their armor marked the figures as drones.

Joining Torrance behind one of the stacks, Gavin's breath caught in his chest as his eyes processed the package over which the other man knelt.

"That's a particle bomb."

"Actually, it's a particle demolition munition," Torrance corrected; his focus on the palm-sized case of tools he had placed on the floor. "Take my gun and hold them off while I get it open."

His mind twisted to determine which part of the directive was more absurd: firing a particle gun in an artillery hold, or opening a particle bomb, by hand, in an artillery hold. Bending to retrieve the other gun, Gavin made a quick scan of their position.

Wall on two sides. One approach from the left. Another from the front. Both narrow. Whether by chance or plan—*likely the latter*—Torrance had selected a defensible point. The soldiers and drones would be hesitant to open fire unless offered a clear, killing shot. With a firearm in each hand, he waited for the rush. The wait was brief.

The first drone stepped into view from the left. Unlike their bulleted predecessors, particle guns had no recoil to decrease accuracy or stability. Even a poor marksman was more apt to hit his target with a particle gun. After a decade and a half with the Ignota, no one would consider Gavin a poor marksman.

Fingers squeezed triggers and a pair of bolts burned through the air and slammed into the drone's head. The machine still stood, though the blasts had distorted its balance and halted its approach. Gavin delivered a second volley, both again taking the drone in the head. The artificial PK raised its arm in an attempt to return fire. A second drone moved into Gavin's peripheral field.

He spread his arms and aimed a gun at each of the drones. Ducking down and away after firing, he said, "I'm barely slowing them."

With unnatural calm, Torrance replied, "Almost done. Just a few more seconds."

Returning to their defense, he found both paths of approach held a single file of drones. Though their weapons were poised at the ready, none fired at him. In rapid succession, Gavin unleashed charged bolts into each line. The drones at the fore suffered the most damage. His original target, having sustained over a dozen headshots, dropped to its knees. There was little relief. As one drone fell, he saw others advancing along the tops of the stacks. The amplified strength of their legs propelling them through jumps across the hold. *It's a damn swarm!*

"Let's move," Torrance urged while rising from his endeavor.

Handing over the borrowed gun, he asked, "Exit strategy?"

"Bomb goes in four. Climb," the warrior replied. A magnetic handle in each hand, Torrance leapt onto the wall and swung and pulled himself towards the open ceiling of the artillery hold. Cursing the lack of warning, Gavin tucked his weapon down the small of his back. Just meters away, A PK-drone quickened its steps.

Grabbing the set of climbing devices from his belt, Gavin bent his knees to launch himself after Torrance. Shoulders pricked with pain as his foot slipped and the full weight of his body dropping tugged on the joints. He had never used the handles in speed, and the result was a clumsy effort. Torrance was advancing; his rhythm of hand-and-foot, hand-and-foot, impossibly graceful.

Struggling, Gavin had climbed a meter when his ankle screamed in agony. Through the blinding white pain, he looked down to find a drone beneath him. The machine's powerful hand was wrapped around his ankle in a bone-breaking grip. Only the tactile fabric of the wetsuit kept his fingers from slipping off the handles. Shouting in rage, he fought as the drone began to pull him down.

Three drops of red-gold heat rained from above, singing his cheek before burning into the drone's wrist. Its grip tightened and Gavin cried out as he felt bone snapping. Barely noticed through the raw pain in his mind, his body felt lighter, almost as if he was floating. Numbed in shock, Gavin realized he was free of the PK's damaged clutch

Feeling the cold spread through his body, it would not be long before his limbs failed to obey the mind. Confused, he heard his brother Jaime shouting down to him.

"Climb, McAvoy!" the figure in black yelled, one hand clinging to the wall, the other firing a particle gun into the PKs amassing below.

Jaime! Jaime?

Thoughts wrestling with reality, a primal instinct, an inherent will of the body to survive, took him. Gavin started to pull himself upward. One foot dangling uselessly, he grunted until he was level with the other figure.

"Keep moving," the masked man ordered. The haze lifted. *Not Jaime. Jaime is dead. It's Torrance.* Strange, he had never noticed how alike the two sounded. "Stay close when we get up."

Unassailed, both men rallied the strength to reach the wide opening to the supply ship's main deck. However, Gavin's body was growing weaker by the second as he expended the last stores of adrenaline. He knew he soon would succumb to the mental paralysis of circulatory shock. Scores of silent, unmoving drones watched from below. He imagined devilish lust in their lifeless metal faces.

Any wonder over the machines' lack of pursuit was explained as he and Torrance dragged themselves over the lip of the cargo hold. Dozens of Peacekeepers, some of flesh and most of steel, aimed ready particle rifles and formed a tight half-circle around the pair, cutting them off from the starboard rail a few meters on the left.

"Freeze!" a human voice ordered.

Ignoring the command, and seeming to ignore the situation's threat, Torrance drew one of Gavin's arms over his shoulder and helped the cell leader to his feet.

"I said freeze!" the PK shouted again. "Take their weapons."

A soldier in full uniform—helmet to boots—moved forward. Gavin could sense the man's reluctance as he lowered the rifle. Hands free, the PK reached behind him and pulled the handgun from Gavin's belt.

"Sowilo," the man whispered as his head passed Gavin's ear. The word was spoken so low he almost doubted it had actually been spoken.

He's a Fifth! the cell leader's mind shouted. Calculations spun. *If we surrender, he'd work to secure our escape.* But the bomb beneath their feet denied them that possibility. In the pain and confusion of the climb, he could not estimate how much longer they had.

There's probably only seconds left.

As the soldier backed away, Gavin seized on the lone solution his mind offered. *He's a Sowilo.* It sickened him how quickly he made the decision.

"My name is Gavin McAvoy," he announced. "There is a particle bomb activated in the artillery hold."

The PKs born of a mother's womb cursed at the revelation. Unlike the drones, these men could feel the fear of death.

The leader of the troops, the man who had ordered the Sowilo to seize the weapons, reprimanded the breach of his men. "It's a bluff. Take them into custody!"

Before anyone could react, Gavin turned to the secret Ignota, who had by then backed well away from him and Torrance.

"It's not a bluff, Sowilo."

The man nodded, almost bowing in respect, as he hooked a pair of fingers around the pins of the two grenades hung on his belt. Crying out, he shouted, "My life for a Founder! *Sic semper tyrannis!*"

Heads turned in a ripple of confusion. Still supported by Torrance, Gavin forced his weight into the man, driving them both left towards the rail just as the flash and concussive boom of the Sowilo's suicide rocked the deck. Whether he was prepared for the act or not, Torrance did not fight his effort. Instead, he moved fluidly, half-dragging Gavin along and over the rail. Falling in a rush of air, the man warned, "Stay under!"

With a final gasp, he hit the water hard, the force separating him from Torrance. His broken ankle screamed as it collided with the icy surface. Fighting the natural instinct to propel up, Gavin forced his arms to dig deeper in the dark lake.

Though muted through the waters, the roar of the particle bomb exploding thundered in an orchestra of a million bass drums. The initial rumble lasted only seconds before another, and then another, each louder than its predecessor, dwarfed the first blast. Not even the lenses of the suit could adjust to the brightness quick enough. Everything became impossibly white as the waters churned and pushed him with greater speed and force than his arms could have ever managed.

Blinded and disoriented, he could not distinguish direction. His chest began to burn with the need for oxygen. The energy behind subsided until his was the only power moving him. *Am I moving up or down?* the voice of panic asked. With dots of vision, tiny black pinpricks stealing into his blindness, he could not wait for his sight to return before he drowned. Relaxing his body, he hoped the natural buoyancy of the wetsuit would be enough to guide him to the surface.

Breathe, his brain called out. The emotion's urgency was at first demanding and violent. The primitive subconscious, ignorant of the danger, or perhaps indifferent to it, warred with his logic.

Breathe! Damn you, open your mouth and breathe! it raged at him again. Then, as if possessed of a sentience all its own, the voice within softened into deception and seduction.

Please, it cooed. *The pain is too great. Just one little breath and it will all go away. We won't hurt anymore.*

Aware of the fracturing of his self, yet unable to overcome it, unable to silence his lung's misguided compulsion, Gavin understood his reality. Understood and accepted it. *I'm drowning.*

Fixing an image of Sonje in his mind—the only true happiness he had known in a decade—Gavin McAvoy, last in the line of a Founder, opened his mouth and surrendered.

You were right. The pain is gone.

CHAPTER SIXTEEN

Sonje Nysgaard

As soon as their suspicions had been confirmed, she knew she would not leave unless the SIDs were destroyed. Even if the demanded price was her life. Still, she felt a moment of guilty relief when Torrance suggested the act before she did. The relationship with Gavin was strained enough without her challenging him while behind enemy lines.

"No. That's not the mission," the cell leader replied. Though he spoke in less than a whisper, the tone's sharp edge was unmistakable.

"Then change the mission," Torrance said, stealing the thought from her mind. Unable to see either man's face, she wondered how close they were to erupting. Sonje was grateful her own expression was likewise hidden.

Not that it matters. He knows how I feel about the SIDs.

Her involvement in the design of the upgrade had been grounded in the best intentions. The new devices exceeded the previous two versions in countless ways: from the strength of the radio frequency that improved its communication speed, to the expansion of early warning medical capabilities. Everything from blood pressure readings to signs of infections would be transmitted to the individual's physician. The potential for further expansion was promising. In time, the chips could be programmed to detect cancers well before noticeable symptoms occurred. The new SIDs would continue the revolution of medicine. And Sonje was proud to be a part of the development. Or had been.

Discovering the chips held a defect had been a devastating professional blow. Recent years may have seen her in a lab more than a hospital, but she was a doctor. She had sworn an oath to save lives. That something with which she had been involved might kill . . . no physician could accept such a truth.

Then the Alliance killed the man who had exposed the defect. They destroyed the Setons, killing the mother and nearly the father as well. The professional responsibility she had felt first had now become personal. Too many had died, and too many might yet, because of the SIDs. Destroying this cache was but a small start to assuaging the outrage she felt towards the Global Alliance.

The men exchanged a few more hushed words before Gavin asked, "How do we do it?"

Her heart leapt with equal measures of fear and exhilaration. Logic brought the fear—they would likely die tonight. But, the prospect of exacting immeasurable vengeance was exhilarating.

Exposing her martial inexperience by suggesting the use of the PKs' few grenades, Sonje voiced no argument when they decided she would maintain surveillance while the men sought a far more substantial explosive. Only once she was alone, tucked into the shadow cast by a tower of stacked cases, did she grasp the moment.

A warhead. They're going to steal a warhead. And set it off. And people will die.

She had not been among the Ignota long enough to view every man or woman in a Peacekeeper uniform as an enemy. If she was under attack, and forced to choose between a PK's death and her own, her conscience would not be conflicted. Not entirely.

But, in detonating a bomb—a warhead—there'd be causalities who had posed no immediate threat. Most of the people aboard the ship, if not all of them, were unaware of the danger stored in this cargo hold. They had enlisted with the military out of a sense of duty, or perhaps in an effort to better their lives, or even for the financial stability the service offered. They did not have the benefit of the knowledge she had unearthed. Did that warrant a death sentence?

Truth, a few months ago I should have been a target of the Ignota. I'm more linked to the SIDs than the PKs on this ship.

As she waited through long minutes, listening to the soldiers playing poker, Sonje sought a means of sparing the men, some way to send them out of the room. Gavin and Torrance, both hardened over a history of strife, would think her foolish. Maybe even weak.

This is war, she told herself. Yet, as much as she wanted revenge, she had thus far only seen the government as an "it." The Alliance, the Council, the Peacekeepers, had all been an anonymous collective, unspecified and nameless. Now, some short meters away, playing a round of cards, sat four men with distinct names and faces. Hearing their laughter, their ribald jokes and easy conversation, she felt a weakening of her resolve.

She almost wished they would discover her, come at her with threat and violence. Then she could claim self-defense and diminish some of her guilt from their deaths. Of course, should they find her, the only death would be her own. She had barely survived a knife fight with an opponent of equal size. *Four PKs, armed with particle rifles,* she laughed.

In a sudden cacophony of activity and sound, chairs grated on the metal floor, the soldiers cursing as they jumped to their feet. From all corners of the hold, a shrill alarm ricocheted and echoed along the walls. Through the mobile comm, Gavin's voice, shouting over the siren, cried, "Get out!"

Startled beyond all sense of self-preservation, she yelled, "What's happening?"

His answer, if there had even been one, was lost in the chaotic din. Realizing she may have compromised her location by shouting, Sonje turned to locate the PKs. The holo-platform gaming table was empty. Moving low along the palettes, she made her way to the end of the row. At the door of the hold, two of the soldiers pulled helmets down over their heads, and positioned themselves to block anyone from entering. *And me from leaving.* The other PKs either were somewhere beyond her line of sight, or had left the area.

With surprising serenity and focus, she returned the black dagger in her right hand to its sheath. Finding the familiar grip of the twin push blades secured to the sides of her torso, Sonje pulled the weapons free. Shaped like spades with a base as wide as her knuckles, the double-edged knives extended from the center of her balled fists. The PKs' armor protected them too well from the slashes and cuts of common knives.

The ambiguity of a moment before, the moral dilemma over a PK's innocence, was now extinct. Stalking forward, synchronizing her quiet steps with the higher pitches of the siren, Sonje closed in from behind. Nearly impenetrable, Peacekeeper body armor had been designed with greater focus on protecting the wearer from enemy gunfire. Kunbo had highlighted the suits' few exploitable areas of weakness during her training. In close quarters, a well-aimed stab could produce fatal results.

Breaking into a run for the last meter, she pushed off the ground. Twisting as she had been taught, Sonje used the momentum of the run and jump, the "cobra punch" Kunbo had called it, to amplify her strike. Left arm swung down across her body, driving the push blade into the unprotected softness between helmet and shoulder guard. Gravity pulled her down, and the PK's body fell with her. The second soldier had just begun to react when her feet hit the ground, knees bending with the drop.

Corkscrewing at the waist with the speed and power earned through weeks of infinite crunches, Sonje hooked her right arm into the turn. Fifteen centimeters of black blade slipped into the unarmored gap over the external oblique muscles. With a surgeon's mind of anatomy, she could picture the severing of the colon, the puncturing of the small intestine. She rotated her fist ninety degrees as she wrenched the push knife out of the abdomen.

Clutching the wound in a futile attempt to prevent his evitable death, the PK crashed to his knees. The alarms swallowed whatever screams he may have voiced. Running out the door, Sonje offered thanks for the small mercy.

While the endless screeching may have shielded her from emotional torment, it was now working to disorient her path to escape. She had never imagined a sound could make thinking so painful. Like most surgeons, she had developed a necessary competence to block out distraction. There were times, either in an operating room or more recently in her lab, when she had focused with such intensity the rest of the world was locked out of her perception. Choosing turns at random, she wished that skill would return to her now.

There!

Some fragment of a memory broke into her panic, and she recognized the stairwell up to the HALO pad. A knot of worry tightened with the realization that no PKs had attempted to stop her. There had been no PKs at all. A fool might attribute it to luck. But, she was certain the empty corridors meant Gavin and Torrance had drawn the crew's complete attention.

At the top of the stairs, she had a full view of the open, and unfamiliar, deck. Puzzled, she thought for a second her retreat had taken her to a different part of the ship. Then she reasoned out the change.

No HALOs.

Sonje threw her eyes skyward but found only the black blanket of night above the lights of the ship.

Do HALOs even fly with lights?

Her training had been focused on direct, hand-to-hand combat. She had no more knowledge of PK machinery than the average citizen. Probably less, and even that small smattering was sourced in the cinema, not tactical intelligence. If the HALOs were close, Sonje did not know what to look for as confirmation.

It would be a quick run of ten meters to the nearest rail. She tried not to think of the drop once she launched herself over the rail. Diving was a far more intimidating task than swimming.

Ten seconds, she calculated, encouraging her inactive body to move. *Ten seconds and I'll be in the water.*

Her hesitation, though, was not fully selfish. Thoughts turned to Gavin. And Torrance as well. Her mind imagined scenes of torture and danger, each increasing in horror. If they were captured, and if she stayed aboard, she might be their only means of rescue and escape. Yet, if the men had managed to leave the ship, and she stayed aboard, she could well be placing herself into enemy custody.

Gavin had warned of this moment. Soon after the events in Washington, when they had been able to explore their feelings, he had worried emotion might compromise reason. That at a critical point the instincts of his heart would overrule those of his brain to a catastrophic result. He had cited Adirene's mad reaction to his brother's death.

Hearing the conflict in his voice, the sparring duality of leader and lover, Sonje had replied, "You were an Ignotum long before you met me. And I joined the cell before I knew my feelings for you. Ignota first. Us second."

He had repeated the four words—a heavy vow neither hoped to be forced to honor—and enveloped her lips with a passionate kiss.

First mission and here I am. The Ignota in Oberlin were waiting. Danica and her father were waiting. Though limited, the intel she had—the SIDs, their quantity, the construction of the cases, the destinations—could aid the resistance in ways her untrained mind could not conceive.

Recalling her earlier admiration for Gavin locking away his feelings towards Torrance at the start of the mission, Sonje swallowed hard, slipped the push lades back into their sheathes, and whispered, "Ignota first."

In an exaggerated lunge that almost caused a fall, she rushed forward. Legs turned over in long strides as the soles of the *jika-tabi* slapped down on the metal deck of the ship. Two seconds, and half the distance covered, was all it took before she caught the attention of a PK. His shout was lost in the fury of her adrenaline, but she could not ignore the blasts of his particle rifle. The solider fired twice, both bolts striking the deck centimeters behind her feet. With an agility achieved through sheer panic, Sonje tucked into a poorly formed hurdle and leapt over the waist-high rail.

Momentum and posture allowed little time for her body to prepare for entry into the lake. The water welcomed with a cruel slap to her flailing legs and arms. Stunned, Sonje gasped in pain, swallowing a mouthful of icy water as she splashed down beneath the surface. Pushing her arms into wide powerful strokes, she forced a path back to air.

Sputtering, pushing out water and gulping air, she oriented her position. Diagonally ahead lay the shore, a kilometer away and past a pair of warships. To the rear, she saw a HALO moving towards her from the ship's mid-deck. The craft beamed a circle of searching light onto the lake's surface. Inhaling, Sonje dove down and away.

She waited until her lungs burned before resurfacing for air. The HALO was closer, scanning the water in tight circles. Though covered in black, she knew a careful eye could spot her head should the craft reach her. Again and again, she dove and surfaced, the intervals between the two growing shorter as her body exhausted.

Assuming she had taken the shortest route to shore, the HALO floated in the air a hundred meters away. Sonje refused to allow any belief of safety into her thoughts. She could not let her mind trick her muscles into complacency. *I'll be safe when I'm in the shelter.*

The current aided her progress, small waves carrying her along in their search for the shore. Nearly past the fleet's guarded perimeter, Sonje was diving under again as a thunderous crack shook the air along the water's surface. Fearing the sound meant they had discovered her, she dove deeper and shut her eyes in anticipation of pain.

Light, intense white light, burned against her closed eyelids. A half-second later, a sound of world-rending cataclysm consumed everything. One thought came to mind, *So this is what dying feels like.*

But then the searing brightness faded, white to red and then gone completely, and the underwater echoes of the world above returned to her ears. The water rumbled, pushing her forward with surprising force. But, that too faded. She opened her eyes and found darkness below, and above an undulating cover of red and orange.

Fire. Kicking to the surface, Sonje spun around to a sight both magnificent and terrifying.

Where the supply ship had been, billows of thick gray and black smoke folded into themselves and rose in a column to an expanding mushroom-cap cloud. The column partially obscured the aircraft carrier, which had floated near the supply ship. What little of the massive ship was visible sat under a dome of blazing red. Other spots of carnage glowed against the heavy smoke stretching across the fleet. As the impossibility of the spectacle settled over her, Sonje pressed a finger to her mobile comm.

"Gavin!" she called out. *He made it off. He wasn't on the ship. He made it off.* "Gavin!"

"Sonje," a voice replied. A surge of hope bloomed—and faded.

"Gavin..."

"It's Corey. You're in comm range. Where are you?"

Fighting back tears, convincing herself the cell leader could not reply because he was out of range, she said, "In the water. Maybe a half kilometer from shore."

"Are you hurt?"

Yes. "No. Corey, what happened?"

"Just get back to shore."

The journey back had been as much a force of mind as it was body. With every stroke, her thoughts had alternated between despair and promise. Exhausted, the former had slowly, but steadily, begun to dominate the latter.

When she reached the shore, it had taken several minutes for Corey and the others to pinpoint her location. She had been confused at first by the scout's instruction to remove her hood and mask before leaving the water. However, the reason became quite clear once she took her first steps on the sand. All around, the citizens of Lorain had traded the warmth of their homes in favor of witnessing the extraordinary scene of chaos unfolding just off the town's coastline.

Without the hood, and the night hiding the knives strapped about her, the skintight wetsuit had elicited only a few questioning looks. The stares were brief, though, as most eyes had returned to the fires in the lake. Shock had still been too new for most to link an oddly dressed *woman* with the explosions a kilometer away.

Secure in the podcar with the scout, Kunbo, and Match Quentin, Sonje took her first warm breath. The African directed the vehicle to begin the return to Oberlin.

"What are you doing?" she exclaimed. "We have to wait. We have to find them. Gavin is . . ."

The weapons master replied, "The deadline has passed, Dr. Sonje. His orders were clear. We must return to Oberlin and inform them of what has happened."

Guilt cut off her reply. *You left him,* a harsh voice accused. *You made the decision to leave him. And now you want them to lessen your guilt.*

To shut out the condemnation, she began to pepper Match with questions while Kunbo sat in silence; the others of the cell following behind in the second pod.

"What happened?" she asked as feeling returned to fingers and toes with prickling comfort.

"Not sure yet," he answered without looking at her. His hands moved furiously, a conductor working through the orchestra of information projected on the pod's display. "About twenty-four minutes before the deadline, there was an explosion on the supply ship. That was followed by two *much* larger blasts. The shockwave was enough to rattle the pod. From the mushroom cloud, I'd guess it was a particle missile."

"Gavin and Torrance were on their way to an artillery hold to steal a warhead," she informed them. The words delivered enough of a blow to break his focus and direct a shocked stare at her.

"*What?*" Corey asked with incredulity.

"We found the SIDs, hundreds of millions of SIDs. Torr—*we* decided to destroy them." She could not place the blame on Torrance.

"Okay. Well, then, mission accomplished, I guess," the scout stammered.

"Is there any way to determine if they got off the ship before the explosion?"

Shaking his head and returning to his task, Match said, "I'm trying to hack into the fleet's comm system. Everything's recorded, so if I can get past the firewalls, we can hear what happened before the blast. I'm hoping no one will notice a small breach in all this chaos.

"The Alliance is so disorganized right now they haven't even stopped the local news from feeding the scene live to national and international outlets."

The pleas of better judgment fell to a whisper as a different demand, one far more strident, cried out in her thoughts. Accepting the enormity of her actions, she said, "Match, can you hack the live feed?"

CHAPTER SEVENTEEN

Aubrey Garrott Hu

Bundled into a long coat of suede and fur, the tans and browns flowing down just past her ankles, she had hoped the garment might spare her the full assault of Beijing's mid-winter cold. She was wrong. The chill seemed a living thing, invading points of weakness—under the hem, down the neck—intent on reaching her skin. Surrounded by actual enemies, those of flesh and bone, Aubrey refused to let the weather conquer her as well.

When she woke that morning, thoughts of the previous night's dinner still fresh, her attendants had informed her of an expansion in her freedoms. The most enticing was access to the large garden off the southern end of the palace. *Supervised access*, she reminded herself. However, the garden's beauty was almost enough to let her forget the pair of servants and squad of Peacekeepers following her every step.

Servants had swept the recent dusting of snow from the circular stepping-stone path weaving through the garden. A small pond, its water still and reflective, sat at the center. Delicate evergreen limbs bent and arched at every height, alive in contempt of the season. At one end of the path, a footbridge crossed over a narrowed section of the pond, and led to a gray-roofed octagonal gazebo. Every aspect of the garden felt ordered. Even the placement of rocks and pebbles was purposeful and precise. Aubrey could imagine how wondrous the space would look come spring.

Crossing the bridge, she lowered herself onto the bench curving around the interior of the gazebo. The PKs took positions nearby; four facing her, four turned away. *They're guarding me as much as they are guarding against me.* Her two servants followed her into the structure and knelt to one side. They were the two youngest from the giggling trio that had dressed her for the dinner with Caput Hu.

Surprised by the maids' posture, Aubrey directed them to sit on the bench. Servants had attended her since birth, and many had become as near to friends as the daughter of a Caput might have. She would never have ordered them to kneel. Nor did she think they would have obeyed if she had.

"Get off your knees and sit properly," she said.

Giggle One and Giggle Two—*I should really find out their names*—shook their heads in wide-eyed refusal. One of the oldest civilizations in the world, the East had returned to ancient customs once the Council had been formed.

Frustrated by the women's foolishness, Aubrey snapped, "I am Caput`e of this House and you will do as I say!"

Hesitant at first, the pair exchanged a quizzical look before deciding a direct command superseded tradition. They moved to the bench and sat. If she did not know better, Aubrey would have thought they were sitting on tacks. Their stiff-backed discomfort was as ridiculous as their kneeling. *Well, at least they obeyed.*

Her mother's voice mocked, "You should never have to remind people of your title. Your position should be in your voice, your eyes, your movement. It should surround you always."

But I'm a Caput`e because we were defeated, Mother. To them I'm a captive, not a Caput`e, she argued back. Aubrey did not need to guess how Roslyn Garrott would have replied. "How they see you is how you see yourself."

Turning her focus back to the servants, she asked, "What are your names?"

The nearer attendant, and the prettier of the pair, said, "My name is Li-hua, *Dianxia*[4]." Disuse heavily accented the English.

"I am Hsiu Mei, *Dianxia*," the second maid added. Unlike her counterpart, Hsui Mei carried more weight on her small frame. Her hair lacked the natural luster of Li-hua, and the thin tattooed brows above her eyes were an unforgiving distraction.

"Are you to be my personal attendants?"

"If it please you, Caput`e," Li-hua answered.

It'd please me if you drowned in the pond.

"We shall see," she replied with intentional indifference. "I want a message sent to my husband. Tell him I am greatly moved by the beauty of this garden. And that I look forward to sharing a meal with him again soon."

Both maids nodded but made no move to deliver the message. Arching one brow, Aubrey asked, "Do you understand?"

Hsiu Mei answered, "Yes, *Dianxia*, but only advisors are permitted to disturb the Caput when he is working. Not house servants."

Narrowing her eyes in her best imitation of her mother, and adding ice to her tone, she said, "Are you saying your Caput`e is a house servant?"

"I . . . no, *Dianxia* . . . the Caput . . .," the girl stammered until Li-hua intervened. Aubrey was not more than ten years older than the maids, but their naiveté and size made them seem like children.

"Take the Caput`e's message to Joseth-liang," she directed her peer. Hsiu Mei all but flew off the bench and crossed the footbridge. Legs and arms jerking awkwardly, it was clear the young woman was fighting the urge to run.

"Joseth-liang?" Aubrey asked.

"Joseth-liang is the commander of the House guard. He will see your message

---

4   *Dianxia* is the East's honorific used for Caputs and their wives. It is similar to "Your Grace" in the West. –M.S.

is delivered, *Dianxia*," the attractive servant explained.

In truth, she did not care if the meaningless communication reached Hu's ears or not. She had made the request to observe the dynamic between the maids, and to test how far her authority reached. Recalling the old adage of sticks and carrots, she transitioned to a tone of sincerity.

"Thank you, Li-hua," Aubrey offered with a warm smile. The attendant bowed her head. "I don't know what the equivalent title here would be, but I am naming you my chief of staff."

"*Dianxia?*"

"My chief assistant. In addition to overseeing the maids and servants and others assigned to a Caput`e's service, you'll also help me learn the language and customs of this place."

The serenity of the girl's face shattered as unbridled horror stole over her expression. Aubrey doubted the girl suspected the true motive behind the promotion. *Her reaction probably has something to do with low birth or some other fool thing. English sensibilities may be dusty, but these people are nearly calcified.*

"*Dianxia,*" Li-hua began her protest, "I cannot accept such an honor. It would not be right. My superiors would be offended if I were to advance above them."

Precisely, she thought with a hidden smile.

"Nonsense. They will celebrate your success," the Caput`e lied. "And if they do not, they will answer to me." Rising with an excited clap of her hands, she added, "Now, the matter is settled. Let's find you something to wear that is more appropriate to your new position."

With a commanding stride that would have made her mother proud, she swept across the footbridge and back towards the palace entrance. Li-hua followed close behind; the girl's dismay was palpable. Aubrey felt a stab of pity for the girl. *She'll likely turn up dead in some staged accident.*

"When you commit to a course of action, do so boldly," Liam had taught. "And once you commit, never falter. Never flinch or shy away once the blood begins to spill. A victor sees it through to the finish."

She pushed aside the pang of guilt and fixed the memory of all the innocents of her House that Hu and the other Caputs had slaughtered. *I will not falter. I cannot falter!*

"I hear you have made some changes."

There had been more than a little surprise when she learned the message to Hu had not only been delivered, but a response—an invitation to dine together the following evening—had been sent in return. Once again, Aubrey sat across from her husband at the long table. While not as decorated as she had been for their first meal, she still approved of the simple red gown and delicate jewels her maids had selected.

"Is that a problem?" she asked without apology and with a hint of challenge.

Smiling as he cut into the thick salmon steak on his plate, Hu responded, "Not necessarily, no. Change can be good, if conducted correctly. But you must understand ours is a very old civilization. A father may go to work in a podcar, watch a film on a holo-set, but then insist his daughter be chaperoned on a date."

Aubrey washed down a bite of fish with a sip of wine. She had grown tired of water and tea, and allowed herself the small alcoholic indulgence. Though she preferred whites, the pinot noir's dark notes of black cherry blended well with the flavors of the salmon. She made a note to have Li-hua schedule a meeting with the House's chef.

"If tradition is so important, perhaps you should have kidnapped an Asian bride."

Laughing soft and warm, Hu said, "Who knows? Maybe I'll adopt the Arab custom and take a second wife. Fawzan has—what? Four now? Or is it five?"

The Middle Eastern Caput was well known for his voracious sexual appetite. Even with four wives, he managed to find the energy for twice that many mistresses. Aubrey found the concept repulsive.

"You could destroy the other Houses and take a trophy from each," she added.

"An interesting goal. Though, I don't believe there are any women in the remaining Houses with the level of acumen I prefer. No, for now I'll focus on the one wife I have. I've a feeling she's going to be more than I bargained for."

There was a definite measure of admiration and appreciation in his words. Unlike the servants, it was clear he did not see her as a weak prisoner of war. In many ways, Hu had spoken to her as a near equal. *Like Father spoke to Mother.* Uncomfortable with the possible implications of his respect, she brought the conversation back to its original topic.

"Are there any particular changes that worry you?"

Shrugging, he said, "Assigning Li-hua as the head of your staff was a surprise. She's inexperienced in anything beyond changing the sheets. I worry she will disappoint you."

"If she does, then I will replace her. For now, I am willing to give her a chance. Besides, in my captivity I haven't had the chance to meet many who might be better equipped. The selection pool was rather small and shallow."

"Your continued references to 'captive' and 'captivity' sadden me," the man said.

Despite the sincerity in his voice, Aubrey could not refrain from a bitter laugh.

"How else should I refer to this?" she said with an encompassing toss of her hands. "That I'm on holiday? Yes, that must be it. I'm on holiday and the PKs following my every move are tour guides!"

Before answering, the Caput studied her for a moment, the tip of his tongue wetting his lips with a quick glide.

"What if I said you were free to leave at any time?" he questioned. "That you could walk out the door right now and no guard would stop you?"

Unsure how to respond, not certain what verbal trap he was setting, she took another swallow of wine. She had expected false opportunities of escape to be presented to her, tests to judge her level of submission. She did not, however, anticipate Hu to offer one so openly.

"Where would you go, Aubrey? House Garrott is gone. And you have been labeled a traitor. How long do you think the other Families would let you live?"

She had already teased along that same string of thought, and reached the same conclusion. If not for Hu intervening, she would have died with the rest of House Garrott. If not for his current protection, she would be sent to her grave. Infallible truths, but bitter all the same. *If he expects me to be grateful...*

"What makes you assume I prefer this life to death?"

"Because you've had a knife with your dinners for two months now, and you haven't buried it in your chest." His reply came so quickly she knew she had been following his intended script.

Seeking a response which did not commit her to any path, she said, "There's little honor in suicide."

The Caput nodded in agreement. "The Cohors Ignota would disagree. They'll use suicide bombers if it advances their cause."

She replied, "I'm no Ignotum. And killing myself now serves no purpose."

"Is that important to you? Serving a purpose."

Aubrey still felt trapped in an orchestrated conversation. Until she could wrestle control away from Hu, she could only deflect with her answers.

"Clearly it is important to *you* that I have a purpose. I don't seem to have much say in the matter."

"More than you believe," he replied. The words could have been referring to either statement. Or both.

A servant stepped into the dining room to refill Hu's empty wine glass and replenish the few sips she had taken from her own. The fellow had barely left the room before the Caput drained the fresh wine in one long swallow. It was the first break in gentility she had seen from him.

"I have a question for you," he said, lifting his eyes from the tabletop with the last word. "There is a chance your answer will be a lie, and I might not know you well enough to detect it. So, in a sign of good faith, I will share something with you first."

Aubrey could not be sure, but she thought she sensed genuine inquietude. The slight hesitation in his words, the swallow of courage he had taken before beginning. *Or it could all be an act. Don't forget, he is the Viper for a reason.*

Drawing a deep breath, Hu said, "Your brother, Tilden, is alive. On the day of the attack against your Family, he escaped in the company of an Ignota cell. The Council is in the process of tracking him down. Near as we can tell, he is being held somewhere in Western Europe. Possibly even in England."

Captured by the Ignota!

With effort, Aubrey managed to keep her expression still. Her mind, however, raced. Did Hu know that she knew Tilden had survived? Was this supposed confession just a way to undermine what little power she thought she held? Or was it genuine? If so, what did he mean to ask her that could warrant divulging such a secret?

Stalling, she said, "How long have you known this?"

"Since the day it happened."

"How do you know it was the Ignota who took him? Perhaps it was members of the House guard taking him to safety."

In response, Hu switched to his native tongue to address the palace's IFaMS unit. A holograph projection sprang up from the center of the table. A compilation of security footage showed her brother, and Isla Carene, racing through the halls of the Family's research center at Inverness. The actress displayed an uncanny familiarity with a particle rifle. One short clip showed her assaulting a uniformed guard before using his gun to hold off approaching drones.

"We believe Carene was planted as an Ignota spy," the Caput said as the images switched to the exterior. Two figures, presumably Tilden and Isla, propelled down the side of the facility. The pair then raced towards the dockyard. They boarded a small boat that then slipped from the camera's view.

Isla Carene was Ignota? Truth, I actually encouraged Til to date her! She had intended to limit the amount of wine consumed during the meal, but her hand brought the glass to her lips. The lush flavors sliding over her tongue helped steady her nerves.

"What evidence do you have that my brother is still alive?"

"The Council assumes two things. First, he is more valuable to the resistance alive. Second, if they kill him, they'll want the world to know."

Neither option was comforting.

"If the Council finds him, they will kill him, yes?" she asked.

Hu nodded.

It seemed both she and her brother were forced to rely on enemies for their safety.

"And what is your question?"

Again, the Caput's hesitation was etched in the grim lines of a subtle frown. Unsure what he might ask, Aubrey readied herself—impassive face, still body. She would have to decide how to respond to the inquiry, but her appearance must give nothing away until then.

"What do you know of The Culling?"

"The Culling?" she repeated in a flat voice. Nothing in her memory recalled hearing the term prior to Hu's ominous mention. *Now, do I pretend to know?* Without even a trace of knowledge to build from, a bluff would be too difficult to maintain. "I've never heard of it," she admitted.

Hu narrowed his eyes, judging if she had spoken in truth. "Your Father never mentioned? Walford? Your brother?" he pressed with greater intensity.

"No. Not to my memory. Why? What is it?"

"It is . . .," he paused, looking away into a shadowed corner, then returning to her stare. "It is the culmination of designs put into place two millennia ago. It is the reason the Council and the Alliance exist." Whatever he had started to say had changed during the pause. *Was he about to reveal more? Or less?*

"You make it sound very much like the foolish old prophecies and conspiracy theories."

With a sad smile, the Caput said, "There's truth at the root of most conspiracies."

The painful memory of the last dinner she had shared with the Family came to the fore of her thoughts. Saunders, her younger brother and the resident pessimist of House Garrott, had argued the same point. She had chided him and his nature of perpetual suspicion.

"You don't intend to elaborate, do you?"

Running a finger around the fine edge of his glass, Hu replied, "There is another matter I had hoped we could address."

Aubrey did not know much of her new home, not the language, not the customs, not the names of cities and sights. Beyond their few conversations, and his reputation, she did not even know her husband. That mattered little, though. She knew men. She knew the meaning of the look in Hu's eyes. And she knew she needed more wine.

To his credit, Yin Xian Hu made no attempt to force her. Though, he had no need to. Whatever he might claim, she was a prisoner—and his wife. Until he found a purpose for her, or until she was free, her sole value lay in the production of an heir.

There were no jitters as he escorted her back to his apartments. She had been fifteen years old her first time with a boy. That first encounter had been brief, with more than a little awkward fumbling. While not unpleasant, Aubrey had failed to see why adults placed such emphasis on the act. However, that view had changed over the years, as both she and her various partners grew in experience and skill. Even still, her most pleasurable trysts were but candles to the blaze Hu kindled in his bed.

His lovemaking, the deft placement of hands—sometimes firm, sometimes soft—the caressing smoothness of his lips on her bare skin, and the intensity of his passion sent her to heights of ecstasy she had never imagined possible. Though she had resigned herself to surrendering her body, she never intended, nor expected, to find enjoyment. And yet each time Hu's hunger renewed, she found herself eager for the banquet. Only as the first rays of dawn stole through the windows' silken drapes did sleep consume them.

The dream was already fading, her awareness drifting into those minutes' fragile tranquility between sleep and wakefulness, when she heard the voices. Before she could register the turbulence in their tone, the doors to Hu's bedchamber burst open. Men in the uniform of the House guard flowed into the room with deliberate vigor. Horrific images of the last time PKs had swarmed where they should not pulled a panicked scream from her throat.

Next to her, Hu said, "Z☐n me huí sh•?"

Pausing for the protocol of a salute, the nearest PK, a man with a thick streak of gray in his black hair, replied in a flurry of foreign words. Had Aubrey been able to translate, she would have been too distracted by another guard pulling her from the bed to exchange the Mandarin for English. Naked and clinging to the bed sheet, she had little power to resist the man's forceful hold on her wrist.

"Shen!" the Caput barked. "She is your Caput`e! Take your hands off her!"

Looking bewildered, the guard complied with the angered command.

Hu softened his voice when he turned to her, saying, "There has been an attack in America against the Alliance. Out of precaution, these men will escort us to a secured level. We will step outside while you dress."

With little available to restore her stolen dignity, and unwilling to appear weak, Aubrey fought back the tumult of her nerves. "That's not necessary," she countered and let the sheet fall from her hands. She crossed the room, guards parting to let her pass. Her expression dared them to steal a glimpse of her naked figure. Whether frightened or scandalized, every man in the room developed a sudden interest in the ceiling.

Collecting her dress from the floor, she pulled the garment up past legs and rear to slip her arms through the shoulder straps. Hu came up behind her, a pair of black silk lounge pants cinched at his waist, and finished the task by closing the long zipper at her back. His breath was warm on her neck as he bent close to her ear.

"Impressive."

In that moment, she understood her mother's lesson. Undressed, unadorned, and exposed for all to see, Aubrey had been clothed in the supremacy of her own power.

Turning to meet his eyes, she said, "Thank you." His gaze was less guarded, warmer than the usual chill calculation. *There's worry there, too.*

The company left the apartments at a brisk pace, a clatter of boots echoing off the marble floors of the palace halls. As the daughter of a Caput, her place would have been a step behind her father. Aubrey positioned herself at Hu's right—matching him stride for stride. At his other side, the PK with the shock of gray spoke in clipped phrases.

Hu interrupted him, saying, "In English, Joseth."

The commander of the House guard cleared his throat in obvious disapproval. Liam Walford had often done the same when disagreeing with her Father. Whatever was happening, the PK did not believe the situation should be discussed in front of her.

"As you wish, *Dianxia*," Joseth-liang frowned. "As I was saying, there is still a great deal of confusion. The carrier strike groups were anchored in Lake Erie, off the city of Lorain, Ohio. The captain of the supply ship, the *Reliant*, issued the Code Bravo alert fifteen minutes ago. The explosion followed a few minutes later. Initial satellite imagery indicate one, possibly two, large scale detonations. We are still waiting confirmation."

"Nuclear?" Hu asked.

"Unlikely," she answered. The Caput gave her a questioning look as Liang's eyes flared with outrage at the interjection. Both men's gait stuttered. Brazenly, and rather smugly, Aubrey explained, "The fleet's conversion to particle weapons was completed three years ago. Only four nuclear reactors still exist in the world, and those are in the process of being decommissioned. Particle warheads, if destabilized and detonated, would look very much like a nuclear blast to a satellite."

"Once we have confirmation, we can rule out the nuclear scenario," Liang dismissed.

Chuckling, she scoffed, "The *Reliant* is attached to the A.S. *Spearpoint* Strike Group. Its length is approximately two hundred and thirty meters long and can reach speeds in excess of thirty knots. The standard crew is two hundred men strong, though it can hold an additional fifty if needed. Six R-14 particle mounts provide its main defense, though it also carries twin short-range missile mounts capable of reaching targets within a kilometer radius. My Family designed those ships, sir, as well as the weapons they carry."

Though she kept her eyes forward, Aubrey could feel Hu's slim smile.

"Ah, my apologies . . . *Dianxia*," Liang offered through grating teeth.

Attempting to alleviate the commander's chagrin, Hu asked, "The Council is being convened?"

"Yes, *Dianxia*."

House Hu's security bunker was quite dissimilar to her Father's subterranean facility. Retrofitted into the architecture of the palace's west wing, meter-thick walls, floor and ceiling formed a substantial metal rectangle. Instead of separate rooms and offices, the space was one wide seamless shelter. With a sweep of her eyes, she saw the essential stations—medical, culinary, command and control—a House under siege would need to function and survive for an extended period. An oval table sat at the center of the facility and was the focus of activity. Several men rose from their seats as the Caput approached.

"Are the Caputs online?" Hu asked, taking his place at the head of the table. He gestured for Aubrey to sit in the empty seat to his right.

"Yes, *Dianxia*," a man in a fine-cut suit replied and handed Hu a Mandarin-collared black jacket. Though he addressed Hu, the fellow's eyes were locked on Aubrey.

Finishing the last button, Hu nodded.

Three squares appeared in the air above the table's perimeter. The faces of the men who had ordered the murder of her Family turned her blood cold. No amount of will could keep the hate from her face.

"What is *she* doing here?" Caput Alexavier Cambrie spat in apoplexy.

"Greetings to you, too, Alexavier," Hu replied. His voice resumed the low sinister hiss she had long associated with him. Every syllable carved from malice. "If being my wife was not sufficient justification, *she* is also one of my advisors. Aubrey's knowledge has already proved useful this morning."

From the hologram on the left, Graziano De Luca, the obese Italian Caput, said, "She is not a member of the Council, Xian."

Sliding his eyes to the man, Hu returned, "Nor are the dozens of people currently around each of us." Then to Fawzan, the eldest on the Council and thus the de facto leader of the body's sessions, he said, "Bashir, shall we begin, or is the presence of my Caput'e the more pressing concern?"

The brown-skinned man, who Kerwen Garrott had once considered an ally, frowned. "This impropriety will be discussed at another time, Xian."

Hu remained silent.

"In service to Truth," the Arab began the invocation, "with remembrance of our duty to the Global Alliance, I convene this gathering of the Council of Four."

As the other Caputs responded, "May our deeds honor Truth," Aubrey felt renewed pain over her Family's death. *Council of Four . . . these men betrayed honor and Truth when they killed my Father!*

"What is the current status?" Hu asked once protocol was met.

Fawzan said, "The supply ship was destroyed. Two warships, the *Hudson* and the *Longshot*, sustained heavy damage. Neither can likely be salvaged. Most distressing, though, is the *Spearpoint* itself. It was moored alongside the supplier. The initial blast caused catastrophic damage to the portside. Evacuations are underway and she'll be under within the next hour."

"Causalities?"

"Too early to determine," the Arab answered. "Though the final count will be high."

Numbers poured into her mind. The carrier alone listed over five thousand in its crew. She did not need a lesson from Liam for her to understand the enormity of the situation. Such a loss of blood and treasure had not occurred since the Alliance and its Peacekeepers had come to power.

"Truth!" De Luca exclaimed. "What is the cost?"

"At least one hundred trillion," the suntanned Cambrie relied.

Double that and you'd be closer, she thought, but kept herself silent.

"Have we determined the type of explosion?" Hu continued on.

"Particle warheads triggered by a smaller bomb," Cambrie supplied.

Aubrey let a triumphant smirk turn up the corners of her mouth. Seated across from her, Joseth Liang balled his visible hand into a frustrated fist.

"Though one is only a shade better than the other, was this an accident or no?" De Luca asked.

Caput Cambrie, who had jurisdiction over the zone, gestured to a man at his side. "We have extracted this from the mobile comms just before the explosion."

"Sowilo."

A few seconds of silence followed the whispered name.

"My name is Gavin McAvoy. There is a particle bomb activated in the artillery hold."

Further silence.

"It's a bluff. Take them into custody!"

"It's not a bluff, Sowilo."

Silence.

"My life for a Founder! Sic semper tyrannis!"

Several shouts, and what she assumed to be gunfire, rang out before the recording burst into loud static and then cut off.

"There are three separate speakers, two of them PKs. The first and last voice was Petty Officer Sosa. The man ordering the arrest was Lieutenant Fitzwallace. The other, the one calling himself Gavin McAvoy, was picked up through the comms of the surrounding PKs."

"Who is this Sowilo person?" asked the fat man.

"Unknown. The name does not appear on any manifest. It might be a code name, or it may not be a name at all but rather a title among the Ignota."

Aubrey's emotions were torn. While a blow of this magnitude against the Council was welcome, that it came from the hands of the Ignota was troubling. As much as she desired vengeance against her Family's executioners, she was still her Father's daughter. The stability of the Global Alliance must be protected and maintained.

"The third man called himself Gavin McAvoy," Hu prompted. "Any way to confirm it was truly him?"

"No," Cambrie said. "We lost what we had on him when that PK traitor attacked the system."

Few had the stomach to name the man, referring to him most often as "the PK traitor." Aubrey's Father had called him a variety of more colorful names. His true name was used so infrequently, she could only recall part of it. *Match something.*

Speaking through a mouthful of food—*the man would probably eat at his own funeral*—De Luca said, "Wasn't it his brother who blew himself up in the Washington fiasco? Not much of a surprise that he'd be a suicide bomber as well. Seems to be quite the upheaval in America lately. Don't you agree, Cambrie?"

Before he could respond to the accusation, a figure stepped into view and leaned towards the Californian, blocking him from view.

"*Dianxia,*" Liang hushed as he handed Hu a tablet.

As her husband studied the glass screen, she watched as dread pushed past the trained apathy of his face.

"Gentlemen," Hu said.

"I'm getting it here as well," Bashir Fawzan added, his own expression stark and raging.

"Put it on the screen," Cambrie instructed as his associate stepped back.

The projected images of the two Caputs slid aside as a fourth display entered the space between theirs and De Luca's. Aubrey's eyes saucered in shock as they took in the scene. Across a dark span of water, great fires burned bright against the night sky. In the air, a thick cloud of black and gray hung low over the lake. Dozens of HALOs hovered beneath the cloud; the lights from the aircrafts barely strong enough to breach the rising smoke. Once the initial shock of seeing the actual disaster faded, she noticed the three lines of white text at the bottom of the video feed.

> THE SIDS ARE BROKEN. THE SIDS WILL KILL YOU.
> WE ARE EVERYWHERE. WE ARE UNITED.
> WE ARE THE IGNOTA.

"Shut it down!" Fawzan shouted.

An unseen voice in his command center replied, "It will take time to isolate the hack, Your Grace."

"Then shut it all down! Kill all broadcasts!"

Slack-jawed, everyone watched in horror through the slow tick of half minute until the feed blinked to black. Even then, the hush endured. No one wanted to be the first to speak. No one knowing what to say. Aubrey could barely find the necessary thoughts to process the event.

Though by very different means, the rebels had scored a victory far more damaging than the destruction of a few military ships. In fact, the physical attack only bolstered the effects of the more psychological campaign. Half the world had seen the broadcast, and the other half would soon wake to the rumor of it. All the gains the Alliance had made since committing itself to the eradication of the Ignota had been diminished. And in some ways, negated. By one simple broadcast, the terrorists had reasserted themselves onto the global stage, shown their strength to be widespread, and exposed the Alliance as incompetent. *Yes, we lost more than ships and SIDs today.*

Her mind seized on a different point of intrigue. *But, why the SIDs?* The Ignota had had an audience of billions. And in their first attempt to speak to the world, they had chosen to warn against a defect that the Council had already addressed and corrected. *Wasted opportunity, no?* she asked herself. *What do they gain by igniting fear of the SIDs? Civil disobedience?* Images of citizens cutting the chips from their hands in protest flashed through her thoughts. *There'd be chaos. But, Liam had always said the Ignota were more than simple anarchists.*

"What—how did this happen?" De Luca's voice brought her out of her thoughts. "How long was that message visible?"

Joseth Liang, scrolling through his tablet, said, "Four minutes, seventeen seconds."

"Merda!" the Italian exclaimed. "That's a Truth-damned lifetime!"

Though it pained her, Aubrey had to agree. Four minutes was long enough for every word of the message to burn into a viewer's memory.

De Luca continued to rage. His jowls and necks jiggled as he vented. She had never seen the man so incensed. Her father had said the man rarely concerned himself with anything long enough to be upset. De Luca was a man of pleasures, and his attention slid from one to another like water on glass.

Cutting into the tirade, the Council elder said, "Graziano! Enough. There's time enough to discover failures and assign blame. But for now, this Council must decide on a response. We cannot continue the blackout much longer. People will grow fearful without information. We must tell them what to believe before the situation gets worse."

Cambrie suggested, "A hoax? Claim the entire thing was a false Ignota propaganda video."

"Word will spread," Aubrey muttered under her breath. Hu turned his head to her words.

"Word *will* spread," he said louder for the rest of the company to hear. "We can't contain this, gentlemen."

"Then what?" Cambrie retaliated. Already his failure to maintain order in America had been questioned. He did not take kindly to his suggestion also being critiqued. "The SID upgrade has already been delayed too long.

Again the focus is on the SIDs. Doesn't he see how much more is at stake? Under Cambrie's watch, the Seton children had escaped, Dr. Sonje Nysgaard had escaped, Philadelphia's streets had become a battleground, Fort Rotterdam had been infiltrated, and now a sizeable portion of the Navy's power was sinking into Lake Erie. *He's ineffective. If a Caput needed to be removed, it should have been Cambrie. Not Father.* In a few shorts months, these four men had managed to bring unprecedented injury to the strength and security of the Global Alliance. She suspected they would even execute their own downfall if given enough time. *But at what cost to the Alliance?*

Until she was better positioned to directly control events—*if that time ever comes,* she added—she was forced to assist her enemies, work through them to protect the

Alliance. To do so, she had to walk the fine line between asset and threat.

Swallowing down her displeasure, she said, "You'll need to admit both the bombing and the broadcast hack were real. Yes, it will show weakness in the Alliance, but that can also be spun to heighten the threat of the Ignota. That, in turn, gives the Council wider scope to act.

"As for the SIDs, have economists cite the risk to the global economy should the Ignota's fear campaign succeed. Something along the lines of: 'If the upgrade is canceled, consumer prices will rise.' Then, raise energy costs by . . . say five percent to reflect the economic damage from the Ignota's attack on the ships and the SID cargo. People don't need to fear the terrorists. They need to hate them. Linking the Ignota with rising prices accomplishes that."

Aubrey was surprised there had been no effort to silence her. At her left, Caput Hu offered no indication of his thoughts. Expressionless, he turned back to the other Caputs.

"She's right," Fawzan acknowledged. "Money is a powerful motivator. Perhaps the only true motivator. I say we accept the recommendation. And every time the Ignota strike, we manipulate the economy so that the people feel the Ignota are attacking them directly."

"Agreed," Cambrie and De Luca said in unison. She wondered how hard the pair was trying to forget the recommendation had been hers. Hu, fingertips pressed together in pyramid before his face, nodded his consent.

To someone beyond the frame of his display, Bashir Fawzan issued a series of commands orchestrating Aubrey's strategy. When he finished, he addressed the gathering. "And what of the Ignota themselves? What response for them?"

Cambrie replied, "Whatever it is, it must be quick and decisive!"

"We have already committed the Peacekeepers to the task of rooting them out, Alexavier," her husband hissed.

"Much good it has done!" De Luca came near to shouting. "Things are worse than ever!"

The Italian's heated demeanor seemed even more turbulent when compared with Hu's pacific poise. "An outcome, if you'll remember, I warned against," he said.

"Your objections to military action against the Ignota are well remembered, Xian. Perhaps better remembered by me than you," the Middle Eastern Caput rebuffed. "Your concern was over perception, not the failure of military strikes. However, we are long past that argument now. For better or worse, it would seem. Moving forward, I suggest operational control be transferred from the generals to Echelon. A scalpel is needed now, not an axe. The bigger question is what to do in the immediate present."

"Strike them hard," De Luca offered. "Make it a spectacle. Let the Ignota, and the world, see the strength of our arms. To hell with a measured response! I say make them tremble!"

"While I tend to agree with Caput De Luca," Cambrie rejoined. "Our efforts against the Ignota have been perhaps too successful. We are running out of known targets."

"*Affanculo!* It doesn't need to be an Ignota target! We tell the world it was, and be done with it. The terrorists will bear the responsibility for the deaths of civilians. And the citizens will hate them for it. Like the traitor's daughter said!"

Aubrey barely registered the insult. Her mind was still grappling with the suggestion of striking civilians as reprisal for the attack on the carrier groups. *That's madness! Beyond the fact it'd likely lead to resentment of the Alliance, innocent lives would be lost.* She held her tongue, waiting for cooler heads to reject the proposal.

"Where?" Cambrie asked.

"As most of their resistance has been centered in America," Fawzan replied, "I suggest the strike be there as well. And since it was your suggestion, Graziano, you should bear the greater portion of the cost."

He's dissuading them in terms they understand, she thought in relief.

Narrowing his eyes, De Luca repeated the other man's question, "Where?"

"New York City."

"A major source of revenue for my House!" the Italian balked, eyes popping through the inflated flesh of his face. Few cities in the world came close to providing the drug- and prostitution-based profits of the failed metropolis. *Fawzan manipulated that well.*

"It wouldn't be for much longer," Caput Cambrie said with an air of prophecy. His meaning confused Aubrey.

"That is still at least two years off. I'd be earning several hundred billion credits between now and then. If I'm to agree, I must be compensated. I want Edge distribution expanded in three markets of my choosing."

Fawzan shook his head, "Two markets, one each in the Americas."

"Agreed."

The ease with which the men bartered almost made her forget the subject of their negotiations. *They're debating the profit lost in massacring millions!* Pitching herself into the dialogue, she said, "This is madn—"

Hu pressed his hand atop hers as he interjected. "Gentlemen, once again I fear we are acting precipitously. There are certainly other locations to consider, other consequences not yet explored. Waiting a day or two would allow us more time to come to a wiser decision."

"Over those two days, we'd look weak," Cambrie countered. "I say we put it to a vote."

Truth, these are people in his zone! How can he agree to this?

"Very well," Fawzan consented. "All in favor of a New York strike?"

"Yes," Cambrie voiced his vote.

"Yes, for two markets in return," De Luca said next.

This is not happening!

"Caput Hu?" the Arab asked.

Aubrey turned to the man seated next to her—his face an unreadable mask. His palm felt cool against the skin of her hand. With just four on the Council, both he and Fawzan would need to vote in the negative to at least forestall this insanity.

"So be it."

The words stole the breath from her lungs. She pulled her hand away as if a snake had bitten her. *The Viper . . .*

With a voice all business, the Council's eldest member said, "We will give the Peacekeepers in the city two hours to evacuate. The carrier strike groups in Lake Erie are within range to conduct a missile strike. And I should think they are quite eager for retribution. In the meantime, our forces on the lake will seal Lorain and question its residents."

"Let's keep ourselves available should we need to reconvene quickly. I recommend remaining in our respective command centers until we can be certain the immediate threat has passed."

As Fawzan concluded the emergency gathering of the Council of Four, Aubrey searched through the many lessons of Liam Walford, and those of her mother, for some means to prevent cataclysm.

She found none.

CHAPTER EIGHTEEN

Milo Chance

"What do you recommend?" he asked the overweight woman as she filled their glasses with water. Besides Milo and Naesha, only a few patrons occupied the small diner's other tables. The patrons made no effort to conceal their prying stares. *Small towns,* he muttered in his thoughts. They had been in quite a few over the last weeks, and the looks had been the same in each. He wondered how much of it was simply the typical speculative interest in outsiders, and how much recent events had shaped the unease.

The crackdown has everyone on edge. The Peacekeeper presence in both rural towns and urban centers had spiked dramatically. *And everyone is wondering where the Ignota will strike next.* He could not fault the locals for being nervous around strangers. Though, the mood in the diner felt closer to hostility than worry. Even the hostess seemed irritated by their patronage.

"Waffles are good," she said in shrill, clipped tones before turning on her heel. Her voice was child-like.

"She's a real charmer," Naesha murmured once the woman had waddled beyond earshot. "I'm almost afraid to order a burger."

"Just go with the waffles," he cautioned. After a long drive, with one stop for lunch along the way, Milo would have preferred a heartier meal. They had stopped at two other eateries in town—both closed—before settling on *Henney's Twenties.* The local grocery, a small independent storefront, had been locked tight for the night. As had most every other business they had passed in Oberlin. Even the town's bar was dark and shuttered—and it was only a little past nine in the evening. With a surprising lack of fast food franchises, the diner with the curt hostess was their only alternative.

"If we want to eat, this is our only option," he added, and tapped in their orders on the glass tabletop.

After a sip of water, Naesha said, "The guys in the corner have been shooting us the evil eye since we walked in."

Milo did not need to turn around to confirm her observation. "So has the couple at the table by the kitchen," he replied behind his hand.

Feigning a yawn and back stretch, she twisted to the direction. The young man and woman across the diner did not look away. If anything, their glare intensified.

"Are we reading too much into it?" Naesha asked once her not-too-subtle spying was done. "I mean, are we looking for something suspect because we know Owen McAvoy was born here?"

The possibility was not without merit. Tired and over-traveled, there was a good chance they were seeing meaning where none existed.

"Maybe," he answered. "Though, it is kind of strange that everything's closed this early. But that might just be how it's done around here."

"I don't trust a place with no fast food," she attempted to joke, but exhaustion robbed it of any real mirth.

Milo grunted in agreement. "Hopefully there'll be a little more life in this place tomorrow. I can stop in at the local PK station; maybe get some information to point us in a direction."

From the kitchen, the portly hostess emerged with a large tray perched on one hand. She walked to their table and began serving the plates of waffles; many years of practice evident in the way she balanced the tray.

"Is there a motel around here?" he asked.

"There's good ones in Cleveland," the woman replied. "Better ones in Akron."

Smiling past the obvious hint, Milo returned, "Well, maybe we'll check those out after we leave here. But, we'll be staying in Oberlin for a few days."

"Why's that?"

Stumbling over the impertinence of the question, he said, "Um, because . . . we're . . . we're doing some research."

In lieu of speech, the woman just fixed him with a level stare. His mother had used a similar look to ferret out answers when he was younger. Back then, a few seconds of that stern glare was all that had been needed to draw out a confession. Older now, and aware of the technique, he found himself confessing once again. *Truth, but mothers are some of the best detectives!*

"We're looking into someone who was born here around the turn of the century. A man named Owen McAvoy."

Quickly—*too quickly,* he recognized—the woman said, "Aren't any McAvoys living in Oberlin now."

"So you've heard the name," Naesha cut in, no trace of a question in the words.

The woman's withering gaze moved to the reporter. "Heard a lot of names over the years. McAvoys, Smiths, Jacksons. People come and go all the time."

Impervious to the woman's power, Naesha replied with a voice all honey and innocence, "Oh, I'm sure you have! But, we're just interested in the McAvoys for now. Owen in particular." Dropping to a conspiratorial whisper, she added, "He was one of the Cohors Ignota."

Milo could feel the temperature of the room drop several degrees. The storm in the hostess' eyes looked ready to thunder. Yet, Naesha kept the schoolgirl grin fixed.

"There are some things a small town likes to forget, miss. Some things are better left in the past."

"That's what I said to my editor!" she exclaimed with a laugh. *She can try all she wants, but this "down home" charm is never going to work,* he concluded. *Though it is hysterical to watch.*

"'Jack' I said. That's my editor. 'Jack, no one cares about some guy from twenty years ago.' But he insisted. Thinks with everything going on, people want to learn more about the Ignota. So here I am in Oberlin, Ohio eating waffles for dinner. These look amazing by the way! I can't tell you how long it's been since I've had some homemade food."

Shoving a forkful of the breakfast cakes into her mouth, Naesha hummed her satisfaction. "Mmm, honey, you have to try them."

Honey? She had called him many things over the last two months, but "honey" was nowhere on the list. Following her lead, Milo broke a wedge off with his fork. The taste was amazing.

"We're from Philly," she continued her prattle. "Everything there is fast food. And it all tastes the same: bad. This here's pure joy on a plate!"

Any hopes the flattery was having the desired effect on the defensive hostess were dashed as she said, "Palm your bill when you're done."

Naesha's ridiculous smile faded as they watched the woman walk back to the kitchen.

"'This here's pure joy on a plate?'" Milo quoted with wry grin. "Who even says that?"

Driving the toe of her shoe into his shin beneath the tabletop, the reporter replied, "Least I was trying to get on her good side. The two of you were staring at each other like you were in a cage fight."

Godwin's voice came over the mobile comm and preempted Milo's response.

"Chance, something has happened approximately twenty kilometers north of Oberlin."

"Something like what?" he asked the drone who was waiting in the podcar.

"Reports are chaotic, but it seems there has been an explosion aboard one of the ships in the Alliance carrier strike groups anchored off the town of Lorain."

"Carrier strike groups? What the hell is a strike group doing in Lake Erie?"

Hearing half the conversation, Naesha looked bewildered. "What's happening?"

From the kitchen, the hostess' voice called out, "We're closing. Now. Pay your tabs."

"Milo, what's happening?" the reporter asked again, more panicked than before.

Tapping through the table's display, he called up the checkout screen and swiped his hand over the scanner. "I don't know," he replied. The display registered the payment and *Thank you. Come again!* appeared across the screen.

Under the watchful eyes of the diner's patrons, none seeming to follow the hostess' order to leave, Milo and Naesha rose and exited through the glass front door. They had parked the DeLuca Corelex at the end of the block; its size and extravagance distinct among the smaller vehicles on the street. In the short walk to the podcar, he briefed Naesha on the few morsels of information. As he talked, two men standing across the wide avenue drew his attention. Though they tried to appear nonchalant, his instincts burned with warning.

"Hurry," he whispered, slipping a hand to his hip to unsnap the holster hidden under the long jacket.

Breathing a bit easier once the vertical doors of the SUV sealed, Milo removed the particle gun from the holster, placing the weapon on the center table console.

"We are being watched," Godwin announced.

"I noticed. Two men on the corner," he explained to Naesha.

"And another pair inside the red podcar parked down the block."

"Probably not the Welcoming Committee. Update?"

"Two carrier strike groups, the Spearpoint and Nemesis respectively, arrived this morning off the coast of Lorain. An intruder alert was issued from the Reliant, which was shortly followed by the explosion. I have accessed the Peacekeeper mobile comm log history. Two individuals were surrounded. One identified himself as Gavin McAvoy."

"So, the son returns to his father's home. If he ever left at all," Naesha said. "Do we head up to Lorain?"

"I would advise against that course of action," Godwin offered. "The Alliance will likely seal off the town once the confusion ebbs."

Nodding, Milo replied, "He's right. And I don't want to have to explain why a Philly PK and his drone just happen to be seven hundred kilometers from home when the attack happened."

As the words came out, he realized he had just classified the Peacekeepers as the enemy. *Damn Delphine! She's got my head all screwed up!* Pushing aside the unsettling shock, he said, "Besides, Godwin can keep track of events from here. That waitress, hell this whole town just screams guilty. Corelex, bring us to the motel on Meadow."

The pod's system engaged and the vehicle pulled out from the parking space. Passing the diner, Milo noticed none of the other patrons had left, but instead had gathered in a group at the back of the restaurant. He also noticed the pair of headlights following behind. *Amateurs,* he mocked, but then considered another possibility. *Maybe they want us to know they're following. Intimidation.*

Whichever, the pod had maintained a steady tail, never falling more than one length behind. When they reached their destination, Milo thought the pursuers might even follow into the square parking lot alongside the small motel. Instead, the vehicle drifted past, and disappeared from view around the corner.

In the lobby, the desk clerk gave the trio a thorough once over. His jaw dropped upon realizing a member of the party was a drone.

"Henney said you'd be coming by," the anxious man yawned. "Didn't mention one of those, though."

Not surprised to learn the nasty woman was *the* Henney of *Henney's Twenties,* Milo replied, "Don't worry. He's housebroken."

Un-amused, the clerk continued, "Just one room? Or two?"

"One's fine."

Completing the transaction, the clerk registering them into Room 4, the trio walked back out into the night to find the appropriate door along the long row of rooms. On the way, Godwin said, *"By saying 'housebroken,' were you implying I am a pet?"*

"No, it was a joke."

"Not a very funny one. Traditionally, less intelligent entities are claimed as pets by those of a higher intelligence. As my processing abilities far exceed a human's, the likely scenario would be that you are the pet to me."

Rolling his eyes, "It was a joke, Godwin."

"One might think a joke is only a joke if it invokes laughter or amusement. Though, I assume the teller's intent must be taken into consideration. Was it your intention to make us laugh by comparing me to a pet?"

"Want to know what I'm comparing you to right now?"

Pausing, his partner said, *"I think I'd rather not."*

"Good call," he said and swiped his palm to open the intended door.

The room itself was small, consisting of a double bed, desk, and side chair, but it was better than sleeping in the pod. Milo instructed the IFaMS unit to power on the holoset sitting atop the dresser. There was no need to change the channel, as every station was covering the explosion. The camera work was choppy and panned from left to right. The modest holoset, perhaps a half-meter square, flickered with age. An off-screen reporter tried to narrate the scene over the deafening sirens and alarms shrieking from the fleet. A hand cut into view, directing the camera to focus on a certain ship, and then another. The vessels looking like a child's toy set on the tiny hologram platform.

Muting the broadcast, Milo turned to his partner. With his access to the PK system, they would receive timelier, and more accurate, details than a local reporter might provide.

"Nearby ships are reporting that the supplier was destroyed. Though, the smoke is making visual confirmation difficult. The carrier Spearpoint *has sustained severe damage and is currently being evacuated. Two other ships, both Class A destroyers, are unresponsive to hails. Rescue boats have launched to collect survivors and assess the damage to the other ships."*

"This is big," Naesha said with a reporter's envy.

The summation was obvious, but he understood the inability to articulate a more exact analysis. Prior to recent events, the Cohors Ignota had only scored minor, infrequent victories—at least as far as the government had acknowledged. *There's probably been a lot more over the years the Alliance has kept secret.*

Again, there was that sense of disassociation.

"They're getting more public, and hitting harder," he said. "The House Garrott suicide bomber, the Washington attack, now this." *I didn't include Philly. Why not?*

"How will the Alliance respond?" Naesha asked from the edge of the bed.

"There's probably a meeting happening right now to answer that very question. I guess first they'd seal the town, like Godwin said. Question anyone and everyone. Nothing like this has ever happened before, so I don't think we can make any accurate predictions."

"Pardon me, Chance, but I can," Godwin offered. *"While you are correct that nothing like this has happened before in the Global Alliance, there have been similar events in history. The Empire of Japan's attack on Pearl Harbor during World War Two bears striking similarities."*

"And that ended with nuclear bombs," Naesha added.

Disliking the direction the conversation was headed, he countered, "That was over two hundred years ago. It was country versus country. This is different."

"Terrorist attacks have been used as reasons to go to war, Milo."

"How many of those turned out to be false flag operations?"

"What does that matter? It still led to war," the reporter replied.

He could feel the argument slipping away.

"The Alliance is not going to declare war on the Ignota. Sure, they'll increase the crackdown, but as far as an actual declara—" the denial trailed off as three lines of text appeared on the broadcast. Reading the short sentences, Milo realized the government would not need to declare war. The Cohors Ignota already had.

The message, and the broadcast itself, lasted a few minutes before the transmission cut out. When the video did not return some seconds later, he called for the IFaMS to change the channel. Silent black met their eyes at every change.

"The Alliance has suspended all broadcasts," the drone informed.

They're trying to control the information.

Moving to the desk, Milo straddled the chair back. "Godwin, give us a whiteboard."

From the horizontal red bar that served as the machine's eye, a beam of light crossed to the opposite wall.

"Okay, what do we know?"

As humans and drone catalogued the details of their investigation, Godwin gathered the information into a well-organized flow chart. Lines connected McAvoys and Torrance, Torrance and Philadelphia, McAvoys and Oberlin, Liam Walford and Torrance and McAvoys, Washington and Ohio, Setons and Nysgaard, Ignota and Alliance, and on and on until the entire display stretched to twice its original size. *Organized yes,* Milo thought, *but still not complete. And still no closer to finding Torrance.*

At some point during the intelligence dump, the holoset resumed its broadcast. Though instead of continued coverage of the Lake Erie attack, most channels had returned to regular programming, and the news networks were interviewing an assortment of economists and policy leaders. Their concerns for economic stability were so alike they were clearly sharing a script. The message was clear; the SIDs were vital to the economy.

"Are they really focusing on the SIDs?" Naesha said. "Navy ships were attacked and the first thing they address are the SIDs? Not global security?"

Milo turned his attention back to the expansive chart. His eyes moved from name to name, event to event.

Setons . . . connected to the SIDs

Washington attacks . . . connected to the SIDs.

Nysgaard . . . SIDs.

Lake Erie . . . SIDs.

Every player, every incident of the last two months, was connected to the SID chips in some way. Some, like Philip Seton and Sonje Nysgaard had a direct link. Others, like Torrance were linked to the chips through the Seton children.

Naesha's right. Why are they talking about the SIDs an hour after the worst terrorist attack in Alliance history?

"How'd we not see it?" he asked, not realizing he had spoken aloud.

"What?"

Exuberant, Milo hopped up from his seat. There were obvious gaps in the evidence, significant weaknesses in the theory, but he felt the familiar stroke of surety. There were moments in every investigation when the mind leapt to unsupported conclusions. Detectives, successful ones at least, possessed an innate sense, a guide, a compass, which led them to the correct assumption. Sometimes, it meant working backwards, filling in the gaps that proved a suspect's guilt. Other times it required looking at the evidence in a new light.

"Think about it," he said. "Philip Seton was the project manager on the SID upgrade. His family was charged as Ignota. Sonje Nysgaard was one of the developmental researchers of the SID upgrade. She was charged as an Ignota. The office building attacked in Washington was Global Tech's headquarters, the company in charge of the upgrade. Two months ago, the Alliance announces a 'minor defect' in the upgrade and delays the launch. Tonight a ship carrying half a billion SIDs was destroyed. The Ignota, instead of boasting their victory, instead of criticizing the Alliance, says the SIDs will kill us. The government responds by citing the economic value of the SIDs."

"What are you saying, Milo?" Naesha asked. Her expression said she already understood his point. She was just waiting for him to say it.

Truth! I'm actually going to say it!

"I'm saying . . . I'm saying the Ignota know the SIDs are somehow dangerous. And the Alliance doesn't want that secret exposed."

That's not all of it.

That's not what it all means.

Say it.

"I'm saying the Ignota are trying to protect us from the Alliance."

No one spoke.

Naesha's eyes offered warm sympathy for the pain such testimony caused him. Godwin, unable to express emotion yet adept at recognizing it, stood frozen in the center of the motel room. *He could arrest me for speaking treason.* But, Milo knew his partner would not. *Well, I'm pretty sure he wouldn't.*

"Someone needs to say something," he blurted once the silence grew uncomfortable.

"So . . .," Naesha began, adjusting the pillow supporting her back against the headboard. "What does this mean for us? As far as the investigation? Do we back off?"

Shaking his head, he replied, "No. I mean, I might be wrong. I might be totally off base here."

"I don't think you're wrong."

"Thanks," he returned, aware of the word's inadequacy. Turning to Godwin, he asked, "What about you? You're the king of probability and logic, am I completely crazy?"

The drone did not reply.

"Godwin?"

"*My apologies, Chance. I was analyzing new intelligence, and while much of it is classified, it seems the Alliance has initiated a military response to this evening's bombing.*"

"Sealing off Lorain?"

"*No. I believe they have launched missiles.*"

CHAPTER NINETEEN

Sonje Nysgaard

There had been no "hero's welcome" when she and the other members of the cell returned to Oberlin. By then, the hacked broadcast had aired and been removed, along with all other programming. The returning party had been whisked into the conference room of the underground shelter. To say the cell leaders were upset would have been a gross under appreciation.

"You had no authority!" Camorata shrieked. "Not to attack the fleet, and certainly not to speak for the Ignota!"

For the third time in as many minutes, she replied, "We acted based on the situation in the field. There was a chance to inflict severe damage with minimal cost." Kunbo and Match had coached the response during the drive down from Lorain. Both men stood behind her seat.

"Except there was no we'," Thompson Fielder corrected. "Gavin made the decision to bomb the ship. He was a cell leader. Issuing a statement was decided by *you*; acting without the authority of a cell leader."

Sonje cursed the man's use of past tense. *They've all accepted Gavin as dead and have moved on! How can they be so cold?* She answered her own question. *They're soldiers.*

Clearing his throat, Kunbo's deep baritone said, "Dr. Sonje did have the authority to act. Gavin named her as his successor should he fall."

"He what?" she asked, snapping her head to the African warrior.

Next to him, Match Quentin added, "It's true. Dr. Nysgaard is now our cell's leader."

They might have just pronounced her head of the Council of Four and she would have been less confused. Gavin had never informed her of such a decision. *He made jokes about me leading a cell, but never this. Never this!*

"If these two vouch for her, that's all I need," announced Marshall. The battle-hungry cell leader had been the only one to commend the hacked broadcast.

Slower to agree, and looking as staggered as she felt, Fielder turned his eyes to each of the men proclaiming Sonje their new leader. Whatever he saw in the stare, the veteran Ignota bowed his head and mumbled, "So be it."

"Fielder! She's only been—," Camorata began to object.

Stoned-faced, Fielder lifted his voice and said, "It's done! And even if it wasn't, we have bigger issues to address. The bombing will keep the Alliance occupied for now. But, they'll restore order soon. We need to decide our next move. Do we order the evac or not?"

"I've already given word to my people," Camorata said; his voice bore a hint of guilt. "We're leaving directly after this meeting."

"So much for working together," admonished Samitha Borden.

Stifling Camorata's retort with a wave of his hand, Fielder asked, "Has anyone else already decided to leave?"

The three cell leaders with whom she was least familiar announced similar resolutions. The divisions among the leaders Sonje had detected days earlier—those who supported Gavin and those seeming to align with Torrance—were reappearing.

With no intention of leaving, and fearing few others would choose to stay, she said, "We are staying. I mean, my cell, Gavin's cell, we're staying. If I escaped, Gavin and Torrance did, too."

Peter Yan, the Sowilo cell leader who had done little more than burn her with the evil eye, said, "My team will remain as well."

Sonje was well aware of the man's misgivings. *I'm responsible for the death of another McAvoy. No,* her mind corrected. *Gavin is still alive! He has to be!*

They had made several attempts to contact him and Torrance after leaving Lorain. However, the short range of the mobile comms used for the mission had limited the efforts. Standard comms, capable of global communication, had an increased potential of the enemy detecting transmissions. With so great a PK presence at the lake, the team had opted for the short burst comms. If Gavin and Torrance still had their comms, the pair would need to be within a half kilometer to communicate.

Sam Borden and Marshall both announced their intention to remain in Oberlin. All eyes then turned to the final two leaders, Ewan Valencia and Rett Sheridan. The youngest of the group, the pair had displayed an affinity for the mysterious Torrance. If they believed him dead, Sonje was certain their cells would leave with the others.

Hoping for the other to speak first, the men finally declared themselves.

"I'll stay," Ewan said, and Rett repeated. If she had not been so worried over Gavin, she might have breathed a sigh of relief.

"All right," Fielder reined back control of the meeting. "We'll leave in shifts to hide our movements. Camorata, if you're people are ready, get 'em gone. Then Massey, then Burke, and then Kellaring. I'll take up the rear. Head west for now."

As the room emptied, cell leaders rushing out to instruct their respective teams, Sonje hung back.

"You're leaving?" she asked Fielder with disappointment.

Soft-eyed, he smiled and said, "Yes. Someone's got to keep an eye on Camorata. Otherwise he'll take the others so far underground it'll be a century before we hear from his cell again."

"You think they're dead," she said.

"I'd like to say I've seen him come through worse, but there hasn't been anything worse. But if there was a man who *could* come out alive, it'd be Gavin McAvoy. And Torrance, for that matter. That one's a survivor."

"Where will you go?" She saw so much of her father in Thompson Fielder—the gruff voice he softened when speaking to her, the infrequent grin reserved for a select few—that the thought of him leaving put another crack in the faulty dam of her emotions.

"It's better if you don't know," he said. "If the Alliance takes Oberlin and . . . well, it's just safer this way."

She nodded and brushed an escaped tear from her cheek.

"I don't know what's coming, Sonje. But, I've been a soldier long enough to feel when something *is* coming. Something big. Something final. And I don't think we can stop it. We've topped the hill, the brakes are out, and the best we can do is hold on and avoid crashing until the road levels."

Laughing, she replied, "That doesn't sound very inspiring."

"The truth rarely is."

As the entire facility had been on alert from the moment the team had left for Lorain, it did not take long for the five departing cells to exit. Within forty minutes, the shelter went from severely overcrowded to eerily quiet.

"What was he thinking?" Sonje asked the two men in her quarters. The weapons master sat across from her in the high-backed wooden chair. Match Quentin had his back to them, his focus on the various screens projected on the holoset platform. There was still no word from Gavin or Torrance.

"He was thinking you were the best suited for leadership, Dr. Sonje," Kunbo answered. "Did you think to become a *combie*? Or perhaps scout or op tech?"

In her time with the Ignota, she had come to learn the roles within a cell were one of the few things every cell had in common. A leader and his second-in-command, a weapons specialist and his *combies*, a pair of scouts, tech specialists, and a medic were the essential, and limited, functions comprising a cell. Failing to meet the qualifications of any other assignment, she had assumed she served as the cell's medic; replacing Ol'Ben whom they had lost two months ago to Adirene's treachery.

"Well, when he gets back that'll have to change," she replied.

Tentative, but purposeful, the African said, "Dr. Sonje—"

Knowing his intent, she rebuked, "I have to think of him as alive, Kunbo. It's too soon to give up."

"I understand."

Do you? she wondered. *I left him. He saved me, and I left him.*

Ignoring the pain that would cripple her, Sonje asked, "What about the PK and the reporter? Any change?"

Expanding one of the small sections of the display with his fingers, Match replied, "No change. Our eyes on the motel report no movement."

Word of the outsiders had increased the already high anxiety within both town and shelter. Their presence, and their interest in the McAvoys, was a threat too close to ignore. *If Gavin comes back, no, when Gavin comes back, we can't have a drone waiting for him.* She feared the remaining cell leaders would be too timid to act. *Especially if I'm the one suggesting it.*

To that end, she and Kunbo had developed a rather simple strategy. And the first phase of that plan was walking down the hall towards her room. *How is this man a covert agent?*

"Place is so Truth-damned empty I got turned around twice," Marshall's voice boomed off the cement walls as he entered.

"Sorry," she apologized. "I'd have come to you but I wanted to stay close to Philip." It was a lie, of course, but a plausible one. Kunbo had advised against her going to the cell leader, instead suggesting a message be sent asking Marshall to come to her. The weapons master had cited some masculine argument of "asserting superiority."

Truth, but the last thing I feel is superiority! The sooner Gavin's back in command the better!

"Has his status changed?" Marshall asked.

She shook her head. Hints to the contrary might get back to Danica, and she did not want to raise the girl's hopes.

"I see," the leader replied. Blustery and bombastic, Marshall was no fool, and he saw through the ruse. "So, what did you want to discuss?"

Swallowing nerves, Sonje said, "The PK and the reporter are still here. And we know they're looking for Gavin, or at least a McAvoy."

"And?" The man leaned against the desk where Match was busy analyzing intel.

"And I think we need to stop them." She wished her voice had not wavered with uncertainty.

With a laugh likely loud enough to be heard all the way in Lorain, he said, "Woman, I'll give you credit, that's for sure. Balls of pure steel! Can't say I blame you thinking I'd be the easiest to win over, either. But you're talking about taking down a drone."

Prepared with rebuttals, she countered, "We have six cells and a handful of particle weapons. If we take them by surprise, the drone won't be a factor."

"Taking out the drone will have the Alliance on our ass in minutes."

Okay, Match, you're up.

Pushing back from the desk, the former PK said, "Maybe not. I've been cryptanalyzing the drone's signal. It's encrypted beyond anything I've seen before. The key size is double the standard Alliance protocol. It makes the Rijndael[5] cipher look like child's play. If I had access to a dozen supercomputers, it'd still take a

---

5   The Rijndael algorithm, also known as the Advanced Encryption Standard (AES) was adopted by most governments in the early twenty-first century. Though its level of security remained reliable, the Cuttlebone algorithm, which doubled the key size of its immediate predecessor, became the new global standard in the year 2089, and remains so today. –M.S.

lifetime to crack the encryption."

"That's not exactly an argument in your favor," Marshall grumbled.

"True. But, it's not the level of encryption that's interesting. Well, not entirely anyway. The Alliance system can process Cuttlebone, the current standard; anything higher would be gibberish to them. Which means this drone is not communicating with the Alliance."

"Who's it communicating with?"

When Match had explained his findings to her, Sonje had been lost in the man's jargon of bits, rounds, and permutations. His current rendition was easier to follow. Though, Marshall still looked puzzled.

"Don't know," Match replied. "But, it's not the Alliance. Their satellites have unique signatures. Whoever, or whatever, the drone is talking to is receiving the intel through a separate, singular string of satellites. It's nearly impossible to block Alliance communications since the messages are delivered to several satellites at once. This drone is transmitting to only one which then sends it out to another, then another, and so on."

Seeing the cell leader's knit brows, Sonje suggested, "Use the shouting analogy you told me."

The op-tech specialist said, "Think of it this way, Alliance communications are like one person shouting to an ever-changing, ever-moving crowd of a hundred people. I can't cover everyone's ears at once to block the shouter. The drone, though, is only shouting to one person, one receiver."

"Which means we can block the drone's signal," she added.

Marshall asked, "Is that what that means?"

"Theoretically . . . yes," Match answered. "Jamming satellite communications is difficult but not impossible. The tech began over a hundred years ago, though much of it is now ineffective against the advanced Alliance systems.

"The problem we have is mobility and size. And, that a jamming signal can be traced to a specific location. Torrance and I developed a sort of 'signal bomb;' a small, portable device which will jam a signal for a short time without being traced."

"And it works?" Marshall asked. His tone had lost some of its earlier doubt, but still did not sound convinced.

"Well, we haven't actually been able to test it in the field. Yet."

"Ha! Balls of steel, I tell you," the cell leader bellowed. "All right. Who do you want me to talk to?"

Knees buckling in relief, Sonje moved to the second phase of the plan.

Despite Marshall's well-known appetite for offensive measures, having the veteran advocating the strategy was a definite boon. His boisterous manner had bent the much younger Rett and Ewan to the cause. Sam Borden had proved more difficult to persuade, but she too had given over. Peter, the last of the leaders to be approached, had readily agreed. Sonje wondered how different the outcome would have been if not for winning Marshall first. However, once the call to action had been agreed to, the scheme progressed at a rapid pace.

Maybe a little too rapid, she thought as she slipped into position behind Patton Rivera and Lance Holton—the two *combies* in the cell—in the alley across from the motel. Somehow their cell had been "honored" with acting as the operation's tip of the spear. Sonje would have preferred an honor closer to the spear's other end. But, Kunbo had insisted she accept the task. He had thus far abided her request to refrain from pronouncing Gavin dead too soon. That had not stopped the African pushing her further down the path to leadership.

The one-level motel, the name *Sleep-Inn* projected along the rooftop, offered ten rooms. In a town the size of Oberlin, out-of-town visitors were usually familial relations, and boarded with their kin. On this night, one podcar was parked in the diagonal spaces along the sidewalk's edge. Sonje, though she knew little about them, could easily recognize the high-end luxury of the silver pod SUV. She sniffed at the ostentation. Her old pod, a model no longer in production, had been more than adequate for her purposes. She wondered what had become of the vehicle. *Probably confiscated with everything in my apartment.*

"Bravo Team, what's your twenty?" Patton whispered.

"We're in position," Rett Sheridan's hushed voice replied over the short-range mobile comm. "Awaiting the go order."

Patton glanced back to her. She needed a second to remember she was in command of the entire op. *At least in name,* Sonje admitted. Kunbo, Match, and the rest of the cell were the true masterminds of the plan.

Marshall and Sam's cells comprised Charlie Team, and were hidden along the neighboring roofs to cut off escape should the other units fail. Peter Yan had joined his cell with Rett's at the rear of the motel, leaving Sonje and Ewan's Alpha Team to strike at the front.

"Simple and clean," Kunbo had declared back in the shelter. She hoped he was right. A blunder would mean—*No, I can't think like that.*

Touching a finger to her earpiece, she murmured, "Close in."

Seventeen darkly dressed shapes stepped into the street. The *combies* from both cells, numbering five men in all, crept forward in a tight knot. Kunbo maintained a protective position at her right, while Match moved on the left. In his hands was the unproven device upon which their success depended. The remaining Ignota formed a staggered fan behind the company. Their firepower was impressive. Most carried the sleek, high-capacity assault rifles common among the cells. Four of the men in the vanguard were armed with the small collection of particle weapons in the shelter's arsenal. Sonje, whose skill with blades far exceeded her clumsiness with firearms, clutched the handle of a single-edged combat knife. A little over two centimeters longer than the standard military issue, the blade offered no protection against a drone, but its weight was comforting all the same.

Heart in teeth, she breathed with each step as the distance to the target shrank. Match slipped his creation, developed with assistance by the absent Torrance, from beneath the padded vest covering his chest. Having spent a career working with biorobotics, Sonje thought the palm-sized cube, with its exposed wires and squat antenna, rather crude in appearance. Given what was at stake, she wished the device looked more up to the task.

The op-tech specialist signaled once they were within the jammer's required four-meter range. The distance, however, was not what troubled her. Match had only been able to provide them with just under two minutes of signal blockage. *When we move, we need to move fast.*

So close to the enemy, she knew there was no allowance for hesitation or second-guessing. Pressing the mobile comm again, Sonje whispered, "Now."

CHAPTER TWENTY

Gavin McAvoy

You were right. The pain is gone, he thought after opening his mouth to the rush of dry water. The searing pain in his chest, the scream of his dying lungs, had flared to new intensity before fading to a dull ache. His head was lighter, free of the crushing pressure of drowning.

So this is death.

Every man, certainly every man of the Ignota, had wondered, had theorized and conjectured, had spent long hours contemplating, what the cessation of life might be like. The disproven and abandoned religions of old had preached on the warm embrace of a white light. Science had mapped the brain, studied the final firings of synapses before the consuming nothingness of medical death. Gavin had thought himself prepared for the experience. Now that it had come, dying was nothing like he had imagined.

Though his eyes saw only white-speckled darkness, the sounds of screaming filled his ears. Shouts of pain and cries of panic carried over a backdrop of—*What? I know that sound. Fire. Could science have been wrong? Had the priests been right? Is this Hell?*

Suddenly he was aware of his legs crossing like scissors beneath him. Beneath the water. As he took another breath—*I'm breathing!*—his confusion clarified. *I reached the surface!*

Acceptance of death succumbed to a primal fight for survival. With his vision slowly recovering from blindness, Gavin had no way of determining the direction of safety. *If I choose wrong, I could be heading away from shore. Or worse, towards an Alliance ship.*

He needed eyes. Reaching to the mobile comm, he said, "Torrance?" His head slipped below the water when his right hand pressed the earpiece.

"Where are you?" came the urgent reply.

Pushing back over the surface, he answered, "Can't see."

"Call out."

Gavin tried to shout the other man's name, but his throat strained so that the word came out in a hoarse gasp. It was enough.

"Hang on," Torrance replied over the comm. "Start heading towards your four o'clock."

Weary limbs struggled against the transition from treading water to lumbering swim. He fought back the panic of moving blindly in the icy lake, having to rely on Torrance's verbal compass. Initially numbed by the water, the pain in his ankle from the drone's grip screamed with renewed agony.

After a few seconds, he felt unseen hands gripping his arms.

"Tie this to your belt," Torrance instructed as he placed a length of cord into his hands. Held afloat by the other man, Gavin looped the tether to his belt, securing it with a tight knot.

"Can you swim?"

"Yeah," he answered, refusing to admit to his exhaustion.

Halfway to the shore, his eyes recovered enough that he could see solid patches of shadow and light through the enhanced lenses of the wetsuit's mask. However, with each stroke across the water he felt the corded link to Torrance growing more and more taut, until finally his progress across the lake owed more to being tugged along than the propulsion of his limbs. Torrance slipped under his arm. The pair' crossed the final meters of swim solely through the rogue's offered strength.

Once upon the sandy edge of a small jut of land, Gavin collapsed to the ground. He pulled off the hood with the last vestige of his will's grit. Chest rising and falling in desperate heaves, he said silent words of thanks for the full return of his vision. Torrance sat to his right, and he could see the weariness in the man's now uncovered face. It was the first time Gavin had seen a crack in the man's unwavering fortitude.

"Thank you." Despite their bitter taste, he could not ignore the obligation of the words.

Nodding in acknowledgment, Torrance asked, "How're the eyes?"

"Mostly recovered," he replied. Sitting up with his arms wrapped across his knees, he added, "That's going to piss some people off."

Some two kilometers northwest, a glowing dome of red burned on the lake. Even at that distance, it was clear the explosion's damage was catastrophic.

"Just a little," Torrance said with a faint hint of humor.

"I can't believe we survi—" he started. Reaching to the mobile comm, he called out, "Sonje? Sonje, are you there?"

"We're out of range," the man said. "She had a better chance of escaping than we did."

While likely true, worry seized him. "We've got to get to Oberlin!" he exclaimed and tried to stand, but his ankle flared and he only managed a clumsy stumble back to the sand.

"No, you need to sit. If your people know what they're doing, they've already issued the evacuation order. By the time we get there, the place'll be empty."

He knew the man was right, though that did little to temper his concern. *It would have only taken her a minute or two to backtrack off the ship.* He had to believe Sonje had reached the water before the blast.

The sound of fabric slicing turned his attention. Though the heavy smoke expanding out from the ships blocked the moon's light, it trapped enough of the illumination from the town's lights to show the long gash running down Torrance's calf.

"You're wounded," he said out of dumb shock. *Truth! How did he manage to carry us both to shore with that leg?*

Wrapping the injury with the black strip cut from his sleeve, Torrance grunted, "Got caught on a piece of metal. We need transportation."

Still in disbelief, he replied, "There's Ignota in Lorain. Not as many as Oberlin, but we'll be able to get a podcar."

Forgetting his own feebleness, Gavin pulled himself up, more cautious than his first failed attempt, and extended a hand to Torrance. The man eyed it before clasping his forearm. The cell leader helped him to his feet with considerable effort. His offer of further assistance was rebuffed.

"I can walk," the man said. In truth, Gavin doubted if he would have even been able to support the man's weight.

Slow and unsteady, the two climbed up a low rise to a tidy backyard behind a shorefront home. A child's plastic playhouse sat across from a worn-down swing set and seesaw, and a weathered privacy fence bordered either side of the yard. The home itself was dark, its owners either away or asleep. Gavin assumed the former. *No way anyone slept through that explosion.*

Torrance unlatched the gate connecting fence to siding and swung the door open on its rusty hinges. The metallic squeal sent a dog into a barking frenzy within the home. Moving down the short driveway, empty save for a pair of bicycles, they reached the street.

Neighbors stood in sporadic circles, peering through the trees at the spectacle on the lake. Those with two-story houses hung out the windows of the upper floor pointing and gawking at the sight. Checking the nearest street sign, Gavin cursed.

"Shit. We're a kilometer from the nearest asset." Dressed as they were, and quite noticeably injured, they would have to pass too many prying eyes. And there was no telling how many might not be Ignota sympathizers.

Ducking back into the drive, Torrance pulled him along. Though they had been relieved of most of their weapons on the ship, the man had managed to keep a few knives hidden. Presenting him with the handle of one such blade, Torrance said, "Shorts and a t-shirt."

Gavin took the knife and began to shear off the legs of his wetsuit. The cold winter air chilled his damp skin and his teeth fought the urge to chatter. A minute passed before he completed the work. Any casual observer would assume he had jumped from bed at the sound of the explosion wearing fitted underwear and t-shirt. Torrance had given himself a similar pair of skivvies, and had sliced open the entire front of his now sleeveless wetsuit. Only the hand-wide bandage encircling the calf looked out of place.

Shivering, though less conspicuous than before, they stepped back into the street. Gavin could see the other man straining against a limp. The first crowd paid little attention to them as they passed, sparing a brief look before returning their gazes to the lake. A man in a heavy bathrobe standing with another group in front of a house shouted out to them.

"You're going to freeze your asses off!" he warned.

In the accented tone of the northern Midwest, Torrance joked, "Tell me about it! Thought we'd get a better view down here. We're heading back home now to watch it on the holoset."

Close enough to no longer need to shout, the man said, "Ain't on anymore. The feed went dead about forty minutes ago. Just a bunch of talking heads on there now."

They're trying to control the story, he said in thought. His father, Owen, had worked in the news business before the Alliance killed him. Only after he had learned of the Ignota, and his father's role in the movement, did Gavin understand the man's muttered complaints about the government's media control. *If I'd only known him, the real him, maybe things would have been different.* For whatever reason, Owen McAvoy had never told his sons about his secret life, or the long legacy of their family.

Overhead, the air stirred into a strong, unnatural wind. The bare branches of treetops bent and swayed against the sudden whirlwind. Seconds later, dozens of low-flying HALOs broke into view, and above them the powerful engines of X.T.E.M. warbirds screamed unseen through the night.

"Fallon," a woman's voice called from the house. "The mayor just announced an immediate curfew. They're closing the roads out of the city. Get back inside now!"

The robed man spat. "Damn Ignota! It'll be martial law here now."

The members of the group grumbled in agreement—some cursing the rebels, others whispering contempt for the PKs—as they broke away and headed to their own homes. In the distance, patrol pod sirens spread across the town. An automated voice blared into the streets from the emergency notification system.

"A state of emergency has been declared for the town of Lorain. Citizens are instructed to clear the streets immediately. Anyone violating the curfew will be detained. Peacekeepers will be conducting door-to-door sweeps to ensure compliance and security. Further instructions will follow."

The message repeated again and again in an endless loop.

"Is there a safehouse here?" Torrance asked as the street became deserted.

Shaking his head, Gavin replied, "There's a network of people who can offer shelter, but there isn't a facility like Oberlin here."

"How big is the city?"

"Sixty, maybe seventy square kilometers."

Bending to adjust the bandage on his leg, the man said, "It won't take long for two carrier groups to drop the net. We need weapons and we need to go underground."

"Vinsy's a Fifth on the local PK force. He'll have a cache of arms."

"Do you trust him?"

More than I trust you. Gavin bit back the comment, and instead responded, "Yes."

They walked a short distance before the blue lights of a patrol pod turned onto the roadway. The curfew announcement had been quickly heeded, and the streets were empty save for the two men. Slowing as it neared, the pod pulled to a stop alongside them. Gavin dared to hope for a familiar face, but he did not recognize the pair of PKs stepping from the vehicle.

"No one is allowed on the streets," the nearest officer confronted. The PKs each angled a flashlight at their faces, forcing the two Ignota to squint to lessen the glare.

"We're down the next block, Officer," Torrance replied.

"Doesn't matter. Orders are to bring in anyone violating the curfew."

Even with the light in his eyes, Gavin could see the second PK resting a hand on his sidearm.

"Lieutenant Parker said we'd have enough time to get back," he said, dropping Vinsy's name in an attempt to prove a common bond.

Unmoved, the PK said, "Well, he told you wrong. Now get on your knees and raise your hands."

"Sir, we don't want any trouble," Torrance offered with the fake accent. "You can even follow us home if you want."

"You're going to find trouble if you don't get on your knees!"

Lowering into a kneel as he lifted his arms, Torrance said, "I really wish we could have worked this out, Officer. You're going to regret this."

"And you just added threatening an officer to your charges," the man shot back. The beam of light shifted and Gavin knew he had drawn his weapon. "Cuff 'em."

On his knees as well, Gavin readied himself, sizing the distance between himself and the lead PK, estimating the height of the man behind the light. The second Peacekeeper placed his flashlight on the ground and moved in behind the Ignota. Gripping Torrance's wrist, the PK twisted the man's arm back.

At the first flash of movement, the cell leader ignored his injury and catapulted to the right—away from Torrance and the soldier now spinning in the air—and slipped the knife from his back, and propelled the blade at the lead PK. His aim was off; the knife striking shoulder not neck as intended. The PK fired a particle shot as the muscles of his arm contracted in pain from the cut. The bolt flew wild, striking a house several meters up the block. A second shot lit the air with a crisp sizzle, passing through the soldier's head.

Perched on one knee, the body of the second PK sprawled on the ground next to him, Torrance lowered the particle handgun. "We need to move. Now," the man said.

With patrols already heavy in the streets, Peacekeepers would respond rapidly to the deaths of two of their own. Gavin took a long stride to the corpse of the lead PK; searching the body's lower legs to find what he had hoped would be there. Pulling the .22 caliber semi-automatic pistol from the ankle holster, he smiled. Despite the power of particle weapons, most PKs still carried a cold steel back-up from their fathers' generation. A glance confirmed Torrance had made a similar search, though he also held the particle gun.

"Tracers," Gavin warned as they set off in a poorly managed jog.

"I know."

Stopping, the man turned back, leveling the advanced weapon at the patrol pod. One . . . two . . . three flashes of amber flew towards the PK vehicle. The final shot breached the pod's energy chamber. With a thunderous roar, the cruiser exploded into a fiery ball. Torrance swept his arm to a second pod, and then a third, until the street was awash in black smoke and red flame. Tossing aside the traceable weapon, he said, "Little bit of cover."

"You played with matches a lot as a kid, huh?" Gavin replied. Wherever the man stepped, a trail of destruction seemed to follow in his wake.

Sirens neared. Blue flashing lights reflected off the street's homes forcing the pair to cut through a yard. In that section of the city, residences were small and closely grouped. Only a meter-wide alley ran between each structure. Though maneuverability was limited, the layout provided adequate cover from both ground and air. Still, they had to tuck themselves against the sides when HALOs hovered above, flooding the area with light before moving on.

Gavin noticed his accomplice's limp growing more pronounced with every stride. Bound to follow the weaving maze of backyards and alleys, they were making slow progress towards their destination. The Ignota leader leapt a short fence between two yards, stumbling to a halt when he saw the motion-activated light attached to the home. He threw out an arm to catch Torrance, but the precaution was too late and the man stepped within the sensor's range, triggering the light.

One bullet brought back the darkness, but the damage was already done. A HALO crested the adjacent rooftop with a gust of air; catching the two men in its lights. Torrance rammed a shoulder into his chest, driving Gavin to the ground. The helicraft fired its front rifles. Massive bolts ripped through the home's rear exterior, covering the men in dust and debris. Bits of burning embers singed his bare legs, but the pain was distant. Under the temporary cover of the explosion, they dragged themselves forward, hands grasping blindly to help the other to his feet.

Lunging and ducking into the next alley, Torrance hefted a nearby rubbish bin and smashed in the window of the neighboring home. Gavin pulled himself up over the sill with relative ease, though the other man struggled for footing with his injured leg. From within, the cell leader gripped the renegade's belt and hauled him in.

At the center of the home's living, a woman stood clutching two toddlers who held tight to her leg. Eyes wide with terror, the woman shifted her gaze a few degrees to the left. Realizing the reason, he turned to Torrance just as another woman pressed into the man's blind spot.

"Behind you!" he shouted in warning.

Torrance spun on his wounded leg. Unbalanced, the man's palm caught the blade of the butcher's knife the woman welded. Grunting from the unexpected pain, he twisted—disarming the woman with a hard smack of his handgun across her wrist. Before the knife hit the carpeted floor, Torrance shoved the woman towards her weeping family.

"Is there a basement?" the man asked.

Both women nodded.

"Go!"

The mothers each took a crying child in her arms and rushed to the kitchen at the back of the house. They had only crossed the threshold into the adjoining room when near-blinding light flooded in through the front and rear windows.

Time slowed and Gavin's skin goosefleshed.

"DOWN!" he cried out.

Both ends of the house exploded inward with round after round of charged particle blasts. Glass shattered. Wood splintered and burned. The floor ripped apart sending clumps of carpet and subfloor into the congested air. Above the sound of destruction, he heard the screams of the women and their children. And then the screaming stopped, though the attack still raged.

Flattened against the floor and hugging the wall, Gavin turned his forearms over in rapid succession, dragging his body deeper into the home's center. The HALOs' weapons still reached there, but the larger portion of the chaos was ahead and behind him. Flames now engulfed both areas, and the fires were spreading with each new amber bolt.

They're going to bring the house down on us. Seemingly in response to his thought, the HALOs' bombardment rose higher, lights and blasts lifting to the ceiling until disappearing. He could hear the second floor erupting above.

"Any suggestions?" Torrance inquired over the mobile comm. There was definite frustration in his voice. Movement in the periphery caught his eye, and Gavin found the man in a parallel position on the other side of the room.

Shifting to access the earpiece, he asked, "The family?"

He saw Torrance shake his head.

Damn.

"This is going to collapse sooner rather than later," he said. The house groaned in agreement.

Thick tentacles of smoke closed in, obscuring Gavin's sight of the man. Throat burning, he could feel the temperature rising to unbearable levels. The nearest exit was through the windows into the alley alongside the home. *Right into the sights of the PKs.*

"We'll have to risk a run," the cell leader replied.

A voice, not belonging to Torrance, said, "Truth! You're still alive. Can you get out the back?"

"Vinsy?" Gavin asked through the comm.

"Yes. Can you get out the back?"

"I . . .," he turned his head but his watering eyes only saw fire and smoke.

"We can," Torrance cut in. "How long?"

The Fifth replied, "Ten seconds."

Pushing up from the floor, the fiery heat even more oppressive in the higher space, he pressed forward. Involuntary tears blurred his vision, protecting his eyes from the air. His mind spared a single thought of regret for discarding the wetsuit's hood. Moving quickly, with conscious effort to avoid the hazy red auras in the smoke, Gavin flinched as angry tongues of fire touched the exposed skin of arms and legs. He struggled to keep balanced as his feet fought the shredded remains of furniture and house.

Past the perimeter of what was once a kitchen, the smoke vanished; driven inside the home by the powerful rotors of the HALO destroying the second floor. Torrance had already reached the cleared space. The lone wolf had not abandoned his hood at the lakeshore. The notice had barely registered when a patrol pod, passenger door raised, crashed through the low gating of the yard. The open door clipped the underbelly of the helicraft.

"Get in!" the uniformed Peacekeeper shouted from the navigator's seat.

With a bounding dive, the two men collided into each other as both fell into the vehicle. Gavin's legs dangled as the pod lurched forward. A shower of sparks from the pod door grinding against the HALO rained down. He battled Torrance's weight to tuck his limbs inside just as the cruiser broke through the next gate. The hydraulic door closed with a hiss.

"Hang on," Vinsy warned. The pod tore through a half-dozen yards before thumping down onto the leveled surface of a street. Expert hands gripped the controls, cutting to the left. Gavin noticed a thin slick of blood dripping down from one of the handles. *He cut his chip out!*

Torrance climbed over the center console to reach the twin rear seats. "Two HALOs closing fast."

"I see 'em. I see all of them," the PK replied. Gavin shifted his stare to the glowing display of the navigation screens. Blue dots, more than he could count, flicked across the display.

"Truth!" he cursed.

"Everyone's out tonight," Vinsy said, and then added to Torrance, "Grab the gear bags under the seats. I raided the search and rescue equipment locker. There's no way out of the city—least not by land."

Gavin's stomach tensed as comprehension spread. Taking the offered bag from Torrance, the cell leader tugged the zipper around the front panel. Inside, as he feared, were the various components of a personal diving apparatus. Lifting the facemask out, he said, "Back in the water."

Edging the patrol pod over the 130k/h mark, the navigator explained, "The tanks hold about an hour of oxygen. Hand props will last just as long under max speed. Head west about fifteen kilometers, then cut to the shore. There'll be some friendlies waiting at the mouth of the channel."

The night flared in burnt orange as the HALOs fired down, several shots striking the street, while one slammed into the pod's trunk. Gavin slipped the diving mask over his face and adjusted the straps as best he could manage through the careening vehicle.

"Pier's ahead," their rescuer warned as the tires echoed off the wooden boards of the pier. Henney's nephew released the controls—there was now only one direction available—and grabbed his own mask.

With no time to secure the propulsion tubes to his forearms, Gavin curled his fingers around each device's throttle bar. He had never used the diving equipment before and feared his first lesson.

The pier behind exploded in timber splinters; the blast's concussive force upended the pod. Throwing his arms wide, he braced his body against the cruiser's frame as it tumbled trunk over hood down the remaining stretch of the dock. Hot bags of air burst around him, somewhat cushioning the tumult while scalding his skin. There was a brief second of silence, the battle sounds of metal and wood muted, before the pod hit the water with a jolting splash.

The patrol pod's security features engaged, blasting off the doors on either side with a release of highly compressed air, and allowing its passengers to escape. Gavin pushed himself clear of the sinking auto. From the light of the HALO over the water's surface, he made out two shadows pulling free from the wreck. Sparing a second to readjust his mask, the cell leader extended his arms and depressed the throttle control on each propulsion tube. Unable to risk activating the headlight on the mask, he found himself swimming through night-dark waters. Again.

CHAPTER TWENTY-ONE

Milo Chance

"Missiles?" he repeated the drone's last word as if he had never heard it before; the meaning hiding in some vacant recess of his mind. The revelation of the Alliance's true nature was still too fresh, too unexplored and too incomplete, for him to accept Godwin's pronouncement without difficulty.

Skeptical by nature and profession, and free from a lifetime of PK service, Naesha O'Geron processed the information more readily. "Where are the missiles headed?" she asked the drone.

"*The projectiles were fired from the fleet in Lorain. I am unable to determine the exact destination,*" Godwin replied. "*That information is currently classified. I am accessing old weather satellites and . . . yes . . . the missiles are traveling east at ninety-four degrees. Speed is . . . approximately seven hundred forty-five kilometers per hour and increasing.*"

"What's in that direction?" the reporter followed-up.

"*Assuming it is maintained, the current trajectory passes over towns and small cities until reaching the island of Manhattan, then the Atlantic Ocean.*"

"They're bombing New York?" Milo won back the ability to speak. "Can you see how many missiles through the weather sats?"

"*I am trying to acc—my signal has been cut off,*" Godwin said with marked surprise. Turning his head to the motel room door, the drone added, "*There are people outsi—*"

In a cacophony of violent action, the door ripped through the jam, sending splinters of fractured wood into the room, just as the window at the rear exploded. From all directions, dark clothed figures rushed in shouting and barking commands. At the door, two men, both mountains of muscle and bone, fired particle weapons at Godwin.

The drone reacted with inhuman speed and impossible strength, grabbing the forearm of the nearest invader. The man shrieked as Godwin forced the limb down, driving sharp edges of bone through flesh. His other metal hand sought the man's neck. The sound of the snapping spine was drowned by the clamor, and followed by the drone swinging the body at the second soldier.

Milo was aware of Naesha's screams as he reached for his sidearm. A hard blow crashed over his back. He had seen the movement behind him early enough to tuck and roll forward with the force of the attack. Weapon in hand, he spun, firing back into the chaos at the rear of the room.

The air crackled with the heat of charged particles. A masked figure pulled Naesha back from the fray. She kicked and screamed at the restraint despite the gun held to her head. Between two blinks, Gavin knew the fight was lost. Even with Godwin's superior skills, there were too many attackers.

"Godwin, stand down!" he shouted to his partner. Immune to the uncontrollable battle lust of human rage, the drone ceased his defense. Several plumes of smoke rose from his metal exterior where particle bolts had struck.

Bent on one knee, Milo raised his arms in surrender, letting the firearm drop to the ground. A tall, lean woman with a tight bun of blonde hair pushed deeper into the room, averting her eyes as she stepped over a crumpled corpse. She rushed to another collapsed body near the foot of the bed. Deft hands searched for a pulse.

"He's alive," she announced. "Get him down to the shelter."

A man, blacker than any he had seen before and looking every bit as dangerous as the stories claimed Deaders to be, kept an uneasy eye on the drone. "What of this thing?" the behemoth asked in a heavy accent.

The woman rose and turned so that Milo could see her face. *Truth, it's her!*

"He's not a threat to you, Dr. Nysgaard," the Peacekeeper pled for his partner. "We're not here to," he began to explain, then confessed, "We know about the SIDs."

Even with her eyes narrowed in suspicion, and the thin lines of worry tugging across her forehead, the woman was beautiful. Milo had seen the digitals released when the doctor had first become a hunted fugitive. Those images had represented her beauty with the same accuracy as a puddle does an ocean.

Another man, holding a device Milo did not recognize, said, "Signal back on in seventeen seconds . . . sixteen . . . fift—"

"The Alliance has launched an attack on New York," he offered. "Godwin, the drone, he can provide you intel."

". . . thirteen . . . twelve..."

"Dr. Sonje," the Deader warned, "we need to destroy it."

Frantic, Milo said, "The Alliance didn't send us. A man called the Soothsayer did."

". . . ten . . . nine . . ."

Naesha, still held immobile by one of the Ignota, added, "He wanted us to find Torrance. We know he's a McAvoy."

The woman's captivating eyes widened in shock. Even the African, who had yet to take his gaze from the drone, turned his head to the reporter.

Seizing on their evident surprise, Milo pressed, "We can help you. All three of us."

". . . six . . . five . . ."

The doctor parted her full lips. Her face gave no sign of the judgment she was about to render. "We'll . . . we'll bring them to the shelter. Match, figure out a way to block the signal again."

Match. Why do I know that name?

The towering ebony soldier looked about to speak, but instead dipped his head. As rough hands pulled Milo to his feet, he wondered how Dr. Nysgaard had become the leader of these Ignota. *Was I right at the start? Was she Ignota all along?*

Progressing down the street, a circle of rebels around each hooded captive, Milo realized the evolution that had begun with that first message from the Soothsayer was now complete. There was no deception in his offer to help Nysgaard and her followers. He had forsaken his oath to the Peacekeepers and the Global Alliance. Worse yet, he suspected the Soothsayer had orchestrated it from the start.

"You've been following the orders of a man you've never seen?" asked one of the men around the table. Five other seats were occupied, and all six Ignota—four men and two women—stared at him with a range of doubt and disgust, belief and pity.

"Yes," Milo replied in as calm a manner as possible. He itched his right palm. Upon reaching the underground facility—down was the only definite direction he had pinpointed during the blindfolded trek to the shelter—he and Naesha had had their SIDs deactivated. The dead chip was still inside him, but he felt as if it had been cut out all the same.

The room, much like the faces staring at him, was austere and expressionless. Dominated by the oblong table at its center, the space had blank walls, free of any adornment. A trio of wall sconces, caged metal around the glowing glass cover, lined the two longest sides and cast a yellow tint to everyone's skin.

"Like I said, I was investigating a drug lord in Philly, when the Soothsayer contacted me. No face, disguised voice. He suggested meeting with Naesha. Which I did. After the drug case was closed, he contacted me again—this time to find Torrance."

"Why did he want you to find Torrance?" the same man asked. Of Asian descent and in his middle years, the man was the second of those gathered to question him.

"I don't know. He wanted me to bring Torrance to him. That's all he said. Look," Milo diverted, "I want to know where Naesha and Godwin are."

After disconnecting the SIDs, the Ignota had separated the three prisoners. Milo had to order the drone to comply.

Dr. Nysgaard cleared her throat. "Until we can verify your stories, we have to keep you apart. I promise you they are safe."

The oldest of the group, a man named Marshall with a voice like thunder, grunted. "You should've blown it up. It killed Patton. And nearly killed Lance. Your own men! And you let it live!"

Whatever authority the doctor possessed in the motel room had been temporary. Three of the men present were handling Nysgaard as though she was the lesser among equals. While not well versed in the command structure of the Cohors

Ignota, Milo assumed the six interrogators were cell leaders. The little he did know also told him that that many cells gathered in one location was an anomaly.

The doctor's eyes watered at the condemnation. Only the Asian fellow came to her defense. "It was her op. And this is not the place for debate."

Are they playing good cop bad cop, or are there real divisions?

The rebuke worked to silence the gray-haired soldier, though his expression still glowered.

"I think we need to get back to these missiles," the second woman asked. In other company, she might have been pretty; shoulder-length brown hair, pleasant smile and tanned skin. Seated next to Sonje Nysgaard, the woman could only be considered plain. "We have no reports of them."

"My partner had just detected the launch when you people busted in," the PK remarked. "Before you killed his signal he said they were on a path from Lorain to New York. But that was what? Thirty minutes ago? They could've changed course."

A fresh-faced youth, who looked better suited to studying for an exam not interrogating a Peacekeeper, turned to the Asian cell leader. "Have we been able to reach Lorain yet?"

"No. Last report was about the curfew. Nothing since."

Milo saw the doctor's lips tighten at the mention of the northern city. *There's a whole lot more going on here,* he assessed. *Way more than a group of terrorists, no, rebels hiding out.*

"Godwin can access the system," he offered.

The old timer slammed his open hand on the table. "Bullshit! We bring that thing in here and you'll order it to kill us!"

"Sir, with all due respect," Milo began. He had experienced more than a few grizzled and jaded veterans while serving with the Peacekeepers. Subtle flattery, moderated bravado, and a healthy dose of formality, tended to pacify the aged bears. "Godwin stood down on *my* order. I fully understand why you're reluctant to trust us. But, again with all due respect, there's shit going down right now bigger than you or me. Godwin's a resource. I suggest you use him."

The woman who had returned the discussion to the missile threat dipped her head low as a smirk broke across her face. By her reaction, he thought he might have struck just the right chord with the old man. *Or she's laughing because I'm about to get my ass beat.*

"I'm inclined to agree," the Eastern Ignota said. "And, I think this technically is still the Doctor's op. So the choice should be hers."

Milo could feel the instant shock rolling off Nysgaard. *She didn't expect support from that one.* The lines of hierarchical command among the PKs were clear and distinct. With the Ignota, he watched them shift and mutate faster than he could process. *It's bordering on dysfunctional.*

When no one objected, Dr. Nysgaard touched her ear and said, "Match, bring the drone to the conference room."

As they waited, the Asian asked, "What proof do you have that Torrance is related to the McAvoys?"

Though it had been the factor that had swayed the Ignota away from destroying Godwin, he wished Naesha had not divulged that particular detail. As much as

PKs worked in unison, there was always a prevailing atmosphere of territoriality. It was his case, and he was not all that eager to hand it over. Not to strangers, about whom he knew little. Unfortunately, Naesha had forced his hand. He would, however, keep the suspected Walford link to himself for the time being.

With evident reluctance, he said, "We found a blood sample in his home, well, a cave really. Godwin tested it. The results show Torrance's mother was a close relative of Owen McAvoy, probably his sister."

"'From the darkness, hidden from the world, the Founder's Blood will come. Trumpets of Fire announce arrival of the Dagaz,'" the questioner murmured in a tone of reverence.

Marshall snorted. "Enough of that, Yan! We don't need your hocus-pocus crap right now!"

The man showed no sign of offense at the censure. If anything, Milo thought he looked relieved. *Truth! Who the hell are these people?*

Godwin's entrance preempted further discussion; the one named Match following him.

"*Are you uninjured, Chance?*" the drone asked.

"I'm fine," he assured his partner. "Godwin, are you able to track the missiles?"

The drone projected the satellite feed on one of the blank walls. Due to the age of the orbitals, the black-and-white video was grainy and pixelated, and it took Milo a second to understand what he was seeing. Manhattan extended a full meter at the center of the display; its many streetlights forming a white-lined grid, the buildings glowing in the squares. To the west, a flickering cloud of static specks, as long as the island itself, approached the metropolis. He realized the cloud was the missiles themselves.

"*I have been monitoring them since the block on my signal was removed. Their original trajectory has remained the same. The projectiles are approximately twenty kilometers west of Manhattan and are dropping altitude. If the island is the target, which it seems to be, they will strike in less than sixty seconds.*"

"Oh my Truth!" Dr. Nysgaard gasped. "We need to do something!"

"There's nothing we can do," the gruff veteran replied.

"Godwin, can you hack them? Intercept them? Put them off course?"

"*No, Chance. The security protocols are beyond my ability to breach.*"

Refusing to accept the horror unfolding before his eyes, Milo stammered, "Can you, I don't know, there has to be some way to—"

The edge of the cloud crossed over the western perimeter of the island. First one, then two, then dozens of tiny dots flared white and expanded as the first wave of missiles fell on the city.

There was order in the chaos. Destruction swept west to east, border to border. The pinpricks of light became too numerous for distinction. Whole sections of the city coalesced into large blinding circles; then those grew larger still until there was but one encompassing light. What had once been the greatest city in the world, in the history of the world, was gone.

Behind him, Milo heard the open weeping of men and women. Only when he ran his tongue over dry lips, and tasted the moist salt of tears, was he aware that he too was crying. Even then, it felt like someone else's reality. Time slowed—or perhaps it had stopped all together, he could not tell—as he continued to stare at the display. Deep gray smoke, a *true* cloud now, spread wide across the projection, blocking even the white death of the missiles.

"Turn it off," a hoarse voiced ordered. A resilient piece of conscious, one that had not been shocked numb, reminded Milo that his partner would heed only his commands.

"Godwin, turn it off," he said, repeating Yan's request. The wall returned to its yellow hue, and he turned his head back to the others. Eyes passed from one stare to another; no one knowing what to say, no one willing to break the silence, but everyone hoping someone would.

It was Dr. Nysgaard who finally did.

"We need to tell the others," she said, words detached from emotion, clinical and precise.

"They've killed millions," Marshall barked with half his earlier gusto. "Those were civilians dammit! Whatever the city's become, those were still civilians. There are rules in war. Rules of engagement! That wasn't a battle; it was a Truth-damn slaughter. They've crossed the line!"

The doctor snapped, "No. We did. We crossed the line. Me, Gavin, and Torrance. We did this. We hit them hard, and they responded. *We* did this."

The multitude of emotions pulsing in the room was too dizzying to evaluate with any accuracy. Especially not when his own feelings ached with such tremendous agony. Marshall's stare at the doctor seemed to suggest some kind of angry sorrow, or perhaps sorrowed respect; but for himself, or the dead, or his fellow leaders, was impossible to tell. The two youngest leaders kept quiet, and Milo believed they joined him in struggling to wade the tides of the ever-shifting power dynamic. The brown haired woman, after dabbing her eyes dry with the sleeve of her shirt, forced a steadiness to her expression that was betrayed by the bedlam in her eyes. Only Yan, whose last words had sounded apocryphal, seemed detached from the others; staring at his folded hands atop the table as his lips formed a continuous monologue of silent words. Match, the man with the familiar name but unrecognizable face, stood next to the hulking drone, biting the corner of his lip while shifting his weight from foot to foot.

"What's next?" Marshall posited. "We can't go out there and announce millions of people were just killed and not have a plan of action. So, what the hell do we do now?"

It was cold. And unfeeling. But, though he had never served in open conflict, Milo knew the man was right. If these six were leaders of men and women, they were duty-bound to offer hope where none appeared to exist. He also knew his own fate, at least for the time being, was linked to what these six people decided.[6]

"I agree," Yan said, breaking off from his muted mumbling. "Morale was low even before tonight. Now almost half the cells have left, we've taken casualties, and a city's been destroyed."

---

[6] What Sergeant Milo Chance did not know then, nor could he have known then, was how history would regard that night's gathering in the shelter beneath Oberlin, Ohio. However, before another month passed, both sides in the war would know it as the first meeting of the Conclave of the Audax. -M.S.

Half the cells left? Milo questioned. He had been shocked to learn that six cells had come together in hiding. He then wondered, *Why'd they leave?*

Continuing, the man said, "And I don't see that we have many options available to us. The broadcast hack, for better or worse, was pretty much an official announcement."

Every eye flashed to Dr. Nysgaard indicating the message had been her doing. *And clearly not everyone's happy about that.*

"It's possible it will rally support for the Ignota," Yan added.

"Which means we can't back down now," the brown-haired woman remarked. "Or it will be seen as an empty gesture. Or that the destruction of Manhattan destroyed the Ignota."

"Sam's right," Marshall nodded toward the woman as he spoke. "For weeks now, I've been saying we can't hide anymore. We need to follow up with another attack. And we need to do it quickly."

Unsure how his advice might be received and expecting to be slapped down, Milo offered, "After tonight, security'll be too high for another big attack."

"Then we go small," the young boyish leader replied. "It doesn't have to be battleships. We can move against less secure targets. Small PK stations, for instance."

"We shouldn't be discussing this in front of him," Marshall growled, remembering the captive's presence. "He's one of them. He's a PK." The title came out as a curse.

Match, who had taken a seat at the table, countered, "So was I."

Milo's jaw dropped. "Shit! You're Match Quentin!"

The craze of the evening's events had occupied so much of his concentration that he had failed to connect the man's name to his infamous history. Though few knew the specifics, the treason committed by Quentin, once a Peacekeeper, was considered the ultimate outrage among those who wore the uniform. *These aren't just any Ignota. I've stumbled into a damn "who's who" of criminals!*

Upon the exclamation of recognition, the former PK returned a mischievous grin and a wink. "At your service," he replied. The two youngest cell leaders snickered over a joke Milo did not understand.

"Just because *you* joined the Ignota, doesn't mean *he* has," Marshall argued.

"Nor does it mean he hasn't," Dr. Nysgaard broke her silence. "If we're to attack PK stations, he and his . . partner," her eyes drifted to the drone, ". . . could be helpful."

He had no intention of assisting the Ignota in killing innocent PKs, but he kept his personal prohibition unvoiced. *We can cross that bridge later.*

The other woman, who he now knew was named Sam, suggested, "Does it really matter now? I mean, the drone has been able to transmit to this Soothsayer person since we brought them down here. Our location is not secret anymore. We can keep them watched, but let's not pretend it matters."

The woman's declaration was certainty not a resounding endorsement of his intentions, but Milo was not going to quibble. Even *he* was not quite sure what his intentions were.

"Sergeant Chance can work with me to create a list of targets," Match said. Out of everyone, the former PK seemed the most willing to accept Milo into the fold. He assumed their similar histories influenced the support. *Even as rebels, the uniform is a bond.*

"Before we talk to the others," Yan leaned forward as he spoke. "I think we need to figure out how our command structure's going to work. Six leaders, in my opinion, is five too many. I know many of us scoffed at the idea of unifying the cells before, but a lot has changed."

Much of the interplay in the room had been too layered in the subtext of strangers for him to gauge the dynamics. But, Milo had interrogated enough suspects in his time to know when deception was afoot. The way Yan had shifted forward to speak, the calculated delivery of each syllable, and the systematic lingering of the man's eyes—holding each person in his gaze for the same amount of time—betrayed the possibility of spontaneity. *This is a rehearsed speech,* Milo thought.

"I propose electing one of us to serve as leader of all the cells. A commander."

Ah, he's a power-grabber. Milo would have thought Marshall, loud and domineering, more likely to suggest assuming control.

"And I suppose you're proposing yourself," the old Ignotum harrumphed.

"No," Yan replied. "I was going to suggest Gavin. We all stayed in Oberlin in large part because we believe he is still alive. He is a natural leader, the Ignota here respect him."

Dr. Nysgaard looked to Match with what Milo could only describe as apprehension.

"I'd have no problem following Gavin," one of the two youngest leaders said; the other agreed.

"Nor would I, except he's not here," Marshall pointed out.

Yan's eyes seemed to smile despite his shrug of appeasement. "True. But, his second-in-command, and his chosen successor, is here. We all trust in Gavin, and he trusts in Dr. Nysgaard. So, until he returns, I say she acts as a sort of interim commander. With the five of us serving as her advisory council."

"You're kidding, right?" the old man returned. "No offense, Sonje, but she's only been with us for two months."

"Which means she's not as entrenched as some of us are. She'll be open to hearing all opinions," Yan countered.

Yeah, this was definitely rehearsed.

The debate continued for a few short minutes. Yan addressed each concern presented, providing a logical reason—sometimes two—why the particular concern was unnecessary. In the end, the five cell leaders voiced a unanimous vote selecting Dr. Nysgaard as their interim commander. Milo watched the woman's face grow paler with every spoken *aye.* By the time the fifth vote came round, he was sure she was fighting her stomach from emptying onto the tabletop.

CHAPTER TWENTY-TWO

Sonje Nysgaard

Within minutes of the meeting's end, every Ignota in the shelter was stunned to speechlessness over the devastation in New York. Now in her quarters, joined by Match Quentin and Kunbo, Sonje struggled to compartmentalize the last twenty-four hours. The attack on the fleet, the explosion, Gavin's disappearance and potential death, the raid on the motel, Patton Rivera's death, the annihilation of Manhattan, and the decision of the cell leaders split her mind in too many directions at once.

Head in hands and seated in the hard folding chair, she asked, "Lance . . . how is Lance?"

"Stable," the weapons master explained. "Broken femur in the left leg, some fractured ribs, but stable."

Hearing the assessment, Sonje realized she had already asked about the injured *combie*. Twice.

"I should check on him," she said, though her body made no move to follow the thought. Her limbs were so cold she wondered if she could even stand through her own will.

"Dr. Sonje, there are medics from the other cells looking after him," Kunbo said. "You have other tasks to focus on now."

I've said that before, as well. And he's replied the same way. She understood her mind was working, trapped really, in a cycle of shock. However, understanding the process and breaking free of it were separate matters. Even as she began the next question, she knew she had asked it already.

"Patton—"

"The coroner in town is handling it," Match interjected with obvious frustration. *That's right. He's being cremated. I knew that.*

"Match," the African intoned.

"No, I'm sorry. We've been going over the same damn thing for an hour now! Doc, I know you're dealing with a lot, but we all are. Thing is, you've got six cells that need instructions."

His biting exclamation was a departure from the looped conversation. The effect was enough to jar her away from the next question—*had there been word of Gavin?*—and she raised her head to ask, "What were they thinking putting me in charge?"

Not entirely under his breath, the rakish op-tech specialist muttered, "Beats the hell out of me."

Seeing Kunbo threaten the man with a glare, Sonje said, "He's right, Kunbo. I'm not trained or prepared to lead our cell." As she talked, her mind pulled further out of the endless sequence of numbness. She had worked through surgeries where everything that could go wrong had. Early on, she had been overwhelmed as systems and organs crashed; trying to meet each crisis concurrently. The residents in charge of her training had instructed she maintain awareness of each, but focus on one at a time. It was difficult, but instinct was fighting to employ the method at that moment. *Except now I'm the patient with everything crashing.*

"While I believe you are more than capable," Kunbo said, "I do not think Peter Yan feels the same. Which makes half of his action suspect."

"Half?" Match asked.

Nodding, the man said, "In war, a tribe needs one chief. Decisions must be made quickly, and a consensus among six requires too much time. Where I do find cause for concern is why Peter nominated Dr. Sonje. There are two possible explanations that come to mind first. One, he believes Gavin is dead and if you are in charge he can influence your decisions and cite your inexperience when you disagree with him."

Her role in Adirene's death had earned her Yan's contempt. However, she had hoped his decision to remain in Oberlin had indicated a cooling of hostilities. Not a reconciliation, but perhaps a ceasefire.

Truth, you're thinking in military terms.

"And the second explanation?" she prompted the cell's master of arms.

"More worrisome. He is Sowilo. You are linked to two Founder descendants. If Gavin still lives, then the cells will be united under one. If Torrance lives," Kunbo's lip curled with distaste at the man's name, "well, his affinity for the Seton children, and you, is obvious."

She did not consider Torrance's temperament towards her as affinity, though it was less hostile than his interactions with everyone else.

"We don't know the PK's story is true," the doctor countered. The moment Milo Chance had announced Torrance's heritage, she knew it was true. *The eyes—the same eyes as Gavin.*

Kunbo answered her empty denial with a raised brow of derision. She had never seen him use such a mocking expression before. It looked rather bizarre on his usually stoic visage. Of course, she knew it was justified.

"Fine," she offered with a minimal roll of her eyes. "So, what do I do? They're going to want action, especially if Marshall pushes it. All I want to do is find Gavin. And Torrance."

Match said, "We can try sending Corey and Ament north on recon. Nothing's come through since the lockdown though, so they might not be able to get very far into Lorain."

The scouts were good, she knew. Gavin had praised them on several occasions over the last few months. Despite his loud rebuke to the opposite, even Corey's bungled decision to take Danica on a mission had only slightly tarnished that esteem. Still, she was not comfortable with sending the pair alone into enemy territory. Too many had been lost already. Jaime, Ol'Ben, Adirene, Patton. And Gavin and Torrance missing. She refused to include them in the list of the dead.

"It's too dangerous," Sonje replied. *I don't care if it sounds weak. I can't live with any more blood on my hands.* Affirming the decision more for herself than the others she said, "I won't send Corey and Ament into danger."

Continuing his knack for appearing at the mention of his name, the young scout rushed into the door of her room. Breathless, he said, "You don't have to. We just got word from Vermillion." Seeing her confusion, he added, "It's a town west of Lorain. Vinsy got Gavin and Torrance out. They're laying low for a day or two before heading here."

Sonje's heart leapt with her body. Proper or not, she threw her arms around the scout and all but strangled him in a relieved hug. In an evening of defeats and frights, the news was all the more sweet.

"And he's okay?" she asked Corey.

"If I say yes, does this hug keep going?" the boy joked before answering. "Yes, they're both okay. A few burns, minor hypothermia, and Torrance had a couple of lacerations. But, they're being looked at right now."

Laughing—with joy for Gavin's safety as well as for the imminent end of her farcical role as leader—the doctor landed a playful jab at his ribs. Across the room, she noticed Kunbo's face kept its dour expression.

"What is it?" she asked.

Turning to the scout, Kunbo said, "Alvins is with them?"

Corey nodded.

"His cover is exposed?"

Another nod.

Confused, she asked again, "What?"

Match rose from his seat and ran a hand through his hair as he replied, "Shit. Vinsy's mother, Henney's sister. The PKs will interrogate her. When they break her, she'll tell them about the shelter, about Oberlin."

"No, she won't," the weapons master corrected.

"Everyone breaks," Match replied.

"Not if they are already dead. Celeste will have ended her life the moment her son broke his cover."

Sonje wanted to scream, to rage and tantrum against the cruelness of life. Their victories, infrequent as they were, and never lasting more than a brief moment, were always followed by death. Suddenly the struggle against the Global Alliance seemed an impossible battle. The Ignota were too few, the enemy too many. And no matter how many victories they achieved, their numbers will fall long before the Alliance's.

"They'll come for Henney next," Match said.

Slipping into command with an ease that surprised herself, Sonje directed, "Get her and her family out of Oberlin. New identities, credits, a pod. Everything. Make them disappear."

Her tone was enough to push Match and Corey into immediate and unquestioning action. The pair departed to carry out the orders. She wished she felt as in control as the men believed she was.

After a moment of silence once they were alone, Kunbo stated, "Henney might not agree to running. Her whole life is here. She might prefer to follow her sister's path."

Flashing to furious, Sonje shouted, "I don't care what she wants! No one else is dying tonight, Kunbo. I don't care if we have to drug her. Hell, I'll do it myself! When she's a thousand kilometers from here, she can do whatever she wants. But tonight . . . tonight she keeps living!"

The resolute giant nodded, saying, "They may still come to Oberlin even if Henney leaves."

Once again, events conspired to overwhelm her mind. Too much had happened, was happening still. Another crisis had swallowed every respite that had allowed a moment of clarity. Constantly reacting was wearying her. And the others as well.

The voices of past mentors rippled in memory, guiding her to focus on one problem before moving to another. This patient, however, was working against her. For every repair made, the patient purposefully inflicted another damage.

"The patient has to stop fighting me," she said.

Thrown by the strange reference, the man asked, "Dr. Sonje?"

It was either sheer genius or mad folly; history would have to judge. For now, though, she needed the patient sedated, distracted long enough to let the body begin to heal.

"Kunbo, other than guns, what kind of weapons do we have?"

As it turned out, the clandestine cells had amassed a sizable arsenal of explosives. The list Kunbo and the other weapons masters in the shelter had compiled counted dozens of rocket-propelled grenade launchers, several cases of hand-held grenades, a complement of anti-personnel mines, basic TNT, and a collection of cruder but just as deadly homemade explosive devices.

Since it had already been suggested, and essentially agreed to at their last meeting, it had not been difficult to gain the support of Marshall, Peter Yan, and the others. Their only qualm had been the immediacy of the action. Yan had questioned if perhaps they needed more time to plan. In a different situation, the concern would have been legitimate. But, Sonje's proposal did not require accuracy. It only required chaos.

Thus, in the waning minutes before dawn, more tired than she could afford to admit, she found herself once again trusting stealth to hide her movements.

The city of Willard was less than an hour west of Oberlin, and resembled its neighboring community. There were two main commercial areas, one at the northern border offering haircuts, realtors, podcar repairs, a consignment shop, and a few locally owned eateries. The second business district, though it was not that formal, lay to the south near the high school, and consisted of fast-food restaurants. In between the two strips, a grid of even streets crisscrossed the length and width of the city. Quiet homes on lazy streets.

Positioned at the corner of an intersection, Sonje crouched beside a leafless tree, hugging to the night's receding shadows. Across from her sat a large municipal building housing the offices of the city's officials, as well as the local Peacekeeper department. Unseen but communicating through the short-range mobile comms were her weapons master, the op-tech genius, the pair of scouts, and the "prisoner" Milo Chance. And the drone, as well.

There had been some debate over the PK's inclusion. And while, she did not completely trust the man, she refused to leave him or the drone in Oberlin while it was undefended. It was a risk bringing either of them into the field, but Sonje would not trust the pair to be left alone with the Setons.

The other cells, fully staffed with the exception of Sam's pair of missing scouts, had divided into teams of five. Each group had driven to small towns and cities no further than sixty kilometers from Oberlin. In total, they would strike a dozen PK stations before sunrise. In addition to the eleven attacks by the cells, several residents of Oberlin had been tasked with an operation within their own city. While giving the Alliance more crises to address, she also hoped to draw focus away from the shelter.

It's their turn to have more problems than they can manage! Though, she knew a handful of small incursions were not beyond the Alliance's ability to investigate or manage. *Then we keep giving them more*, she told the voice of her mind's doubt.

She had to remind herself that Gavin would be assuming command upon his return. In half a day, she had brought about a wider public presence of the Ignota, captured a PK and his drone, and somehow managed to get him elected as leader of the unified cells. All of which he had argued against. *Well, not the PK and drone*, she tried to mitigate. Still, it was unlikely in the extreme that he would be pleased with her actions. *Just wait 'til he finds out Torrance is his cousin.*

"Eyes check," Kunbo's baritone whisper shook her from distraction.

"Southeast is clear," Corey replied over the comm.

"North side clear," the second scout confirmed.

Swiveling to check the rear, she raised a hand to her ear and said, "Southwest corner is clear."

"Moving in with the package," the weapons master informed.

"Looping the camera feed," Match, stationed with the drone and PK a block away in a pod of their own, confirmed the hack of the building's exterior cameras.

The "package" was in truth three separate units of explosives; each equipped with a remote-detonation trigger. Kunbo had designed the devices himself, and promised a high-intensity explosion blast with a localized radius. "Powerful and compact" had been his description of the bombs. More than enough to destroy three of the patrol pods parked outside the municipal building.

Moving with greater agility than his wide frame should have allowed, Kunbo's dark form slipped into view, crossed the avenue, and dropped low to place the first bomb. She counted the long seconds nervously. If anyone exited the building, the man would have little potential to hide. The night's goal was one of sideline subterfuge, not direct engagement.

Sergeant Chance had made his feelings about killing Peacekeepers clear. While some of the others viewed the refusal as evidence of his ambiguous loyalties, Sonje understood. Like her, he was new to this struggle. And she had not yet abandoned the hope of winning bloodlessly despite all that she had already seen. Seen and mourned.

A shift in the fading shadows revealed Kunbo stalking to the second target vehicle. Once again, the mountain dipped down to plant destruction.

Glancing up, she found the sky had begun to brighten. Inky black had turned to navy, with even lighter blue hues to the east. A soft rustling behind her drew her attention. Well before she saw the headlights, she recognized the sound of tires rolling over macadam. The pod came up along a cross street and slowed before turning right at the intersection. Drawing closed into her body, Sonje whispered the warning into the comm.

"Pod heading to the station."

As the vehicle passed her, she cringed at the red emblem painted onto the black door.

"It's a patrol pod," she told the team in a gasp.

"Match, emergency extraction," Corey added.

"Stand down," the African replied.

She could overrule him, order the retreat, but she knew Kunbo was not one to make rash decisions. *If he thinks he can complete the mission, I have to trust him.*

The cruiser glided into an empty space two spots over from the Ignota's position. Vertical doors rose in unison. In the quiet of dawn, the PKs' chatter carried through the air. The uniformed men stepped out from the pod, stretching with the weariness of a long shift. They lingered for a minute before making their way up the steps of the building.

Sonje held her breath. *Don't turn around. Don't turn around.* She repeated the wish a dozen times before both figures disappeared through the front doors. Kunbo wasted no time. She watched him duck behind the third target.

"Ament, go," she commanded the scout covering the rear of the building.

"Copy that."

A half-minute later, the scout was driving their second pod towards her position. Headlights off and passenger door lifted high, the vehicle approached, stopping just long enough for Sonje to enter. Turning left, Ament navigated them towards the weapons master. The African stepped away from the parked patrol pods just as they reached him. A few seconds later, Corey joined them inside the pod.

"Cargo's loaded," Ament informed Match.

From the other pod, the op-tech replied, "Okay. Head on home. We'll be right behind you."

Three blocks from the building, Sonje turned back to Kunbo and gave him a nod. The man tapped a brief code into the small tablet held in his hands. Staring out the rear window, she saw a spout of a fire push skyward above the rooftops, then expand as the second and third devices detonated. The thunder of the explosions followed.

It was simple. Basic. And compared to the destructive scale in Lake Erie and New York, it was barely even a *minor* attack. Nor would the Alliance suffer any great financial pain from it. But, Sonje found satisfaction in the night's work.

Righting herself in the seat, feeling the exhaustion of a frantic chain of events, she muttered, "We are everywhere."

To which Kunbo replied, "We are united."

CHAPTER TWENTY-THREE

Liam Walford

Madness! It was the only word his stunned mind could find to describe the events unfolding on the small holoset. When news of the Lake Erie attack broke, the crew had gathered on the bridge and huddled around the projection. While the sailors passed around their theories and commentaries, Liam counted the many errors made by the Council.

A military escort of that size should never have been used to protect the SIDs. It sends the wrong message.

Even denied the encompassing breadth of reports from his intelligence network, he knew the SID delay had birthed rumors. The people needed to *want* the upgrades. Battleships had the marked impression of *force*.

And it provided a large, inviting target to the rebels.

That he, and the rest of the world, had been able to watch the chaos of fire and smoke was the second mistake. Billions of people could now testify to the weakness of the Alliance's security.

Then the damned Ignota message!

The only effort he could praise was the economic spin the talking heads had used to counter the warning against the SIDs. In fact, he would have advised the exact response had he been counseling his late Caput. Yet, the announcement of the strike against Manhattan had extinguished that one bright moment of success.

Minutes ago, Benton Wakefield, the Council's Minister of Information—a fool of a man Liam had never liked—had addressed the world in a breaking newscast. He spouted some drivel about intelligence pointing to a widespread Ignota operation based on the island. The Council had acted quickly in order to prevent further terrorist attacks. One did not need to be privy to the inner workings of government to hear the lie in Wakefield's words. The strike had been an aggressive and unnecessary display of retaliation.

Madness! Liam thought again. No matter how degenerate the victims were, few would applaud government-sanctioned murder. *How long before the first digital of a dead child emerges?* he wondered.

Before turning to leave, the old spy asked Captain Dimas to send for him should further developments arise. The captain agreed with a grunt. It was not lost on Liam that the ship had only recently departed the now-destroyed island of Manhattan. Captain and crew had likely lost friends in the bombardment. Though, the former was probably more concerned over a loss of revenue. *Leaders must be practical.*

A brisk pace brought him to the small quarters he shared with his assistant, Mitchall. The half-room was even further cramped by the addition of Gal. They had confined the Irishman beneath their watchful eyes since the enlightening night on the deck. Eyebrows had been raised as to the reason the red-haired man now slept in their room. Liam did not respond to the intrigue, instead letting the crew create whatever salacious gossip they wished. As they were sailors, he was certain their tales would be prurient in the extreme.

"Well?" Mitchall asked when he entered. His apprentice sat at the edge of one cot, while their "friend" curled himself into a sullen ball on the other bed.

"No exact numbers, but between the lines it would seem Manhattan is no more." Liam snapped his fingers at the Irishman who sulked off the cot and down onto the floor.

He had interrogated the fellow within the limits of their situation. No visible injuries, nothing broken. Though, Gal would have more than a few nightmares of drowning in the coming months. A psychoactive compound had loosened his tongue, but there was little learned.

Recently turned twenty, the boy's first contact with the Soothsayer had occurred four years ago. He had been in service to the faceless mystery ever since. There was nothing remarkable about his early orders—mostly acting as a courier of sealed packages to different locations across Europe. At first study, Liam found nothing revealing about the locations. Most were empty warehouses and abandoned homes.

Gal's thread had not twined with the Garrott's until recently, when the Soothsayer instructed him to place a cryptic message in the home of the abducted Chief Engineer of Garrott Industries. Days and days passed with no contact from his master, until last week when he was sent to Manhattan to follow the spymaster and his apprentice.

While the questioning had yielded little of the Soothsayer's identity or intent, Liam was forced to offer the shadowed man greater respect. Operating for four years without detection and locating Liam when the Alliance had not were impressive feats in their shared world of espionage.

Respect yes, he mused, *but one does not share in our world and expect to live.* He needed more intelligence if he hoped to neutralize the Soothsayer.

Reclining on the now-vacated cot, he returned to the present.

"If this escalates much further, I fear we may face a rapidly destabilizing region," he said to Mitchall. "Even without escalation, the same may be true."

"And Cambrie barely had a hold on things before," the younger man added.

"Precisely why we must pass through the Dead Continent quickly, and reach," he paused with a glance to Gal, then finished, "our final destination."

Though he trusted their ability to keep the captive secured, there was no need to speak too openly in front of the youth.

"As to that," Mitchall replied, "have you given any more thought to *how* we're to cross a continent of hostile savages?"

Having recovered somewhat from his bout of seasickness, or perhaps simply grown used to it, the assistant had resumed his familiar questioning. Liam viewed the man's return to self as an unfortunate blessing.

Frowning at the impertinence, the spymaster replied, "I have indeed."

Captain Dimas had required a great deal of convincing, but he had managed to find the gruff sailor's price. Points the crewman, however, had not been told of the arrangement yet. The events in America had forced a postponement to the conversation.

The idea had first tickled his intrigue days ago when they had boarded the ship. Points' intellect had impressed Liam. Coupled with a criminal past and years of hard labor, the boy was an interesting candidate. True, Points was a fair bit older than the preferred age of a new trainee; but with his network gutted, Liam knew he had to work with what was available.

As expected, Mitchall second-guessed the decision.

"We know nothing about him," he argued.

"On the contrary. We know he is quite intelligent. We know he is loyal to those who have helped him. We know he has few ties to the outside world."

We just don't know if he will agree, he added in thought.

"And even if none of that were true, we need an able body to help us in the DC. Our journey would have been a challenge without having to watch him," his chin jutted to the man on the floor, "but now that we *are* so burdened, another set of eyes, and arms, is preferred."

"You mean to tell him who we are?"

Liam had not settled that question in his own mind. Their cover story—foolhardy scholars seeking to educate the Deaders—would not explain why the Irishman was under guard, or why they would be heading to England with all possible haste.

"I will tell him what is necessary," he replied.

Ultimately, as they would discover, they needed to tell Points very little. Very little and everything.

"When did you recognize us?" Liam asked, barely hiding his surprise.

"As soon as you boarded, sir," the sharp-toothed sailor replied. "Well, at least you, sir. I read the diginews most days; probably the only one on the *Espado* that does. I recognized your face from an article about the assassination attempt at the Garrott party."

"And who have you told?" Mitchall inquired. The menace in his voice earned a reproachful look from the spymaster.

"No one, sir."

"You must have assumed there would be a reward if you turned us in," he asked with more moderation than his assistant.

"I was running from a past, too. And the Captain would have gotten a reward if he'd turned me in, though probably not as large as the one for you," Points explained. "But he didn't. It wouldn't have been right for me to do to you what wasn't done to me."

Liam studied the boy's eyes as he spoke, watched the steady rise and fall of his chest, saw the steadiness of Points' hands and feet. He did not need a serum to know the sailor was being truthful.

Truly a diamond in the rough, he mused in cliché.

"You are a remarkable young man, Zlatan," he complimented, purposely using his true name.

"Thank you, sir."

Though door to the room was closed, allowing for freer discussion, Mitchall leaned against it in the event a wayward crewman grew too curious. The spymaster and sailor sat across from each other on the twin cots. On the floor, Gal kept his head bowed in disinterest, but Liam could tell by the tilt of the man's head that he was absorbing every word.

"What I am offering you is dangerous. There are people hunting us—Alliance, Ignota, and others. Powerful and ruthless people, Zlatan. Simply being in our presence would be sufficient guilt for your execution.

"If we manage to survivor, however, I can ensure you never need to work another day in your life. Or if you choose to stay on with us after the DC, I can offer you access to a world of which few can even dream."

Though he wanted the boy to agree, he would not hide from him the inherent dangers of that decision.

"Captain Dimas—," Points began.

"Has agreed to be handsomely compensated for your resignation." The captain had been willing to part with other members of the crew for a lower price. Apparently, the man reciprocated the youth's respect and loyalty. "Though I should say the bargaining was a challenge. Dimas thinks very highly of you."

That brought the hint of a smile to the boy's face. Liam knew the appreciation of one's mentor was unquantifiable.

Sensing Points still wavered, the old spy said, "If the salary is not adequate, I am willing to negotiate."

"It's not that, sir," Points replied. The opening offer had been five million credits upon agreeing, and another ten should they escape the DC intact. For a cargo shipman, fifteen million credits was several lifetimes of earnings.

"It's just, well, I've never been a big fan of the Alliance. Nothing personal," he said with an apologetic raise of his hands. "Work on a ship long enough, and you see how corrupt it all is. Bribes and payoffs just so we can do our work. Even the legitimate work. And now with New York . . .," he trailed off.

"As you can assume, Zlatan, I'm not too big a fan of the Alliance lately either," he offered. "The Council killed the only true Family I've known. If we succeed, we will be remaking the Council and the Alliance."

He did not mention there were some things that would not change. The Culling, for one. Liam had long ago understood its necessity. There were few things he believed in more strongly. But, the boy was right. Some things did need to change. *And Tilden will be that change. He can be the one guiding star in this darkness.*

The youth lifted his eyes to meet Liam's. After a moment of silent searching, he said, "Okay."

CHAPTER TWENTY-FOUR

Tilden Garrott

The celebratory atmosphere over the success at Cerne Abbas continued for several days. And understandably so. The cache's worth had surprised even him. In addition to access codes for bank accounts holding more than two billion credits—a sum which could finance an individual cell for a century or more—the retrieval mission had also netted six crates of XG-15 charged particle rifles, two crates of particle handguns, and several dozen sets of the Ex-Cal design body armor worn by Peacekeepers.

Tilden had not intended to guide his captors to such an impressive score. Clearly, his father had added to the stores hidden beneath the foundation of Cerne Abbas' oldest building. There were other holds tucked away across Europe with far greater prizes. Even an underground hangar with a small fleet of HALOs in Ireland. But, he would not allow the terrorists access to that arsenal.

Nor do I need to, he smiled in quiet thought.

Since the return to the base, they had treated him with almost collegiate acceptance. His guards were more lax in their supervision, calling him by name and sharing swigs of poorly distilled scotch. Isla's visits came more frequently, as did her smiles. The only unaltered constant was the reproachful glares and harsh words from the cell's leader, Cleland Bain. But Tilden had not expected one successful mission to win over the old bastard. In fact, he admired the man for remaining immune to his subterfuge.

And it will be his undoing, he added.

"Another round, *mon ami?*" Etienne asked from across the round tri-pedal table. Though the question was directed to Kieran, the third man seated in the cell, Tilden refocused his eyes.

That evening's pastime was poker, an older Americanized version. He'd had little experience playing the game; his societal level disdained it as a crude man's amusement. Though after a few nights' play, Tilden wondered if perhaps his enlightened peers had misjudged it. There was a certain art in manipulating opponents with deception, bullying them into missteps with a tall stack of holographic chips. He quickly found himself winning more hands than he lost.

"Aye," replied the cell's scout. In his early thirties, Kieran was an avowed lover of all things alcoholic. Through innuendos, he'd learned the scout's drinking had run him afoul of Bain on more than one occasion. The man's skill, however, was such that even the occasional drunken spell was forgiven.

The Frenchman poured four fingers of scotch into each man's cup. Tilden's head already spun—it had begun to spin after the third glass and by the sixth he was drunk—but he was well past the ability to refuse. Only his artificial eye prevented his vision from completely blurring.

That had taken some getting used to. His living eye was susceptible to the full effects of inebriation. As were the biological nerves and receptors attached to the implant. But the implant itself was immune. The result was a disturbing field of vision to which he was still working to adjust.

As the scout dealt the next hand, Tilden raised his glass. A small voice in his mind warned him to watch his words.

"To the hospitality of the Ignota," he toasted; tongue tripping over the words. The intoxicated smile on his face hid the malice in his meaning.

Careful, the voice warned. He heard the scolding clearly. Tilden could not remember if his conscience had always been so distinct. Since the abduction, it had seemed to take on its own identity. Even his dreams were divided. More often than not, he saw himself in the dreams; an entity, an actor, separate from his subconscious. But, at the same time, under his control. In quiet moments of reflective interpretation, he assumed it represented his situation.

Two months of running an inner dialogue of plans I can share with no one. I show one face to these Ignota, and keep another hidden from them.

It was exhausting, but necessary. With the recent introduction of liquor to his diet, he'd discovered the internal division diminished with each drink.

"To the Ignota," Kieran replied, slurring less than the heir. "An' t'Tilden fer makin' us da richest cell n'da Ignota!" the man added with a laughing shout.

The three men took a healthy swallow. Despite the numbness of his tongue, the honey-gold liquid still burned down his throat.

"Maybe now you can buy a better bottle," he joked to his two companions. After the laughter died down, he said, "In truth, I owe you lot my life. I'd be dead and buried if not for you."

"It was Isla's quick thinking which saved you," Etienne corrected.

"Aye! To Isla!" the fair-skinned Irishman called for another toast.

Glasses once again in the air, Tilden added, "To Isla, and her wise leadership." The two Ignota repeated his words without criticism.

Even intoxicated, he still held enough awareness to relish the small victory.

The game ended when the last drop of scotch fell from the spent bottle. Red-eyed and stumbling, the pair of Ignota dragged the table from the cell before leaving him to sleep off his dizziness on the cot. His body needed no encouragement to slip from consciousness.

Senses too deadened to even dream, Tilden did not hear the activity in his cell until rough hands pulled him up from the cot. Blinking in confusion, the contents of his stomach threatened sickness as his body crashed against the far wall. A hard punch landed on the side of his face. The blow spun his head into the concrete wall.

"You son of a bitch!" Bain's angry voice growled at him.

Stunned, not yet sober, and in sudden pain, Tilden was unable to defend himself from a second, and then third, strike along his jawline.

"Stand up!" the cell leader ordered, tugging him to his feet.

Tilden tried to force his eyes to focus through the nauseating double vision. The attempt was successful enough to reveal Cleland Bain's face pressed close and twisted with animalistic rage.

"Do you know what your people did?" the man snarled. Warm flecks of spit frothed and flew from his mouth. Tilden's mind was too busy registering the taste of blood in his own mouth to notice the moisture hitting him. "Is that what you fuckers get off on? Killing innocent children?"

A swift blow to his gut punctuated the questions. The battle with his stomach was lost and a night of scotch forced its way out. Bain cursed as bile and liquor splashed over them both, further fueling his enflamed fury. One hand around his throat kept Tilden against the wall, while the cell leader's right fist fell again and again against his face.

"Sick fuckers!" Bain repeated as each attack landed.

Other voices sounded over the sharp ringing in his ears. He saw Isla's face rush forward behind the right shoulder of his attacker.

"Sir!" she cried with alarm. Her hands reached for the leader's swinging fist to prevent the next punch. Bewitched in his own madness, Bain changed the momentum of his arm and drove his elbow into her chest, sending Isla to the ground with a gasp.

Two figures moving too fast for Tilden to identify pulled Bain away. With the removal of his "support," the Garrott heir crumpled in a rapid slide down the wall to the floor. Looking up, he saw Etienne and Lars grappling with their leader.

"Get your fucking hands off me!"

The men restraining Bain made repeated pleas for the man to calm down, but the old warrior refused to oblige. He kicked at Lars' knee, forcing a scream of pain out of the scout. Trained to fight, Bain used the momentary release to pull the handgun from the holster on the injured man's thigh.

Tilden managed a warning shout. "He's got a gun!"

The Frenchman moved quickly, throwing his weight into Bain's side before the man could raise the gun. The pair collided against the bars of the cell.

From his position, he could not see if the commanding officer had been disarmed. Etienne's head flew back from what Tilden assumed had been a head butt from Bain. The large man staggered, but kept a loose hold on his combatant.

With a limping lunge, Lars returned to the fracas, grabbing Bain's wrist with both hands. Isla, drawing air with deep heaves, was picking herself off the ground. She held one hand to her chest, and the other closed around the gun at her hip.

In the tiny room of stone, cement, and concrete, the blast of a firing gun boomed and echoed. Tilden flinched at the sound. Heedless of the pain, he swung his head to the trio of men, then to Isla's hand. Her weapon had just left its holster.

He pulled his eyes back to the men. No longer struggling, Bain submitted to the Frenchman's restraint. The pair stepped back, the pistol dropping from the cell leader's grip.

Shocked to full sobriety, he watched Lars collapse to his knees. The scout pressed his hands against the center of his chest where a dark stain expanded down his gray t-shirt. Wide-eyed and growing pale, the man lowered his head to the wound. As he did, a long trickle of blood fell from his lips. Isla Carene's frantic call for help had barely finished when all life left the man's eyes and his body slumped forward.

Chaotic action filled the next moments. Etienne escorted his compliant prisoner out of the cell; depositing Bain in the one adjacent. With freefalling tears, the former actress turned Lars' body over and pressed her hands over the wound to stem the pulse of blood that was no longer flowing. Others, Kieran and the cell's medic, pushed into the cell with faces confused and despairing.

Tilden watched. And as he did, his thoughts raced. He had been trying to erode Cleland Bain's influence on the cell; undermine the man's leadership through casual remarks and subtle manipulations. However, the cell leader had just self-inflicted more damage in three minutes than Tilden would have been able to achieve in months.

Go to her, the voice instructed. *Support her.*

Crawling across the floor, flexing his jaw as he went, relieved to find it was not broken, he wrapped his arms around the woman. As he tugged her away from the corpse, he whispered, "Shh, he's gone. He's gone, Isla. You have to be strong. They can't see you weak. You need to be in control."

While he doubted Bain's actions would be easily forgiven, Tilden pushed the woman to fill the power vacuum. The sooner she assumed control, the less opportunity Bain would have to reassert himself in the aftermath. Martial matters may not be his forte, but he had been well educated in power—and the succession of power.

Fighting the weakness and pain in his own body, the heir used what little strength was left in him to help Isla to her feet. Once sure she'd not stumble or fall, he took his hands away. Seeing the remaining members of the cell aligned a pace away, Tilden hushed, "They need to see you in command. Give them an order."

Her eyes turned to his. He saw a brief vacancy in the wells of green before a return to self flashed in the emerald irises. Isla stepped from him, moving closer to the gathered Ignota.

"Have the body prepared for burial," she commanded.

Three days had passed since the ceremony. Of course, he'd not been invited to attend. An exclusion which suited him just fine. He was too exhausted to feign mourning a dead enemy. Playing the sympathetic confidante consumed too much of his focus for him to waste any on a corpse.

"Liam always said leadership was a punishment for the well-intentioned," Tilden said as he stood by the window, staring out across the long fields of grass.

Three days, and he'd still not taken in his fill of light and openness. Though the funeral had been restricted, the perimeters of his captivity had expanded. During the day, he was now free to roam the upper levels of his prison.

He had been quite surprised to discover the "prison" was an old farmhouse, with its vegetable cellar converted into a jail. Three stories tall, the building breathed antiquity. The many rooms were small, in the style of an English country home, and well maintained. Wide wooden planks, polished to a reflective sheen, stretched across the floors, and echoed even the softest step. The furnishings were old as well. No piece had been built more recently than the end of the last century. Beyond electricity and running water, there were no other elements of modernity.

While banned from stepping outdoors, and still forced to sleep underground (locked in his cell, but without a guard), he knew his status among the terrorists was a vast improvement.

Especially compared to Bain, his mind smiled. The group's leader had not been out of his cell since the shooting. Tilden worked to ensure the man remained there.

"A leader is forced to make decisions which would break lesser men," he said, then added, "or women."

Isla sat on the opposite side of the second-floor study. Once, her presence would have filled a stadium. Now, the upholstered chair seemed to swallow her. She turned a glass cube paperweight over and over in her hands. As the prism caught the sunlight, shades of red, blue, and violet danced along the floor and walls.

They had spoken frequently over the intervening days. And though she'd not asked directly, he knew she was seeking his counsel.

And why wouldn't she? his second-self asked. *I was groomed to lead. These Ignota were trained to follow.* Still, he was careful to only share his encouragement when they were alone. It would negate his efforts if the others thought he had too much influence on the woman.

"I think it may be breaking me," she confessed. "I know something has to be done. We can't sit here inactive. There's a revolution starting out there."

No one had provided him the full details of current events, but he had pieced together enough to know major shifts were occurring in the world. The catalyst for the newest unrest was an Ignota attack in America, to which the Alliance had responded with the full destruction of Manhattan. An act that had also been the impetus for Bain's savagery three nights earlier. It seemed the man was father to a handful of bastard children who lived on the island.

Used to live, he corrected. As much as he despised the Council for the crimes against his Family, he was also impressed with the scope of their response to the Ignota threat. He had once argued to his Father that the Council had allowed the terrorists to exist for too long. And now the Ignota had sparked revolution. Or so Isla claimed.

While he assumed hopeful subjectivity tainted her view, he did not deny the terrorists needed to be eradicated. *When I lead the Council . . . when I am the Council, every last one of them will be hunted down. Their bodies will be displayed in warning. I will kill every enemy of House Garrott!*

For now, though it sickened him, he needed at least this one cell alive. *What was it Liam said?* "Deal with the devil, but never forget what he is."

Turning from the window, pushing the contempt from his eyes, he said, "Are you familiar with *The Art of War?* The treatise of the ancient general Sun Tzu?"

Shrugging and shaking her head, Isla replied, "I've heard of it. But never studied it."

Truth! These people expect to win a war against the Alliance? The Asian text had been one of the cornerstones of his education under Liam Walford. The Chief Advisor of House Garrott had believed the work should be the principle guide for those in power.

"Sun Tzu," Tilden continued without deriding her lack of education, "believed that a general must be temperate. The general who cannot control his anger will blunder, and his men will die without any gain in advantage."

"And Cleland doesn't control his anger," Isla replied. "That's not the issue. Not really. No one would question forcing him to step down. But I know Cleland. He won't accept it. And is that even the appropriate punishment? He killed Lars. It was an accident in a moment of anger but Lars is dead. Is a demotion a good enough penalty?"

Assuming the questions were not rhetorical, and believing he'd laid sufficient groundwork over the last three days, he risked an outright recommendation. "You could send him away. Force him to leave the cell."

Isla returned a mirthless laugh. "That's not his style, walking away like a scolded dog. Part of me wishes Etienne had—"

He tried not to react as she let the comment trail off. His heart raced and fluttered against his ribcage. Bain brought low and banished was as much as he'd dared hope to achieve. But with her unguarded thought, she had Tilden wondering how much further he could push.

Crossing the wood floor between them, he dropped to one knee and took her hands in his.

"If you ask it of me, I will do it," he said, hoping his voice was love-struck. "No one needs to know. It will look like an accident . . . a suicide."

"Tilden," she answered, her face all eyes. "No. I can't—"

"You saved my life, Isla. You helped me see the Alliance for what it truly is. If you believe this man is a threat to what the Ignota hope to achieve, let me take care of it. Let me do this for you."

"Tilden," she said again. "What you're suggesting, when I said I wished . . . that would have been different, but this, it's murder."

He sneered at her hypocrisy. *How many died the night you allowed a suicide bomber into my home?*

"Or is it justice?" he asked. By the look on her face, he knew he was coming close to going too far. However, he was too incensed with the promise of victory, and the hatred he harbored for Bain, to draw back. Besides, he had never seen her this weak, this insubstantial to the task faced. He had to leverage the moment.

She pulled her hands away as she rose from the chair. Kneading her brow with her knuckles before tucking a lock of dark hair behind a petite ear, Isla turned to him and said, "Justice has a court, a jury. This is execution."

"Some luxuries do not exist in war," he replied with another of Liam's many axioms. "In war, a leader is sometimes forced to act quickly, decisively, and, on occasion, is forced to act harshly."

He searched her face for any sign of revulsion over his words. There was none. If they had been speaking of anyone other than Bain, she might have flinched away from the thought. However, he suspected the cell leader's bullying and contemptible nature had at least opened her mind to contemplating his suggestion.

Moving to where he'd stood moments ago at the window, her voice cracked as she asked, "How? How would you do it?"

He was fortunate the woman had her back to him. Otherwise, she would have seen the malevolent smile breaking across his face. She was his now. He had won. By agreeing, Isla Carene had tethered herself to him more than she realized.

The body was discovered the next morning. By the level of rigor mortis, the cell's medic, Colton Sawyer, estimated Bain had taken his life shortly after midnight. A pool of blood had spilled from the deep gashes in each wrist, soaked through the cot to cover a sizeable section of the floor. Isla did not look at Tilden when she came down to the underground jail.

He told them he had heard nothing in the night. Which was true. Bain's evening meal had been laced with a potent sleep aid. The bastard had not even been conscious when Tilden used the key she'd given him to enter and exit the locked cells. There'd been no struggle when the heir curled Bain's hand around a knife and sliced the sleeping man's wrists.

Tilden had never killed before. He was amazed at how easy it had been. Easy and exhilarating. The rush was unlike anything he'd ever felt. Though his list of enemies was still long, striking Bain's name from it was quite pleasing.

There's still much more to do, his inner voice remarked.

Yes, I know, he answered, not realizing he was now replying to the voice directly, as he watched the body being taken out. *This is only the start.*

CHAPTER TWENTY-FIVE

Gavin McAvoy

Close to twenty-four hours of rest had been quite restorative, but his body still argued for more. As it was, he'd spent the first half of his recuperation shivering uncontrollably. While the swim from Lorain to Vermillion had been swift, the icy water seemed to have seeped into his bones. Even now, a brief chill stole over him from time to time. Though they were coming far less frequently.

His burns had been superficial, and after treatment, he looked like he had been in the sun too long. In the span of an hour, he had been burned and frozen. Such extreme exposures were a shock to his system that had sapped much of his strength.

Even his ankle, which he had assumed had been broken by a drone's hand, had proved to be a bone bruise. The swelling and pain had all but subsided while he had slept.

Torrance, of course, appeared in better condition despite having more severe injuries. The wounds on the man's leg and hand had been sealed and dosed with accelerant. Pink scars were already forming and would be fully healed in another day or two.

The two men, wrapped in blankets, reclined in separate chairs that had been placed in front of the fireplace. The heat from the crackling wood massaged their fatigue. Alvins "Vinsy" Parker rested in one of the bedrooms on the second floor of the home. Word of his mother's suicide, and aunt's escape, had been received hard. Gavin respected the man's desire to mourn in solitude.

News of Vinsy's family, and their collective sacrifices, was but a fraction of Gavin's troubles. Upon waking a short time ago, he had been informed about the retaliatory attack on New York City. The Alliance's savagery was unprecedented. And he knew he shared in the guilt.

For the moment, and somewhat selfishly, his thoughts were focused on the recent events in Oberlin. An hour ago, he had spoken with Sonje over a secure mobile comm. The concern in her voice was obvious as she explained the situation. Each revelation increased his agitation tenfold.

The Ignota had declared themselves to the world. Half the cells had left the shelter. The remaining cells had united, and named him as the leader. A Peacekeeper and a drone had been captured—the latter killing Patton Rivera in the process. Ten attacks against PK stations had been carried out in neighboring communities. And he had the distinct feeling Sonje had not told him everything.

She's created a Truth-damned mess! he cursed. Worse, everything she had done in his absence had come from Torrance's playbook. He had guilt in that too, though. He was the one to name her his successor, even after knowing she'd agreed with the rogue's recommendations.

Taking a sip of coffee from the mug in his hands in the hope of quieting some of his anger, he looked to the man seated a meter away. "If you're able, I'd like to use the morning commute tomorrow to get back to Oberlin."

Staring into the flames, Torrance nodded. The unspoken truce between the pair, which they had silently declared prior to the supply ship mission, seemed to be holding.

In the kitchen, he could hear the low murmuring of the home's owners. Craig and Juliana Packard, both in their late-twenties, had been married for half a decade. He was an emergency room nurse at Amherst Hospital, and she was a teacher at the local high school. Husband and wife had been Fifths prior to meeting, and, after settling in the city of Vermilion, continued their service to the Ignota together. Gavin had only met them twice before arriving at their doorstep in the middle of the night. Upon his first introduction, he'd not needed to see the rune symbol in their wedding bands to know the couple was Sowilo. Over the years, he had become much attuned to the way cultists swooned after hearing his name. With so much on his mind, he enjoyed the wide berth they were giving him. From the way they stared at Torrance, he assumed the man's reputation was what kept them away.

Whatever their reason, I'm happy not dealing with Sowilo foolishness.

"You agree with what she's done?" he asked Torrance. There was no doubt to whom he referred.

Eyes of icy sapphire turned from the fire to him. Gavin remembered his confusion on the ship, and in the lake, when he'd thought his brother Jaime was with him. Free now to study Torrance without the threat of pursuing enemies, he was surprised how much the man's features resembled those of his late brother.

His edges are harder, though. Like chiseled stone. Jaime's were softer—a river rock.

"I do," Torrance replied. "You won't win this on your own. If the other Ignota are smart, they will join together."

It was the same argument he had made in the shelter.

"What about escalation?"

"Escalation?"

"We attacked their fleet, they destroyed Manhattan," the cell leader answered. "What's next? We strike another military target, they bomb London? LA? Both?"

The warrior's eyes narrowed.

"Maybe."

With a touch more challenge in his voice, he asked, "And that doesn't bother you? Millions of people dying doesn't bother you?"

Chuckling low and shaking his head, Torrance asked, "How do you see this ending, McAvoy? Tomorrow the Alliance announces surrender? They admit the error of their ways and beg forgiveness? If you can find a way to fight and win a war without anyone dying, let me know how. Until then, you need to figure out just how much you're willing to sacrifice. Is destroying the Alliance worth the death of millions? Because that's the price. If you can't accept that, then what the hell are you doing?"

The fireplace was no longer the source of heat in Gavin's blood.

"It's not that black and white. These are people's lives, not some tally sheet we add to and hope the balance comes out in our favor. Can't you see that? Or do you just not give a shit? Are you so fucked up that you really don't *feel* anything?"

Expressionless, the man from the woods stood, letting the blankets fall back onto the chair to reveal a borrowed set of shirt and pants, as he replied, "Emotions are a weakness. Especially in war."

"Then why'd you protect the Seton kids?" he accused. "There couldn't have been a strategic advantage in that. Wasn't it just emotion?"

"I had my reasons. I still do," the man returned. Standing by the fireplace, one arm leaning against the mantel, Torrance had his face towards the flames and away from Gavin's sight.

He knew he should let it drop, knew he would be crossing a line, but the entirety of events conspired against his better judgment. The cell leader said, "Because of your past? Because of the scars on your back? Sonje told me what they're from. She said you were whipped as a child. Is that why you protect the kids? Is that why you don't give a damn about anyone else?"

The speed with which Torrance turned, the strength he displayed hoisting Gavin from the chair, would have been impressive for a man in peak condition. For one healing from hyperthermia, burns, a leg and hand wound, not to mention exhaustion . . . it was quite simply stunning.

Gavin reacted, bringing his arms up and using his forearms to strike the other man's elbows and force the joints to bend. The hold broke, and neither man moved to another attack. Instead, they stared at each other, arm's length apart, challenging like lions.

Low and cold, Torrance said, "You should be glad it was me getting whipped and not you."

The words held meaning beyond the explicit, but he was too impassioned to decipher them. Part of him wished Torrance would initiate a brawl. Gavin knew he'd lose, yet his anger and frustration needed a release.

"Gavin—" Juliana's timid voice was barely heard over the pounding in his veins.

"Yeah," he answered, not breaking the contesting stare.

Taking a careful step into the living room, the woman said, "There's a problem."

He laughed at the absurdity of the understatement. Torrance dropped a long blink and turned back to the fire. Though he'd not backed down, Gavin felt no victory.

"What's the problem?" he asked after a beat and a deep breath. As he shifted, his foot tapped against the coffee mug he had dropped in the scuffle. A sip of coffee had been in the container when it fell, but Gavin still apologized to his host as he picked it up.

"It's fine," Juliana replied.

"An Echelon team just landed in the city," her husband explained as he came in from the kitchen.

Wiping his hands on the thighs of his jeans, he said, "Echelon? Not troops?"

"They're pretty distinctive," Craig returned.

Every generation, every government had its version of the elite soldier. Before the Global Alliance, it was America's Navy SEALs and Army Delta Force who had earned the world's recognition as the "best of the best." Though, the Central Intelligence Agency's Special Activities Division, which recruited from both groups, was superior, the clandestine nature of the division prevented its members from receiving proper credit.

For the last sixty years, the men and women[7] of Echelon—or "Echers" as they were called—were the undisputed holders of that crown now. Trained in languages, combat, counter-terrorism, propaganda, intelligence gathering, direct and covert action, and unconventional warfare, Echelon agents were a global force few lived to speak of. That a team was in Vermilion, and openly so, was more than troubling.

"PKs and drones would be better," he thought aloud. "What's their current position?"

"They were seen heading up to the channel."

"They know we came ashore here," Gavin declared. He may not have been trained in the specifics of Echelon's operational directives, but their movements were rarely accidental. The prospect of running—or worse . . . swimming—made him want to scream.

"If you want to leave for Oberlin now, we can give you our pod," the nurse offered.

From the fireplace, Torrance said, "Surveillance drones are already in the air. Echelon wanted their arrival to be noticed, to spook us into moving. They'll be watching everything."

The man's assured tone prompted Gavin to ask, "You've gone up against them before?"

"Once. A weapons deal went bad. Echelon got wind of it and sent an operative to investigate. These aren't just well trained soldiers. These guys are chemically enhanced. They hit harder and fight longer than the average man."

Back in college, before he'd ever heard of the Ignota, Gavin had been friends with one of the university's football players. Simon Orlange had ignored the long-established ban on performance-enhancing drugs, and within one season had become a star player. The increased attention led to officials discovering the illegal source of his skill. But Gavin well remembered the strength his friend had gained. *If Echelon agents were equally enhanced . . .* it was a frightening revelation.

He asked, "How do you know this?"

---

[7] Approximately thirteen percent of Echelon's ten-thousand-plus members were women at that time. –M.S.

"I autopsied the body." The reply's frank delivery suggested Torrance could have ended it with "obviously."

Really wish I didn't know that.

"Okay. So, they're elite, but still beatable?"

"That was only one agent. And I barely survived. There's four on a fireteam. Direct confrontation would be suicide."

If his memory was correct, Gavin had never heard the man admit to even a fraction of weakness.

"On the plus side, if they die, the Alliance won't know right away," the man continued. "Echers aren't chipped; they're basically ghosts who can operate off the grid. The Alliance doesn't worry about them breaking ranks because the drugs they're pumped with are addictive. Without the drugs, an agent will die."

Well, that's at least something in our favor.

"We can't stay here," the cell leader replied. "Sooner or later, they'll sweep the houses like the PKs did in Lorain."

"There's another way out of the city," the woman of the house interjected.

"Juliana!" her husband spun with the sharp rebuke.

"But Peter said—"

"What way?" Torrance cut her off before she could explain further.

The married couple stared at each other for several seconds, arguing with eyes not words, before Craig Packard surrendered with a resigned sigh and shake of his head.

"Not long after the Founders separated, a tunnel was built at the bottom of the lake," the nurse informed.

"To where?" Gavin asked.

"Pelee Island. About forty kilometers northwest of Vermilion."

Sparsely populated—less than two hundred people were permanent residents—the Canadian island was the largest land mass in Lake Erie. Its long-established wineries and the seasonal pheasant hunting were the main attraction for visitors to Pelee. But even at the peak of the tourist seasons, the island was quiet and secluded. Though he and his cell had been based in the region for over a decade, this was the first mention of a tunnel to reach his ears.

"What's on Pelee?" he asked.

After another exchange of furtive glances with his wife, Craig said, "It is a Sowilo community."

Gavin cringed and balled his hands into fists. That the quasi-religious sect kept such secrets from the rest of the Ignota was irritating. That they were his only means of escape was even more irksome.

"How many cells are on the island?" he questioned through a clenched jaw.

"You misunderstand, Gavin. There are no cells on the island. It is a community."

"Fine. How many are in this *community*?" He tried, and failed, to keep his distaste from the word.

Juliana placed a stalling hand on her husband's arm.

"Everyone on the island is Sowilo," she explained. "Not everyone is militant, but all the men, women, and children on Pelee are believers."

Truth! There's got to be three hundred people living there!

"You mentioned Peter. Peter Yan knows about the island?"

"He does," the teacher answered. "I understand why you're angry. But, we know how the others view the Sowilo. The secret was kept so we would have a place of our own, free from judgment."

His anger was too strong for him to find the words to reply. Yan had kept a place of safety hidden while eleven cells overcrowded the shelter in Oberlin.

"Where's the tunnel entrance?" Torrance asked.

Twenty minutes later, Gavin, Torrance, and Vinsy stood at the door of the Packard home, thanking their hosts for the much needed shelter and medical treatment. The PK had been reluctant to join the escaping party. Still in the early stages of grief, the man had wanted to stay behind to exact revenge for his mother's death. Gavin, unwilling to lose a friend to a foolish act, had all but ordered him to follow.

The night was naturally cold, and unnaturally quiet. Word of Echelon agents had spread quickly. In the middle of a winter's night, a city—even one as small as Vermilion—should have had some night owls about. But, every house in sight was cloaked in darkness. No window showed the glow of a holoset tuned to some late-night entertainment. Every porch light was off.

The coastal city's lighthouse, and the tunnel entrance hidden beneath it, was a few minutes' walk away. Given the deserted streets, Gavin decided against traveling by pod. If Torrance was correct, and there indeed were surveillance drones above, a podcar would be noticed. Three men on foot without SIDs had a better chance of passing the aerial cameras unseen.

Strict silence was observed as they made their way; keeping their footfalls soft and light and steady. The cell leader was less concerned with reaching the lighthouse than with what they would find once there. Echelon's agents were last seen at the channel leading into Vermilion's marina.

We'll be less than two hundred meters from them. Torrance's warnings of the agents' strength and ability repeated in his mind.

Turning left onto Washington Street, the trio passed down the last row of houses. To their right, he saw the Vermilion Lighthouse, a disused piece of nostalgia, through the leafless branches of the tree line. Torrance took point, ducking across the lawn of a large shorefront home. Gavin noticed the man compensating for a limp—which then reminded him of his own healing ankle. Of the three, Vinsy was in the best condition, but he lacked the training of the other two men.

He's a PK, he tried self-reassuring. *He can handle himself if it comes to a fight. Truth, please don't let it come to a fight!*

Torrance waved them forward after his brief inspection of the area. Brown, dried-out grass crunched beneath their feet, but the sound did not carry. Ahead, the cell leader saw a dozen tree trunks separating the residential property from the perimeter of the old building that once housed a maritime museum. Now a bed and breakfast for the occasional tourists, the structure was empty and quiet in the off-season.

Keeping tight to the building, the men inched around its northern face. Twenty meters away, the lighthouse rose up from a swell of sand. The sight of a HALO resting on the short stretch of beach adjacent to the beacon overshadowed any relief at reaching their destination.

Unlike typical HALOs, which were emblazoned with the red symbols and military markings of the Global Alliance and Peacekeepers, this craft was entirely black. Nor did it have the open-center bays the standard models used for troop dispersal. Solid and enclosed, the hulking vehicle was in the style of those used for dignitaries and Caputs.

Craig was right. It's damn distinctive.

"Three o-clock," Torrance hushed in a barely audible whisper.

Sliding his eyes to the appointed location, he saw two figures standing near a tripod. One man was operating the round, head-sized device perched atop the stand. Gavin assumed it was a three-dimensional camera.

"Where are the other two?" Vinsy asked.

"We need eyes on them," the cell leader replied. They could reach the lighthouse unseen if they swung wide to reach it. But, to enter it, they would be exposed. If Echers discovered them near the lighthouse, they would also find the tunnel. Beyond their own consequence, he had to protect the hundreds of lives at the other end of the underwater passage.

The two visible agents were some seventy meters away. Nodding to the silenced 9mm in Torrance's hand, he asked, "Can you . . ."

"Not accurately at this range."

"HALO," the PK directed.

From the far side of the craft, a third Echer stepped into view.

Where's number four?

"We make for the lighthouse," Gavin suggested. "Hold to its west side. Then we'll see what we can see."

Single file, the trio pushed off the museum's wall and crept forward in the darkness. The angle of their approach shielded them from the agents. *But we can't see them either,* his instincts cautioned. By the time he reached the curved side of the beacon, his heart was drumming in his ears.

The pair of agents with the tripod had not moved from their task. Blocked by the HALO, only the shadow of the third Echer was visible. The fourth member of the fireteam was still missing.

"There's no way we're getting in the door without them seeing us," Gavin assessed in a frustrated rasp.

"From here I can take out the two with the camera," Torrance said. Even shaving twenty meters off the distance, it would take an impressive amount of skill to bring the men down with the small weapons the Packards had given them. Gavin was known as an exceptional marksman, but he doubted he'd be able to make the shot. He'd have to trust the man was not boasting.

"Still leaves three and four, wherever he is," he replied.

Gavin felt Vinsy shifting behind him.

"Tell my aunt what I did," the PK said. There was no mistaking the dark resolution in his voice.

Confined by their tight huddle, he was unable to get a firm grip on the PK to pull him back. Vinsy made a fast deliberate dash towards the HALO. Rising to his feet to chase after his friend, Gavin felt a hand restraining him.

Torrance pressed him back against the lighthouse, and said, "He made a choice. Don't waste it."

The dislike he'd felt for the man over the past months could not compare to the violent hatred now burning through his body. In his years in the resistance, he had known men who were bloodthirsty, men who perhaps even found joy in killing the enemy. But in all those years he had never met a man more cavalier about others dying for him.

He's an abomination. And she loves him, even if she doesn't know it. That the realization flashed in a moment of dire danger did not lessen its pain, or its truth. The cell leader relaxed his muscles, signaling no further resistance to Torrance's restraining hand.

"Be ready," the man said as he turned back and aimed his weapon.

Only seconds had passed since Vinsy broke away. *To die*, his thoughts added in mourning. The unsilenced firing of several rounds announced the PK's plan. Torrance's weapon coughed twice, and the two Echers in view dropped to the sand. From the parking lot of the bed and breakfast, a single particle bolt scorched the air. Vinsy's painful cry tore into the night.

Torrance shifted his stance and fired three rounds in the direction of the bolt's origin. A return volley of charged shots flew out of the darkened lot to strike the side of the lighthouse just above their heads. The sweet, rich scent of burned and burning wood was nauseating.

"Conserve your rounds," the man from the woods instructed. "Echers are overconfident. He'll come to us."

Proving the assumption true, a second wave of amber splintered the other side of the structure. The angle confirmed the remaining agent had reached the northern face of the museum.

With a forceful tug, Torrance pulled him around the lighthouse, away from the second attack. The effort was too late. Behind him, the Echer leapt forward, grabbing the front of Gavin's shirt. He swung his right arm around to aim the Beretta in his hand. The agent's forearm slashed up to block him. A bullet fired into the lake as the weapon flew from his grip. Gavin had no time to counter before a foot drove into the side of his knee, wrenching the joint into a damaging angle. The shout of pain was cut off as the Echer landed a debilitating blow to his windpipe. Unable to stand, unable to breathe, Gavin's face met the sand within a blink of the violence's onset.

His lungs' need overrode all other awareness. Gasping, his mouth filled with sand, choking him and further preventing the intake of air. A consuming flare of agony, spreading out from his ruined knee, met his attempt to stand. Digging his fingers into the sand, Gavin managed to pull himself a half meter along the beach. His teeth bit into the side of his cheek as he twisted his body over onto his back. Blood and sand mixed across his tongue into a thick clump that he both swallowed and spat in a struggling effort to breathe.

Through the all too familiar white flecks of looming unconsciousness, he saw

Torrance and the Echelon agent engaged in combat. The blond renegade had his body diagonally squared against his opponent. The Echer's arms and legs cut, kicked, and slashed in an endless series of martial skill. Even if Gavin's mind had not been in a cloud of pain and asphyxiation, he would not have been able to track the agent's fast roundhouses, uppercuts, hooks and butterfly kicks. The man's fighting style switched just as rapidly: one second Karate, then Jujitsu, followed by Krav Maga and Muay Thai.

Torrance was successful in deflecting most of the strikes; arms and legs flying to intercept the blows a quarter-second before they reached his body. More than once, the Echer managed to slip past the man's guard to force a grunt from him. The trickles of blood from lips, nose, and brow streamed together to cover much of Torrance's face in crimson. With each dizzying flurry, the agent kept him on the defensive and was driving him back.

The Echer glided over the sand as though it was ice. In quick succession, the enemy dipped low for a leg sweep, pushing up through the turn with middle roundhouse, and finishing with high kick to Torrance's head. The triple strike battered the man to the ground.

Gavin watched the agent advance on the prone figure. Showing no signs of exertion, the Echer pulled a knife from the sheath strapped to his thigh. Lungs still burning, and knee crying out at the slightest movement, Gavin stumbled to his feet. Knowing a return to the ground was eminent, he used the brief second of stability to propel his body towards the soldier. The distance between them was too great, and he only succeeded in colliding his shoulder with the Echer's calf. His punishment for interfering was quickly delivered. The agent spun ninety degrees to deliver a sharp kick to the side of his ribcage. The popping break of bones was barely felt amid the other injuries.

Curling into the fetal position, Gavin prepared for the next strike. A cloud of sand rained down as Torrance threw a fistful of the grains towards the agent's face. Cursing, the Echer squinted and shook his head to clear the temporary blindness from his eyes.

The cell leader rolled out of reach during the reprieve. His torso, already spasming with each rotation, struck something hard in the sand. From his periphery, he saw Torrance fighting his way to his feet. The blond man limped across a meter of beach to reach the agent.

Already recovering from the dirty tactic, the Echer met Torrance's approach with his knife at the ready. Holding the hilt in a reversed grip, he slashed the air to keep Torrance at bay. Favoring the previously wounded leg, the man from the woods feinted left, then lifted a high kick to the agent's outstretched wrist. Slowed by injury and exhaustion, the attack was anticipated. The agent stepped to the right and ducked beneath the kick.

Gavin reached under his body for the rock or debris that was jabbing into his spine. Fireworks of exhilaration burst in his mind as his hand found the cool metal grip of Torrance's silenced 9mm handgun. Shifting his weight to free the weapon, he swung the gun out and up. Squeezing the trigger again and again, he fired four rounds into the head and neck of the Echer. Given the ferocity of their opponent, he almost expected the agent to turn and attack. Instead, his body pitched away with the force of the bullets.

Wiping the coating of blood and sand from his face with his sleeve, Torrance shuffled over and extended an arm to him. Shaking his head, Gavin said, "Knee's dislocated."

The renegade turned away and limped over to the lighthouse. He wondered if the man might leave him behind. His fears were assuaged as he watched the other man snap two pieces of wood from the lighthouse's damaged exterior. From there, Torrance made a methodical search of the two downed agents nearby. Having collected a small cache of items, he returned to the cell leader.

"Bite this," he said as he handed Gavin a belt.

Lifting the nylon strap to his mouth, and folding it double, he slipped it between his teeth. Torrance's hands made a quick survey of the injured joint. With no warning, the man pulled and twisted. Screaming through the belt and clenched jaw, his vision turned white as his leg made a sickening pop. The intense flash of pain subsided, leaving behind a throbbing ache.

Torrance placed a strip of wood on either side of the leg. Taking a second belt, he tightened it around the limb just beneath the knee. The cell leader took the other strap from his mouth and secured it around the lower thigh himself. Repositioned and immobilized, the injury was field-treated as best it could be until they reached Pelee Island. Though he knew he should count himself lucky to have even survived a battle with an Echelon fireteam, Gavin hoped there was little nerve and tissue damage.

"Your turn," Torrance lowered himself to the sand and tossed over an emergency wound kit and finger-sized flashlight taken from the dead agents. The cell leader removed and assembled a small plastic syringe filled with alcohol. Holding the light with his mouth, he pressed the plunger to clean the gash above the man's right eye. Torrance hissed as the clear liquid flushed out the wound.

That's for the knee, jackass.

Tearing open a sterile gauze pad packet, he dabbed the cut dry, pinched the torn flesh together, and applied a thin line of accelerant. He waited a minute before taking his hand away then repeated the process on the matching split over the left eye.

Pieced back together to a survivable degree, the men helped each other to their feet. Gavin was again forced to rely on the other man's strength to help him reach the lighthouse.

Once inside, and aided by the small beam from the flashlight, they found the trapdoor at the center of the concrete floor. Torrance pulled the handle ring and lifted the door along its hinges with a cloud of dust and a squeak of old timber. Directing the light down into the opening to reveal a ten-rung metal ladder, Gavin groaned. Letting the other man descend first, he dropped the flashlight down and followed after. With only one bendable leg to support his weight, his arms bore the brunt of the effort.

A series of antiquated control panels and instrumentation encircled the lower chamber. Following the Packards' detailed instructions, Torrance located the various levers and dials needed to expose the tunnel's hidden entrance. A small panel at the bottom of one bank of panels sprung open once the last control was adjusted. The access was just wide enough for a man to crawl through on his stomach.

Maneuvering through the opening was simpler than the one-legged trip down the ladder. The outer board strapped to his leg collided with the side of the passage only once. The painful contact reverberated from ankle to hip.

With Torrance's help, he stood upright in the dark tunnel. The damp air was thick with the pungency of old, still water turned sour. Along the left wall, the flashlight found a brass sconce holding a slender torch of wood and oil-soaked cloth. Striking a match taken from a box tucked into the sconce, Torrance lit the torch.

The tunnel was narrow, just wide enough for two people to walk abreast. There was a noticeable slope downward as the passage continued beyond the red glow of the torch. The walls themselves were comprised of uniformly segmented sections of concrete and stone, and were sealed at the seams. Some seams glistened were Lake Erie had found thin and weak areas. A steady drip . . . drip . . . drip echoed from the darkness ahead.

"Not exactly an architectural wonder," he commented as Torrance manipulated the levers on the wall behind them, closing the entrance to the tunnel.

"Better than swimming," the man replied.

Even with the great distance before them, and the slow pace forced by their injuries, Gavin had to agree. He'd spent enough time underwater in the last few days.

The two men began the trek in silence. They would be crossing over forty kilometers of tunnel before reaching Pelee Island. If not for their wounds and exhaustion, they might have completed the trip in nine or ten hours. Shuffling along as they were, and requiring numerous breaks, he knew they would be lucky to arrive in twice that time. Every time they came upon a fresh torch in a sconce, they allowed themselves several moments of rest.

The Packards had provided them with light provisions: a small supply of water and pre-packaged military meals. During their fifth or sixth rest stop—he had already lost count—they admitted to their exhaustion. Torrance was barely able to hold the torch higher than his head, and Gavin's injured leg throbbed and burned with greater intensity at every step.

They set no watch after stretching out on the cold hard floor. If the enemy followed, neither man had the ability to run or defend their position. Early warning would do them no good. Seconds after he closed his eyes, Gavin fell into a heavy dreamless sleep.

When he woke, he noticed the torch in the scone had burned out. Yet there was still light in the tunnel. Disoriented, the cell leader jerked upright and was reminded of his broken ribs.

"Torrance!" he hissed when he saw long beams of light bouncing along the walls several dozen meters away.

The other man reacted much as he had expected; springing to his feet within seconds, gun ready and aimed. A trio of voices carried over the still air. Lights and voices were advancing faster than human speed.

Sliding himself to the wall for support, Gavin lifted his own weapon.

"They're coming from the island," he whispered to his companion upon realizing the direction.

Before a half-minute passed, the white lights drew close and then slowed.

"*Sic semper tyrannis,*" a voice behind the lights called out the Ignota's motto. "We were sent to find you."

"Sent by whom?" Torrance challenged.

A second voice answered, "Brother Trig sent us once Craig and Juliana Packard told him you were coming."

Both men lowered their weapons as the strangers approached. As they neared, Gavin saw the source of their speed. Three young men, none older than twenty, rode bicycles with headlights attached to the handlebars.

We're being rescued by kids on bikes, he thought in wonder.

The boys introduced themselves—Drew, Collan, and Ivan—though he forgot which name belonged to which youth. Spinning their cycles on the back wheels to reverse direction, they waited for Torrance and the cell leader to mount before pedaling the remaining kilometers of the tunnel.

Even with the additional weight of their passengers, the boys crossed the distance with incredible speed. An hour after waking, they had reached the other end of the underwater tunnel.

Would've taken us half a day on foot. Almost makes up for feeling like an idiot riding on the back of a kid's bike. Almost.

Not surprisingly, the entrance on Pelee Island was also located beneath a lighthouse. However, what he had not anticipated was the gathering waiting for them outside the beacon. Three dozen people—some still clinging to their mothers' breast, others stooped low with age—stood with expectant eyes as Gavin and Torrance were led out of the round interior of the lighthouse into the bright day.

Though largely silent, a few murmured to a neighbor.

"It's him."

"From the Darkness . . ."

"The Founder's blood has come."

". . . hidden from the world."

"The *Dagaz* has come."

He'd heard much of the "prophecy" from his brother, who had learned of it from Adirene. It was a poorly constructed set of quatrains babbling a series of signs and events that would mark the coming of the Sowilo savior, their *Dagaz*. Conveniently, the events were just vague enough, just pliable enough, to bend and affix to anyone.

As soon as the Packards had explained the truth of Pelee Island, Gavin had had a knot in his stomach. One Sowilo fawning over him was bearable. Hundreds of them at once . . . *We need to get fixed up and leave ASAP.*

While he was familiar with Sowilo adoration—it was one of the burdens of having the name McAvoy—he had never before heard any of them refer to him as the *Dagaz*. No doubt Sonje's recent antics had inspired this new bit of stupidity.

From the bicycle boys, he had learned that this Brother Trig fellow was the island's head, a sort of unelected mayor and spiritual leader. Gavin's first task would be to ensure the man understood—without any confusion or equivocation—

that he wanted no part of the Sowilo or their Truth-damned prophecy.

One of the elderly men in the crowd stepped forward and bent at the waist with a reverential bow. Once tall before age had compacted his frame, the man had brown-splotched skin that clung tight to lean muscle and bone. All hair had departed his scalp, and his face, eyebrows included, was clean-shaven.

"Our doctors will see to your injuries," the old man offered. Not waiting for a reply, the man turned and hobbled up a wooden ramp. Neither Torrance nor Gavin could manage much speed, so the old Sowilo's slow pace was welcome. The crowd merged into a column and trailed after like a parade or funeral procession. Their stares had begun to make him feel uneasy and he was relieved when their guide ushered the pair into a podcar. However, it became evident he had not escaped the faithful entirely.

During the ten minute drive to the community's hospital (which in truth was little more than an oversized clinic), they passed countless islanders standing on the sidewalks and gawking at the vehicle.

"Will Brother Trig be at the hospital?" he asked the old man. The sooner he could put a stop to the nonsense, the better.

"He should be there when we arrive," the senior replied.

The Pelee Island Medical Facility was located on the northern end of the island. Its two stories were painted in a crisp white and looked very much like a large home. Inside, Gavin and Torrance were led to neighboring rooms for examination.

With a little help from a nurse, he climbed onto his room's medi-bed and stretched out on the cold glass surface. A soft blue light filled the room as the machine performed its battery of scans and tests. The pulsing light and the medi-bed's low hum calmed and lulled him near to sleep.

"Mr. McAvoy," a man's voice brought him back to full wakefulness.

He'd not even realized the examination had ended. Sitting up, wincing at the pain in his chest, Gavin took the man's offered hand.

"I'm Dr. Alexi Fedorov," the man said. By the receding hairline and thin wrinkles around his eyes and lips, Gavin guessed him to be in his early fifties.

"Gavin McAvoy."

Smiling, the doctor replied, "Yes. I know. Your body has taken quite a bruising, Mr. McAvoy."

"Gavin's fine," he corrected. *At least he's not calling me* Dagaz. "How bad is it?"

"You were lucky. With a knee dislocation, there is almost always damage to the ligaments and tissues around the joint. The severity of the damage varies from patient to patient. In your case, both the anterior cruciate ligament, or ACL, and the posterior cruciate ligament, PCL, escaped with minor tears. I can repair them with a minimally invasive procedure.

"As for the vascular tissue, I don't see any cause for concern. Though, I would like to perform an angiogram just to be certain. Barring any complications, I'd say you're looking at full recovery in two to three weeks.

"You also have three broken ribs. The fractures are clean and not in danger of damaging any organs. We can either let the bones heal naturally, or we can inject a BGS to abbreviate the recovery time."

Gavin had had an injection of a bone growth serum a few years earlier to treat an arm he managed to break during a rooftop fall. The process itself had been painful as the serum needed to be injected into the bone marrow. The days following had also been agonizing as his body worked to repair the injury faster than his nerves could handle. As it had been explained to him then, the mild pain spread out over months of natural healing were condensed it into a week of excruciating discomfort. It was a daunting and, in his opinion, necessary price to pay for recovering in a fraction of the natural time.

"There've been some advances since then. The post-treatment pain is not as bad as it once was," Fedorov promised after Gavin told him of his last experience. "Though, yes, you can expect a period of somewhat intense discomfort."

The man's pause did little to mitigate his apprehension.

"Fine. Just do it."

Pulling the shirt over his head and down onto his wrapped chest, Gavin watched the doctor and a nurse finish attaching the brace to his knee. The local anesthetics used on both injury sites kept him from feeling much pain.

Just wait 'til they wear off, his mind teased.

"Normally, I'd prefer keeping the leg immobilized for a day or two, but given the circumstances I doubt you'd agree to that," Dr. Fedorov said after cinching the last strap.

"You'd be right," the cell leader replied with a smile. The doctor may be a Sowilo, but he'd focused on the task without any of the cult's mystic rantings. For that, Gavin was grateful.

Standing, Fedorov said, "The brace will limit the movement of the knee while bearing the impact from walking. Don't expect to run with it on, though."

He slid off the medi-bed, adding weight to the leg and testing its stability.

"Well?" the physician asked.

"Feels good."

"If you can avoid fights with Echers for a few weeks, it will continue to feel good," Fedorov warned. "In the meantime, Brother Trig has asked for you to be transported to his home for dinner."

The mention of food brought a rumble from his stomach.

"Where's Torrance?" he asked. If he was going to suffer through a meal with a Sowilo leader, he did not intend to do it alone. Hopefully, the rogue's reputation would keep Brother Trig off balance.

The doctor inclined his head, keeping his eyes on the floor, and replied, "The . . . He is waiting for you outside."

Let's hope he has the same effect on Trig, he thought as he took the bottle of painkillers from the doctor and moved out of the room.

Torrance rose from a chair in the hospital's lobby. Like him, the man had been given a set of borrowed clothes. The cuts above his eyes had been re-treated, and his face and hair had been washed free of dried blood.

"We're having dinner with this Trig guy," Gavin murmured as they walked out into the pre-dusk afternoon. Once again, a crowd had formed. This new gathering was several times larger than the vigil at the lighthouse. The cell leader clenched his jaw in frustration.

A different podcar, with a different navigator, drove them to the Sowilo's home. Set well off the road down a long, paved driveway, the farmhouse was large but modest. Pale green shutters bordered the many windows of the pastel yellow home. Similar to much of what he'd seen of the island, the architecture spoke of days long gone. He was not surprised by the date on the plaque beside the front door. 1924.

Almost two hundred and fifty years old, he calculated. In the residential technology boom at the start of the century, many homes had been rebuilt to accommodate the advances. The Sowilo's farmhouse, however, seemed to survive the global renovation trend unaltered.

A servant, a butler he assumed, greeted the two men at the door, bowed, and escorted them to the dining room. Gavin made a quick study of the interior's furnishings. Everywhere his eyes fell, he found antiques as old as the home itself.

"Welcome," a familiar voice hailed them as they stepped into the dining room. At the far end of a long table, the old man from the lighthouse rose from his seat. No longer wearing the simple pants and shirt from earlier, the hairless figure was now dressed in a knee-length coat of deep purple. The construction of the garment cinched at the waist before widening at the hip. A diagonal zipper extending from right shoulder to left knee sealed the coat. Its high stiff collar made a complete circle around the man's head so that his chin was barely visible. Leather patches capped both shoulders in a darker, almost black, shade of plum. The dye of his plain pants repeated the color.

"I see our doctors have improved your condition."

"You're Brother Trig," the cell leader said. He did not appreciate the earlier deception. "Why didn't you tell us before?"

Sincere regret frowned across the man's expression. "Forgive me. You needed medical attention, and I feared an earlier introduction would have forestalled that. Please sit. I'm told you've not eaten in quite some time."

Turning his attention to the servant, Trig said, "Please tell Ezra we are ready."

Still bothered by the gameplay, but incredibly hungry, Gavin took the seat on the host's left, while Torrance went round the table to sit at the man's right. The anesthetics were beginning to fade. With a muted grunt, he gripped both chair arms to steady himself as he lowered his body to the cushioned seat.

Trig remained standing and lifted a glass decanter of red wine. After pouring first for Torrance, then for Gavin, the old man reclined again.

"It is a blend made here on Pelee," he said with pride, inhaling the wine's bouquet. "There's white too, if you prefer. But, this is our masterpiece."

"Red's fine," the cell leader answered. If he had been in more comfortable surroundings, he'd have preferred a harder drink—bourbon ideally. Instead, he settled for the offered wine. Though in no way a sommelier, Gavin took a small sip and admitted agreement with the Sowilo's boastful claim. The island vintage was leagues beyond others he'd tasted.

As he set the glass back down, he noticed Torrance had not touched his own glass. The man sat with eyes narrowed; stare focused on Brother Trig. His body was tensed and ready to pounce should the need arise.

While he understood some of the man's wariness, he also knew there was little cause for concern. *The Sowilo may be a nuisance,* Gavin thought, *but they'd never harm a Founder's descendant.*

A stout gentleman, who he assumed to be Ezra, bearing a heavy tray of plates, entered the room and offered the three seated men an appetizer of lightly dressed greens. His hands shook as he placed the first dish, Torrance's dish, on the table. The man's nerves calmed as he served the remaining two plates. His task complete, the man exited.

Gavin lifted an eager forkful. With every bite, the crisp snap of vegetables in his mouth renewed his flagging energy. Swallowing his third taste, he decided it was time for Brother Trig to answer his questions.

"Craig and Juliana Packard said that the people on Pelee are all Sowilo."

Trig nodded, adding, "And have been for nearly a century. Three generations of believers call Pelee Island their home."

"Yet, all of you have managed to live here in secret, hidden from the rest of the Ignota, that whole time?"

Though it was brief, Gavin caught the man's eyes flash to Torrance and then back to him. "Living in secret is sometimes necessary," he replied. "It allows us to avoid persecution, to grow strong, to understand our purpose."

There was a piety in the man's voice that both calmed him and worried him. As the cell leader had learned through his brother, a devout Sowilo often became lost in his faith.

"Thank you for revealing yourself when you did," Gavin afforded the man just gratitude. He disliked the idea of such secrets among the Ignota, but he knew Trig and his followers could have kept themselves hidden.

"There are no thanks needed," the old man returned. "It has become clear that the long war against the Alliance has turned in our favor. The *Dagaz* has finally come to lead us to victory."

Brother Trig spoke with passionate sincerity.

He believes in it completely, Gavin reflected. He'd intended to be forceful, but the Sowilo's age and soft demeanor made it difficult. Forcing his words and tone to gentler degrees, the cell leader said, "Brother Trig, I am not a Sowilo. I do not believe in the *Dagaz* or their prophecy."

The sadness his words caused was clear in the old man's eyes.

"I know. But, your brother did, yes?"

"Yes."

"And he died believing it?"

"Yes."

"Died because he believed?"

"Yes. But, I'm not Jaime. And if he was here now, he'd tell you I'm not your *Dagaz*. I may be the great-grandson of a Founder, but that just means my family's been fighting the Alliance for a long time. And that's all it means. I appreciate you taking us in," he gestured to the silent Torrance across the table, "but I want no part of your religion."

"Hmm," Trig hummed as he lifted his wine glass and drained it of the red liquid. "How far back does your knowledge of your family's history extend, Gavin?"

In truth, he knew little beyond the vague details that others had told him. And that had come after his father's death. There were many nights, lonely and quiet nights, when he grew angry at his father's secrecy. Guilt always followed those emotions. *How can I be angry with the dead?*

"I know my father, Owen McAvoy, served as a Fifth while working at a news station in Cleveland where we grew up. He was discovered when I was nineteen and executed with my mother. He had one sister, Regan, who died two years before I was born. Their father, Nolan, also died before I was born. And, Seamus was my great-grandfather and a Founder."

As he spoke, he watched Torrance lower his head; on the tabletop, the man's powerful hands clenched into fists.

"And that is all you know?" Brother Trig asked.

"I've heard about some of the information my father provided the resistance."

He could tell the aged Sowilo was using the questions to lead him to some predetermined destination. "I assume you know more?" Gavin turned the conversation around.

Before the cell leader received an answer, Ezra returned to collect the salad plates. The portly fellow, sweating despite the cool temperature of the room, replaced the empty dishes with ones stacked with thick slices of roast beef smothered in aromatic brown gravy. Again, Torrance was served first.

"Meeting you today marked the fourth generation of McAvoys I have known," Brother Trig continued once the servant left. "I was a boy of sixteen when I met Seamus. He had been fighting the Alliance for over thirty years by then, and he bore the scars of those difficult decades. My own parents had joined the resistance not long after it had begun."

Raising his right hand, palm turned towards his guests, the Sowilo said, "My skin has never known a SID."

Gavin's eyes showed his surprise. He had never heard of an Ignota living in the open without a chip. Even being secluded within a community of rebels on an unimportant island, publicly living without a SID was highly dangerous. If the claim was true, the cell leader wondered if that did not explain Trig's position among the Pelee Sowilo.

Their host paused to eat a piece of the roast; gesturing with a fork for his guests to do the same. More captivated than hungry—*This man knew my entire family!*—Gavin cut into his meal during the silence. Torrance moved for the first time in minutes, taking up his own fork and knife. However, his actions seemed slow and distracted.

"Seamus was a hard man, made so by endless strife, but he was also fair and kind to those in need of his protection," Trig continued after swallowing. "It was from him that I first learned of the Sowilo."

Gavin's hand froze halfway to his mouth; the second bite of roast beef dripping gravy from the fork.

"He was . . . he was a Sowilo?" he asked in disbelief.

"In a manner of speaking, yes. As was his son, though the fervor of their faith differed greatly. Seamus believed his fellow Founders had made a mistake in separating as they did. He agreed with the need to spread the truth and recruit, but he feared a divided resistance was doomed to failure. He believed the Ignota would *need* someone to unite them once again. His son, however, was more extreme.

"Nolan was a few years older than me, and we became friends. He shared his father's hardness, but I can say that where Seamus was kind and just, Nolan was dark and vengeful." The man's gaze shifted into the empty air just past Gavin's shoulder. His face bore the look of a man recalling unhappy memories. Pulling back into the present, he said, "They shared the same brilliant blue eyes, as well. Seems all the McAvoys do."

Something itched at the back of Gavin's mind. So much information crowded together in his thoughts that he was unable to discern which of Trig's revelations had triggered the sensation.

"Your grandfather believed that not only did the Ignota *need* someone to unite them, but that Fate would send them someone. He also thought he could help nudge Fate along."

This time the old man's eyes lingered on Torrance for several long seconds. Gavin could feel unknown mysteries unraveling in his thoughts—truths he did not know existed circling his awareness.

"Shall I continue?" Brother Trig directed the question to the blond renegade, the man from the woods. "Or will you tell your own tale, *Dagaz*?"

Torrance lifted his head. His eyes turned first to the old man, and then he met the cell leader's confused stare. In that glance, when he saw the blue in his eyes, the eyes that had reminded him of his brother, Gavin understood.

"You're a McAvoy," he said.

Parting his lips, the man confirmed, "Yes."

Gavin shook his head to clear the fog of surprise, working his mind to choose one question from the many flooding into it.

"How?"

"My mother was Regan McAvoy. Your . . . our grandfather tasked her with infiltrating one of the Houses. When her true identity was discovered, she was thrown out. She died giving birth to me that same night."

A sickening prospect twisted his stomach. Pieces of the puzzle flew together to form a horrifying likelihood. First, it was Torrance's heated words delivered in the Packard's living room, words which had made little sense. Then Brother Trig's last comment . . . *"he thought he could help nudge Fate along."*

"It was him," he said with disgust catching in his throat. The image of a scarred back burned in his eyes. "Nolan McAvoy was the man that raised you. My grandfather was the one who . . ."

Torrance showed no emotion as he nodded.

"Is he . . ."

"No," the man from the woods answered. "He died in '48."

There's sadness in his voice, Gavin thought. *He mourns the death of the man who tortured him.*

Addressing their host for the first time, Torrance asked, "How did you know who I was?"

"Peter Yan contacted me two nights ago. The Peacekeeper captured in Oberlin has been searching for you. He and his companions met a woman, a Delphine

Porter I believe he said, who directed them to your home in Philadelphia. A sample of your blood was found and tested."

A fire of anger burned in the man's eyes. "Did they harm her?" he growled.

Trig shook his head. "No. Though she took her own life after she spoke with them."

"Who's Delphine Porter?" Gavin inquired.

Torrance replied, "She was, she was a friend."

The word sounded strange on the violent man's tongue.

Though dry and on land, Gavin felt as if he was once again struggling to stray afloat in unforgiving waters. For so long he had wanted to know the story of his family. Orphaned at nineteen, told impossible secrets that had destroyed what he had thought to be truth, the cell leader had been forced to settle for passing scraps of information. From them, he had built a new reality—a reality of the great McAvoys and their proud Ignota heritage. Now, once again, the truth was exposed as so many lies.

His family had not only been Founders of the resistance, but had also begun the crazed devotion to a prophesized savior. His grandfather's zealotry had led to the tortured creation of the monster seated across from him.

I'm not the descendant of heroes. I am the descendant of extremists, of torturers.

"You can see why the Sowilo often live in secret," Brother Trig said.

Gavin realized he had spoken the private horror aloud.

Enraged by the guilty legacy of his last name, he slammed his fist to the table, upturning the wine glass, and shouted, "You defend what he did? Taking a child, whipping him, beating him, turning him into . . . into a *thing* . . . a heartless savage?"

The red wine seeped and expanded across the fabric, staining the white lace of the tablecloth.

"He did what was necessary." Shockingly, the rebuttal had come from the victim himself.

"You don't even see it! You're defending a monster because he made you into one, too!"

With a soft, ancient voice, a voice holding greater command than most men could muster through shouting, the old Sowilo said, "Nolan McAvoy was a cruel man, and his actions may have been reprehensible, but they cannot be undone now. Through his cruelty, the *Dagaz* has finally come to us! Whatever wrongs were done in the past, we should rejoice for our future. With the *Dagaz* leading us, we are at the precipice of victory. The Sowilo will weep with tears of joy as word of His arrival spreads."

"The *Dagaz* is a myth created by men!"

"As are all myths, Gavin. Some are created to explain the inexplicable, while others are to inspire, and still others are made to kindle hope in the hopeless. They sustain us through the dark times with the promise of a coming dawn. A hero, sent either by the disproven gods, or by Fate, or by necessity, is needed to win a long war. Already the believers are mobilizing."

"What do you mean 'mobilizing'?" Torrance asked.

Gavin noted the alteration in Brother Trig's tone when he answered the man's question. A diminutive tone of adoration replaced the previous command.

"Hidden from the larger network of the Ignota, and thus well hidden from the Alliance, communication among the Sowilo has not suffered under the government's attacks. When I learned of your existence, *Dagaz*, I sent word to others, who will in turn tell others, and so on. Soon, every Sowilo in the world will know you have come."

"To what end?" Gavin interjected into the old man's portentous sounding response.

Timeworn eyes, filled with renewed vigor, turned to him in assessment. "To what end? The end is victory," Trig replied. Shifting his sight again to Torrance, the man said, "*Dagaz*, I am giving you an army. Faithful men and women who will give their life for yours should you ask it of them."

Though Gavin felt revulsion at the offer, Torrance was unfazed.

"How many?" the blond renegade asked. "How many Sowilo are there?"

"Our numbers are great, *Dagaz*. Over the years, we have proselytized in every corner of humanity. Certain peoples have been more receptive to our effort. They do not even know their beliefs come from the Ignota. Instead, they have adapted their pre-existing faith to include the *Dagaz* and His promise of victory."

Hearing the unspoken, Gavin said, "The Dead Continent, that's who you mean."

Nodding, Trig remarked, "Yes. Unlike the rest of the world, the Great Revelation, which was trumpeted by the Global Alliance, did not shatter the faith of the Africans. Relative to the history of mankind, it was not that long ago that their tribal beliefs adjusted to accept Christianity and Islam. Once they were cut off from the world, thrown back into divided tribes and warlords, many eagerly accepted a newer belief as part of their religion."

"And they will join the Ignota?" Torrance asked.

Offering a frown of ambiguity, the Sowilo replied, "As I said, many do not know the *Dagaz* is part of the Ignota. And despite our efforts, the DC is still fractured with warring tribes. But, it is my belief that once they learn the prophecy has been fulfilled, you can unite them."

Searching for any way to impede the progressing insanity around him, and choosing to temporarily ignore the atrocity of manipulating an entire region through religion, Gavin said, "Even Kunbo will tell you the warlords of the DC will never surrender their power. Especially not to an outsider. His own brother ordered his death because he believed Kunbo was a threat to his position."

The butler entered from the hall, approached Trig, and whispered into the old man's ear. Nodding at the hushed message, the old man turned to Torrance and asked, "With your permission, *Dagaz,* there is something I must see to."

Only after Torrance indicated his consent did the Sowilo lift himself out of the seat. With small shuffled steps, the old man exited the room.

Freed from their host's presence, Gavin said, "You can't possibly believe in this? A prophesized savior coming to lead his people to victory?"

Torrance answered with a disparaging look. "And if I did, it wouldn't matter. This people choose to believe. So, let them. If what he says is accurate, then there's a new army willing to fight the Alliance."

"With you as its general." He filled each word with accusation.

Laughing, the other man replied, "Is that what bothers you? You're worried they'll no longer look at you as the great Gavin McAvoy, blood of a Founder?"

The comment stung more than he expected. *Is there truth to that?*

"What worries me is what you would do with an army of devoted followers. You've made no secret that you only care about yourself. Would you even pause before sending them into battle? Or maybe ordering thousands of suicide bombers to attack the Alliance?"

"How long did you pause before sending Sonje into the Global Tech building? It took a second before telling the Sowilo on the supply ship who you were. You knew he'd kill himself to save you. We're not that different, McAvoy. Only, I accept the sacrifices that need to be made, while you hide from them."

Pushing back from the table, Torrance rose and limped out of the room; leaving the cell leader alone to suffer with the truth.

CHAPTER TWENTY-SIX

Danica Seton

Everyone seemed to have a purpose. A purpose that prevented everyone from paying much attention to her. At least that's how it had felt to her over the past few days.

She was relieved Dr. Nysgaard and the others had returned from the mission on Lake Erie. Gavin McAvoy and Torrance had not come back yet, but the most recent reports said the two men were hiding on some island to the north. News of the attack on Manhattan had hit her hard. Her grandparents lived in the city, and Danica did not think she could bear losing more family. She felt guilty relief when Dr. Nysgaard told her the bombing had been centered on the narrow island. The city's other boroughs—Brooklyn, Queens, Staten Island, and the Bronx—had passed that night of death and destruction unscathed. If Brooklyn survived, it was likely her grandparents had as well.

Part of her had hoped everything would return to normal, or the new normal of living underground, once the mission had been completed. Instead, events developed at a dizzying pace. On each of the last three days, Dr. Nysgaard had led the cells—*or is it one cell now?* she wondered—on guerrilla missions in nearby cities and towns. And while the missions themselves were small and relatively without risk, Danica was of course excluded from them.

"Not that I would've been much help anyway," she complained to the unconscious figure in the bed. Lately, her father had been the one person always available to listen. Still in a coma, conversations with him did little to pass the time. Even Sonje, who had been her willing confidant over the past two months, was now too busy planning and leading.

"Everyone's got a job," Danica said. "Except me."

"Looking after your dad is a pretty important job."

So used to being alone, the intrusion of another voice made her jump and squeak in surprise. Her pulse, which the shock had already quickened, beat even faster when she saw Corey Branson standing in the doorframe. The two had not spoken since before the lake mission.

"Sorry," he said, running a hand over the brown stubble of his shaved head. "I didn't mean to scare you. Can I, um, come in?"

"Yeah, sure," she replied as she tried to make nonchalant adjustments to her appearance. Clothed in loosing fitting cotton pants and shirt, there was not much she could fix.

Taking the empty chair and turning it so that he sat with his arms folded over the back, he worked through another apology. "I'm sorry I haven't come around a lot. It's just been, you know, really busy and all. Sonje's got us working pretty hard."

"It's okay," Danica said. It wasn't. She was still angry at his brusqueness at their last meeting, and his absence since. But, it was a challenge to hold on to anger when she could smell his crisp clean scent.

"No, it's not, but thanks." His smile made her stop trying to be mad. "I was kind of a jerk the last time we talked. So, I guess I'm sorry for that, too."

Laughing, she told him, "Yeah, you were. But, there was a lot going on, so I understand." Hoping to absolve any guilt he might have, she changed the topic to one where no apologies were required. "How come you're not getting ready for a mission?"

"They're all closed up in the conference room. I think it has something to do with Gavin and Torrance."

Though she had been keeping to herself, the whispers and murmurs of the last twenty-four hours or so had been impossible to miss. Most of it she did not understand. Something about a *dah-gahs* and a prophecy. From the tone of those behind the whispering, it was clear few were pleased with either one. Only Peter Yan, one of the cell leaders, expressed a noticeable measure of joy.

He had come to her father's room last night; asking all sorts of questions about Torrance. What she knew of his home. His past. Every word or movement she had heard or seen him make. Some of her answers made Yan mutter what sounded like poetry under his breath. Only once she had told and retold every detail did he leave.

"The prophecy?" she inquired, bringing her thoughts back to the boy seated by her.

Seeming surprised with her knowledge, he said. "I didn't know you heard about that."

Danica shrugged, "People kind of forget I'm around and I hear them talking about it. I didn't mean it like that," she added upon seeing Corey's pained face. She had not intended the comment as an accusation. "Maybe 'forget' isn't the right word. I'm not really part of the Ignota. And I pretty much keep to myself. So, I guess it's more like they 'overlook' me being around."

Corey smiled again, wider this time. "That's the first skill a scout needs to master—how to be overlooked, not noticed."

"It doesn't feel like being a scout," she added with a laugh.

"If you'd like," he replied, "I could teach you. You know, show you a few tricks and stuff."

Blushing, and hating herself for it, she said, "I'd like that."

Truth, he could offer to teach me to skin cats, and I'd say yes. Her nose scrunched with the unpleasant thought. *Well, maybe not cats.*

"Why the face?" he asked.

Please don't say cats, her conscience cautioned.

"I was thinking about, the, um, the prophecy." *Okay, good recovery.*

Now it was Corey whose face displayed disgust.

"Don't waste your time thinking about that," he told her. "It's just some made up bullshit for crazy people. One of those crazy people killed Ol'Ben, and tried to kill Sonje."

When Danica had located Dr. Nysgaard in Washington, the woman was a bruised and bloody mess. Only later did the girl learn the attacker had been a member of the cell.

"And they believe Torrance is a . . . dahgahs?"

"The *Dagaz*," he corrected. "And yes. Well, at least Peter does. Apparently there are some more Sowilo on Pelee Island who do too."

The scout's mood soured at her mention of the man. The bruising around his eye may have faded, but his anger and wounded pride had not diminished.

"I know it sounds crazy," she confessed, "but Marcus says Torrance is important. Like really important."

She had not told anyone about the conversation between her and her brother. Not only had there been little opportunity to share it with anyone, Danica had also worried what others might think of the boy's bizarre *insights*. She had taken to calling them *insights* because *premonitions* and *predictions* sounded too much like prophecy. Given the mood in the shelter, she did not want Marcus associated with that.

"I may not like the guy," Corey replied in understatement, "but he did save your lives. So, it's not a shock that your brother looks up to him."

Danica bit her lip as she wondered how much of her concerns she should share with the scout. After days of solitude, not all of which had been of her choosing, she decided to trust him.

"It's more than just that. I thought it was just idolizing a hero at first. But now, I don't know. Marcus is acting different. It's not that he *believes* Torrance is important. It's like he *knows* he is. Like he has some sixth sense about it. When we were captured by the PKs, when it looked like Torrance had betrayed us, Marcus was totally calm. He said he knew Torrance would save us. And he was right."

Corey looked troubled, and she regretted her words.

"Are you saying he's psychic or something?"

"I asked him that and he said no. That it's just something he feels, like instinct."

"There are Sowilo down here. Peter Yan is one. Could be your brother's just heard a lot of their talk."

She appreciated his efforts to rationalize rather than judge. She had not considered the possibility that Marcus had been influenced by those who believed in the prophecy. It was a valid point except there'd been no Sowilo in the prison cell at the military base.

"What do you believe?" Corey asked the inevitable question she had been dreading.

Struggling with an answer she had not yet formed for herself, she replied, "I don't know. He's my brother. He's all I have left. And he seems so sure. What am I supposed to say? That I think he's crazy?"

"Do you, Dani?" Marcus asked as he walked into the room.

His sudden appearance brought looks of conspiratorial guilt to the older pair's faces. Dressed in a pair of dark blue denim and a heavy gray sweater with wide cuffs, his sandy brown hair tousled, Marcus looked much like any other thirteen year-old. The only difference from his peers was the unnatural calm of his face and the sharp understanding in his eyes.

Unfolding her legs from beneath her, Danica leaned forward in her chair. "Marcus, we were just—"

"It's okay if you do," her brother said. He took slow deliberate steps to the end of their father's bed, placing his hands on the cot's foot rail. "I'd probably think so too if I was you."

"No one thinks you're crazy, little man," Corey offered. "Your sister's just worried about you."

The boy's eyes shifted to the scout. His head tilted like a dog hearing a whistle. Danica could feel her brother weighing the scout, assessing him, comparing him to some unknown standard.

"She does not have to worry about me."

Corey continued, "Well, some of the things you've been saying—"

"Were private," Marcus interjected. He turned his gaze to his sister. She saw feelings of pained betrayal in the stare. And it chilled her.

Speaking quickly to prevent the scout from further agitating the moment, she asked, "Are you here to see Dad?"

The question should not have been necessary, but her brother had been an infrequent visitor to their father's bedside.

"Yes," he answered and looked to the bed with a small smile. "I wanted to be here when he wakes up."

Danica squinted in confusion at the hint of . . . of something in his voice. *He said when, not if.*

She spun out of the chair and jumped to the bed.

"Dad!" she cried.

Philip Seton was blinking as his eyes adjusted to the light. A dry tongue moved across even drier lips. With a weak voice, strained from disuse, he said, "Dani."

"Dad, it's me! Marcus is here, too."

The patriarch's mouth cracked into a thin smile. He lifted his ruined hand to wipe the tears from his daughter's cheek. "Shh. Don't cry, honey. I'm okay," he rasped.

Danica placed her hands over his bandaged hand and held it to her face. Though she had been sitting by his side every day for the past two months, he had only now returned to her. Now that he was awake, her mind admitted how fearful she had been that he would never again say her name. Her heart expanded with immeasurable relief.

"I'll get Sonje," Corey said, heading to the door.

"Corey," she called after him. "Don't tell her about . . ." Letting the words trail off, she cast her eyes to her brother who had not moved from the foot of the bed. The scout followed her gaze, and then nodded before finding the doctor.

"Sonje's here?" her father asked.

"Yes." Unsure what to do until Dr. Nysgaard arrived, and fearful he might overexert himself, Danica repeated what she had heard in holofilms. "Don't try to talk. Save your strength, Dad."

"He is fine," Marcus said. He may have shared his words as comfort, yet to her the remark brought more ominous attention to his foresight.

Not now, a guiding voice told her. *Focus on Dad.*

"Dr. Nysgaard will be here in a minute," she told him. "She's been looking after you. She promised me you'd wake up. Everything's going to be okay now, Dad."

After the first mention of the doctor's name, Philip had become anxious and unsettled.

"I have to tell her," he mumbled as he strained to sit up.

"Dad, please stay still. She's coming."

Corey must have run with all his speed, and brought the woman back with him just as fast. Dr. Nysgaard entered the room in a rush; her hands finishing the work of pulling her hair into a ponytail. From a small table by the door, she grabbed a stethoscope. Without apology, she pushed past Danica to reach her patient.

"Philip, it's Sonje Nysgaard. Do you remember me?" she asked while shining a penlight into his left, then right eye.

"Yes," her father croaked. "Sonje, I know what—"

"Can you tell me your children's names?"

Frustrated but too debilitated to express it, Philip used his good hand to grab ahold of the woman's wrist. The clear tube of his IV pulled free of the catheter in his arm.

Straining to be heard, he said, "Sonje, I know what . . . the SIDs are for! They're going to cull the population."

For the better part of an hour, a congestion of bodies had overtaken what little space her father's room offered. The leaders of the other five cells, as well as Match Quentin, the African Kunbo Fofana, two medics from different cells, and the Peacekeeper, reporter, and drone had all responded to Dr. Nysgaard's summons. As each figure arrived, the Seton siblings, and Corey, were pushed closer and closer together until the three had little room to breathe at the head of the bed. Danica might have welcomed the forced closeness to the scout had her focus not been consumed with concern for her father.

His voice had gained some strength once Dr. Nysgaard removed the feeding tube from his nose. Though still thin and pale, her father looked less fragile now that he was propped up in the cot. Danica was worried the endless questions from those gathered in the room were too much for him to handle so soon after waking. However, each time she had suggested the Ignota allow him to rest, Philip protested and said he was fine.

Danica knew part of her protective feelings were selfish. No one, not even Dr. Nysgaard and her medical ministrations, had spent more time caring for and looking after the man. She had eaten nearly every meal at his side, spent nearly every night sleeping in the chair next to his bed. *She* was the one who had shaved the stubble from his face twice a week. *She* was the one who had changed the bags filled with urine and feces. *She* was the one who had stretched and flexed his legs and arms to prevent atrophy. For weeks, it had been her and her alone. And now that he was awake, everyone had swooped in to claim him for themselves.

They need to know what he knows, the rational pieces of her mind told her. *I know,* she responded. *But, that doesn't make it any easier.*

"And you're certain it was Alexavier Cambrie?" one of the cell leaders asked. The oldest of the fugitives, she only knew him as Marshall. Whether that was his first or last name, she could not say with certainty.

Philip nodded.

"Yes. It was a day or two after they arrested me. After they did this," he said, raising his crippled hand. "He came into the room during an interrogation."

Even though she was sure her father had minimized the extent of his torture, the few details he did share had brought tears to her eyes.

"I was drugged and barely conscious, but I knew his face."

"You didn't recognize who was with the Caput?" Sam Borden asked.

"No. From the way they talked, I'd say he was subordinate to the Caput. An advisor, I think. I might be able to identify him if I saw him again."

"And that's when you heard about the culling?" Dr. Nysgaard had asked very few questions during the interview.

Sounding tired, he replied, "Again, I was heavily sedated from the interrogation—which is probably why they talked so openly in front of me. They kept asking me what exactly I knew about the flaw in the SID upgrade. The other interrogators only wanted to know how I detected the defect, who else knew, where the children were. But, Cambrie's questions were all about the SID itself. I don't know how many times I told them I didn't know what specifically was defective before they stopped . . .," Danica saw him look at her in the pause, ". . . questioning me."

Repeating the most crucial aspect of his debrief, her father continued, "That's when they agreed I wasn't a threat, but still needed to find the holocard to prevent anyone else from digging deeper. Cambrie said he was worried about the Council being exposed before the implantations were finished.

"The advisor told him they were only weeks away from implanting the upgrade globally. After that, the Council could speed up the Culling, or if they *were* exposed, do it all at once. Cambrie said that would lead to open revolt, as well as a health crisis with over eleven billion bodies rotting as the 'select' struggled to burn and bury them."

Though it was the third time her father had shared it with the room, a moment of uneasy, disbelieving silence followed the conclusion of his story.

Peter Yan, who had questioned Danica the night before, said, "Can it be true? I mean, could the Council really intend to kill billions of people?"

"They just killed two million plus in Manhattan," the gruff old cell leader reminded them.

"But *billions*?" Yan returned, stressing the word. "And why? What would be the point?"

"I might be able to answer that."

The drone's oddly human voice was made even more unsettling by its lack of a discernible mouth. Danica had caught a fleeting glimpse of the machine just after its capture. The fluidity of its movements, despite its bulk and metallic construction, had amazed her. Over the last two days, the drone, and the man and woman taken with it, had attained a higher level of trust from the Ignota. Her mind, however, held too many fresh memories—her mother's murder, her own capture, her father's rescue—to consider trusting a government super soldier.

"Godwin," the human PK attempted to quiet his partner.

"Let him talk," Sonje interjected with unequivocal authority.

The man nodded for the drone to proceed.

"Thank you, Dr. Nysgaard. Regarding Mr. Yan's question, there have been many studies—most conducted during the twentieth century—which suggest a critical point in time when the planet cannot sustain humanity's population growth. Beyond simple overcrowding, the studies focused on food and water shortages, environmental pollution, and poverty.

"While those studies are relatively recent, the concept of population control is far older. The philosopher Aristotle, born some twenty-five hundred years ago, advised abortion and exposure of infants should a populace grow too large to sustain.

"Throughout history, many cultures have been known to kill infants born with defects in order to ensure that the limited resources were available to the strongest. Others believed a large population was directly linked to increases in crime.

"More recently, societies have advocated the use of contraception and abstinence. Though the latter was encouraged for mostly religious reasons, the result is the same.

"In the late eighteenth century, Thomas Malthus, a learned man and Church of England clergyman, believed war, famine, disease, and natural disasters were 'positive checks' on society's overpopulation. A hundred years later, an American biologist advocated involuntary, government-regulated sterilization through water and food contamination. He equated humanity's population growth to a cancer needing to be stopped."

"And you think that's what the Alliance is doing? Controlling population growth?" Dr. Nysgaard asked the drone.

Danica watched the woman and machine interact from her small space near her father. She was not alone in her scrutiny; everyone seemed to be captivated.

Though she was shorter and far leaner than the drone, Dr. Nysgaard did not seem inferior. In fact, Danica thought the woman cast an aura of greater strength than the machine. *Truth, I'd be cringing if everyone was watching me like that!* As much as she had complained to Corey about feeling unnoticed, she knew it was preferable to the alternative.

"It is possible. History is also filled with conspiracy theories proposing such things. Groups real and fictional have been accused of working towards what was known as the New World Order. The Illuminati, the Freemasons, the Council on

Foreign Relations, the Templar Knights, and endless secret societies have all been victims of these conspiracy theories. One of the alleged tenets of the New World Order was maintaining a population in balance with nature."

"Maintaining balance? You make it sound almost noble," the Nordic doctor sneered.

The drone shook his head as he replied, *"To them it is. Understand, Doctor, I am not advocating such methods. But, most of those who have advocated for population control in the past—whether forced or natural—have done so believing themselves benevolent. They see it is a necessary step in the preservation of mankind. Admittedly, there have been other individuals with a less benign reasoning."*

Dr. Nysgaard's eyes narrowed. "Which was?"

"Simply put: control. A smaller population is easier to control."

"That sounds more like the Alliance," Marshall said in his usual shout. Danica could see the veteran disliked agreeing with the drone.

"And it explains the extreme security measures protecting the SIDs," the shorthaired Sam Borden commented. "As well as the extreme response to our attack on the SIDs."

"Attack?" Philip asked with obvious confusion. Danica realized no one had yet told him how much the world had changed during his months of sleep. His face had registered significant shock just learning he was hidden away with several dozen members of the Cohors Ignota.

With a physician's voice for breaking bad news, Dr. Nysgaard detailed some of the events that had led to their current situation. From the infiltration of the Global Tech building, to the rescue at Ft. Rotterdam, to the more recent Lake Erie and New York City bombings, the woman provided a stunning overview. Philip Seton's eyes widened with each revelation.

His mouth hung agape for several seconds before saying to his former colleague, "This is all because of us?"

"Hell no!" Marshall exclaimed. "This was started by them. And it will be finished by us!"

Her father flinched at the volume of the Ignota leader's declaration. Everyone else, even the Peacekeeper and reporter, had grown accustomed to Marshal's bellowing.

"Philip," Dr. Nysgaard said, "as impossible as it sounds, you've woken up to a war. I felt all the confusion, the shock, and the guilt you're feeling now. I still feel it. But if you're right, the Alliance is going to use the SIDs to . . . . You and I worked on the chips. We need to stop them."

Danica watched as indecision and fear, obligation and paternal instinct, fought in her father's tired eyes. *He just woke up!* she thought. *Why can't you leave him be?* A part of her, a foolish and naïve hope, had believed that once their father stirred from his coma, her family's role in the crisis would be at an end.

Snuffing out that dim flicker, her father said, "Okay."

"Okay," Dr. Nysgaard repeated with a soft smile. "There's an island to the north that can offer us better protection. We had just agreed to relocate there when Corey came to get me. Now that you're awake, transporting you will be easier."

"Happy to help," Philip replied. His attempt at laughter brought forth a short coughing spasm. Danica offered him a glass of tepid water to calm the fit. "Thank you, honey," he smiled and said after catching his breath.

Dr. Nysgaard checked her patient's vitals once again, and then turned to address the Ignota. "Match, send a message to Pelee and this Brother Trig. Tell him to have the ferry ready to pick us up in Sandusky at eight tomorrow morning."

Danica ignored the buzz as everyone filed out of the room to prepare for their exodus. In that moment, all she needed was her father. Once more, her life was being uprooted. Familiarity was again being left behind. And the future was still a shadowed unknown. Only now, he was awake to help her face it. She knew all the worries would return. But in that moment, in those fleeting minutes she wished would never end, she thought together they just might be strong enough to face them.

CHAPTER TWENTY-SEVEN

Aubrey Garrott Hu

Perhaps it was a further streak of his cruelty. Perhaps it was some sick pride. Or perhaps he was so detached from the horror that he did not even understand. Whichever, Aubrey found herself absorbed with the holoset. The device, delivered to her chambers the morning after the Manhattan bombing, was the newest privilege her captor had bestowed upon her. In the days that had followed, she had watched hours of news coverage. Only select images had been allowed to air, mostly aerial footage of the devastation. Distant enough for weaker stomachs, but near enough to see what destruction the hands of the Alliance had wrought. Despite the strength she wished to project, she could not stem the steady stream of tears.

Pressing a wet tissue to her puffy reddened eyes, Aubrey again mumbled, "Three million."

The number was conservative. In truth, another half million or more had been killed in the attack.

The analysts and pundits, all in the employ of the Alliance, followed well-developed talking points. The military spokespeople rehashed the strategic importance of eliminating a "hotbed of terrorist activity." Retired General Logan McAllister and others made the rounds of the morning shows and the evening news programs.

McAllister was highly decorated and highly favored by the Council. Fiercely loyal, the old veteran never questioned the words his superiors ordered him to say. Aubrey had met him several times and found him to be a sycophantic dog. Then, she had understood his purpose. Now, his obvious lies sickened her.

"Holoset off," she ordered. The three dimensional image disappeared at the command.

Rising from the black velvet divan, Aubrey gathered a handful of fallen tissues and deposited them in the wastebasket beside the vanity table. Despite the room's heat, she pulled the fabric of her heavy robe closer to her body, and walked over to the windows of the far wall. Her breath fogged the glass pane as she stared out into the gardens.

The snow had begun just before yesterday's sunset. It'd been heavy at first, but had subsided to a soft flurry. A white blanket coated the grounds and walkways. As a child, she had always loved the stillness of a winter storm. Snow seemed to soften the world; envelop it in an echoless beauty. Her mood today, however, only allowed her to feel its cold as she watched the flakes float down.

Compounding the empty heartache carved out by the deaths of millions, Aubrey felt an oppressive melancholy for her own predicament. Seeing the power and brutality of the Council—how quick the four men had been to exact their ruthless, disproportionate response—had her questioning the chances for overcoming her imprisonment.

I'm one person. A powerless prisoner, she rued in silent thought. *Those men can destroy cities with one word. They have armies. Spies. Weapons.*

Liam Walford, of course, as well as her mother, would chide her for such defeatist thinking. The Chief Advisor would quote some arcane text, share some parable of one man overcoming many. Caput`e Roslyn Garrott would have smiled while reminding her daughter that though weapons were powerful, they were conceived first in the mind. "Cleverness and cunning are the most powerful weapons," she would have said.

"And then given me a slap," she added to the empty room. "I'm wallowing, and I know it." Essentially, her frustration was frustrating.

Knowing the servant was waiting just outside her chambers, she summoned the woman.

Li-hua entered and shuffled over to her mistress. Aubrey had ordered the woman to wear western clothing, but she still walked as one encumbered by a kimono.

"Yes, *Dianxia?*"

Having called for her as a distraction, Aubrey paused to create an excuse.

"I wish to have a lesson," she informed her new chief assistant. Since the bombing, the Caput`e of House Hu had kept to herself; only interacting with the staff out of necessity for food and wardrobe.

"Of course, *Dianxia,*" the little woman replied with a reverent bow. "A lesson on what?"

Gesturing for Li-hua to follow her and sit in the leather chairs by the hearth, Aubrey said, "I've noticed preparations have begun for the Spring Festival."

It seemed an odd timing for the event given the snow on the ground.

"Yes, *Dianxia.* The New Year's celebrations are two weeks away."

Despite global unification, and the adoption of the standard calendar, the Chinese continued to celebrate their ancient traditions. As a child, her Father had taken the Family east to witness the first day of the merriment. As it was a state visit, she had only seen the parades and displays organized for the previous Chinese Caput. The louder, more inebriated entertainments of the lower classes had been far beyond her view within the palace known as The Forbidden City. Still, the colors and costumes, the fireworks and puppetry, had mesmerized her.

"I assume my husband and I have some role in the ceremonies?" She added a slight emphasis on the word *husband.*

Shaking her head, Li-hua answered, "The Caput prefers to remain here. He has not attended the celebrations at *Zijin Cheng,* the Forbidden City, since succeeding his Father."

Of course not, she thought. *Easier to order the people dead if you don't have to see them!*

"Then, what activities are held here?"

"There is a great feast on the first day. The servants and the Family dine together in the Great Hall. The Caput gives us gifts to mark the occasion."

"I see. Many years ago, I attended the start of the New Year. Someone then told me that the festival is because of some mythical monster. *Nuon*?"

"*Nián shòu.* The old stories say it was a horrible monster that would steal and kill children. Every spring the villagers would tremble as they waited for the *nián shòu* to come again. One year the villagers' shaman, or *xi☐n,* told them how to frighten away the beast. When it came, they banged pots and drums and lit fireworks to scare it. Others waved red robes. It is said the *nián shòu* was driven from the village and never returned again."

"Until now," she murmured. In her mind, Aubrey had given the monster Hu's face. Even her distraction reminded her of the evil the Council had called down.

"*Dianxia?*"

Standing, the Caput'e said, "I've suddenly grown tired, Li-hua. Thank you, but we'll continue the lesson another time."

Dismissed, the Asian woman retreated from the room.

Aubrey idled the remainder of the day in solitude. She passed several hours watching the holoset. The coverage of Lake Erie and Manhattan was decreasing. No doubt the Council had ordered a return to "normalcy." Other times, she paced the length of her chambers as she sought answers. When her dinner arrived, she ate because her body required it, not because she had any real appetite.

Near midnight, Aubrey slipped beneath the blankets and satin sheets of her bed. She fought her mind for some time before winning sleep.

The difference was subtle. A waft of chilled air slipped over the skin of her shoulder, bare save for the thin silk strap of the nightgown. It was that breath of a breeze that had woken her. Frustrated to rouse after struggling so hard for slumber, Aubrey curled her arm around the down pillow; plumping it against her cheek. Then, she felt it.

Her spine tingled with the sense of being watched. Just as one can enter a familiar room and *feel* something out of place—a picture askew, a chair misaligned—she knew someone was in the room with her.

She kept her breath in the even shallow rhythm of sleep. Turned on her side, her view of the dark chamber was limited. Aubrey scanned her memory for anything nearby she could use as a weapon. Other than the small figurines arranged on the bed stand, there was little available for defense.

Perhaps it is Li-hua, she thought while straining to hear any sound of movement. She knew it was unlikely that the timid servant would be skulking about her mistress' chambers in the middle of the night. *An assassin then?* If her husband wanted her dead, he would not need to send a killer cloaked in shadows. *One of the other Houses?* Hu had said the other Caputs had been against sparing her life.

She wondered if the guards outside the chambers would arrive in time if she called out for them.

"You think I am a *nián shòu*?" hushed a familiar voice.

Cursing at whatever game Hu was playing, Aubrey slid along the satin sheets and reached for the lamp beside the bed.

"No lights, please," her husband whispered. "Even here, I cannot be sure who watches."

She debated before acquiescing to the request. "How did you get in?" the Caput`e demanded. If the man was worried about unwanted eyes, he would not have used the main door.

"There are passages," he replied in his unsettling hiss.

Eyes adjusting to the night, and following the sound of his voice, she placed him a few meters to the right of the bed's end. "What do you want?" Aubrey asked. She was surprised to find herself whispering. *Why is he hiding in his own home?*

"I've been watching you the past few days," he admitted with no trace of shame.

"Only the past few days?" she shot back. She assumed she had been under constant surveillance since arriving at the Summer Palace.

"True. Then, let me say I've been watching with heightened interest as of late. You have mourned the deaths in the West a great deal." He spoke the last as though it was a question.

"That is what one does when one witnesses the murder of innocents."

"Unless that *one* is a ranking member of a Family," the invisible Caput retorted.

"Not every Family is as comfortable with murder as you," she answered with open contempt.

From the darkness came amused laughter. "If only that were true. Tell me, Aubrey, if there was a truth so horrible, so unsettling it might bring you to despise all those you love, would you wish to know it? Would you wish for that truth to be revealed? Or would you prefer ignorance?"

There was bleak gravity in his tone. *What game is he playing?* she wondered. *Is this some test of my loyalty? My submission?*

Seeking to stall, she replied with a Shakespearian quote, "'There is no darkness but ignorance.'"

Hu met her response with flat laughter. "Fitting, but not an answer," he called her on the stalling tactic.

"If such a truth existed," Aubrey began, trying to determine Hu's goals, "then yes, I would wish to know it."

For a long moment neither spoke. The stillness grew thick and pressed against her mind. *Has he left?*

"Then I will show it to you."

Aubrey jumped at the voice. No longer wrapped in the shadows of the corner,

Hu had moved to the side of the bed. Near enough to see his distinct outline, and the hand he had extended to her, she pulled the covers off with a soft rustle of fabric. Standing, she ignored his hand.

"The path is concealed and I cannot risk a light," he explained. "I do not want you to stumble."

She placed her hand in his. Warm and strong, she recalled how it had felt cupping her breasts during their one night together. Her face flushed with unwanted warmth. Pushing the memory aside, she allowed him to lead her across the room towards the fireless hearth. Hu blocked her limited night vision with his body as his free hand moved about the right side of the mantel. A breeze of cool air followed a tiny click. When the crisp flat wood floor beneath her feet became rough and cold—*concrete*, she assumed—it was clear they had entered the hidden passage.

Why let me know of the passages? she questioned as he led her along a narrow hall. *Does he think I am defeated and won't try to escape? Or can they only be accessed by him?* There was another possibility that chilled her even more than the air and floor. *Will I not live long enough to use them?*

The passage narrowed even further, forcing the pair to walk sideways in a single file. Wishing she had donned her robe before leaving, her skin pricked and tightened from the cold.

They turned left once, then again, and then right through the hidden access. While she was not familiar with the layout of the palace, she was certain they were moving inside the walls between rooms.

"We are going down a stairwell," Hu spoke for the first time since drawing her out of the bed. "It is spiral. Place your right hand against the center to balance yourself. There are fifty-seven steps."

Is that how he moves without aid? He memorized the route?

As the passage was impossibly black, she could only trust in his directions. Her feet met the edge of the first step. She let one foot drop through the air until it reached the next platform. The space between the steps was not steep. With one hand sliding along the hard stone wall, Aubrey descended in a tight circle. At a landing she could not see, Hu helped her across another few meters before opening a doorway into a well-lit room.

A glass-topped holotable, perhaps ten or eleven meters long and half as wide, dominated the rectangular room. Six leather chairs lined each length of the table, and a thirteenth sat at the head. At the opposite end, a massive glass panel covered the far wall. Smaller panels hung along the sides of the room in polished wood frames. A Caput's daughter, she recognized the space as a combat information center.

"Are you going to make me watch another massacre?" she asked.

Hu's face looked saddened by the remark. "Just the opposite," he said. "Please sit."

Though days earlier he had ordered the death of millions, the Caput showed gentility as he pulled out the seat for her. Lowering herself into the comfortable leather, Aubrey let the room's warmth alleviate much of her chill. Still, she wished she was wearing more than the thin silk nightclothes.

Hu took the head seat at her right.

"When I asked what you knew about the Culling," he said in a normal tone, "you denied any knowledge of it.'

"Which is still true," she answered.

Nodding, he continued, "I believe you, Aubrey. However, it still comes as a surprise that one who was considered to be the next Chief Advisor of House Garrott would be unaware of it."

The list of those who knew her Father and brother had planned on her succeeding Liam Walford was short. Yin Xian Hu should not have been part of that small number.

"And what is the Culling?" she asked.

Narrowing his eyes in indecision, Hu's lower lip pulled into his mouth and under his teeth. With a deep sigh, he said, "It is the reason the Houses exist. It is the reason the Alliance and the Council exist. It is a plan conceived over two millennia ago. It is . . . global massacre."

In another setting, with a different bard, Aubrey might have leveled an accusation of melodrama. But everything about Hu, from the worry in his eyes to the pinched furrow in his usually expressionless face, indicated there was no hyperbole in the statement.

"Show her," the Caput ordered when she did not respond.

An endless array of images appeared on the panel. Plaster busts, marble effigies, and oil paintings covered the screen—the same man depicted in each. Close-cropped hair, just long enough to show the hint of curls, fell atop a strong brow. Hard, angular lines formed cheeks and jaw, with a proud nose at the center of the face. In several of the depictions, the figure wore a breastplate emblazoned with a lion. A thin band of woven leaves and branches rested upon his head.

Many of the works featured on the screen had been part of her Father's personal collection. The Family's Chief Advisor had lectured on the ancient man's accomplishments.

"You recognize him?"

Nodding, Aubrey said, "Julius Caesar."

"Yes," her husband confirmed. "Assassinated a few decades before the start of the common era. Do you know why?"

An excellent student in her youth, she replied, "The Roman Senate feared Caesar was growing too powerful. And in doing so, their own power was being limited and reduced."

On the screen, a rich painting recounted the ruler's final moments. A red-robed Caesar, down on one knee in mid-fall, was surrounded by his betrayers. The men of the Senate held knives aimed at his body.

"So history tells us," Hu narrated. The skepticism in his voice was evident. "In truth, the Senate had learned of Caesar's true plans. For the Senate, his efforts to consolidate power were not nearly as egregious as his belief in *populi angustus*, a limited populace. A skilled general, Caesar had expanded the borders of the empire through many great conquests. But in his wake millions were killed."

Paintings of ancient armies and wars and burning cities flashed across the screen.

"For him, conquered land meant resources which would provide his subjects bountiful lives. However, he knew those resources were finite. In order for all to live richly, the population must be checked at certain levels. When the Senate discovered his intentions, they conspired to kill him."

Aubrey had never heard of the alternate history Hu had laid out.

"If that is true," she voiced the question, "how is it that no one knows this story?"

"Because Caesar's plans, and his acolytes, did not die with him. Those who came after, those who rose in power and influence, hid the truth. Caesar's fall had shown the weakness in precipitous overreach. They understood their goals could not be achieved in the span of one lifetime. Or even several lifetimes. So, they waited.

"As knowledge of the world's size and the resources it offered grew, it was decided that the doctrine of *populi angustus* could be forestalled. Calculations of how great the population could become were made in secret. Yet all the while, those who believed in the doctrine expanded their influence on world events. In time, there was a global government working in the shadows. Among them were kings and queens, popes and sultans, and eventually presidents and prime ministers. They called themselves 'Caesareans.'"

"As in Cesarean section?" Aubrey asked.

Smiling, he replied, "Many believe, incorrectly mind you, that Caesar was born through that procedure and thus gave birth to the term."

The screen showed the surgery across vast stretches of time: from the cave paintings of long forgotten people to the modern operating rooms of the twenty-second century

"And that is not true?"

"No. For obvious reasons, women who gave birth via surgical means in the ancient world never survived. Yet, Caesar's mother lived long enough to become his advisor in his adulthood; making the tale impossible.

"The term can, however, be traced to a Roman law, *Lex Caesarean*, which translates to 'imperial law.' At the time, it was believed sacrilegious to bury a pregnant woman. The law called for an infant to be cut from his dying or dead mother's womb.

"Further evidence suggests the term is actually derived from the Latin verb, *caedere*."

"*Caedere*," Aubrey repeated.

"'To cut.' Today, in other cultures, the procedure is translated as 'the emperor's cut,' or 'imperial cut'."

"Just as the swastika was once a symbol of good before the Nazis adopted it, 'caesarean' found its way into the modern lexicon with an altogether different meaning. For the Caesareans, the followers of *populi angustus*, it is the doctrine of cutting life to save life."

"The Culling," the daughter of House Garrott murmured.

"Exactly. Which brings us back to more recent history. While most Caesareans bid their time until the Culling was absolutely necessary, others sought to force it. Like Caesar himself, their efforts failed. Some spread plagues, others relied on war. A German in the first half of the twentieth century nearly succeeded."

The face of Adolph Hitler grew large at the end of the room.

"Supported by the leaders of certain industries, and some evidence suggests the Roman Catholic Church, the Fürher came frighteningly close to achieving Caesar's dream. In the end, Western powers realized Hitler's mental instability. Coupled with their own jealousies, the Allies aligned and ended his conquest.

"But once again, lessons were learned. Caesar and Hitler's fall proved that one man could never enact *populi angustus*. Knowing the population was nearing its allegedly climatic size, the Allied leaders leveraged the world's fears into the creation of the United Nations. A coalition of world nations ostensibly charged with maintaining global order."

"But they were really working towards *populi angustus*," Aubrey said. The lack of doubt in her voice surprised her. Too much of what Hu said synced with her understanding of global politics.

"Yes," the Caput replied. "And from there events sped rapidly. NATO, the World Bank, the World Health Organization, the European Union, the African Union, the Western Alliance, and then the Global Alliance. Less than one hundred years after Hitler's defeat, the world was governed by a united, totalitarian power.

"And unlike Hitler, and Caesar before him, the Alliance had a new means to enact their secret doctrine. They did not need war or plague to reduce the population. They had a tool which could be more exact. They could cull selectively; spare those individuals they determined to be beneficial to the continuation of humanity, while excising those they viewed undesirable."

Clarity burst in her mind. Even before the glass panel called up the image, she said, "The SIDs. The Alliance will use the SIDs to cull the population. There was no defect in the chips."

Hu offered a grim nod of concurrence. "They work perfectly . . . for their intended purpose. The deaths which occurred during the final testing were deliberate. Through an unlikely series of happenstance, Dr. Sonje Nysgaard stumbled upon what she believed to be a defect. And thus, we come to the present situation."

Aubrey recalled the man's warning about learning the truth. *If there was a truth so horrible, so unsettling it might bring you to despise all those you love, would you wish to know it?*

Knowing what the answer would be and knowing it would be true, she said, "And my Father knew about this. He was part of *populi angustus*. He was a Caesarean."

"As was my Father," Hu acknowledged. The screen returned to the image of Caesar's murder.

Just above a whisper, with a tear sliding down her face, she said, "*Sic semper tyrannis.*"

"The famous words supposedly uttered by Caesar's assassins. And the adopted motto of the Cohors Ignota; though I doubt many of them are aware of their two thousand year old history. In many ways, the Senators were the first Ignota."

Though the realization should have brought revulsion, Aubrey looked into the Caput's eyes and said, "You're an Ignotum."

"As are my advisors, and most of the palace staff as well. Though I was far down the line of succession, I was still uniquely positioned to infiltrate the highest levels of the Council. Through acts which earned me the 'Viper' epithet, I rose to

Caputhood."

She knew that among those "acts" was the murder of his own Father. Hu seemed to read her thoughts through her expression.

"I confronted him that night," he confessed; the pain of the memory written in his stare. "Begged him to turn against the Council, begged him to help me stop what they planned. His commitment to the doctrine, however, was stronger than the love he had for a second-born son. It was the same with my brother—"

"And *my* Father?" Aubrey asked with heat. Her conscience searched for some way to redeem her memories of a loving father. It angered her that she could muster no skepticism towards Hu's tale. *I could have swayed him,* she argued. *I could have convinced my Father.* "Was he given a chance before you conspired to kill him?"

More sympathetic than acerbic, Hu replied, "Beyond his own ability to decide right from wrong? But, yes, before the end, I gave him a choice."

Had he rejected it? She had last seen Kerwen Garrott two nights before the Council moved against the House. With the exception of Tilden, the Family had shared a dinner together. *Our last dinner together.* Even then, her Father had been called away with news of the chief engineer's—Aubrey's eyes widened as several memories combined into revelation.

"Xian," she said. "Enlightened one . . . *xiān* . . . shaman. You're the Soothsayer!"

His gray-hazel eyes did not blink.

"I am. Even among the Ignota, I could not risk exposure. Over the years I have built a substantial network of contacts; all of whom know me only as the Soothsayer."

Considering, Aubrey added, "And many would be unwilling to trust a Caput if they knew."

"Precisely."

Breathing as Liam had taught her, she organized her thoughts. The enormity of what she had just learned made the task quite difficult. However, too much was at stake to let insecurities and emotions run unchecked.

"I have two questions," she proposed in measured efficiency.

Smiling, Hu replied, "Only two?"

"I'm sure more will come. But, we'll start with these. Why did you spare me? And why reveal yourself to me now?"

The Caput drew his hands together, twining his fingers into a perch for his chin. "Regarding the latter question, I have brought you into my small circle of confidants because I believe you share my disgust for what the Council intends. As I said earlier, I've watched you. There was no falsity in the tears you've shed over the New York bombing. Further, I believe you knew nothing of the Culling.

"As for why now, events have unfolded faster than I had anticipated. The Ignota in the West have grown bold. The attack on the naval ship was an unprecedented offensive. This Torrance figure has become a rallying point for the cause. Unfortunately, the Ignota are operating without a full understanding of the enemy. They need to be guided."

Though he seemed to be laying himself bare, Aubrey searched for signs of hubris in the man's mention of guiding the Ignota. The infamy of Yin Xian Hu depicted of a man who desired power above all else. *Is he simply securing a position of power should the Ignota win?* It was a thought for later exploration.

Continuing, Hu said, "However, their increased visibility has attracted the ire of the Alliance. The Caputs are determined to eradicate the resistance entirely—by whatever means necessary. If the Ignota are destroyed, the Council will rule unopposed. I fear the time is coming when House Hu must declare itself and offer the rebellion the full weight of our support."

Prior to the destruction of her House, the animosity between the ruling Families had been limited to petty squabbles and secret manipulations. The Council's success had been dependent on the public appearance of unity. Thinking tactically, Aubrey said, "War between the Houses. Three against one."

"I had hoped to bring down the Cambries in the coming years. But, again, the Western Ignota have made waiting impossible. My House is powerful, more so than the other Caputs believe or wish to admit. However, it would not survive long against three Houses. And there are still Caesareans in my own House who would support the Council. If . . . ." Hu paused, then corrected, ". . . *when* we openly join the battle, it must be done correctly and only in conjunction with an organized Ignota."

Her education in warfare had been limited, and what little there'd been was couched in hypotheticals. Even so, any fool knew a House engaged in civil strife could not stand against a unified Council. Aubrey had spent the last two months conjuring ways to bring down the Caputs and avenge her Family. Now, one of the guilty was offering her an opportunity to do just that. *The enemy of my enemy . . .*

Returning to her first, and still unanswered question, she said, "And your decision to spare me?"

Hu inhaled and lifted his head from his clasped hands. "You already know part of the reason. If time had permitted, you'd be placed on the Council and your House re-established."

He had told her those plans over their first dinner.

"The other part?"

"Your Family designed the SIDs. If a way to remove the chips' threat exists, it would likely rest with the Garrotts."

She had not yet begun to process the feelings of guilt and anger over her Family's role in executing the *populi angustus* doctrine. Though she had voiced neither acceptance nor rejection of Hu's impossible testimony, the depths of her heart knew its veracity. Now, he had placed the lives of—

"How many?" she asked. "How many are to be culled?"

"Caesareans have set the ideal population level at five hundred million. To achieve that figure, over eleven billion need to die. The deaths were to be spread over a decade, and blamed on an incurable plague so as not to arouse resistance from the survivors. Not that it'd matter, half a billion people spread out across the world would pose no threat to the incredible might of the Alliance."

Aubrey countered, "Even a plague killing that many would be questioned."

"In only two years, the Black Death[8] reduced Europe's population by nearly

---

8 Believed to have originated in Asia before spreading to Europe, the Black Death (1348-1350 C.E.) was attributed to rats and the *Yersinia pestis* bacterium. –M.S.

sixty percent. No one questions its origins."

"It was the Caesareans?"

Hu nodded.

"As I warned, it is a horrible truth."

Turning to the far wall, and its now-blank glass panel, Aubrey rubbed the ache spreading across her temple. Nothing in Liam's teachings had prepared her for—*for whatever this is,* she added in thought. Schemes and manipulations had been the crux of his lessons. *Not millennia-old conspiracies aimed at killing billions!* Had her life progressed as planned, she would have been tasked with advising her brother against the other Houses. But, the prospect of open war between the Families—actual military conflict—had been so far removed from the plausible. Now she was faced with exactly that. Worse still, it seemed the terrorists she had been raised to despise were on the just side of the battle. *Nothing prepared me for this.*

In memory, she could hear her teacher's voice. "Your enemies will not wait for you to be ready." Knowing what she did, Aubrey wondered who Liam had considered the enemy. Likely, it was the man now sitting beside her at the table.

"What do we do?" she asked, placing clear emphasis on the pronoun.

With a swelling smile of gratitude, Caput Yin Xian Hu replied, "We prepare for war."

CHAPTER TWENTY-EIGHT

Milo Chance

The journey north to Pelee Island was completed without incident. Each cell had left Oberlin in different directions, and then converged in the city of Sandusky, Ohio to travel by ferry to the island. Besides being in the company of dozens of Ignota, Milo had no complaints with the trek.

Even the discomfort of their presence, and their many stares of suspicion, was mollified by the new accommodations. The residents of the secluded community had opened several of the island's various bed-and-breakfasts, inns, and rental cottages (which had been closed for the off-season) for the new arrivals.

There had been some debate over where to house the former PK, the reporter Naesha O'Geron, and the drone. Though Sonje Nysgaard and those closest to her had accepted the trio into the Ignota, or at least as guests of the Ignota, theirs was a minority opinion. In the end, the blonde doctor had prevailed in convincing the others that the three did not need to be locked away. Given the town's lack of a jail, Milo was not sure how that would have been accomplished anyway.

His new home, The Anchor & Wheel Inn, consisted of a centuries old main building designed as a boarding house, as well as a smaller guesthouse, a pair of cottages, and a beach house. With its ability to sleep ten, the beach house had been the obvious choice for Nysgaard and her ragtag party.

Sharing one of the beach house's queen-bed rooms, Milo and Naesha were sprawled on the hand-stitched quilt covering the bed top. Godwin stood like a statue, guarding the room's door.

"I know we should be focused on what's next," Naesha sighed, "but this mattress just won't let me care about it."

Milo laughed. Their mutual agitation from months on the road, which had been put aside once the Ignota had taken them, was relinquished when their weary bodies met the soft cushion. While the shelter in Oberlin had been a significant improvement over sleeping in his pod, it paled compared to the comfort and quiet of the room in the beachfront home.

"I say we lock the door and stay in here until it's all over," he jested. At first feeling he had been swept up in a sea storming with confusion, he had come to accept that he was inextricably linked to his circumstances. *My SID's been removed, I'm quartering with the Ignota, and I'm half a kilometer away from one of the most wanted men in the world . . . and I'm apparently on his side.* Even if he left now, if the Ignota let him leave, Milo understood he could not return to his former life. There would be questions he could not answer—and some he *would* not answer. He had no doubt he'd be accused of aiding known criminals. *Or worse—conspiring with them.* In resignation, he admitted both charges were true.

"Do you get the feeling we've bitten off more than we can chew?" Naesha asked. The smooth skin of her arm pressed against his own. Though they had been at odds several times along the way, he knew her company was a blessing.

Turning on his side, Milo bent his arm to prop his head against a loose fist. *Truth, she's beautiful!* he thought as he met her eyes. "Is it too much?" he answered question with question. "You agreed to help me find Muerte. But now, we're on an island with the world's most wanted terrorists. Is it too much? I mean, we can't go back, but if you want we can try to leave, to disappear—"

"You, me, and Godwin?" the reporter teased. "Not an easy group to hide."

That she had included the drone in their future plans meant a great deal. The PK had grown rather fond of his inhuman partner since the pair's first days together.

"Besides," she continued, "I'm still a journalist, and this is going to be the story of the century. We just need to live long enough for me to write it."

An impatient knock at the door ended the conversation.

"Yeah?" Milo inquired while rising from the bed.

"It's Match. We're meeting," a voice outside the room informed them. Like Milo, the legendary cyber-terrorist had once been a Peacekeeper. The shared background had provided the foundation for an unspoken bond between the two men.

"On our way," Milo called out.

The island's diminutive size had developed among its residents a penchant for walking as opposed to driving. In fact, he had only seen a handful of podcars since arriving. City-born and bred, Milo could not imagine the dullness of an island childhood. Bundled into borrowed coats and gloves, the party made its cold kilometer-long march to the home of Brother Trig.

Milo maintained a purposeful lag to remain towards the rear of the pack. His investigative senses wanted to study his new companions now that everyone was in unfamiliar territory.

At the head of the group walked Dr. Nysgaard. He still wondered how the woman had come to command six Ignota cells. From the stricken look he had seen in her eyes over the past few days, it was clear she wondered the same.

By her side, as always, was Match Quentin and Kunbo, the giant African whose full name required more gymnastics than most tongues could manage. Both men seemed to serve as advisors, though the Deader's protective demeanor also suggested he was the doctor's bodyguard. Milo had never seen the man fight, but his size was enough of a deterrent. Though Nysgaard was tall and lithe, she looked like a tiny stick alongside the ebony mountain.

The cell's two scouts and the Seton children walked a few paces behind the lead. During his time with the Ignota, Milo had had little interaction with the Setons. His most prolonged contact had been in the crowded room of their awakened father. Even then, Philip Seton's startling words had kept him from studying the children.

The girl walked timidly; hands twined with the scout on her left. A wool winter hat covered her head of short auburn hair. Her brother was on her right. Milo had lived among the rebels long enough to hear the whisperings about the child. "Quiet." "Reserved." "Peculiar." Those were the more complimentary descriptions. They were also the least frequent descriptions. "Damaged" was what he'd heard most often.

Filling out the rest of the group were the five other cell leaders. Loud Marshall, whose stride was more akin to a march, stepped beside the less bombastic Samitha Borden. Even Marshall's footsteps echoed more than anyone else's. The two younger leaders, Marrett and Ewan, kept pace together with inaudible words passing between them. Last of all, and perhaps the most serene, was Peter Yan. His face was a mask of composed elation. Whatever awaited them in the meeting with Brother Trig, Yan alone appeared untroubled.

Down a long paved driveway, the eclectic assemblage reached the yellow farmhouse. Dozens of quiet onlookers filled the home's front lawn. As the citizens turned towards the approaching Ignota, Milo saw the same look of euphoria in each person's eyes. His skin prickled as the crowd parted, allowing Nysgaard to lead the party forward.

At the center of its large wrap-around porch stood an old man—*ancient's more like it,* Milo thought—who smiled and waved them forward. The man wore a purple coat with a bizarre collar. It reminded Milo of the plastic shield his parents had used on the family dog after the vet had neutered the poor mutt.

"Welcome, my friends," the old man said. The voice was far stronger than the body suggested it would be. "I am Brother Trig."

In pairs, the visitors climbed the wooden steps, greeting Trig and filing into the house. When it was their turn, the former PK introduced Naesha and the drone. Though Milo stumbled a bit at the sight of the old man's hairless head and face, Trig barely blinked upon meeting Godwin.

"My home is protected," Brother Trig informed them. "Your connection to the system will be blocked inside."

"That's fine." Expecting some measures of security, Milo still appreciated their host's candor. *I just didn't expect a rural island to have the tech to cut Godwin off completely.* He looked forward to a day without a surprise.

Brother Trig ushered the last of the guests inside and closed the front door. Milo thought he heard a chorus of sighs from the front yard.

Following the other Ignota, he entered the sizeable dining room.

"Please sit," Trig's voice requested from behind.

Milo gave a small nod to his partner. Preferring to stand, the drone slipped into the far corner of the room. Godwin may once again be blocked from the system, but the PK had instructed him to record the meeting. The corner provided the drone an unobstructed view.

As everyone began taking seats, Milo's own view of the room cleared. His stomach clenched when he saw the two men placed to the left and right of the table's head. One man he knew immediately. Though older than his college digitals, Gavin McAvoy was still recognizable. *Which means the other one is—*

Blond hair hung in long, shoulder-length strands. Black shirt and pants made pale skin even lighter. Blue eyes, fierce and cold, scanned everyone and everything. Milo shivered when they fell on him.

A childhood memory boiled to the surface of his thoughts. The zoo exhibit had received national attention and he had begged his parents to take him. White lions were a rare sight and young Milo had not wanted to be the only one of his friends to miss out.

He'd stood for over an hour watching the beast loll in the warm summer sun. Even dozing, the animal's majesty and power were palpable. At one point, the lion rose to its feet, shook its mane, and paced towards the paying gawkers behind the thick protective glass of the observation room. He remembered the moment when the great cat's blue eyes settled on him. The gaze all instinct; impartial and emotionless. And that had made the look all the more frightening. A lion did not hate the gazelle it killed, but that mattered little to the gazelle. Torrance's stare carried the same penetrating weight.

Delphine Porter's parting words echoed in his memory. "If ever your paths should cross, if ever his life rests in your hands, I ask that you consider what I've told you today," the woman had requested. Now faced with the man, Milo could not help but feel it was *his* life placed in Torrance's *hands*.

At the head of the table, there was a silent exchange as Brother Trig offered the seat of prominence to the blond man. Torrance shook his head in refusal. The oddly dressed old man relented and settled into the chair. His advanced years showed in the slow lowering of his body.

"I hope you all have had time to rest after your journey," Trig began. "Should you need anything during your time here, please do not hesitate to ask."

A murmur of sincere appreciation rounded the table.

"Thank you for taking us in," Dr. Nysgaard spoke for the group. "We understand the risk our presence poses for the island."

Hand gesturing dismissal, Trig replied, "We have lived under the threat of discovery for a long time. There are many safeguards in place to shield us from the Alliance's suspicion. Though, the coming months will test those safeguards."

"How so?" Marshall asked.

"Our tourist season is still a few months off. Until then, the arrivals of the others will need to be managed and hidden."

"How many others?" the doctor quizzed.

"Regionally, several thousand," Trig estimated. "There are communities around the world—in China, Nicaragua, Spain, Iran and others—where the Sowilo will gather. But many will want to make a pilgrimage here to see the *Dagaz*."

Milo blinked at the surprising number. "The Alliance is going to notice several thousand SIDs converging on a small island," he said. The looks from Marshall and Peter Yan made him regret mentioning the Alliance. *They don't need more reminders of my career. Former career.*

"The Sowilo who travel will not be chipped much longer," Trig responded.

"That's suicide!" Marshall boomed. "As soon as they cut out the chips, PKs will be all over them!"

The old man smiled at the loud cell leader. "The Peacekeepers are not equipped to hunt such a great number. Plus, I assume the rest of the Ignota intend to continue their strikes; further occupying the Alliance's attention."

"You said there'd be several thousand regionally," Nysgaard interjected. "How many Sowilo are there in the world?"

"Let me ask you this first," Trig directed his words to the entire room. "How many Ignota do you believe exist?"

Scanning the table, Milo watched each man and woman make quiet calculations in their heads. There was the sense of a class of students unwilling to incorrectly answer their teacher.

"Four generations of recruiting," the old man continued. "Four generations of people like Gavin McAvoy," he gestured to the man seated at his left, "who, in just the last few months, has brought five new people into the struggle."

"A hundred thousand?" Nysgaard was the first brave enough to guess. "Two hundred thousand?"

Brother Trig shook his head. "The problem with a de-centralized resistance is the loss of its own history. I have dedicated my life to preserving our past and recording our present. An Ignota historian, you might say.

"The world's population nears twelve billion. In my most conservative research, the Ignota represent one quarter of one percent of the world."

Better with words than numbers, Milo waited for someone else to complete the math. It was the doctor who finished first.

"Thirty million?" she said in a breathy gasp. "There are thirty million Ignota?"

"Likely more," Trig replied. "It may be closer to double. And the Sowilo, at least ten times greater."

Though he was lost in the full meanings of Sowilo and *Dagaz*, the PK's own breath caught at the possibility of three hundred million people ready to rebel against the government.

"Gavin said you're in communication with the Sowilo," Dr. Nysgaard said, meeting McAvoy's eyes.

Milo had learned the two were involved, but at the moment that fact was far from evident. He knew relational tension when he saw it. *And these two are definitely having some issues,* he assessed. Though seated only several chairs apart on opposite sides of the long dining table, the doctor and the Ignota seemed distant.

"He said you told him the Sowilo will join the rest of the Ignota and fight the Alliance?" she asked.

Pursing his thin weathered lips, the bright gleam in their host's eyes dimmed. *He's worried about something,* Milo understood.

"What you were told is partially correct," Brother Trig returned with slow precise words. "The Sowilo will fight," the old man paused, then added, "for as long as the

Dagaz asks them to fight."

Guffawing, Marshall exclaimed, "You've got to be fuckin' kidding me!"

"Marshall," the shorthaired Sam Borden attempted to stem the veteran's anger. "Don't—"

"Like hell I won't!" the Ignota fired back. Leaning forward, pointing a finger at the old man, he let his rage spew forth. "We're not handing over command to the Sowilo! You people have been hiding safe and sound while we're out there getting killed! And you," he shifted his rant to Peter Yan, "we spent the last two months crowded under Oberlin and you knew this place existed and didn't say shit!"

The Asian cell leader replied, "It was not the time to reveal ourselves."

"Well, isn't that convenient? I suppose the time's right now that you've got your Truth-damned *messiah*?"

Judging by their reactions, Milo knew everyone in the room felt the venom in the title. Match Quentin had explained to him some of the significance of this *Dagaz* figure. He had never heard of a mystic faction among the Cohors Ignota. *One of the many things I didn't know I didn't know,* he thought.

"The coming of the *Dagaz* has changed many things," Yan replied, voice soft but firm.

"If you think it's going to change who's running the show, you're all out of your fucking minds!" Marshall spat back.

"Gentlemen, please," Brother Trig said as he raised both hands in a calming gesture. Despite his obvious age, Trig's voice carried marked authority. "We are all part of the same resistance. We share the same goals, fight the same enemy. The Sowilo have no wish to claim power or command."

"No. You just want one of your own in charge," Marshall replied.

During the heated exchange, Milo kept his eyes fixed on Torrance. It was clear the man detested being the focus of the debate. Knowing what he did of Torrance's past—raised in isolation, responsible for himself, reliant on himself—the PK could not imagine how the change in anonymity affected him. Once again, the memory of the white lion came to mind. Proud and powerful, the beast was not meant to be confined; not meant to be the target of ogling spectators.

"What does it matter if we're all fighting for the same cause?" Sonje Nysgaard offered. "If we all agree on a course of action, the Sowilo can believe what they want."

Speaking for the first time, Gavin McAvoy said, "Because that's not how war works."

"Then we make it work," Nysgaard replied with a touch of frustrated pleading in her tone.

"What happens when we can't agree? When Torrance argues one plan, and the rest argue another?" McAvoy conjectured. Milo suspected the debate between the cell leader and the doctor was not a new one.

"He's right," Samitha said. "We'd have two factions following two different leaders."

"Exactly," Marshall supported the statement.

The youngest of the Ignota leaders, Ewan Valencia, added, "The cells would follow Gavin, but I doubt many will accept orders from a Sowilo."

At that, everyone began to speak at once. Most opinions expressed were in opposition to the minority voices of Nysgaard and Yan. Schooled under the hierarchy of the Peacekeepers, Milo understood the need for an explicit chain of command. However, he chose to keep his views to himself. His status among the Ignota would draw suspicion to any counsel he offered.

Drowned by the din, few seemed to hear Torrance's almost inaudible insertion into the dispute.

"The archer and the arrow," the blond figure seated at Trig's right said. On the third repetition, the arguing party realized he had spoken.

"What?" Marshall asked.

Cold blue eyes stared down the long table, subduing the veteran's ire. Milo wondered if anyone had ever silenced Marshall so effectively.

"A commander to lead the Ignota, and a general to carry out his campaign," Torrance expanded. "The archer and the arrow. One aims, the other kills."

Brother Trig said, "Ah, the Sowilo might not—"

"If I'm their *Dagaz*," Torrance cut the old man off, "the Sowilo will do as they're told. You've shown me the full prophecy. It says the *Dagaz* will bring victory. It doesn't say he will lead them to it."

Withering under the weight of his savior's stare, Trig struggled to find the courage to argue. "Well, the prophecy can be interpreted diff—"

"And I'm choosing to interpret it this way."

Face blanching, the man bowed his bald head and said, "Yes, *Dagaz*," and then fell silent.

"Is this an arrangement you can agree to?" Torrance asked McAvoy across the table. His demeanor suggested the exclusion of everyone else in the room. "Will you lead the Ignota?"

There was an air of challenge in the question.

Several heartbeats thumped as the two men, both of a Founder's blood, stared at and through each other. Like the others at the table, Milo was holding his breath as he waited for the cell leader to speak.

"Yes," Gavin McAvoy said.

WHAT FOLLOWED AFTER

Sitting in the dark room, Milo held the small leather-bound book in his hands. Decisions had been made quickly after McAvoy assumed command of the Ignota. Like everything else, he'd had much to add, but his input had not been requested. As Naesha slept in the bed, Milo sat in silent contemplation.

I'm a local PK, he thought. *I'm not cut out for this world revolution stuff.*

He smiled.

Then how'd I end up in the middle of one?

The sheets rustled as Naesha stirred and found him missing from the bed.

"What are you doing?" she asked, her voice husky from sleep.

Standing, he crouched beside the bed.

"Nothing," he whispered. Lifting the book to her sight, he said, "I think I should return this. Before he leaves."

"Mmm, okay," the reporter yawned. "Did you ever figure out what it is?"

Milo looked back to the book.

"His conscience."

"What?"

Leaning into to kiss the smooth skin of her forehead, the PK said, "I'll explain later."

Rising and crossing to the door, he stopped. With one hand on the door handle, Milo turned.

"I love you," he said.

"I love you, too," Naesha replied. "Hurry up and get back to bed."

Smiling again, he promised, "As soon as I can."

Outside the room, Godwin kept a constant vigil. Though Naesha seemed unbothered by the drone's presence, he could not "perform" while his partner was in the room.

Closing the door behind him, he said, "Thanks, Godwin."

Machine and man read the many meanings hidden between the lines.

"I still do not think this is a wise decision," the drone shared again.

"I know. But, it's a necessary one."

Milo left his friend in the hall and took deliberate steps to Torrance's room downstairs. He knocked twice.

The blond man, stripped to the waist, opened the door.

"I know you're busy," the PK stammered, "but I wanted to talk to you before you left."

The man's penetrating eyes studied him. Not speaking, Torrance pulled the door open and turned back into the room. Milo assumed an invitation had been extended.

He followed Torrance inside. Barely brighter than the entryway, the room's dim light was enough to reveal the many scars on the man's back. Milo's stomach twisted at the sight. Days ago, he had discovered the instrument that had left the marks.

Covering himself with the black shirt he picked up from the half-packed gear on the bed, Torrance turned to face him with his arms folded across his chest.

"I, um, I found this," he extended his arm to offer the book, "when we were searching . . . when we were in your . . . home."

Torrance took the tome from him.

"You know what it is?"

Nodding, he said, "I had Godwin translate it. Sun Tzu's *The Art of War*."

Lowering into one of the twin armchairs by the window, Torrance gestured for him to sit as well. Even seated, the threat of his strength was evident.

"The man who raised me," Milo's white lion began and then paused. A humorless smile twitched at the corner of his lips. "My grandfather gave it to me. It belonged to his father. Are you familiar with it?"

Reclining, the PK replied, "I'd heard of it, but never read it until a few days ago."

"What did you think of it?"

"As a theory, it's interesting. As a way of life . . . I don't know."

Torrance turned the book over in his hands. There was affection in the touch.

"So, you met Delphine?" the blond man asked.

"I did."

"How was she?"

Choosing his words with care, he answered, "She seemed to care about you a great deal. But, she was also haunted. By what she'd done. Or not done, really. And by what you might have become."

One brow arched over an icy blue eye.

"And what have I become?"

Milo looked to the book in the man's lap.

"Before today, I didn't think I knew."

"But you do now?"

It was difficult not to let the dangerous stare defeat his courage.

"In your home, the things we saw. What Delphine told us about your past. That book. And then today when you mentioned the archer and the arrow," Milo laid out the evidence. "He raised you to be a weapon; raised you to be unfeeling, without remorse, cold and calculating. But he failed."

The muscles along Torrance's jaw flexed as he clenched his teeth.

Already past the point of timidity, Milo pressed on. "He failed because no matter what he wanted you to become, you're still human. I've dealt with sociopaths, psychotics, the whole spectrum of crazy criminals. Their brains are damaged;

yours isn't. That's why you protected the Seton kids. And that's why you let Gavin McAvoy lead the Ignota. If your grandfather had made you a weapon, you would've never let someone else lead this army."

The man replied, "There wouldn't have been an army if I hadn't."

"I don't believe that, and I don't think you do either."

"Then what's your theory?"

"You're holding it," Milo said as he cast his gaze to the book once more. "A commander and a general, like you said. According to Sun Tzu, 'a Commander stands for the virtues of wisdom, sincerity, benevolence, courage, and strictness'. Even if the Sowilo believe you're their *Dagaz*, you know you can't be those virtues. You need to be the general. You need to be the butcher; unfeeling, without remorse, cold and calculating. Brother Trig says the Sowilo will die for you. But what he doesn't say is that they'll eventually hate you for it. And when they do, they'll have Gavin McAvoy to love."

Rubbing his hand along a hairless chin, Torrance gave a soft laugh. "Well, that's . . . that's one hell of a theory."

Smiling in return, Milo said, "So's gravity."

Torrance straightened his legs and stood from the chair. "We're leaving soon and I have to finish packing."

Standing, the PK said, "I want to go with you."

"Where we're going a drone is going to stand out."

"He's staying," Milo said. It had taken a great deal of convincing, and a firm order in the end, before Godwin had agreed. He needed to know there would be someone protecting Naesha. And to keep her from following him into yet another danger.

The white lion stared at him; both in the room and in his memory.

"We leave in an hour."

Milo nodded once and headed for the door.

"Why?" Torrance asked, stopping the PK midstride. "With everything you just said, why do you want to come?"

The former Peacekeeper, now a resistance fighter, turned to say, "An old woman asked me to look out for you. I wasn't ready to tell her yes then, but I am now."

"You're pissed with me," Sonje said after he rebuffed her attempt at a civil conversation. "You're actually pissed with me!"

Sitting in the old-fashioned swing hanging from the back porch of Brother Trig's house, Gavin replied, "I'm not in the mood to fight."

The doctor softened her tone, saying, "Then talk to me."

The night was crisp and their breath fogged in the glow of the white porch light. Though the island's temperature was a few degrees warmer than the coastal towns, there was no mistaking the season. Bundled into a heavy wool parka, the fabric a darker green than the home's shutters, Sonje leaned against the porch's railing with her arms folded. The pose was as much for warmth as it was a mark of her current mood.

"About what?" he asked.

"Gavin," she warned.

"You had no business volunteering," he admitted the root of his frustration. "Do you have any idea how dangerous it is over there? Do you?"

There was not a person alive who had not heard the rumors of the Dead Continent. Warlords, human traffickers, the PK blockade. But, she knew Gavin had earned his experience firsthand. He had helped Kunbo escape the bounty placed on the weapon master's head. Whatever Sonje thought she knew about the DC, Gavin had witnessed the reality.

"I'll be with Kunbo and Match," she said. "And Torrance and Peter, for that matter. And, I'm not totally defenseless. Even Kunbo says I'm advancing quickly."

"Truth, Sonje! We're not talking about going into the Global Tech building. You're walking into a war zone with a set of knives in your pocket. There are millions of men there who would sell a blonde Westerner to the nearest warlord in a heartbeat! Did you even stop to think about that? Of course you didn't. You volunteer for these things without any hesitation."

She had little ground to argue against that particular point. In a break from her methodical scrutiny—a habit of every successful doctor and researcher—she had rushed headlong into every event over the last few months. Flying to meet Philip Seton. Joining the Ignota. Infiltrating Global Tech. The raid on the supply ship. Capturing the PK and his drone. And now the mission to the DC. *Truth, with that list even Gretchen would call me reckless.* Which was saying something given her sister's long history of impulsivity.

"My instincts haven't been too wrong so far." It was a weak counterpoint, and her voice lacked conviction.

Turning away from the darkness beyond the porch, Gavin looked up at her. "Is it instinct that's sending you to the DC?"

Confused, she replied, "What else would it be?"

"You tell me," he said without emotion.

"I, I don't know what you're trying to suggest. Sure, part of me wants to be there for Kunbo. He's been there for me, and I know what going back there means for him. Someone needs to keep an eye on Yan, too. His priority is the Sowilo. He'll be at Torrance the entire time; positioning the Sowilo and himself."

"And what about Torrance? Is he part of your *instinct*?"

"My inst—what are you talking about? With all that he's done, including saving your life, and mine, and the kids, knowing who he really is, why do you still hate him?"

"Why don't *you*?"

Sonje's eyes widened in disbelief. "Oh Truth," she said just above a whisper. "Tell me that's not what this is about. A petty rivalry is one thing. It was actually kind of cute. But now you're being ridiculous!"

Standing up from the swinging bench, Gavin remarked, "I don't think I am. I think there's a part of you that's in love with him."

"In love—wow! And you're basing that on what exactly? The five conversations I've had with him in the past two months? Or all the times I *haven't* been alone with him?"

"My instincts haven't been too wrong so far," he quoted her in return.

Swallowing her rising anger, she said, "Well, they are now."

Sonje unfolded her arms and extended her hand to his, but he stepped back and away from her touch.

"I can't," he rasped.

"Gav—"

The tears welling in his eyes brought the same to hers.

"I have to be able to think clearly, Sonje. When I was out there with him, there were times when jealousy almost blinded me. I can't let that happen. When you and I met, it was a different time; things were simpler. At least by Ignota standards. Now . . . now everything's gotten so much bigger. The decisions I'm going to have to make . . . my feelings can't get in the way."

Beneath the gloves, beneath the parka, her body shook with an internal chill. Her stomach ached, twisted with the threat of emptying its contents. *Empty,* she told the organ. *Then it will feel like the rest of me.*

The home's backdoor creaked open, followed by the flimsy screen door banging against its frame.

"We're ready to go," Kunbo's baritone called out to the pair.

Blinking back the tears, refusing to let them drop, Sonje took a stuttering breath before turning and walking across the porch to the weapon master and the open door. Part of her wished Gavin would call her name; make some move to draw her back. She knew that once she reached the door the opportunity for reconciliation would be impossible. The others were waiting, and their departure was tightly scheduled.

Sonje faked a smile as she passed the tall African. As her foot crossed the threshold into Brother Trig's house, she felt a small piece of her heart die.

Gavin had not called out for her.

The morning was almost over by the time she woke to greet the day. Danica had stayed up quite late to send off the party heading to the Dead Continent. She had been one of a handful standing on the steps of Brother Trig's farmhouse to bid them farewell. Her father, still struggling with extended periods of walking or standing had exchanged his goodbyes with Dr. Nysgaard from his bed at the inn. Even Marcus, who she thought was certain to see Torrance off, had instead opted to head to bed after dinner.

Danica had shed many tears as she hugged and said goodbye to the doctor. Even more had fallen when she wrapped her arms around Torrance's chest. The man had shown uncharacteristic affection when he patted her on the back. He had also promised to return. If not for her father's sudden revival, the loss of the doctor and Torrance might have been unbearable.

She had stayed a half-minute longer after the two podcars disappeared down the property's long, winding driveway. Other vehicles waited to take her and the others back to their respective inns and lodgings. Once in the room she shared with her brother, Danica had kept the lights off, slipped beneath the covers of her twin bed, and drifted off to sleep.

Awake now, and an hour short of noon, she padded down the hall to one of the shared bathrooms. Given the late hour, she did not have to wait for anyone else to finish. She took a quick shower and dressed herself in donated jeans and a sweater. The habit of bringing her clothes with her to the showers had begun during her time with the Ignota. Modesty—and teenage insecurity—prevented her from walking through the underground shelter in a towel.

Danica spent what remained of the day with her father. With little else to do, and the weather not suitable for outdoor rehabilitation, Philip Seton paced the halls and climbed the stairs to strengthen his weakened muscles. By his side for each step, she wished her father would not push himself so hard. She could see the beads of sweat forming on his brow and darkening a "V" on the back of his button down shirt.

"Dad," she cautioned during his fifteenth lap of the downstairs common rooms, "why don't we take a break?"

"Can't," he replied in between gasping breaths. "Have . . . to get . . . stronger."

His stubborn determination was understandable. As much as her world had changed over the last months, she'd at least been conscious to process each change as it occurred. Philip had woken up to an impossible alien reality. She could not fault him for fighting to at least reclaim familiarity with his own body.

"You are getting stronger. A couple days ago, you were in a coma," she said, with just a touch of teasing. While he might not have looked like the man he was in her happier memories, he had made a remarkable transformation since waking from his long sleep. With every passing hour his coloring had improved, his voice grew less hoarse, and the dark circles under his eyes had faded. If not for his thinness and the crippled hand, he looked healthy. Though his frame would fill out in time, repairing the hand seemed to be on indefinite hold due to the departure of Dr. Nysgaard.

Too winded to talk and walk, Philip chose the former and came to a stop. Steadying himself with a hand on the wall, he said, "I won't let anything . . . happen to you again. I have to get stronger."

For the first time in a long while, Danica felt like she was the center of someone's attention.

"I put you and your brother at risk," he continued in lamentation, "If I had stopped and thought, then your mother—" His words broke off as a sob pulled on his throat.

Already on the edge of emotional overload, Danica swept under her father's arm and held him. In all the many sensations she had experienced since the PKs had torn into her home, she could not recall ever blaming her father. If she had, then she knew it was wrong.

"It's not your fault, Dad," she cried into his shoulder.

"If it wasn't for Torrance, I would have lost you, too," Philip wept as he held his daughter. "I'm your father and I put you in danger, and he was the one who protected you."

Danica had not seen much interaction between her father and her quiet guardian. Of course, Torrance rarely interacted with anyone. The one time she'd witnessed the two together, Philip had gripped the other man's wrist from the bed and thanked him for protecting his children. In typical fashion, Torrance had nodded and detached himself from her father, physically and emotionally. It was clear Philip's gratitude had now become guilt.

"You did protect us," she argued. "You threw yourself at the PKs so we could escape." Unlike him, she remembered every detail of that horrible night.

After a time, father and daughter regained control of their sorrows and fears. Drained in both mind and body, Philip asked her to help him back to his room. Dr. Nysgaard had warned that he would need frequent naps as he recovered. A simple task for a healthy person would prove exhausting for him until he rebuilt his strength and endurance.

Closing the door of his room behind her, Danica left to let her father sleep. Dinner was just a few hours away, and she wanted to speak with her brother before the meal. With Torrance gone, and their father awake, she refused to accept Marcus' continued absence. The man needed his children and there was no reason for her brother to stay away.

First checking their shared room and finding it empty, she made a quick search of the rest of the inn, but reached the same result. Growing more frustrated by the minute, Danica headed to Brother Trig's farmhouse. When she did not find her brother there—no one she had talked to recalled seeing him lately—frustration became panic. The boy had likely decided to wander through the town, but her imagination created several scenarios where Marcus was injured, laying in a field or ditch, and waiting for help.

Truth, I'm Mom now, she thought.

After an hour of unsuccessful searching, aided by Corey and his fellow scout Ament, Danica's stomach began to knot. When a second hour passed, the search party expanded to include nearly every Ignota who had traveled from the Oberlin shelter. By dusk, the entire island sought some sign of the youngest Seton.

Danica had thus far managed to keep her father excluded from the panic. Still fragile, she had not wanted to burden him with what she hoped would end in a story of humorous overreaction.

"I think you need to tell him," Gavin McAvoy advised her. The pinks and reds of sunset had muted to very dark blues. "Marcus is probably sitting in the middle of a farm, but your Dad needs to know we can't find him."

Returning to the inn in the company of familiar faces, Danica wrung her hands as she prepared to inform her father that his youngest child was missing.

"This is going to kill him," she whispered to Corey. The scout kept a supportive arm around her shoulders.

Trying to forestall the moment, Danica's mind convinced her that one more check of her room would prevent the need to deliver the news to her father. Like many faced with an abhorrent task, she placed all her dying hopes into the surety that Marcus would be sitting on his bed, safe and sound. In that last-ditch effort, the voice of reason was crowded out and shouted down.

Shaking, she turned the door handle. She spoke the command to turn on the room's lights. Of course, the space was empty, but she still called out the boy's name.

Fighting back tears—crying was all she seemed to do that day—Danica said, "What if he's out there and he's hurt? It's getting colder and—"

"We'll find him," the scout promised. "I'm sure he has a coat on—"

A different revelation evolved in her thoughts. Leaving the protection and comfort of Corey's arm, she strode to the shared chest of drawers.

"Dani?" Corey questioned the sudden change in her demeanor.

Pulling open the drawers, she found none of the clothing the locals had provided Marcus. A folded piece of paper rested inside the bottom compartment.

Angry, knowing its message, Danica read the note aloud.

"'Remember the turtles.'"

Three words with a meaning Marcus knew she'd understand.

"What does that mean?" Corey asked.

Learning the truth was even worse than she had imagined, she said, "It means he followed Torrance to the Dead Continent."

"I still do not see the value in bringing him along," Mitchall groused. The referenced "him" was the crewman Points; who stood a meter away from Liam's protégé. Among some of his less favorable qualities, Mitchall Kingston was an unapologetic snob. It was a trait rarely on display as the man's service to House Garrott most often found him interacting with his betters. But when given the chance, as was now the case with the crewman, Mitchall made no effort to mask his superiority.

Points, however, did not show sign of insult.

With some work, he'll be useful, the old spymaster thought to himself. *Need to do something about those teeth.* The daggered dentistry would draw far too much attention if he hoped to use the young man as a spy. *After the DC, though.* The intimidating look might be beneficial when dealing with the continent's warlords.

Deflecting with a barb, Liam replied, "Your lack of foresight is forgiven."

With their destination visible to the naked eye, he had no time to indulge his assistant's misplaced hauteur. Of greater concern was Gal. While he believed the lad's induced testimony, Liam held back trust in the Soothsayer's agent. They were soon to enter hostile territory, and he feared a double-cross.

Mitchall had advocated slitting the boy's throat as soon as they disembarked.

It would make things easier, Liam weighed the option, as he had done numerous times over the last two weeks. But as the sole tangible link to the mysterious Soothsayer, Gal might prove invaluable.

The Ignota, the Alliance, the Council, the Deaders, the Soothsayer. So many enemies on the board.

As Chief Advisor, he had dealt with multiple adversaries before, but then he'd had more resources. His current inventory was lacking. And, like it or not, Gal was part of that limited portfolio.

"If you stray so much as a pace away, speak a syllable out of turn, or in any way jeopardize our safety," Liam warned the youngest member of the quartet, "I will hand you your own entrails."

He'd delivered similar threats throughout the voyage, always with a different organ at stake for his own amusement, but never with any less vehemence. Gal had confessed to knowing the spymaster's reputation. There was no chance the boy believed the threats empty.

"Aye, sir," the red-haired youth replied with a quivering Gaelic lilt.

Your Lordship, Liam corrected in his mind. With just Tilden before him in the line of succession, Liam was the Heir to House Garrott. *An unwanted truth,* he added as he rubbed his temple to rid himself of the thought.

A knock turned all four heads. Mitchall opened the door to reveal the ship's chef, Cookie.

"Captain says to tell you we're nearing the barricade," the man informed them.

The former Chief Advisor thanked him for relaying the message. The party of four hoisted their meager belongings onto their backs and set out for the main deck of the *Espado do Mar.*

The plan had been to arrive in Mauritania, but Gal had admitted to revealing the destination to the Soothsayer. Fearing an unwelcome greeting party sent by the mysterious figure, Liam had persuaded Captain Dimas to change course and instead deliver them to Senegal.

The ship itself would not make port in the small African nation. No crafts of considerable size were allowed to breach the barricade. Instead, the quartet would board a smaller Alliance boat to reach the shore. There was a risk Liam might be recognized during the short journey to shore, but it was doubtful a low-level PK sailor would take much interest in fools wanting to die on the DC.

Unlike their point of departure, the temperature off eastern Africa was dry and hot. Stiflingly hot. Within a minute of standing on the deck, tiny beads of sweat were already slipping down to the small of Liam's back. He could already feel Mitchall readying his first complaint.

Ahead, and stretching left and right further than the eye could see, was the naval barricade itself. Great warships sat idle in the rolling waters. As ships were retired from active service, and replaced by their more modern descendants, they had made one final journey to join the DC blockade. Relics from all the great superpowers were now tasked with ensuring no one left the continent. *Sovremmeny* and *Luda* class destroyers from Russia and China. *Rajput* guided missile ships from India. *Ticonderoga* cruisers from America. Once feared marvels of their times, now little more than floating guard posts.

Captain Dimas came down from the bridge to speak with his departing passengers. And to collect the second half of his payment.

"They're droppin' a swifty t'collect ya," he explained in his typical coded jargon. "Be here in a few ticks."

Liam could already see an inflatable boat pulling away from a destroyer and cutting a path to the *Espado.*

"Thank you, Captain," the spymaster offered as he pressed his hand to the SID scanner to deposit two million credits into the man's account. Liam had been prepared for a more contentious journey, but Dimas and his crew had provided the opposite.

In an uncharacteristic show of concern, though coming after the transaction was complete, the captain said, "Ya sure yer wantin' to step th'sand? Deader country's more sharks than op'water. No safety hiding there."

"That seems to be true everywhere, Captain."

"True talk," the tattooed man replied.

Though the government-controlled media did its best to mask it since the destruction of Manhattan, hints of global upheaval had been abundant in the news. Liam could only imagine the true extent of the Ignota's increased rebellion. *If full war breaks out,* he thought, *the DC might actually be a haven.*

Even if it was, Liam did not intend to tarry on the Dead Continent longer than necessary. Once ashore, he intended to cut northeast through Mauritania and Algiers to reach Tunisia. From there he hoped to bribe their way across the narrow stretch of sea to Sicily. The Strait of Gibraltar offered the shortest route out of the DC, but it was also the most guarded. Tunisia, though adding another thousand kilometers to their escape, was the safer option. If that failed, he would try crossing the land barricade into the two countries not included in the DC isolation: Libya and Egypt.

Fawzan's territory, Liam mused as he watched the boat approach. While he had contacts in the Arab Caput's domain, he preferred to reach the more House Garrott-friendly lands of Europe without delay. Even with Caput De Luca residing in Italy, Liam would feel more secure if he could avoid the Middle East. With the destruction of his House, he worried foreign agents might be unwilling to help him. Or worse, seek Fawzan's favor by handing him over to the Alliance.

The Alliance craft slowed as it neared the *Espado*'s portside and then cut its engines once it rubbed alongside the cargo ship. One of Dimas' crew tossed a rolled ladder over the side; its rungs unfurling as it dropped to the water.

More familiar with the descent, Points bid his farewell to the captain and headed down the ladder first. The barrel-chested Dimas gave Liam a respectful nod and handshake before the old spymaster swung himself onto the ladder. As he did, Liam shot a last warning glare at Gal. This would be the youth's first chance to betray them to the Alliance, and Liam wanted to boy to remember his earlier threats.

Once the four men were huddled into the available space in the bow of the rigid inflatable, the small boat's engine roared to life and made a wide half-circle back to shore. The PKs did not speak; not to the passengers, nor to each other. The armed squad had already taken measure of travelers and had deemed them non-threatening. Still, Liam kept his head turned away.

The boat bounced hard through the waves. Liam smiled as he watched his assistant clench his jaw against a return of seasickness. Dark blue waters faded to lighter hues as they sped to the rocky shore. To the left, a derelict lighthouse rose from the shallowing waters, white froths forming as the waves broke along the rocks surrounding it. With piers, docks and port landings long since destroyed, the PKs brought the inflatable as near to the shore as was safe.

"Last chance," one of the soldiers said. The single star and bar insignia marked him as an ensign.

Keeping his face to the shore, Liam replied, "Thank you, but we're sure."

"Then off you go."

The passengers slipped over the side into knee-deep water. The inflatable reversed. Before it turned around, he heard one of the soldiers snicker, "Dead men swimming."

Trudging along, the men marched forward until their soaked boots met dry sand. The bottom centimeters of their footwear collected a coating of tan grains, which further added to the uncomfortable weight. With a hand to shield his eyes from the oppressive sun overhead, he squinted to observe the surroundings.

Remnants of a resort, weathered by a century of abandonment, dotted the beach. A favorite destination of European travelers, the once pristine Club Med resort was now less than a shade of its former self. Rotted wood cabana loungers, frames of stripped straw beach umbrellas, and pedal-boats spoke of a time when Senegal teemed with millions of tourists seeking to enjoy the country's famed beaches and national parks. Those tourists, of course, had been well skilled in ignoring the starvation and slums in cities further inland.

"Well?" Mitchall asked while wringing out water from his pant legs.

"Well, now we look for natives and find ourselves transportation north," he replied.

And hope they don't decide to kill us instead, he added.

In one of the guest rooms of the large Victorian mansion, she sat rocking in the antique chair by the window. Outside, yesterday's snow covered the bare branches of the trees lining the street. Less than a kilometer away, on the very same street, stood the White House Museum.

Tilting the chair back and forth, the wood creaking with each motion, she kept her overlapped hands on the lower part of her stomach. The scars had long since faded, a credit to the doctor's surgical skill. But even his skills could not heal her largest wound.

Dr. Tessari had invited her into his home two months ago. A prolonged hospital stay would have invited unwanted questions into her identity. During her convalescence, he had prepared her meals, helped her with physical rehabilitation, and nursed her back to visible health. Even now, he was two floors below putting the finishing touches on her midday meal.

No matter how much she ate, though, there was an emptiness within that no amount of food could defeat.

Only my son could fill that void, she thought. *He should be growing inside me now.*

Except he wasn't. A traitor had taken him from her, murdered him.

That woman had killed the father, and then she'd killed his son.

She should be angry. She should be filled with fury. But, the emptiness consumed all her emotions. She felt no joy in being alive. She felt no rage in her loss.

There was only emptiness.

The Emptiness. Its power was so great, seemingly omnipotent, she had taken to believing it was its own entity. A living void eating her from the inside out. And she saw no way to fight it.

Tessari had tried to draw her out. He'd spent hours and days talking to her, encouraging her to allow her mind to heal with her body. When his efforts failed, he'd brought in a counselor, another Ignota Fifth, to assess and console her.

The counselor, a gentle woman in her mid-fifties, had explained the process of grief and grieving. She'd told her what she was feeling was normal for a woman who had just loss an unborn child.

He wasn't just a child. He was the child.

She had not said that to the doctor or the woman. In fact, she'd not spoken since first waking in the hospital months ago. The memory of that moment was now a constant companion.

The baby . . .," she whispered, drawing her hand to her abdomen.

Frowning, the doctor replied, "I'm sorry. I did all I could, but . . . I couldn't save him."

He'd had to sedate her to end her screaming.

Oh, how she wished she could find the will to scream again!

The will to hate.

Even the will to end her life.

Instead, she sat. Sat and rocked.

Her catatonia, or prolonged emotional shock as Tessari called it, did not however prevent her from understanding what was happening in the world beyond the mansion. Though he had spared her the worst details, for fear such devastating news might drive her further inward, the doctor had told her about the recent attacks in Lake Erie and Manhattan. The Ignota had declared itself, and the Alliance was worried.

Such news should have excited her. But, The Emptiness would not allow it.

Still holding the space of her son's murder, she kept her gaze on the foggy panes of the window when Dr. Tessari entered with her lunch tray.

"Tomato soup and grilled cheese," he said. Swapping the trays on the lampstand, the doctor pulled over an armchair and sat opposite her.

"Adirene," he began, speaking to her profile, "there's been a development." The tone of his voice was even more nervous and expectant than when he had informed her of the attacks.

"Brother Trig has sent out an announcement through our network."

Like her, the doctor was a believer.

"The *Dagaz* has come to the Sowilo."

Hearing the name of the prophesized savior roused The Emptiness to awareness. Adirene turned form the window to meet Tessari's eyes.

"It's the man called Torrance. The one who saved the Seton children. Brother Trig says the beginning of the prophecy has been fulfilled! They're calling him 'the man from the woods.'"

The Emptiness within her sneered. *Blasphemy! I carried the Dagaz in my womb! Jaime's son was our savior!*

Parting her lips to speak for the first time in months, she said, "Founder's blood."

Tessari blinked in surprise at her brief oratory. Believing the news was encouraging her, he continued. "They say he is, that he's a descendant of Seamus McAvoy. And cousin to Gavin McAvoy."

The strength of The Emptiness' storm increased as it tried to consume her. It condemned Brother Trig, a man she'd admired, for falling under the spell of an imposter.

"Gavin McAvoy," she repeated.

"Yes," the doctor replied, eager to build on the resurrection of her mind. "Brother Trig tells us to be ready. That we're to unite behind Torrance. He will lead the Sowilo. And Gavin will lead the Ignota. Him and a woman; that Swede doctor. Sonje Nysgaard."

The Emptiness raged.

And she understood what it was.

For two months, she had fought to keep it from consuming her. But now she knew that was not the path to victory. She had to surrender to It. She had to *let* it consume her. She had to *become* its instrument.

The Emptiness, living inside her, feeding off her, growing stronger every day, was her son. A traitor may have killed his body, but the spirit of the true *Dagaz* continued on within his mother. His blood had been her blood. And it still flowed through her veins. The blood of a Founder flowed through her veins!

This man from the woods, propped up by the traitor Nysgaard and the weak-minded Trig, was an imposter.

With energy and a sense of purpose she'd not felt in ages, Adirene rose from the rocking chair.

"We must go to Brother Trig."

END

THE EPIC CONTINUES IN:

TEARS OF THE SOWILO